2016

PUSHCART
PRIZE XL
BEST OF THE
SMALL PRESSES

EDITED BY BILL HENDERSON
WITH THE PUSHCART PRIZE EDITORS

Note: nominations for this series are invited from any small, independent, literary book press or magazine in the world, print or online. Up to six nominations—tear sheets or copies, selected from work published, or about to be published, in the calendar year—are accepted by our December 1 deadline each year. Write to Pushcart Fellowships, P.O. Box 380, Wainscott, N.Y. 11975 for more information or consult our website www.pushcartprize.com.

Acknowledgments
Selections for The Pushcart Prize are reprinted with the permission of authors and presses cited. Copyright reverts to authors and presses immediately after publication.

Distributed by W. W. Norton & Co.
500 Fifth Ave., New York, N.Y. 10110

Library of Congress Card Number: 76-58675
ISBN (hardcover): 978-1-888889-79-6
ISBN (paperback): 978-1-888889-80-2
ISSN: 0149-7863

For Philip Levine
(1928–2015)

INTRODUCTION

Feel free to skip this introduction. I skip most introductions. I'd rather read the book, then come back to the introduction to see what I have missed. But I might ask that you stay put for a bit before proceeding to the brilliance that awaits you—69 poems, stories, essays, and memoirs from 52 presses.

Recently it hit me—40 years (or XL if you prefer) is a long time. How has it happened that the *Pushcart Prize* is still here and still thriving?

A little history—back in 1974 I was in Berkeley, California. I was an about-to-be fired "senior editor" at a major trade book publisher. I deserved to be fired. My heart wasn't in commerce, because there is very little heart in that enterprise. Profit was all and the continued search for profit in literature is not in my bones. Those who live for money die by money.

At the Mediterranean Café I scribbled a note in my journal "why not a best of the small presses." I let it drop for a year, coming back to that notion in the summer of 1975 in a seaside cabin on Long Island. I tried out my idea on dozens of literary icons—Paul Bowles, Anaïs Nin, Ralph Ellison, Joyce Carol Oates and others, all listed as Founding Editors on the masthead in this edition. Bless them. An ex-editor, a would-be novelist, I had one credit—Pushcart's first book, *The Publish It Yourself Handbook*. Published weekends on a minimal budget it sold 75,000 copies in several editions.

The handbook advised oft-rejected authors to ditch non-responsive and non-responsible publishers and publish their own work. Above all avoid vanity publishers it exhorted. The handbook said it was most important that writers not leap into self-publishing on their first rejec-

5

tion. Take time, take care, and above all care about what you write—don't fire it off lightly into the digital ether, as is the custom today.

But I digress.

What happened next with my best of the small presses idea was astonishing and continues to amaze me. The Founding Editors said OK, good idea, and off Pushcart sailed on a venture that brings us to this introduction decades later.

It turned out that many employed in the commercial book and magazine industry were also made queasy by the profit driven world. They too longed for an alternative that valued mind and soul over bucks and three martini lunches—people like Tom Lask and Harvey Shapiro at *The New York Times*, John Baker and Sybil Steinberg at *Publishers Weekly* and editors at *Booklist, Kirkus, Village Voice, Library Journal* and dozens of newspapers and magazine rose up in support of this quixotic effort. Many did not expect it would last more than a year, maybe two. After all, Pushcart had no grant funding, no institutional cash, no Federal support or family fortune (still doesn't). PP was to be issued from a one room apartment and later a backyard shack (still is). Not much of a chance there in the cold world of big boys and girls.

But the Prize refused to die, and I know the reason, hidden from the conglomerates. There is a heart, mind, soul, and defiance out there in small press land that refuses to let commerce kill the spirit of our writers, editors and readers.

And so we come to the point of this introduction. Thank you. That's it. Thank you.

This is not my personal thank you so much as gratitude from the thousands of writers who have been honored by reprint or mention in these pages over the decades, the hundreds of presses that were able to make nominations each year, the 200 plus Contributing Editors who make suggestions for every edition and the annual Guest Editors who have the opportunity to select from more than 8000 submitted works.

My personal thanks to W.W. Norton & Co. for distributing our Prize over most of its life. Norton is a stellar publisher—independent since 1923, employee owned, dedicated, serious, and despite these virtues, a major publishing force.

And finally thanks to my wife Genie who has been with Pushcart for almost the entire run, enduring her financially-challenged, holy fool of a husband for all of it, and to our beautiful and whip-smart daughter Lily who keeps us sane and in touch with an electronic universe that I often find appalling.

Forty years. What's changed?

In conglomerate and vanity publishing it's gotten far worse. Most of the fabled old independent book publishers are mere shells of their former glory or long gone. Vanity ghouls snap up lost writers for a nifty profit and no benefit. Magazines and newspapers are expiring in the insane excitement of a digital world that values "creative disruption" with an almost nihilistic glee.

Leon Wieseltier, former editor of *The New Republic*, describes the situation in the January 18, 2015 issue of *The New York Times Book Review*:

"Amid the bacchanal of disruption, let us pause to honor the disrupted. The streets of American cities are haunted by bookstores and record stores, which have been destroyed by the greatest thugs in the history of the culture industry. . . . Words cannot wait for thoughts, and first responses are promoted into best responses, and patience is a professional liability. As the frequency of expression grows, the force of expression diminishes: Digital expectations of alacrity and terseness confer the highest prestige upon the twittering cacophony of one-liners and promotional announcements. It was always the case that all things must pass, but this is ridiculous. . . . Meanwhile the discussion of culture is being steadily absorbed into the discussion of business. Where wisdom once was, quantification will now be. . . ."

I am tempted to include the entire essay. To me it is one of the essential statements of social and cultural decay at the hands of the tech slathered elite. At the same time, in the small press world, far from the rapacious, empty, dollar and factoid cosmos, all is just fine -- and getting better. Back in the 70's, 450 pages was a good PP selection, now this fat volume isn't nearly enough room to encompass a fair sampling of how very good many (not all for sure) of our writers are today. Perhaps when we lost the opportunity to publish for much of the commercial world we gained our own souls.

The future for small press writers, editors and readers is bright. For those who live for cash, there is no future. In fact there isn't even a present.

Every year I ask our Guest Poetry Editors, who choose half the contents of our collection, to describe the state of contemporary poetry as they see it.

Kim Addonizio is both a poet, an editor, and a novelist. She has won

7

accolades from the National Endowment for the Arts, the Guggenheim Foundation and Pushcart Prize. Her recent poetry collections include *Tell Me* (2000), *What Is This Thing Called Love?* (2004) and *Lucifer At The Starlite* (2009). Her novels include: *A Box Called Pleasure* (1999), *My Dreams Out In the Street* (2003), and *Little Beauties* (2005).

Kim writes: " I was privileged to read and cursed to choose . . . In the end these are the poems I choose, culled from the myriad poems that spoke to me. I hope they speak to you in various ways, by virtue of their muse, or beauty, or weirdness, or harsh truths, with wit or surprise or stealth."

David Bottoms is the Poet Laureate of Georgia and the editor of *Five Points*. He has won a Ingram-Merrill Award, an NEA Fellowship, the Walt Whitman Award and recognition from the American Academy and Institute of Arts and Letters.

His poetry collections include *Vagrant Grace* (1999) and *Waltzing Through the Endtime* (2004), plus the novel *Easter Weekend* (1990).

David comments: " If I had to characterize in a word my experience with judging the Prize, the word would be 'overwhelming.' I was absolutely stunned at the wealth of submissions I received, a testimony that poetry is surely alive and well. I was delighted to find that serious poetry is being written and being written well."

My profound thanks to Kim and David and all our Guest Editors, and to the hundreds of helpers listed on our masthead, and to the donors to our Endowment. Also gratitude for their international support to Phil Schultz and his Writers Studio and to Cedering Fox and her Word Theatre for their annual celebrations of the Prize. Finally, as always, to you the reader, thank you for keeping the faith with our small presses. To you goes all our gratitude. Without you, nothing.

Love and wonder . . . Bill

THE PEOPLE WHO HELPED

FOUNDING EDITORS—Anaïs Nin (1903-1977), Buckminster Fuller (1895-1983), Charles Newman (1938-2006), Daniel Halpern, Gordon Lish, Harry Smith (1936–2013), Hugh Fox (1932-2011), Ishmael Reed, Joyce Carol Oates, Len Fulton (1934-2011), Leonard Randolph, Leslie Fiedler (1917-2003), Nona Balakian (1918-1991), Paul Bowles (1910-1999), Paul Engle (1908-1991), Ralph Ellison (1914-1994), Reynolds Price (1933-2011), Rhoda Schwartz, Richard Morris, Ted Wilentz (1915-2001), Tom Montag, William Phillips (1907-2002). Poetry editor: H. L. Van Brunt

CONTRIBUTING EDITORS FOR THIS EDITION—Steve Adams, Dan Albergotti, Dick Allen, John Allman, Idris Anderson, Antler, Tony Ardizzone, Renée Ashley, David Baker, Kim Barnes, Ellen Bass, Rick Bass, Claire Bateman, Bruce Beasley, Marvin Bell, Molly Bendall, Karen Bender, Pinckney Benedict, Bruce Bennett, Marie-Helene Bertino, Marianne Boruch, Michael Bowden, John Bradley, Fleda Brown, Rosellen Brown, Michael Dennis Browne, Ayse Papatya Bucak, Christopher Buckley, E. Shaskan Bumas, Richard Burgin, Shannon Cain, Kathy Callaway, Bonnie Jo Campbell, Kara Candito, Richard Cecil, Kim Chinquee, Jane Ciabattari, Suzanne Cleary, Michael Collier, Jeremy Collins, Martha Collins, Lydia Conklin, Stephen Corey, Eduardo Corral, Lisa Couturier, Philip Dacey, Claire Davis, Chard deNiord, Jaquira Diaz, Stephen Dixon, Frances Driscoll, Jack Driscoll, John Drury, Karl Elder, Elizabeth Ellen, Angie Estes, Kathy Fagan, Ed Falco, Gary Fincke, Maribeth Fischer, Robert Long Foreman, Ben Fountain, H. E. Francis, Seth Fried, Alice Friman, Sarah Frisch, John Fulton, Richard Garcia, Frank X. Gaspar, Christine Gelineau, Nancy Geyer, Gary Gildner, Elton Glaser, Mark Halliday, Jeffrey Hammond, James Harms, Jeffrey Harrison, Tim Hedges, Robin Hemley, Daniel

9

Lee Henry, David Hernandez, William Heyen, Bob Hicok, Kathleen Hill, Jane Hirshfield, Jen Hirt, Edward Hoagland, Andrea Hollander, David Hornibrook, Christopher Howell, Maria Hummel, Karla Huston, Colette Inez, Mark Irwin, David Jauss, Bret Anthony Johnston, Fady Joudah, Michael Kardos, Laura Kasischke, George Keithley, Brigit Kelly, Thomas E. Kennedy, Junse Kim, David Kirby, John Kistner, Richard Kostelanetz, Wally Lamb, Fred Leebron, Sandra Leong, Dana Levin, Philip Levine, Daniel S. Libman, Gerald Locklin, Jennifer Lunden, Bill Lychack, Alexander Maksik, Paul Maliszewski, Matt Mason, Dan Masterson, Alice Mattison, Tracy Mayor, Robert McBrearty, Rebecca McClanahan, Davis McCombs, Jill McDonough, Erin McGraw, Elizabeth McKenzie, Brenda Miller, Nancy Mitchell, Jim Moore, Ottessa Moshfegh, Joan Murray, Kent Nelson, Kirk Nesset, Mike Newirth, Aimee Nezhukumatathil, Celeste Ng, Risteard O'Keitinn, Joyce Carol Oates, Dzvinia Orlowsky, Peter Orner, Kathleen Ossip, Alan Michael Parker, Benjamin Percy, C. E. Poverman, D. A. Powell, Kevin Prufer, Lia Purpura, James Reiss, Donald Revell, Nancy Richard, Laura Rodley, Jessica Roeder, Jay Rogoff, Rachel Rose, Mary Ruefle, Maxine Scates, Alice Schell, Brandon R. Schrand, Grace Schulman, Philip Schultz, Lloyd Schwartz, Salvatore Scibona, Diane Seuss, Anis Shivani, Floyd Skloot, Arthur Smith, Anna Solomon, David St. John, Maura Stanton, Maureen Stanton, Paul Stapleton, Pamela Stewart, Terese Svoboda, Barrett Swanson, Ron Tanner, Katherine Taylor, Elaine Terranova, Susan Terris, Joni Tevis, Robert Thomas, Jean Thompson, Melanie Rae Thon, Frederic Tuten, Lee Upton, Nance Van Winckel, Inara Verzemnieks, G. C. Waldrep, BJ Ward, Don Waters, Michael Waters, LaToya Watkins, Marc Watkins, Charles Harper Webb, Roger Weingarten, William Wenthe, Philip White, Jessica Wilbanks, Joe Wilkins, Eleanor Wilner, Sandi Wisenberg, Mark Wisniewski, David Wojahn, Carolyn Wright, Robert Wrigley, Christina Zawadiwsky, Paul Zimmer

PAST POETRY EDITORS—H.L. Van Brunt, Naomi Lazard, Lynne Spaulding, Herb Leibowitz, Jon Galassi, Grace Schulman, Carolyn Forché, Gerald Stern, Stanley Plumly, William Stafford, Philip Levine, David Wojahn, Jorie Graham, Robert Hass, Philip Booth, Jay Meek, Sandra McPherson, Laura Jensen, William Heyen, Elizabeth Spires, Marvin Bell, Carolyn Kizer, Christopher Buckley, Chase Twichell, Richard Jackson, Susan Mitchell, Lynn Emanuel, David St. John, Carol Muske, Dennis Schmitz, William Matthews, Patricia

CONTENTS

MISS ADELE AMIDST THE CORSETS

fiction by ZADIE SMITH

from THE PARIS REVIEW

"Well, that's that," Miss Dee Pendency said, and Miss Adele, looking back over her shoulder, saw that it was. The strip of hooks had separated entirely from the rest of the corset. Dee held up the two halves, her big red slash mouth pulling in opposite directions.

"Least you can say it died in battle. Doing its duty."

"Bitch, I'm on in ten minutes."

"*When an irresistible force like your ass . . .*"

"Don't sing."

"*Meets an old immovable corset like this . . . You can bet as sure as you liiiiive!*"

"It's your fault. You pulled too hard."

"*Something's gotta give, something's gotta give, SOMETHING'S GOTTA GIVE.*"

"You pulled too hard."

"Pulling's not your problem." Dee lifted her bony, white Midwestern leg up onto the counter, in preparation to put on a thigh-high. With a heel she indicated Miss Adele's mountainous box of chicken and rice: "Real talk, baby."

Miss Adele sat down on a grubby velvet stool before a mirror edged with blown-out bulbs. She was thickening and sagging, in all the same ways, in all the same places, as her father. Plus it was midwinter: her skin was ashy. She felt like some once-valuable piece of mahogany furniture lightly dusted with cocaine. This final battle with her corset had set her wig askew. She was forty-six years old.

"Lend me yours."

"Good idea. You can wear it on your arm."

And tired to death, as the Italians say—tired to *death*. Especially sick of these kids, these "millennials," or whatever they were calling themselves. Always on. No backstage to any of them—only front of house. Wouldn't know a sincere, sisterly friendship if it kicked down the dressing-room door and sat on their faces.

Miss Adele stood up, untaped, put a furry deerstalker on her head, and switched to her comfortable shoes. She removed her cape. Maybe stop with the cape? Recently she had only to catch herself in the mirror at a bad angle, and there was Daddy, in his robes.

"The thing about undergarments," Dee said, "is they can only do so much with the cards they've been dealt. Sorta like Obama?"

"Stop talking."

Miss Adele zipped herself into a cumbersome floor-length padded coat, tested—so the label claimed—by climate scientists in the Arctic.

"Looking swell, Miss Adele."

"Am I trying to impress somebody? Tell Jake I went home."

"He's out front—tell him yourself!"

"I'm heading this way."

"You know what they say about choosing between your ass and your face?"

Miss Adele put her shoulder to the fire door and heaved it open. She caught the punch line in the ice-cold stairwell.

"You should definitely choose one of those at some point."

Aside from the nights she worked, Miss Adele tried not to mess much with the East Side. She'd had the same sunny rent-controlled studio apartment on Tenth Avenue and Twenty-Third since '93, and loved the way the West Side communicated with the water and the light, loved the fancy galleries and the big anonymous condos, the High Line funded by bankers and celebrities, the sensation of clarity and wealth. She read the real estate section of the *Times* with a kind of religious humility: the reality of a thirty-four-million-dollar townhouse implied the existence of a mighty being, out there somewhere, yet beyond her imagining. But down here? Depressing. Even worse in the daylight. Crappy old buildings higgledy-piggledy on top of each other, ugly students, shitty pizza joints, delis, tattoo parlors. Nothing bored Miss Adele more than ancient queens waxing lyrical about the good old bad old days. At least the bankers never tried to rape you at knifepoint or sold you bad acid. And

20

then once you got past the Village, everything stopped making sense. Fuck these little streets with their dumbass names! Even the logistics of googling her location—remove gloves, put on glasses, find the phone—were too much to contemplate in a polar vortex. Instead, Miss Adele stalked violently up and down Rivington, cutting her eyes at any soul who dared look up. At the curb she stepped over a frigid pool of yellow fluid, three paper plates frozen within it. What a dump! Let the city pull down everything under East Sixth, rebuild, number it, make it logical, pack in the fancy hotels—not just one or two but a whole bunch of them. Don't half gentrify—follow through. Stop preserving all this old shit. Miss Adele had a right to her opinions. Thirty years in a city gives you the right. And now that she was, at long last, no longer beautiful, her opinions were all she had. They were all she had left to give to people. Whenever her disappointing twin brother, Devin, deigned to call her from his three-kids-and-a-Labradoodle, goofy-sweater-wearing, golf-playing, liberal-Negro-wet-dream-of-a-Palm-Springs-fantasy existence, Miss Adele made a point of gathering up all her hard-won opinions and giving them to him good. "I wish he could've been mayor forever. FOR-EVAH. I wish he was my boyfriend. I wish he was my daddy." Or: "They should frack the hell out of this whole state. We'll get rich, secede from the rest of you dope-smoking, debt-ridden assholes. You the ones dragging us all down." Her brother accused Miss Adele of turning rightward in old age. It would be more accurate to say that she was done with all forms of drama—politics included. That's what she liked about gentrification, in fact: gets rid of all the drama.

And who was left, anyway, to get dramatic about? The beloved was gone, and so were all the people she had used, over the years, as substitutes for the beloved. Every kid who'd ever called her gorgeous had already moved to Brooklyn, Jersey, Fire Island, Provincetown, San Francisco, or the grave. This simplified matters. Work, paycheck, apartment, the various lifestyle sections of the *Times*, Turner Classic Movies, Nancy Grace, bed. Boom. Maybe a little *Downton*. You needn't put your face on to watch *Downton*. That was her routine, and disruptions to it—like having to haul ass across town to buy a new corset—were rare. Sweet Jesus, this cold! Unable to feel her toes, she stopped a shivering young couple in the street. British tourists, as it turned out; clueless, nudging each other and beaming up at her Adam's apple with delight, like she was in their guidebook, right next to the Magnolia Bakery and the Naked Cowboy. They had a map, but without her glasses it was useless. They had no idea where they were. "Sorry! Stay warm!"

they cried, and hurried off, giggling into their North Face jackets. Miss Adele tried to remember that her new thing was that she positively liked all the tourists and missed Bloomberg and loved Midtown and the Central Park nags and all the Prada stores and *The Lion King* and lining up for cupcakes wherever they happened to be located. She gave those British kids her most winning smile. Sashayed round the corner in her fur-cuffed Chelsea boots with the discreet heel. Once out of sight, though, it all fell apart; the smile, the straightness of her spine, every-thing. Even if you don't mess with it—even when it's not seven below—it's a tough city. New York just expects so much from a girl—acts like it can't stand even the *idea* of a wasted talent or opportunity. And Miss Adele had been around. Rome says: enjoy me. London: survive me. New York: gimme all you got. What a thrilling proposition! The chance to be "all that you might be." Such a thrill—until it becomes a burden. To put a face on—to put a self on—this had once been, for Miss Adele, pure delight. And part of the pleasure had been precisely this: the buying of things. She used to love buying things! Lived for it! Now it felt like effort, now if she never bought another damn thing again she wouldn't even—

Clinton Corset Emporium. No awning, just a piece of cardboard stuck in the window. As Miss Adele entered, a bell tinkled overhead—an actual bell, on a catch wire—and she found herself in a long narrow room—a hallway really—with a counter down the left-hand side and a curtained-off cubicle at the far end, for privacy. Bras and corsets were everywhere, piled on top of each other in anonymous white cardboard boxes, towering up to the ceiling. They seemed to form the very walls of the place.

"Good afternoon," said Miss Adele, daintily removing her gloves, finger by finger. "I am looking for a corset."

A radio was on; talk radio—incredibly loud. Some AM channel bring-ing the latest from a distant land, where the people talk from the back of their throats. One of those Eastern-y, Russian-y places. Miss Adele was no linguist, and no geographer. She unzipped her coat, made a noise in the back of her own throat, and looked pointedly at the pre-sumed owner of the joint. He sat slumped behind the counter, listening to this radio with a tragic twist to his face, like one of those sad-sack cab drivers you see hunched over the wheel, permanently tuned in to the bad news from back home. And what the point of that was, Miss Adele would never understand. Turn that shit down! Keep your eyes on the road! Lord knows, the day Miss Adele stepped out of the state of Florida was pretty much the last day that godforsaken spot ever crossed her mind.

Could he even see her? He was angled away, his head resting in one hand. Looked to be about Miss Adele's age, but further gone: bloated face, about sixty pounds overweight, bearded, religious type, wholly absorbed by this radio of his. Meanwhile, somewhere back there, behind the curtain, Miss Adele could make out two women talking:

"Because she thinks Lycra is the answer to everything. Why you don't speak to the nice lady? She's trying to help you. She just turned fourteen."

"So she's still growing. We gotta consider that. Wendy—can you grab me a Brava 32 B?"

A slip of an Asian girl appeared from behind the curtain, proceeded straight to the counter and vanished below it. Miss Adele turned back to the owner. He had his fists stacked like one potato, two potato—upon which he rested his chin—and his head tilted in apparent appreciation of what Miss Adele would later describe as "the ranting"—for did it not penetrate every corner of that space? Was it not difficult to ignore? She felt she had not so much entered a shop as some stranger's spittle-filled mouth. RAGE AND RIGHTEOUSNESS, cried this radio—in whatever words it used—RIGHTEOUSNESS AND RAGE. Miss Adele crossed her arms in front of her chest, like a shield. Not this voice—not today. Not any day—not for Miss Adele. And though she had learned, over two decades, that there was nowhere on earth entirely safe from the voices of rage and righteousness—not even the new New York—still Miss Adele had taken great care to organize her life in such a way that her encounters with them were as few as possible. (On Sundays, she did her groceries in a cutoff T-shirt that read THOU SHALT.) As a child, of course, she had been fully immersed—dunked in the local water—with her daddy's hand on the back of her head, with his blessing in her ear. But she'd leapt out of that shallow channel the first moment she was able.

"A corset," she repeated, and raised her spectacular eyebrows. "Could somebody help me?"

"WENDY," yelled the voice behind the curtain, "could you see to our customer?"

The shopgirl sprung up, like a jack-in-the-box, clutching a stepladder to her chest.

"Looking for Brava!" shouted the girl over the radio, turned her back on Miss Adele, opened the stepladder, and began to climb it. Meanwhile,

23

the owner shouted something at the woman behind the curtain, and the woman, adopting his tongue, shouted something back.

"It is customary, in retail—" Miss Adele began.

"Sorry—one minute," said the girl, came down with a box under arm, dashed right past Miss Adele, and disappeared once more behind the curtain.

Miss Adele took a deep breath. She stepped back from the counter, pulled her deerstalker off her head and tucked a purple bang behind her ear. Sweat prickled her face for the first time in weeks. She was considering turning on her heel and making that little bell shake till it fell off its goddamn string when the curtain opened and a mousy girl emerged, with her mother's arm around her. They were neither of them great beauties. The girl had a pissy look on her face and moved with an angry slouch, like a prisoner, whereas you could see the mother was at least trying to keep things civilized. The mother looked beat—and too young to have a teenager. Or maybe she was the exact right age. Devin's kids were teenagers. Miss Adele was almost as old as the president. None of this made any sense, and yet you were still expected to accept it, and carry on, as if it were the most natural process in the world.

"Because they're not like hands and feet," a warm and lively voice explained, from behind the curtain, "They grow independently."

"Thank you so much for your advice, Mrs. Alexander," said the mother, the way you talk to a priest through a screen. "The trouble is this thickness here. All the women in our family got it, unfortunately. Curved rib cage."

"But actually, you know—it's inneresting—it's a totally different curve from you to her. Did you realize that?"

The curtain opened. The man looked up sharply. He was otherwise engaged, struggling with the antennae of his radio to banish the static, but he paused a moment to launch a little invective in the direction of a lanky, wasp-waisted woman in her early fifties, with a long, humane face—dimpled, self-amused—and an impressive mass of thick chestnut hair.

"Two birds, two stones," said Mrs. Alexander, ignoring her husband, "that's the way we do it here. Everybody needs something different. That's what the big stores won't do for you. Individual attention. Mrs. Berman, can I give you a tip?" The young mother looked up at the long-necked Mrs. Alexander, a duck admiring a swan. "Keep it on all the time. Listen to me, I know of what I speak. I'm wearing mine right now, I wear it every day. In my day they gave it to you when you walked out of the hospital!"

"Well, you look amazing."

"Smoke and mirrors. Now, all you need is to make sure the straps are fixed right like I showed you." She turned to the sulky daughter and put a fingertip on each of the child's misaligned shoulders. "You're a lady now, a beautiful young lady, you—" Here again she was interrupted from behind the counter, a sharp exchange of mysterious phrases, in which—to Miss Adele's satisfaction—the wife appeared to get the final word. Mrs. Alexander took a cleansing breath and continued: "So you gotta hold yourself like a lady. Right?" She lifted the child's chin and placed her hand for a moment on her cheek. "Right?" The child straightened up despite herself. See, some people are trying to ease your passage through this world—so ran Miss Adele's opinion—while others want to block you at every turn. Think of poor Mama, taking folk round those god-awful foreclosures, helping a family to see the good life that might yet be lived there—that had just as much chance of sprouting from a swamp in the middle of nowhere as any place else. That kind of instinctive, unthinking care. If only Miss Adele had been a simple little fixer-upper, her mother might have loved her unconditionally! Now that Miss Adele had grown into the clothes of middle-aged women, she noticed a new feeling of affinity toward them, far deeper than she had ever felt for young women, back when she could still fit into the hot pants of a showgirl. She walked through the city struck by middle-aged women and the men they had freely chosen, strange unions of the soft and the hard. In shops, in restaurants, in line at the CVS. She always had the same question. Why in God's name are you still married to this asshole? Lady, your children are grown. You have your own credit cards. You're the one with life force. Can't you see he's just wallpaper? It's not 1850. This is New York. Run, baby, run!

"Who's waiting? How can I help you?"

Mother and daughter duck followed the shopgirl to the counter to settle up. The radio, after a brief pause, made its way afresh up the scale of outrage. And Miss Adele? Miss Adele turned like a flower to the sun.

"Well, I need a new corset. A strong one."

Mrs. Alexander beamed: "Come right this way."

Together, they stepped into the changing area. But as Miss Adele reached to pull the curtain closed behind them both—separating the ladies from the assholes—a look passed between wife and husband and

Mrs. Alexander caught the shabby red velvet swathe in her hand, a little higher up than Miss Adele had, and held it open.

"Wait—let me get Wendy in here." An invisible lasso, thought Miss Adele. He throws it and you go wherever you're yanked. "You'll be all right? The curtain's for modesty. You modest?"

Oh, she had a way about her. Her face expressed emotion in layers: elevated, ironic eyebrows, mournful violet eyes, and sly, elastic mouth. Miss Adele could have learned a lot from a face like that. A face straight out of an old movie. But which one, in particular?

"You're a funny lady."

"A life like mine, you have to laugh—Marcus, please, one minute—" He was barking at her, still—practically insisting, perhaps, that she *stop talking to that schwarze*, which prompted Mrs. Alexander to lean out of the changing room to say something very like: *What is wrong with you? Can't you see I'm busy here?* On the radio, strange atonal music replaced the ranting; Mrs. Alexander stopped to listen to it, and frowned. She turned back to her new friend and confidante, Miss Adele. "Is it okay if I don't measure you personally? Wendy can do it in a moment. I've just got to deal with—but listen, if you're in a hurry, don't panic, our eyes, they're like hands."

"Can I just show you what I had?"

Miss Adele unzipped her handbag and pulled out the ruin.

"Oh! You're breaking my heart! From here?"

"I don't remember. Maybe ten years ago?"

"Makes sense, we don't sell these any more. Ten years is ten years. Time for a change. What's it to go under? Strapless? Short? Long?"

"Everything. I'm trying to hide some of this."

"You and the rest of the world. Well, that's my job." She leaned over and put her lips just a little shy of Miss Adele's ear: "What you got up there? You can tell me. Flesh or feathers?"

"Not the former."

"Got it. WENDY! I need a Futura and a Queen Bee, corsets, front fastening, forty-six. Bring a forty-eight, too. Marcus—please. One *minute*. And bring the Paramount in, too! The crossover! Some people," she said, turning to Miss Adele, "You ask them these questions, they get offended. Everything offends them. Personally, I don't believe in 'political correctness.' " She articulated the phrase carefully, with great sincerity, as if she had recently coined it. "My mouth's too big. I gotta say what's on my mind! Now, when Wendy comes, take off everything

to here and try each corset on at its tightest setting. If you want a de-
fined middle, frankly it's going to hurt. But I'm guessing you know that
already."

"Loretta Young," called Miss Adele to Mrs. Alexander's back. "You
look like Loretta Young. Know who that is?"

"Do I know who Loretta Young is? Excuse me one minute, will you?"

Mrs. Alexander lifted her arms comically, to announce something to
her husband, the only parts of which Miss Adele could fully comprehend
were the triple repetition of the phrase "Loretta Young." In response,
the husband made a noise somewhere between a sigh and a grunt.

"Do me a favor," said Mrs. Alexander, sighing, letting her arms drop,
and turning back to Miss Adele, "put it in writing, put it in the mail.
He's a reader."

The curtain closed. But not entirely. An inch hung open and through
it Miss Adele watched a silent movie—silent only in the sense that the
gestures were everything. It was a marital drama, conducted in an-
other language, but otherwise identical to all those she and Devin had
watched as children, through a crack in the door of their parents' bed-
room. God save Miss Adele from marriage! Appalled, fascinated, she
watched the husband, making the eternal, noxious point in a tone Miss
Adele could conjure in her sleep (*You bring shame upon this family*),
and Mrs. Alexander, apparently objecting, (*I've given my life to this
family*); she watched as he became belligerent (*You should be ashamed*)
and she grew sarcastic (*Ashamed of having a real job? You think I
don't know what "pastoral care" means? Is that God's love you're giv-
ing to every woman in this town?*), their voices weaving in and out of
the hellish noise on the radio, which had returned to ranting (*THOU
SHALT NOT!*).

Miss Adele strained to separate the sounds into words she might
google later. If only there was an app that translated the arguments of
strangers! A lot of people would buy that app. Hadn't she just been
reading in the *Times* about some woman who had earned eight hundred
grand off such an app—just for having the idea for the app. (And Miss
Adele, who had always considered herself a person of many ideas, really
a very creative person—even if she was fourteen pounds overweight—
a person who happened never to have quite found her medium; a per-
son who, in more recent years, despite her difficulties finding suitable
undergarments, had often wondered whether the new technologies
had caught up with precisely the kind of creative talents she herself had

long possessed, although they had been serially and tragically neglected, first by her parents—who had let shame blind them—and later by her teachers, who were the first to suggest, fatally, that Devin was smarter; and finally in New York, where her gifts had taken second place to her cheekbones and her ass.) You want to know what Miss Adele would do with eight hundred grand? Buy a studio down in Battery Park, and do nothing all day but watch the helicopters fly over the water. Stand at the floor-to-ceiling window, bathed in expensive light, wearing the kind of silk kimono that hides a multitude of sins.

Sweating with effort and anxiety, in her windowless East Village cubicle, Miss Adele got stuck again at her midsection, which had become, somehow, Devin's midsection. Her fingers fumbled with the heavy-duty eyes and hooks. She found she was breathing heavily. ABOMINATION, yelled the radio. *Get it out of my store!* cried the man, in all likelihood. *Have mercy!* pleaded the woman, basically. No matter how she pulled, she simply could not contain herself. So much effort! She was making odd noises, grunts almost.

"Hey, you okay in there?"

"First doesn't work. About to try the second."

"No, don't do that. Wait. Wendy, get in there."

In a second, the girl was in front of her, and as close as anybody had been to Miss Adele's bare body in a long time. Without a word, a little hand reached out for the corset, took hold of one side of it and, with surprising strength, pulled it toward the other end until both sides met. The girl nodded, and this was Miss Adele's cue to hook the thing together while the girl squatted like a weight lifter and took a series of short, fierce breaths. Outside of the curtain, the argument had resumed.

"Breathe," said the girl.

"They always talk to each other like that?" asked Miss Adele.

The girl looked up, uncomprehending.

"Okay now?"

"Sure. Thanks."

The girl left Miss Adele alone to examine her new silhouette. It was as good as it was going to get. She turned to the side and frowned at three days of chest stubble. She pulled her shirt over her head to see the clothed effect from the opposite angle, and in the transition got a fresh view of the husband, still berating Mrs. Alexander, though in a violent whisper. He had tried bellowing over the radio; now he would attempt to tunnel underneath it. Suddenly he looked up at Miss Adele—not as far as her eyes, but tracing, from the neck down, the contours of her body. RIGHTEOUSNESS, cried the radio, RIGHTEOUSNESS AND RAGE! Miss Adele felt like a nail being hammered into the floor. She grabbed the curtain and yanked it shut. She heard the husband end the conversation abruptly—as had been her own father's way—not with reason or persuasion, but with sheer volume. Above the door to the emporium, the little bell rang.

"Molly! So good to see you! How're the kids? I'm just with a customer!" Mrs. Alexander's long pale fingers curled round the hem of the velvet. "May I?"

Miss Adele opened the curtain.

"Oh, it's good! See, you got shape now."

Miss Adele shrugged, dangerously close to tears: "It works."

"Marcus said it would. He can spot a corset size at forty paces, believe me. He's good for that at least. So, if that works, the other will work. Why not take both? Then you don't have to come back for another twenty years! It's a bargain." She turned to shout over her shoulder, "Molly, I'm right with you," and threw open the curtain.

In the store there had appeared a gaggle of children, small and large, and two motherly looking women, who were greeting the husband and being greeted warmly in turn, smiled at, truly welcomed. Miss Adele picked up her enormous coat and began the process of re-weatherizing herself. She observed Mrs. Alexander's husband as he reached over the counter to joke with two young children, ruffling their hair, teasing them, while his wife—whom she watched even more intently—stood smiling over the whole phony operation, as if all that had passed between him and her were nothing at all, some silly wrangle about the accounts or whatnot. Oh, Loretta Young. Whatever you need to tell yourself, honey. Family first! A phrase that sounded, to Miss Adele, so broad, so empty; one of those convenient pits into which folk will throw any and everything they can't deal with alone. A hole for cowards to hide in. Under its cover you could even have your hands round your wife's throat, you could have your terrified little boys cowering in a corner—yet when the bell rings, it's time for iced tea and "Family First!," with all those nice church-going ladies as your audience, and Mama's cakes, and smiles all round. *These are my sons, Devin and Darren.* Two shows a day for seventeen years.

"I'll be with you in one minute, Sarah! It's been so long! And look at these girls! They're really tall now!"

On the radio, music again replaced the voice—strange, rigid, unpleasant music, which seemed to Miss Adele to be entirely constructed

29

from straight lines and corners. Between its boundaries, the vicious game restarted, husband and wife firing quick volleys back and forth, at the end of which he took the radio's old-fashioned dial between his fingers and turned it up. Finally Mrs. Alexander turned from him completely, smiled tightly at Miss Adele, and began packing her corsets back into their boxes.

"Sorry, but am I causing you some kind of issue?" asked Miss Adele, in her most discreet tone of voice. "I mean, between you and your . . ."

"You?" said Mrs. Alexander, and with so innocent a face Miss Adele was tempted to award her the Oscar right then and there, though it was only February. "How do you mean, issue?"

Miss Adele smiled.

"You should be on the stage. You could be my warm-up act."

"Oh, I doubt you need much warming. No, you don't pay me, you pay him." A small child ran by Mrs. Alexander with a pink bra on his head. Without a word she lifted it, folded it in half, and tucked the straps neatly within the cups. "Kids. But you gotta have life. Otherwise the whole thing moves in one direction. You got kids?"

Miss Adele was so surprised, so utterly wrong-footed by this question, she found herself speaking the truth.

"My twin—he has kids. We're identical. I guess I feel like his kids are mine, too."

Mrs. Alexander put her hands on her tiny waist and shook her head.

"Now, that is *fascinating*. You know, I never thought of that before. Genetics is an amazing thing—amazing! If I wasn't in the corset business, I'm telling you, that would have been my line. Better luck next time, right?" She laughed sadly, and looked over at the counter. "He listens to his lectures all day, he's educated. I missed out on all that." She picked up two corsets packed back into their boxes. "Okay, so—are we happy?"

Are *you* happy? Are you really happy, Loretta Young? Would you tell me if you weren't, Loretta Young, the Bishop's Wife? Oh, Loretta Young, Loretta Young! Would you tell anybody?

"Molly, don't say another word—I know exactly what you need. Nice meeting you," said Mrs. Alexander to Miss Adele, over her shoulder, as she took her new customer behind the curtain. "If you go over to my husband, he'll settle up. Have a good day."

Miss Adele approached the counter and placed her corsets upon it. She stared down a teenage girl leaning on the counter to her left, who now, remembering her manners, looked away and closed her mouth.

Miss Adele returned her attention to the side of Mrs. Alexander's husband's head. He picked up the first box. He looked at it as if he'd never seen a corset box before. Slowly he wrote something down in a note pad in front of him. He picked up the second and repeated the procedure, but with even less haste. Then, without looking up, he pushed both boxes to his left, until they reached the hands of the shopgirl, Wendy.

"Forty-six fifty," said Wendy, though she didn't sound very sure. "Um . . . Mr. Alexander—is there discount on Paramount?"

He was in his own world. Wendy let a finger brush the boss's sleeve, and it was hard to tell if it was this—or something else—that caused him to now sit tall in his stool and thump a fist upon the counter, just like Daddy casting out the devil over breakfast, and start right back up shouting at his wife—some form of stinging question—repeated over and over, in that relentless way men have. Miss Adele strained to understand it. Something like: *You happy now?* Or: *Is this what you want?* And underneath, the unmistakable: *Can't you see he's unclean?*

"Hey, you," said Miss Adele, "Yes, you, sir. If I'm so disgusting to you? If I'm so beneath your contempt? Why're you taking my money? Huh? You're going to take my money? *My* money? Then, please: look me in the eye. Do me that favor, okay? Look me in the eye."

Very slowly a pair of profoundly blue eyes rose to meet Miss Adele's own green contacts. The blue was unexpected, like the inner markings of some otherwise unremarkable butterfly, and the black lashes were wet and long and trembling. His voice, too, was the opposite of his wife's, slow and deliberate, as if each word had been weighed against eternity before being chosen for use.

"You are speaking to me?"

"Yes, I'm speaking to you. I'm talking about customer service. Customer service. Ever hear of it? I am your customer. And I don't appreciate being treated like something you picked up on your shoe!"

The husband sighed and rubbed at his left eye.

"I don't understand—I say something to you? My wife, she says something to you?"

Miss Adele shifted her weight to her other hip and very briefly considered a retreat. It did sometimes happen, after all—she knew from experience—that is, when you spent a good amount of time alone—it did sometimes come to pass—when trying to decipher the signals of others—that sometimes you mistook—

"Listen, your wife is friendly—she's civilized, I ain't talking about your wife. I'm talking about *you*. Listening to your . . . whatever the

31

hell that this—your *sermon*—blasting through this store. You may not think I'm godly, brother, and maybe I'm not, but I am in your store with good old-fashioned American money and I ask that you respect that and you respect me."

He began on his other eye, same routine.

"I see," he said, eventually.

"Excuse me?"

"You understand what is being said, on this radio?"

"*What*?"

"You speak this language that you hear on the radio?"

"I don't *need* to speak it to understand it. And why you got it turned up to eleven? I'm a customer—whatever's being said, I don't want to listen to that shit. I don't need a translation—I can hear the *tone*. And don't think I don't see the way you're looking at me. You want to tell your wife about that? When you were peeping at me through that curtain?"

"Now I'm looking at you?"

"Is there a problem?" said Mrs. Alexander. Her head came out from behind the curtain.

"I'm not an idiot, okay?" said Miss Adele.

The husband brought his hands together, somewhere between prayer and exasperation, and shook them at his wife as he spoke to her, over Miss Adele's head, and around her comprehension.

"Hey—talk in English. English! Don't disrespect me! Speak in English!"

"Let me translate for you: I am asking my wife what she did to upset you."

Miss Adele turned and saw Mrs. Alexander, clinging to herself and swaying, less like Loretta now, more like Vivien Leigh swearing on the red earth of Tara.

"I'm not talking about her!"

"Sir, was I not polite and friendly to you? Sir?"

"First up, I ain't no sir—you live in this city, use the right words for the right shit, okay?"

There was Miss Adele's temper, bad as ever. She'd always had it. Even before she was Miss Adele, when she was still little Darren Bailey, it had been a problem. Had a tendency to go off whenever she felt herself on uncertain ground, like a cheap rocket—the kind you could buy back home in the same store you bought a doughnut and a gun.

Short fused and likely to explode in odd, unpredictable directions, hurting innocent bystanders—often women, for some reason. How many women had stood opposite Miss Adele with the exact same look on their faces as Mrs. Alexander wore right now? Starting with her mother and stretching way out to kingdom come. The only Judgment Day that had ever made sense to Miss Adele was the one where all the hurt and disappointed ladies form a line—a chorus line of hurt feelings—and one by one give you your pedigree, over and over, for all eternity.

"Was I rude to you?" asked Mrs. Alexander, the color rising in her face, "No, I was not. I live, I let live."

Miss Adele looked around at her audience. Everybody in the store had stopped what they were doing and fallen silent.

"I'm not talking to you. I'm trying to talk to this gentleman here. Could you turn off that radio so I can talk to you, please?"

"Okay," he said, "so maybe you leave now."

"Second of all," said Miss Adele, counting it out on her hand, though there was nothing to follow in the list, "contrary to appearances, and just as a point of information, I am not an Islamic person? I mean, I get it. Pale, long nose. But no. So you can hate me, fine—but you should know who you're hating and hate me for the right reasons. Because right now? You're hating in the wrong direction—you and your radio are wasting your hate. If you want to hate me, file it under N-word. As in African American. Yeah."

The husband frowned and held his beard in his hand.

"You are a very confused person. I don't care what you are. All such conversations are very boring to me, in fact."

"Oh, I'm *boring* you?"

"Honestly, yes. And you are also being rude. So now I ask politely: leave, please."

"Baby, I am out that door, believe me. But I am not leaving without my motherfucking corset."

The husband slipped off his stool, finally, and stood up.

"You leave now, please."

"Now, who's gonna make me? 'Cause you can't touch me, right? That's one of your laws, right? I'm unclean, right? So who's gonna touch me? Miss Tiny Exploited Migrant Worker over here?"

"Hey, I'm international student! NYU!"

Et tu, Wendy? Miss Adele looked sadly at her would-be ally. Wendy was a whole foot taller now, thanks to the stepladder, and she was using the opportunity to point a finger in Miss Adele's face. Miss Adele was tired to death.

"Just give me my damn corset."

"Sir, I'm sorry but you really have to leave now," said Mrs. Alexander, walking towards Miss Adele, her elegant arms wrapped around her itty-bitty waist. "There are minors in here, and your language is not appropriate."

"Y'all call me 'sir' one more time," said Adele, speaking to Mrs. Alexander, but still looking at the husband, "I'm gonna throw that radio right out that fucking window. And don't you be thinking I'm an anti-Semite or some shit . . ." Miss Adele faded. She had the out-of-body sense that she was watching herself on the big screen, at one of those screenings she used to attend, with the beloved boy, long dead, who'd adored shouting at the screen, back when young people still went to see old movies in a cinema. Oh, if that boy were alive! If he could see Miss Adele up on that screen right now! Wouldn't he be shouting at her performance— wouldn't he groan and cover his eyes! The way he had at Joan and Bette and Barbara, as they made their terrible life choices, all of them unalterable, no matter how loudly you shouted.

"It's a question," stated Miss Adele, "of simple politeness. Po-liteness."

The husband shook his shaggy head and laughed, softly.

"See, you're trying to act like I'm crazy, but from the moment I stepped up in here, you been trying to make me feel like you don't want someone like me up in here—why you even denying it? You can't even look at me now! I know you hate black people. I know you hate homosexual people. You think I don't know that? I can look at you and know that."

"But you're wrong!" cried the wife.

"No, Eleanor, maybe she's a divinity," said the husband, putting out a hand to stop the wife continuing, "maybe she sees into the hearts of men."

"You know what? It's obvious this lady can't speak for herself when you're around. I don't even want to talk about this another second. My money's on the counter. This is twenty-first-century New York. This is America. And I've paid for my goods. Give me my goods."

"Take your money and leave. I ask you politely. Before I call the police."

"I'm sure he'll go peacefully," predicted Mrs. Alexander, tearing the nail of her index finger between her teeth, but, instead, one more thing went wrong in Miss Adele's mind, and she grabbed that corset right out of Mrs. Alexander's husband's hands, kicked the door of Clinton Corset Emporium wide open, and high-tailed it down the freezing street, slipped on some ice and went down pretty much face first. After which, well, she had some regrets, sure, but there wasn't much else to do at that point but pick herself up and run, with a big, bleeding dramatic graze all along her left cheek, wig askew, surely looking to everyone she passed exactly like some Bellevue psychotic, a hot crazy mess, an old-school deviant from the fabled city of the past—except, every soul on these streets was a stranger to Miss Adele. They didn't have the context, didn't know a damn thing about where she was coming from, nor that she'd paid for her goods in full, in dirty green American dollars, and was only taking what was rightfully hers.

Nominated by The Paris Review

SINGER

by MAXINE SCATES

from CAVE WALL

They listen to something they can't hear
until they open their mouths, skinny whistler
in a tuneless childhood where every scrape, every
skinned knee, every door slammed
on a spilled or misbegotten dream leans toward us
cloaked in smoky bar light or circled in stage light,
Amália Rodrigues singing the losses of Fado
in a language we don't understand
but can because no one was happy there
and neither were we. They tell us what we
want to know and what we don't, static popping,
Bessie Smith singing to Clara Smith singing
it back, *We don't know why we are here.* They're
not asking why, they're just saying that's how it is,
earth turning, their voices spinning a thread
through the galaxy, life going on, every stray dog
howling at the moon. If they live long enough,
if the car doesn't crash on a Mississippi backroad,
if Garland's last pill isn't one pill too many,
their voices thicken, their vocal cords scar
with the notes they keep reaching for because they know
we've been waiting, listening without knowing
why we were listening until we heard them,
our sirens, our chorus, their voices heard
for the first time in the honied voice

of someone we knew, the shot thrown back
at the kitchen table, the lipstick on the rim of the glass,
the first voice that told us sorrow was a well so deep
we'd never hear the rock hitting water, that song,
their song, never a song of ships so much as someone
going away, a lament, never a song sung around fires,
the one that keeps telling the endless march to victory,
but the other song, Hecuba's wail, the song of junked cars
and roofs tarped against rain, song of the broken branch
we gave them, its fragrant blossoms, asking
please sing why it's broken, sing why we broke it,
why do these blossoms fade?

Nominated by Brigit Pegeen Kelly and Cave Wall

VISION

by TIFFANY BRIERE

from TIN HOUSE

1.

For three nights, my mother hasn't slept. Since her cousin died, his spirit has visited her each night, for hours at a time. He appears from the waist up on the north wall of her bedroom, facing her directly, blinking but not speaking. He doesn't frighten her; on the contrary, she hopes that one of these nights he will claim her, escort her to the other side, where he now resides. She prepares me for this possibility.

My mother suffers from more than one autoimmune disease. The pain—which plagues her joints and shoots throughout her back and legs—has outwitted medical intervention. When I hold her hand (its appearance is that of a claw, palm curled inward, digits at odd angles, the whole hand functioning as a single unit) I feel clusters of marbles all along her knuckles. To hold her hand is to let it rest in mine as I rub my thumb across her paper-thin skin. Her back painfully hunched, she walks only to get from one chair to another, her legs giving in to spasms.

We share an apartment, and on the morning after the third visitation, I make her a cup of tea, strong and sweet. I find her sitting up in bed, more distracted and distant than usual. When I hand her the tea, she looks at me with the kind of adoring expression you give a child who has done something unexpected and delightful. I bring my daughter into the room, and for the rest of the day, we engage my mother with nursery rhymes, picture books, and puzzles.

In the evening, my husband returns from work at the pharmaceutical company where he is a biologist. He brings my mother another cup of tea, chamomile, then sprawls across her bed to ask about her day.

No one has ever spoken to my husband about visions or the ubiquity of the dead. He is of German descent, not West Indian, but over time he's learned that this intimacy with the dead—for him, unimaginable and unreal—is woven into the fabric of my family. He's a scientist for a reason, drawn to black-and-white explanations of the world. But there, in my mother's bed, he holds her hand, willing to consider all things possible.

2.

I'm an undergraduate conducting research in a neurophysiology lab. We study diabetes and epilepsy in rodents, diseases we induce with drugs that kill off the pancreas and alter the brain's chemistry.

On this day, I'm decapitating rats. "Rapid decap" is the preferred method. I use a rudimentary guillotine. I position the rat with one hand and bring down the angled blade with the other. The rats protest little. By this point they are obese and lethargic, side effects of the drugs. Their tails are thick and limp. They are soaked in their own urine, and the sugar they leak fills the small procedure room with a sweet, clingy odor. When the blade returns to its resting place, there is a satisfactory click that I feel rather than hear. I move quickly to isolate the brain and preserve its tissue. This is done with forceps, a process of removing skin and skull to expose the chestnut-like organ within. I discard the bodies in a red biohazard bag. Still innervated with electrical impulse, the bodies twitch, causing the bag to shape-shift, to crackle intermittently.

I'm not alone. There is a graduate student helping me, and if not for his presence, I may faint. I'm not cut out for this work, but this realization is years down the road. Now, I'm the sole undergrad in a lab full of grad students, and I have something to prove.

The grad student is a muscular redhead with the neck of a football player and hazel eyes. He teaches the practical section of the physiology course I'm taking and a group of us girls comments on his appearance: his long, curly hair tied down with a bandanna; his wholesome overalls; his rugged, midwestern good looks. The other girls are jealous of the long hours the grad student and I spend alone in the lab, the longer hours we spend at bars and on golf courses.

I'm isolating a brain, facing away from the grad student, when I feel a hand on my back. Fingers graze my skin, a firm palm presses against my shoulder blade. I take a deep breath and close my eyes, savoring the seconds that compromise the integrity of the organ I'm harvesting.

I've anticipated this moment: the grad student and I acting on—in the midst of this gruesome study—our attraction for each other. He has seen me struggling with the day's work, and this hand on my back is a release. When I turn around, I'm ready for whatever he has in mind.

But he's across the room. And it's clear from his posture, the way he's settled in his chair, that he hasn't been on his feet for some time. The hand on my back remains a moment longer before setting me free. It will visit me again at dawn on the day of my wedding and at one astonishing moment on the morning I give birth.

What does the hand hope to show me? That is always the question. My unlikely career path? My growing anxiety over its moral implications? The grotesque nature of the work I do?

Or perhaps it hopes to reassure me, to gesture to this grad student—this gentle, enthusiastic man—whom, sooner than I could ever imagine, I will wed.

3.

My parents don't save photographs. There are very few from their childhoods—my father's in Guyana, my mother's in Jamaica. They don't believe, as I do, in the value of mementos. What they have, what they cling to, are stories that always begin with the words *Back home.*

Three of my grandparents die before I'm born. The fourth, my maternal grandmother, at the end of her life, is locked away in religion. By the time I meet her, she is residing in the Jamaican countryside, at my uncle's house, and I am permitted to speak to her through a gate and only for a few minutes. A few years later, she too passes away.

I've been raised with the belief that the deceased are always with us, that their presence can be felt. Through stories, I have come to know my ancestors. In my dreams, they are very much alive. There are many guiding forces in life, many ways, genetic and otherwise, in which the past adheres to the present.

My paternal grandmother had a tattoo on her right arm, a mark placed on indentured servants who were shipped from India to work the sugarcane fields in Guyana. The tattoo was her name in Hindi. To me she is a mystery, a black-and-white photograph that I had to borrow from an aunt. My grandmother was "coolie," as the Guyanese say, East Indian. She wore saris and bangles and parted her hair down the middle to sweep it back in a low bun. I have her eyes.

Now when I see my own arm, the tattoo that on my eighteenth birthday marked my freedom, I think only of the tattoo that marked her servitude. Through this ink, I feel the connectivity of flesh.

4.

I'm a child, impressionable, and my mother's explanations of the world are bigger than skyscrapers and dinosaurs. She says that our ancestors are always with us, that our dead relatives inhabit our lives. They are disappointed when I misbehave, pleased when I'm obedient. I can speak to them, aloud or silently, and they will hear me. Eternity, she says, is fluid.

I'm haunted by her words, never quite able to behave naturally because of this omniscient audience. My mother says I shouldn't feel disconnected from the dead but, rather, bound to them. She says the fabric of humanity is ancient and unfathomable. She says life is infinite and eternal. She says when I meet my ancestors, I will recognize their faces and know them by name.

In other words, heaven is family.

5.

I take a secretarial job at a hospital to make money while I'm in college. I'm assigned to the hematology-oncology floor. On heme-onc, patients are given private rooms and have access to services not offered on other floors: aromatherapy, yoga, and massage. Some days a pianist plays in the lounge; other days, a clown goes room to room.

I'm one of the weekend secretaries. I sit at the nurses' station and handle admissions and discharges, relay orders, answer phones, and man the call box. When patients have requests, they press their call button and talk to me through the intercom. When the request is simple, I don't bother the nurses. I bring the pitcher of ice chips, the blanket, or the menu. In their rooms, you're pulled into the patients' worlds—children's drawings and get-well cards, headscarves and earrings, self-help books and classical music.

On heme-onc you see the same patients again and again. A complication—such as a fever, an infection, a spike or drop in blood count—and they're admitted to our floor. The emergency department calls up and lets me know a familiar patient is returning, and I make sure that the room has been cleaned and the television is functional. The family members turn the corner before the stretcher, and you see

41

that their shoulders are heavy with portable radios, books, photographs, and linens from home.

The nurses all want the leukemics. They negotiate over acute and chronic myeloids. They say *my patient* and *my leukemic* and trade assignments as if they are baseball cards. *I'll give you Cunningham for Howard, Chakrabarti for Williams.* They maneuver for the ones who are young and very sick, because everyone loves a fighter.

No one, however, wants the anemics.

The sickle-cell anemics are what the doctors call "frequent flyers." Their multivolume charts are heavy, wrapped tight with thick rubber bands. When their nurses aren't looking, one has sex with her brother-in-law and another sneaks whiskey from a mouthwash bottle. And because I'm young like them and black like them, they let me in on their secrets.

We get a frequent flyer, a thirtysomething sickle-cell patient, admitted with a port-a-cath infection, the result of injecting heroin through the direct line to his heart. He's lost most of his legs—both are amputated above the knee—and he's scheduled to lose more.

He calls the nurses' station and tells me to come. The volume on his television is turned up high, and there are clothes all over the floor. He is jaundiced, but because his skin is dark, I can tell this only from looking at his eyes, which are yellow where they should be white. He's sitting up in bed, basketball shorts covering what's left of his legs. Like my mother, pain transforms him. He tells me he could strangle someone, that he was promised his morphine an hour ago. *C'mon man, c'mon man,* he says. He tells me that I better find his nurse and drag her in here. He's bare-chested and sweaty, and when he pounds his thighs with his fists, he wants to see me jump. He wants to fill the room with the scent and heat of pain, so that it's no longer his alone.

A few hours later, when he's comfortable and feeling more like himself, he shows me a school photo of one of his sons. The backdrop is autumnal and artificial, meant to evoke harvest.

He talks to me about this son and the others, about the sports they play, their report cards, and their talents. His boys, I've been told, haven't inherited his disease.

I don't interrupt him. I don't return to the nurses' station, where the intercom is ringing. I listen quietly as he describes his family, witnessing a different transformation now: from condition to man.

6.

At Yale, genetics becomes my religion. I'm a graduate student, studying kidney disease in lower organisms, namely mice and fish. Ash Wednesday arrives and my forehead is a blank canvas. My father, a devout Catholic, reminds me of the importance of going to mass. My uncle, one of my father's many brothers, is an atheist and a professor. I remember him teasing: *What if your land of milk and honey is right here?*

What attracts me to genetics isn't purely the validation of thought or the process of discovery, but, rather, what it symbolizes. Our genomes contain our complete ancestral history, a record of where we've been. The history of our evolution has been transcribed and it lives in every one of our cells. And perhaps more inspiring than this record are the vast open regions that represent where we, as a species, have yet to go. These regions are wide open, ready to be filled with fortitude and endurance.

Genetics, like storytelling, is a search for core truths, for what informs the human condition. At its best, it tells an artful story, a narrative meant to inspire and enrich our lives. But it also invokes the worst about living: misfortune, pain, and truncation.

The genetic code is a language, written in a four-letter alphabet. I spend hours at the computer, interpreting its narrative. I read in one gene the story of an ancestor, common to both man and fish, an ancestor of the sea from which man descended. I read in another gene our similarity to other unlikely species—fish and dogs, rats and mice— similarities that make them suitable models for studying human disease. I read in a third gene our connection to chimpanzees: beyond both species having nurturing relationships and problem-solving abilities, we share somewhere near 98 percent of the same genetic material. The blueprints that govern us are nearly identical.

And it's this that preoccupies me: the connectivity of all living things, past and present. What is passed on? Is this record all that remains after we're gone, or is there something more?

And can a single narrative—one single truth—encompass all the forces at work in our lives?

7.

On a Tuesday morning, my father goes to work. He arrives, as he always does, on the E train, which has a stop in the concourse beneath his building. He goes up to the trading floor, boots the computers, and heads to his office in the next building.

He is many floors above the city when a loud seismic boom draws people away from their desks and into doorways. He makes his way to a window of his office building and sees that the adjacent building, its twin, is swaying.

He doesn't know what has happened, but thinking only of the chaos and traffic that will ensue, he and a friend ignore the order to stay put and make the decision to leave. Outside he watches an airplane disappear inside a tower of steel. Around him, clusters of people are—as he is—hands-over-mouth transfixed, stunned and silent. He sees bodies fall from the sky, and he and his friend run, until they find themselves on a train and headed off the island.

At home, my father frets over the welfare of the children who were in the building that morning, at the on-site day-care facility. When he finds out that all of them—more than forty infants and toddlers—made it out alive, his body absorbs the news, releasing tension in the small muscles of his neck. He retreats to the den, draws the curtains, and curls up in the loam of quilts and sheets, further blanketed by the glow of the television. Two days later, he has a stroke.

On my wedding day, my father and I are in the back of the limo, waiting for the ceremony to begin. The night before was the first time he'd seen my mother since their divorce. He doted on her all night, bringing her drinks from the hotel bar and whispering in her ear. He is remarried, but when my mother is in the room, no one else exists.

Outside, a storm rages. Wind shakes the limo. My father tells me he's seen the face of God. I ask him to tell me another story. I ask him not to say anything that will make me cry. God's face, he tells me, is round and full of magnificent, soothing light. He says he spoke to God, that he bargained for his life, offering up his service and devotion, his cigarettes and his alcohol, in exchange for the chance to walk me down the aisle. This is the closest he has ever come to expressing his love.

There are forces at work on my father, forces that are slowly exposing his fragile nucleus. Terror, disease, heartbreak. I have seen him lose everything that matters to him, including my mother. I have seen him kiss the dead. I have yet to see him cry.

He made his deal with God after suffering a massive heart attack, years before the towers and the stroke. The night before his open-heart surgery, he spoke of his father, who was fifty-four when he died—same age as my father at the time—from complications during surgery.

The vision came to my father while he was on the operating table. As I sat in the waiting room, I couldn't help but picture him, somewhere beyond the electrified doors, lying there in a cavernous operating theater. I imagined him in his most vulnerable state: his chest cracked wide open, God and steel rebuilding him.

8.

I harvest organs. I'm taught different methods of immobilization. Cervical dislocation—the pinning of a mouse across its shoulder blades followed by a quick yank of its tail—is one I won't try. Ether doesn't require any manipulation of the mouse, but it has been deemed unsafe for researchers. Ketamine is what we use in our lab.

There is a sweet spot in the belly where the needle slides in smoothly, at an angle that doesn't hit an organ and cause the mouse to buck. When the ketamine is successfully administered, the mouse tumbles out of your hand, staggering in the first minutes before falling still on its side or belly, its inhalations sharp and pronounced. When you hit the sweet spot, it's a good omen.

Once the animal is sedated, there is nothing you can't do to it. I study cystic disease, and because the mouse has been engineered, I hope to find cysts on its kidneys and liver. I pin the mouse, belly up, to the Styrofoam board I use for my dissections. With forceps, I pinch the loose skin below the abdomen, pull it up into a tent, and reach for my scissors.

I cut from the groin to the neck, across the shoulders, then hip to hip, so the final product is an incision in the shape of the letter *I*. The body speaks indisputable truths. To examine the workings of a body is to experience the logic, the divine order, of nature. When the flaps of skin are pinned down, you have a window into the animal, its mechanics more intricate, more intelligent—yet cruder and messier, so more difficult to appreciate—than the clean, articulated movements behind the face of a watch.

I perform harvests not surgeries, and at some point during the removal of organs, the mouse will die. I have performed countless harvests alone, but it's much easier when someone stands over your shoulder, someone interested and experienced, his or her excitement contagious, so much so, your nerves masquerade as anticipation. You peel away layers of fat and see what you have, the person beside you—hand on your back—rooting for cysts.

God is taking my mother in pieces.

First her kidneys, now her eyes—her organs are failing her. She loses perspective, colors, and words on the page. It seems to happen over-night: one morning I discover her left eye has drifted off center. I'm suddenly aware of the shape of her eyeball, elliptical and oblong, the distinct pointedness of the pupil. I no longer know how to look her in the eye. I have a choice: stare into the eye that is dying or the one that still has life.

With the loss of her vision, her prayers increase in frequency, and I buy her a large-print Bible in the hopes it will sustain her. She doesn't want anyone operating on her eyes. She says, in the strange and beau-tiful way she has of phrasing things, that she had always thought her eyes would outlive her.

She talks at great length about her childhood and tells stories I've never heard. She misses her parents, her father more so, and when she says that all she wants is to see him again, I can't know for certain which world she'd prefer to see him in.

Several times in my life, a deceased relative has visited me in a dream. I remind my mother of one of these times, of one particular dream:

It's my wedding day. It looks and feels like the wedding day of my memory, except that in this version, there is no turbulent weather; the mansion's French doors are wide open, and long, white drapes billow in the breeze. As I walk from room to room, I'm met by family.

I enter a room, and there, before me, are my maternal grandparents, who died long ago. My grandmother is in a white dress, my grandfather in a white suit and fedora. And though I never met my grandfather, I recognize him. He says: Tell your mother I am proud of her.

Upon waking from this dream, I phoned my mother to relay his mes-sage. As I described the details, she cried. When she was calmer, she told me that it was her father's birthday.

My mother hears the end of this story now as if for the first time. For a short while, she feels the presence of her father, and there is distance between her and her suffering. In the following days, her prayers main-tain their frequency, but now they are inflected with hope.

She decides to fight for her vision. While she prays to retain what's left of her sight, she seeks out doctors who hope to save her eyes with surgery. This is her treatment plan: God and medicine.

10.

On a Saturday afternoon, I'm sitting on the living room floor reading, my daughter napping nearby, when I feel the hand on my back. My husband is behind me on the sofa. But he's not within arm's reach, and the hand remains as I stare upon my husband's face.

When I tell my husband that the hand has visited me again, when I describe again the sensation of the palm and the articulated digits, he listens. He doesn't try to explain it away, to interject with a scientific explanation that would undermine its significance to me. The hand is a gift, a force that solidifies moments, that suggests I pause and take inventory. My husband accepts it for what it is: a piece of the larger narrative of my life. He knows that my understanding of this world comes a sliver at a time, in fragments and not as a whole.

At the opposite end of our apartment, my mother is resting. She's in her bedroom, as she tends to be, behind a closed door. She's able to sleep once again; the spirit of her cousin no longer visits her. There are nights when he comes to her in dreams, but for the most part, he's gone. And though his spirit has never spoken to her, this vision was an answer to her prayers. Someone has heard her call for death and responded: *Soon, soon.*

Nominated by Jaquira Diaz and Inara Verzemnieks

SNOW WHITE

by CHLOE HONUM

from TAB

Queen, you were starlight
obsessing over an empty cradle,
then over the door to the cradle room,
then over the hallway to the door.

I too feel my life is moving backward.
I spend hours recalling
how I reeled, as if from dream
to dream, when you knocked,

how crows swooped and dived
like black fire behind you.
The prince tells me I moan
for you in my sleep—

good star, bad mother, lone tree
in a vast field on which the seasons hang
their sheets, wet and colored
with all the illnesses of beauty.

Nominated by TAB

YELLOW CLAW

by LUCIA PERILLO

from AMERICAN POETRY REVIEW

For weeks a backhoe has been working
where the shore drops into the bay: it claws
then lifts a yellow clawful
of rubble. Other times
the claw's being used as a sledge.

Inside the cab we already know there's a man,
his orange shirt visible
a long way off. The cab swings in circles
but the man never dizzies. We know this
because we never see the claw spazzing out.

How strange a translation is the world
of the mind behind the world!
The sky already darkening,
the man's belly growls, his big fat belly,
and the future he spreads with the claw's rusty teeth,

every hillock and divot, is really mashed potatoes
and gravy, the day's fixation, as he shapes the land,
tamps it in. Someday a bone will be broken here
in the bad dip, layer within the layer
someday to be sifted

and sifted again, though they slip through the mesh.
Photons, neutrinos, the governing waves—
mashed potatoes and gravy:
ever since the doctor forbade it
how he craves the salt.

Nominated by Marianne Boruch and American Poetry Review

TELREF

fiction by EDWARD McPHERSON

from THE GETTYSBURG REVIEW

Sam and Kat, Kat and Sam, as unassuming as their three-letter names but, to their minds, violent with potential. In the spring of 1998, they met in St. Louis, when they both had to board a bigger bus. Two kids in zipped pullovers smoking and picking at their fingers as they watched the driver fling their bags into the belly of the coach as if they weren't their only belongings in the world. Sam stretched his legs across two seats; when Kat came down the aisle, he dropped his feet and said, "Been saving a seat." Both were eastbound, heading away from somewhere they didn't talk about. Tulsa and Topeka—what was there to say? They weren't New York City. As the now dank and belchy bus crawled out of the Lincoln Tunnel and wound the ramp into Port Authority, after twenty-three hours and fifty-five minutes of ragged conversation, Kat finally got up the nerve to say, "You know, I'm a good kid from a bad home. I've got no place to crash." Sam handed her his last piece of gum and said, "Me neither." He cocked his head at a sign that read, "To all points," with an arrow pointing up. "Welcome to Xanadu," he said.

Both had a few years of college and a little cash in their bags. They knew no one (no friends, no relatives, no couches to surf), but they found a hostel in Hell's Kitchen, then a place in Bed-Stuy, where— despite two broken windows and a split lip for Sam the first week— they'd somehow stuck it out for three years. They soon discovered other people, but theirs was first love, and Kat had always been told, "Dance with the guy who brought you."

She could scrub up and immediately found work waitressing at a hip hotel where her tattoos were appreciated. The city would always have room for another pretty face. She was most at home singing bar karaoke with her friends. Sam never went with her; he knew old songs were dangerous, yanking heartstrings that no longer served any purpose. For as long as he could remember, he had been moody, reserved, but deep down he just wanted things solved, boxed in, put away, dealt with—he had little patience for problems or issues that lingered.

At first Kat's outbursts startled him, like sudden summer lightning. Things would be fine, and then one day she'd be beating his chest: "You can't stay out all night without calling!" She would twist her head back at an impossible angle, as if she meant to break it. "Three years—what are we doing?" Sam's heart would race, and he'd glance around the kitchen like he'd been caught by a pop quiz. His only thought would be to get her to stop crying. He'd say, "We're happy, baby. You and me. That's all we need." One night she grew quiet and said, "I feel like an empty trashcan," and he'd tried to gather her in his arms, but she slipped away. "You're broken," she said through the closed bedroom door. "You were born a gene short, and that makes your heart two fucking degrees colder than most." Outside the kitchen window, something small and airy threw its body against the glass.

Still, he carefully cataloged the little barbs that pricked him from waking until night, the missed trains, jammed umbrellas, and hidden potholes in the street, the minor setbacks that gathered like nettles to give his unhappiness weight. He read voraciously and complained about everything. Did she know Helen Keller wore brilliant blue prosthetic eyes after becoming a celebrity—actually had her true ones plucked out, because one was disfigured? Or had Kat seen the recent report on the Gowanus Canal, which now contained trace amounts of gonorrhea? He knew his fits were stupid and small, but still it bothered him that Kat left dishes in the sink and lost change in the bed. He was constantly surprised by how she could wound him in places he thought were shut off, inaccessible to the public, like those graffiti tags deep in the subway tunnels that always brought him up short—what ghosts left them?

In a bit of dumb luck, Sam had found the perfect job their first month in town. He'd gone down to the vintage clothing store that stuck out on their block like a fruit stand on Mars with the idea he might be able to get a few bucks for his grandfather's old buckle. The guy behind the counter had raised one pierced brow and said, "Hot dog—cowboy chic!" before paying him eighty dollars. That was Duke, and he became their first friend. Duke had a boyfriend named Mehdi whom Sam came to like, though Duke was constantly annoyed that Mehdi wouldn't sleep over more often, and—when he did—Duke said he behaved like a tourist whose luggage had gone missing, borrowing Duke's toothbrush and oversized shirts as if to prove he was game and didn't sweat the small stuff.

Duke lived in a studio off McCarren Park that his father had bought him after he graduated from NYU, one of those hastily converted warehouses filling up with slumming trustafarians like him. Duke chose to open his store in Bed-Stuy because he thought Williamsburg soon would be on the way out. Still, he had connections he could call on when he wanted, like the friend who headed the "Young Lions," the junior philanthropic group that supported the public library. They were, he told Sam, "just a bunch of obnoxious twenty-something socialite dick-farts-in-training," for whom the library threw elaborate costume balls (Hemingway's Cuba! Dante's Disco *Inferno*!), letting them fool around drunkenly behind the stacks in the hopes of one day getting big money. This friend—whom Sam thankfully never met—landed him the job at Telref.

The phone rang, and Sam picked it up. A voice said, "Memorandum, May Day 2001: for nearly seven months, I have been the victim of covert surveillance."

Sam said, "That's not a question," and hung up.

From the next desk, Martin, a large gray-haired man, said, "Another nut job?"

"That's all I get," said Sam. "These days, my line's nothing but a shit storm of crazy."

Martin gave him a funny look. He said, "Hey, doc, it's Friday. You coming to happy hour? Been a while since we've seen your face." Martin was a West African immigrant who had moved to Manhattan and gotten a library science degree before spending two decades working his way up to become head of Telref. He had memorized most of *Paradise Lost* and skated in the roller dance party that roved through Central Park on the weekends. Wandering the Mall one Saturday, Sam had spotted Martin in a spandex singlet grooving in ecstatic slow motion with a glass of water perched on his head. Sam didn't say hi.

Across the room, a girl lowered her phone and covered the receiver. "Hey, guys—what's the rat population in Manhattan?"

Martin and Sam answered in unison: "A shitload."

The girl said into the phone, "A shitload. No, ma'am, that's not a technical term. It's an estimate. What I'm telling you is that no one really knows."

Sam hated that question, one he got all the time. Vermin were political—like crime or bed bugs—and reports tended to ebb and flow with election cycles. Megan would learn that. She was new to Telref, having recently moved from Boston, that city with training wheels, where she'd left behind a longtime boyfriend she said used to make hateful offhand comments and then leave her to stew. She was still getting over the guy. Later that year, she would wake up one night and drive to Boston—and him—leaving Sam and Martin to joke about "disaster sex," "catastrophe couples," and "apocalyptic bootie calls." Still, she never came back.

Megan hung up the phone. "Thanks, boys," she said and blew them an air kiss. That morning, like most mornings, Megan had asked Sam, "Honey, do you need to talk?" Meanwhile Martin had taken one look and said, "Get off the cross, doc. We need the wood." Martin was a true believer.

At first they had teased Megan, the newcomer, telling her they had in their possession a secret set of encyclopedias compiled long ago just for them, an alternate history of the world that the upstairs librarians knew nothing about. She would have to prove herself worthy to see it. Sam had read Borges. Of course. He worked in a library; they all had read Borges. Megan caught on when she realized all Sam and Martin did away from their desks was play honeymoon bridge or flick around tiny paper footballs.

The Telephone Reference Service was established by the New York Public Library in 1968, back when a dedicated call center seemed cutting edge and most of the inquiries came from secretaries trying to sound out a word their boss had used in dictation. Through the years, the number remained the last-ditch resource for fact-checkers, journalists, recluses, writers, perverts, and lunatics, their own personal oracle available five days a week, nine hours a day, just dial ASK-NYPL. Lately, of course, the department had been shrinking; you no longer had to be a trained librarian, just a warm body with time on your hands and modest powers of research. The real librarians looked down on them as glorified receptionists. Still, even with the Internet, Sam fielded about a hundred calls a day. Most were lame: Who killed Kennedy? Where is Jimmy Hoffa? What's my wife's birthday? And so there had to be rules: no medical advice, crossword clues, interpretation of dreams, or helping with homework. Recently, management had instituted a "no philo-sophical speculation" rule, but that one was largely ignored. His first day, Sam had heard Martin laugh and say, "God's grace? Sure it exists. It's what allows me to handle people like you."

Sitting in their cramped office off the main floor, the operators had five minutes to dedicate to each question, which was meant to rein in the researchers more than the callers. Sam would have been happy to lose an afternoon tracking down a rare Bolivian mushroom, or the number of manholes in Cleveland, or where Lady Di had bought her bras. The callers wanted answers, pure and simple; Sam's job was to cut through the dross. If he couldn't settle the request, he had to pass on the name of someone who could. Five minutes and on to the next. Question, answer, question, answer—the hours passed quickly.

Every morning Sam walked up Fifth Avenue to mount the sweeping steps of the main branch, flanked by the twin marble lions, Patience and Fortitude, which he first recognized from *Ghostbusters*. He worked in a mausoleum, the collected bones of Astor, of Lenox, of Carnegie. It fit his sense of living late in his time in a city where everything even-tually was plowed under to make room for everything else. In a degen-erate culture, nothing could be done to fuck things up further. They were all pretty much off the hook.

Still, Sam appreciated, even felt somewhat entitled to, the library's grandeur: the illuminated ceiling in the gilded reading room (fifty-two feet up and the size of a football field—a question they got all the time), the burnished pneumatic tubes swishing call slips through the eight floors of dark, dusty stacks stretching below Bryant Park, and the men's room urinals so grand—massive marble blocks big as beds—that it was like pissing on a Cadillac.

And—against all odds—he truly loved his job. At the end of the day, he would bring facts to Kat like a rat collecting shiny spoons for the nest. Did she know that—in proportion to its body—the hummingbird had the largest brain in the animal kingdom? That the city's power lines could circle the globe four times? She would shoot back ones he thought she made up: "Or that fifty-seven percent of men change their sheets before the first date?"

Their weekends were quiet and lazy—they found thrills on the cheap—but after reading an article on human photosynthesis, Kat began insist-ing they leave the apartment more often. She cited stale air, poor

55

vitamin D, and a case of the "winter blues." And so it was on a first Saturday in June that Sam found himself at the counter of a neighborhood diner. The place was packed. They squeezed into their seats and ordered the breakfast special. They sat in silence until the food came. Sam closed his eyes and kneaded his temples; his head was splitting. Then he looked up. "You loved him," he hissed out of the blue. It was a longstanding game: whispering lines from old film noirs just loud enough for other patrons to hear.

"No, I hated him," Kat said. The words sent a crackling of urgency across plastic plates of cold eggs.

"You loved him, you hated him—and now we're stuck good." Sam took a sip of coffee. "What's done is done, baby, and it's got to be straight down the line."

"You don't trust me?" Kat waved the waiter away.

Sam buttered his last triangle of toast. "You've never had your face on straight—not one day in your life."

Kat put down her fork. "You're one to talk, mister. You waltzed home pretty late last night."

Sam looked up. She was off script. He said, "What's it to you?"

"I'll kill her," Kat said. "Clean and simple—a morgue job. If they even find the body."

"Don't talk crazy," he said and reached for the check.

"I love you, too, dummy. We're on this trolley together, remember. Next stop: the grave."

Sam plunked down a tip, and they made a wordless exit.

When they first moved into their building, the downstairs door was broken, but the inner one seemed like it would hold firm for a while. There was a rumor that two winters ago some junkie had OD'd in the vestibule. Sam and Kat weren't sure what to believe, though it was clear that someone was peeing in the recycling. Up four flights of chipped tile steps that sloped dangerously down—"drunk-proof stairs," they called them—was a brown door with a shattered peephole that led to their tiny apartment, with its noisy radiator they had no control over and a bathroom so narrow they had to brush their teeth standing in the tub. Upstairs, a fearless six-four giant—who surprisingly worked underground as a sandhog—bent the floor nightly as he carried his dishes from his TV tray to the sink. They didn't have a TV, but on summer weekends they listened to the boy across the alley announce pro-wrestling matches in his room. Down the block was a playground with a few old pieces of equipment with a vague nautical theme and a faded mural dedicating the park "to fish and children and all things that need water."

They knew the city broke people like them every day. Almost immediately Sam had his Discman jacked, and one evening, while closing up the shop, Duke was attacked by kids he had watched only years before swing on the playground, kids who called him a faggot while beating him with a board with nails driven through it. They didn't even bother to rob him. When Sam came by the hospital a few days later, the bruises ran thick and ropey beneath Duke's skin, making his face look like a watermelon. The neighborhood was appalled, the kids went to juvie, and Duke started walking the long way to work.

The first fall they arrived, they told and retold the story of the young cousin of Kat's coworker, Maureen, until it finally came back to them slightly disfigured but essentially still true months later at a bar. The girl, whose name they never remembered, was new in town and nervous to be making her first trip alone on the subway. But job interviews were hard to come by, and Maureen told her not to be silly—nothing ever happened at rush hour. And so the girl printed her resume, put on brave lipstick and heels, and boarded the train into Manhattan. All was fine until the doors opened on her stop, and she found the platform blocked by a bum's upended bare ass, which was gloriously growing an enormous shit tail. The next day the girl went back to wherever she came from.

Another weekend and Sam and Kat were sitting in a bar that had archery. The room was below street level and black with smoke; the booths smelled sweet, either from whiskey or piss. Sam and Kat's conversation was punctuated by the rhythmic *thwack* of arrows burrowing into something.

"A little dark for target practice," Kat said. "How can you hit what you can't see?"

Sam said, "It's the other way around—what you hit is what you get."

Kat put down her drink. "I'm nervous to get up and go to the bathroom. I can see the headline: 'Talented, Unwed Girl Taken Out in the Crossfire.' "

Sam laughed. "Oldest story there is."

Kat said, "You know I won't always be sitting here."

Sam said, "I know—you're going to the bathroom." He turned to the door. A low, ugly man walked in carrying a crossbow. Sam said, "There goes the neighborhood."

Kat said, "You just don't get it, do you? I'm not asking for much, just a little encouragement. It's like I'm the first woman to land on the moon—only to find a sign saying, 'Go back where you came from.' "

Sam transferred at Jay Street from the A train to the F. He was late to work, but by now the others were used to covering for him. Last week, Martin had looked up and said, "Love is like a shark. It must move forward or it dies."

Sam asked, "West Africa?"

"No. Woody Allen."

This morning, Sam had forgotten his book, so he stared at the MTA signs with their black-and-white typeface. (Helvetica, he thought, formerly Standard Medium—same as on the space shuttle.) The train's AC wasn't working; sweat ran down his neck. Next to him sat a wan couple whose kids were climbing over the seats and pressing their tongues to the glass. Unprovoked, one of them let out a bloodcurdling scream. The passengers jumped in unison; Sam smiled, lest anyone think he was judging.

Two pixieish girls got on at York.

"Oh my God, Suzy! What's new?"

"Well, I'm engaged."

"You're shitting me! That was quick. Gimme the story!"

"He's a young thirty-eight and runs a hedge fund in Connecticut. On our first date he took me to Bouley. I drank so much I ended up puking. He must have liked that because he called the next day."

"Wow."

"Yeah. We're getting married at the Botanical Garden in August."

At West Fourth, the car filled with more commuters and transfers. Sam gave up his seat to a woman who was either pregnant or fat. A man got on wearing a string of keys around his neck and a bright button on his jacket that read, "Happy Anniversary! Thirteen Years of Attitude Adjustment." The man didn't move to the middle but stood blocking the door. At the last minute, a woman jumped on and gave him a pretty good bump. They got into it. Thirteen years down the drain.

The conductor opened his cabin door to see what was up, but before he could read the situation, the train came screeching to a halt. Anyone not holding onto a pole ended up in someone's lap. The air smelled like metallic brake dust. A voice erupted from the squawk box, "Twelve nine! Twelve nine!" and the conductor, a pale, rangy guy with a slight lisp, said, "Aww, fuck-fuck-shit."

Sam asked, "What's going on?"

The conductor said, "Twelve nine. Body under train."

The pixies gasped. Mr. Attitude Adjustment looked confused, as if he'd been upstaged.

"A jumper," the conductor said. "Folks, we won't be going anywhere for a while."

A man in a tan suit said to no one, "I've lived in this city forty-one years and of all the goddamn days."

The conductor wiped his nose on his sleeve and said, "I see this four to five times a week. You just don't hear about it because we got a PR department. Don't want to give people ideas. Jumping's messy—but efficient."

Ten minutes later, the passengers filed through the front car, which was halfway into the station. People on the platform were quietly retelling what happened, either to each other or to the cops and paramedics standing idly by. Flashlights crisscrossed beneath the wheels of the train. Sam heard a little girl say, "She flung out her arms like she was doing jumping jacks."

"Explain it to me again," Kat said. It was past noon, and they were still goofing around in bed.

He looked at her and the lock of dark hair that fell over her face. He had always loved her brown eyes. He said, "There are facts, and then there are *facts*, and then there are FACTS."

"Like what?" She brushed her hair back.

"Okay. First level: unimportant facts. You might say 'trivia.' "

Kat said, "Oh, I would never."

Sam smiled. "Well, they're lightweights. Cool, but so what? So butterflies can see yellow, red, and green; so the ballpoint pen first sold for $12 in 1945; so cows can go up stairs but not down; so the most popular name for a boat is *Obsession*; so you can't kill a mouse in Cleveland without a hunting license; so the first toilet shown on TV appeared in *Leave It to Beaver*."

Kat said, "Got it, got it. Continue, professor."

Sam said, "Second level. A little weightier. The stuff of science teachers, lifeguards, and all solid citizens. Might even save your life one day.

When taken intravenously, nutmeg is a poison. To kill germs, you should wash your hands as long as it takes to sing 'Happy Birthday.' You can't pump your own gas in New Jersey. The termites of the world outweigh humans ten to one."

Kat said, "Hmm, most useful. Termites of the world, unite!" She made a halfhearted poke at his crotch. "Beware the uprising!"

Sam stifled a laugh. "Third level. Those that might create what they call a sense of moral obligation. In other words, the ones that go bump in the night. The exact names and numbers of the dead. The location of sailors lost at sea. The percentage of children killed by indifference or foul play in any given year. The knowledge that parents don't treasure their children in equal measure, and that even when true, 'I love you' is rarely enough."

Kat groaned. "Oh, brother. That last one came from a commercial."

Sam shook his head. "Billboard. In SoHo."

Kat propped herself up on an elbow. "What I want to know is if you laid all those facts end to end, would they be enough to reach all the way from me to you?"

In the summer, Kat caught the eye of some big shot at the bar, and he offered her a job at Windows on the World. It wasn't like that, she told Sam. More money. Better hours. Breakfast and lunch service with a chance at dinner if everything worked out. "Come on, baby," she said. "I'm headed right to the top!"

On a clear day she could make more than in a month at her old gig. When she first saw the view, she thought she could trace the curve of the globe. She had never before wanted to come to work on the Fourth of July. Cloudy days meant cancellations, but she didn't mind it when things slowed down, and she got to hang around in the back with the rest of the waitstaff, who came from thirty different countries and were already taking bets on next year's World Cup. It was a running joke after the tips were distributed to slap each other high five and say, "God bless America." One day Kat had her picture taken with Hillary Clinton. Her ears popped as she soared 107 floors to the tip of the tower. She told Sam the ride lasted a full sixty seconds. How many restaurants had a gift shop *and* a million dollars in wine?

The captain, Jesús, was supporting a wife and baby girl back in Ecuador. Because Kat reminded him of his little sister, he let her bring home leftover racks of lamb from lunch, which she would stick in the fridge until Sam walked in for dinner. One day, one of the Wall Street execs left one of the girls his number and two tickets to *The Producers*, which she scalped for more than $500 apiece and took anyone who wanted out for all-night drinks in Tribeca. Sam hadn't answered his phone, so Kat hit the town right from work in her smart tailored jacket and shiny brass pin.

At Telref, Megan told Sam, "You know, maybe the greatest compliment we can pay something or someone is to be devastated by them."

Martin looked up from his call and rolled his eyes. Sam ignored them both. The night before the three of them had gone to a poetry reading given by one of Megan's roommates in a bar where everything—ceiling to floor—was painted red after an Eggleston photograph. The reading was for a collection of breakup verse called *Fuck Cupid*. Kat had been working an extra shift and wouldn't be home until late.

It was Sam's first reading, and he'd been appalled by the audience, the way everyone made little grunts of assent from time to time to show that they were on the same special wavelength as the reader. The end brought applause and a vigorous nodding of heads. Sam gave a loud hoot.

Megan leaned over and said, "Behave yourself, mister."

Sam said, "Why? Can anyone tell me what she was talking about up there?"

Megan reached for his hand. "I think her point was that two can be miserable better than one."

Hours after the reading, drunk in a dive bar, Sam watched some fatty with a shaved head and tattooed eyelids wave his fist at the tap. "Gimme another lager," the big guy demanded.

Sam crisply informed him, "That's not a lager—that's an ale."

The skinhead barreled up to him. "Time to go home, mopey motherfucker." Then everything went black. Sam woke up on Megan's couch, rolled over, and threw up in the trashcan. He left Kat a voicemail: "Don't worry. I passed out at Martin's."

On the last day of July, Sam got off work early. The city was laying new fiber-optic cables and had severed some crucial connection to the library. When the lines all went dead, Martin said, "That's our cue," and they snuck out the back, imagining the riot going on upstairs at the public computers.

Sam got off at Utica and was walking up Malcolm X Boulevard when a boy no more than twelve or thirteen peddled by on a bike. The boy cast his eyes back and forth across the street as if he were playing a game of hide-and-seek he was determined not to lose. Sam looked at the boy's bright orange backpack and thought, Shouldn't you be in summer school? But he said nothing, which afterward would seem fortunate to him. A block later he heard a loud popping sound and thought, Firecrackers, even here the kids light firecrackers. But they weren't firecrackers, he realized, when he saw the boy in the bright orange backpack tucked behind the rim of a beat up DeVille taking potshots with a small snubbed handgun at a group of his peers across the street.

The kids sprinted up the avenue, ducking behind a van before returning fire. Afternoon crowds burst apart like startled birds. Sam hit the pavement, putting a parked cab between him and the action. He stretched flat on the ground, his mind strangely blank. The hot concrete close up. The cracks, he thought, who fills those in?

Meanwhile, tiny guerillas had appeared out of nowhere, and now two distinct gangs were scurrying behind cars, winding their way up the wide avenue. In the distance, a siren careened toward them. Sam raised his head and locked eyes with the kid in the backpack, who had not moved from his original position just two cars down from Sam. He had a slight bruise above one eye, and his little-boy lips were set in a thin grim line. Sam had only two thoughts: What I am seeing is not real. And, These kids have seen too many cop shows.

Miraculously, no one was hurt. When the police sped up, lights blaring, the boys scattered down alleys and side streets on their way, Sam imagined, to hide in the park. He got up, brushed off his chest, and calmly walked home. When he was halfway down his block, his legs started to shake.

The city was tearing itself to pieces.

When Kat got home, the apartment was already dark. She crawled into bed.

"Rough day?" she asked.

Sam held her, saying nothing, by the light of the streetlamp.

In mid-August, Kat turned twenty-four, and Sam surprised her with a party just for two. He told her to meet him after work at Martin's apartment. It was the kind of neighborhood where parents sent birthday presents by bike messenger. Kat arrived after her afternoon shift, and Sam led her to the roof. He had made dinner, a simple cold couscous that Martin had coached him on, even going as far as to cover Sam's calls while he went shopping. After inspecting the ingredients, Martin had given him the spare key and said, "Now get going, doc, and make that pretty lady proud. I won't be back before midnight."

Sam had set the teak table and lit some citronella. Money was tight, but at Kat's place sat a pair of packages wrapped in green paper. After dinner, she opened them to find two matching black hoods.

"What are we, ninjas?" she asked.

At the edge of the roof stood a six-pack and a bucket of water balloons. They spent the rest of the hot night launching them at unsuspecting passersby. Drop, watch the bomb fall, then step back into the shadows. If they were lucky, and if they felt the person deserved it, they could get the same victim twice by sneaking over to the next roof and dropping another balloon. Only one person ever saw them, and he shouted bloody murder.

As they clutched each other—sweaty, sudsy, and doubled over with laughter—Sam said, "Forget him. Did you know the average person will make and lose 363 friends in a lifetime?"

Kat smiled and said, "Or that in Iowa it's illegal to make love to a stranger?"

Sam stuck out his hand. "Hi. I'm Sam."

"Tell me something I don't know," Kat said and pulled him down to the still-warm tar of the roof.

The phone rang at Telref. Martin answered, waited for a reply, then put down the receiver. He shrugged. "Wrong number, I guess."

Megan picked up her phone. After a moment, she hung up. She turned to Martin. "Is something going on with the lines? This has happened twice to me this morning."

Martin smiled. "What—you got a heavy breather? Pass them to me. I *love* a heavy breather."

Megan said, "Nope, it's silence and then 'click.' "

Martin tilted back in his chair. "I guess no one's willing to speak up these days."

Sam's phone rang. All eyes turned to him. He picked up. "This is Telref."

A familiar voice said, "I'm looking for answers."

Sam stared down at the pencil on his desk. He tried not to look surprised, but the back of his neck was hot. He felt dumb for not seeing this coming. Their old game—as with all things, she was just taking it to the next, obvious level.

After a minute, he said, "That's what I'm here for. I'm the answer guy."

The voice said, "I've been trying to get through for some time."

Sam said, "Well, our operators are busy. We're in pretty high demand." There was a pause. Then he said, "Please, Miss, what is your question? You only have five minutes—then I have to hang up." He could almost picture her huddled in a whitewashed bathroom stall or ducking down in some dark-paneled phone booth while well-heeled patrons padded by. Did places like that still have phone booths? He didn't know.

She said, "What I want is some information on the progress of love."

"Oh," he said. "You mean the paintings? By Jean-Honoré Fragonard? I think they're hanging in the Frick. I believe the cycle goes: *The Pursuit, The Meeting, Love Letters, Reverie, The Lover Crowned, Love Pursuing a Dove . . .*"

"Yeah, okay. Sure. So how does it end?"

"No one knows the exact order. Perhaps with *Love Triumphant.*"

"Or perhaps not. What about *A Fool for Love*—is that part of the story?"

"Sure—*Love the Jester.* That's in there too. Right next to *Love the Avenger.*"

"How do you know what painting you're looking at?"

"It's quite clear by the context."

There was a long pause. Sam heard her sob twice. Then she said, "Listen, why are we still together?"

Sam couldn't think of what to say.

She was fighting to hold her voice steady. "What I'm asking is, are we just a habit? A product of circumstance? How do you know when it's time to end a good run?"

After a moment, Sam said, "I don't know the answer to that."

"Then who does?"

Sam looked at his watch. "I'm sorry. Your five minutes are up."

That day in September that had started out so clear, Kat woke to find Sam was gone. They'd had a fight the night before: more than three years since Port Authority, and where were they going? What had changed? Everything and nothing.

Kat had stood in the kitchen and banged a pot on the stove.

"Stop it," Sam said. "You're being silly. Don't take it out on the cookware."

Kat was crying. She said, "You didn't used to be mean."

"Are you kidding? That's what we liked about each other."

Kat looked at him. She said, "It was always us against *them*."

Sam threw back his head and regarded the ceiling. "Did you know the average person stays with their bank two years longer than with their romantic partner?"

Kat stopped crying and put down the pot. She stared at the dinner dishes, then looked at Sam sadly. "When did we become average?"

"I'm just saying—do you realize the odds of us having already lasted this long? That means something. That's nothing to sneeze at."

Kat said, "What makes you happy?"

"You, me, my job."

"Really? The way things are?"

"Yes, the way things are makes me happy."

"Is that a fact?"

Sam smiled. "Yes, that's a fact."

The pot hit the floor. "I am so fucking sick of FACTS!"

Sam said, "What do you want then? Lies?"

Kat said slowly, "I don't care about her; I don't even care about the truth." She slumped in a chair. "All I want is to see an *emotion*."

They went to bed, where they sat still and stubborn in the shadows, neither wanting to be the one who gave in to sleep. In the morning, still angry, Sam hadn't bothered to wake Kat. She had already overslept. Let her miss her shift, he thought, if she can't bother to set an alarm. Days and then years later, he would struggle with the fact that this thoughtlessness was perhaps the greatest act of his life.

Kat woke to the sound of every TV on the block tuned to the same channel and knew something was wrong. She crept upstairs and knocked on a neighbor's door. She stayed there curled up on the couch watching the news until Sam found her that afternoon, having left the library and walked across the bridge into Brooklyn. Eight or nine miles had never felt so far. No cell phones were working that day. He had never seen the streets so wide, so empty of parked cars.

Sweaty, out of breath, he rushed through the door. He said, "Sometimes 'I love you' just isn't enough."

She said, "Billboard. In SoHo."

"So what?" he said. "You know that it's true."

In the days ahead, they would read the accounts, one after another, that appeared in the papers. There was an hour and a half between the impact of the plane and the north tower's collapse. Kat pictured Jesús looking down and seeing flames licking up the side of the building. No one knew about the plane half-buried, half-vaporized seventeen floors below. His nose burned with the chemical smell seeping from the carpet that had started to bubble. Soon smoke turned the room from day into night. There was no word from the Tower Fire Command, which, as they had drilled again and again, was supposed to tell them which exit to use. At that point all four stairwells were already gone. Because of the expensive broadcasting equipment, the door to the roof was permanently sealed shut.

The staff realized first what kind of situation they were in. They rushed to the windows some of them had cleaned only hours before, carefully wiping off the smudges and prints—as they did every morning—but only after first pressing their noses against the glass. Not once had their stomachs gotten used to the sight. Now, in the distance, white boats bobbed like gulls on the Hudson. Someone soaked a thick linen napkin in a pitcher of water and put it over her mouth, inhaling for a brief instant the sharp smell of lemons. Between 8:46 and 10:28, the temperature in the restaurant reached two thousand degrees. Long before then, one of the prep cooks, Roshan, the ace reliever who wasn't even supposed to be on duty that day, heaved a heavy padded chair through one of the plate-glass windows. Everyone was surprised at how easily it broke.

As if a spell was shattered, one of the Wall Street guys leapt out headfirst. No one could bear to look down. Thinking of his baby girl, Jesús took the hand of the accountant, a small-spirited man who had often accused the staff of stealing. Together they stepped out over the abyss, and the air, for a second, caught and cradled them, because how could it not?

That night, after dinner, after news, after seeing the last of their neighbors come home covered in dust, Sam and Kat crawled into bed. They left the window open above them, as if to keep the street company. Kat sobbed, and he hugged her body to his, and they listened to emergency vehicles wail in the distance.

Sam said, "It's getting cold. Want me to close the window?"

Kat said, "I can't sleep. Tell me something, anything."

Sam said, "I can't think of anything. There's nothing to say."

Kat said, "Please."

They watched the curtain billow in the blue night. Beyond, they could make out a few stars.

Sam said, "You know the light that reaches us is already dead."

"That's not exactly comforting."

"But here I am, here you are, here we are—still breathing."

Kat looked at him.

Sam said, "It's going to be okay. You know we're going to make it."

Kat said, "Sure. Straight down the line." She kissed his forehead. Eventually she slept.

Sam thought of the black smoke still raining upon Brooklyn, how it would settle on every roof, park, and pond, collecting in dim corners and on the sills of cracked windows, small specks of dark matter that wouldn't brush off.

He pulled the covers to his chin. Kat shifted and surfaced halfway from sleep. She said into the pillow, "Do you know where we're going?"

Only his heart dared to answer back its own quiet lie.

"Sure, I do," he whispered.

And together they lay there in the dark.

Nominated by E.S. Bumas, Tracy Mayor and Gettysburg Review

SNAPSHOT

by KURT BROWN

from I'VE COME THIS FAR TO SAY HELLO (TIGER BARK PRESS)

Ten men on a postcard   clinging to the cables
of Brooklyn Bridge   they look   *one can't help it*

like insects glued to the struts of some unspeakable web

some things will die with us   memories   words
almost everything will die with us unspoken

it's nearly gone   the sound of waves
pummeling the beach   a seagull's sharp demands

a hundred years   if we had them
won't matter   much less the years we've had

those men   suspended in air   dry leaves
caught in a fence before the wind hauls them away

what do they say   in their best suits
perched nonchalantly above the flames of the East River

what matters is that we have been here at all

waves heave up and burst in bright concussions of foam
seagulls weave above it   slandering

in the distance   flags of smoke that never touch land

why not speak of what we know
instead of dangling   always   above the ineffable

on the opposite side   no address   no message

what matters is that we have been here at all

so they say   but what does the wind say
after the men are gone   blowing through those empty cables

Nominated by Tiger Bark Press

THE AGE OF SKIN

by DUBRAVKA UGRESIC

from SALMAGUNDI

> *Now, for a long while Snow White lay in the coffin and never changed, but looked as if she were asleep, for she was still as white as snow, as red as blood, and her hair was as black as ebony.*
> — *Brothers Grimm, "Snow White and the Seven Dwarfs"*

1.

I always recoil when I hear that withered (yet more rapacious than ever) line about life writing novels. Let's get one thing straight: if life really wrote novels, there wouldn't be any literature. Literature might be on its deathbed, but its pervasive frailty can't be ascribed to any historical victory of life over literature—taking that honor is the destruction so beautifully wrought by those invested in the literary enterprise: publishers with rapacious appetites for money, indolent editors, backscratching critics, unambitious readers, untalented writers with rapacious appetites for fame. As far as the relationship between literature and life goes, this is how things stand: the underlying premise of every literary act is gossip. We all want to know what others are doing, even if it's just what they had for breakfast. Has anything changed in the time of new media? Ah, no, our appetite for gossip has only increased. Reality literature, literature that records the minutest details of one's private life, has today reached its apex. What was once limited to the hagiographies of saints has, over time, evolved into biography, autobiography, and memoir. Once induced, an appetite for gossip is hard to sate. And besides, by now we've all become saints. We sling our skin on hooks, our internal organs on ready display, each of us an exhibit in the window of our own butchery.

2

Like other linguistic communities, the Slavs have a respectable number of phrases connected with skin. One can have thick skin, slip one's skin, drive someone out of their skin, or save one's skin; one can be of flesh and blood beneath the skin, can skin someone alive, or feel something on one's own skin; one can pay like a wolf with its skin (hide), get under somebody's skin, sell one's skin, or be in someone's skin; one can be a wolf in sheep's skin (clothing), pack on the skin (pounds), or else strip to one's bare skin. Skin is something so very intimate, and in terms of intimacy, lords it over metaphors of the heart. While our heart may readily love all of humanity, only our skin loves us.

In Slavic languages one doesn't have two words for the two types of skin that one has in English (skin, leather), German (haut, leder), Dutch (huid, leer), Spanish (piel, cuero), or Italian (pelle, cuoio). Slavs use the same word for the skin that covers one's body and the leather from which shoes are made. Perhaps this absent difference is a question of civilization—or perhaps even explains the poor man's fascination with real leather?

In the second half of the twentieth century, former Yugoslavs traveled to Trieste, in neighboring Italy, for shoes, handbags, and jackets (of real leather, of course). Later they hotfooted it to cheaper Istanbul, hauling leather sartorial goods back to Yugoslav flea markets. The guy with the gold cross and leather jacket was quite the catch. But it wasn't long until cheap imitations dimmed the shine of real leather. The wee men and women in leather jackets took a slide down into the so-called "trash," before leather slipped even further down, into subculture, whence it rose again to become a "czaress," a fetish, a cult.

3

Like all humanistically oriented intellectuals, at the feet of hard science I fall to my knees in genuflection. No one impresses me more than a mathematician, a physicist, an astronomer, or a statistician; unlike the rest of us, they're folk who know their stuff. And so it was when a Croatian newspaper recently ran a story with the curious headline "Countries of fatties like Croatia are a burden on the planet." It turns out that among the heaviest countries in the world, America takes top spot, while Croatia, tucked in behind Kuwait, takes third. Leanest are the African and Asian countries, North Korea first among flyweights. The article cited a new study published in the journal BMC Public Health, which claims that the average earthling weighs 62 kilograms (with the average American earthling hitting the scales at a significantly heavier 80.7 kilograms). Fatness is unevenly distributed: Americans make up only six percent of the world's population, but account for a third of earthlings' excess body mass. Professor Ian Roberts says that today researchers are as worried about the amount of flesh to feed as they are the number of mouths. "Everyone accepts that population growth threatens global environmental sustainability—our study shows that population fatness is also a major threat. Unless we tackle both overpopulation and fatness—our chances are slim," said Professor Roberts. The problem, thus, is body mass—human flesh.

Disciplines such as demography, ecology, medicine, and socioeconomics have all lent their weight to the stigmatization of the fat. With the discovery of the AD-36 virus, modern medicine would have us believe that the fat are contagious. In the wake of her U.S. tour, plus-sized British singer Adele came in for criticism on a regional American TV channel. A fitness instructor, full of the kind of righteous rage fitness instructors specialize in, claimed that Adele was a danger to American society because she was sending little American girls the message that it's OK to be fat. Who knows, maybe sometime in the near future a similar message will declare it open season on the fat, and send some future Adele back to where she had the audacity to let her divine voice first sing—in the ghetto of the poor, who are all fat because they're poor, and poor because they're fat.

4.

In a particular historical moment, men in black leather jackets were capable of anything, it's just that they've since been forgotten. The book called *Lenin's Embalmers* is an unusual testimony to the skin of the famous revolutionary, a symbol of one of the greatest, most fascinating, and certainly most catastrophic social experiments in human history. Ilya Zbarsky was the son of Boris Zbarsky, the Soviet biochemist who (together with a fellow scientist named Vorobyov) embalmed Lenin's corpse. For almost twenty years, Ilya Zbarsky, himself a biochemist, worked in the specialist team at Lenin's mausoleum in Moscow. His account is a fantastic glimpse into the long life of a mummy, and the lives of those employed to preserve it.

The descriptions of saving Lenin's skin are most compelling, as is the pervasive anxiety that it might disintegrate. We can but imagine what the squadron of experts felt when in late March 1924, barely two months after Lenin's first embalming, a specially formed commission asserted that

> [t]he corpse had turned sallow, with more marked discoloration around the eyes, nose, ears and temples. Wrinkles and a purplish stain had appeared over the frontal and parietal lobes of brain. The skin had sunk in over an area roughly a centimeter in diameter, at the place where the skull had been opened to extract the brain. The tip of the nose was covered in dark pigments, and the walls of the nostrils had become paper thin; the eyes were half open and sinking into their sockets; the lips had parted, leaving the teeth clearly visible; brown spots had appeared on the hands, and the fingernails were tinged with blue.

After this catastrophic report, Lenin's lungs, liver, and other internal organs were extracted, and his eyeballs replaced with artificial ones. The interior of the body was cleansed with distilled water and a powerful antiseptic, and then treated with a solution of formalin, potassium acetate, alcohol, glycerin, and chloride. This time around they managed to save Lenin's skin, and with it, their own, although one didn't make it. Among the many unresolved deaths of the era is that of comrade Vorobyov, the pioneer of Soviet embalming. One of the most bizarre details in the book relates to Nadezhda Krupskaya (Lenin's wife), who, visiting the mausoleum in 1938, admitted with a woman's bitterness that Lenin remained as youthful as ever (!), while in the meantime she had visibly aged.

With the end of the Second World War, the team of scientists was bolstered, research conditions improved, and the 1939 team of four was increased to 35 leading scientists, medical historians, anatomists, biochemists, and medical doctors, their research centered on skin structure, subcutaneous cell tissue, and the auto-decomposing factors that cause cell disintegration. Between 1949 and 1995 the Lenin mausoleum internationalized its activities, embalming the bodies of Georgi Dimitrov, Klement Gottwald, Ho Chi Minh, Agostinho Neto, Linden Forbes Burnham, Kim Il-Sung, and the Mongolian dictator Khorloogiin Choibalsan. By the end of the last decade of the previous century

73

these mummies had all been cremated. Stalin, who had lain beside Lenin a full nine years (1953–1961), had gone the same way.

Even with the disintegration of the Soviet Union, the mausoleum team continued its work, but was soon transformed into a high-end undertaker, offering pricey mortuary services to the Russian nouveau riche, for the most part, mafiosi. The same Stalin-era concoction of fluids is used, the same eight liters of "balsam" injected into the dead arteries. The balsam is so effective that the body remains in perfect condition up to a year after burial. Ilya Zbarsky claims that following a balsam injection the dead man's skin miraculously changes from the pale blue hue of a corpse to an ivory white. Today the Lenin mausoleum sells wooden "Made in the USA" coffins, and Russian models crafted from precious crystal. The most popular model is the "Al Capone," a coffin based on a mausoleum staff member's recollection of something he saw in *The Godfather*.

As for Lenin's mummy, Russians have been squabbling over its fate for the past twenty years, the debate over whether the mummy should be buried or kept "alive" reignited on slow news days. Things always seem to hit a deadlock, with only a slim minority ever in favor of one or the other option.

5.

Peter van der Helm, the owner of an Amsterdam tattoo parlor, has figured out a way to monetize the skin of the dead. Around thirty of van der Helm's clients have bequeathed their inked skin to his company "Walls and Skin." In the hope that their skin may one day adorn an art collector's walls, each client has even paid a few hundred euro to be involved in the project. When they die a pathologist will remove the skin bearing a designated tattoo, before sending it on to a laboratory for processing. "Everyone spends their lives in search of immortality and this is a simple way to get a piece of it," said van der Helm. One client, Floris Hirschfeld, who has an image of his deceased mother tattooed on his back, explained his involvement with the rhetorical "people have stuffed animals in their house, so why not skin?" Or as van der Helm himself summed things up, "Vincent van Gogh was a poor man when he died. You and I can't buy a Van Gogh. Tattooing is the people's form of art."

This story appeared in Dutch in the news media sometime in the wake of King Willem-Alexander's address to the Dutch citizenry in mid-September 2013. Television viewers followed the royal coach's traditional journey to the palace, where on the golden thrones of the Ridderzaal sat Willem-Alexander and his wife Máxima, two of the "fleshier" representatives of the European royal houses. The Dutch king announced to his subjects that the welfare state was dead, and was to be replaced with the "society of participation." In this new society, Dutch subjects will assume full responsibility for their futures and need to create their own "social and economic networks." In other words, they need to save their own skins.

6.

Given the plethora of forms and shades coloring the contemporary cultural landscape, differentiating the wood from the trees is no mean feat. But if we look a little more carefully, holding our snippiness about the omnipresence of popular culture in check, we'd have to confess that in this landscape, one stripped of divine hierarchies, human flesh predominates. The human-body-in-danger has long been a staple of popular culture: all kinds of "foreigners" sink their teeth into human skin—aliens, vampires, zombies, cannibals. It's a staple in genre novels, comics, video games, and film, and alongside the more svelte corpus of serious work there is a somewhat different domain within which one can clearly discern a foundation for contemporary human fears. Suzanne Collins's trilogy *The Hunger Games* (an American version of Koushun Takami's novel *Battle Royale*) owes its popularity to its extreme message: if the human subject wishes to survive, he or she must kill another human subject. In a world divided into clones known as "donors" and "normal people," Kazuo Ishiguro's novel *Never Let Me Go* (along with its cinematic adaptation) offers a similar message. The protagonists of the film *The Island* offer yet another iteration, Ewan McGregor and Scarlett Johansson playing "harvestable beings," human clones being prepared for "organ harvesting."

Most people are able to discern their present lived reality in the themes of popular culture, and many also foresee their coming futures. Packaged in a protective religious-philanthropic cellophane, the hunt for human organs is well underway. Out in the field, the borders of the permissible are shifting on a daily basis. Once demarcated by the harvesting of organs from deceased donors, the border has shifted to encompass the culling of organs from living donors and, if survival is at stake, selling one's own. In most cases of organ harvesting, only the donor is (partially) revealed, the recipient remaining concealed. Via their illegal fixers and dealers, the anonymous recipient buys or steals an organ that he or she needs, untroubled by ethical doubts. The borders of the permissible shifted again in the recent case of a Chinese two-year-old found lying in the dust with his corneas removed. Stories about organ theft no longer come from out of space. Today it could be one's next-door neighbor who, for a little cash, might lift a fresh kidney or cornea in easy reach. Medical practice itself is shifting the borders, aiding and abetting the rich in their vampiric bleeding of the poor. Vampirism—by what other name should one call the transfusions of young blood for rejuvenation of the elderly offered at expensive clinics?

Popular culture, which represents a new mythological field, helps its consumers wield an unwieldable reality, to reconcile themselves with it, accept it, register it, avoid it, or possibly even rebel against it—each to his own. As always, popular culture does this incomparably more efficiently than anyone or anything else. Some thirty years on, Hannibal Lecter, the antagonist of Thomas Harris's novel (which owes much of its popularity to Anthony Hopkins's brilliant screen performance) has lost his repugnant hue and gained an almost romantic one. His fellow antagonist, Buffalo Bill, who was besotted with human skin as tailoring fabric, today has his own artistic "followers," Jessica Harrison among them. In her *Handheld* series, Harrison exhibits pieces of furniture that can be held in the palm of one's hand, the pieces as if crafted from real human skin. In her *Skin* project, Shelley Jackson invited participants to permanently tattoo a word of a story she was writing, a kind of reversal of Buffalo Bill's morbid obsession, all in the glorification of an artistic collective—and the glorification of mortal art. Yes, "mortal art." Here we should perhaps remember "moral art," and Balzac's novel *The Magic Skin* (also known as *The Wild Ass's Skin*), in which a piece of shagreen magically fulfils the every wish of its greedy owner. Yet for every wish granted, the skin shrinks, taking a little more of the owner's life with it.

7.

Borders have dissipated: what is art and what is reality, what is the imitation of life and what is life (not to mention the imitation of imitation) is no longer clear. Whatever the case may be, few fates appear more wretched than when our everyday lives play like B-grade horrors.

On a day in February 2014, I was witness to a scene that played out in a Zagreb tram. Zagreb is the capital of Croatia. Croatia is a new member of the European Union and a "burden on planet earth." All in all, it's a tiny country of four and a half million people, with that final half being unemployed.

A fuller-figured woman in late middle age sat slumped in the tram, her clothing somewhat dowdy. Beside her stood a slip of a man, taking her measure with a snarled and twitchy gaze.

"Some folk are living it up, eh . . ." said the man noncommittally, his glare ugly and with ill intent.

"I don't understand . . ." said the woman quietly.

"Some folk are living it up . . ." the man repeated, turning the volume and aggression up.

"I don't understand what you're trying to say . . ." the woman repeated, although from the expression on her face it was clear she knew exactly what the man wanted to say.

"Just saying that some folk are living it up . . ." the man insisted. The woman lowered her head, as if trying to shrink from the inside out.

"I'm fifty kilos, a qualified engineer, and I'm unemployed . . ." the man said, giving the woman a right tongue lashing now, unconcerned as to whether other passengers could hear him.

"It's not my fault. Why don't you talk to the authorities?" the poor woman murmured and stood up to get out.

It was a torturous scene. Fifty kilos of human flesh was attacking ninety kilos of human flesh, convinced that the ninety kilos of flesh couldn't possibly be hungry. And though the woman's age probably made her the embittered man's older sister, or perhaps even his mother, and though I'm sure he'd swear that there was nothing of the sort involved, in his protest the discerning ear would have caught an undertone of sexual inadequacy.

The innocent woman in the tram obviously irritated the man, like an apparition from his deepest subconscious, a banal symbol of his loserdom (the fat are rich, the thin poor). He would have gladly beat her, have gladly snapped her neck, watched her blood flow, gladly wounded that ninety kilos of flesh, twice as heavy as his own, lacerated that hulking body slumped in the seat of the tram, indifferent to his suffering. (It's not my fault. Why don't you talk to the authorities?)

Many postcommunist transitional societies have turned their citizens into zombies. As Dutch king Willem-Alexander put it, in the twenty-first century we await the "society of participation." "Self-management" is probably what linguistically inventive followers of contemporary trends would say. Both "participation" and "self-management" are euphemisms for a message that is as sharp as a scalpel: today, the individual has been reduced to his or her bare skin.

For years a team of experts conscientiously preserved their master-piece, their mummy. For years the most celebrated modern mummy in the world was nourished and protected by this team, and for a time symbolized the belief that a society of liberty, equality, and fraternity was possible. Today, for all of a few hundred euro, tattoo parlors—miniature replicas of Lenin's mausoleum—have their customers believe that their tattooed skin is a work of art deserving of eternity.

Yes, we live in the age of skin. Our age—the corpse to which we are pressed—isn't in the greatest shape. The corpse's skin grows darker, new purple blotches surfacing, the cranium, from which the brain has been extracted, has shattered and taken the skin with it, threatening dark pigment spreading everywhere, the nails turned completely blue. We exhaust ourselves, there is never enough balsam, we cover the dead spots with liquid foundation, and our bodies too. There's an odor spreading everywhere, seeping into our clothes, our hair, our lungs, there's nothing that will get it out. There are so many of us, we're like ants, our number inconceivable, in no state to determine the size of the corpse we serve. Perhaps we should abandon a thankless task; perhaps we've long done our duty. Perhaps it's time to open the door and drag the corpse out into the sun. Perhaps the sunlight will faithfully find its target and light a spark, the corpse bursting into flames of its own accord. Fire, they say, is the most efficient means of disinfection.

TRANSLATED FROM THE CROATIAN BY DAVID WILLIAMS

Nominated by Salmagundi

MUDFEST

by MARIANNE BORUCH

from AMERICAN POETRY REVIEW

Some kid in the class,
a boy usually. Do we have to, Sister?
And the nun once: no. She turned and slowly *no, you don't
have to do anything
but die.*

A room's hush
is a kind of levitation. So the end of a rope frays. So mortality
presses its big thumb into clay early, 6th grade,
St. Eugene's School, mid-century.
It's a mudfest, ever after. Free, yay! is what some heard
howbeit the gasp
primal, a descending, an unthinkable click.

Forget what she'd no doubt been programmed
to say, as postscript, as speaking-of: but we live forever,
don't we, children? in God's sweet light?
She didn't. Too old, too mean, too tired, too smart,
maybe shocked at her own relish, her bit coming hard.
I'm just saying there are
charms on the bracelet from hell.

An ordinary question, the boy's whatever it was, and did we
have to?

He was stunned. I could tell.
And he must have walked home in the falling leaves distracted,
disturbed, pushed off for a time
from the anthill.

As for the other ants, we had our work.
It gleamed like truth is said to, in the dark before us—
grains of edible filth or just
sand and splintered glass. To carry.
Carry it down.

Nominated by David Hernandez, Jane Hirshfield, Mark Irwin,
Donald Revell, Eleanor Wilner

THE BRANCH
WAY OF DOING

fiction by WENDELL BERRY

from THE THREEPENNY REVIEW

Danny Branch is older than Andy Catlett by about two years, which matters to them far less now than when they were young. They are growing old together with many of the same things in mind, many of the same memories. They often are at work together, just the two of them, taking a kind of solace and an ordinary happiness from their profound knowledge by now of each other's ways and of how to do whatever they are doing. They don't talk much. There is little to explain, they both are likely to know the same news, and Danny anyhow, unlike his father, rarely has anything extra to say.

Andy has always known Danny, but he knows that, to somebody who has not long known him, Danny might be something of a surprise. As if by nature, starting with the circumstances of his birth, as if by his birth he had been singled out and set aside, he has never been a conventional man. To Andy he has been not only a much-needed friend, but also, along with Lyda and their children, a subject of enduring interest and of study.

Danny is the son of Kate Helen Branch and Burley Coulter. His family situation was never formalized by a wedding between his parents, who for various and changing reasons lived apart, but were otherwise as loving and faithful until death as if bound by vows. And Danny was as freely owned and acknowledged, and about as attentively cared for and instructed, by Burley as by Kate Helen. "He's my boy," Burley would say to anybody who may have wondered. "He was caught in my trap."

And so Danny grew up, learning by absorption the frugal, elaborate housekeeping of his mother through the Depression and afterward, and grew up also, from the time he could walk, in the tracks of his father, which led to work, to the woods, to the river, sometimes to town. Danny learned as they went along what came from work, what came, more freely, from the river and the woods, what came even from the easy, humorous talk of his father and his friends.

The whole story of Burley Coulter will never be known, let alone told. Maybe more than his son, he would have been a surprise to somebody expecting the modern version of *Homo sapiens*. He loved the talk and laughter of work crews and the loafing places of Port William, but he was known also to disappear from such gatherings to go hunting or fishing alone, sometimes not to be seen by anybody for two or three days. Everybody knew, from testimony here and there, from gossip, that he had been by nature and almost from boyhood a ladies' man. Little girls had dreamed they would grow up and marry him, and evidently a good many bigger girls had had the same idea. But he remained a free man until, as he put it, Kate Helen had put a bit in his mouth and reined him up. But nobody had heard much more than that from Burley himself. He was full of stories, mostly funny, mostly at his own expense, but they never satisfied anybody's curiosity about his love life. He never spoke disrespectfully of a woman. He never spoke of intimacy with a woman. And so Port William speculated and imagined and labored over what it believed to be his story, receiving the testimony of many of its own authorities: "Why, he did! I know damn well he did!" And Burley quietly amused himself by offering no help at all. It is possible, Andy thinks, that Burley was the hero of a work of fiction, of which he was hardly innocent, but a work of fiction nevertheless, composed entirely in the conversation of Port William.

Burley knew the way questions followed him, and he enjoyed the chase, preserving himself unto himself sometimes, like a well-running red fox, by arts of evasion, sometimes by artful semi-truths. Those who thought to catch him were most apt to catch a glimpse as he fled or perhaps flew, a mere shadow on the horizon. When he stood and faced you, therefore, as he did stand and face the people he loved, his candor would be felt as a gift given. But in ordinary conversation with the loafers and bystanders of Port William, he could be elusive.

"Where was you at last night, Burley? I come over to see you, and you wasn't home."

"I stepped out a while."

"Well, I reckon your dogs must've stepped out too. I didn't see no dogs."

"My dogs do step out."

"Reckon you all was stepping out off up Katy's Branch somewhere?"

"A piece farther, I reckon."

"Well, now, where?"

"Well, till full day I didn't altogether exactly know."

"If I couldn't hunt and know where I was, damned if I wouldn't stay home."

"Oh, I knew where I was, but I didn't know where where I was was."

Danny, his father's son and heir in many ways, always has been a more domestic man, and a quieter one, than his father. In 1950, two years after the law allowed him to quit school and he started farming "full time" for himself, he married Lyda, and the two of them moved in with Burley, who had been living in the old house on the Coulter home place alone ever since his mother died.

For seven years Danny and Lyda had no children, and then in the following ten years they had seven: Will, Royal, Coulter, Fount, Reuben, and finally (*"Finally!"* Lyda said) the two girls, Rachel and Rosie. Lyda, who had been Lyda Royal, had grown up in a family of ten children, and she said that the Lord had put her in this world to have some more. Like Danny, she had grown up poor and frugal. "If my daddy shot a hawk that was killing our hens, we ate the hawk."

She was about as tall as Danny, stoutly framed but not fat, a woman of forthright strength and presence whose unwavering countenance made it easy to remember that she was blue-eyed. She and Danny are the best-matched couple, Andy thinks, that he has ever known. That they had picked each other out and become a couple when they were hardly more than children and married before they could vote seems to Andy nothing less than a wonder. He supposes that they must have had, both of them, the gift of precocious self-knowledge, which could only have seemed wondrous to Andy, whose own mind has come clear to him slowly and at the cost of much labor.

For a further wonder, Danny and Lyda seem to have understood from the start that they would have to make a life together that would be determinedly marginal to the modern world and its economy—a realization that only began to come to Andy with the purchase of the Harford place when he was thirty. It was already present in Danny's mind at the age of sixteen, when nearly everybody around Port William was buying a tractor, and he stuck with his team of mules.

Marginality, conscious and deliberate, *principled* marginality, as Andy eventually realized, was an economic practice, informed by something like a moral code, and ultimately something like religion. No Branch of Danny's line ever spoke directly of morality or religion, but their practice, surely for complex reasons, was coherent enough that their ways were known in the Port William neighborhood and beyond by the name of Branch. "That's a Branch way of doing," people would say. Or by way of accusation: "You trying to be some kind of Branch?"

To such judgments—never entirely condemnatory, but leaning rather to caution or doubt or bewilderment, for there was a lot of conventional advice that the Branches did not take—it became almost conventional to add, "They're a good-*looking* family of people." The good looks of Danny and Lyda when they were a young couple became legendary among those who remembered them as they were then. Their children were good-looking—"Of course," people said—and moreover they looked pretty much alike. Danny and Lyda were a good cross.

Their economic life, anyhow, has been coherent enough to have kept the Branch family coherent. By 2004, Branch children and grandchildren are scattered through the Port William neighborhood, as Lyda says, like the sage in sausage. They stick together—whether for fear of Lyda, or because they like each other, or just because they are alike, is a question often asked but never settled. Wherever you find a Branch household you are going to find a lot of food being raised, first to eat and then to sell or give away, also a lot of free provender from the waters and the woods. You are going to find a team, at least, of horses or mules. But there are Branches catering to the demand for heavy pulling horses. Some keep broodmares and sell anything from weanlings to broke farm teams. If a team will work cheaper or better than a tractor, a Branch will use a team. But with a few exceptions in the third generation, they also can fix anything mechanical, and so no Branch has ever owned a new car or truck or farm implement. Their habit is to find something that nobody else wants, or that everybody else has given up on, and then tow or haul it home, fix it, and use it.

As they live at the margin of the industrial economy, they live also at the margin of the land economy. They can't afford even moderately good land, can't even think of it. And so such farms as they have managed to own are small, no better than the steep-sided old Coulter place where Danny and Lyda have lived their married life, no better even than the much abused and neglected Riley Harford place that Andy and Flora Catlett bought in 1964.

The Branch family collectively is an asset to each of its households, and often to their neighbors as well. This may be the surest and the best of the reasons for their success, which is to say their persistence and their modest thriving. When the tobacco program failed, and with it the tobacco economy of the small farmers, and when, with that, the long tradition of work-swapping among neighbors, even acquaintance with neighbors, was petering out, the Branches continued to swap work. They helped each other. When they knew their neighbors needed help, they went and helped their neighbors. If you bought something the Branches had for sale, and they were always likely to have something to sell, or if you hired them, they expected of course to be paid. If, on the contrary, they went to help a neighbor in need, they considered their help a gift, and so they would accept no pay. These transactions would end with a bit of conversation almost invariable, almost a ritual:

"Well, what I owe you?"

"Aw, I'm liable to need help myself sometime."

The old neighborly ways of Port William, dying out rapidly at the start of the third millennium, have survived in Danny and Lyda Branch, and have been passed on to their children. The one boast that Andy ever heard from Danny was that he had worked on all his neighbors' farms and had never taken a cent of money in payment. After his boys grew big enough to work, and he knew of a neighbor in need of help, instead of going himself he would sometimes send a couple of the boys. He would tell them: "If they offer you dinner, you can eat, but don't you come back here with any money."

This uneasiness about money Andy recognizes from much else that he has known of the people of Port William and similar places. Free exchanges of work and other goods they managed easily, but transactions of money among friends and neighbors nearly always involved an embarrassment that they had to alleviate by much delay, much conversation, as if to make the actual handing of cash or a check incidental to a social occasion. It was not, Andy thought, that they agreed with the scripture that "the love of money is the root of all evil," but that from a time even older they held a certain distrust against money itself, or the idea of it, as if a *token* of value were obviously inferior to, obviously worse than, a *thing* of value. And so a man, understanding himself as a neighbor, could not accept money as in any way representative of work or goods given in response to a need.

The Branches, then, would have things to sell. They would work now and then for wages. At convenience or if they had to, they would spend. But their aim, as often as possible, was to have a choice: something they could do or make or find instead of spending money, even of earning it.

Of the source and the reasons for this Branch fastidiousness, Andy is still unsure. For himself, he has finally understood that, however it may be loved for itself, money is only symbolic, only the means of purchasing something that is not money. To live almost entirely, or entirely, by purchase, as many modern people do, is to equate the worth of every actual thing with its price. The symbol thus comes to limit and control the thing it symbolizes, and like a rust or canker finally consumes it. And so buying and selling for money is not simply a matter of numbers and accounting, but is a dark and fearful mystery.

Do the Branches know this? Because he so imperfectly knows it himself, Andy has not known how to ask Danny or Lyda if they know it. He knows only that they, and their children too, seem to be living from some profound motive of good will, even of good cheer, that shows itself mainly in their practice of their kind of economy. The Branches are not much given to explaining.

And so in addition to being included in their friendship, benefiting from it, knowing them well, and loving them in just return, Andy has studied them with endless liking and fascination, feeling always that there is yet more that he needs to know. He believes that the way they live, and the way they are, can be summed up, not explained, by a set of economic principles, things Danny could have told his children but probably never did, or needed to. Andy, anyhow, after many years of observing and pondering, has made a list of instructions that he hears in Danny's voice, whether or not Danny can be supposed ever to have said them:

1 – Be happy with what you've got. Don't be always looking for something better.
2 – Don't buy anything you don't need.
3 – Don't buy what you ought to save. Don't buy what you ought to make.
4 – Unless you absolutely have got to do it, don't buy anything new.
5 – If somebody tries to sell you something to "save labor," look out. If you can work, then work.
6 – If other people want to buy a lot of new stuff and fill up the country with junk, *use* the junk.
7 – Some good things are cheap, even free. Use them first.
8 – Keep watch for what nobody wants. Sort through the leavings.

9 – You might know, or find out, what it is to need help. So help
   people.

Andy heard Danny say only one thing of this kind, but what he said
summed up all the rest.

When he was just old enough to have a driver's license, Reuben,
Danny and Lyda's youngest boy, raised a tobacco crop and spent almost
all he earned from it on a car. It was a used car—Reuben, after all, was
a Branch—but it was a fancy car. Lyda thought the car was intended
to appeal to a certain girl. The girl, it turned out, was more impressed
with another boy's car, so Reuben got only his car for his money, plus,
as his mother told him soon enough, his good luck in losing the girl.
Though all in vain, the car was bright red, and had orange and black
flames painted on its sides, and had a muffler whose mellow tone an-
nounced that Reuben was more rank and ready than he actually was.

Andy and Danny were at work together in Andy's barn when Reuben
arrived in his new-to-him car. He had promised his help, and he was
late. He drove right up to the barn door, where his red and flaming
vehicle could hardly have looked more unexpected. He gunned the
engine, let it gargle to a stop, and got out. Maybe he had already had a
second thought or two, for a touch of sheepishness was showing through
his pride. Danny favored his son with a smile that Reuben was not able
to look away from. Reuben had to stand there, smiling back, while, still
smiling, his father looked him over. When Danny spoke he spoke in a
tone of merriment—the epithet he used seemed almost indulgent—but
his tone was nonetheless an emphasis upon a difference that he clearly
regarded as fundamental: Some people work hard for what they have,
and other people are glad to take it from them easily. What he said
Andy has remembered ever since as a cry of freedom: "Sweetheart, I
told you. And you'll learn. Don't let the sons of bitches get ahold of your
money."

Nominated by The Threepenny Review

ADVERTISING

by JOHN CHALLIS

from BUTCHER'S DOG

All night they have been touching meat,
thrusting trolleys stuffed with cheek,
shoulder, ear and leg, and now the day's
come back to life they're closing
Smithfield market; sewing up the partly
butchered, washing off the blood.

I watch them from my office vantage
as they strip their overalls. I button up
my collar for handshake after handshake,
to present our creative for clients to dissect.

The past lowers like a theatre set.
Axes swing for human heads, the gallows
start their jig, and men sell unwanted wives:
the horseshit is piled high beside meat labelled fresh.

Nominated by Butcher's Dog

SH'KHOL

fiction by COLUM McCANN

from ZOETROPE: ALL-STORY

It was their first Christmas in Galway together, mother and son. The cottage was hidden alongside the Atlantic, blue-windowed, slate-roofed, tucked near a grove of sycamore trees. The branches were bent inland by the wind. White spindrift blew up from the sea, landing softly on the tall hedges in the back garden.

During the day Rebecca could hear the rhythmic approach and fall of the waves against the shore. At night the sounds seemed to double.

Even in the wet chill of the December evenings, she slept with her window open, listening to the roll of the water sweeping up from the low cliffs, rasping over the run of stone walls, toward the house, where it seemed to pause, hover a moment, then break.

On Christmas morning she left his present on the fireplace, by the small tree. Boxed and wrapped and tied with red ribbons. Tomas tore the package open, and it fell in a bundle at his feet. He had no idea what it was at first: he held it by the legs, then the waist, turned it upside down, clutched it dark against his chest.

She reached behind the tree and removed a second package: neoprene boots and a hood. Tomas stripped his shoes and shirt: he was thin, strong, pale. When he tore off his trousers, she glanced away.

The wetsuit was liquid around him: she had bought it two sizes too big so he could grow into it. He spread his arms wide and whirled around the room: she hadn't seen him so happy in months.

She gestured to him that they would go down to the water in a few hours.

Thirteen years old and there was already a whole history written in him. She had adopted him from Vladivostok at the age of six. On her visit to the orphanage, she had seen him crouched beneath a swing set. His hair was blond, his eyes a pellucid blue. Sores on his neck. Long, thin scars on his lower back. His gums soft and bloody. He had been born deaf, but when she called out his name he had turned quickly toward her: a sign, she was sure of it.

Shards of his story would always be a mystery to her: the early years, an ancestry she knew nothing about, a rumor that he'd been born near a rubbish dump. The possible inheritances: mercury, radiation sickness, beatings.

She was aware of what she was getting herself into, but she had been with Alan then. They stayed in a shabby hotel overlooking the Bay of Amur. Days of bribes and panic. Anxious phone calls late in the night. Long hours in the waiting room. A diagnosis of fetal alcohol syndrome gave them pause. Still, they left after six weeks, swinging Tomas between them. On the Aeroflot flight, the boy kept his head on her shoulder. At customs in Dublin, her fingers trembled over the paperwork. The stamp came down when Alan signed. She grabbed Tomas's hand and ran him, laughing, through arrivals: it was her forty-first birthday.

The days were good then: a three-bedroom house in Stepaside, a series of counselors, therapists, speech experts, and even her parents to help them out.

Now, seven years on, she was divorced, living out west, her parents were gone, and her task had doubled. Her savings were stretched. The bills slipped one after the other through the letter box. There were rumors that the special school in Galway might close. Still, she wasn't given to bitterness or loud complaint. She made a living translating from Hebrew to English—wedding vows, business contracts, cultural pamphlets. There was a literary novel or two from a left-wing publisher in Tel Aviv: the pay was derisory, but she liked stepping into that other-ness, and the books were a stay against indifference.

Forty-eight years old and there was still a beauty about her, an olive to her skin, a sloe to her eyes, an aquiline sweep to her nose. Her hair was dark, her body thin and supple. In the small village she fit in well, even if she stood at a sharp angle to the striking blondness of her son. She relished the Gaeltacht, the shifting weather, the hard light, the wind off the Atlantic. Bundled up against the chill, they walked along the pier, amongst the lobster pots and coiled ropes and disintegrating fishing boats. The rain slapped the windows of the shuttered shops. No tourists in winter. In the supermarket the local women often watched them: more than once Rebecca was asked if she was the *bean cabhrach*, a word she liked—the help, the nanny, the midwife.

There was a raw wedge of thrill in her love for him. The presence of the unknown. The journey out of childhood. The step into a future self.

Some days Tomas took her hand, leaned on her shoulder as they drove through the village, beyond the abandoned schoolhouse, past the whitewashed bungalows toward home. She wanted to clasp herself over him, shroud him, absorb whatever came his way. Most of all she wanted to discover what sort of man might emerge from underneath that very pale skin.

Tomas wore the wetsuit all Christmas morning. He lay on the floor, playing video games, his fingers fluid on the console. Over the rim of her reading glasses, Rebecca watched the gray stripe along the sleeve move. It was, she knew, a game she shouldn't allow—tanks, ditches, killings, tracer bullets—but it was a small sacrifice for an hour of quiet.

No rage this Christmas, no battles, no tears.

At noon she gestured for him to get ready: the light would fade early. She had two wetsuits of her own in the bedroom cupboard, but she left them hanging, pulled on running shoes, an anorak, a warm scarf. At the door Tomas threw his duffle coat loose around the neoprene.

—Just a quick dip, she said in Irish.

There was no way of knowing how much of any language Tomas could understand. His signing was rudimentary, but she could tell a thing or two from the carry of his body, the shape of his shoulders, the hold of his mouth. Mostly she divined from his eyes. He was handsome in a roguish way: the eyes themselves were narrow, yes, but agile. He had no other physical symptoms of fetal alcohol, no high brow, no thin lip, no flat philtrum.

They stepped out into a shaft of light so clear and bright it seemed made of bone. Just by the low stone wall, a cloud curtained across and the light dropped gray again. A few stray raindrops stung their faces.

This was what she loved about the west of Ireland: the weather made from cinema. A squall could blow in at any time and moments later the gray would be hunted open with blue.

One of the walls down by the bottom field had been reinforced with metal pipes. It was the worst sort of masonry, against all local tradition, but the wind moved across the mouths of the hollow tubes and pierced the air with a series of accidental whistles.

Tomas ran his hand over the pipes, one by one, adjusting the song of the wall. She was sure his fingers could gauge the vibrations in the metal. Small moments like these, they crept up, joyously sliced her open.

Halfway toward the water, he broke into a Charlie Chaplin walk—feet pointed out, an imaginary walking stick twirling as he bent forward into the gale. He made a whooping sound as he topped a rise and caught sight of the sea. She called at him to wait: it was habit now, even if his back was turned. He remained at the edge of the cliff, walking in place, rotating his wrist. Almost a perfect imitation. Where had he seen Chaplin? Some video game maybe? Some television show? There were times she thought that, despite the doctors, he might still someday crack open the impossible longings she held for him.

At the precipice, above the granite seastack, they paused. The waves hurried to shore. Long scribbles of white. She tapped him on the small of his back where the wetsuit bunched. The neoprene hood framed his face. His blond hair peeked out.

—Stay where it's shallow now. Promise me.

She scooted behind him on her hunkers. The grass was cold on her fingertips. Her feet slid forward in the mud, dropped from the small ledge into the coarse scree below. The rocks were slick with seaweed. A small crab scuttled in a dark pool.

Tomas was already knee-deep in the cove.

—Don't go any farther now, she called.

She had been a swimmer when she was a child, had competed for Dublin and Leinster both. Rows of medals in her childhood bedroom. A championship trophy from Brussels. The rumor of a scholarship to an American university: a rotator cuff injury had cut her short.

She had taught Tomas to swim during the warmth of the summer. He knew the rules. No diving. End to end in the cove. Never get close to the base of the seastack.

Twice he looked as if he were about to round the edge of the dark rock into the deeper water: once when he saw a windsurfer, yet again when a yellow kayak went swiftly by.

She waved her arms: Just no more, love, OK?

He returned to her, fanned the low water with his fingers, splashed it high around her, both arms in a Chaplin motion.

—Stop it, please, said Rebecca softly. You're soaking me.

He splashed her again, turned away, dove under for ten seconds, fourteen, fifteen, eighteen, came up ten yards away, spluttering for air.

—Come on, now. Please. Come in.

Tomas swam toward the seastack, the dark of his feet disappearing into the water. She watched his wetsuit ripple under the surface. A long, sleek shadow.

A flock of seabirds serried over the low waves in a taunt. Her body stiffened. She edged forward again, waited.

I have, she thought, made a terrible mistake.

She threw off her coat and dove in. The cold stunned the length of her, slipped immediately along her skin.

The second she climbed from the water, she realized she had left her phone in the pocket of her jeans. She unclipped the battery, shook the water out.

Tomas lay on the sand, looking up. His blue eyes. His red face. His swollen lips. It had been easy enough to pull him from the cove. He hadn't struggled. She'd swum up behind him, placed her hands gently behind his shoulders, pulled him ashore. He lay there, smiling.

She whipped her wet hair sideways, turned toward the cliff. A surge of relief moved along her spine when she glanced back: he was following her.

The cottage felt so suddenly isolated: the small, blue windows, the bright half-door. He stood in a puddle in the middle of the floor, his lips trembling.

Rebecca put the phone in a bag of rice to soak the moisture, shook the bag. No backup phone. No landline. Christmas Day. Alan, she thought. He hadn't even called. He could have tried earlier. The thought of him in Dublin now, with his new family, their tidy house, their decorations, their dramas. A simple call, it would have been so easy.

—Your father never even phoned, she said as she crossed the room.

She wondered if the words were properly understood, and if they were, did they cut to the core: *your father, d'athair, abba*? What rattled inside? How much could he possibly catch? The experts in Galway said that his comprehension was minimal, but they could never be sure; no one could guess his inner depth.

Rebecca tugged the wetsuit zip and gently peeled back the neoprene. His skin was taut and dimpled. He lay his head on her shoulder. A sound came from him, a soft whimper.

She felt herself loosening, drew him close, the cold of his cheek against her clavicle.

—You just frightened me, love, that's all.

When darkness fell, they sat down to dinner—turkey, potatoes, a plum pudding bought from a small store in Galway. As a child in Dublin, she had grown up with the ancient rituals. She was the first in her family to marry outside the faith, but her parents understood: there were so few Jews left in Ireland, anyway. At times she thought she should rebuild the holiday routines, but little remained except the faint memory of walking the Rathgar Road at sundown, counting the menorahs in the windows. Year by year, the number dwindled.

Halfway through the meal they put on the party hats, pulled apart the paper crackers, unfolded the jokes that came within. A glass of port for her. A fizzy orange drink for him. A box of Quality Street. They lay on the couch together, his cheek on her shoulder, a silence around them.

She cracked the spine on an old blue hardcover. Nadia Mandelstam.

Tomas clicked the remote and picked up the game stick. His fingers flitted over the buttons: the mastery of a pianist. She wondered if the parents had been gifted beyond the drunkenness, if one day they had looked out of high conservatory windows, or painted daring new canvases, or plied themselves in some poetic realm, against all the odds—sentimental, she knew, but worth risking anyway, hope against hope, a faint glimmer in the knit of neurons.

Christmas evening slipped away, gradations of dark outside the window.

At bedtime she read to him in Gaelic from a cycle of ancient Irish mythology. The myths were a sort of music. His eyes fluttered. She waited. His turmoil. His anger. Night rages, the doctors called them.

She smoothed his hair, but Tomas jerked his shoulder and his arm shot out. His elbow caught the side of her chin. She felt for blood. A thin smear of it appeared along her fingers. She touched her teeth with her tongue. They were intact. Nothing too bad. Perhaps a bruise tomorrow. Something else to explain in the village store. *Timpiste beag.* A small accident, don't worry. *Ná bac leis.*

She leaned over him and fixed her arms in a triangle so that he couldn't bash his head off the wall.

Her breath moved the fringe of his hair. His skin was splotchy with small, dark acne. The onset of an early adolescence. What might happen in the years to come, when the will of his body surpassed the strength of her own? How would she hold him down? What discipline would she need, what restraint?

She moved closer to him, and his head dipped and touched the soft of her breast. Within a moment he was thrashing in the sheets again. His eyes opened. He ground his teeth. The look on his face: sometimes she thought the fear edged toward hatred.

She reached underneath the bed for a red hatbox. Inside lay a spongy black leather helmet. She lifted it out. *Kilmacud Crokes Are Magic!* was scrawled in silver marker along the side. Alan had worn it during his hurling days. If Tomas woke and began bashing again, it would protect him.

She lifted his head and slipped it on, tucked back his hair and fastened the latch beneath his chin. Gently, she pried open his mouth and set a piece of fitted foam between his teeth so they wouldn't crack.

Once he had bitten her finger while asleep, and she had given herself two stitches—an old trick she had learned from her mother. There was still a scar on her left forefinger: a small, red scythe.

She fell asleep beside him in the single bed, woke momentarily unsure of where she was: the red digits on the alarm shining.

The phone, Rebecca thought. She must check the phone.

She went to the fridge for a bottle of white wine, stoked her bedroom fire, put Richter on the stereo, settled the pillows, pulled a blanket to her chest, opened the bottle and poured. The wine sounded against the glass, a kindling to sleep.

In the morning Tomas was gone.

She rose sleepily at first, gathered the blanket tight around her neck. A reef of light broke through the bare sycamores. She turned the pillow to the cool side. She was surprised by the time. Nine o'clock. The wine still lay on her breath, the empty green bottle on the bedside table: she felt vaguely adulterous. She listened for movement. No video games, no television. A hard breeze moved through the cottage, an open window perhaps. She rose with the blanket around her. The cold floor stung her bare feet. She keyed the phone alive. It flickered an instant, beeped, fell dead again.

The living room was empty. She pushed open the door of his room, saw the hanging tongue of bedsheet and the helmet on the floor. She dropped the blanket from around her shoulders, checked under the bed, flung open the cupboard.

In the living room, the hook where the wetsuit had hung was empty.

The top half of the front door was still latched. The bottom half swung panicky in the wind. She ducked under, wearing only her nightgown. The grass outside was brittle with frost. The cold seeped between her toes. His name was thrown back to her from among the treetops.

The sleeves of grass slapped hard against her shinbones. The wind played its tune over the pipes. She spied a quick movement at the edge of the cliff—a hunched figure darting down and away, bounding along the cliff. It appeared again, seconds later, as if out of the sea. A ram, the horns curled and sharp. It sped away along the fields, through a gap in the stone wall.

Rebecca glanced down to the cove. No shoes on the rocks. No duffle coat. Nothing. Perhaps he had not come here at all. Good God, the wetsuit. She should never have bought it. Two sizes too big, just to save money.

She ran along the cliff, peered around the seastack. The wind blew fierce. The sea lay silver and black, an ancient, speckled mirror. Who was out there? There must be a coast guard boat. Or an early morning kayaker. A fishing craft of some sort. The wind soughed off the Atlantic. Alan's voice in her head. *You bought him what? A wetsuit? Why, for crying out loud?* How far might he swim? There were nets out there. He might get tangled.

—Tom-as! Tom-as!

Perhaps he might hear her. A ringing in his ears, maybe, a vibration of water to waken his eardrum. She scanned the waves. Snap to. Pull yourself together for fucksake.

She could almost see herself from above as she turned back for the cottage: her nightdress, her bare feet, her hair uncoiled, the wet wind driving against her. No phone, no fucking phone. She would have to get the car. Drive to town. The Gardaí. Where was the station, anyway? Why didn't she know? What neighbors were home? You bought him what? What sort of mother? How much wine did you drink? Fetal alcohol.

The wind bent the grass-blades. She stumbled forward over the low wall, into the garden, a sharp pain ripping through her ankle. At the back of the cottage the trees curtsied. The branches speckled the wall with shadows. The half-door swung on its hinges. She ducked under, into his bedroom again. *Kilmacud Crokes Are Magic!* Still the phone did not work.

At the kitchen counter she keyed the computer alive. The screen flared: Tomas at six in Glendalough, blond hair, red shorts, shirtsleeves flapping as he sauntered through the grass toward the lake. She opened Skype, dialed the only number she knew by heart. Alan answered on the sixth ring. Jesus. What had she done? Was she out of her fucking mind? He would call the police, the coast guard, too, but it would take him three or four hours to drive from Dublin. Phone me when you find him. Hurry. Just find him. He hung up into a sudden, fierce silence.

Rebecca put her head to the table. When she closed Skype, the background picture of Tomas appeared once more.

She ran to her bedroom, struggled into her old wetsuit. It chafed her body, tugged across her chest, scraped hard against her neck.

A menace of clouds hung outside. She scanned the horizon. The distant islands, humped and cetacean. The sweep of headland. Gray water, gray sky. Most likely he'd swum north. The currents were easier that way. They'd gone that direction in summer. Always close to shore. Reading the way the water flowed. Where it frothed against rocks, curved back on itself.

A small fishing boat trolled the far edge of the bay. Rebecca waved her hands—ridiculous, she knew—then scrambled down along the cliff face, her feet slipping in the moist track.

Halfway to the beach she stopped: Tomas's tennis shoes lay there, neatly pointed toward the sea. How had she missed them earlier? She would remember this always, she knew: she turned the shoes around, as if at any moment he might step into them and return, plod up to the warm cottage.

No footprints in the sand: it was too coarse. No jacket, either. Had he left his duffle behind? Hypothermia. It could come on within minutes. She had bought the wetsuit so big. He was more likely to be exposed. Where would he stop? How long was he gone now? She had woken so late. Wine. She had drunk so much wine.

She pulled a swimming cap hard over her hair and yanked the zip tight on her wetsuit. The teeth of it were stiff.

Rebecca waded in, dove. The cold pierced her. Her arms rose, rose, rose again. She stopped, glanced back, forced herself onward. Her shoulder ached.

She saw his face at every stroke: the dark hood, the blond hair, the blue eyes.

Out past the seastack, she moved along the coast, the sound of the waves in her ears, another deafness, the blood receding from her fingers, her toes, her mind.

A novella had arrived from the publisher in Tel Aviv eight months before, a beautifully written story by an Arab Israeli from Nazareth: an important piece of work, she thought.

She had begun immediately to translate it, the story of a middle-aged couple who had lost their two children. She had come upon the phrase *sh'khol*. She cast around for a word to translate it, but there was no proper match. There were words, of course, for *widow*, *widower*, and *orphan* but none, no noun, no adjective, for a parent who had lost a child. None in Irish, either. She looked in Russian, in French, in German, in other languages, too, but could find analogues only in Sanskrit, *vilomah*, and in Arabic, *thakla*, a mother, *mathkool*, a father. Still none in English. It had bothered her for days. She wanted to be true to the text, to identify the invisible, *torn open*, *ripped apart*, *stolen*. In the end she had settled upon the formal *bereaved*, not precise enough hardly, she thought, no mystery in it, no music, hardly a proper translation at all, bereaved.

It was almost noon when she was yanked in by the neck of her wetsuit. A coast guard boat. Four men aboard. She fell to the deck, face to the slats, gasping. They carried her down to the cabin. Leaned over her. A mask. Tubes. Their faces: blurry, unfocused. Their voices. Oxygen. A hand on her brow. A finger on her wrist. The weight of water still upon her. Her teeth chattered. She tried to stand.

—Let me back, she shouted.

The cold burned inside her. Her shoulder felt as if it had been ripped from its socket.

—Sit still now, you'll be all right. Just don't move.

They wrapped her in silver foil blankets, massaged her fingers and toes, slapped her twice across the cheek, gently, as if to wake her.

—Mrs. Barrington. Can you hear me?

In the blue of the skipper's eyes she thought she saw Tomas. She touched his face, but the beard bristled against her hand.

The skipper spoke to her in English first, then Irish, a sharpness to his tone. Was she sure Tomas had gone swimming? Was there any other place he might be? Had he ever done this before? What was he wearing? Did he have a phone? Did he have any friends along the coast?

She tried to stand once more, but the skipper held her back.

The wind buffeted the cabin windows, whitened the tops of the waves. A few gulls darted acrobatically above the water. Rebecca glanced at the maritime maps on the wall, enormous charts of line and color. A furnace of grief rose up in her. She peered out past the stern, the widening wake. The radio crackled: a dozen different voices.

She was making the sounds, she knew, of an animal.

The boat slowed suddenly, pulled into a slipway. A fine shiver of spray stung her face. She did not recognize the area. A lamplight was still shining in the blue daytime: a faint glow, a prospect of dark. Onlookers huddled by their cars, pointing in her direction. Beams of red and blue slashed the treetops. Rebecca felt a hand at her shoulder. The skipper escorted her along the pier. One of her blankets slipped away. She was immediately aware of her wetsuit: the tightness, the darkness, the cold. A series of whispers. She was struck by the immense stillness, the silence, not a breath of wind. *Sh'khol.*

She turned, broke free, ran.

When they pulled her from the water a second time, she saw a man hurrying toward her, carrying his cell phone, pointing it at her, watching the screen as he filmed her rising from the low, gray waves: she would, she knew, be on the news in just a few hours.

—Tomas, she whispered. Tomas.

A sedative dulled her. A policewoman sat in a corner of the room, silent, watching, a teacup and saucer in her hands. Through the large plate-glass window Rebecca could see figures wandering about, casting backward glances. One of them appeared to be scribbling in a notebook.

The Gardaí had set up in the living room. Every few moments another phone rang. Cars turned in the narrow laneway outside the cottage, their tires crunching on the gravel.

Somebody was smoking outside. She could smell a rag of it moving through the house. She rose to shut the bedroom window.

Something has ended, she thought. Something has finished. She could not locate the source of the feeling.

She paused a moment and strode across the floor toward the door. The policewoman uncrossed her legs but did not rise from the wicker chair. Rebecca strode out. The living room fell quiet, except for the static of a police radio. A wine bottle on the table. A discarded party hat. The scraps of their Christmas dinner heaped in the sink, swollen with dishwater.

—I want to join the search parties.

—It's best for you to stay here.

—He can't hear the whistles, he's deaf.

—Best stay in the cottage, Mrs. Barrington.

She felt as if she had chewed a piece of aluminum, the pain in her head suddenly cold.

—Marcus. My name is Marcus. Rebecca Marcus.

She pushed open the door of Tomas's room. Two plainclothes police were sifting through his cupboard drawers. On his bed was a small plastic bag marked with a series of numbers: strands of hair inside. Thin and blond. The detectives turned to her.

—I'd like to get his pajamas, she said.

—I'm sorry, Miss. We can't let you take anything.

—His jammies, that's all I want.

—A question. If you don't mind.

As the detective approached, she could smell the remnants of cinnamon on him, some essence of Christmas. He struck the question sharply, like a match against her.

—How did you get that bruise?

Her hand flew to her face. She felt as if some jagged shape had been drawn up out of her, ripping the roof of her mouth.

Outside, the early dark had taken possession of everything.

—No idea, she said.

A woman alone with a boy. In a western cottage. Empty wine bottles strewn about. She looked over her shoulder: the other guards were watching from the living room. She heard the rattle of pills from the bathroom. An inventory of her medicine. Another was searching her bookshelves. *The Iron Mountains. Factory Farming. Kaddish. House Beautiful. The Remains of the Day.* So, she was under suspicion. She felt suddenly marooned. Rebecca drew herself to full height and walked back toward the living room.

—Ask that person outside to please stop smoking, she said.

He came down the laneway, beeping the car horn, lowered the window, beckoned the guard over: *I'm the child's father.*

Alan had lost the jowls of his occasional drinking. The thinness made him severe. She tried to look for the old self that might remain, but he was clean-shaven, and there was something so deeply mannered about him, a tweed jacket, a thin tie pushed up against his neck, a crease in his slacks. He looked as if he had dressed himself in the third person.

He buried his face in Tomas's duffle by the door, then sank theatrically to his knees, but was careful to wipe the muck when he rose and followed her to her bedroom.

The policewoman in the corner stood up, gave a nervous smile. Rebecca caught a glance at herself in the full-length mirror: swollen, disheveled.

—I'd like to be alone with my wife, Alan said.

Rebecca lifted her head. *Wife*: it was like a word that might remain on a page, though the page itself was plunged into darkness.

Alan repositioned the wicker chair and let out a long sigh. It was plain to see that he was seeking the brief adulation of grief. He needed the loss to attach itself to him. Why hadn't she woken? he asked her. Was the door to her bedroom open or closed? Had she slept through her alarm? Had Tomas eaten any breakfast? How far could he swim? Why didn't you get him a wetsuit that fit? Why didn't you hide it away? Did you give him his limits? You know he needs his limits.

She thought about that ancient life in the Dublin hills, the shiny kitchen, the white machinery, the German cars in the pebbled driveway, the clipped bushes, the alarm system, the security cameras, the *limits*, yes, and how far the word might possibly stretch before it rebounded.

—Did he have gloves on?

—Oh stop, please, Alan.

—I need to know.

The red lights of the clock shone. It had been twelve hours. She lay on the bed.

—No, he had no gloves, Alan.

She could not shake the Israeli story from her head. An Arab couple had lost their two children to two illnesses over the course of five years: one to pneumonia, the other to a rare blood disorder. It was a simple story—small, intimate, no grand intent. The father worked as a crane driver in the docklands of Haifa, the mother as a secretary in a corrugated-paper firm. Their ordinary lives had been turned inside out. After the children died, the father filled a shipping container with their possessions and every day moved it, using the giant crane and the skyhooks, to a new site in the yard, carefully positioning it alongside the sea: shiny, yellow, locked.

—He feels invincible, doesn't he?

—Oh Jesus, Alan.

The search parties were spread out along the cliffs, their hopeless whistles in the air, her son's name blown back by the wind. Rebecca pushed open the rear sliding doors to the balcony. The sky was shot through with red. A stray sycamore branch touched her hair. She reached up. A crushing pain split her shoulder blade: her rotator cuff.

Cigarette smoke lingered in the air. She rounded the back of the cottage. A woman. Plainclothes. The whistles still came in short, sharp bursts.

A loss had lodged itself inside her. Rebecca gestured for the cigarette, drew long and hard on the filter. It tasted foul, heavy. She had not smoked in many years.

—He's deaf, you know, she said, blowing the smoke sideways.

A tenderness shone in the detective's eyes. Rebecca turned back into the house, pulled on her coat, walked out the front door and down toward the cliffs.

A helicopter broke the dark horizon, hovered for a moment right above the cottage, its spotlight shining on the stone walls, until it banked sharply and continued up the coast.

They went in groups of three, linking arms. The land was potholed, hillocked, stony. Every now and then she could hear a gasp from a neighboring group when a foot rolled across a rock, or a lost lobster pot, or a bag of rubbish.

The stone walls were cold to the touch. The wind ripped under a sheet of discarded plastic. Tiny tufts of dyed sheep wool shone on the barbed wire: patterns of red and blue.

Along the coast small groups zigzagged the distant beaches in the last of the light. Dozens of boats plied the waves. The bells on the ancient boats tinkled. A hooker went by with its white sails unfurled. A fleet of kayaks glided close to the shore, returning home.

The moon rose red: its beauty appeared raw and offensive to her. She turned inland. The detectives walked alongside. Rebecca felt suspended between them. Cones of pale torch beam swept through the gathering darkness.

At an abandoned home, roofless, hemmed in by an immense rhododendron bush, a call came over the radio that a wetsuit had been found, over. The male detective held a finger in the air, as if figuring the direction of the wind. No, not a wetsuit, said the voice, high alert, no, there was something moving, high alert, stand by, stand by, there was something alive, a ripple in the water, high alert, high alert, yes, it was a body, a body, they had found something, over, a body, over.

The detective turned away from her, moved into the overgrown doorway, shielded the radio, stood perfectly still in the starlight until the call clarified itself: it was a movement in the water, discard, they had seen a seal, discard the last report, only a seal, repeat, discard, over.

Rebecca knew well the legend of the selkie. She thought of Tomas zippering his way out into the water, sleek, dark, hidden.

The female detective whispered into the radio: For fucksake, be careful, we've got the mother here.

The word lay on her tongue now: *mother, máthair, em.* They went forward again, through the unbent grass, into the tunnels of their torches.

Alan's clothing was folded on the wicker chair. His knees were curled to his chest. A shallow wheeze came from the white of his throat. A note lay on her pillow: *They wouldn't let me sleep in Tomas's room, wake me when you're home.* And then a scribbled, *Please.*

They had called off the search until morning, but she could hear the fishing boats along the coast, still blasting their horns.

Rebecca took off her shoes, set them by the bedroom fire. Only a few small embers remained, a weak, red glow. The cuffs of her jeans were wet and heavy from the muck. She did not remove them.

She went to the bed and lay on top of the covers, pulled up a horse-hair blanket, turned away from Alan. Gazing out the window, she waited for a bar of light to rise and part the dark. A torchlight bore past in a pale shroud. Perhaps there was news. At the cliff he had twirled the imaginary cane. Where had he learned that Chaplin shuffle? The sheer surprise of it. The unknowability. Unspooling himself along the cliff.

From the living room came the intermittent static of the radios. Almost eighteen hours now.

Rebecca pushed her face deeper into the pillow. Alan stirred underneath the sheets. His arm came across her shoulder. She lay quite still. Was he sleeping or awake? How could he sleep? His arm tightened around her. His hand moved to her hair, his fingers at her neck, his thumb at the edge of her clavicle.

That was not sleep. That was not sleep at all.

She gently pushed his arm away.

Another torch bobbed past the window. Rebecca rose from the bed. A gold-backed hairbrush lay on the dressing table. Long strands of her dark hair were tangled up inside it. She brushed only one side of her hair. The damp hem of her jeans chilled her toes and she walked toward the wicker chair, covered herself in a blanket, looked out into the early dark.

When dawn broke, she saw the door open slightly, the female detective peeping in around the frame, something warm in the flicker that went between them. Alan stirred, pale in the bed, and moaned something like an excuse. His pinkish face. His thinning hair. He looked brittle to her, likely to dissolve.

In the kitchen the kettle was already whistling. A row of teacups were set along the counter. The detective stepped forward and touched her arm. Rebecca's eyes leaped to catch hers, a brief merged moment.

—I hope you don't mind. We took the liberty. There's no news yet.

The presence of the word *yet* jolted her. There would, one day, be news. Its arrival was inevitable.

—We took one of Tomas's shirts from the wash basket.

—Why? said Rebecca.

—For the dogs, the detective said.

Rebecca wanted suddenly to hold the shirt, inhale its odor. She reached for the kettle, tried to pour through the shake in her hands. So there would be dogs out on the headland later. Searching for her son. She glanced at her reflection in the window, saw only him. His face was double-framed now, triple-framed. He was everywhere. Out on the headland, running, the dogs following, a ram, a hawk, a heron above. She felt a lightness swell in her. A curve in the air. A dive. She gripped the hem of the counter. The slow, sleek slip of the sea. A darkening underwater. The shroud of cold. The coroner, the funeral home, the wreaths, the plot, the burial. She felt herself falter. The burst to the surface. A selkie, spluttering for air. She was guided into a chair at the table. She tried to lean forward to pour the tea. Voices vibrated around her. Her hands shook. Every outcome was unwhisperable. She had a sudden thought that there was no sugar in the house. They needed sugar for their tea. She would go to the store with Tomas later. The newsagent's. Yes, that is where she would go. Inland along the bend of narrow road. Beyond the white bungalow. Crossing at the one traffic light. Walk with him past the butcher shop, past the sign for tours to the islands, past the turf accountant, past the shuttered hotel, the silver-kegged alleyway, into the newsagent's on Main Street. The clink of the anchor-shaped bell. The black-and-white linoleum floor. Along the aisle. The sharp smell of paraffin. Past the paper rack set up on lobster pots, the small blue and orange ropes hanging down, old relics of the sea. She would walk beyond the news of his disappearance. Bread, biscuits, soup. To the shelf where the yellow packets of sugar lay. We cannot do without sugar, Tomas, second shelf down, trust me, there, good lad, get it, please, go on, reach in.

She wasn't sure if she had said this aloud or not, but when she looked up again the female detective had brought one of Tomas's shirts, held it out, her eyes moist. The buttons were cold to the touch: Rebecca pressed them to her cheek.

From the laneway came the sound of scraping branches. Van doors being opened and closed. She heard a high yelp, and then the scrabble of paws upon gravel.

She spent the second morning out in the fields. Columns of sunlight filtered down over the sea. A light wind rippled the grass at the cliff edge. She wore Tomas's shirt under her own, tight and warm.

So many searchers along the beaches. Teachers. Farmers. School-children holding hands. The boats trawling the waters had trebled.

At lunchtime, dazed with fatigue, Rebecca was brought home. A new quiet had insinuated itself into the cottage. The policemen came and went as if they had learned from long practice. They seemed to ghost into one another: almost as if they could slip into one another's faces.

She knew them, somehow, by the way they drank their tea. Food had arrived, with notes from neighbors. Fruit bowls. Lasagna. Tea bags and biscuits. A basket of balloons, of all things: a scribbled prayer to Saint Christopher in a child's hand.

Alan sat next to her on the couch. He put his hand across hers. He would, he said, do the media interviews. She would not have to worry about it.

She heard the thud of distant waves. The labored drone of a TV truck filtered down from the laneway.

A Sunday newspaper called, offering money for a photograph. Alan walked to a corner of the cottage, cupped his phone, whispered into the receiver. She thought she heard him weeping.

Pages from the Israeli novel were strewn across her desk. Scribbles in the margins. Beside the pages, Mandelstam's memoir lay open, a quarter of the way through. Russia, she thought. She would have to tell them in Vladivostok, let them know what had happened, fill out the paperwork. The orphanage. The broken steps. The high windows. The ocher walls. The one great painting in the hallway: the Bay of Amur, summertime, a yacht on its water, water, always water. She would find the mother and father, explain that their son had disappeared swimming on the western seaboard of Ireland. A small apartment in the center of the city, a low coffee table, a full ashtray, the mother wan and withdrawn, the father portly and thuggish. My fault. I gave him a wetsuit. All my fault. Forgive me.

She wanted the day to peel itself backward, regain its early brightness, its possibility, its pour into teacups, but she was not surprised to see the dark come down. It was almost two days now.

Alan sat in the corner, curled around his phone. She almost felt a sadness for him, the whispered *sweetheart*, the urgent pleading and explanations with his own young children.

That night, lying next to him, Rebecca allowed his arm across her waist. The simple comfort of it. She heard him murmur her name again, but she did not turn.

At daylight she totaled up the hours: forty-eight.

Rebecca rose and walked out into the morning, the dew wet against her plimsolls. The television truck hummed farther up the laneway, out of sight. She stepped across the cattle grid. The steel bars pushed hard into the soles of her feet. A muddy path led up the hill. The grass in the middle was green and untrodden. Moss lay slick on the stone wall.

A piece of torn plastic was tangled in the high hedges. She reached in and pulled it out, shoved it deep into her pocket: she had no idea why.

Water dripped from the branches of nearby trees. A few birds marked out their morning territory. She had only ever driven this part of the laneway before. It was, she knew, part of an old famine road.

Rebecca stood a while: the hum from the TV truck up the road seemed to cancel out the rhythm of the sea.

She leaned into the hard slope of the road, opened the bar of the red gate, stepped over the mud. The bolt slid back perfectly into its groove. She walked the center grass up and around the second corner to where the TV truck idled against the hedges. Inside, silhouetted against a pair of sheer curtains, three figures were playing cards. The curtains moved but the figures remained static. Across the front seat a man lay slumped, sleeping.

A small group of teenagers huddled near the back of the truck, sharing a cigarette, their breath shaping clouds of white in the cold. They nudged each other as she approached.

She stopped, then, startled by the sight. Alone, casual, adrift. He sauntered in behind the group, unnoticed. A brown hunting jacket hung from his shoulders. A hooded sweatshirt underneath. His trousers were rolled up and folded over. The laces of his boots were open and the tongues wagged sideways. Steam rolled off him, as if he had been walking a long time.

His mouth was slightly open. His lip was wet with mucus. Mud and leaves in the fringes of his hair. Under his right arm he carried a dark bag. The bag fell from his arm, and he caught hold of it as he moved forward. A long, gray stripe. The wetsuit. He was carrying the wetsuit.

He had not yet seen her. His body seemed to drag his shadow behind him: slow, reluctant, but sharp. *Sh'khol.* She knew the word now. *Shadowed.*

The door of the TV truck opened behind her. Her name was called. Mrs. Barrington. She did not turn. She felt as if she were skidding in a car.

She was aware of a bustle behind her, two, three, four people piling out of the truck. The impossible utterance of his name. Tomas. Is that you? Turn this way, Tomas. A yell came from the teenagers. Look over here. They had their phones out. Tomas! Tomas! Turn this way, Tomas.

Rebecca saw a furred microphone pass before her eyes. It dipped down in front of her, and she pushed it away. A cameraman jostled her. Another shout erupted. She moved forward. Her feet slipped in the mud.

Tomas turned. She took him in her arms with a surge of joy.

She held his face. The paleness, the whites of his eyes. His was a gaze that belonged to someone else: a boy of another experience.

He passed the wetsuit to her. It was cold to the touch and dry.

The news had gone ahead of them. The cheers went up as they rounded the corner toward the garden. Alan ran along the laneway in his pajamas, stopped abruptly when he saw the television cameras, grabbed for the gap in the cotton trousers.

Rebecca shouldered Tomas through the gauntlet, her arm encircling him tightly, guiding him to the front door.

In the cottage, a swathe of light dusted the floor. The female detective stood in the center of the room. Her name badge glinted. Detective Harnon. It struck Rebecca that she could name things again: people, words, ideas. A warmth spread through the small of her back.

A smell of turf smoke came off Tomas's clothing. It was, she later realized, one of the few clues she would ever get.

The cottage filled up behind her. She saw a photographer at the large plate-glass window. All around her, phones were ringing. The kettle whistled on the stove. A fear had tightened Tomas. She needed to get him alone. The photographer shoved his camera up against the windowpane. She spun Tomas away as the flash erupted.

Morning light stamped itself in small rectangles on the bedroom floor. Rebecca closed the window blinds. The helmet was lying on the bed. His pajamas were neatly folded and placed on a chair. She ignored the knocking at the door. He was shivering now. She held his face. Kissed him.

The door opened tentatively.

—Leave us be, please. Leave us be.

She touched the side of his cheek, then shucked the brown jacket from his shoulders. A hunting jacket. She checked the pockets. A few grains of thread. A small ball of fur. A wet matchbook. He lifted his arms. She peeled the sweatshirt up over his head. His skin was tight and dimpled.

A piece of leaf fell from his hair to the floor. She turned him around, looked at his back, his neck, his shoulder blades. He was unmarked. No cuts, no scrapes.

She looked down at Tomas's trousers. Denims. Too large by far. A man's denims. Fastened with an old purple belt with a gold clasp. Clothing from another era. Gaudy. Ancient. A bolt of cold ran along her arms.

—No, she said. Please, no.

She reached for him, but he slapped her hand away. The door rattled again behind her. She turned to see Alan's face: the stretched wire of his flesh, the small brown of his eyes.

—We need a detective in here, she said. Now.

In the hospital it was still bright morning and the air was motionless in the low corridors and muddy footprints lay about and the yellow walls pressed in upon them and the pungent odor of antiseptic made her go to the windows and the trees outside stood static and the seagulls cawed up over the rooftops and she stood in the prospect of the un-imaginable, the tangle of rumor and evidence and fact, and she waited for the doctors as the minutes idled and the nurses passed by in the corridors and the trolleys rattled and the orderlies pushed their heavy carts and an inexhaustible current of human misery moved in and out of the waiting room every story every nuance every pulse of the city hammering up against the wired windows.

The water poured hard and clear. She tested its warmth against her wrist. Tomas came into the bathroom, dropped his red jumper to the floor, slid out of his khakis, stood in his white shirt, clumsily working the buttons.

She reached to help, but he stepped away, then gestured for her to leave while he climbed into the swimming togs. So, he wanted to wear shorts now while she washed him. Fair enough, she thought.

The house was quiet again. Only the sound of the waves. She keyed her new phone alive. A dozen messages. She would attend to them later.

After a moment she returned to the bathroom with her hands covering her eyes.

—Ta-da! she said.

He stood there, pale and thin in front of her. The swimming shorts were far too tight. Along his slender stomach she could see a gathering of tiny, fine hairs that ran in a line from his belly button. He hopped from foot to foot and cupped his hands over the intimate outline of his body.

He had been untouched. That is what Detective Harnon had said. He was slightly dehydrated but untouched. No abuse. No cuts. No scars. They had run all manner of tests. Later the detective had asked around the village. Nobody had come forward. There were no other clues.

They wanted him to come in for evaluation the following week. A psychologist, she said. Someone who might piece together everything that had happened, but Rebecca knew there'd never be any answers, no amount of probing could solve it, no photographs, no maps, no walks along the coastline. She would go swimming with him again, soon, down to the water. They would ease themselves into the shallows. She would watch him carefully negotiate the seastack. She would guide him away from the current. Perhaps some small insight might unravel, but she was aware she could never finally understand.

The simple grace of his return was enough. *I live, I breathe, I go, I come back, I am here now.* Nothing else.

Rebecca tested the water again with her fingers. She helped Tomas over the rim of the tub. Goose bumps appeared on his skin. His ribs were sharp and pale. He fell against her. The wet of his toes chilled her bare feet. She threw a towel around his shoulders to warm him, then guided him back toward the water. He finally placed both feet in the bath, and let the warmth course up through his body. He cupped his hands in front of his shorts. She put her hand on his shoulder and, with gentle insistence, got him to kneel.

He slid forward into the water.

—There we go, she said in Hebrew. Let me wash that mop.

She perched at the edge of the bath, took hold of his shoulder blades, ran a pumice stone over his back, massaged the shampoo into his hair. His skin was so very transparent. The air in his lungs changed the shape of his back. She applied a little conditioner to his scalp. His hair was thick and long. She would have to get it cut soon.

Tomas grunted and leaned forward, tugged at the front of his shorts. His shoulders tautened against her fingers. She knew, then, what it was. He bent over to try to disguise himself against the fabric of his shorts. Rebecca stood without looking at him, handed him the soap and the sponge.

110

Impossible to be a child forever. A mother, always.

—You're on your own now, she said.

She moved away from him, closed the door and stood outside in the corridor, listening to his stark breathing and the persistent splash of water, its rhythm sounding out against the faint percussion of the sea.

Nominated by Zoetrope and Dana Levin

BROKEN CUP

by MARGARET GIBSON

from BROKEN CUP (LSU PRESS)

I've forgotten how it broke, the great cause
or the petty cause that cracked the handle
into two pieces and left me without
a cup for morning coffee. In the cabinet
there were others of white porcelain,
with steeply elegant lines, cups that matched
their saucers. But my cup was Mexican,
squat, and as round as Rivera's peasant
bent before the wall of callas
he carried on his back, his burden of blossoms.
Hand-painted, my cup was carnival
purple and yellow, flowers that honored earth,
birth, death, geometry, symmetry, riot,
good sex, good coffee, the sun rising hot.
I banished it, broken, to my desk and used it
for paperclips. Now I've rescued it, fit
and glued the pieces back together.
Still I'm afraid to lift it, even to wash it by hand
in hot water—it is that fragile.

You brought the cup to me from Puerta Vallarta,
that seaside trip you took to help
your daughter past heartbreak—a little hotel
by the sea, with bougainvillea
and a great deal on cocktails as the sun

rolled its dying splendor onto the Pacific.
I think I was jealous; I was jealous. I hoped
you drank margaritas and missed me—
most likely Dos Equis with a squirt of lime.
The cup gave me Mexico each morning,
on the cheap. I loved it. *I loved it,
it broke. I ignored it, I cast it aside*—
sounds like a classic sitcom-bad marriage.
Sounds like the wary caregiver who reads
The Thirty-Six Hour Day, heart empty.
Who really wants to know about this despair?
I have minimizing friends who tell me,
*It's not so bad—just a little accelerated
forgetting, such as we all have these days.*
O Ancient of Days, that was once a name
for God, for something so deep within the self
it's beyond us. Even so, it is possible,
I want to tell them, to love what is broken.
Possible, urgent, and necessary.
And so for love of thee and me,
I take my broken cup and set it down
before me on a yellow place mat. I make
toast with ginger jam and real butter,
coffee whose beans have flourished
on a mountain in Peru, I hope near Machu Picchu.
I sit down in my Japanese bathrobe,
in my Navajo beads, with bare feet; I sit
without ire or envy, without fear or despair,
and drink and eat. Slowly. Very slowly,
savoring all I can remember of that first
night we met, the good talk, the dancing
until we were too tired to do anything else
but take the dancing to bed—the miracle
of unintended meeting, the first of what
was to be years of meeting, moments
I hope to remember when I lie down to die,
my beautiful love, your head of unruly hair
and unruly thoughts unraveling
into a silence that will lengthen . . . or may
break off, as this handle did, in two pieces.

Who knows how love will hold, or if we will
ever be all right. Who knows what wrong
tastes like or how much emptiness the cup
will hold as we share it—who knows?

And if it is the cup of suffering,
drink it down—or better, may it pass from you,
and you live easy and go gently
where you will, or where you must. I'll go
with you, grateful for plum-colored flowers
so close to bruising, coffee, sunlight, earth;
the journeys we took together—and the long one
left us to walk until we lie down near
clear water, shade trees, green pasture.
In that place, there will be nothing unspoken,
nothing forgotten or feared. Day or night,
whatever the hour, it will be all shining,
our whole and broken bodies full of light.

Nominated by Dick Allen and Jane Hirshfield

WANDERLUST

fiction by LALEH KHADIVI

from THE SUN

We are Inna, Yulia, Victoria, Yana, Snezhana, Tamara, Olesya, Nadesha, or Lena. We come from Saint Petersburg, Moscow, Kursk, Barnaul, Kharkov, Odessa, Yekaterinburg, Stavropol, or Novosibirsk. Our hobbies are running, skating, biking and/or sailing, aerobics, dance and/or kickboxing, stretching and/or chess. We were born under the signs of Aquarius, Pisces, Virgo, Capricorn, Gemini, Cancer, Sagittarius, Scorpio, Taurus, Libra, Aries, or Leo. Some of us are 1.6 meters tall; some of us are 1.8 meters tall. We believe in God, or we are Orthodox, or we are spiritual, or it is not important. Our English is preliminary (need a translator) or conversational or excellent or fluent. We smoke occasionally; we never smoke. We drink occasionally; we never drink. We have been married once; we have never been married; we are divorced. We have no children; we have one child. Here we are in photos. Have a look. We are at the beach. We are in a hay-filled barn. We are in front of a fireplace, wearing the sort of fur cap you might recognize from *Doctor Zhivago*. See our lovely skin, our shimmering eyes of blue or black or brown, our long hair of any imaginable shade. Gaze at our narrow shoulders and slender waists, our full mouths and delicate necks. Go ahead. See us and dream. Click and click and click until we are a single, many-headed woman, a blur of smiles and eyes that call to you and announce: We are a sensitive, funny, outgoing, warm, sweet, intelligent, sexy, disciplined, professional, resolute, stubborn woman from Russia looking for a tall, ath-

115

letic, confident, successful, witty, kind, financially stable, generous man from anywhere else.

And, yes, we swear we are the women we claim to be, just as we were all once girls. At six, seven, eight years old we watched television all day to see a wall in Berlin—a cold, gray city not unlike our own cold, gray city—tumble and tumble and tumble again. When we asked our mothers what was happening, they shook their heads and tried to explain it to us in terms we could understand: *Tsk. Just an old bear, like any old bear in the forest, darling—shot a hundred times over a hundred years and just now feeling the pain of the bullets.*

But what will happen to the poor bear, Mama? Who will take care of her? we asked, worried as girls of six, seven, eight will worry for the animals in children's books.

We will see, our mothers answered. *We will see.*

So we waited and watched our mothers and fathers, and the mothers and fathers of our friends, and our teachers, and the bus driver, and the checkout clerk, and we scanned them for signs of anxiety about what might happen and clues as to how we should prepare. If the adults around us paced, smoked cigarette after cigarette, and asked each other, *Where will we get our food? Who will pay our pensions? What jobs will there be if there is no state?* then we were anxious, too, nervously chewing gum, explaining the coming hard times to our stuffed animals and imaginary friends: *You must behave very well so we won't be thrown out on the streets and made to eat from the dumpster and to wash ourselves in the subway bathrooms, where rats drink.* If the adults were indifferent and shouted at each other, *One government, another government—this is Russia, always Russia!* then we walked around with a brave attitude and entertained our friends by proclaiming, *Who cares! Nothing is going to change! Worry is for babies!* If our parents were the kind to celebrate, to watch news of the politburo's collapse with smiles on their faces and tiny glasses of vodka in their hands, to hold our chins and whisper, *Just imagine what is going to come now! Things will be so much better for everyone. All this time we waited . . .* , then we pulled our chins away and walked alone around our changing world and wondered, *If not this, then what? What is better than this?*

* * *

By fourteen, fifteen, sixteen we were old enough to understand that little uncertainties tucked themselves into bigger uncertainties, like our famous nesting dolls. In those early years we watched as the first reformist president became more and more of a buffoon in the eyes of our parents and grandparents, teachers and neighbors. We learned that we were a people without a guide in a dark time. What we'd once understood as the strong, unassailable state was now a long, nervous joke as leaders fell and the congress collapsed and banks shut our parents' accounts and community-store shelves emptied as the hyper-marts and malls opened, filled with a quantity and variety of food and clothes and toys such as we had never imagined. Skyscrapers rose in the cities, and the first generation of oligarchs clogged the Moscow streets with their imported cars. We learned that money was a goal unto itself. And just as we turned fourteen, fifteen, sixteen and started to look about for answers to questions we dared not ask—What makes a woman a woman, a man a man?—we saw our mothers, defiant or supplicant but always dignified, and our fathers, men who'd been giants in our girlhoods, massive from labor, open throated with song and laughter, now given to silence and drinking, drinking and anger, anger and sorrow. At the same time, the magazines and televisions and billboards showed us another kind of man and woman and family: smiling, fit, often at the beach, often in America.

At fifteen, sixteen, seventeen we dangled a shoe over the precipice of girlhood. Our hearts began to beat with heat and want and a lust for love. Our girlhood bodies slipped from us like old sweaters, and what had grown beneath was often stunning and confusing in equal measure. Our lips and lashes, breasts and legs filled and extended, and we woke each morning and found ourselves changed.

Some of our mothers watched over it all with a knowing eye and gave advice: *If a man invites you for a lift in his car, refuse. Don't take money from a man for a soda or a snack or anything. If they try to talk to you when you walk down the street, don't listen to them. Keep your eyes on the sidewalk.* Other mothers accosted us in the shower and in dressing rooms, taking in an eyeful and asking, incredulous, *How did this happen? Only your great-aunt looked like this. Those lips, like pillows. That ass . . .* And we were unsure whether to hold our heads up in pride or drop them in shame.

117

It was only a matter of time before others noticed the changes as well. Our brothers and fathers made remarks; our sisters ran their hands over our breasts and giggled or gasped. But no one noticed more than the men from our apartment block, our fathers' friends from the office or the factory or the field, and our brothers' forever-sweating classmates, who now found reasons to stop and talk to us, to pause for an extra second and ask, *Are those Levi's you're wearing? So easy to come by these days. They look good.* Sometimes we were followed by leering men who lived on the streets or in the train stations, and their gaze stuck to us like greasy fingerprints. Other kinds of men looked at us, too, men we had never seen before, Russia's new type of men in silk suits and crisp English raincoats, their hair gelled so that it didn't move. Sometimes they were bald and driven around by chauffeurs who knew to slow down as they passed a group of us walking home from school. Sometimes they were young and handsome and surrounded by two or three women. We noticed their curious, hungry stares and returned them with curious, hungry stares of our own.

By twenty, twenty-one, twenty-two we had entered a new century, a new millennium, and we were no longer scared little girls and cared not at all about what had happened to that bear in the woods. Political leaders, popular songs, and state-sponsored advertisements told us that it was up to the young to rebuild Russia. The future was ours.

A few of us believed this and tried out for jobs that required us to wear the ugly uniforms of store clerks and fastfood servers, and the work made us grumble and slouch. Some of us chose to forgo work and clung to boyfriends who turned into husbands and then into fathers like our own: taciturn and drunk, or belligerent and drunk, or depressed and drunk, or some odd combination of them all, depending on the day of the week and the weather and the sport results. Nevertheless, by twenty, twenty-one, twenty-two some of us were married. There were marriages of love, marriages of duty, marriages of boredom or lack of imagination. One of us married a short, odious neighbor she had never liked, simply because he stood a good chance of inheriting his grand-mother's elegant pre-revolution vacation cottage on the Volga River. *It's simple*, she explained. *We will have children. I might have affairs. And nine months of the year we will be miserable and cold. But for the three months of summer I will live in paradise, jump straight off the porch into the water, and eat fresh berries every day. You are crazy if you think life can be more than that.*

For those of us crazy enough to think that life could be more, if only just a little bit, there was university. We went to earn degrees that would get us jobs that paid well. We longed to put our hands into our pocketbooks and pull out a plane ticket to Greece, a bra made of French lace, a pair of designer Italian shoes like the ones we saw in a magazine. Some of us were too impatient for classes, tests, and degrees, and we walked around at twenty, twenty-one, twenty-two asking ourselves: *Why can't I go live in the world, be a part of something more than this confused, old-fashioned place?* We researched exit visas, one-way tickets to New York, English lessons. *I can stay with Uncle Pyotr in Queens! When I was six, seven, eight, he always told me I was his favorite. . . .* The more impatient among us found work at the restaurants, clubs, and hotels built to host British, German, and American businessmen. These men were nice to us, flirtatious and funny when they answered our questions: *What is it like there? Can I have my own apartment? My own car? For how much?* They assured us the prices were very reasonable, letting their hands come to rest on our hips, our shoulders, the backs of our necks. *You would be so happy in*—and they named a place we could not point to on a map.

In the manner of prayers being answered, the machines that would grant us our exodus appeared. We found them in our brothers' bedrooms, at university libraries, in the offices where we worked, and most readily in the hundreds of new Internet cafes, where teenage boys left behind sticky keyboards. Just like that we could type in the name of a town, a city, a country, and just like that there was a map, information in Russian, photographs of the main streets. The proprietors of the cafes took great care in explaining to us the mechanics of the Internet, which, they told us with confidence, was going to change everything: *Because of the Internet this computer you sit in front of is connected to almost every other computer in the world. With the click of a mouse, you can contact your uncle Pyotr in America. Amazing, really.* We agreed. Amazing. And the moment they left us alone, we took out the pieces of paper hidden in our purses and pockets and typed in the ad-

119

dresses given to us by friends: *Listen, go to this website. Lena's sister tried it, and now she lives in Switzerland. She is married to a banker. They have a maid.* We typed slowly and carefully: RussianBride.com. UkranianDelight.com. YourRussianLove.com. And, just like that, there we were—or, at least, versions of ourselves: women of eighteen, twenty-two, thirty-one who looked like us and wanted what we wanted. We sat before this machine—one part oracle, one part mirror—enchanted by the possibilities and all wishing the exact same wish.

The questionnaires were easy: Forty-five kilos. Blue, brown, black. Slender, well shaped. Rock, classical. Thrillers, romances, mysteries. Responsible, independent, calm, open-minded, kind. Some of us didn't believe it would lead to anything. Some of us spent hours with Russian/English dictionaries, poorly translating our deepest desires and personal details: *I have golden hair and diamond blue shade eyes. One day I would like to manage a hospital for sick children who are tired.* Lucky for us the questions were few, and we devoted most of our energy to our photographs. Casual shots, the sites requested. Alone, if possible. Fine clothing helps present a flattering picture. No nudity. We all had old photographs tacked to the walls of our bedrooms: pictures of our second, third, fourth birthdays, our grandmothers holding a cake, our mothers smiling beside us, our thin chests in homemade sweaters that were too big and then, a few photos later, too small. There were the school photographs, groups of us in the same grade, serious and unsmiling under the flag of the USSR; and then the later photos where we stood at eleven, twelve, thirteen under the flag of Russia. Some of us had photos taken on trips to the Urals or the Black Sea, our pale bodies fading into the gray landscape, our expressions sour or wanting. These photos wouldn't do. Those of us who could afford it had professional photos taken. Others saved money for the photographers' fees, or begged our weak-willed fathers for it. If we could not bear to explain ourselves, we stole the money from our mothers' purses.

It was not unusual for the photographers we hired to pull us aside and ask in confidential whispers, *Maybe you want to wear a little less?* as they tugged at our black hose or thumbed the collar of our turtleneck sweaters. For some of us the photographers raised an eyebrow and asked if we wanted to put shawls around our shoulders: *Aren't you cold? You must be so cold. Perhaps it is better to show only the face, the beautiful smile. Let us show the world that our Russian women are true ladies: honorable and respectable.* Sometimes, if we arrived alone, they watched as we put on makeup, and they casually mentioned that they were willing to offer their top-level services, the finest photographs and most elegant prints, if we spent a private hour or two with them in the darkroom after the shoot. Those of us who did not hire a photographer begged our boyfriends to take our pictures. *Of course!* they replied. *Let us pose together. I can borrow my father's tripod and use the timer. You are looking very pretty these days. It is a good time to take your picture.*

No, we said. *Take one or two of me by myself first.*

With the help of the cafe owners our images floated into the computer, and suddenly there we were: RussianDoll5399.Bride_to_Be21482. Miss-lady953. The cafe owners peered over our shoulders and smoked: *You look nice.* Yes, we agreed, seeing our face, body, birth date, height, eye color, favorite color, wishes, and dreams as if for the first time. The cafe owners took our rubles and stared at us with confused expressions: *I don't understand it. Why can't you be happy here with a Russian man? Your father and grandfathers were Russian men. Why not marry your own, stay close to your family, make children for this new country? Is it so bad here that you have to behave like the terns or the turtles and travel thousands of miles to find your mate? I don't understand it. . . . There are so many of us here to love you.*

Some of our mothers found out when we told them, and some of them found out when our brothers or sisters dragged them to the computer cafes to show them our web page: *She says she is 1.8 meters tall. See, Mama, that is a lie.* And when we came home for dinner, our mothers greeted us with slaps and insults, or tears of shock, or enormous embraces and confessions: *If I were your age, I would do the same thing! Yes! Why not? I may still do it. I am only forty-three, forty-four, forty-five. Your father won't even notice I am gone.* Many of us didn't tell our mothers, or anyone, and if a man we had been e-mailing paid us a visit or sent us an airline ticket and secured us a visa, then our mothers wasted no time in calling us sluts and whores as they cried in our doorways while we packed. We stayed strong. We shouted back at them, *I am going because I am in love, and that is better than this!*

What did we know of love?

We knew love as we'd first discovered it at five, six, seven. The love we'd learned from storybooks. The love the mermaid had for the prince, so strong it lured her out of the sea to her death on the land. There was the love we learned in school: the love for our mother country, the adoration we pledged to farmers, cosmonauts, and soldiers we had never met. There were our first loves: the boy in history class who rarely spoke, or the neighbors' son down the hall who played heavy-metal music and never looked us in the eye. Some of us let these loves drive us crazy, as girls do when they are eleven, twelve, thirteen. After that, love changed, turned into a strong chemistry, irrational and hasty, that left us dry in the throat and hot between the legs. We sat closer to the boys on the bus, let them hold our hands, wished for more but did not know how to name it and so could not properly ask, *Could you please love me?*

What did we know of love?

Our parents kept framed photographs of their wedding days in their bedrooms, and we stared at their rigid bodies and expectant faces and opulent hairdos and asked, *Is this love?* The man and woman in the photo said nothing, while down the hall our fathers farted loudly and our mothers slowly put the dishes away.

A few of us knew the love professed by boys who followed us like hapless dogs: *I will do anything you like.* We laughed at them. What could they offer us? These were boys we had known our whole lives, boys we had seen naked at the lake, wrestled with and touched and held before we'd even noticed they were boys. We wanted nothing to do with them. Then there were the few of us who, at fourteen, fifteen, sixteen, had gone all the way, had felt our first or second or third raptures, had said the words and heard the words and knew romance as it has been known since the beginning of time. For them the questionnaires were a small torture. We posted photos of ourselves wearing conservative clothes and dim smiles and made no mention of looking for "Mr. Right" or "dreaming of love." We had found it and lost it, and at that age we thought it was something that happened only once in life.

＊　＊　＊

We spent hours at the computer cafes, waiting for the responses to come. We browsed the Internet while we waited, hopping from site to site to distract ourselves. We clicked aimlessly on photographs of singers and actors we admired. There were newspapers and travel guides. There were websites of naked women on their hands and knees in the position of dogs. There were women with enormous, plastic-looking breasts and hairless parts who made unbelievable faces as men maneuvered into them. We saw websites with photos and videos of women playing with themselves until they reached a closed-eyed ecstasy. Was this love? We quickly turned off the screens and shut down the computers and called the cafe owners over to tell them the machines had broken. We left in a hurry, nerves raw, wondering where we would end up and what *love* would mean there.

To see if any responses had come in, some of us went in pairs and trios and held hands as if the screen were about to reveal the faces and names of our future husbands. Some of us sat alone in front of the computer and swore we would tell no one what we were about to find out. And every last one of us was disappointed. The men were old, some older than our fathers. They were bald or had unforgivable hair. Their bodies were fat and misshapen or thin and without form. If they were British, they had bad teeth, and if they were American, they wore the white grin of the wolf in the fairy tale of Little Red Cap.

Those were the ones who sent pictures of their faces. Most of the messages came to us with a single photograph of just a section of a man, usually from the belly button to the knees, sometimes standing, sometimes sitting, always naked. We turned away from the computer. *Where is his face?* we muttered in disbelief. Later in our lives it would become a joke: *Where is his face! Ha, ha.* Some of us flipped desperately through our Russian/English dictionaries, looking up words and phrases: *plaything . . . erotic . . . a Russian doll for all my needs.* And some of us, even more desperate, hired translators, discreet girls we knew and trusted who excelled at languages: *It says here he is divorced. He has four children. He is looking for stimulation only; no commitment. He thinks you are very beautiful, like Julie Christie in* Doctor Zhivago. *He would like to feel your skin by a warm fire. . . .* We told the translators to write back: *I am a good Russian girl, and you are a piece of shit not worth stepping on with my dirtiest shoe.* And some of us wrote back ourselves: *Yes, I can be your Russian kitten, but first we must meet. You may send a ticket for me to this address. . . .* And if we were too upset by the impoliteness of the invitations, we didn't bother with a response and simply took the tissues offered by the cafe owners, who patted our shoulders affectionately as we cried: *What is the point? Who was I to think life could be better elsewhere? I am a fool.* The cafe owners spoke to us in gentle tones: *There now. What is so bad about your life here? We have no war. The worst of the poverty is gone, we hope. And just look at you! You are young and beautiful, and if you want work, there is much work for the young. If you want love, there is love here—my son . . . myself. . . .* And with that, even the saddest of us left the cafes more determined than ever to write our own futures, futures better than those that seemed only a repeat of generations long past.

After a while our hungry ears started to hear success stories. They were few and far between, but we listened greedily to tales of the good fortune that had reached out from the computer screen and swept up a friend of a friend of a friend. One girl met a man from Australia: *He flew all the way to Novosibirsk to meet me. Can you believe it? He is tall and tan and has a job in marketing. He bought me a ticket to visit him after just two days here! He has tattoos covering both his arms, and at first it bothered me, but now it is OK. You should see them. They are very different from the tattoos on prisoners here. They don't have anything to do with the Mafia or murder. They are pretty even, like art.*

Another girl bragged that she'd gotten e-mails from a man wealthier than Richard Gere in *Pretty Woman: He arranged everything—my visa through the consulate, the first-class ticket. They gave me champagne on the flight, and when I arrived at the airport in New York, his chauffeur was there to pick me up. The apartment was on the top floor of a glass building, and whatever I wanted came to me: food, clothes, cigarettes. I never had to leave. When he arrived, I was amazed by how professional he looked. White hair, a suit, very fit. We had sex immediately. And then again, and once more. When we woke up in the morning, I told him I wanted to go to the famous streets—Broadway, Fifth Avenue—but he said no, that we should stay in the room; New York was too dirty and dangerous for me. When I asked him again, he yelled at me,* Do you want to get me in trouble with my wife? You can leave tomorrow! I don't need this! *My ticket back was not first class. But I don't mind. He won't be mad forever. I am sure he is planning a way for me to return. I am sure of it.*

Other women, other stories: *I met his family, and none of them would talk to me. They called me rude words under their breath. I could tell by the way they said them. After a while it was hard to pretend I didn't hear. What could I do? I was stuck. I couldn't even find where I was on a map.* And still other stories: *Yes, we married! I am a citizen now, and everything is wonderful. I have my own car, my own bathroom. He is gone most of the week, and when we see each other, he does not like to talk to me or touch me. I am learning that this is just his way. I will get used to it.*

We used the good parts of the stories to keep our hopes up. Many of us began to answer responses from men who did not on first glance appeal to us. We found ourselves having romantic long-distance conversations with kind old grandfathers and men who resembled the janitors from our elementary schools. We spent more time at the computer cafes and less time at home, and our parents and siblings grew accustomed to our absence, and soon they began to treat us as if we were not there at all. Our mothers stopped asking us where we'd been, and our brothers and sisters were not interested in having us with them when they went to concerts in the town square on perfect summer nights. And so we stayed even longer at the cafes, improving our English by chatting with anonymous men who wanted to talk about only one thing. We lived and moved and ate and held ourselves back from the love of family, the love of lovers, the love of ourselves. We were careful to love only the idea of a future we could not know.

For many of us there came a day when we caught sight of a woman at the market near our house who was five or six years older than we were, cursing at a baby or a small child, at the weather, at the price of cereal, and we ran to the computer cafe and scoured our correspondences. Of the men we had kept communications with, there was one who seemed smart enough, funny enough, and not so perverted that we would be afraid. He was not our fantasy, but he looked like a man who would support us should we arrive in his life tomorrow. We started to write him warm notes. We dug around inside ourselves for some glimmer of affection with which to express our intentions: *Yes, I would very much like for you to visit. Yes, I am available to travel to see you. Yes, I can leave Russia right now. I am very excited.* As we typed, we pushed back the dark stories of the men who beat up girls on their arrival, tied them to beds, refused them phone calls, food, daylight. We told ourselves, *I am different. I am stronger. I know how to get out of a bad situation. I can always run away if I have to.* And this is what we were thinking as we smiled prettily and wheeled our bags out of customs and searched for the face we hoped was searching for ours.

For some of us it is our first time. We tell the men this, or we don't. Regardless, they take us in whatever way they know how. They take us nervously. They take us quickly. They take us with anger, curiosity, exhilaration, or humility, and we let them and wait for them to finish and wonder, *Was that it?* Some of us beg for them to stop, saying it hurts, and if they are kind, they ask, *Where does it hurt?* But we can't pinpoint it, because the pain is not just in our bodies but somewhere deeper, where we cannot reconcile the strange sheets, the strange sky outside the window, the strange man doing strange things to us, and we are overcome with sadness. For still others the first time is a welcome surprise, and we lock easily into an ancient rhythm of pleasure that may one day belong to us both.

Some of us don't last a week. We are scared or harassed or bored or had a plan to leave the man from the very start. We wait until he is out of the house and take whatever won't mark us obviously as a criminal and hit the streets of Boise or Dallas, Tampa or Los Angeles, and we are full of exhilaration and terror. We find work where we can and live day to day and try not to think about the past. The jobs we get are at the bottom: cleaning offices, washing laundry, taking care of children, taking off our clothes on stage for the dead eyes of truck drivers and men in the military. Many of us came from houses where our mothers often walked around naked, and the exchange of currency for nudity strikes us first as a fortuitous joke and then as a tiresome occupation. In the end we make enough to live on, and our English improves from all the between-dance conversation: *Yes, I am from Russia. Yes, I want to be a lawyer, a dress designer, a business owner.* The men are impressed by our optimism and determination: *You know, you are just like the pioneers who came here all those years ago, so brave,* they tell us. *America needs more women like you.*

If we stay with the man for a few years, the children come. We have one and then another and, if things are going well, maybe a third. We speak to them at the playground in happy, singsong Russian while the American mothers and Filipina or Jamaican nannies stare. We can't help ourselves. Russian is the only language in which we can properly tell our children we love them. And love them we do, so much it makes us homesick. Some of us combat the constant longing for our mothers, our sisters, our holidays, our foods by forcing ourselves to become Americans alongside our American children. We sing the ugly patriotic songs, learn the Pledge of Allegiance and the correct spellings of *Wednesday* and *February* for their tests. When it comes to math, we teach them the Russian way, and, though they protest, their scores are always the highest in the class. There are some among us who come to resent our children, who chide them when they reply to us in English instead of Russian, when they look too much like their fathers. We try not to blame them for how marooned we are in America, but we are quick to discipline and even quicker to anger. Frustrated by our own cruelty, we lock ourselves in bathrooms as clean as any Russian kitchen and let the mirrors tell us what we refuse to tell ourselves: We hate this life. The children we detest chain us to men we do not love or even care for. *Go ahead then*, our reflections tell us. *Leave. It is* OK. *Leave it all: the family, the home, the nest. You have done it before; you can do it again.* And a few of us do as we are told.

Either way, the children age. They take on American personalities and American nicknames given to them by their fathers and schoolmates and aunts. If we stay long enough, they eventually leave us, returning home dutifully on holidays or vacations, and after some years they ask questions: *What was Russia like? What was my grandfather like?* Some of us claim we don't remember, though not one of us has forgotten. At fifty-four, fifty-five, fifty-six we realize that the world is made up of two kinds of people: those who, like our husbands and mothers and grandmothers and great-grandmothers, stay where they are, and those who leave. We left seeking food, heat, mates—something our instincts told us to do. Did we want beautiful objects nestled in a beautiful life? Yes. Were we perhaps inspired by our own beauty to crave a life different from the one in which we were born? Yes. Were we wrong to want that?

At fifty-four, fifty-five, fifty-six we are locked to this foreign soil, crying into strange rivers and swimming in enormous seas and dreaming in a language we did not speak as girls. If you had asked us at five, six, seven, *What is your life going to be like?* not one of us would have said, *I will drive a Honda. I will be a pharmacist. I will go by an American version of my name.* No. All of us would have responded as Russian girls of that time did: *I will live in a cottage in the woods. I will make friends with the bears. I will go to space with the cosmonauts. I will be happy and strong.*

Nominated by The Sun

WELCOME TO THE JUNGLE

by MORGAN PARKER

from PRELUDE

With champagne I try expired white ones
I mean pills I mean men

I think I'm going crazy sometimes really
you think I'm joking I'm never joking

All Men Have Been Created Equally
To Shiver At The Thought Of Me

is something I used to think but forgot
or got drunk tried smoking something new

put on a wig made a scene threw up
in someone's living room cooked

too much food every time can someone just
give it to me when I get home

I know the answer is probably cleavage
cleavage all the boys I know

holding my arms down taking off
my bracelets with their white hands

129

I've pissed on a sidewalk in midtown watched
a Joan Crawford movie at dawn

art is nice but the question is how are you
making money are you for sale

people in movies are always saying
I can't live like this! packing a little bag

or throwing down their forks I mean it
one of these days my whole body might just

go away like just standing in line
at Whole Foods or Purgatory I wish I were

a dream for you to suck on
once I got four tattoos

cut off all my hair
died my hair blonde

had a party had fifty parties
looked for Jupiter and Venus in the smog

painted and repainted my nails
what can they do for you sir

the question is where the fuck
is the sun the answer is tip-toe

into the park at midnight pretend
it's green like home

Nominated by Prelude

JESUS RAVES

by JORDAN KISNER

from N + 1

Five PM at the Sloppy Tuna and the Christians are party ready. The house music started bumping around 11 AM—because it is Saturday in Montauk, and summertime—but five o'clock is the golden hour, when everyone is sundrunk and loose and beautiful. Girls in cutoff shorts and bikini tops throw their arms around boys in Wayfarers, and sway. The dance floor is jammed and everything is spilling, the effect being that it seems to be raining PBR, and the mixture of sweat and sand and other people's beer feels gritty and intoxicating on the skin. The light comes through the crowd slantwise because the sun is setting just past the railing that separates the dance floor from the beach, and while the heat and the stick and the pressing in of bodies is uncomfortable, the visual is stunning: a jungle of skin and light and air thick with energy that is not quite joie de vivre and not quite a collective, ecstatic denial of mortality but something ineffable and in-between.

Pastor Parker Richard Green is standing near the entrance, by the railing where there's a view of the water, drinking a beer. He's 26 and almost aggressively healthy looking. Tawny of skin, blue of eye, blond of crew cut, he looks like he's straight from the manufacturer, a human prototype intended to indicate the correct proportion of biceps to shoulders. His brow is square and his jaw is square, and maybe even his whole head is kind of square, but he's pulling it off.

Next to him is Jessi Marquez, also blond, also tawny. Her face is familiar from stock photographs of sunkissed girls with highlights—wispy hair, round blue eyes, a smile to please—but mysteriously hard to place, as though the lens tilted. Her chin is soft, not angular; her teeth are

131

slightly crooked. On her wrist she has tattooed GRACE, and her right shoulder reads AND THEN SOME, because she wants to remember that God will provide everything you need . . . and then some.

Parker and Jessi have managed to locate the girl in the dancing mass who seems most out of control. She's coke thin, maybe heroin thin, and dazey and wild, jumping up and down and waving her stick arms. They're discreet about it—they stand near her group of friends on the dance floor and catch her as she bounces back and forth—and because they don't invite her to church directly, and Parker, in his board shorts and sleeveless T-shirt, is no one's vision of a pastor, she doesn't realize. If she knew she were speaking to a pastor and his bride-to-be, she might not be screaming into his ear, "I love you so fucking much I'm going to jizz all over your fucking face no really I am Imma come and rub it all over your fucking face."

"You're like my new favorite person," Jessi tells her. "You're like a composite of all our friends. We're gonna be best friends. Give me your number." Cokethin stops running in circles for a minute and does this, and then shouts, "Text me you have to text me right now so I have your number too."

"I am," Jessi says. "I am texting you. You're gonna come out with us tonight and then you're going to spend all day with us tomorrow." Tomorrow, Sunday.

"I'm gonna text you did you text me you have to text me."

"I *already* texted you. I texted you two minutes ago."

Cokethin accepts the challenge. "I texted you an *hour* ago."

"I texted you *yesterday.*"

"I texted you years ago."

"I texted you before you were even born! I texted you when you were in your mother's womb!" With this Jessi wins. Cokethin screams for good measure and then announces, "I'm going now but I'll see you guys later because you're my new best friends kbye," and whirls away off the dance floor and into the road.

They stare after her and then laugh. Satisfied, Jessi leans over and says to Parker, "Now *that's* how you make a Christian."

Parker laughs and shrugs. "Yeah," he says. "In Montauk, that's pretty much how it works."

It was Facebook that delivered me to Liberty Church. A friend from college posted a video that caught my eye; it looked like a trailer for a

Sundance short or a promotional video for a well-funded line of men's accessories. I clicked, and was met with sweeping shots of the New York City skyline and two beautiful faces: Paul and Andi Andrew. They could be J. Crew models, but they are pastors, and the video was the story of their church, of how they left ministry positions at one of the most powerful megachurches in the world, Hillsong Sydney, and moved to New York, where they knew no one, because God asked them to.

I closed the video and wrote my friend an email. "Tell me about your church?" He responded immediately, because he is a good friend, and invited me to come check out Liberty for myself, because he is a good evangelical.

I used to be a good evangelical, too. I was 9 when I "got saved" at Bible camp, which is the evangelical way of saying I accepted Jesus Christ as my Lord and Savior and asked him to come live in my heart forever. For five years after that I prayed all the time; I read the Bible and had earnest if one-sided conversations with Jesus about it; I tried to make other converts. And then, more or less suddenly when I was 14, I stopped believing. It was upsetting for a while, and then high school took over in the way that it does, and I forgot about it.

I had roughly the same interest in "getting right with God" as in readopting my other pubescent passions—scrunchies, the Backstreet Boys—but I tagged along to services the following Sunday anyway. No one seemed to mind when I refused to pray and sat off to the side taking notes. "It's just great that you're here!" they said, and, "Have you eaten? Come grab dinner with us later!"

When Paul and Andi founded Liberty in New York in 2010, they "planted," or established, not one church but two: Liberty Church Tribeca, which launched at Tribeca Cinemas in 2010 and subsequently moved to the Scholastic Center on Broadway; and Liberty Church Union Square, which meets Sunday nights at the Union Square Ballroom. The Tribeca and Union Square communities will be joined by Brooklyn and London outposts in 2014. By 2020, the Andrews plan to have ten churches spread across New York City. This is, for the most part, the evangelical model: constant acquisition of souls, constant efforts to "grow the kingdom of God." Hillsong, the Andrews' old church, boasts tens of thousands of members spread over twenty-nine congregations worldwide. C3 Church, which just opened on North 3rd Street in Williamsburg and is one of Liberty's closest contemporaries (the pastors are friendly, though the churches aren't officially affiliated), has 300 churches all over the world and pulls in roughly 100,000 worshippers every Sunday. By 2020, C3 is aiming for a thousand churches and a weekly attendance of half a million.

The Andrews are fond of saying that while each new church they plant will adopt the culture of its neighborhood, they'll all carry "Liberty DNA." The phrase leapt out at me when I first heard it: tracing lineage in modern evangelicalism is a convoluted, exhausting project. From the strict fundamentalism of the early 20th century to the birth of Liberty Church there have been too many inheritances and rebellions to count. Mutations in identity, politics, and theory multiplied as fundamentalism gave way to the charismatic Pentecostalism that swept glossolalia across the South, inspired a movement toward rigorous Christian intellectualism in the Midwest, and spawned hundreds of other subdenominations: congregationalism, neo-evangelicalism, global evangelicalism; revivalist communes and the Jesus People and Young Life youth ministry; the rise of the Christian right and Falwell's Moral Majority and antiabortion rallies in the '80s; holy laughter revivals in the '90s; the progressive megachurches and the not-so-progressive megachurches; the Michele Bachmanns of the world and today's startlingly liberal emerging church movement.

Despite all the dizzying bifurcation, contemporary evangelicalism comprises a broad but basically recognizable continuum of inherited doctrine, and it was easy to identify Liberty's theology as more traditional than cutting edge, a near relation to the woodsy California Bible camp where I memorized John 3:16 and prayed for the unbaptized. The pastors at Liberty believe that the journey to both righteous living and eternal salvation begins when you accept Jesus into your heart and "give your life to God." They preach from the Scriptures. They tithe. They consider themselves disciples of Christ, and refer to themselves as warriors for God in a war against Satan, who is not a metaphor but a very real demon intent on destroying each of them personally.

They also believe that grace is real, that peace is real, that everyone is deserving of love and forgiveness—and that those things are real because of and through Jesus. Liberty has an active volunteer organization and gives lavishly to impoverished New Yorkers and orphanages in Zimbabwe, regardless of religious or political affiliation, so that everyone can know God's goodness. They "place his name above cancer." They perform healings, witness to miracles.

But there the traditionalism ends. The first time I went to Liberty I thought I'd gotten lost and stumbled into a concert: the house band was blasting anthemic power ballads in advance of the service. There was an iPad on the pulpit. The congregants I met were photojournalists and DJs and brand developers and models. They drink liquor and go clubbing and take notes during sermons on their phones and Instagram the service, which is allowed because all the pastors are doing it too.

Evangelicals have been debating for years to what extent one can be both "in the world" and "of the world." How to balance holiness with worldliness? It's the pastors who primarily define a church's culture, and Liberty's pastors relish the collision of Christianity and a kind of youth-oriented hypermodernism. Liberty has a Pinterest account and a Twitter account. Andi wears leopard-print jeans and quotes Kanye in sermons. Her younger brother Parker, who serves as Union Square's community pastor, knows how to dougie. Steve Trayner, who co-pastors Tribeca with his wife Rhema, works in fashion and rocks a leather jacket and a side fade; Rhema, who has the glossy bangs and punk-polished styling of a downtown gallerist, interrupted the call to tithe to ask the front row if they were into her black nail polish.

"It's adorbs," Parker hollered back.

Last May, Liberty popped up in my Facebook newsfeed again. This time it was a photo of a beach at sunrise: thick, white foam hugging a shoreline that stretched to the horizon, a mirror of slick-wet sand reflecting abundant cloudscapes. The image was sepia toned and dreamy, as though someone had run it through the Walden filter on Instagram. Underneath, text in a bold sans serif read:

Liberty Church Montauk
You're Invited
Join us every Sunday beginning May 26 for . . .
THE WORLD'S FIRST POP-UP CHURCH

Near the bottom, in print so small I had to look twice to see it, there was an asterisk: "DJ will start spinning at 1 PM."

Funny things, lucky things started happening in the twenty-four hours before I left to visit the Montauk pop-up, things that should have gone wrong but didn't. As soon as I realized I wouldn't be able to make the trip without a car, a car materialized. I couldn't afford a hotel room at peak season rates, but with hours to spare, just as I was resolving to sleep in the backseat of the car, a friend of a mother of an elementary school friend appeared, with a big house and a spare bedroom only ten minutes from the bar that houses Liberty's pop-up.

I drove up with Leah, a 23-year-old songwriter and freelance videographer I'd met through Liberty in the winter. We were introduced at a friend's apartment and within minutes I decided that she was one of the strangest, most luminous people I'd ever know. She's physically striking—a former model, she is tall and lanky with long, dark hair and eyes so green that every time they focus on you your breath catches. There's a glowiness particular to people whose hearts are, to quote Psalms, secure in the Lord, and she's got it. She moves through the world expecting adventure and goodness and beauty, and mostly the world obliges: she met Ellie Goulding's bass player at a coffee shop and, four hours later, was hanging out with the band backstage at a concert; she gave a ride to a friend and wound up dancing all night with strangers in a candlelit barn in the middle of the forest; she struck up a conversation in a hotel lobby and found herself in a transcontinental courtship with a famous rock star. (First, she asked him if he was a follower of Christ. He was.)

The drive offered the opportunity for her to catch me up on the latest, which was primarily that she was freaking out about whether the rock star was sufficiently into her and that she'd received the gift of the Holy Spirit after a trip to California. Leah was worried that the rock star might be too nervous to kiss her for fear of violating their shared morals. "And I'm not really that way! I mean, I am, but I'm also like . . . down to hang out and make out." She gave a giddy little laugh and reached over to touch my knee conspiratorially. "You know?"

As she was talking, a pair of headlights appeared out of the darkness in my rearview mirror and grew steadily until, within seconds, the car was right on top of us. The road was deserted and there was room to pass, but the driver followed us this way for more than a mile, the headlights boring menacingly through the rear windshield.

"Go around," I said under my breath. "I'm already doing 80 in a 55. Go around." The car inched closer and closer until, now afraid, I nudged us up to 85 and then pulled away into the next lane. When the car pulled even with us, the lettering on its side became visible: NEW YORK HIGHWAY PATROL.

"Oh god." I pumped the brake.

136

"What?"

"That's a cop. The guy who's been tailgating us is a cop. I'm thirty over the speed limit."

But the state trooper pulled away from us and disappeared into the dark, and that was all. "Whoa." Leah's voice was soft. A stillness fell over the front seat. The road's white median lines continued to disappear rhythmically under the car like before, but the air felt altered, uncanny.

"What *was* that?" I demanded of no one in particular, and then, "What is going on today?"

Leah, more accustomed to this sort of thing, was too polite to answer.

At Leah's request, we headed straight to Ruschmeyer's, where Parker and Jessi and a few other Liberty congregants were already partying. Ruschmeyer's is one of Montauk's scenier nightlife spots, and accordingly is both a breathtaking idyll and a high-octane frat hellscape. The ocean is so close you can see moonlight glint off the water from the bar area; outside, paper lanterns dangle over a wide garden, hung from branches so curved they form a leafy ceiling. When we arrived the air was skin temperature and perfumed by the blooms on the nearby bushes, and young women in microshorts and breezy polyblend blouses stood like stalks around the lamplit lawn in their stilettos.

Inside, gin and tonics were flying. It smelled like college. No one could move because the dance floor was packed to the walls with aggressive fun-having and the only recourse was to throw elbows or simply give up and hump your neighbor. The DJ never played more than a third of a song before cross-fading to another, so Nelly slid into Usher slid into Kanye without ever risking a second of boredom from the dancing throng. In the line outside Leah had been telling me she hates the way modern dating commodifies love. "It turns people into products for consumption. You just try one out, like you'd try out a vendor, until you get bored and then go shopping for another one." The girls ahead of us in line looked surreptitiously over their bare shoulders.

Once we gained entrance, Leah was not two steps onto the dance floor when an enormous linebackerish guy in a collared shirt appeared from nowhere and snatched up her hand, whirling her around and pinning her ass to his hips. "What's your name," he shouted.

"Leah!" she obliged him, smiling and throwing her arms in the air and swaying her pelvis in time with his in a way that was both compliant and neglectful. He was getting what he wanted, but for her, he might as well have been a lamppost.

The music swelled and the collared shirt took the opportunity to lean in closer and bellow "WHERE ARE YOU STAYING." Leah smiled the smile of a woman practiced at gentle demurral. "With friends," she answered, and delicately disentangled herself.

The linebacker shrugged and scanned the crowd for another. He didn't have to look long, and neither would Leah, had she been looking. Men appeared hoping to dance, ready to buy cocktails she would later give away; men appeared and appeared. One roughly shoved a plainer girl out of the way when she obstructed his view of Leah dancing. We found Jessi and Parker and the rest of the crew smack in the middle of the dance floor, unperturbed by the pressing in or the stickiness of the drinks spilling everywhere. This was their element: a crazy party and, looked at the right way, an opportunity to minister.

It was mid-July, the summer's apogee, right in the middle of the pop-up's life span. Jessi and Parker worried a little about the ebb and flow of things: the weekend of Jessi's birthday a week earlier, they had nearly forty people at the Sunday service; other Sundays attendance dwindled and they redoubled their efforts to reach people on the beach and in the bars. Not long ago, Jessi had seen a girl sitting on one of the picnic benches outside Ruschmeyer's crying, and went over to her. "It was actually this kind of big moment for me personally," Jessi told me. Her voice, high and slightly grainy with a young girl's wide vowels and upward lilt, amplified a little. "Because I'd been doing a lot of questioning about what we were doing out here, and having doubts. And I'd said to God that day, Show me You want me here, and I will be obedient. And I saw this girl sitting on a bench crying and God was like, There you go." Jessi asked what was wrong.

Boy problems. The girl seemed receptive to Jessi's consoling, but her friends circled, suspicious. Eventually one of them came out and asked: Who are you? Why are you being so nice? "I said, I just know that God wants you to be happy. We all go through this stuff so He just gave me a heart of compassion for you." The girls were touched; for Jessi, the moment was a victory and a confirmation.

This particular Friday there was more dancing than ministering. Leah swung her bangs from side to side, twerking and spinning and, when the attentions of ambient men became too intense, putting others in the center of attention. "Go Parker, go Parker," she encouraged, stepping back to nudge Parker toward the middle of the tight circle of bodies. Parker stepped forward, shuffling and preening good-naturedly as if to say, "Let me show you how this is done." He paused a moment to work the spotlight, waiting for the beat to drop, and crooked a come-here finger at Jessi, who advanced toward him, grinning. He took her hand and spun her slowly until her butt came to rest against his hips. She leaned forward in her low-cut maxi dress and as the beat dropped her body hit a ninety-degree angle, her back arching in time so that her backward gyrating met his forward thrusting with a kind of breathtaking symmetry. No one could look away. As the whoops and hollers rose above the music, they began to laugh.

Jessi Marquez got saved at four in the morning on St. Patrick's Day, 2009. She'd been clubbing. At the time she was clubbing a lot, working as a promoter, and things were falling apart: a breakup, a crappy apartment, a pervasive sense of hopelessness. "I was doing cocaine and had really bad depression and was taking Xanax and Adderall and all these prescription drugs. I came home and started bawling crying. You know the kind of crying where you can't hold it in? Where you feel like your guts are actually going to come out? It was like that. I felt like I couldn't cry hard enough." She crawled into her bedroom and lay on her bed wailing. Suddenly, she started crying out to God, though she'd never done that before.

"God," she said, "if you exist, I hate you. Why are these the cards that I was dealt? I hate my life. You have to take the pain away." Almost immediately, silence came crashing over her bedroom and the noisy midtown street outside her window. The sirens went quiet and a stillness came into the room. Abruptly, she stopped crying. "I was sitting there and I was trying to make myself cry and nothing would come out. I started laughing. And I just went to sleep."

She woke up the next morning thinking, "Well, if God is real and He has relationships with people, then that's all I want." She quit her job, sold all her things, and left on a yearlong missionary trip with no plans to return. At the end of the year she accepted a ministry job in Australia and was readying to move when she started having dreams. Every night for more than twenty days she was haunted by vivid dreams about New York. "I was waking up bawling crying and—this sounds really weird—I could feel the pain of the people I was dreaming about. God said to me in a dream, 'Would you go? I came into your room and saved you, now will you go and save them?' "

First she said, emphatically, no. "I was terrified about coming back. I had found all this joy and hope and I remembered what my life had been like here." But God kept asking, and eventually she said yes. She returned to New York, connected with Liberty Church, and founded FreelyBe, an event-planning company that pairs nightlife events with nonprofits that receive a portion of each event's revenue. She started integrating: old life, new life; partying, God.

"If you look at Jesus's life, he did missional Christianity," Jessi said. "He went where people were broken. It's so cheesy, but what would Jesus do? I really do feel that Jesus would, like, be hanging out with the homeless in Union Square." She inclined her chin toward me and smiled a little lopsidedly. "I think Jesus would be hanging out in the clubs."

The Liberty kids spent most of Saturday on the beach, listening to the new OneRepublic album and getting tan. When I arrived, it was like I'd stumbled across a group of extras from *90210*: Jessi, voluptuous and tan in her bikini; Jessi's friends Gracie and Monica, bleached blondes with curled and lacquered eyelashes; Leah, with her waist-length hair and constellation freckles; assorted sturdily built boyfriends. Parker padded around in bare feet, aviators, and a muscle tee. "You look like you belong in the Hamptons, Parker," Gracie said. "You look rich." It was true.

When Leah saw me, she jumped up to give me a hug. "Jordan! I had an epiphany last night. I want to tell you about it."

I plunked my bag in the sand and started stripping off layers.

"So last night," she continued, beaming with excitement, "I realized that I think I'm a feminist."

Jessi and Gracie let out groans. "Ugh, Leah, don't say that," said Monica.

"Leah, ew," Jessi shook her head. "You are not a feminist." Leah laughed, enjoying her small rebellion. I glanced around at the expressions of distaste.

"OK," I said, "what makes you think you're a feminist?"

"Well last night I was thinking again about the thing with this guy—"

"With the *rock star*," Jessi interrupted, grinning.

Leah smiled and shrugged. "Anyway, I started thinking about why guys never want to make me their girlfriend. What is it about me that makes guys want to be really good friends with me but not date me? And so I started thinking about, like, the things in men that are universally attractive. The things that everyone wants in a boyfriend, like a guy who will pay for everything, or a guy who wants to take care of you —"

"Wait," I interrupted, "but not all girls want guys to take care of them."

Her face went blank. "What?"

"I mean, not *all* girls want that stuff, like a guy who will . . ." I looked around at the others for confirmation, but they looked mystified. Jessi squinted skeptically.

"What do you mean?"

"Well, lots of the girls I went to college with don't like it when a guy insists on paying for things, and they don't want to be taken care of. They want to . . . take care of themselves."

"Maybe some girls feel that way," Leah suggested diplomatically, "but to me that suggests that maybe they have some other . . . bigger problem with men, you know?"

I suggested we get back to the epiphany. "Right!" she said. "Anyway, I was thinking about the things that are universally, or"—she nodded deferentially in my direction—"that *basically* everyone finds attractive about men. And then I was thinking about what those qualities are in women, like what are the qualities in a woman that make her attractive to men. And like, I don't have any of them."

I stared at her. This was ludicrous. "Qualities like what?"

"Well, I don't have that impulse to nurture or take care of people. I hate cooking, and I don't really care about, like, house stuff. I just want to make art and, like, think about things, and travel and talk to people." She giggled, as though finding herself ridiculous.

At this, Jessi propped herself up on her elbows and shook her head. "But Leah, God doesn't call all of us to be the *same*. Imagine how stupid it would be if we were all perfect domestic homemakers who liked to cook. God calls us to be individuals. You are beautiful and you are wonderful and someone will totally love you just the way you are. Like, just be Leah."

Gracie tipped her head back and hollered, "Let Leah be Leah!"

Parker sauntered over, looking concerned. "Where's the boom box? Did we bring the boom box?"

Jessi rolled over. "Parker, Leah thinks she's a feminist. Will you tell Leah she's not a feminist?"

Parker's eyebrows shot up. "Oh come on, Leah. I feel like that might be a little extreme."

One of the blondes said, "I feel like that might be a little *weird.*"

There was a pause.

"Does anyone want to come with me to get the boom box?" asked Parker. When no one moved from her towel, he shrugged and plodded away across the sand.

The plan had been to barbecue, but by four o'clock the burgers were still frozen and wouldn't grill up right, so Parker dumped the scalding coals in the sand and the group prepared to scatter. Everyone was tired and hungry and sandy and thirsty, but agreed to hit up the Sloppy Tuna for a drink or two, "make some friends," and then go home to shower and regroup before the nighttime round.

"We haven't done much outreach this weekend," observed Gracie.

"I know," Jessi lamented. "We haven't handed out any flyers or anything."

We lugged the cooler and the grill back across the sand and stood around awhile in the parking lot, checking Instagram and waiting for the truck that was coming to ferry everything back to the hotel. Tired of waiting, Leah and I went to the café on the corner, Coffee Tauk, which offered spirulina-enhanced lemonades, organic health bars, and air-conditioning to the visiting Manhattanites.

We sat and sighed, brushing sand off. Leah pushed her bangs from her forehead. "Wait, have I told you about 365 Epiphanies?" She swiped to unlock her iPhone. "It's this file that I keep on my phone because I'm always having these epiphanies, like all the time, and I never have time to sit down and really write about them. So I started this file where I keep track of them, one for every day of the year."

We did the math to see which day we were on, somewhere near 200, and then she told me about her latest entry, which was also about the rock star. "I was praying about it and I just realized, maybe I'm looking at this on entirely the wrong scale. We're so used to thinking about relationships in terms of whether or not our desires can be fulfilled. Like: Does he want me in the way that I want him? Will I get what I want? But there's just a much bigger plan at work. Maybe the value we're supposed to bring to each other's lives is huge—maybe I'll say

142

something that will inspire his work, maybe we're supposed to bring each other closer to God—but I can't see our purpose for each other because I'm fixated on my own idea of how it's supposed to be. And that's just such a narrow way to think about love."

I groped for a response.

"It would be easier except I have Eros for him." she sighed.

At Liberty's regular services in the city, the sermon always ends the same way: the call for souls. The congregation closes their eyes while the pastors speak to the unsaved. They address themselves to anyone new to Liberty or new to Christianity, anyone who may have walked away from religion, or anyone hurting and desperate to change his life. And to those people they offer an opportunity: to get right with God, to give their lives to Him *right then*. This is, the pastor says, the biggest decision of your entire life, the passage to new life and eternal life, and all you need to do is raise your hands. Come on, the pastor says, just raise your hands right where you're sitting.

All over the room, members of Liberty's operations team—event staff who handle practical details, like setting up and tracking how many souls Liberty saves—watch closely over the bowed heads. As the hands go up, hesitantly, one after the other, the ops team scans the crowd and tracks them, pointing to blind converters: There's one. There's another. They look around at each other urgently, catching souls, counting and recording as a group who and how many.

There are hands going up all over the room, the pastor says, and it is so good. Come on, put your hand up. Now we're going to pray together, and as you pray this, Jesus Christ is coming to live inside your heart. You are connected to God after you pray this prayer, and it all changes.

The hands come down and, one phrase at a time, the pastor feeds the words to the assembled:

Lord God, tonight, I give my life to you.
I believe that Jesus Christ died on the cross and rose again in my place so that I
could have everlasting life.
Tonight I say I want to be a Christian, a follower of Jesus Christ, placed in
community and flourishing.

In Jesus' name:
Amen.

And then they open their eyes.

The leopard-print jeans have everything to do with this moment. As does the iPad glowing on the pulpit and the fonts on the projector overhead and the choice of a venue with an enormous, shiny bar in the lounge area. Because if Liberty's success, both worldly and other-worldly, rests on its ability to deliver people to God, to "grow His kingdom," then its most important task is to become the kind of club that people want to join.

This is why the pastors refuse flatly to talk politics. When asked about gay marriage, Paul Andrew replied that he wants Liberty to be known by what it's for, not against. Rhema Trayner told a congregation in the spring, "Doctrine is not a point of unity, and no one will ever have perfect theology. I don't come to church because we agree on every single issue. I come to church because we are family." I asked my friend Tim, a member of Liberty's house band since the earliest meetings, if it was really possible that a church that believes in healings and pre-marital abstinence has no agenda about abortion or contraception or homosexuality. Tim, who works for Reuters and also DJs at clubs all over downtown Manhattan, suggested gently that I was missing the point. "To be fair, I don't know," he said. "But I do know that the only person never welcome to come to Liberty is someone who is physically dangerous," he told me. "That's the only kind of person not allowed in the building."

It's all so likeable. A church designed to make people feel comfortable, included, and inspired. A church that wants to demonstrate at every turn that following Jesus will expand your life, not restrict it. Come on, they say. Just raise your hand.

I had a friend who underwent a dramatic and—to me—baffling religious conversion the year we turned 21. His Jewish ancestry, dormant for so many years, was suddenly rioting forth, and in a matter of months he'd acquired a yarmulke and tzitzit, begun keeping strict kosher, and had withdrawn from what had been his social life. He started hanging around the local Chabad house. A rumor circulated that he'd attended a ritual slaughter of a goat in Williamsburg.

We'd had an intimate, tumultuous friendship, and his conversion was bewildering for both of us, like body snatching. It also imposed an expiration date: if he hewed to conservative Jewish imperatives about male-female interaction, he'd be unable to spend time alone with me, or hug me hello or touch me at all. The door was closing. For several months leading up to that moment, he would come to my room in the evenings bearing one or another kosher dessert and try to explain what was happening to him. Sometimes he wanted to talk about theology, like the role of sex in a Jewish marriage, or why conversion was completely irrelevant to Judaism. ("You are either one of God's chosen people or you are not. There's no use in trying to be one if you're not, or in trying to reject it if you are.") Sometimes he wanted to talk about what he was leaving behind.

These conversations were lonely, a series of loving but hopeless attempts to map a barrier we couldn't see and wouldn't overcome. There were flashes, though, of the old intimacy. One night he arrived with honey cake wrapped in brown paper napkins and settled on my floor. He rested his back against the door, and confessed that he was feeling conflicted. Soon he would have to choose between the two communities and philosophies of Judaism he'd become involved with: Chabad and conservative orthodoxy. The orthodoxy, he explained, was a little more intellectual, more theologically rigorous. It felt to him, for whatever reason, like the more legitimate choice, the serious choice. But Chabad had joy, zeal, animus. He felt like he *should* join the orthodoxy, but he looked at me with pleading eyes and said, "But at Chabad, Jordan, they dance. They *dance*."

That was the last thing he ever said to me that I truly, instinctively understood.

Sunday morning came mild and hazy. At the secluded beach a half mile from the bar where Liberty's service would take place, there was a minor miracle at around half past ten: the sky broke without ever darkening, yielding fat droplets that seemed to come down one at a time in the sunshine. The shoreline was deserted, and when the rain stopped again the sun kept shining, no evidence but a gloss on the stones that anything had happened.

Church was slated for 11 AM, but when I arrived at 10:40, the bar—named, rather baptismally, WashOut—was empty. Plastic cups littered the tables and the ground, abandoned mid-rager the night before. An empty pizza box sat near the door. Outside, an aboveground swimming pool draped in PBR flags incubated in the sunshine, beer mixed with rainwater in pools on the bar, and melted daiquiri in the spinner turned to hard candy.

As I picked my way through the back deck looking for a clean, dry place to sit, a black sedan with tinted windows drove up. The driver rolled down his window and called across the parking lot, "Are you all open?"

"I don't work here."

"Oh." We considered each other for a moment.

"They don't look open," I offered, squinting at the back window, trying to discern the shadowy passenger sitting there, "but there's about to be a church here."

The driver thought he'd heard me wrong. I confirmed that this morning WashOut was a house of God, and he conferred briefly with his fare. They sped away.

Parker, Jessi, Leah, and a few others arrived in a shiny black Escalade a few minutes before 11 and began arranging chairs and pulling water from the bar tap into plastic cups for the visitors. They seemed subdued but composed, clutching coffees and freshly showered. Jessi was wearing glasses for the first time all weekend; Parker looked tired but clean and calm in flip-flops and a pressed chambray shirt.

Cokethin was a no-show. Actually, very few people came to claim their waters: only a Midwestern couple on vacation and a local woman whose enthusiasm for the pop-up caught everyone off guard with its intensity. "I've been praying for you," she confided, opening her eyes wide. "I'm just hoping and praying for a revival in Montauk because the Devil has really taken hold here. It's gotten bad in the last few years."

Parker nodded, his eyes straying to the pile of individually wrapped Rice Krispie Treats Jessi was laying out on the welcome table. "Well yeah. It's been hard planting here. It's hard ground."

She seized on this. "The Devil doesn't want you here. He wants to *kill and destroy* you. And me and everyone else."

Three people represented Liberty Montauk's smallest crop yet, but if Parker and Jessi were disappointed they didn't show it. Parker talked cheerfully about wanting to do Saturday night bonfires next summer, maybe services on the beach. And on the horizon, more pop-ups: spring break in Florida.

But there were beginnings here. Parker's housemates in Montauk, for example, were "basically all Christians now."

"How many is that?" I asked.

"Four, since the beginning of summer," Jessi said, and I turned to Parker.

"So that's four guys in seven weeks who are Christians now?"

Parker's head listed slowly to the left, the words appearing to stall in his mouth. "They're all starting to discover their faith," he said, diplomatically.

Once they determined that no one else was coming, everyone shuffled around and sat down in the two rows of wooden chairs Leah had arranged. Jessi opened with a prayer, quoting Matthew 18:20: *Where two or more are gathered in my name, there am I with them.* "You call us to be light in the dark places, Lord God," she added, "and we know you have such a heart for Montauk."

After thanking her, Parker settled himself on a stool, hooked one flip-flopped foot behind a rung, and took a breath. "A while ago, I had a job transporting kids who were addicted to drugs to rehab," he said. "We used to wake them up at three in the morning and be like, 'Surprise! You're going to rehab.' I didn't stay at that job very long because I got a knife pulled on me, and a gun one time, but actually I really liked the car rides with those kids. I'd talk to them all night."

He'd been thinking about that job since he got to Montauk. Watching the way the visiting summer crowd partied, the way they drank and used drugs and hooked up, reminded him of something he realized on those car trips. "The deepest human desire is to be known completely and also loved. What people display, the partying, the craziness, is not the problem. It's a symptom. The problem is that they feel they aren't loved."

A few people nodded. "That's good," Leah encouraged him softly.

Parker spoke without notes, but in his hand he held a Bible, the one his mother had given him to carry as he shuttled the addicted teens. He flipped it open to First Corinthians 13 and read aloud:

> If I have the gift of prophecy and can fathom all mysteries and all knowledge, and if I have a faith that can move mountains, but do not have love, I am nothing. Love is patient, love is kind. . . . Love never fails. But where there are prophecies, they will cease; where there are tongues, they will be stilled; where there is knowledge, it will pass away. For we know in part and we prophesy in part, but when completeness comes, what is in part disappears. . . . For now we see only a reflection

as in a mirror; then we shall see face to face. Now I know in part; then I shall know fully, even as I am fully known. And now these three remain: faith, hope and love. But the greatest of these is love.

He set the book down and looked around at the few of us gathered there. Then he said quietly, "Think about a love that is so powerful, so immensely powerful that it does not even need to exert effort to create a universe, because He *is power.* Now think about that kind of power, the greatness of the power that put the stars in the sky and spoke light into being before the sun even was, and now think about that power focused into love for one human person. You. God valued you so immeasurably much that He sent a king to die for you. The King died for you. And He adores you."

The room was still. Our eyes were fixed on Parker, who seemed to be radiating both vulnerability and ease, as though these words were at once the most intimate and the most self-evident he'd ever spoken. Imagine the way God loves you, he told us. You are completely and totally known. He sees the depths of your heart and your silliest foibles and your most monstrous thoughts and your most generous acts, and He takes it all and He delights in you and loves you, totally and finally.

Right then, something happened that I wasn't expecting, which is that I remembered what it feels like to be a Christian, or what it felt like for me. There's a membrane between imagining God's love as a thought experiment and experiencing it as absolute reality, and if you slip across it the entire known universe breaks open and then reorders itself to be more whole and beautiful than you thought was possible. I had forgotten. It's a tragedy you can't truly explain what this feels like, the safety and wonder and rest and joy and shattering humility and crazy peace, because when you feel it all you want is for everyone else to feel it too. It's like you've been let in on the most magnificent secret and all you want is to bring everyone else along, because if everyone knew the secret it could solve every problem in the world. This is what Christians call, in a terrific understatement, "the Good News." This is also called grace. Sitting in that converted bar, I got maybe seven seconds of a vivid memory of grace, and the echo alone was enough to remember why people who know the Good News do wild things to spread it: they're filled up with a love so great it demands to be given away.

When the world clicked back into its familiar alignment, the bar actually looked different. The light was coming in softer, and the room glowed hopeful and clean. Parker was talking about miracles.

As soon as the sermon ended, Jessi and the other girls dumped the untouched waters in garbage bins and pecked at their iPhones. Everyone decided on burritos for lunch. The bar resolved, slowly, back into a bar. Before long, the Christians climbed back into their enormous truck and headed toward the coast. +

Nominated by N + 1

LOVE POEM

by MICHAEL MARBERRY

from THRUSH

Darling dumbfucked Darling grumpers Darling
goddess of regret and every graywinged whoring

after longwronged Darling Darling now newer
now improved a sad song played in chords of D

minor oft burgled Darling Darling even oftener
endangered or objectified Darling in the artstuffs

where's your sexkind's goldurn hizzouse Darling
if not symbology a permafrost or nympho anti

rampart Darling our literatures only painting you
a crazy razer of attics and/or raiser of pants tents

Darling have i done no better by you (so doubtful)
Darling have i come some piece hither since being

shit tongued and iffy i don't mean to be the ways
i am and am but Darling you are and Darling but

Nominated by Thrush

ARTIST'S STATEMENT

by JAMES HANNAHAM

from GIGANTIC

As a black artist of color with an Irishman's name, I feel it is necessary to let the viewer know that I am black. By using such a methodology, I may allow the reader to begin the process of dismissing my work for its highly specialized racial content, or conversely, the procedurality of praising it excessively for its Negro-specific performativity with regards to the blactification of subject matter, and in the case of academic and/or funding institutions, commence the compartmentalization and commodification of my identity as well as the inherently intrinsic angry political nature of the work for the consumption of those sympathetic to, or pitying of, what they may or may not perceive to be my apparent st(rug)gle(s).

The telegraphication of my blactitude primarily serves to advertise the packageability of my work, such that those with limited experiential firsthandedness of a melanin-enhanced schema, due to their dearth of Afrogenetic materiality, may believe themselves to have acquired said firsthandedness to the extent that they may now expound upon their knowledge base, by, for example, instruction of Caucazoid Others in the use of linguistic frissons of an Ebonic nature during the course of gala benefits, dinner parties, and the like. Hence, those of an elevated socioeconomic stratum may frequently see fit to circumlocutorily beslaver themselves by the manual juxtapositioning of remunerations and/or the conferral of accolades and compensatory numismatical plethoras within my metacarpus.

* * *

However, the medium of visual art—being primarily uncoupled from the physicality of the body and hence what Clarinda Mac Low calls "the tyranny of the visual," that is to say in this case, the cognitive dissonance created by the Gaelicity and presumed nonblackness of the patronymic and baptismal moniker in question as opposed to the African American *corpus mei* (not accounting for the requisite renegement, or re-nigg-ment, if you will, of any probable European genetic elenchus)—becomes problematized by the assumptional nature of the subjectivity. Insomuchas reader supposition trends toward the normative cloud, thus postulating the hypothesis of apparent pallidity which is then ascribed and projected onto the part of the originator, no linguistic challenge to this customary standard can possibly forthcomb from the substantive quality inherent to the materiality of the art object, being itself composed primarily of black figures (text) upon a background of whiteness. Ergo (or "nergo," to reconfigure the term in an anagrammatical pseudo-Nubianism), it becomes incumbent upon the expositor herself to telegraph the projected mahogany nature of his (in this case) epidermal externality. As in one of my recent works, a poem entitled "Daffodils":

Ise walkin my ass
down Eastern Parkway, mindin'
my business or
                              whatever

smokin' a blunt, drinkin'
a 40, and
it's all spring and whatnot?

And sud'nly I'm like Oooh, snap! Lookit! What's
them li'l   yellow flowers
that's sproutin' the hell up

all over this bitch? (29)

Nevertheless, even as the modality heretofore aforementioned bespeaks what Aimé Césaire and others referred to as "Négritude," the conundrum becomes repostulated: In the absence of embodiment, how

152

may corpo(reality) become fleshtified in terms of spectrumular mani-festation (albeit a similarly ocular occurrence) for the purpose of com-munitizing the reader, who, in the Nietzschean sense, transmogrifies herself into what Sartre would call a *voyeur*, if we are to assume his customary Francophone linguistic stratagem, nevertheless a voyeur of her own intrinsic, viscerous images within the visual construct of her own self-evisceration? If, as Homi Bhabha suggests in *Re-Marking the Savage*, the phenomenon "of" textualization deracinates race, is not the subaltern deformed within the environment of that cellulocity into a series of gesticulations designated as corresponding to preexisting tropes of blaculation, or even individual blaculas, so as to render (norma)tive any conceptualizations of such? Such would desiccate the reification inherent in the refutation of additional homies deficient with regard to Bhabha, babka, or even rugelach. Take this sentensification emanating from within my third dance-novel, the Audelco Award–losing *Why We Greasy*:

> *The man ate a slice of sweet potato pie.* (323)

Based on normative conceptualizations, this gesturally Negrossified delineation transmits a portrayal of representation quite incommen-surable with the contextualized archive, as you will see. If you will, the geography of demonstrative variability may resensitize the voyeuristi-cism inherent in the essentialized, disembodied (yet black) body of this "absence of a nonpresence" within the compository representa-tion. To wit:

> *"The man" ate a slice of sweet potato pie.* (325)

Here, through a reconfiguring of mere punctuational morphology, we may decant the phylogenetic ethnology assumed by the internalized cinematic acumen within the structural body of the nontextualized Other. Paradoxically:

> *The man ate himself a slice of sweeet potato pie.* (327)

In the tertiary reconfiguration above, yet another eventuality becomes emergent, not that of discourse, nor of bibliophilic culpability, but, based on the secondary alabastration in the praxis of the textuality, a contingency of narrational racification, insomuch as the personage in question, by applied verb-tense reflexivity and alphabetical augmentation, becomes emancipated from the circumstance of the oppressed to the locus of the gaze itself, insofar as we posit, in this repositioning, a juxtaposition that negligeés any sense of authorial absolutism, as Bourdieu might not put it.

Hence, the excavation of such Negronial anomalies inherent in the text itself becomes self-reflexive, as the black body, despite its absence from these tropes, becomes objectified (though lacking cor/poreality), dominated, and Ferberized by the methodology within which it is circumducted. It is this tracheotomy with which, in my work, I mean to bludgeon (*matraquer*), in Frantz Fanon's phrase, not only the patronymically presumptive and patronizing gaze posited by its hetero-, homo-, questioning and lesbionic normative space in all its trans-, man-, and womanifestations, but also the hegemony of the hagiographic ideology within the tradition of the Afroristic hyperebony *weltanschauung*, that "sameness within an otherness," as it is said Said said.

Nominated by Gigantic

THE AUTISTIC SON

by SCOTT MORGAN

from TAR RIVER

I.

He drew his name in black Sharpie, blocky
angular letters. On everything, his name.

He built Lego monsters in the doctor's office,
swarmed his fingers over them like larvae

while we discussed therapies. Once in a while
he would look up at us, the doctor would write

that down, he would go back to his creation
and sometimes speak for it, a low monotone

growl creasing his lips. The doctor wrote that down too.
Sometimes he would tell us its name, enumerate

its powers, the doctor would ask for more, he would
deny, the doctor would write that down, he would put

the Legos away and draw his monster on a sheet
of paper, blocky name on the top. He was 7.

The doctor, who worked for the state, drooped his lips,
told us we could expect nothing more.

II.

To clean the wound I pressed alcohol to my gut
with a clean cloth. Absolute commitment

his grip on the box knife. I called his mother
to help me take it from him, his face furious

red, whole body shaking as his mother held
one arm to her chest and I beat the other fist

against the desk until the knife slipped out
and he stopped fighting, dropped his face down

on the desk. His mother called the hospital;
I helped him put on his shoes to go.

III.

It's 6:30, so he wants to go to bed, wants
tucked in, wants me to play Medal of Honor

on his computer until he falls asleep
to the weather channel. He's 17; in another

year his mother and I will take him to court,
tell the judge our boy will never drive a car,

shouldn't draw his name to anything legal.
While he was gone the doctors shuffled his meds,

we replaced the chipped computer desk, the scars
on his arms and fingers healed, and we

redecorated his room. He likes the black furniture,
the red accent wall. He eats his dinner one item

at a time, wears only cotton, cannot start
his own shower water. He's asleep before

I've shot my first Nazi, but I will stay and listen
to the snoring, surrounded by his Lego Monsters,

his Rob Zombie posters, his crabby self-portrait,
his name drawn on everything, in black Sharpie,

in blocky, angular letters.

Nominated by Phil Dacey and Tar River

MAP-READING

fiction by RICHARD BAUSCH

from VIRGINIA QUARTERLY REVIEW

They were to meet at the Empire Hotel lounge on West 63rd Street and Broadway, across from Lincoln Center. She told Benton she would be wearing a blue woolen hat shaped like a ball and a lighter blue top coat. "They have a great wine list," she said. Then, through a small nervous laugh: "I'll be early, and get us a table *away* from the piano." A pause, and then the laugh again. "Believe me, it's good to be away from the piano." She sounded good over the telephone. A soft rich alto voice, full grown. She was now twenty-two. Benton was fifty-one. A half-sister he had never had a conversation with in his life. Kate. Katie.

Her letter, last month, said that she was living in New York now, and had made the adult decision to get in touch with him. She had included an address and phone number. He sent her a postcard: *Welcome to the big city. I don't get into town much, but we should get together.* He hoped she would leave it at that. But she had called him. Their sister, Alice, had given her the number. "I was kind of worried that you wouldn't pick up."

"Don't be silly," he told her. He knew Alice would've given the number with the air of someone expecting nothing less from him.

That was Alice.

He took the train into the city and spent the night and most of the day in the apartment of a friend on East 86th Street. The friend had left for work early in the morning. Benton, a high-school teacher, occupied himself with grading papers and reading *The Great Gatsby*, yet again, to teach. At four o'clock he went out into the rainy street to look for a cab. The rain was cold. There was surprisingly little traffic. He began to walk, hurrying toward Park Avenue. An easterly wind started up. His umbrella shielded only his head, and by the time a cab stopped for him, his front was soaked.

"West Sixty-Third," he said, shivering. "And Broadway." The thought occurred to him that this was life in the world: getting yourself drenched even with an umbrella. He had always been inclined to gloomy reflections. Friends remarked on it. With several of them he had formed a casual club that never met, called *The Doom Brothers Club.*

He sat in the cab and tried to shake the icy rainwater from his coat. The cab was not moving. Horns blew. The rain rushed from the ragged sky, and the windshield wipers made a nerve-racking screech every time they swept across.

He used the newspaper he'd been carrying to absorb some of the water. He was shivering. The cabbie, without being asked, turned the heat up. Benton looked at the back of his head. Dark hair, dark, deeply lined neck. A beetle-browed round little man of fifty or sixty. "I'm soaked."

The cabbie was silent, shoulders hunched at the wheel. You could hear a Middle Eastern voice singing on the radio, though it was turned so low you wouldn't be able to distinguish words even if you knew the language. He looked out at the people hurrying along in the windswept rainy street, and murmured the name, "Katie." She had called herself Katie. "Hi, this is Katie," she'd said over the telephone. "Thank you for answering."

He had seen her only once, when she was three years old, in Memphis. He had traveled there alone expressly to meet his father's new wife and child. His father got a room for him at the Peabody Hotel and they met down in the big lobby that afternoon, shortly after Benton arrived from the airport.

"How's your sister and brother-in-law, there, Tommy," the old man said.

"Oh, they seem fine."

"Haven't heard a thing from her yet, you know."

The divorce was done, and though their mother had met someone else—a real-estate man named Eddie—and seemed happy, this was a sundered family, and Alice wanted nothing to do with the old man or his new wife. Alice and her husband were devout Catholics, and in fact this devoutness was a matter Benton himself had been at pains to overlook:

Alice had problems with Benton, too. She wanted him to repent. She believed it would bring him true happiness. He had always been fortunate enough to see happiness as one of the forms of emotional weather. It would always change. He had learned this without words when he was very small and knew that something about him was different. His sister was too simple for the world itself, he had told her once, and she answered, "Unless ye be like little children, ye shall not enter." She actually used the word *ye*. She actually meant that he would not enter.

Nothing for it.

And that afternoon in Memphis, sitting in the lobby of the Peabody Hotel, seeing the cute little girl with soft blue eyes and black, black hair, he felt his own nearness to this member of the broken family as a shock. He could not quite take in her existence. He discovered an odd reluctance to look at her. The greatest likelihood was that there would never be any close relationship between them.

His father's young wife appeared tired and worried. When she wasn't dealing with the baby, she kept wringing her hands in her lap.

Here he was, doing his own kind of judging.

They sat around a low table, and aside from a gentle awkwardness nothing seemed particularly out of order.

His father said, "You think she looks a little like her older sister?"

"Can't see it."

"Alice remembers growing up in my house like it was paradise. And she resents that I broke it up."

Benton said nothing.

"Well. Anyway."

As five o'clock neared, the old man decided they should stay and watch the famous Peabody Ducks make their anticlimactic waddle along the red carpet from the fountain to the elevator that would take them up to their penthouse home. They all waited and had more drinks while the crowd gathered. The young wife, Della, wanted to know how he liked teaching, what sort of students he had. She had done some elementary-school teaching, she told him, but then that was different. "High school must be so much more demanding."

"Well," he told her, "these days none of them read, and neither do their parents."

"Not like us," said the old man. He had spent his working life as a contractor, building houses. He read history.

"You always had something to read."

"I wasn't being sarcastic."

"I read to him sometimes, now," Della said. "His eyes hurt him."

"Have you had them examined?" Benton asked him.

"Dry eyes," said the old man. "But you like reading to me, don't you, Della."

"Sure." She was mostly concerned with the little girl, now. Katie wanted to get into the fountain with the ducks.

The old man had already had something to drink earlier, and while they waited for the ducks he had three whiskeys on ice. He always drank more than you thought he should, and seldom showed any effects from it. Benton looked at the high ceiling, and at the gathering crowd. Finally the fanfare played, and then the march, and the famous ducks were prodded along into the elevator going up. The doors closed. Much of the crowd dispersed. And the three-year-old girl pulled down into herself, wanting the birds to come back. It was a long afternoon and evening, Della trying to manage a cranky child and an increasingly gregarious husband. Benton, watching her, thought of fine crystal: the kind that broke when sound waves got too high. By the time they walked across the street to Automatic Slim's for dinner, the old man had made friends with several of the barmaids and waiters. At the restaurant, nobody had much appetite. The old man ordered a bottle of Sancerre, and drank most of it alone.

"We don't go out much," Della said, wrestling with the girl.

"Must be hard to find the time."

"We stay home and enjoy this one, mostly." She kissed the top of the child's head.

"You don't need a TV with a kid this age," said the old man. "All the entertainment you need. It's a comedy show just watching them move around. Used to get the same kick watching you and Alice."

The child climbed into her mother's lap, and whined low about something.

"Past Katie's bedtime," the old man said. He got up and made his unsteady way to the restroom.

"He doesn't usually drink *this* much," said Della. "I think he wants to celebrate your being here."

"I've never seen him drunk, but I've seen him drink more than this. I wouldn't worry." He smiled at her.

"Oh." She looked down. "I wasn't—I didn't mean to say anything."

"It's fine," Benton told her.

She gave him a strange, evaluative look.

"What is it?" he asked her.

"Do you see your coming here as a peace trip?"

He realized that his father's young, anxious wife had also drunk more than was usual for her. "Not necessarily," he said. "I think we're okay. I mean we've had the usual troubles, I guess. It's Alice he must be thinking of."

"He was surprised—but very happy you wanted to come." She seemed about to cry. She held the child and nuzzled the little fat neck.

The old man strolled back to the table and pulled out his wallet. "We should get."

"I've already paid," Benton said.

"Well—if you're sure."

He watched them get themselves into the car, with Della behind the wheel. They drove off toward Union Avenue, and he waved, without being able to see whether or not they waved back.

In the lobby bar, he met another young man who was looking. They had some drinks together and then went upstairs. The man, Peter, smiled gently when Benton told him about teaching high school. He said he was a med student at the university. Epidemiology.

"Of course," Benton said.

"Not what you think," said Peter. "My interest is influenza."

He left before light, and Benton slept a little more, and took a Xanax when he woke. His father called. "We'll have breakfast at the Peabody— pretty good buffet up in the Penthouse. We'll meet you there in half an hour."

"I've got a flight at three-thirty."

"Plenty of time."

You could not argue with the old man.

The Peabody Penthouse had five long tables, each one laden with dozens of foods to choose from. The city looked gray out the windows. Pale with what he said was a little hangover, drinking black coffee and a Bloody Mary, the old man asked Benton about girlfriends. The old man would not let it alone.

"Actually, there are several candidates," Benton answered, not wanting to quarrel over anything, and hoping he sounded casual enough.

Della looked at him with interest. He wondered what his father had said to her. She was not quite three years older than Benton himself.

Finally, after a shallow hour of avoiding the subject of why his son was not apparently interested in some one woman, the old man drove his wife and daughter away, Della making the little girl wave from her child's seat in back.

He'd kept that image for a time. The little sister's uplifted hand in the window of the car. The very heart of possibility. And as the years went by he thought of her now and then, imagining her growing into a teenager, growing up in that house with Benton Sr., with his judgments and his temper, and Della, who had seemed so fragile and worried. But he could never see Katie as anything but that little girl. Alice's children, two little boys and a girl, were not much older than she. How strange to think that the little girl straining to put her hands in the water of the fountain in the lobby of the Peabody was another sister. And grown now.

Alice lived in Brooklyn. Because he brought the children stuffed toys and performed little magic tricks for them—disappearing coins and multiplying veils—he was a favorite uncle. He loved them, and had learned to discount Alice's load of sorrow at his life, just as she and her husband had brought themselves to the point of being glad to have him in their home.

Many times when he was with them and the children he felt good. It was a little like throwing something back at the darkness all around. As there were pockets of the Middle East that were still locked in the eighth century, so also many places, most places, in his own country were still mired in 1955. He had said this as a joke at their dinner table one night, and she got up and went into the other room, holding a napkin to her face. Her husband, Lew, a kindly little man with white hands and tufts of furry black hair on the backs of his fingers, shook his head and concentrated on his steak. He worked as a salesman of hospital supplies.

"I thought it was funny," Benton said. "She knows I'm joking with her."

"She's been moody," said Lew. "Means so much to her. We keep praying for you."

"I'm just fine," Benton said. "Really. Just fine. Couldn't be better."

"She worries."

"Tell her not to worry."

Their father and Katie's mother, as far as he knew, were both alive and well in Memphis. He knew from her letter that Katie had finished her degree at Boston University, and had been in New York now for more than a year. He and his father hadn't spoken in years—not even to argue

163

anymore. Everything between them had been broken for so long. But she was a grown someone, blood kin, and he was curious and nervous, too. Actually quite nervous. This struck him as having unexpectedly to do with his father. He could not explain it to himself otherwise.

He used to meet a man named Clovis at the Empire Hotel lounge, and sometimes Clovis would already have a room. Benton's life had been spent going from one to another of these kinds of affairs—his own kind of serial monogamy: everything carefully arranged and brokered for safety. He was all right with it. While you did not have a choice about your sexuality, there were many choices about how you lived the life given to you. He liked living alone. He went out when he wanted to, and he kept his private affairs to himself. It had been close to a year now, since the last. The high school at which he taught English was in Clifton, New Jersey. There was a woman in Clifton he saw platonically. They went to movies together, or to dinner, or just out for drinks in the late afternoons after meetings. They seldom spoke about their personal lives.

At the hotel restaurant, he found a band playing loud, while a woman stood on the piano stool wearing a skirt whose hem came only to the top of her thighs. She bent over to slam the keys, exposing her whole backside in black frill-bordered panties. Her playing was fast, loud, highly skilled, and aggressive. Benton understood that it was not really about the playing, but about the standing on the piano bench in that way, wiggling to the boogie-woogie. He stood in the entrance and looked for the ball-shaped blue woolen hat, and there it was, in the far corner, near the windows looking out on 63rd Street. He went to the table and she stood, tall and slender, with a face that replicated her mother's. He could not convince himself it wasn't Della.

"Hi," she said.

"Hello."

There was a moment of deciding whether or not to embrace. "I'm afraid I got soaked," he said, and she helped him off with his coat. Finally he took the step toward her and she put her arms out.

"Mom told me to look for a tall man with ocean-blue eyes."

They sat across from each other. "I could just have looked for your *mom.*"

"People say that." The piano player's antic singing was filling the place, so they had to shout to be heard.

"You see why I wanted to sit away from the piano."

"She's good."

Katie smiled and took off the hat.

"It's hard to believe you're here," he said.

"I have a vague memory of you, you know. Those Peabody Ducks."

"You wanted to get right in that water with them."

The waiter came. He had a faintly sour expression—someone just awakened from a nap. Benton asked if red wine would be all right, and she smiled. He ordered a bottle of Bordeaux, and an appetizer of steamed calamari for himself. She asked for a prawn cocktail. He looked at her hands, the bones of her wrists. She was very thin.

"So, how are your parents?" he asked.

She looked at him. "The same. They never change."

"Does Dad know you're seeing me?"

Her smile was quick, and then it was gone. "We don't talk that often."

"I haven't spoken with him in forever. I don't know how long."

"We haven't been much of a family, have we?"

"I'm pretty certain that's been his choice, wouldn't you say?"

"Well, people make allowances, don't they?"

"You'd say that of him?"

"I don't know. He likes things smooth."

"Pardon?"

"I meant he never talks about what he feels. Never anything about himself. The world is

going to hell—you know."

"Tell me about *your*self."

She hesitated. The waiter brought the wine and then had some trouble opening it. Benton said, "You want me to do that for you, son?"

But the waiter got it open, thanked him anyway, and poured the taste. The wine was soft and tannic. "Good," Benton said, nodding.

The waiter poured it, set the bottle down on the table, and walked away. Benton lifted his glass and shouted against the music, "To families everywhere."

"I'll drink to that." There was something barely controlled in her voice, a tension that gave it the faintest tremor. Probably it was having to talk so loud to be heard.

Again, he said, "Tell me about yourself."

"Not much to tell. I grew up an—an only child. Graduated from Boston. I have a job in public relations at Harper."

The music stopped, and the singer was talking about taking a break.

"You're in publishing?" Benton asked, happy about the quiet.

"Well, no. Marketing, really."

"But in publishing."

"Lowest of the low rungs on the ladder, you know. I'm just starting."

"Well, but that's great. Do you think you might want to get into the editorial side of it?"

"I took a publishing course in Vancouver last summer. So, sure, maybe. I don't know if I'm smart enough."

"How did you do in the course?"

"It was fun. I did well."

"Then there you are."

"And you teach English, I think?"

He regarded her, taking in the kindly smile.

"Mom said she was pretty sure you teach English."

"I've been at the same school since before you were born. In New Jersey. Clifton."

"I have a friend from New Jersey. She's an older woman. Mom's age. But nice. I met her in Vancouver, if you can believe that."

"Small, small world," he said. But he thought about how immense it was, how a man could have a sister he has seen only once in her life.

They were quiet, sipping the wine.

He poured more for them. "So you're working in publishing, and living in New York."

"I went and saw Alice in Brooklyn."

He waited.

"I wanted to meet her. So I just went over there. And she let me in. She was pretty nice. I met her husband, Lew. I liked him. I liked them both."

"I don't see much of them since their children moved out."

"Alice was stiff but nice."

"Ridiculous, after all this time. She's like the Taliban."

"Well."

"She is—you're her sister, for God's sake."

She gave him a strained look, then gazed out the window.

"Nothing against Alice," he said. "Nor any other Christians anywhere, elsewhere."

"You both hate him."

"Alice grieves for his soul. Alice is still angry at him. Alice can hold on to anger. Believe me, you've never seen anything like it. She's like a character in a Southern Gothic novel. And me, well, to be absolutely

166

truthful, I never think about him. He—we never could agree on some things. Let's put it that way."

"Alice grieves for his soul. And is angry."

"You see, Alice and Lew are of a particular *kind* of Christianity. Christ as the celestial cop."

"She showed me pictures of Dad when he was younger, with your mother. Your mother was very pretty. Alice cried showing it all to me."

Benton said nothing.

Katie stared into her wine. "She's just this lonely old Brooklyn lady with a big mole on her neck who wears a scarf to church and shops with a metal wagon."

"Well," Benton felt compelled to say, "don't give her any political power."

The other shook her head and drank.

"You'd think the divorce just happened."

She said, "I saw the wagon off the back stoop when I went out there to smoke a cigarette. Lew was so sweet to me but I had the feeling he spends most of his time watching sports and waiting for her to bring him drinks and food. I had dinner with them. There's a crucifix in every room of the house."

"Oh, it's definitely a Catholic house."

"They seem happy enough together."

"Habit."

"Does that invalidate it?"

"Not at all. That's absolutely the truth of it. Habit or no, it's still a form of domestic bliss."

"You sound bitter."

"Maybe I am, a little. Since that form of happy also allows for some pretty terrible habits of thought."

"Do you still go—"

He shook his head. "Not since I left home for college."

"Alice and Lew said grace. We held hands and it was like we were a family."

"You didn't have that at home."

"Not once." She laughed that soft laugh he remembered from her voice on the phone.

"No," he said. "The old man's never been much for it. The source of his problems lies elsewhere."

"I used to wish I had whatever it is that makes them so calm. Did you ever wish you had that?"

"No."

"Well, your mother was a pretty woman."

"She still is. And like I said, she's happy, too. At seventy-three, with her second husband. And of course Alice didn't like him at first. Mother was living in sin."

"The phrase is funny, isn't it. 'Living in sin.' Isn't everyone living in sin?"

"Living in the weather of the world." He smiled. And then he caught himself wondering how much she knew about him.

" 'Living in sin.' It always struck me as a phrase religious women used. Almost exclusively."

He said. "Someone should do a linguistic study."

"And you never were like that—that they were living in sin—about him and my mother."

"Never. Of course not."

"And Alice is all right with it now."

"Well, Mom got a dispensation on some technicality, making her marriage to Dad invalid in the *church*. Which made bastards out of Alice and me. But it saved the whole thing for her and she could accept the old boy—Eddie's his name—still without really liking him much. Alice is a bit judgmental by nature. Which, of course, she got from Dad. I think Eddie's all right, really. And he treats her like a queen."

"Funny." She took more of the wine. "This is the strangest place."

"Here?" he said.

"Earth." She grinned.

"And we walk up and down on it?"

She nodded, looking off. Then: "I didn't know where to go."

"Excuse me?"

"Nothing. Tell me about your life, brother of mine."

The wine was evidently going to her head. She took more of it.

He looked for the waiter. "How long does it take to put steamed calamari and a prawn cocktail together?"

And as if what he had said called her forth, the singer walked over in her tight, brief, black skirt and fishnet stockings. He saw the black bow tie at her neck, the puffed white sleeves of her blouse. "Too early?" she said to Katie.

"This is Lanelle," Katie said.

Benton offered his hand.

"Too early," said Lanelle, sitting down.

He stared.

168

The waiter came over and gestured. She nodded. He went off. She turned to Benton and grinned. "They know what I like here between sets."

"You sing and play wonderfully," Benton said, and tried not to have it sound as empty as it did sound. He couldn't take his eyes from her face. There was something slack in it, a kind of indolent watchfulness. He added, "I mean that. I'm very impressed."

"Lanelle's my roommate," said Katie. "That's why I wanted to meet here."

Benton glanced at her, then regarded Lanelle again. "You in publishing, too?"

She laughed. "Not so's you'd notice. But it's a pleasure to meet Katie's brother, Tommy. Long-lost brother, I should say. I think it's great."

"Maybe we'll all go get something in Chinatown after your last set," Katie said. She sounded younger, hopeful, and faintly pleading.

"Sounds like fun." Lanelle gave Benton an appraising look. "You like Chinese?"

"Very much."

"We *love* Chinese." She touched Katie's wrist. "Don't we."

"I think I've got MSG in my blood," Benton's sister said.

He leaned slightly toward her. "Am I to understand something here?"

"Funny," Katie said, without the slightest inflection.

"Are you—are you on speaking terms with Dad?"

She moved her index finger around the lip of her glass, staring at it. "Like you are, sure."

"Well, I'll be," he said.

Lanelle touched his wrist now. "It's true, though, isn't it? You see it on the news now. People talking the wave of the future, and famous people coming out and marriages in some states and you start thinking it really is changing. But there's always the individual cases. Right?"

He nodded, and drank the wine.

She went on: "People like us still have to map-read."

"Excuse me. Map-read?"

She looked at Katie. "I'm ten years older than your sister, here."

"You don't look it."

Now she gave him a sweet smile, charming and perfectly empty. "Well. Thanks for the compliment. But really—come on. Haven't you been reading the maps all these years? From your own kind of closet?"

The waiter brought her a whiskey, neat, with a little cup of espresso. She drank the whiskey in a gulp, then sipped the espresso.

"We live together as husband and wife," Lanelle said. "Her family— and mine, too—don't really know what to do with it."

"So you—you read the maps."

"We navigate the waters, yeah. But we're out there in the sunny blue."

"I see."

"For love."

"Yes," Benton said.

Lanelle repeated it. "For love."

He said, "I'm with you."

She finished her espresso, set the cup down, then stood and walked off. Benton saw her stop at another table and lean over to speak to the woman there.

"You teach English," Katie said to him. "What grade?"

"Twelfth."

"Do the people you work with know?"

He watched Lanelle go on out of sight beyond the bar. "I'm sorry?"

"Do they know about you."

After a brief pause, he said, "Some of them, of course. Friends."

"Crazy, isn't it."

"It's the territory," he said. "You know. Our schizoid country."

"You should do something where you don't have to worry."

"I'm fine, really."

"You're my brother," she said, and raised her glass. "Here's to my one brother. And I didn't know this about you until a couple of years ago." She smiled, but there were tears lining the lower lids of her eyes.

"You all right?"

"Isn't it strange to have better treatment from people—just people— than you ever got from your own family?"

"You mean the parents," he said.

She did not answer. She was pouring more of the wine.

"I think I know what you mean," he said. "You mean all of us."

"We should get another bottle."

"You mean me."

"I wish I'd known about you, and if you'd called now and then, just to be in touch, if we'd been in touch, I think I might've. Because what if you were there when I figured it out? I mean things might not've been so hard."

He nodded helplessly. "Right. That's absolutely right. I'm sorry."

"I went through a lot of hell, growing up. An awful lot of—just—you

170

know, hell." She had turned to the waiter, one hand up. The hand shook slightly, the smallest tremor while she made a little waving motion. It went all the way to the bottom of his heart.

"God," he said. "I'm so sorry."

But the music had started up again, and it was clear that she hadn't heard him. She was watching Lanelle move through the room, languid and sultry, mic in hand, singing "Angel Eyes."

Nominated by Virginia Quarterly Review

PORN

by DOROTHEA LASKY

from THE PARIS REVIEW

All types of porn are horrific
I just watched a woman fuck a hired hand
In her marble kitchen while her friends looked on
The title of the movie was *Divorce Party*
And throughout his big cock, her skinny thighs
Her friends shouted, Nah girl, now you're free

But no she's not she's in a movie
And now I am crying
Because the man looks like an ex-boyfriend
Or my half brother
My boss
A monster
Someone who left me in the dark
Someone who darkened me
A million times over

I've only fucked 7 guys in my whole life
But I've watched more porn than you ever will
Hours and hours
A woman and a dog
Three women
A hairy fruit
Four bending over backwards
Vomit sex

The underplay
Of tendril
In motion

I watch porn
Cause I'll never be in love
Except with you dear reader
Who thinks I surrender
But who's to say this stanza is not porn

Calculated and hurtful
All my friends say I'm free
And yes, maybe I am
But are you free
No, you'll never be
I've got you in my grasp
I've got you right here in my room
Once again

Nominated by The Paris Review

FOUR-WAY STOP

fiction by GEORGE SINGLETON

from THE GEORGIA REVIEW

G.R. prided himself on both historical and traditional figures. He felt as if he knew quite a bit about pop culture, too, at least in movies and music. This was Halloween at his and Tina's front door, out from normal suburban neighborhoods. He'd already pointed at masks and said Batman, Iron Man, Superman, Spiderman, Incredible Hulk, and common zombie. Clown, ghost, Pocahontas, ninja, Iraqi War Special Forces Seal. He'd correctly identified Reagan, Bush, Napoleon, and Rush Limbaugh. Ballerina, pro wrestlers (Andre the Giant, Lex Luger, Ric Flair, The Undertaker, Macho Man Randy Savage, Hulk Hogan, Dusty Rhodes, Rey Mysterio Jr.). Football players (Cam Newton and Peyton Manning). G.R. waved at parents waiting on the roadside in cars, gave a thumbs up, said how he liked the way their little Lady Gagas looked, their Mileys, their MacBook Airs and cans of Red Bull. "Goddamn, how many miniature Snickers we got left? We got any of those Reese's Cups?" G.R. said to his wife. "I don't remember Halloween being like this the last few years. The churches must've quit having parties. I thought parents got scared off by razor blades and white powder."

Tina sat in the den, with the door open to the living room where her husband stood at the front door. "I told you to wear a bloody bandage on your head like some kind of Civil War amputee. That might scare some of them away," she said. "Do I need to go back out? We already spent almost fifty damn dollars. Please don't tell me I got to go back out. These kids aren't even from around here. Some of them aren't even

174

kids." She picked up the channel changer and moved from one food network program to another. She went from a tips on vinegar barbecue show to one on noodle making in southeast Asia. Tina wore flannel pajama bottoms with giraffes printed on them, and a T-shirt advertising WSPA because she called first to the station one morning when she knew the trivia answer, which happened to be "avocado green shag carpet."

"We might," G.R. said, and then looked out the door and said, "Jesus! Jesus! Two Jesuses! Are y'all with each other?" Two young men limped up the walkway, both burdened with crosses fashioned from four-by-four lengths of pressure-treated pine normally used for flower-bed edging.

G.R. yelled out, "Jesus and Jesus! Y'all are the first biblical characters we've had tonight. Good job, boys!" He focused on the teenagers, but handed over a couple small Butterfingers and Milky Ways to a young hobo and Snow White who elbowed in. They didn't say "Trick or Treat" or "Thank you," but he didn't mind. To the two Jesuses he said, "Man, this has to be tough," for they had to hold their arms out to the side, with plastic orange pumpkins strapped to their wrists, which were strapped to the wood.

"We're not Jesus," the kid on the left said. "I'm Impenitent Thief."

"Penitent Thief. Sorry," said the other kid.

G.R. looked at them and thought, Did a Mormon family move nearby? Are these boys Jehovah's Witnesses? He said, "Say all that again, what y'all just said?" He didn't say, Aren't y'all a little old to be trick-or-treating? but thought it. He also thought, It's almost ten o'clock, and remembered seeing a news item one time about how the last visitors on Halloween often case a house.

The thieves' father slid out of the shadow of the tea olive bush and said, "It's what they wanted. They wanted to go out one last time. What can you do as a father?"

G.R. said, "Jesus. Jesus Christ." He said, "I doubt I have anything y'all might want," and he stared. "I mean, I got candy, that's it." The father had long brown hair and a beard, and when he stood between his boys it looked like a painting G.R. saw one time in a book in the hospital emergency room's waiting area. "We ain't got no manna, or silver."

"I'm allergic to peanuts," said Impenitent Thief.

G.R. dumped what he had left in both boys' candy receptacles, and turned off his porch light once they trudged back to the road. He didn't think, at first, about how he didn't see a car out there for them, and the next house stood a quarter-mile away. He tried not to think about how his own son kind of looked like Penitent Thief.

At ten o'clock Tina went to bed without saying goodnight, leaving G.R. in the den. He turned to the early local news on the right-wing channel he normally watched in order to stay in tune with the enemy's movements. The anchorwoman came on saying, "Some people are calling it a Halloween miracle," then went on to say how she'd get to that story right after the weather forecast.

The weatherman said, "It's forty-five degrees outside now, and I got your miracle right here, Amy—it's going to be in the mid-seventies tomorrow, but rain will be moving in over the weekend, with lows near freezing. Near freezing! So much for global warming!"

"Thanks, Pete. That sounds wonderful to me. As you know I was brought up in Portland, so a little rain doesn't bother me at all."

G.R. wished that he hadn't poured out all the candy. He got up, went to the refrigerator, and thought about eating whatever Tina cooked earlier in the day that involved diced kidneys. He took out two cans of beer and heard Amy say, "And now for the Halloween miracle."

When he got back in the den he looked at the TV screen and saw Jesus and the two thieves. He yelled back to Tina, "Hey, those guys were here," but she didn't respond.

"They was here, and then they wasn't," a woman being interviewed said to a reporter. "I seen them, and then they vanished. Like, I don't know, I thought maybe I blunk my eyes, but Maura here seen them, too, and she says she didn't blink none either."

The camera swung to Maura, the woman's daughter, still dressed up in her costume. G.R. said out loud, "Vampire."

"I come back from my boyfriend's momma's boyfriend's party and they was standing right dare," said Maura, pointing to the front stoop. "I said, 'Y'all ain't right,' and took me a picture using my cell phone." She held the phone up close to the camera.

Her mother said, "I normally don't do Halloween, you know. Something tode me this year, though, to go out to Big Lots and get me bunch of them little Skittles packs. I did. We had a bunch of kids show up, and then right at the end come Jesus and them two robbers, you know. I gave them one Skittles pack each, and then they disappeared. We all lit up out here! Ain't no way to just take off without no one noticing."

The camera turned to the reporter. He looked, to G.R., like the kid on *The Addams Family*. G.R. couldn't tell if the guy wore a costume or not. "Amy, I'm on Old Roebuck Road—and three other people say they had the same experience but they didn't want to be on camera. If anyone out there witnessed Jesus and the two thieves, we'd like to hear about it. Back to you."

G.R. said, "I witnessed it," to himself, then louder to Tina in the bedroom, "I witnessed it. Hey, I might've witnessed a Halloween miracle, honey."

He drank his beer and accidentally hit LAST on the channel changer. A man wearing a toque looked straight at G.R. and said, "Never, ever, underestimate the remarkable flavors of sweetbreads."

G.R. called the station to say he'd seen them, too, but the line was busy for five minutes straight. He finished his second beer, went back to the refrigerator, extracted the rest of the six pack, and went out to his truck. He looked at his watch and tried to remember when his last trick-or-treaters came by—9:45, he figured. Now it was 10:20. He knew that people walked at about three miles an hour because Tina's doctor had put her on a regimen. G.R. thought that anyone sporting a cross couldn't make more than a mile and a half at most, and then if they stopped at houses working a late-shift Halloween, it wouldn't even be that far.

He thought, If I can find these guys and deliver them to the TV station, maybe I'll get on the news. What would Tina think about that? What would she think about turning on the television in the morning and seeing G.R. standing there next to Jesus and the two thieves?

He thought, Maybe I can tell our story.

Near the end of Old Roebuck Road, a quarter-mile before it teed into 215, stood a useless four-way stop. On three corners stood pastures, and then there was a cement block convenience store where sheriff's deputies hung out waiting for people to ease through without holding their brakes properly. G.R. had his truck window down. He'd called out "Jesus! Jesus!" about every fifty yards, driving twenty miles per hour, his high beams on.

At first he thought he heard the pop-pop-pop of a pistol from be-hind the store, but then realized the sound was planks of lumber dropped upon one another. He sat at the four-way a good half-minute longer than needed, a can of open beer between his legs, before re-leasing his clutch and rolling into the store's shallow parking lot, and then around back where, sure enough, Jesus and the two thieves stood around a fifty-five-gallon drum, the crosses standing upright in it, Jesus holding a lit Zippo in one hand and some wadded newspaper in the other.

G.R. pulled up beside them and turned off his headlights. The three men stood motionless. "Y'all was on the news just now," G.R. said. "They said anyone could find y'all, call up the station and let them know."

"We haven't done anything wrong," the father said. He said, "We were hungry. Candy isn't the best for a body, but it's better than noth-ing." The boy who introduced himself as Penitent Thief apologized again, but his brother said, "And then we'll eat this crap, get cavities, get diabetes, and die."

G.R. got out of his truck. He said, "Is the store closed? What time does this store close? I don't come down this way very often any-more." He thought, Certainly they'll have cans of sardines or some-thing inside better than candy. He thought, I don't have enough beer to share.

"Name's Darmon. You can have your candy back if you feel like we duped you," the father said. He lit the newspaper and dropped it into the drum. His two sons stepped closer and held out their palms.

G.R. put his beer can on the roof of his truck. "Okay, listen. You men were at my house. I don't know if I looked away, or what, but you dis-appeared. And then this woman came on TV and said y'all disappeared from her. People out there think you're really Jesus and the two thieves."

"People see what they wish to see," Darmon said.

G.R. said, "Yeah." He said, "Yeah, I know what you mean." Without the crosses on their backs, and without the porch light providing a shadow, these three men looked like normal unemployed construction workers. They looked like hobos, grifters, Irish Travelers. If they would have shown up without the accoutrements, G.R. thought, he would've pointed at all three and yelled out, "Welder," or "Landscaper," or "Shriner."

"It's a long story," said the father. "Last year we had a roof over our heads. Now we don't."

"Mom does," Penitent Thief said. "She's at the shelter, but there wasn't enough room for all of us."

Impenitent Thief reached into one of the plastic jack-o'-lanterns and pulled out the packs of M&Ms. "We got to remember she likes these best, tomorrow."

G.R. reached into the back of his truck and wrestled out two logs he'd picked up at some point where Duke Power workers had trimmed trees that neared electric lines. He had prided himself on not buying half-cords of delivered wood for three years. He said, "I could give y'all this." He said, "Wait a minute. I could give y'all this, and you'd have heat for the night. Or I guess I could drive you around and show you how to find wood, so you can have heat for a lifetime. Ha-ha-ha. You know what I mean?"

Then he dropped the tailgate and held out his right hand to help both Penitent and Impenitent into the back. Darmon got in the passenger side, after sliding the beer over.

For a couple seconds G.R. thought about taking them straight to the TV station. He thought about saying, "Don't worry. I was never a soldier."

At the four-way stop sign he stopped, again, too long. Darmon said, "You got it both ways."

G.R. said, "This is right where our son got killed three years ago."

After he pulled out the push mower, riding lawn mower, edger, leaf blower, and then the stacked rakes/shovels/post-hole diggers/limb cutters/rolled-up extension cords/rolled-up extra garden hose/boxes of Christmas decorations, there was enough room inside his storage shed to house three stray men temporarily. G.R. manhandled a roll of hurricane fence he didn't need, and a roll of barbed wire he thought he might need some day, then humped out a number of clay flowerpots Tina said she'd one day use to plant lemon trees and ficuses. He moved bags of potting soil, pine-bark mulch, playground sand, and lime. "I'm embarrassed that we have all this shit," he said.

"You have a nice house," said Darmon. "What you got here, two acres?"

G.R. said, "Y'all can stay here tonight. One and three-quarter acres. Y'all can sleep here tonight. But you'll need to leave before my wife gets up. She just won't understand, you know. It's one of those things. Hey, who wants to eat some kidney pie?"

G.R. went tiptoeing back inside the house, picked the casserole dish out of the refrigerator, opened a drawer for three forks. He placed the dish on the dining room table, got a roll of paper towels out of the closet, and listened for Tina's snoring. He said, "Tina" in a normal speaking voice. She didn't answer. The bedroom television aired nothing, which meant the remote's timer had shut it off. As he stepped out on the back porch he heard one of the boys say, "That wouldn't be right," which made G.R. wonder if his father or brother had just said, "We can break in later."

"I heard all that," G.R. said when he approached the shed, a hundred steps away, in hopes of calling a bluff. "Don't get any ideas about breaking in later. I have no money hidden."

Penitent Thief said, "What? We were talking about what to do if we needed to use the bathroom. Peeing won't be a problem, but in case one of us has to go number two. I was saying it wouldn't be right to use the wheelbarrow."

"We can use one of the jack-o'-lanterns," Darmon said.

"And these paper towels," said G.R., handing over the kidney pie. "Here, my wife said for y'all to eat this," he lied. "Well, anyway, y'all stay warm. Put some charcoal in that hibachi and light it up, but keep the thing outside the shed. I wouldn't want y'all to asphyxiate."

Darmon said, "We appreciate everything. Listen, I'm sorry about your son. I appreciate what you're doing for mine. For me and mine."

G.R. said, "There's a pull cord for a light in here. Let me go back inside and see if I can find some blankets." He started back to the house, then turned and said, "There's a smashed-up car over there on that side of the property. Don't sleep in it."

"This kidney stuff ain't bad," said the Impenitent son. He said, "Is there a hose out here? Would you mind if we drank some water?"

"Right over there. Help yourself. If I think about it, I'll bring out some plastic cups."

G.R. had not stood in his son's bedroom more than a half-dozen times since the accident. Tina sat at the desk daily. G.R. couldn't. He sat outside—no matter the season—from dawn until dusk most days. Although he didn't have to return to work after the settlement, G.R. wouldn't have gone back anyway. He ran through images of his boy turning a double play in high school, of his throwing a stick to the dog, of his sitting down at the desk to work out algebra problems. G.R. knew that he would've ended up just like Jesus and the two thieves had the insurance company not agreed to pay seven million dollars for their client's negligence. Seven million dollars didn't seem like all that much money, G.R. and Tina thought, but they agreed with their lawyer that they didn't want to fight longer. If Sam had lived to be eighty, that would mean the seven million came to a hundred grand per year and some change. Good money for something like a minister or teacher. Not much for what Sam could've done in life had he indeed made the pros.

G.R. went into his son's bedroom and stripped the mattress. Then he opened the closet and pulled out an extra folded-up blanket.

"The water's running," Tina said at 5:00 AM. She nudged G.R. "Did you turn on the washing machine or dishwasher?" G.R. didn't answer. She said, "Someone's outside running our hose." She sat up and elbowed G.R. hard in his upper ribs.

G.R. opened his eyes and stared at the pebbled ceiling he had wanted to scrape smooth since buying the house. He felt Tina looking at him. G.R. thought, Work, and then remembered he didn't have to show up at Kohler. He didn't need to check the kiln's temperature. He didn't need to tell anyone not to mess up.

And then he remembered Jesus and the two thieves out back. I got Jesus and his two thieves out back! G.R. thought. From Halloween. I should've called the TV station about this. I could've gotten on there and said some things about Sam.

The running water turned off. G.R. said, "It was the refrigerator. It was the freezer, making ice."

"No it wasn't," Tina said, throwing off the covers and getting up. "I know that noise. I know every noise this house can make. I remember the ones it used to make, too." She grabbed her bathrobe.

G.R. turned on the bedroom television to drown out what sounds a thirsty thief or son of God might likely emit from the business end of a tangled hose. That same chef came on talking about the organs and glands of farm animals. By the time G.R. got out of bed, his wife had turned on the porch lights already, and grabbed a flashlight she kept in the china cabinet. "Wait a minute, wait a minute," G.R. said. "Let me go out first," but she'd opened the back door and stepped out, shining a beam.

"It's just a homeless man and his boys," G.R. yelled out too loud. "They're just staying for the night, honey. I felt sorry for them."

Tina held the light on the three men. She said nothing, and they stood motionless, twenty feet away, all three of them with their hands above their heads—though the two boys held theirs out to the side. Darmon said, "We couldn't sleep, and we thought we'd water your plants. If you water things at dusk they tend to get mold. What time is it, anyway?"

Tina turned around and looked at her husband. She kept the flashlight pointed toward Darmon and his sons. "What the hell are you doing to us? Why can't you do anything right? First Sam, and now this. And everything that's happened in between."

"That was a fine casserole you baked," one of the sons said. "We appreciate the food you cooked, ma'am."

Tina stared at her husband. She said, "What?"

"I gave them your kidney pie," G.R. said. "They were hungry. I couldn't let them live off of Skittles and Snickers, you know. Didn't you hear me yell out to you to turn on the news and see the Halloween Miracle? It was these fellows here I was talking about."

Tina asked G.R. how much he'd had to drink and went back inside. She turned off the back porch floodlights. Darmon said, "We didn't mean to get you in trouble." His Penitent Thief son said the same.

"Y'all have to forgive her. She doesn't know how she comes off sounding. I keep waiting for her to turn a corner, but it doesn't seem to be happening."

Darmon said there was no need to explain. He asked if G.R. needed help putting the lawn mowers back in the storage shed, and thanked him for his kindness, and said they should be walking toward the shelter, anyway, in order to give some candy to his wife. The Penitent Thief handed over folded blankets and linens and apologized for any scuff marks. G.R. said he'd be looking out for them as the evenings got colder, and reminded Darmon to look for already cut firewood beneath power lines.

G.R. returned inside and went straight to his son's room. He unfurled the sheet and blankets, then lay atop the bed. G.R. fell asleep praying for his wife to revert back to being the gamesome woman she'd been before the accident. He pushed his head deep into his dead son's pillow, and wondered what kind of willpower it would take to suffocate himself.

Four hours later he heard the doorbell ring. Tina answered. Before he could get up he knew already that a merciless and committed person stood there—if not the Impenitent Thief, then another. He thought about how he would finally be able to tell his family's story to anyone watching the early local news.

Nominated by Stephen Corey

MY FATHER'S LAUNDRY

by SUE ELLEN THOMPSON

from THE SUMMERSET REVIEW AND *THEY* (TURNING POINT)

When my mother died, my father discovered
he could not fold a fitted sheet. Patiently,
I showed him the appropriate technique,
but in the months, then years, that followed,
I would find the bottom sheets he'd laundered
spread out on the guest room bed,
where they remained until one
of his three daughters came to visit.

He could operate the washing machine, the dryer,
he could roll a pair of socks until one
disappeared inside the other,
but those fitted sheets defeated him—
or else that bedroom was the place
he went to say, *I can't do this without you.*

Nominated by Lisa Couturier and Summerset Review

FATHER JUNÍPERO
ADMONISHES A BIRD

by POE BALLANTINE

from THE SUN

We do not find the meaning of life by ourselves alone—we find it with another.
— *Thomas Merton*

I met Dabber Jansen in 1979 on a trip to Arcata, California, to see my ex-girlfriend, who was his girlfriend at the time. He was at work driving a truck for Eureka Fisheries when I arrived, and my ex warned me before he got home that Dabber was a redneck. To my surprise, the "redneck" turned out to be a self-styled radical intellectual, like me. Dabber was thirty. I was twenty-three. He and I stayed up long after my ex had gone to bed, drank all the liquor in the house, and discussed Planck's constant, *The Marriage of Figaro*, and the influence of Joseph Campbell on the work of John Steinbeck. Fattened on the milk of the beatnik revolution and disenchanted with science, law, organized religion, journalism, politics, and the military, we both viewed Art as the last noble pursuit. About four that morning, Dabber dragged out his manual Royal typewriter and inserted a piece of paper into the roller, and, along with a few pickled poems, a friendship was born.

After Dabber broke up with my ex and lost his job at Eureka Fisheries, he moved into a small trailer park next to a cow pasture and enrolled at Humboldt State University on the GI Bill. (He'd been in the Navy for six years.) There were about ten other trailers in the park and a few empty lots with naked cement pads. Cows grazed in sunlight filtered by the mighty redwoods, and the university sat above it all in the mist. Dabber's salmon-pink trailer had porthole windows, a worn linoleum floor, and plaid covers on the beds. There were books everywhere, and on the fold-down kitchen table sat his typewriter, upon which he composed pornography for publication—mostly confessional letters purported to be by women.

185

In between traveling stints and jobs that never lasted, I visited Dabber and sometimes stayed for weeks at a time, hiding out and reading books and drinking his homemade hard cider beside that meadow. He was a fine host. We drank deeply in the evenings, debating and philosophizing and working on screenplays we never finished. We assumed that writing drunk freed us from conventional restraints, that liquor was some ethereal panacea you poured into your throat, and out your fingers came the music of the gods. We'd heard of many great writers who composed drunk, who fell into magnificent other-states and sometimes also fell from boats or bridges or balconies or in front of their students or down staircases before they passed with alarming alacrity into immortality.

Having taken most of the literature classes Humboldt State had to offer, and restless to get traction in the world of art, Dabber decided to transfer his credits to the University of California in San Diego and pursue a filmmaking degree. Like me, he had grown up in San Diego, so it was a pleasure for him to haul his trailer out of the foggy northern woods and into his sunny filmmaking future.

He set up camp in a crowded trailer park on Morena Boulevard not far from Interstate 5. I was living and working in San Diego at the time, still eyeing the mantle of the Great American Novel without making any noticeable strides in its direction. Dabber and I were the sort of unshaven stragglers you'd see jabbering animatedly at one another at the Del Mar racetrack, newspapers under our arms, jumbo cups of beer in our hands, and a flask of whiskey between us. We'd often see the celebrated wino poet Charles Bukowski, who also frequented the major Southern California tracks. He was always standing alone either up under the eaves or at one of the bars, or down by the benches on the west end. Bukowski was the kind of writer I thought I would be one day, an uncompromising iconoclast who needed at least two bottles of wine in him before his muse would speak. The dream of genius continued to elude me (after two bottles of wine I'd be staggering around the kitchen making a hamburger), but that only made me cling to it more tenaciously.

I felt assured of my potential greatness. I had bushels of brilliant ideas for novels and stories. I had notebooks filled with notes. My mind never ceased working. Words spoken to me were immediately transcribed across the top of my brain in ten-point type. I was, however, concerned about my inability to get the ball rolling. I nurtured a lazy fantasy that someone—a teacher, agent, wise man, magic sprite, eccentric uncle, or professional life coach—would somehow appear and show me the way. So instead of simply parking myself in front of a typewriter for three to four hours daily, I continued to seek counsel in science and psychology and the convoluted corridors of academia. When those failed, I moved on to religion, choosing my disciplines so poorly that on several occasions I looked around to find myself in a room with a voluble proselytizer representing a belief system such as Nichiren Shōshū, Scientology, or est. I briefly belonged to a cult whose name I can't remember that was run by a mute, tyrannical survivalist who kept hitting his bulldog.

For a long time I believed in the capital-т Truth and thought that, once I'd laid my hands on it, I would find not only the source of my angst but the key to the mysterious Door of Action. I pored over ancient Asian sutras, fasted for days, meditated, abstained from vice, took vows of silence, and lived voluntarily among the poor—a series of gimmicks that left me standing pretty much where I had started.

Eventually I decided that Art alone was the best way to get to Truth—not to mention that as an artist you could attract women, set your own hours, be your own boss, drink too much, and be a total jerk if you wanted to. Also artists are often canonized and worshiped within their own lifetimes, whereas the saints always have to wait until after they're dead.

With an answer of sorts now resolutely in hand, I still couldn't summon the discipline to sit every morning at the typewriter and grind out something more than a letter to a friend. So I was happy to oblige when Dabber suggested we pack up his hand-painted 1964 Chevy Impala and try to track down one of the gods of our literary pantheon, Richard Brautigan. We were both star-struck by this Mythic Lonesome Otherworld Poet, whose sacred sadness seeped palpably from the pages of his books and whose muses were solitude and an ever-ready case of George Dickel sour mash.

It was the snowy autumn of 1984 when we formulated our plan to meet Brautigan at his ranch in Paradise Valley, Montana. We weren't going to stay, just maybe shake his hand and tell him how much his work meant to us. (*Trout Fishing in America* was, in my youthful opinion, the most original novel ever written.) A few days before we were to leave, we heard on the radio that Brautigan's body had been found. He'd ended his life with a .44 Magnum blast to the head. So if you want to catch a Mythic Lonesome Otherworld Poet while he's still alive, map your route and leave right now.

For a graduate project Dabber directed a short film from a script of mine called *Voyeur*, about a woman pursued by a mysterious observer who turns out in the end to be nothing more than her own vanity. Dabber shot a loose interpretation of my treatment, which didn't turn out as well as either of us had hoped. Nevertheless he was awarded his degree, along with the question that accompanies all art degrees: What now?

Our reply was: Not much. Oh, we could still talk. We could still paint pictures on the wind. But disciplined pursuit of a realistic goal wasn't on the agenda.

One night, after drinking a bellyful of hooch and giving the usual lip service to the goddess Athena, we hatched a scheme to go to Mexico to make a movie. I would once again write the screenplay. Dabber would handle the rest. We weren't sure what our movie would be about. Dabber wanted a road movie; I was thinking something more mystical. Carlos Castañeda was a fascinating chap, I pointed out. The rumor was he'd fabricated the "anthropology" books that had made him famous, but if this was the case, what good drugs the man must have had! Maybe we could get our hands on some of that peyote and tap into our own reservoirs of genius. Dabber proposed we marry the two ideas, travelogue and mysticism, and so we packed up the trailer with canned food, bundles of peso notes (the Mexican economy had recently crashed), fishing poles, a chamois to strain the water and rust from the Mexican gasoline, and loads of *Playboys* and lantern fuel for barter, and we set out across the border to make a run deep into the heart of Castañeda Country.

To avoid the blistering stretch of barren Sonoran Desert where most of Castañeda's books are set, we aimed down the narrow Baja highway that threads back and forth between the Sea of Cortez and the Pacific Ocean. About midway down the peninsula we planned to catch the ferry to the Mexican mainland and maybe find some of that cactus fandango that had turned Castaneda into an animal and allowed him to fly, travel in time, separate himself from reality, and eventually write bestsellers and become a kooky recluse living in a big house in LA.

Dabber seemed the ideal traveling companion: wry, generous, easygoing, intelligent, and reliable; an old-fashioned anarchist in the nonviolent tradition of Tolstoy; and the possessor of the sort of indecipherably complex aesthetic principles one might have overheard at a painter's studio in Montparnasse circa 1922. We had never taken an extended trip together, however, and we soon discovered that our traveling styles were incompatible. Dabber the ex-trucker liked to drive straight through to a destination, no messing around. I liked to linger and explore, to get to know places and speak with the locals and sit in their bars and admire the women. I preferred no schedule, whereas Dabber, no matter how much liquor he might have consumed the night before, was ready early each morning for the long haul to the next dot on the map.

One evening we were parked on a deserted Pacific beach when three sneering, drunken, foul-mouthed locals rolled up in an old green pickup. They made obscene gestures and said they wanted to fuck our girlfriends. Dabber, who spoke no Spanish, didn't seem to realize we were in danger of being assaulted or robbed or worse. I persuaded the men in my crude Español that we didn't have any girlfriends—or anything else worth their time—and finally the driver spit out the window, turned his truck around, and drove off down the empty beach. Afterward I berated Dabber for not at least going into the trailer for a knife while I'd had them distracted.

Once we'd gotten properly under each other's skin, we could fashion an argument from any subject. Congenial debates dissolved into contention. Dabber believed that the universe was an accident, that all matter and everything we knew had been "created" somehow in one mass explosion. Matter had been degrading since then and could not be replaced, and therefore the stock market would collapse and the world would soon end. This position had always amused me, but now I felt compelled to refute it and assert my own cosmology, citing regeneration and grace and the impossibility of an accident sustaining itself in aesthetic harmony for more than 4 billion years.

From there the discussion degenerated to our romantic prospects. One of Dabber's goals, besides the miraculous materialization of a movie from our ideas and dreams, was some kind of sexual conquest, and in my unsympathetic (and unsolicited) opinion it was pitiful to presume you would have success with women in another country when you couldn't get laid in your own. Due to the zigzagging, shoulderless, unfinished highway, the frequent unavailability of gasoline in stations placed eighty miles apart, and all the dead horses, abandoned dogs, and automobile wrecks along the way, we were lucky to make two hundred miles a day. At night we'd drink and disagree in the usually empty government-sponsored trailer parks where we camped every evening.

When we got to Santa Rosalía, the wait for the ferry to the mainland was four days. We had no timetable for our return to the States, so I thought we should submit to some R & R, hang out on the beach, and dally in the *mercados* and cantinas. I offered to hire us a boat for a day of sportfishing, but Dabber balked at paying what amounted to fifty dollars to fish. He wanted to scrap the Castaneda angle and push south along the Baja. So south we went.

By the time we'd reached the end of Mexican Federal Highway 1 at the southern tip of the peninsula, we were bitter and snapping at each other and had not produced a single credible movie idea. The whole business unraveled one afternoon, ostensibly over a liter of milk, and Dabber drove stubbornly home, hauling the trailer, while I stayed on in San José del Cabo, in a quirky little trailer park run by expats, where I had my chance to drink on the beach, practice my Spanish, and get to know the people, including a tennis pro who loved to give the OK sign and a friendly female physician from Reno, Nevada. I flew back to the States a week later.

Dabber and I didn't see each other again for many years. I had found that constant travel suited me and also fit my idea of what a writer's life should be. I moved about the U.S., working odd jobs and never living in one place for long. In the evenings I actually parked my lazy ass in front of a typewriter and began producing work, though nothing very good, as I was still looking for inspiration through intoxication. It wasn't until I ended up alone in a motel room about to put an end to my suffering that I realized I was going about it all wrong. From that point I approached the page with a (mostly) clear head and gradually, over a period of years, began to make gains, even achieving some modest success.

Meanwhile I was making solo forays into Mexico. Quite to my surprise, I returned from one such trip with a Mexican wife, who bore me an even bigger surprise: a son. By then Dabber and I had mended our friendship. We corresponded often and saw each other every few years.

Now, in 2008, my wife, Cristina, our seven-year-old son, Tom, and I are on a two-week vacation in San Diego, and we've decided to take a day trip to visit Dabber in Vista, where he lives with his mom.

My wife and son are gaga over California. Tom ranks Disneyland second only to our local landfill back home in Nebraska for entertainment value, and though he is drawn to the ocean, the spectacular multi-million-dollar homes sliding down the dissolving seaside cliffs in northern San Diego County are what really ring his bell. My wife, who is originally from a provincial town in the middle of Mexico, likes the beaches, the endless shops (purses and shoes especially), the restaurants, and the great-paying jobs available for bilingual applicants. She thinks I should apply. (I earn an average of seven thousand dollars a year as a writer.)

Tom was red-flagged for autism in kindergarten and later cleared of the diagnosis by a specialist. His school psychologist gave us the option of labeling him with Asperger's or a learning disability or attention-deficit disorder, all of which we rejected due to my dislike for pigeon-holes and tags. Tom is finicky, hypersensitive, ritualistic, and asocial among kids his own age, and he rocks whenever he sits, but he is also a natural pianist and consistently wins praise for his watercolor and crayon renderings.

So far on this trip the thundering interstates of California have mesmerized Tom, as have the colossal curving bridges, the insane Indy 500 traffic, the drivers shaving and eating burritos and yapping on their phones as they hurtle pell-mell toward their destinations. He's marveled at the stoplights with their left-turn arrows and the pedestrian crossings with their red-or-green hands instead of WALK and DON'T WALK, like we have back home. Most amazing of all to Tom are the many Mexicans. "I don't like Mexicans," he will tell anyone who happens to be listening, including my wife's Mexican family. (Fortunately none of them speaks English.) Tom has remained a bigot even though I've told him he's half Mexican and that 150 years ago, before the Mexican-American War, California belonged to Mexico, and all the Anglos who came here to settle had to agree to (a) become Mexican citizens, (b) submit to Catholicism, and (c) give up their slaves.

As cars rocket past us doing ninety, I glance over at Cristina and recollect all the long nights I've spent in cramped rooms with nothing to hold but a paper dream. Until I met her, I had rejected the idea that I officially belonged to the human race. I was a different breed: the artist. I had to be independent and unsettled and unnerved and exposed to as much danger and misery as possible. Good writers bleed, I believed, and not just metaphorically or when it's convenient for them.

Once Cristina got that ring on my finger, she laid down the law: no more smoking, carousing, and being a mopey old hobo who didn't care if he died. A Catholic, she knew the rules of family, community, and sanity. No amount of money, talent, or fame was going to save me from despair, she said. Neither was there any law in her book against artists marrying, having a family, joining the human race, and being responsible adults. I began to reconsider my beloved Jack Kerouac, who was so steadfast in his adolescent stands against society and conformity that he had no choice but to die young and unhappy. Wouldn't it have been better if he had put down the bottle before it was too late and begun to write about his new sober, reflective life?

Dabber and his ninety-year-old mother, Ellen, live about six miles inland from Oceanside, California, at the top of a knoll at the end of a private lane. Tall and crinkly eyed and slow of gait, Dabber comes out to greet us as we pull into his driveway. He is sixty now, with preternaturally lit blue eyes and no hair left on his head. After a divorce and the death of his father, he returned to this house where he was raised to take care of his mom. He never made another film after *Voyeur*, but he satisfies his creative urges by painting, making ceramic tiles, brewing beer, and devising complex thoroughbred-handicapping schemes.

By Dabber's own admission he is a failed artist, a failed husband, and a long-distance father to his son, who he says "turned out pretty well by default." Uncle Dabber, as Tom knows him, also describes himself as a failed alcoholic who always fell asleep before the party started.

Dabber makes me a martini, almonds in the olives, spirits carefully measured. (One time he bought new martini glasses and kept pouring drinks from the frozen blue Sapphire bottle until we got so shellacked I couldn't remember how we'd made it to the restaurant or that I'd proposed to the waitress. We discovered later that the new martini glasses held twice as much as normal.) Even devout dreamers learn through age and experience that inebriation is the consequence and not the cause of artistic talent. You cannot drink yourself to greatness, but many greats drink themselves into the grave. I have come to believe that true genius is a kind of character defect, a mental illness marked by nervousness, delusion, self-infatuation, social immaturity, and chronic pain—what Brautigan likened to "steel spider webs" in his mind. The only relief comes from creating, becoming intoxicated, or sticking your head in an oven and turning on the gas.

This is the coldest summer in San Diego in seventy-seven years. Even inland, where it's routinely a hundred degrees in July, the five of us huddle in the pale sun at the backyard picnic table, resisting the sensible solution of warmer attire. My wife, who thought highly of Boone's Farm when she first arrived in the States but now prefers a dark, dry red, sips modestly from her glass of Chariot Gypsy ($4.99 a bottle). Dabber would never spend more than five dollars on a bottle of wine lest his mother, a child of the Depression, reprimand him.

Ellen Jansen is ninety, thin and sharp-tongued, especially with Dabber, whom she routinely blasts as if she were a Luftwaffe pilot strafing a French village. Ellen has confided to me on two separate occasions how disappointed she is that, with so many gifts and opportunities, her only child has ended up as no more than her caretaker. Dabber handles her criticisms with wounded aplomb, bent like a French peasant by the daily attacks. An amateur day trader who's been without official employment for the last fifteen years, he is still waiting for the stock market to collapse and invests accordingly. He insists that one day we will wake up and there will be no government, and no one will miss it. This sort of talk infuriates Ellen, who has seen America at its apex and knows damn well we could get back there if we wanted to. I would tell her that all great civilizations blossom, exhaust themselves in war, and go to seed, regardless of the will of their citizens, and that whether or not the U.S. topples into the dust forever or rises again like Byzantium to become the new America for a thousand years, we should be grateful that we were lucky enough to witness a true Golden Age. But I don't want to raise her ire.

Scrawny gray rabbits lope about in the shade of an acre of citrus and pepper trees. Coyotes are coming into the bankrupt cities of California now, Dabber says. He's right. I think I've seen them in broad daylight, walking on their hind legs, wearing transparent green visors, and waiting patiently in line at the ATMS. A coyote was staring into Dabber's bedroom window the other night, he tells us—the same night he saw the UFO. It was nothing more than a sighting, he admits, unable to conceal his disappointment: no epiphany, no anal probes, no waking up naked in Texas.

We talk about the miles of boarded-up north-county homes sliding down the beachfront cliffs (California literally falling into the ocean) and the voters' recent rejection of a referendum to offer the homeowners support of any kind. We talk about Swami Yogananda's Self-Realization Fellowship, just down the hill from where my parents live, and lament that after all our years of earnest philosophical exploration and reading *Thus Spake Zarathustra* and the Tao Te Ching, we remain unenlightened. We talk about the undocumented Mexicans Dabber used to hire but doesn't anymore, out of respect for the high number of unemployed U.S. citizens. There is so little work in California now that Mexican immigrants are returning to their homeland in droves.

"And that's a good thing," Ellen says. Tom nods in full agreement.

I would tell Ellen that if we would let these eager young men and women work openly at jobs that most of us won't take anyway, like picking crops, butchering cows and pigs, and roofing houses, we could refill the Social Security coffers in five years. But, again, I don't want to raise her ire.

"The economy is so bad," Dabber says, "I can't even afford cross-packed Norwegian sardines —"

Before he can finish, Ellen blasts him for wanting to spend three dollars on a can of fish.

Dabber fires back: "I said nothing about *buying* Norwegian sardines. I said that I *can't* buy them."

"This place is boring," Tom declares. *Boring* is his new favorite word. Everything is boring these days: books are boring, sports are boring, Norwegian sardines and bickering adults are boring.

"Well, let's go find something to do," his mother says.

They wander around the property, scuffing up clouds of dust. Water rationing has created a dead-lawn motif throughout Southern California. Along with the numerous bank-foreclosure notices tacked onto FOR SALE signs, it makes for a bleak landscape. Tom inspects the two old pickup trucks parked under the pepper trees and peers into the windows of the trailer that Dabber and I trundled through Mexico in so long ago.

After exploring the Jansens' modest, oddly laid out house, my son returns wide-eyed, claiming to have seen a ghost, which is unlike him. I ask for details, and he describes a dark man with "skinny" eyes and a frown. Another ghost, a "foggy" woman, was standing behind him. Without missing a beat, Ellen says it was the former owner, who built the house in the fifties and died of a heart attack before he could finish it. She doesn't know who the woman was.

"Probably the one who gave him the heart attack," says Dabber.

Cristina attempts to teach Tom to say, "They were ghosts," in Spanish: "Eran fantasmas."

She has been trying for the last two years to raise Tom to be bilingual, but his bigotry prevents it. "I don't want to be a Mexican," he'll say, arms folded. "I am an American, and I only speak English."

Cristina admits it was a mistake not to teach Tom Spanish in his first five years, when he could have absorbed the language without resistance. But she spoke no English when she first came to America, and she feared that if we stuck to Spanish at home, Tom would be speaking better English than she did by the time he was four. She also believes privately (as the television communicates daily) that to be a Mexican in America is to be a second-class citizen. Her shame about being Mexican has been compounded by the indelicate remarks of a few yahoos back home. The boy has picked up on all of this.

"No," Tom replies with several consternated glances over his shoulder. "They were *ghosts*."

To ease his vexation, Ellen breaks out a game of tiddlywinks that uses taut-legged plastic frogs instead of disks. Cristina, with her strong but delicate hands (she was a dentist in Mexico), is skilled at this game, launching her blue frogs in marvelous arcs into the cup. Tom, with the yellow frogs, seems appeased. Ellen takes the green frogs and looks to be having fun, gushing lovingly over both Cristina and Tom. While the three tiddle and wink at the picnic table, Dabber pours himself and me another martini and offers to show me the painting he recently finished, which he believes was responsible for the death of a young man named William.

Dabber's crowded bedroom has a TV, two simultaneously running computers upon which he ciphers his apocalyptic investment schemes ("Market's going down to six thousand this week," he somberly advised me earlier), and a window from which you can see the ocean on a clear day. His two bookcases are filled with DVDs (nothing after 1979) and his unchanging literary canon.

Dabber's paintings are in an expressionist-primitive style, usually with mountain and horse-racing motifs. The painting that purportedly killed William has rhinestones and tiny dice stuck in the paint. There is a Mexican graveyard in the corner with a single white flower. Dabber told the kid, the twenty-year-old grandson of a friend of his mother's, to touch the flower, and a week later the boy went joy riding in a stolen car and died in a wreck.

No doubt we are in the presence of True Art, I admit, for such an achievement, like witchcraft, calls for sacrifice and suffering. Art nearly killed me on many occasions, I say, and I am sorry that it chose to take a friend of his mom's. I tip my glass to my lips, but no liquid comes, so I eat the two olives stuffed with almonds.

Dabber is pleased with my assessment. He says the painting reminds him of the Brautigan story about the graveyard of the poor, where the epitaphs read, "Had His Ass Shot Off in a Honky-Tonk," and so forth. He intends to print William's name in small letters by the flower he touched. Dabber then touches the flower himself in an affectionate way and invites me to touch it, too.

195

On a card table is the old Royal typewriter upon which we never wrote anything worth a hoot, a piece of paper rolled up into it. For the past twenty years Dabber has been incubating a novel about his truck-driving experiences. I know it will be good, if he ever finishes it.

The other three are still playing frogglywinks when we return, and it's so cold outside at 4 PM that Dabber finally rounds up flannel shirts and sweaters for everyone. He refills my glass, lights the gas barbecue, pours briquettes onto the flames, and drags out a beautiful slab of marinated salmon.

"Yuck," Tom says, warming his hands over the fire. "What is that?"

"It's your dinner, junior," I say, "and you should be grateful that Uncle Dabber has gone to all this trouble."

"I don't want it," Tom says.

"You know, Tom," I say, "sometimes you act like a seven-year-old child."

"I *am* a seven-year-old child," he replies, delighted.

Dabber checks the fire and then sets up a croquet game with three goal stakes, one a ceramic statue of a tonsured man dressed like a friar. I don't know whom the figure represents, but he seems annoyed by a bird on his arm. "Father Junípero Serra admonishing a bird," I announce: " 'You crap on my bald head one more time, buddy, and it's a potpie for you.' "

Dabber laughs. "It's Saint Francis of Assisi," he says. "Patron saint of animals."

The actual Father Junípero established the first Spanish missions in California and caned his subjects, the Indians; that's all I recall about him. I remember more about the leper-hugging Francis, whom I studied on my aborted path to illumination.

Three short, dark, mustached men in wide-tooled leather belts and cowboy boots and white straw hats emerge at the top of the hill and saunter down the lane to the fence. Dabber goes over, but he speaks no Spanish, and they speak no English, so my wife translates. They are from Chiapas, she explains. They are looking for work: landscaping, home repair, welding. They will do anything.

"Sorry, no work," Dabber says. "You're too late. California is finished. Try Oregon." He points north. "Oregano," he says.

They smile, bow their heads, and turn back up the road. Cristina, sipping from her glass of Chariot Gypsy, watches them go. My son glares after them.

Dabber drapes the salmon filets over the fire, sending up the lazy, luscious scent of roasting fish flesh. Tom will not eat the salmon, he insists, or any of the other fine dishes Uncle Dabber has prepared.

"Do you want a hot dog, Tom?" I ask.

"I only want hot dogs from my real home," he says.

So I boil a hot dog in water seasoned with onions and garlic and a capful of cider vinegar, as it would be prepared in his "real" home. It passes muster.

Our table is set: salmon, roasted corn, grilled *pasillas*, romaine salad with garden tomatoes. Under duress, my picky son nibbles at an ear of corn.

When Dabber appears again with the bottle of gin, I realize I've had too much and wave him off. Saint Francis has a yellow croquet ball perched between his ceramic feet. I recall that he was a rake before he converted, and in his early days he sought to become a martyr. I was a rake for much longer than Saint Francis, and I sought to become a martyr, too. But that is where the similarities between us end. My goal was not sanctity or the betterment of humankind but the adulation and vindication of fame—which, I now know, would have brought me little but torment and sorrow.

I look down the table at my son, working on his third hot dog, and hope he will not be like me. If he chases after Art, I'll show him pictures of Hemingway sitting drunk with broken eyeglasses in his bathtub and Brautigan's corpse being eaten by maggots on his couch. I'll tell him what it took me thirty years to discover: that great artists more often than not lead lives that are shabby, bizarre, dissolute, and self-destructive. So if you want to be a teacher, Tom, or to sell insurance, or to fly around the country setting up grocery stores, that'll be all right with me. I like having you around. You and your mother are the sole reason I am alive today.

Nominated by Nancy Geyer

TEMPLE GAUDETE

by LISA RUSS SPAAR

from IMAGE

> *Deus homo factus est*
> *Natura mirante.*

Is love the start of a journey back?
If so, back where, & make it holy.

Saint Cerulean Warbler, blue blur,
heart on the lam, courses arterial branches,

combing up & down, embolic,
while inside I punch down & fold a floe

of dough to make it later rise.
On the box, medieval voices, polyphonic,

God has become man, to the wonderment
of Nature. Simple to say: there is gash,

then balm. Admit we love the abyss,
our mouths sipping it in one another.

At the feeder now. Back to the cherry, quick,
song's burden, rejoice, rejoice.

O salve & knife. Too simple to say
we begin as mouths, angry swack,

lungs flooded with a blue foreseeing.
Story that can save us only through the body.

Nominated by David Wojahn

THE WEAVE

fiction by CHARLES JOHNSON

from THE IOWA REVIEW

News item, July 12, 2012. Hair theft: Three thieves battered through a wall, crawled close to the floor to dodge motion detectors, and stole six duffel bags filled with human hair extensions from a Chicago beauty-supply store. The Chicago Tribune *reported Saturday that the hair extensions were worth $230,000.*

"So what feeds this hair machine?"

—*Chris Rock*, Good Hair

Ieesha is nervous and trying not to sneeze when she steps at four in the morning to the front door of Sassy Hair Salon and Beauty Supplies in the Central District. After all, it was a sneeze that got her fired from this salon two days ago. She has a sore throat and red eyes, but that's all you can see because a ski mask covers the rest of her face. As she twists the key in the lock, her eyes are darting in every direction, up and down the empty street, because she and I have never done anything like this before. When she worked here, the owner, Frances, gave her a key so she could open and straighten up the shop before the other hairstylists arrived. I told her to make a copy of the key in case one day she might need it. That was two days ago, on September first, the start of hay fever season and the second anniversary of the day we started dating.

Once inside the door, she has exactly forty seconds to remember and punch in the four-digit code before the alarm's security system goes off. Then, to stay clear of the motion detectors inside that never turn off, she gets down on the floor of the waiting room in her cut-knee jeans and crawls on all fours past the leather reception chairs and modules stacked with *Spin, Upscale*, and *Jet* magazines for the salon's customers to read and just perhaps find on their glossy, Photoshopped pages, the coiffure that is perfect for their mood at the moment. Within a few seconds, Ieesha is beyond the reception area and into a space, long and wide, that is a site for unexpected mystery and wonder that will test the limits of what we think we know.

Moving deeper into this room, where the elusive experience called beauty is manufactured every day from hot combs and crème relaxers, she passes workstations, four on each side of her, all of them equipped with swiveling styling chairs and carts covered with appliance holders, spray bottles, and Sulfur8 shampoo. Holding a tiny flashlight attached to her key ring, she works her way around manicure tables, dryer chairs, and a display case where sexy, silky, eiderdown-soft wigs, some as thick as a show pony's tail, hang in rows like scalps taken as trophies after a war. Every day, the customers at Sassy Hair Salon and the wigs lovingly check each other out for some time, and then after long and careful deliberation, the wigs always buy the women. Unstated, but permeating every particle in that exchange of desire, is a profound, historical pain, a hurt based on the lie that the hair one was unlucky enough to be born with can never in this culture be good enough, is never beautiful as it is, and must be scorched by scalp-scalding chemicals into temporary straightness, because if that torment is not endured often from the tender age of four months old, how can one ever satisfy the unquenchable thirst to be desired or worthy of love?

The storage room containing the unusual treasure she seeks is now just a few feet away, but Ieesha stops at the station where she worked just two days ago, her red eyes glazing over with tears caused not by ragweed pollen, but by a memory suspended in the darkness.

She sees it all again. There she is, wearing her vinyl salon vest, its pockets filled with the tools of her trade. In her chair is an older customer, a heavy, high-strung Seattle city councilwoman. The salon was packed that afternoon, steamed by peopled humidity. A ceiling fan shirred air perfumed with the odor of burnt hair. The councilwoman wanted her hair straightened, not permed, for a political fundraiser she was hosting that week. But she couldn't—or wouldn't—sit quietly. She gossiped nonstop about everybody in city government as well as the 'do Gabby Douglass wore during the Olympics, blathering away in the kind of voice that carried right through you, that went inside like your ears didn't have any choice at all and had to soak up the words the way a sponge did water. All of a sudden, Ieesha sneezed. Her fingers slipped. She burned the old lady's left earlobe. The councilwoman flew from her seat, so enraged they had to peel her off the ceiling, shouting about how Ieesha didn't know the first thing about doing hair. She demanded that Frances fire her, and even took things a step further, saying with a stroke of scorn that anyone working in a beauty salon should be looking damned good herself, and that Ieesha didn't.

Frances was not a bad person to work for, far from it, and she knew my girlfriend was a first-rate cosmetologist. Even so, the owner of Sassy Hair Salon didn't want to lose someone on the city council who was a twice-a-month, high-spending customer able to buy and sell her business twice over. As I was fixing our dinner of Top Ramen, Ieesha quietly came through the door of our apartment, still wearing her salon vest, her eyes burning with tears. She wears her hair in the neat, tight black halo she was born with, unadorned, simple, honest, uncontrived, as genuinely individual as her lips and nose. To some people she might seem as plain as characters in those old-timey plays, Clara in Paddy Chayefsky's *Marty* or Laura Wingfield in *The Glass Menagerie*. But Ieesha has the warm, dark, and rich complexion of Michelle Obama or Angela Bassett, which is, so help me, as gorgeous as gorgeous gets. Nevertheless, sometimes in the morning as she was getting ready for work, I'd catch her struggling to pull a pick through the burls and kinks of her hair with tears in her eyes as she looked in the mirror, tugging hardest at the nape of her neck, that spot called "the kitchen." I tell her she's beautiful as she is, but when she peers at television, movies, or popular magazines where generic, blue-eyed, blonde Barbie dolls with orthodontically perfect teeth, Botox, and breast implants prance, pose, and promenade, she says with a sense of fatality and resignation, "I can't look like that." She knows that whenever she steps out our door, it's guaranteed that a wound awaits her, that something will tell Ieesha that her hair and skin will never be good enough. All she has to do is walk into a store and be watched with suspicion, or have a cashier slap her change on the counter rather than place it on the palm of her outstretched hand. Or maybe read about the rodeo clown named Mike Hayhurst at the Creston Classic Rodeo in California who joked that "*Playboy* is offering Ann Romney $250,000 to pose in that magazine and the White House is upset about it because *National Geographic* only offered Michelle Obama $50 to pose for them."

Between bouts of blowing her nose loudly into a Kleenex in our tiny studio apartment, she cried the whole day she got fired, saying with a hopeless, plaintive hitch in her voice, "What's wrong with me?" Rightly or wrongly, she was convinced that she would never find another job during the Great Recession. That put everything we wanted to do on hold. Both of us were broke, with bills piling up on the kitchen counter after I got laid off from my part-time job as a substitute English teacher at Garfield High School. We were on food stamps and got our clothes from Goodwill. I tried to console her, first with kisses, then caresses, and before the night was over we had roof-raising sex. Afterward, and for the thousandth time, I came close to proposing that we get married. But I had a failure of nerve, afraid she'd temporize or say no, or that because we were so poor we needed to wait. To be honest, I was never sure if she saw me as Mr. Right or just as Mr. Right Now.

So what I said to her that night, as we lay awake in each other's arms, our fingers intertwined, was that getting fired might just be the change of luck we'd been looking for. Frances was so busy with customers she didn't have time to change the locks. Or the code for the ADT alarm system. Naturally, Ieesha, who'd never stolen anything in her life, was reluctant, but I kept after her until she agreed.

Finally, after a few minutes, Ieesha enters the density of the storeroom's sooty darkness, feeling her way cat-footed, her arms outstretched. Among cardboard boxes of skin creams, conditioners, balms, and oils, she locates the holy grail of hair in three pea-green duffel bags stacked against the wall, like rugs rolled up for storage. She drags a chair beneath the storeroom window, then starts tossing the bags into the alley. As planned, I'm waiting outside, her old Toyota Corolla dappled with rust idling behind me. I catch each bag as it comes through the window and throw it onto the backseat. The bags, I discover, weigh next to nothing. Yet for some reason, these sacks of something as common and plentiful as old hair are worth a lot of bank—why, I don't know. Or why women struggling to pay their rent, poor women forced to choose between food and their winter fuel bill, go into debt shelling out between $1,000 and $3,000 and sometimes as much as $5,000 for a weave with real human hair. It baffled me until I read how some people feel that used things possess special properties. For example, someone on eBay bought Britney Spears's chewed gum for $14,000, someone else paid $115,000 for a handful of hair from Elvis Presley's pompadour, and his soiled, jockey-style shorts went on sale for $16,000 at an auction in England. (No one, by the way, bought his unwashed skivvies.) Another person spent $3,000 for Justin Timberlake's half-eaten French toast. I guess some of those eBay buyers feel closer to the person they admire, maybe even that something of that person's essence is magically clinging to the part they purchased.

As soon as Ieesha slides into the passenger seat, pulling off her ski mask and drawing short, hard breaths as if she's been running up stairs, my foot lightly applies pressure to the gas pedal and I head for the freeway, my elbow out the window, my fingers curled on the roof of the car. Within fifteen minutes, we're back at our place. I park the car, and we sling the bags over our shoulders, carry them inside to our first-floor unit, and stack them on the floor between the kitchenette and the sofa bed we sleep on. Ieesha sits down on a bedsheet still twisted from the night before, when we were joined at the groin. She knocks off her shoes run down at the heel and rubs her ankles. She pulls a couple of wigs and a handful of hair extensions from one of the bags. She spreads them on our coffee table, frowning, then sits with her shoulders pulled in, as if waiting for the ceiling to cave in.

"We're gonna be okay," I say.

"I don't know." Her voice is soft, sinus-clogged. "Tyrone, I don't feel good about this. I can't stop shaking. We're *not* burglars."

"We are now." I open a bottle of Bordeaux we've been saving to celebrate, filling up our only wineglass for her and a large jam jar for myself. I sit down beside her and pick up one of the wigs. Its texture between my fingertips is fluffy. I say, "You can blame Frances. She should have stood up for you. She *owes* you. What we need to do now is think about our next step. Where we can sell this stuff." Ieesha's head jerks backward when I reach for one of the wigs and put it on her head, just out of curiosity. Reluctantly, she lets me place it there, and I ask, "What's that feel like? A stocking cap? Is it hot?"

"I don't know. It feels . . ."

She never tells me how it feels.

So I ask another question. "What makes this hair so special? Where does it come from?"

Hands folded in her lap, she sits quietly, and, for an instant, the wig, whose obsidian tresses pool around her face, makes her look like someone I don't know. All of a sudden, I'm not sure what she might do next, but what she *does* do, after clearing her throat, is give me the hair-raising history and odyssey behind the property we've stolen. The bags, she says, come from a Buddhist temple near New Delhi, where young women shave their heads in an ancient ceremony of sacrifice called Pabbajja. They give up their hair to renounce all vanity, and this letting go of things cosmetic and the chimera called the ego is their first step as nuns on the path to realizing that the essence of everything is emptiness. The hair ceremony is one of the 84,000 "dharma gates." On the day their heads were shaved, the women had kneeled in their plain saris, there in the temple *naos*, and took two hundred forty vows, the first five of which were *no killing, no lying, no stealing, no sexual misconduct*, and *no drinking of alcohol*. They didn't care what happened to their hair after the ceremony. Didn't know it would be sewn, stitched, and stapled onto the scalps of other people. But Korean merchants were there. They paid the temple's abbot ten dollars for each head of fibrous protein. After that, the merchants, who controlled this commerce as tightly as the mafia did gambling, washed the hair clean of lice. From India, where these women cultivated an outward life of simplicity and an inward life free from illusion, the merchants transported the discarded, dead hair halfway around the planet, where, ironically, it was cannibalized as commerce in a nine-billion-dollar hair-extension industry devoted precisely to keeping women forever enslaved to the eyes of others.

As she explains all this, Ieesha leaves her wine untasted, and I don't say anything because my brain is stuttering, stalling on the unsyllabled thought that if you tug on a single, thin strand of hair, which has a life span of five-and-a-half years, you find it raddled to the rest of the world. I didn't see any of that coming until it arrived. I lift the jar of wine straight to my lips, empty it, and set it down with a click on the coffee table. When I look back at Ieesha, I realize she's smiling into one cheek, as if remembering a delicious secret she can't share with me. That makes me down a second jar of Bordeaux. Then a third. I wonder, does the wig she's wearing itch or tingle? Does it feel like touching Justin Timberlake's unfinished French toast? Now the wine bottle is empty. We've got nothing on the empty racks of the refrigerator but a six-pack of beer, so I rise from the sofa to get that, a little woozy on my feet, careening sideways toward the kitchenette, but my full bladder redirects me toward the cubicle that houses our shower and toilet. I click on the light, close the door, and brace myself with one hand pressed against the wall. Standing there for a few minutes, my eyes closed, I feel rather than hear a police siren, and our smoke alarm. My stomach clenches.

Coming out of the bathroom, I find the wig she was wearing and the weaves that were on the coffee table burning in a wastebasket. Ieesha stands in the middle of the room, her cell phone pressed against her ear.

"What are you doing?" Smoke is stinging my eyes. "Who are you talking to?"

Her eyes are quiet. Everything about her seems quiet when she says, "911."

"*Why?*"

"Because it's the right thing to do."

I stare at her in wonder. She's offered us up, the way the women did their hair at the temple in New Delhi. I rush to draw water from the kitchen sink to put out the fire. I start throwing open the windows as there comes a loud knock, then pounding at the door behind me, but I can't take my eyes off her. She looks vulnerable but not weak, free, and more than enough for herself. I hear the wood of the door breaking, but as if from a great distance, because suddenly I know, and she knows, that I understand. She's letting go of all of it—the inheritance of hurt, the artificial and the inauthentic, the absurdities of color and caste stained at their roots by vanity and bondage to the body—and in this evanescent moment, when even I feel as if a weight has been lifted off my shoulders, she has never looked more beautiful and spiritually centered. There's shouting in the room now. Rough hands throw me facedown on the floor. My wrists are cuffed behind my back. Someone is reciting my Miranda rights. Then I feel myself being lifted to my feet. But I stop midway, resting on my right knee, my voice shaky as I look up at Ieesha, and say:

"Will you marry me?"

Two policemen lead her toward the shattered door, our first steps toward that American monastery called prison. She half turns, smiling, looking back at me, and her head nods: *yes, yes, yes.*

Nominated by The Iowa Review

VERNACULAR OWL

by THOMAS SAYERS ELLIS

from POETRY

For Amiri Baraka

    Old Ark,
how funky it was, all those animals, two of every kind,
and all that waste, the human shit somebody had to clean up.
Somebody, some love you hugged before fear,
the fear of an in-sani-nation, the No Blues, ruined your bowels.
Go devil.
Public programs
like
Race.
Dems a Repub
of Dumpster Molesters.
Private
like
the Runs.
God evil.
Somebody had to clean that shit up.
Somebody, some love who raised you, wise.
Feathered razors for eyebrows,
alto,
tenor,
Wasn't no branch.
Some
say
a tree,
not

for rest either.
For change.
          We a wild life,
                   long-eared
              and short. Prey,
             some prayed for
          the flood. And were
                  struck by floating,
            corporate quintets
           of Rocks & Roths,
          assets bond Prestige.

First
Organizer
ever
called a
Nigga,
      Noah,
but not
the last
Occupier of Ararat
. . . got thick
on
Genesis
and electric cello, cell-phone-shaped UFOs
fueled by the damp,
murdered clay
of divinity-based
Racial
Mountain
Dirt.
      Somebody had to clean that shit up.
Some native body,
beside the smooth water,
 like a
brook

      Gwen say,
"I had to kick their law into their teeth in order to save them."

Chaser if
you straight.

Ark Old
Ark New
Ark Now

Only   Only
  Sidney P   Simple JessB
would   would
___Spencer T   ___Dizzy G
to turn   to accent
the dinner   the p's
cheek.   not the ". . . nuts."

Change the record, Record Changer.
Name _____
Change
the changing same.

             Something only you could Art Messenger
  & dig in any chord.
High water, like the woods of secrecy,
always a trail a ways a coming.
God devil.
Move the *d*.
Go devil.
The Mosque watchers know.
Also de wind, de wind
and de Word, spoken and written,
hidden in love
with the intestines
of Testament.
 Eyes like
 a woman's fist,
her hard facts—not the crying,
domestic consonants
 "of non being."
Soprano,
piano,
or the cultural cowardice

of class,
in any chord
of standardized sheet music, low coup risks slit.
 Though flawed, too,
by penetrable flesh,
some blue kind.
 Unlike
a pretty shield,
loaded free.

                    Wasn't just Winter
                    or lonely. Those.
                    Wasn't just Sundays
                the living did not return.

   Crouch if you a bum or one of Mumbo Jumbo's reckless,
poisonous reeds. A neck-crow-man-servant *n*
 a jes' grew suit.
Us am,
an unfit
second
Constitution.
 Us am, an Af-Am ambulance full of . . .
broke-down,
as round as we bald.
 Obeying
hawkish
eagles.

            Why the young Brothers so big, what they eatin',
why they blow up like that, gotta wear big white tees, gotta wear white
skin sheets, like maggots, like lard, the domestic oil of death and klan
sweat, who blew them up, doctored, who pickin' them off like dark
cotton, make them make themselves a fashion of profitable, soft
muscular bales, somebody got to clean this shit up.

   All us, us animals,
on one floating stage
we knew
was a toilet,

the third oldest in the nation, unreserved.
Wasn't no bank
or branch.
  Yes we Vatican, despite Alighieri's medium rare, rate of interest.
It
was
confirmation,
 Some say
black fire
wood.
   Some love that changed our screaming
   Atlantic bottoms
when all we
 could be
was thin olive sticks
with battered whore-ti-cultural beaks, and eastern screech.

            Flushed, too, every time the *Yew Norker*
or one of Obi-Wan Kenobi's traitorous X Jedi Clampett hillbillies
fresh prince'd us . . .

                    The real religion,
                    our "individual expressiveness"
                      wasn't dehuman-u-factured
                    by a Greek **HAARP**
                      in a Roman uni-dot-gov-versity.
                    Where we Away
                    our Steel, "flood"
                      means "flow."
                    Where we Tenure
                    our Ammo, "podium"
                      means "drum."

Flood,
flow.
Podium,
drum.
Flood,
drum.
Podium,

flow.
Drum,
podium.
Flood,
flow.

    Used to be a whole lot of chalk around the Ark,
then anger, then angels, their wings made of fried white dust,
fallen from when the board of knowledge was public and named
after a stranger or crook, an anti-in-immigrant-can'tameter
stretched across the teepee-skin, chairs of class

        where we clapped
    the erasers,
     fifty snows old,
    like we were
    the first Abraham,
     where we clapped
    the Race Erasers
    and drove away
    from K James V and K Leo PB
    in shiny Lincolns,
    sprinkling holy sheeple from the sky,
    their
    powdery
    absolute
     Rule.
    Just add oil-water.
    Belongs
    to humanity.
    Just add sugar-rubber.
    Belongs
    to civilization.
    Gold.
    Days.
    Nights.
    Ounces.
    A forty.
    Mules move.
    A forty.

Move.
Move.
Move
mule.

       Whatchamacall "how we here," where
we fear, how we hear how we sound and how sometimes [time is
some] even our own sound fears us, and remembers the first us,
confronting Columbus with thunderbolts, when "was-we" not good
citizen sober, voting and drowning, and rotting like the armed guts
of our young?

                Now a daze,
                tribe-be-known,
                the devil
                the best historian we got.
                Anyhow.

Nominated by Celeste Ng and Poetry

FEAR ITSELF

fiction by KATIE COYLE

from ONE STORY

On a trip with their U.S. History class to a presidential wax museum in a nearby city, three girls make up a game they call Categories, the rules of which are perfectly simple. First, one girl suggests a type of person or thing—Beatle Wife, *Pride and Prejudice* Sister, Greek Goddess, Mode of Fortune Telling. Second, each girl tries to identify one another within said category. That's it. That's the extent of the game. As they play, one girl feels like crying and another feels like screaming and another wants to stop playing Categories altogether, because no one wants to be the Yoko Ono, and no one wants to be the Mary Bennett. But they never officially quit. They are sixteen. They've been best friends since grade school. They are Kara (The Mean One), Ruthie (The Funny One), and Olive (The Smart One). All three are mean and funny and smart, but Kara is probably the most of each.

By noon, their classmates have scattered across the museum to smoke and take inappropriate pictures of themselves with Millard Fillmore. The girls, cursed with a sense of moral superiority correlating directly to their social inferiority, find a corner of the lobby in which to become invisible. After an hour, they've exhausted ideas for Categories, even Alcoholic Beverages (which none of them have drunk) and Women of the Bible (which none of them have read).

"What else, what else," says Kara.

"Maybe we should walk around the museum for a little while?" says Olive, Old-Fashioned and John the Baptist's Mom. Olive can tell Kara's getting bored, and when Kara gets bored, she gets nasty. "We *do* have to write a response paper. . . ."

213

"We could write it in haiku and Olsen would accept it," says Kara. Their teacher, Mr. Olsen, is fresh from college, bright-eyed and weirdly-bearded. He has a habit of rewarding substandard effort with high grades for the sake of irony.

Ruthie laughs a bit too loudly at this. "Imagine him reading the haikus out loud to Cassidy Fontana. 'Listen to *this* one, honey. I think I'm really getting through to them.' And she's all, 'You're so *Mr. Holland's Opus*, baby. Take me now."

Cassidy Fontana is a creation of the girls' collective imagination: Mr. Olsen's beautiful, hypothetical girlfriend, the primary audience for his sardonic puns and excessive interest in mumbly indie rock bands. At the beginning of the school year, all three indulged in fantasizing about Cassidy, who, if the Category was Girlfriends, would be the coolest possible option, the one none of them would feel confident enough to claim. But now it's November, and Ruthie alone won't let it go. While Mr. Olsen reads *A People's History of the United States* out loud to their class, Ruthie writes awkward erotica about his afterschool trysts with this imaginary woman. *'You be the robber baron and I'll be the anarchist,' Cassidy moaned in ecstasy as Mr. Olsen slid himself inside her.* She passes one fevered page at a time to Kara and Olive, and though the dread that Mr. Olsen will one day notice is a constant sickness in her stomach, she can't stop.

Kara was the one who came up with the name "Cassidy Fontana"— alluring and perfectly unreal—but now she stares at Ruthie through half-closed eyes, sleepy with disdain. "Sometimes it feels like Cassidy Fontana is just an excuse for you to think about Olsen's dick."

Ruthie's mouth pops open in protest, but Olive, the oldest of four sisters and a natural diffuser of conflict, quickly rattles off a list of prospective Categories before the argument can snowball. "Sandwiches? European Cities? Pink Ladies?"

There's a pause. Then Ruthie's eyes widen; she points. In the center of the lobby is a reproduction of LBJ taking the Oath of Office, one hand raised beside a wax ear, the other resting on an invisible Bible. Beside him is Jackie O., blank-eyed in her bloodstained pink suit.

"First Ladies!" cries Kara.

"No good," says Olive. "By default I'm Michelle Obama. Or Sally Hemings."

"Laura Bush," says Ruthie. "*Black* Laura Bush. Do you accept?"

Olive thinks this over. "Laura Bush is a librarian. And possibly a secret feminist. I'll consider it."

"Ruthie should be Jackie O., since she's the most virginal," says Kara. Kara always makes Ruthie the most virginal one—Joan of Arc when the Category was Historical Figures, and "Only the Good Die Young" when it was Billy Joel Songs. It doesn't matter that, as Ruthie constantly reminds her, all three of the girls are virgins—that none of them have so much as kissed a boy.

"What about Kara?" Olive prompts, before Ruthie can object.

There's a beat of silence, and then Ruthie says, "Eleanor Roosevelt."

"What does *that* mean?" Kara cries. Ruthie always identifies Kara as the ugliest thing in any given Category. Kara has already been named Ursula (Disney Villainesses), *Rocky* (Oscar-Winning Films of the 1970s), and Tugboat (Modes of Transportation).

Ruthie sighs. "Eleanor Roosevelt helped write the Universal Declaration of Human Rights. She practically *was* president. Easily the best First Lady."

"Right," Kara says. "It has nothing to do with the fact that bitch was horse-faced as fuck."

"Eleanor Roosevelt is a compliment. It means you're strong," Olive says. "And by the way? I find it upsetting that you can dismiss a woman's entire body of work just because she didn't fit a patriarchal society's definition of beautiful."

Kara snorts. "God, Olive. You sound like a lesbian."

Olive's stammering retort ("And what exactly does a lesbian *sound* like, Kara?") is interrupted by a man clearing his throat nearby. Mr. Olsen stands beside them in his jeans and tweed blazer, twisting a strand of beard between two fingers, watching them with eyebrows raised.

"Hey, dudes," he says.

"Hey," say Kara and Ruthie and Olive.

"This museum's pretty cool, huh?" He takes a step. "I mean, in a totally lame way."

Ruthie shoots Kara a quick, smiling glance—a peace offering that lasts no longer than a second. Though Kara can feel her friend's eyes on her, she does not turn her head.

"Still." Mr. Olsen puts his hands in his pockets. "Maybe you should walk around a bit? Take some notes? You might learn something! Probably not, though."

Kara and Ruthie and Olive begin to shuffle away in a tight pack—staying, even during an altercation, no more than an arm's span apart. They stop when Mr. Olsen clears his throat again.

215

"Separately," he says.

Olive looks to Ruthie who looks to Kara. If anyone could challenge Mr. Olsen's authority at this moment, it would be Kara, who regularly calls him a "man-child" to his face, in front of other students. Each time she does it, a shivery thrill goes up the spines of Ruthie and Olive—they know it's mean, but they love watching their fierce friend make this tiny man squirm. Even Ruthie, who—it must be said—continues to talk about Cassidy Fontana as an excuse to think about Mr. Olsen's dick, gets off on how cruel Kara is to him. They wait for it now, the delicious snap of Kara's retort. But Kara has already begun to stalk away, down a corridor over which hangs a sign reading *In Times of War*. . . . Ruthie and Olive have no choice. They separate.

The war corridor holds Dolley Madison in flight, a portrait of Washington held tight to her wax breast; Abraham Lincoln at a podium, the Gettysburg Address crackling through a speaker behind him; and Kara's huge, insurmountable anger. She is sick to death of her only two friends. She used to have more; they used to be a group of six or seven. But when high school started, the other girls drifted away to drink beers in the basements of thick-necked football players, to give blowjobs in the backs of mini-vans. They didn't invite Kara or Ruthie or Olive to join and the remaining three never figured out how to invite themselves. Now they're stuck with one another.

Kara never actually forgets that she's a virgin; she just believes that the larger she makes Ruthie's virginity, the more impossible it is to miss, and the smaller her own becomes. The problem is that Ruthie and Olive carry their virginity around as if it is a gift, a choice, whereas for Kara it is an impossible oppression, so much dead weight. Kara is not as skinny as Ruthie and Olive, not as take-off-your-glasses-and-let-down-your-hair secretly beautiful as Ruthie and Olive. And every time Ruthie compares her to Eleanor Roosevelt, to a tugboat, it's as if she is saying, *No one will ever love you.*

"Fuck!" Kara shouts into the abandoned corridor.

She hears a laugh just beyond Woodrow Wilson. She imagines one of her asshole classmates, Rob Rafi or Andrew Atwell or somebody, hiding and watching and laughing at her.

"Fuck *you*!" she calls out.

"That's not very ladylike," says the laugher, and Kara knows she does not know him. A figure in a wheelchair moves out of the line of presidents and towards her. She's embarrassed by the wheelchair, the expletive.

"Sorry!" she calls before she can see his face. "I thought you were someone I knew."

"You usually scream 'fuck you' at people you know?" asks the figure. He's directly in front of her now, illuminated by the spotlight hanging over Lincoln. The funny thing is, he looks like Franklin Delano Roosevelt. Same jaw, same hairline, same round glasses perched on the same strong nose. Between his teeth is a long black cigarette holder. Kara does not recognize the look the man gives her. His mouth grins but his eyes are dead, two expressionless blue glass beads. She feels a wave of cold spread from her center, some combination of curiosity and fear.

"Are you an actor?" asks Kara. "I didn't know they had actors here."

"Sure, honey," says the man who looks like Roosevelt. "Let's call me an actor."

Kara thinks this is a weird answer, but the fact that he's called her 'honey' keeps her from caring. No one has ever called her 'honey' before, not in the smirking way FDR just did. Kara thinks she likes it. "How long have you worked here?"

"Hell, I don't know," FDR replies. He tugs at a gold chain attached to his vest and opens the watch hanging at its end. Kara notices that inside there's just a blank white face, no numbers. "Five years? Ten? However long this wing has been open."

"Well," says Kara. "It's a great museum."

"Yeah, you really seem to love it." FDR's voice gets flinty but he never stops smiling. "Such a filthy little mouth on such a pretty little girl."

"Oh!" Kara is flustered. "It's not the museum. I got in a fight with my friends. It's no big deal. Just girl stuff."

FDR nods once. "Human stuff."

"Human stuff," Kara agrees. "You're right. I never thought of it that way. Not just girl stuff. Everyone can be unhappy."

"Are you unhappy, honey?"

It's an easy question, but to answer it truthfully is difficult. Kara takes a moment to evaluate what she thinks of as her life—her parents and school, but mostly Ruthie and Olive, her own fat face in an endless stream of mirrors. Whiskey Sour, Lot's Wife. Tugboat. Eleanor Roosevelt.

217

"I'm lonely," she says.

FDR reaches out and takes Kara's hand. Immediately she knows something is wrong. His skin is neither warm nor cold. It feels nothing like skin. It feels slippery and malleable, like a melted candle.

"I'm lonely, too," he says.

At two p.m., the class boards the bus for the trip back to Meadow Ridge. Mr. Olsen stands at the door, making checkmarks next to the names of students as they enter. Ruthie stumbles as she and Olive climb aboard, but Olsen doesn't notice—he's too busy perfecting a casual slouch.

"Basically," Ruthie hisses to Olive, continuing a conversation they never stop having, "Kara is toxic." She likes the feel of the word in her mouth. It sounds spiky and diseased. Here on the bus, though, where Kara already sits by herself near the back, staring out the window pensively, Ruthie has to admit she looks pretty harmless.

"Where've you been?" Ruthie asks, sliding into the seat beside Kara. She doesn't apologize, and neither will Kara. The girls let the moments where they hate each other happen, and once they've happened, they don't remark on them again.

"We looked everywhere for you," Olive lies, sitting in front of them. Actually, she and Ruthie went to the museum cafeteria and ate hot dogs.

Kara turns her head from the window slowly, as if she doesn't want to tear herself from the view. She looks at Olive's affable face, framed between the two gray seats, and Ruthie's, frowning and still hungry. Kara appears utterly at peace, and the sunlight that streams into the window behind her lights up her head like a halo.

"I *met* someone," she says.

That afternoon is play practice. Mr. Olsen is directing *The Crucible*, and because their school lists 'all-inclusiveness' in its mission statement, everyone who auditioned got a part. Kara and Ruthie and Olive were cast with twenty others as "Hysterical Village Girls." They have one big scene, where they wail and claw at one another in the courtroom and scream the same words: "Begone! Begone!" They don't particularly like acting, but they do like this scene—how loud they're allowed to be, how frightening. Waiting in the wings for their cue, Kara and Ruthie and Olive inhale the sawdusty backstage smell and let their brains go fuzzy; they wake up to their open mouths and sore throats when Olsen bounds onstage with some new direction.

When the girls are not needed onstage, which is most of the time, they help build the sets. They paint backdrops, cut plywood with a buzz-saw, and construct John Proctor's jail cell, using a blowtorch to bend the metal bars. When there's no work for them, they sit in the lobby outside the auditorium and play Categories. But today they talk about FDR.

"So he's made of wax?" asks Ruthie. On the bus ride home she got swept up in Kara's exhilaration and managed to momentarily forget her toxicity—at one point Kara squealed, made a prolonged "Eeee!" sound, and Ruthie couldn't help but join in.

"Yes," says Kara. "At least, I think so. It doesn't seem like the kind of thing you can *ask* a person, you know?"

"Remember those candy wax lips we used to get on Halloween?" Ruthie says. "Do you think that's what kissing him would be like?"

"I'm not going to take a bite out of his lips."

Ruthie giggles. Kara's mouth is a prim line but her eyes beam. Everything looks beautiful to her right now: the fluorescently lit lobby, the red-leaved branches scraping the window, her friends in their starchy costume bonnets.

"Listen." Olive has been quiet a while. "Are we going to pretend this is normal? I'm sorry," she says, because Kara instantly gets that look in her eye, the murderous one, "but there's nothing sexy to me about a wax figurine. This isn't a supernatural romance novel. In real life, people don't have relationships with vampires and zombies."

"Maybe you don't think it sounds sexy, but you weren't there," says Kara. "And anyway, no offense? But you don't always have the best judgment about these things."

Olive bites the inside of her cheek. Last year, she had a crush on Nicholas Dawkins, a gawky, big-eared junior. Kara and Ruthie teased her, but they couldn't ignore the nods he'd give Olive in hallways, the way he'd linger by her locker on Fridays to talk A.P. Chemistry. Olive asked him to homecoming and he said maybe—shyly, she thinks, like he was really going to think about it—but after a week with no answer, Kara told her she was being played and confronted him in the cafeteria with Ruthie, saying if he didn't treat Olive right he'd have to answer to them. Nicholas never spoke to Olive again, and Kara and Ruthie still consider this their finest, bravest, most legendary act of friendship.

"I'm just saying," Olive says. "You barely know him."

Kara rolls her eyes. "I know plenty."

"Like?"

"Polio? The New Deal? 'The only thing we have to fear'?"

"But is it *actually* Franklin Delano Roosevelt?" asks Olive.

"Are you even listening?" Kara snaps.

"I was *listening*," Olive snaps back. "What I'm asking is—is it the spirit of Franklin Delano Roosevelt imbued in this wax figurine? Or is it just a wax figurine that's come to life?"

Kara thinks. Besides his admission of loneliness—the thought of which, and the memory of his hand touching hers, sends something soaring in her stomach—she can't recall many specifics. She remembers the hack of his laugh in the empty corridor; the blue blankness of his eyes. The way he appeared there at exactly the right moment, to her and her alone. Kara has a prickly awareness that Olive's trying to take something away from her by asking the question. Kara won't let her: she remembers FDR's sweetness, and something else, too—some force of character emanating from him as he sat in front of her. Massively confident. Sexy/dangerous. She feels it now. Whatever it is, she thinks, it's presidential.

"It was him," says Kara confidently. "It was FDR."

It's easy to be happy with Kara, when Kara is happy. Ruthie and Olive are at first devoted listeners to their friend's smitten wonders: do they think FDR would come to homecoming? Do they think he'd like her hair up or down? Do they think he minds that she can walk, that she's not made of wax? The details of Kara's infatuation become more and more minute as the days pass. But her moods swing less violently now, and her wax president boyfriend proves a more fascinating topic of conversation than endless rounds of Categories. By Wednesday, something has shifted in Kara—she walks taller, spaces out during class and conversation, wears an infuriatingly permanent half-smile. When Ruthie passes her a page of Olsen-Fontana smut in History, Kara writes a note at the top: *Can you write one about me and FDR?* It's an alarming request Ruthie pretends not to have noticed. She itches to diagnose Kara with something awful—Narcissistic Personality Disorder? Borderline?—but it seems possible all Kara suffers from is love.

Olive worries that love gives Kara a sense of authority she does not deserve. On Wednesday, when the three of them walk out into the cold sunshine after school and see Nicholas Dawkins driving by in his beat-up station wagon, and Olive's hand raises involuntarily in a wave that's really more of a Nazi salute, and they all see Nicholas cringe as he passes, Kara turns to Olive with a look of sympathy.

"You guys never really had that *spark*, did you?" she says.

And Olive wants to retort. She wants to say, "At least Nicholas Dawkins has *bones*." But what's the point? Kara's thing with FDR is bigger than a high school crush. It gives her an otherworldly sheen, a glamour. It turns her into an adult. It turns her, Olive realizes with dawning horror, into Cassidy Fontana.

For months, the girls have waited for a movie that opens on Friday. It's a revamp of *The Castle of Otranto* set in high school, starring an actor whose prominent cheekbones and long eyelashes render him androgynous enough to be attractive to them. "Opening night," Kara and Ruthie and Olive confirm every time they see the trailers on TV. They'll love every second of it, and at the end they'll pretend they were only loving it ironically. Ruthie went so far as to order tickets in advance.

"*Otranto High*, 7:50," she reminds Kara on Thursday afternoon.

"*Otranto High*, 7:50," Kara repeats. The girls sit outside the auditorium—Ruthie and Olive with their homework, Kara with an issue of *The Economist* she is reading to impress FDR. They are waiting to be called to the stage when Kara glances at her cell phone, and sees a text message from a number she doesn't recognize:

i miss u

Who is this? she replies.

Ten minutes later, a response arrives: *lol ur crazy*

Normally, Kara would obliterate this digital stranger for having wasted her time—even now, she imagines the rude things she could say. *Eat a dick, moron. Leave me alone.* But loving FDR has softened her. *I think you have the wrong number*, she texts back, adding a smiley face. Then she puts down her phone and tries to get Ruthie and Olive to help her analyze everything FDR said to her as well as the way he said it—she imitates for her friends his gently teasing tone.

Olive focuses on her textbook, and after a while Ruthie's eyes glaze over. "Why don't we go watch rehearsal?" she finally suggests, cutting Kara off mid-sentence. The girls move to the dark auditorium; they watch Abigail Williams and John Proctor read from scripts.

"I have once or twice played the shovelboard," says the dark-eyed senior playing Abigail, "but I have no joy in it."

The buzz from Kara's phone is so loud, Proctor stumbles over his line at the sound.

y r u mad?

I'm not, Kara texts back. *I just don't know who this is.*

This time the answer comes quickly: *met u at the museum, kara.*

If Kara had to visualize the effect this message has on her, she'd picture her heart ripping itself from the veins that hold it steady to hammer alarmingly at her ribcage. *I didn't know you had a phone*, she texts.

got it from the lost n found, FDR replies, *when do i c u next.*

Kara puts the phone down and tries to concentrate on the play, to pretend everything is normal, as though she does not have to remind herself to breathe. She wipes her sweating palms on the legs of her jeans. She's trying to think of a good response, but the only flirtatious banter she's had with the opposite sex has run a little too heavy on banter. She wants to do this right. Something is happening, finally, to her. Her phone buzzes again.

kara r u there kara? i need to c u kara when do i c u

Tomorrow! Kara sends back, and she nearly laughs out loud.

When she looks up, her face lit white by the glow of her phone, Ruthie and Olive are watching. She sees identical concern in her two friends' faces, twin grimaces of love and frustration furrowing their brows, and hates them for it.

On Friday Kara Googles "Franklin Delano Roosevelt favorite drink" and finds a page that claims it's Scotch, but when she surveys her parents' liquor cabinet she's so nervous she grabs a half-empty bottle of coconut rum instead. She stops at a convenience store before getting on the parkway and buys a disposable lighter, Diet Coke, and trail mix. Her eyes graze over the colorful boxes of condoms hanging in rows behind the cashier's head, but she cannot work up the nerve to ask for one. It needs to happen sooner rather than later, but she can't make her mouth say the words. In the car, she feels like laughing and crying. "This is only a first date," she tells herself.

She arrives at eight p.m. The museum has been closed for hours and the janitors have already made their rounds. Kara parks in the employee lot. She pushes open the unlocked back door FDR texted her about. She turns on her flashlight and makes her way through a hallway that opens up into the lobby. Kara is the best kind of nervous. What she's doing feels utterly surreal, partly because she's told no one else she's doing it. She considered telling Ruthie and Olive, of course, but in the end it seemed sweeter to hold the plan inside her, secret and safe and all her own. Still, she pictures her friends now, glancing at the time on their phones, waiting for her outside the movie theater, wondering how much of *Otranto High* they've already missed, and Kara regrets not telling them. Not because she's stood them up, but because she wants someone to call later to describe how good she's feeling.

In the *In Times of War* . . . corridor, the lights are on, and FDR is waiting.

"Hi," says Kara.

"Right on time!" FDR marvels. "So you're not one of those dummies who's always getting herself lost."

"Ha ha," says Kara as she comes closer, and then, "What?"

In the last week, she's almost forgotten what FDR looks like. He wears the same dark suit he wore when they first met, the same red tie. He has the bright white rectangular grin of a wind-up monkey. For days she's scoured the internet for pictures of the thirty-second president, but none of them capture him exactly as he looks now. The pictures show a man tall but bowed, with weak-looking legs and liver-spotted skin. This FDR has those, but also glossy blue eyes, and thick black lines etched into his face. He looks older than Kara remembered. Less real, too. She doesn't quite know how to proceed. Should she kiss him? She thinks it might be too soon to kiss him.

"Pull up a seat," says FDR. "Get comfortable."

Kara looks around for a chair, but there are none. She sits at his feet and opens her backpack. She pulls out two red plastic cups and the bottle of coconut rum. "I know you like Scotch, but this was all my parents had."

FDR just grins. "I can't drink. I don't have a throat."

"Oh, my God," says Kara. "I feel so dumb. I didn't even think of that."

"That's okay," FDR says.

Embarrassed, Kara fills her cup, half rum and half Diet Coke. The result tastes like sunscreen. FDR watches her sip.

"I've never really been on a date," says Kara. "I know how pathetic that sounds. But I've never met anyone like you before." She waits for FDR to respond, but he doesn't. "I guess this isn't new for you."

"No," says FDR, "it isn't. There was another girl a few years ago. She went to school in Cherry Hill. I can't remember her name. Maybe Tina?"

"Another high school girl?" Kara is surprised, but she tries to play it cool. She knows Roosevelt had affairs when he was alive—she's spent lots of time on Wikipedia this week.

"Now that I think about it, there was another one before that. Cute," he says, inspecting Kara. "Thinner than you. But they both went to college. You won't do that, will you, Kara? You won't go away and leave me?"

Kara is confused. "I've already started looking at schools."

"Well, stop," says FDR.

They're silent a while. Kara can hear the buzz of electricity from the spotlights over each president. She stares at the *MISSION ACCOMPLISHED* banner hanging behind George W. Bush at the end of the hall. She stares at the open door.

"What are you looking at?" FDR snaps. "Are you looking at Lincoln?"

Kara shakes her head. "No, I—"

"If you're here for Lincoln, you can get up and go. I don't appreciate having my time wasted by dummies who just want a shot at boning Lincoln."

"I'm not here for Lincoln," Kara says. "I'm here for you."

The muscles in FDR's face relax. He hasn't stopped smiling. "Damn right you are."

Kara watches him a long moment, waiting for him to blink. He never does. She tries to remember that she's having a good time.

"Hey!" she says suddenly, happy to remember her surprise. She reaches into the convenience store bag and pulls out the lighter, flicking it until a flame appears. Kara moves the flame toward the cigarette at the end of FDR's holder, but FDR quickly rolls away.

"What the hell do you think you're doing?" he shouts. "Are you some kind of an idiot? I'm made of wax, retard!"

"Oh, God!" Kara drops the lighter and starts to cry. "Oh, God, I'm so sorry. I wasn't even thinking. I just thought you might miss cigarettes."

She's kneeling in a wax museum on her first date, crying in front of the only man who has ever called her pretty. She is sixteen—too old for this to be happening this badly. *You are a tugboat*, Kara thinks. She wipes her nose on her sleeve and FDR wheels towards her again.

"Hey," he says. "Hey, dummy. Calm down. I'm not mad anymore." He puts his wax hand on her shoulder and whistles through his square teeth. "Boy oh boy, are you lucky you found me. Other guys wouldn't put up with that kind of crap, you know. But I love you, Kara. Even though you are a dummy."

"You love me?" Kara looks up into his beady eyes. "Oh, FDR."

FDR grins down at her. "What's an 'FDR'?" he asks.

The next day, Saturday, is dress rehearsal for *The Crucible*. Kara walks into school a little past noon to find Ruthie and Olive sitting on the floor, waiting. Ruthie's dour-faced under her white bonnet, makeup-less, her eyes ringed and tired. She scrambles to her feet when she sees Kara. Olive's expression is stony; she takes her time. Kara pretends she hasn't noticed them and slips into the drama classroom, but her friends are on her heels.

"Are you okay?" asks Ruthie. "Why didn't you meet us at the movies last night?"

"Did you have *sex*?" asks Olive.

Kara shushes her. The classroom is filled with their co-stars—stretching, doing vocal warm-ups, buckling their pilgrim shoes, paying no particular attention to the girls. They step into the large closet where Kara's costume hangs, and Ruthie closes the door behind them.

"Well?" Olive asks.

"I don't see how it's any of your business," says Kara.

Ruthie sighs in relief. She can tell by Kara's tone—quiet and strange, not clipped and smug—that she didn't. Olive only gets angrier—all morning she's imagined, in gory detail, the things that could have happened to Kara last night, and now it burns to see her in one piece and still a virgin.

"What happened?" Olive asks.

"Nothing," Kara shrugs. "He asked me to visit him. We just hung out and talked." She ignores the look Ruthie and Olive exchange. "It was, if you must know, really nice."

"How did you even get in?" Ruthie asks.

"There's a back door near the employee parking lot they always forget to lock. FDR told me about it. He knows everything that goes on in there."

"Are you, like, boyfriend and girlfriend now?" asks Olive.

Kara says nothing. She slips the scratchy brown Puritan dress off its hanger, and struggles to pull it over her head.

"Why didn't you tell us?" Ruthie asks. "We could have come with you."

"Oh, yeah," said Kara. "That would have been great. 'Hey, FDR, I'm so excited for our date; by the way, my friends think I'm a child so they've come, too.' "

"It's just moving so fast," Ruthie says. "We don't even know the guy."

"Maybe it would be easier for you if he wasn't a former president of the United States?" Kara's smile is frosty. "Maybe you'd prefer him to be, like, a History teacher or something?"

Ruthie feels her face go hot. Earlier that day—as inspired by Kara's new boldness as she was itchy not to be left behind—she had stepped into Mr. Olsen's classroom wearing a clingy blue dress she didn't have the nerve to wear to homecoming. Ruthie had planned what to do the night before, re-reading key sections of the 254 pages she'd written about Mr. Olsen and Cassidy Fontana. She was going to touch his face and whisper, "You dumb hipster fuck," and then he was going to lay her flat and do things to her, more explicit versions of things she wrote about him doing. But Mr. Olsen only looked up from his laptop and said, "What's up, Rachel?" She could smell the coffee on his breath. She could see a little white glob of donut frosting caught in his mangy beard. "My name is *Cassidy*," she'd said, before stumbling out of the room.

Ruthie felt stupid then but now she feels even stupider. She looks to Olive—this is the part where Olive usually intercedes, changes the subject, protects them both from themselves—but Olive stares pointedly in another direction, her jaw clamped shut. She looks like she has given up. She looks like she is going to burn down the school.

Kara's phone buzzes then, and when she takes it out of her bag, she watches three texts arrive from FDR in rapid succession:

Miss you, says the first.

C u soon, says the second.

Send me a pic of ur boobs, says the third.

Kara quickly shuts off her phone. "Well," she says at last. "We can't share FDR, if that's what you're thinking."

"What?" Ruthie exclaims. "What's *wrong* with you?"

"I don't know what to tell you." Kara laughs a high, mean laugh, a laugh with no laughter in it. "Maybe you're happy being best friends with people you hate. Maybe you're happy being alone. But I'm not." She ties her costume apron around her waist. Ruthie and Olive stare at her.

"I don't hate you," says Olive.

"We're not worried because we *hate* you," Ruthie says.

Kara shrugs, reaching into the cubby where her bonnet sits. She pulls out the bonnet, and something falls out of it and onto the floor. Ruthie glances down and screams.

"What is that?" she shrieks. "Is that a finger?"

Kara looks. At her feet is a man's ring finger, still circled by a gold wedding band. She can tell instantly that it's wax. It's fallen out of her bonnet along with a couple of roses. The roses are dead. Ruthie's still screaming. Olive grips Ruthie's arm, her face furrowed in disgust. Kara swallows. She crouches to sweep the items back into her bonnet, murmuring, "It's just a gift, it's just how he shows he cares," as the rose petals come loose and crumble in her hands.

Mr. Olsen has them run through all of Act Three. For once the girls are onstage for most of rehearsal, writhing and screaming "Begone!" and beating their breasts. But they're distracted. Kara stands as far away from her friends as Mr. Olsen's blocking will allow. She ignores the exhortations they hiss at her. The finger has terrified Ruthie and Olive so much that Ruthie can ignore her discomfort in Mr. Olsen's presence, and Olive can stop pretending she doesn't care. Kara's relationship with FDR is, clearly, flipping weird as all get out. She can't accuse her friends of being jealous now, because they aren't. They're angry and curious and thoroughly grossed out. Kara is gray-faced and jumpy the whole rehearsal, and once when Olsen snaps at her for being distracted, she *apologizes.* When it's over, she runs for her car, still in costume, clutching the wax finger to her chest.

"She's going to go see him," says Olive, as they watch Kara drive away.

"You know what we have to do, right?" Ruthie says. "We have to go to the museum and confront FDR. Like when me and Kara talked to Nicholas."

"You think?" Olive's face goes sour, as it always does when she remembers the incident.

"Absolutely. He needs to know what he's dealing with—otherwise he'll do whatever he wants to her. That's how older guys are," Ruthie explains with a sigh. "They underestimate you. They assume you've got no one looking out for you. They assume you're nothing."

Olive thinks Ruthie is full of shit, but she knows they need to save Kara. Olive has always been the responsible one, unfailingly good and self-sacrificing. In *Little Women* Characters, Olive was Marmee. In *Articles of Clothing*, she was Mom Jeans. It's far preferable to being the ugly one or the prude, but it's boring, too—nobody falls in love with the mom. Olive stares after Kara and raises two fingers to her mouth. She sucks on the imaginary cigarette she holds there.

"Okay," Olive says. "Let's roll."

It is a rush—making the plan, telling the necessary lies, taking the train into the city that night. The girls stow two weapons in Ruthie's bag—a hammer Ruthie finds in her dad's toolbox, and a blowtorch stolen from *The Crucible*'s tech crew. "Just in case," Ruthie says, and Olive begins to understand why her friends took down Nicholas Dawkins: this act, this rescue mission, is the most powerful performance of love Olive has ever attempted.

The night is especially dark, the moon obscured by clouds. Ruthie and Olive realize—once they push open the same unlocked door through which Kara entered the museum—that they haven't brought a flashlight. Ruthie grasps Olive's hand. Olive takes her phone out of her pocket and turns it on; it casts a short span of blue light in front of them, enough to make their way down the back hallway. They don't know where in the museum they are until the clouds shift outside and moonlight pours in through the large front windows of the lobby. Jackie O. looms up in front of them, gaunt and widowed and waxen.

Olive nods at the *In Times of War . . .* sign, visible for only a second before the moon goes dark again. "In there," she says.

They creep through the corridor, Olive shining light on the faces of the presidents they pass. She stops at Lincoln. His arms are frozen in some eternal gesticulation.

"Wait," says Ruthie. "Look at his hand!"

Olive looks. Lincoln's left ring finger has been cleanly lobbed off.

"It wasn't even *his*," Olive says. The girls exchange a look of disgust. They keep moving.

When they finally reach FDR, they're surprised by how old he seems. He's perched in his chair like a grandfather, and far from lifelike. He looks more like the Penguin from *Batman* than a former president of the United States.

"Um," says Olive. "Excuse me, sir?"

FDR doesn't move. His gaze fixes on some point beyond them.

"Is he asleep?" Ruthie whispers. "Does he sleep with his eyes open?

"I can't tell." Olive stretches a tentative hand forward, waves it in front of FDR's blank eyes. Nothing happens.

The girls hear a shuddering noise, like a door opening—it's distant, but the silence around them has been so tense that Ruthie, startled, drops her bag at FDR's feet. The hammer clonks to the floor. Olive shut her phone off quickly, snuffing out their only light.

"What was that?" she hisses.

"I don't know!" Ruthie inches her way down the corridor, arms outstretched in front of her, shaking for fear she'll actually brush against someone. She doesn't. Her eyes adjust to the dark lobby, and when she discerns nobody moving within it, she turns on her heel and wanders back to Olive, using the sound of her friend's nervous ragged breathing to guide her.

"I don't see anybody," she says to Olive.

"Okay," Olive says. She turns on her phone again, casting its blue light. She and Ruthie take in each other's alarmed faces. Then they look at FDR.

His grinning head is tilted upwards. He's looking at them; there is no mistaking this. And in his left hand, he is holding Ruthie's hammer.

Ruthie's scream is something low and gurgling and feral. She pulls at Olive's arm, trying to drag her away, but Olive can't move. Her mouth is open and her eyes are perfect circles. Suddenly, the lights come on. Ruthie's scream dies in her throat. She and Olive turn to the opening of the corridor, where Kara stands, hand poised over the light switch, her *Crucible* bonnet askew.

"What the hell is going on?" Kara says.

FDR places the hammer calmly in his lap. "Friends of yours, dummy?" he asks.

It's shocking for Ruthie and Olive to hear this wax figurine speak, but it's even stranger to hear someone call Kara "dummy." They see their friend's face flush as she approaches.

"Not anymore," says Kara.

FDR sizes the two girls up, gazing at them for a moment too long. His expression never changes, yet both Ruthie and Olive feel a strange wave pass over them, a sense that their own bodies no longer belong to them.

"Pretty," he grins at Kara. "Why hasn't any of that pretty rubbed off on you?"

Kara's hand is wrapped around Lincoln's severed finger. She's holding it so tightly that her arm trembles.

"Hey," says Ruthie faintly, in protest.

The girls had assumed FDR would be handsome, or magnetic—at

the very least, kind of nice. But it's beginning to dawn on them that he's completely horrible. That whatever Kara has with him is nothing they want.

"You guys should probably go," Kara says after a moment, not looking at them.

"Don't be like that," FDR says. "I thought we could play your game. Categories, right? You want to play Categories with me? Kara told me the rules—you're each a different thing in the category, and Kara's always the Ugly One. Isn't that right?" His eyes shift to Kara. "You're the Ugly One. Right, dummy?"

"Hey!" says Olive this time. "You can't talk to her like that."

FDR's head begins to bob, the cigarette holder between his teeth bouncing up and down. It's as if he's laughing, but they don't hear any laughter. "Oh, little girl. Of course I can."

Olive and Ruthie look at Kara.

Kara tries to smile. She tugs at the string of her bonnet. "It's okay," she tells them. "He's just joking around. I'll call you tomorrow."

Olive sucks her teeth a moment, then shakes her head. She picks Ruthie's bag up off the floor. Ruthie's so embarrassed for Kara she can't quite look at her. Plus, she needs to retrieve the hammer from FDR's lap; it's her dad's only hammer. But she doesn't want to ask. She leans in as quickly as she can and takes the hammer by the handle, but FDR grabs her around the wrist before she can pull back. Ruthie whimpers. FDR laughs again.

"Little girl," FDR taunts softly. He lets go.

Olive takes the hammer from Ruthie and drops it in the bag, where it clangs against the blowtorch. She and Ruthie begin to walk down the corridor, but they haven't gotten very far—only to a bemused William McKinley, shrugging over the Spanish-American war—before Olive stops, and turns.

"Kara," she says. "Come with us. We'll get pizza or something."

Olive sounds gentle, but firm. Her voice makes Ruthie's courage return. Ruthie remembers how she felt, standing beside Kara in the cafeteria last year, shouting at Nicholas Dawkins—strong. Bigger than human. Like if she wanted, she could breathe fire. She stares at Kara now, mortified in her bonnet, and thinks of Mr. Olsen calling her 'Rachel.'

"Come on, Kara," Ruthie says. "Let's go." And then she adds: "What would Cassidy Fontana do?"

But it's the wrong question, because all three know what Cassidy

Fontana would do. Cassidy Fontana would stay at home in slinky clothes, laughing and sighing and waiting to be fucked. Cassidy Fontana would do what she has always done. She would do exactly what Kara is doing.

"No," says Olive. She takes a few hesitant steps toward FDR's wheelchair. Kara is wild-eyed and frightened. But Olive keeps moving toward them. "Don't be Cassidy Fontana." She reaches into Ruthie's bag and pulls out the blowtorch. "Be Eleanor Roosevelt."

The girls don't know whether FDR doesn't understand what they're saying or just doesn't care; he continues to chomp down on his cigarette holder without expression. But Kara takes the blowtorch and turns it over in her hands, gazing at it like it's some kind of a talisman. She looks at Ruthie. She looks at Olive.

"Begone!" Olive screams suddenly.

And Ruthie joins in. "Begone! Begone! Begone!"

They use their loud, screechy stage voices. Olive stomps and Ruthie waves her fists wildly. Both of them have their teeth bared, and they wear the exact expressions they get right before Kara says something awful to Mr. Olsen, something she should really get detention for but somehow never does; they look at her like she's the most powerful creature in the world. Kara loves that look. She drinks it in now.

Kara adjusts the blowtorch and stands up straight. Then she extends one arm and releases the trigger, and with her other hand she pulls the plastic lighter from her pocket and flicks the wheel in front of the gas. A line of blue fire emerges, melting the tip of FDR's cigarette. Fat white drops of melted wax spill onto FDR's lap and he starts to yell through his teeth, rolling his wheelchair backwards, but whether it is from fear or basic anatomical inability, he can't turn his head. He backs into the wall. Kara follows until FDR's cigarette holder has melted down, then his teeth, then his lips. She holds the blowtorch steady until FDR no longer has a mouth, just a smooth seal of white wax across the bottom of his face. She drops Lincoln's finger, which she's been squeezing so tightly it's now misshapen, to the floor, and she turns the torch on that, too.

"What kind of a gift is a *finger*, you freak?" Kara yells at FDR as it turns into a small, flesh-colored puddle. Ruthie and Olive stand behind her and cheer.

Outside the museum, Kara hands Ruthie the keys to her car and crawls into her own backseat. When Olive gave her the blowtorch every nerve in her body went wild with adrenaline; she could feel the blood coursing through her veins. But now she's tired and her head hurts. The three girls are silent as they drive.

Olive and Ruthie are stunned by what they've done. Olive touches her imaginary cigarette to the end of the blowtorch, then lifts it to her lips. *Begone*, she thinks, blowing imaginary smoke out the open window. Ruthie has already started re-writing Cassidy Fontana in her mind. Now Cassidy Fontana smears on poison lip gloss and kisses Mr. Olsen until his mouth burns away; she takes off on the back of an eagle to become an avenging Amazon, a terrifying virgin princess. As they hit the parkway, Olive turns on the radio and Ruthie picks up speed and they let the cold wind whip around their faces as they sing along to the worst pop song they have ever heard, their favorite.

When they played the Category of Musical Components, Olive was a drumbeat, Ruthie was a synthesizer, and Kara—the loudest, the only one they'd ever want to speak for them—was vocals. Now Olive and Ruthie bounce and shimmy, approximating dancing as closely as they can without unbuckling their seatbelts, and Kara leans her head back. She can feel Ruthie's eyes on her in the rearview mirror, so she mouths along with the lyrics. But she doesn't sing. She doesn't make a sound.

Nominated by Sandra Leong and One Story

FIRST SNOW

by ANDREA HOLLANDER

from SPILLWAY

My friend said the first snow always felt
immaculate—she couldn't wait to play in it.

But she didn't grow up near a highway where
any accumulation turned gray before your eyes.

And she didn't have a father like mine, a man raised
by his mother's images of the worst catastrophes.

This afternoon, as the first flakes fall onto the streets
of this city I just moved to, how can I forget

those warnings he gave me throughout my childhood
never to eat it, the way he forbade me to play

in anyone else's yard, told me that snow,
no matter how inviting, could be hiding something—

a broken beer bottle, a rake left on a lawn, a sinkhole.
Like those irresistible phrases

my ex piled on—how beautiful my eyes, my hair,
how much he loved, he said, to contemplate

my body. I should have suspected something
sharp and dangerous

below that gleaming landscape.

Nominated by Alice Friman, Susan Terris and Spillway

THING WITH FEATHERS THAT PERCHES IN THE SOUL

by ANTHONY DOERR

from GRANTA

1. THE HOUSE

I am driving my twin sons home from flag football practice. It's September, it hasn't rained in two months and seemingly half of the state of Idaho is on fire. For a week the sky has been an upturned bowl the colour of putty, the clouds indistinguishable from haze, enough smoke in the air that we taste it in our food, in our throats, in our sleep. But tonight, for some reason, as we pass St Luke's Hospital, something in the sky gives way, and a breathtaking orange light cascades across the trees, the road, the windshield. We turn onto Fort Street, the road frosted with smouldering, feverish light, and just before the stoplight on Fifth, in a grassy lot, I notice, perhaps for the first time, a little house.

It's a log cabin with a swaybacked roof and a low door, like a cottage for gnomes. A little brick chimney sticks out of its shingles. Three enamel signs stand on the south side; a stone bench hunkers on the north.

It's old. It's tiny. It seems almost to tremble in the strange, volcanic light. I have passed this house, I'm guessing, three thousand times. I have jogged past it, biked past it, driven past it. Every election for the last twelve years I voted in a theater lobby three hundred yards from it.

And yet I've never really seen it before.

2. JERRY

A week later I'm standing outside the little house with a City Parks employee named Jerry. A plaque above the door reads THIS CABIN WAS THE FIRST HOME IN BOISE TO SHELTER WOMEN AND CHILDREN. The outer walls are striped with cracked chinking and smudged with exhaust. The ratcheting powerheads of sprinklers spatter its back with each pass. An empty green bottle of something called Übermonster Energy Brew has rolled up against its north wall.

Jerry has to try three keys before he manages to push open the front door.

Inside, it's full of old leaves and hung with the pennants of cobwebs. Little fissures of light show through the panelling.

No furniture. It smells like old paint. Through the dirty steel mesh bolted over a window I can watch cars barrel past on Fort, sedans and Suburbans and pickups, maybe every third one piloted by a sunglasses-wearing mom, a kid or two or three belted into the back seat. Any minute my own wife, ferrying my own kids to school, will come charging past.

'How many people ask to come in here to look at this?' I ask Jerry.

'In four years,' he says, 'you're the first.'

3. BOISE BEFORE BOISE

Take away the Capitol building, the Hoff building, the US Bank building. Take away all eighteen Starbucks, all twenty-nine playgrounds, all ten thousand street lights. Take away the parking garages, Guido's Pizza, the green belt, the fire hydrants, the cheat grass, the bridges.

It's 1863 in the newly christened Idaho Territory and we're downtown. There are rocks. Magpies. The canvases of a dozen infantry tents flutter beside a cobble-bottomed creek.

Into this rides a man named John.

John has a gnarly, foot-long beard, a wagon full of tools and a girl back in Colorado. Born in Ireland, he has sailed around the globe; he's been to London, to Calcutta, around Cape Horn; he has heard the whump of Russian artillery, saw men die, won a medal.

For years he was a sailor. Now he's a prospector.

He's something else too. He's in love.

236

John stops at the tents and asks the infantrymen who they are, where he is, what they call this place.

Camp Boise, they say. Boise Barracks. Fort Boise.

John unpacks his wagon. To his south a green river slides along. To his north the shadows of clouds drag over foothills. All this time he's thinking of Mary.

Mary is seventeen years old. Big-nosed, wavy-haired, as Irish as he is. Good with a needle, good at seeing into people too. Her eyes, curiously, are like the eyes of a grandmother. As if, though she's half his age, she knows more about the world than he does. She too has seen a measure of the planet: born in Cork County, sent to the New World at age nine, enrolled at a convent school in New Orleans, married a man in Philadelphia at age fifteen. Gave birth to a girl. That marriage caved in, God knows why, and Mary found John in Louisville, or John found Mary, and they got married and rode two thousand miles west into the unknown, into Colorado, and now he's here, another thousand miles farther on, in this place that is not yet a place, to look for gold.

John is almost forty years old. Try for a moment to imagine all the places he might have slept: hammocks, shanties, wickiups made of willows, the lurching holds of ships, the cold ruts of the Oregon Trail. Curled on his side next to a mountain stream with his mules hobbled and elk bugling and wolves singing and the great swarming arm of the Milky Way draped over them all.

John rolls away rocks, uproots sage. Cottonwoods are bunched along the river, plenty of them. They're lousy with caterpillars, but they're lightweight, and they're close. He cuts his logs and drags them to a flat area beside the creek and uses the blade of a broad axe to wrestle their crooked shapes into straight lines.

A simple rectangle in the sand. Three feet high, then four, then five. Into the spaces between he jams clay and leaves and sticks. He leaves two low doors and two windows to cover—or now—with paper. Later, maybe, he can put in real window-glass, if window-glass ever makes it all the way out here along two thousand miles of ruts and raids and storm.

If he's lucky. If this place is lucky.

He starts on the roof. Mary is coming from Colorado in a train of fourteen wagons. Already she could be pregnant. Already she could be close.

He fashions wooden pins for door hinges. He installs a stove. He nails fabric to the insides of the walls. Just get here, Mary. Get here before winter.

4. HOPE

Three hundred yards from the spot where John O'Farrell raised what would become the first family home in Boise, my wife and I used to pick up drugs from a fertility clinic. We wanted to start a family but we weren't getting pregnant. Month after month. We went through the expected stuff: tests, doubt, despair. Then I got a chance to move from Boise to work at Princeton University for a year.

Then we got pregnant.

Then we found out it was twins.

Hope, wrote Emily Dickinson, *is the thing with feathers—*

That perches in the soul—
And sings the tune without words—
and never stops—at all.

All autumn in New Jersey we worried the pregnancy wouldn't last, biology wouldn't work, the foetuses wouldn't hang on. But they did.

When my wife went home early to Idaho for Christmas, I stood in our rented New Jersey apartment, in the shadowless grey light of a snowstorm, and let myself believe for the first time that it was actually going to happen, that in a couple of months we would open the squeaky back door and carry in two babies.

The apartment's walls were blank, its stairs were steep. It was not, I realized, ready. Was not a home.

Who hasn't prepared a welcome? Set flowers on a nightstand for a returning hospital patient? Festooned a living room for a returning soldier? Stocked a refrigerator, washed a car, laid out towels? All of this is a kind of hope, a tune without words. Hope that the beloved will arrive safely, that the beloved will feel beloved.

I stood in that little apartment in 2003 thinking of my wife, of the two unknown quantities siphoning nutrients out of her day and night. How she never complained. How she ate Fruit Roll-Ups by the dozen because they were the only food that didn't make her feel sick. Then I drove alone to a shopping mall, not something I've done before or since, and bought foot-high fabric-covered letters–A, B and C–and a night light shaped like a star and something called a Graco Pack 'n Play Playard and set it up and then stayed up till midnight trying to figure out how to fold and zip it back inside the bag it came in.

When you prepare a welcome, you prepare yourself. You prepare for the moment the beloved arrives, the moment you say: I understand you've come a long way, I understand you're taking the larger risk with your life.

You say: Here. This might be humble, this might not be the place you know. This might not be everything you dreamed of. But it's something you can call home.

5. QUESTIONS

Mary O'Farrell leaves Colorado in the summer of 1863. Lincoln is president; the Emancipation Proclamation is five months old. Across the country, in South Carolina, Union batteries are bombarding Fort Sumter and they won't let up for two years. On the long road north does she remember what it was like to be a nine-year-old girl and leave her home in Ireland? Does she remember the birds she saw at sea, and the light heaving on the immense fields of the Atlantic? Does she hear in her memory the Latin of Irish priests; the Gaelic of her parents; the terror when she showed up for her first day of school in New Orleans, and heard those accents, and saw faces that were utterly different than every face she had known before? Does she think of her first husband, and their first night together, and does she ponder the circumstances under which she—a sixteen-year-old with a newborn daughter—left him? Does she think of that decision as a failure? Or as an exercise of courage? And was it that same courage that kept her from turning back when she saw the storm-racked brow of the Rockies for the first time, and is it courage that keeps her going now, Pike's Peak at her back, her daughter at her knees, very possibly a new, second child growing in her uterus, the wagon pressing into newer, rawer country, the bench bouncing, wheels groaning—courage that keeps her from weeping at the falling darkness and the creaking trees and the unfettered miles of sage?

It takes Mary four months and four days to reach Fort Boise. Here there are no telegrams, no grocery stores, no pharmacies. There aren't even bricks.

On legs weary from the road she walks into the little house John has built for her. Stands on the dirt floor. Sees the light trapped in its paper-covered windows.

239

John stops beside her, or in front of her, or behind her.

How many thousands of questions must have been coursing through that little space at that moment?

Is it good enough, does she like it, did I make it all right?

Where will I cook, where will we sleep, where will I give birth?

Will I find gold and will winter be awful and how will I feed us?

Have we finally come far enough to stop moving?

6. HOME

Whatever magic John threads into the walls of their house, it works. Fort Boise survives the winter; the O'Farrells survive the winter. John embarks upon a remodel: he replaces the gable ends with board and batten siding; he cuts shingles for a proper roof.

Around them civilization mushrooms. By the time the O'Farrell cabin is a year old, Boise has a population of 1,658. There are now sixty buildings, nine general stores, five saloons, three doctors and two breweries.

John buys wallpaper to cover the interior planking. He builds a fireplace from bricks.

Meanwhile, Mary does not need a fertility clinic. In the years after she arrives in Idaho, she gives birth to six more kids. She loses three. She also adopts seven children.

Their home is two hundred square feet, smaller than my bedroom. There are no SpongeBob reruns to put on when the kids get too loud. No pizzerias to call when she can't think of what to cook; there is no telephone, no freezer, no electricity. No internal plumbing. No premoistened baby wipes.

But it's fallacy to imagine Mary O'Farrell's years in that tiny house as unrelenting hardship. Her life was almost certainly full of laughter; without question it was full of noise and energy and sunlight. One day she convinces two passing priests to start holding Catholic Mass in her house and they celebrate Sundays there for four consecutive years.

By 1868, Boise boasts four hundred buildings. Ads in the *TriWeekly Statesman* from that year offer coral earrings and 18-carat-gold ladies' watches and English saucepans and hydraulic nozzles and 24-hour physicians' prescriptions. A stage line boasts that it can bring a person to San Francisco in four days.

This is no longer a place of single men: by the end of that year, Boise has two hundred children in four different schools.

Eventually John shifts from the unpredictability of crawling into mining tunnels to the rituals of farming: a more sunlit profession. Soon enough he starts construction on a colonial revival at Fourth and Franklin, a real house, made of bricks.

But before it's done, before they move in, John rides to a store downtown and buys panes of glass and carries them home and fits them into strips of wood and builds real French windows for his wife, so she can sit inside their cabin and look out, so the same golden sunshine of a summer evening that every person who has ever lived in this valley knows can fall through the glass and set parallelograms of light onto the floor.

7. PROBABLY I'M WRONG ABOUT A LOT OF THIS

Maybe John O'Farrell had some help raising the walls of his cabin. Maybe Mary hated it when she first saw it. Maybe they weren't devoted to each other the way I want to believe they were; maybe I'm trying to fashion a love story out of cobwebs and ghosts.

But listen: To live for a minimum of seven years with a minimum of seven kids in two hundred square feet with no toilet paper or Netflix or Xanax requires a certain kind of imperturbability. To adopt seven kids; to not give out when snow is sifting through cracks in the chinking; to not lose your mind when a baby is feverish and screeching and a toddler is tugging your skirts and the hairdryer wind of August is blowing 110-degree heat under your door and the mass production of electric refrigerators is still fifty-five years away–something has to hold you together through all that.

It has to be love, doesn't it? In however many of its infinite permutations?

John and Mary are married for thirty-seven years. They live to see a capitol dome raised and streetcars glide up and down the streets. Out in the world Coca-Cola and motion pictures and vacuum cleaners are invented.

On 13 May 1900, the page 8 'Local Brevities' section of the *Idaho Daily Statesman* includes the following items:

The rainfall during the 36 hours preceding 5 o'clock last evening was 1.72 inches.
The May term of the supreme court will begin tomorrow.

241

Mrs. John O'Farrell is lying at death's door. The physicians have
given up all hope.

The second stanza of Emily Dickinson's poem reads like this:

And sweetest—in the gale—is heard;
And sore must be the storm—
That could abash the little bird
That kept so many warm—

Sore must be the storm indeed. John outlives Mary by only a few
months. According to his obituary,

Mr. O'Farrell was one of the pioneers of Idaho,
having come to this section in the early sixties.
He was well and favorably known throughout
Idaho and the northwest.

And then there's this:

Mr. O'Farrell's wife died last spring and he never recovered
from the blow.

8. WHAT LASTS

Through the decades the house John built for Mary has been softened
by lawn sprinklers and hammered by sun. The cottonwood it was built
from makes a weak and spongy lumber, nonresistant to decay, prone to
warping, and to keep the house from collapsing, Boiseans have had to
come together every few decades and retell its story. In the early 1910s,
the Daughters of the American Revolution collected $173 to move and
reroof it; in the 1950s, a dance was held to raise funds; seven hundred
people showed up. And at the turn of the last century, folks who live in
the houses around the O'Farrell Cabin raised $52,000 to help the ar-
chitect Charles Hummel repair the logs, doors, windows and roof.

And so it stands, 150 years old, the same age as the city it helped
establish.

As unassuming as Boise itself. Invisible to most of us. The first fam-
ily home in our city. On a given night John might have lain in here on

a home-made cot dreaming of his years at sea, Anatolia, cannon-fire, the churning Pacific; four or five or six or seven kids might have been hip-to-hip under quilts, breathing in unison, their exhalations showing in the cold; owls would have been hunting in the gulches, and dogs barking in town; Mary might have been sitting up, hands in her lap, drowsing, watching stars rotate past her new windows. Out the door was Boise: place of salmon, place of gold, place to buy supper and a saddle and have the doctor stitch you up before heading back out to try to wrench another quarter-ounce of metal from the hills.

Fifteen decades have passed. It's late September now, and smoke from a dozen fires still hangs in the valley, hazing everything, as I drive to a windowless grey warehouse not too far from the O'Farrell cabin. Inside, stored in an amber-coloured gloom, are rows of fifteen-foot-high shelves loaded with artefacts. There's Native American basketry in here and antique typewriters and a covered wagon, and Nazi daggers, and scary-looking foot-powered dental equipment probably eighty years old. There are prisoners' manacles and nineteenth-century wedding gowns and optometry kits and opium scrapers brought to Idaho by Chinese miners who have been dead for more than a century.

From the arcane depths of these shelves a curatorial registrar for the Idaho State Historical Museum named Sarah retrieves four items and lays them out on white Ethafoam.

A miner's pick. A long metal spike called a miner's candlestick. A tin lantern. And an ornate wooden candlestick painted white and gold.

Each is inscribed with a little black number and looped with a paper tag. Each, Sarah tells me, belonged to the O'Farrells.

Did Mary carry this lantern into town on some winter night? Did her adopted sons carry the candlestick during Mass, sheltering its flame with one hand, like the altar boys I knew in childhood? How many times did John swing this pick, hoping to feed his family, hoping to strike gold?

All four objects sit mute in front of me—points of light dredged out of the shadows, incapable of testimony.

What lasts? Is there anything you've made in your life that will still be here 150 years from now? Is there anything on your shelves that will be tagged and numbered and kept in a warehouse like this?

What does not last, if they are not retold, are the stories. Stories need to be resurrected, revivified, reimagined; otherwise they get bundled with us into our graves: a hundred thousand of them going into the ground every hour.

Or maybe they float a while, suspended in the places we used to be, waiting, hidden in plain sight, until a day when the sky breaks and the lights come on and the right person is passing by.

Outside the warehouse, the air seems smokier than before. The sky glows an apocalyptic yellow. Beneath a locust tree at the edge of the parking lot, doves hop from foot to foot. My hands tremble on the steering wheel. I start the engine but for a long minute I cannot drive.

It's not that the stuff is still here. It's not that the house still stands. It's that someone keeps the stuff on shelves. It's that someone keeps the house standing.

Nominated by Kim Barnes

PICTURE OF
A RIVER

by JULIA STORY

from SIXTH FINCH

They could eat food but it made them decay. I read about it, then put the book down and slept for five hours. I dreamed the river took the dead in a type of passageway, on its way to somewhere else, or toward other people. People were stacked up on the weedy shores, swaying like haphazard piles of books. I saw a picture like this once. In Sunday school Mrs. McIntire passed the postcard around so we could see the rapture: cars crashing on earth, skeletons floating up to heaven, men and women in suits on fire, Jesus' head floating like an egg in the sky. He looked a combination of mean and sorry. Underneath it all in hell the people worked with shovels and picks, hundreds of them on different levels and more descending, their mouths tiny straight lines. The worst thing that could happen was a lifetime of physical labor underground. There were flames but they were small. There was a river full of small boats, and the mouths of the people in the boats were screaming, as if moving through the water instead of shoveling for Satan gave them time to think about eternity. The river here, in the book and in my head, moves part of me to another part of me. There was a river in my town: it did nothing. Time in its own way, awake and asleep, makes something slow I can barely see. It waits like the river of my childhood. It takes the dead away from the dead.

Nominated by Sixth Finch

PARADISE COVE

fiction by LISA LEE

from PLOUGHSHARES

The beach house in Bodega Bay was supposed to be our escape, but it was just another place for us to be uncomfortable together. Every summer, we used to spend a couple weeks there. My father drove us in his coral car, a BMW sedan so glossy it was almost as if it wasn't there; all you could see were the objects and colors reflecting off of it. Every three months my father waxed the car with his shirt off, his white stomach puffing out. For over an hour, his hands moved in little circles, pressing down on the surface of the car with soft round pads, white swirls and spirals spreading slowly across the paint. In the twenty-five years that my father owned the car, it never broke down, so attentive was he to the lifespan of parts, wires, and tubing, and the degradation of the distinct interior workings of the machine. He was proud of the car, and ever since I was small, I was too.

I was almost thirty when he gave it away. He didn't sell it. As far as I knew, Korean immigrants did not sell possessions. They gave away the things they no longer needed, and even the things they still had a need for, simply to be generous, to help someone out who had less, to family or to Koreans in the community, and this was a trait that I had always respected about my people, this sense that we should help each other, that we were part of a large extended network, connected by collective traumas passed down through generations. No one wanted such an old car, and while I didn't want to see it go, I didn't have anywhere to put it, or the income to insure or maintain it, since I was trying to pay off my law school debt. The day my father donated it to charity, I was in my apartment, opening and closing the fridge, making sandwiches, baking bread, screwing the lids of jars on too tight so I couldn't open them again later.

The beach house was another achievement, acquired after three luxury cars and one regular one, a new house in the hills, and the country club. I was embarrassed about it and didn't mention it to people who didn't already know.

When we first got the house, we would go there often on the weekends, stay for weeks at a time during the summer, and twice we went for Christmas, packing into the car, wearing fishermen's sweaters and fleece pullovers, until my parents decided they would rather stay home in the winter or go skiing in Tahoe. We always took the coral BMW. The interior was black leather, conditioned with lotions and detailing solutions until it was slick and shiny as a seal. I complained that it was too slippery, and I'd demonstrate this by letting myself fall dramatically from a sitting position to a tangle of arms and legs on the floormat. "Put on your seatbelt," my father said.

My father drove, my mother sat in front, and Kevin and I piled in the back. We fought over the dividing line that separated his half of the backseat from mine. After we spent some time jabbing our elbows into each other's ribs, our mother would tell us to quiet down. She would point her finger at me and say, "Don't talk back to your brother." Men were always right, they always had the authority, and she imposed this on me, though living according to that rule was at the root of her unhappiness, even if she never knew it. That, and the tendency to compare herself to everyone else, her husband to other husbands, and her children to other children, in order to measure her own success.

Kevin and I put the center console down between us, and with our elbows we fought over who got the space on top of it, until we tired and retreated to our respective sides. There was plenty of room in the backseat for three or four children, but we both craved the few inches of elbow room that would make one of us feel like the person who was winning. After about half an hour, we'd prop up our travel set of Connect Four on the center console and play for a while. We'd only last a couple games because Kevin couldn't stand to lose, and even when he won he was angry, calling me stupid.

The farther we got from Napa and the closer we got to Bodega Bay, the cooler and thicker and cleaner the air became. I could tell when we had crossed the border from country land to beach land when the trees at the side of the road turned to brush, dotted with little patches of white sand, and the air grew dense with salt. We could see the ocean from the car, the sun shimmering off the water that was constantly in motion, rolling, causing the sun's reflection to turn with it. Kevin and I would ask for taffy when we passed the market, but our parents rarely bought it for us. When they did allow it, we got only a small bag, and we bickered over who got which flavors. I usually ended up with most of the cinnamon-flavored taffies. He caved in like that, always giving up what he wanted, because our parents taught him that men should give up things and women should be given things. I remembered that later, the unfairness to both of us, how one person was given power and authority but forced to sacrifice personal desires, while the other person was made powerless but given the right to material things.

On our way through town, we'd drive past downtown, a two-way street with a little market, a post office, and an antique store with an old wagon wheel on the front lawn. Our house was in a gated community on the beach, and all the properties were maintained by the organization that the homeowners paid dues to. One side of the neighborhood abutted the water, and the other side, a rolling 18-hole golf course. At least once on every visit, we'd have brunch at the clubhouse, as if it was a chore, sitting uncomfortably in the wood-paneled dining hall with exposed beams, barely looking at each other, maintaining the most stilted conversations as the other diners stared at us, the only nonwhite people in the room. I used to get upset about it, and I'd sit there, keeping it inside, though my face was red, fists balled up like wads of paper, frustrated that our parents kept putting us in this position, the Asian family getting stared down by a bunch of white people, and that we were supposed to pretend that everything was normal. My parents and brother, in their discomfort at trying to maintain the guise of fitting in, would shift their attention to me and tell me that I was acting spoiled. For a minute, I would relax my hands, lean back, smile, try to act less spoiled. My parents and brother didn't smile and their shoulders were hunched, as if it was chilly.

One summer when I was sixteen, we stopped in for Sunday brunch, and our waitress was a woman in her twenties with frizzy red hair and too much eye makeup. I thought that she was a townie, though I myself was a townie in Napa, where we lived year-round. Her nametag said Celeste.

"Can I take your order? Would you like to start with drinks or appetizers?" Celeste's skin was nearly translucent and covered in ginger-colored freckles. She did not smile at us, though she glanced around the dining hall several times while she stood at our table, and I noticed that she was smiling at everyone else. She nodded agreeably at the people sitting at the table next to us, and flashed her teeth at the other waitstaff passing by. There was a small gap between her two front teeth. When she looked at me, or Kevin, or my mother or father, her face turned hard and she looked annoyed.

"Chink," I blurted out.

Celeste stared at me. "What?" she said. There was a crease between her eyebrows.

"You heard me. I called you a chink."

"*Jane*," my father said in a low voice.

"Shut up," Kevin said to me.

"What happened?" my mother said, looking up from her menu, her eyes roving around the table. Since everyone was looking at me, her focus finally settled on me. "What did you do?" she said to me, her tone sharp.

I picked up a white cloth napkin, shook the complicated folds out of it, making an elaborate gesture with my hand as I flourished it, and I laid it down in my lap, smoothing out the creases. "Origami," I said.

I looked up at Celeste, who was still staring at me. There was a little dot of spit right in the groove above her upper lip. Her mouth moved, forming words that did not vocalize.

"Um, OK," Celeste said slowly. "I'm going to give you a few more minutes." She turned around and walked away, fast, her arms pumping. I could hear her starched white shirt brushing against her black half-apron.

I could tell when someone didn't like me because of my race, which might not seem that important, but it's everything, almost. The difference between knowing and not knowing when something is unjust is almost everything.

Back at the house, my father liked to sit on the backyard deck, smoking cigarettes and reading a book. He read mass-market paperbacks, one to two a day, the kinds of books that you would never see on a college reading list. Stephen King, Michael Crichton, John Grisham, Nicholas Sparks. My father was not educated, at least he would never be considered so in the US, having dropped out of Yonsei University when he was twenty-one because he was conscripted into the army for a year, then immigrated to America, and never returned to finish school. Even though Yonsei was a prestigious school in South Korea, in America this did not mean anything, and still wouldn't have even if he had graduated. Whenever I move to a new city and visit my local convenience store or greengrocer, if it's owned and run by a Korean man, I always wonder what he left behind in Korea, if he regrets coming to America, if he has a graduate degree from a university in Seoul, what it's like to stand behind the counter selling candy, cigarettes, fruit, condiments, and beer all day, every day, the days and months and years falling on to you slowly and all at once.

I knew that it made my father feel bad that he didn't have a college degree, and I tried to convince him he should go back to school, but he said it was too late for him because he was old and it didn't matter. Whenever he wasn't working or playing golf or washing his cars, he had his nose in a book, English language only, and only the kinds of books that most people I knew would scoff at. I was pretty sure he didn't know that, but I knew that if he did know, he wouldn't care.

The deck had privacy. He would lie down on the hammock, shaded by a big oak tree. It was his favorite spot in all of Bodega Bay. The neighbors couldn't see him and nobody bothered him when he was out there alone. When he retreated to the hammock, my mother would walk my brother and me down to the beach. Kevin and I would bury her in the sand, chase each other into the ice-cold water, climb up onto giant porous rocks jutting out of the ocean, and we would duck, shielding our faces with our arms when the waves crashed against the rocks and splashed over us. We would wade back to the shore, lie down on the pebbly sand, and sunbathe until we got headaches. During this summer ritual, my mother told me once that she wished my brother had gotten some of my luck. I asked her what she meant. She said, "It's OK that he's not handsome. He's not a girl, so it's OK. But I wish he was smart. He's going to grow up and he'll be a man and he should be the one who gets to be smart, not you. I wish he was talented. Everything is so easy for you. But he tries so hard and he's never the best."

I didn't think it was true. That somebody was better. I believed that we were the same, and that getting good at something was a matter of whether or not you thought you could, and that what people thought of you was a matter of what you could make them think. It was all a game. In high school, I learned that everything is about maintaining a façade. Faking confidence, making people believe that you are special, making it look easy. Kevin couldn't do that. It was as if he had a disability, and his disability was not knowing how to lie. Back then, that was the only difference between us.

We all had the sense that this was our last time at the beach house. It was hard for all of us to get there. A rocky inlet of the Pacific on the coast of Northern California between Sonoma and Marin, Bodega Bay was far enough away to be inconvenient. A trek for Kevin and Sanghee, who lived in San Jose, where Kevin was a police officer, and for me in San Francisco, where I worked as an intellectual property lawyer. My parents were a bit closer in Napa, but they were sixty now and got grumpy when they had to be in a car for more than an hour, as if they had regressed into children who couldn't sit still. For these reasons, the house had been rented out, and for this one week, it was between leases. *Paradise Cove*, read the title of the listing above the details about the rental house.

That was the last time I saw my brother. I had just started as a junior attorney at La Rose and Associates and Kevin had been a cop for a few years. By then he was married to Sanghee, who had been joining us on our summer breaks in Bodega Bay ever since they began dating in college. Through the course of a single dinner Sanghee would ask me if I had gained weight, then tell me that I should stop running because my legs looked too muscular, and wonder aloud why my face and chest were so flat. Sanghee was fat, her hair was permed and dyed an orangey-brown, her eyebrows were drawn on, lips outlined, the outside corners of her eyes were extended with black liquid liner into little curlicues, her clothes were too small and exposed too much, and she shopped at Forever 21, but she had a collection of Louis Vuitton bags. "Why don't *you* have one?" she asked me. "Can't you get someone to buy one for you?" During our interactions I kept my mouth shut. Sometimes Kevin would nudge her with his elbow. I wondered if this woman-on-woman bullying was about being Korean. Sometimes if I was talking she would say to Kevin, "Tell your sister to shut up." I didn't share my dating life with them, and Sanghee was fond of making pronouncements that I must not be able to find someone who would date me, that it was either because I wasn't pretty enough or because I was a high maintenance pain in the ass. I've never met a Korean woman who wasn't called both high maintenance and submissive, polar opposites, yet still sometimes

251

uttered in the same sentence. She would brag about how her sister was marrying a doctor. "Why don't *you* get one?" she said. A doctor husband, she meant.

But Sanghee didn't marry a doctor. She married my brother, a cop. Sanghee idolized Kevin. "My handsome husband," she said. "He's so handsome and smart and such a good husband," she said. "I'm so lucky," she said. "I don't even have to work. He's such a good provider." She had wanted to be a chiropractor, but Kevin stopped her from enrolling in the classes. "You're not going to be able to handle it. It's too hard for you," he said. She cooked all of his meals for him, washed and ironed his clothes, kept house.

It made me happy to see her doting on him, to see him enjoy the attention, because those were the only moments that I saw him smiling. He seemed grateful, even, to be the center of someone's life, to hear someone say, "For the *best husband!*" as a casserole was plopped on the dinner table.

That last time we were all together at the beach house, my father was lying on his back on the couch. It was morning. Earlier that summer, we had buried his younger brother, Steven, who had died of a heart attack. When we got to the house, we found a big ruby-colored stain left by the renters on the carpet in the living room. My mother spent the first hour trying to scrub it out, spraying it with bleach and lemon. My father stared up at the ceiling, telling story after story about Steven, as a child in Seoul, how he was taunted by other kids because his skin was so white and his hair was red. "His hair turned dark when he got older but he could never get along with anyone. He always thought people were making fun of him. The other kids thought he must be a war child, half American, but he wasn't! He was one hundred percent Korean, like us!" Kevin and Sanghee were sitting on the couch opposite him. My father kept craning his neck to look at me as he spoke, propping up a bit on his elbows from the position on his back, so that he could see me. I was sitting on a big square pillow on the floor, slightly out of his view. "Jane, do you remember when Steven was teaching you to ride a bike, and when he was showing you how to do it, he fell off his own bike? We laughed for so long." My father let himself fall back down, so his body was reclined completely with his head resting on a pillow. "Huh," he sighed. "Steven always knew you were the smart one, Jane. He knew from the start. That's why he was nicer to Kevin."

I looked at Kevin. I hoped he hadn't heard that, but obviously he had. He was sitting right there. Kevin stared deeply into his teacup. Sanghee set hers back down on the table, too hard. My mother brought in a fresh pot of tea and placed it on the coffee table on top of a tray. On her way back to the kitchen, she gasped so loudly I thought maybe a burglar was in the house.

"OHMANA!" she screamed. She was hunched over, inspecting the bottom corner of the mirror in the hallway. Kevin and I jumped up and rushed to see what was wrong.

"There's a crack!" she said. "Oh no oh no oh no oh no! What do I do?"

Kevin took a few steps back. His eyebrows were raised, mouth open a little.

"Do you see this?" my mother said. "The mirror. It's cracked." She pointed at it, then whipped around, and pointed her finger at me. "Did you do it?"

"Of course not," I said. "Why are you freaking out?"

She pointed her finger at Kevin. "Did you do it?"

He shook his head.

"You're lying. You did it. Somebody did it! I know you did it."

"I didn't," Kevin said. "I didn't do it."

"It was probably the renters," I said. "Remember the stain on the carpet?"

"We can't stay here!" my mother said. "How many times do I have to tell you? Broken glass is bad luck, especially mirrors! We have to leave. We can't come back again. What is wrong with these people?"

I went back to the living room and sat down in the rocking chair. Kevin put his hand on our mother's back, while talking to her in a low, soft voice. She was taking deep breaths, interspersed with squelched sobs, and I could smell her sweating from fifteen feet away. "Maybe you should go lie down," I heard Kevin say after a while. He walked her to the bedroom. I worried that she would get excited again, because all of the mattresses had deep indentations, sunken in with the outlines of bodies larger and heavier than our own, and all night we slept as if we were lying in hammocks. She had barely commented on them. "I thought you bought extra firm," she had said to my father.

My father fell asleep on the couch, though it wasn't even noon yet. Sanghee put a blanket over him. Kevin went out to the back deck and I followed him there. The sunlight filtered through the mist, thick with dew. It made me feel clean. Kevin stood on the deck, his hands on the railing, and he was looking out past the yard where you could see the unnaturally green hills of the golf course and the mountains beyond that. He had on a blue baseball cap that had an embroidered shield on it: *San Jose Police Department.* I could see the bulge under his jacket on his right hip where there was a gun in a holster. Even if I hadn't looked, I'd know it was there. He always wore it. There was probably another gun under his jeans at his ankle, and a knife in his pocket. *Ready for anything*, he used to say. *You have to be ready.*

I could tell from his posture, the tension in his shoulders, that he was angry. I wished that he didn't have to have so much pain, that there was somewhere else that he could put it. I felt that his pain was part of me, and if I could take some of it, then we might both feel better. I wanted us to be in it together, so we could be on the same side, but he didn't know that the same thing that was happening to him was happening to me too, and I didn't know how to tell him.

Kevin turned around to face me. I cleared my throat. I took a step toward him and I wanted to touch him but I knew I couldn't. I was about to say something meaningless, to kill the silence, but he beat me to it.

"You're such a fucking bitch." His mouth got tiny. I was not surprised at his anger; I never was anymore, waiting for it, expecting it, and though I was not surprised, I was afraid. "Did you hear me. You're a fucking cunt, you fucking vagina."

"What did I do?"

"You're so stupid. You're such a baby. You always get everything you want. You're just a stupid woman. You don't know anything. Everybody fucking loves you even though you're so stupid. It's because you're a woman. Women don't have to do anything. It's so much easier to be a woman. But I would never want to be a woman, because I feel sorry for you, because you're all so weak and pathetic. A man can always overpower a woman. Women are always getting abused by their husbands and they can't do anything about it."

"Yeah, life is easier for women," I said. I didn't even know if I was being sarcastic or agreeable.

"All he cares about is *you*. You don't even care about him. *I'm* the one who's a nice person. *You're* a bitch. Why doesn't anybody know it. I feel sorry for you because you're so pathetic." Then he came at me, elbows and knees pointing out, a figure with all sharp angles, charging at me like a bull, his face blank as a napkin, an expression of aggressive emotionlessness that he learned from watching Steven Seagal movies, the blankness meant to be frightening. When this happens, I'm under the impression that he's either going to beat me up or at least punch me in the face, and I'm supposed to think this, because the second he can sense my fear, the moment I take a step back, he knows he's won. His goal is to intimidate. He wants to know that you are afraid of him. I'd seen him practice this move, in the backyard, when we were in high school, around the time when our father chopped up his tennis rackets with an axe. He pushed me hard, the blank face turned into a snarl, trying for the most menacing look he could muster.

"You're a stupid bitch," he said. "Why are you surprised!" he was shouting now. "You're so stupid. I can't believe you're always so surprised!" He pushed me two more times, palms out, pressing on my shoulders, firmly, not with all his force, but hard enough for me to lose my balance. I put my hands out behind me and grabbed the balcony so that I wouldn't fall. I didn't say anything at first, afraid that he'd become more agitated. But somehow the situation had already escalated, and I didn't know how to stop it.

"What are you talking about?" I said.

"Our mother! You know who I'm talking about. You're such a fucking idiot. I can't believe people think you're smart when you're so fucking stupid."

I put my hands up, trying to block him from pushing me again. "I didn't do anything," I said. "What is wrong with you?"

"Why are you always surprised when she totally loses it! How you think it's going to be fine, and you think that wasn't so bad, that was a nice time, but then one little thing goes wrong, and then she loses it like we're all about to fucking die! Or when she promises you something and acts nice to get you to do something she wants, but then she screws you over and then denies that she ever promised you anything! Why are you so fucking surprised that she's a fucking bitch!"

"You're insane," I said. "You're talking about yourself." My voice was firm, but my legs were shaking.

He pushed me so hard, it was like an open-fisted double punch on each shoulder. I fell back, my feet kicking up in front of me, and I landed on my butt and slid down the seven wooden steps leading from the balcony into the backyard. On impulse I reached my hands up and tried to grab the railing, which was a mistake because the wood splintered into my fingers and palms. I tumbled onto the lawn, my arms and legs splayed out. I stayed down. I looked at my hands, which were bleeding. My butt was numb.

"What the *fuck*," I said to myself. I looked up at Kevin standing at the top of the stairs. He didn't look sorry. He was still on the balcony, peering down at me, and he did not look satisfied. "What the *fuck* is wrong with you?" I shouted. "*Who's* the asshole?"

It was like he didn't even hear me. His eyes glazed over for a moment and he turned away. He looked at me again, and walked down the stairs very slowly, his boots dropping heavily on each step, then swishing through the grass. He came up right next to me and half-kneeled with one knee touching the ground, and he was so close I could see that the fabric of his jeans was wearing thin at the knee. I thought that maybe I should get him a new pair of jeans.

His fingers touched the grass near my shoulder. "Remember when I asked dad for a sleeping bag and he said no but then a week later he bought you a new sleeping bag?"

"Are you serious?" I tried to sound unafraid and I kept my shoulders open, but inside everything was gathered close together. "The only sleeping bag I can remember him giving me is when I was ten." I was sitting up. My voice was deep and measured. "I don't even have it anymore. Mom uses it when they go camping."

"Why did he get it for you? You didn't even want it. I was the one who wanted it."

"I don't know," I said. "I don't remember."

Kevin's denim jacket was open, the bottom right hem pulled back and held in place with the inside of his wrist. His fingers rested on the gun that was holstered to his hip. He was still kneeling and his other hand hung at his side, lazily, knuckles grazing blades of grass. I didn't know if he was touching the gun absentmindedly, or if he was getting up the nerve.

Nominated by Sandra Leong and Ploughshares

THE JOINS

by CHANA BLOCH

from THE SOUTHERN REVIEW

Kintsugi is the Japanese art of mending precious pottery with gold.

What's between us
often seems flexible as the webbing
between forefinger and thumb.

Seems flexible, but it's not;
what's between us
is made of clay,

like any cup on the shelf.
It shatters easily. Repair
becomes the task.

We glue the wounded edges
with tentative fingers.
Scar tissue is visible history,

the cup more precious to us
because
we saved it.

In the art of *kintsugi*,
a potter repairing a broken cup
would sprinkle the resin

with powdered gold.
Sometimes the joins
are so exquisite

they say the potter
may have broken the cup
just so he could mend it.

Nominated by Andrea Hollander

THE KNOWLEDGE GALLERY

fiction by JOANNA SCOTT

from CONJUNCTIONS

I.

"You saved nothing?" I asked, unable to contain my disappointment. I'd been hoping that a woman of her advanced age would have a diary or two in a drawer, maybe index cards or even notes scrawled on the backs of those old envelopes used for Baronial Cards.

She idly tapped the tassel on the window blind to set it swinging. "My dear, multiply two by zero and it would be nothing. If, rather, you mean anything, then yes, the last of it went into recycling when I moved here."

"You have no manuscripts? No letters?"

She observed me, then lifted her head to direct her gaze downward, through the bottom half of her bifocals. "I see you're writing with a pen. On paper. The old-fashioned way. But surely you haven't forgotten that until quite recently, paper was discouraged as an indulgent, poisonous consumption. The taxes on a single ream . . . who could afford it? And if you could afford it, you didn't want your enemies to know. My generation was particularly suspect—thus the public statute requiring accreditation from EcoGreen before we could receive Social Security. Writers, of course, were notorious. Have you heard of Olivia Gastrell?"

I scribbled the name, adding it to a list that was growing ever longer with each writer I interviewed. "Gastrell—with two *l*'s?"

She reached for a glass of water on her bedside table and took a sip. "You haven't read her? Surprising, given your interests. She came late to fiction, published her first novel, *Fortunate Odyssey*, when she was fifty-two. She would have won a Hermes with *Say What You Mean*, but she skipped the ceremony and thus forfeited the award. Not that she needed honors to buck her up. My dear friend Olivia. She was nearly eighty when she hired movers to transfer her papers to a storage unit. Two hundred and five pounds of cellulose pulp—that was two hundred pounds over the personal legal limit. The movers were obligated to file a report. The authorities seized and destroyed everything. She had to pay a fine . . . I don't remember how much, but it was significant."

"Is she still alive?"

She sucked in her lips as she considered her response, then looked toward the door, seeming to will the interruption that came a moment later, the sharp knock startling me to the point that I bounced up from my seat, then fell back.

"Come in!"

The nurse, a bald little man lithe as a dancer, entered holding a paper cup. "M&M time!" he announced, rattling the pills deposited inside the cup. "You need more water, hon?"

"I have plenty, lovey, thank you." She picked out the pills and tossed them both in her mouth, then made a show of taking a swig of water from her glass. "This young lady has come for a chat. So if you'll excuse us . . ." She nodded in the direction of the door.

The nurse hesitated. "You'll let me know if you need anything. . . ."

"Absolutely, sweetheart. Now go, shoo, shoo." She waited until he had closed the door behind him, then leaned over, opened the drawer of the table, and extracted a box. Cracking the lid, she removed the two pills that she had craftily pretended to swallow and added them to a substantial collection of pills in the box. "Don't tell," she said. Her imperious smile was clearly designed to remind me that I was a minion beholden to her goodwill. "Now where were we?"

"Olivia Gastrell."

"Ah, yes. She once told me that she had an ancestor who chopped down a mulberry tree that was said to have been planted by William Shakespeare. To this day, the name Gastrell is banned in Stratford-upon-Avon."

"And Olivia, is she—"

"Fort Worth. I'll let her know you're coming." Suddenly her gaze was harsh, boring into me, daring me to react. I didn't know what to say. I was embarrassed and resentful at being forced into extending my inquiry yet again. Didn't she realize that I was there to preserve the reputation of Eleanor Feal? But in the evasive manner that I'd come to realize was typical for the writers I'd tracked down so far, Eleanor Feal didn't want to tell me about herself. She wanted to tell me about Olivia Gastrell.

It was the same outcome, interview after interview. I aimed to reconstruct a writer's work from scratch but ended up being directed by each of them to the beginning of someone else's story. After six months and twenty-seven separate interviews, I had failed to recover a single book.

II.

There was a welcome coolness in the breeze that skimmed the river. As I crossed the pedestrian bridge, I saw the sleek back of a beaver swimming toward the shore, pushing a newly felled branch that looked like a rack strung with pieces of green silk. In the shallows, a magnificent heron stood patiently, as if awaiting its delivery. The beaver drew nearer, still pushing the branch, changing its course only at the last moment, swimming upstream to some other destination.

I leaned against the iron rail and watched for several minutes. The heron remained stock-still, the current swirling around its legs, its yellow eye unblinking, the blue plume extending from the back of its head like a pomaded spike of hair. I was hoping the bird would rise into the air—I wanted to see the slow beat of its wings as it flew overhead. But it just stood there, so I walked on. Hearing a splash, I turned just in time to witness the heron lift its dripping head from the water and with a deft movement drop the fish that had been clamped in its beak headfirst into its gullet.

There in the heart of the city, the natural world was thriving. Along the path curving across campus, chipmunks scampered ahead of my footsteps. It was early May, and the air was redolent with the fragrance of lilacs. Petals from the magnolias flitted like butterflies in the breeze. The sun, as if summoned by the carillon chiming in the bell tower of the Knowledge Gallery, peeked shyly out from behind a flat-bottomed cumulus cotton ball.

I was in good spirits that day, contemplating the lovely campus and the equilibrium of a planet that had fully recovered from its long fever. The climate was healthy again, thanks to the ingenuity of our scientists. We were like angels dining on wind and light and water. Life itself seemed infinitely renewable.

I was sorry to have to go inside, but I had research to do, and the Knowledge Gallery was scheduled to close early, as it often did, for a special administrative function. The building, a five-story former library with sloping floors that spiraled around a hollow interior, seemed to be more useful as a party house than a location for scholarly research. Still, the resources were vast, with thousands of databases that could be accessed by anyone with a VPN account. There were technical advisers on hand to resolve any problem with a device. Numerous work spaces were furnished with white boards, televisions, self-service espresso machines, and more Macs than there were students enrolled in the university.

If the gallery had one acknowledged problem, it was the noise. Most of the work spaces opened up to the echo chamber of the central gallery. From the main floor, you could easily overhear the conversation of two people on the fourth floor. On a given day you might hear biology students comparing lab results, research advisers explaining how to modify a search, two young lovers setting up their next date. And always in the background was the tap tap tapping of hundreds of fingers on keyboards.

After a year as a graduate student on campus, I'd found a relatively quiet space at the back of the Rare Books Department, behind the cases used to display simulated manuscripts. Most of the furniture in the building was manufactured with repurposed metal or plastic, but in the Rare Books Department there were four beautiful antique tables made of oak. I loved the earthy smell and the rosy heartwood grain of those tables. And I appreciated the serenity of the department. Few visitors came to see the simulations, since everything in the cases was viewable in more detail in online exhibitions.

On this particular day I was verifying references for the second chapter of my dissertation and hoped to start assembling notes for chapter three. My subject was Avantism—a recent literary movement based in the US. Focusing on six writers who identified themselves as Avantis, I intended to argue that Avantism had its roots in once popular fiction of the early twentieth century and drew especially from the work of a little-known Spanish writer named Vicente Blasco Ibáñez.

In terms of its basic elements, Avantism was as diverse as literature itself. There were mysteries, tragedies, farces, fictional biographies, and biographical fictions. One novel used an encyclopedic structure, with chapters arranged alphabetically by subject. Another built its narrative out of a collage of quotes taken from other Avanti texts. Some authors concentrated on providing rich scenic details; others strove to give their characters an expansive interiority. All of the manuscripts were handwritten. Finished books were produced by expert letterpress printers on wove pearlescent paper, with painted cloth bindings.

What united the Avanti authors, besides the care they took with the printing of their books, was their dystopian imaginations. All the Avanti novels I'd read, plus those I knew of through hearsay, were set in an apocalyptic future, when civilization had deteriorated either into anarchy or tyranny. The plots involved characters struggling with the most basic hardships—there were famine and flood stories, homesteading stories set in harsh lands, stories about super flus and climate change, and stories about the total devastation of a final world war.

The Avantis prided themselves on scorning publicity. They had no websites, sent no tweets, and were rarely photographed. Their work appeared only in hard copy. Once all publications became electronic, the Avantis refused to publish at all, sharing manuscripts only among themselves. The general public was indifferent. By the time I'd narrowed down the subject of my dissertation, few people had ever heard of the Avantis; fewer still had read any of their books.

As a scholar of Avantism, I had to be a clever detective. I was constantly testing the strength of various search engines against the defenses of the Avanti writers. They'd resolved to hide themselves from scholars. I was determined to write their history. By then I'd spent two years on research and had a fellowship that would support me for two more years. In the end, I hoped to have a notable dissertation that would secure me enough interest from foundations to fund a web appointment as a digital humanities scholar.

I was twenty-five years old and confident that all was going according to plan. I agreed with my peers that we were living in a golden age. Except for the endless skirmish in northern Nigeria, the world was at peace. Every question had an answer . . . until the morning when I was typing the final sentences of chapter two of my dissertation on my laptop, writing the words—

What words? Maybe something close to these words I'm writing now, surely involving dependent clauses, nouns, an article, an adverb, whatever, I'll never know because I can't remember the specific words, only the experience of watching the loop of a *b* break away from its stem, an *o* dissolve, an *a* sink to the bottom of the screen and disappear, replaced by symbols: ⊆Σφℜξω, and on and on in a blur where there had once been sentences.

I was the second student in line at the Question & Information desk on the ground floor of the Knowledge Gallery. While I stood there waiting my turn, I noticed that the letters on the digital sign above the desk had been replaced by a video of cascading roses. Naive as I was, I didn't connect the roses to the symbols on my laptop screen.

The first student was an undergraduate woman whose PowerPoint had frozen—a coincidental glitch that the techie, himself an undergraduate, managed to repair simply by turning the student's tablet off and on again.

"Hi," he said to me. He had a scruff of a beard, icy-blue eyes, and a bowl of doughnut holes next to his Mac. "What's up?"

I tried to contain my panic. "It looks like I just crashed. All my files—I can't . . . I mean, I can access them, but everything has been scrambled."

"Let's take a look."

I opened the laptop and touched the screen to activate the light. The symbols were still there, a wallpaper of shapes that reminded me of snorkeling: sea grass waving, jellyfish drifting, minnows darting away from my submerged hand.

"Cool," said the techie.

"Can you fix it?" I implored.

"Mmmm." Still staring at the screen, he reached for the bowl, blindly fumbled for a doughnut hole, and popped it in his mouth. He chewed in concentrated silence, pressing various keys and studying the screen for the results that didn't come. While I waited, I reminded myself that a crash was no more than an inconvenience. With every file automatically saved to the Cloud, everything could be recovered. Still, it would take time to restore the files to my hard drive, and more time if I had to buy a new computer entirely.

The Q & I desk was positioned at the rear of the ground floor. It was early, and workstations still had empty chairs. But among the students scattered throughout the Knowledge Gallery, a new kind of sound emanated, a flurry of murmurs and exclamations competing with the rattling of keyboard taps and the burbling of espresso machines.

"Oh just, what, you gotta be kidding!" said a boy loudly from across the room.

"Shit, shit, shit!" called someone from a cubicle on the second floor.

I heard chairs scrape along the laminated floors. I heard a phone buzz and then a thump that sounded like a small bird flying into plate glass. I looked toward the nearest window. The sun was still shining, the magnolia blossoms still dancing in the breeze. At the Q & I desk, the techie tapped my keyboard with impressive speed, then stopped and studied the screen.

"I don't really understand why they call them holes," he said at last.

"What?"

"If it were up to me, I'd call them centers." I realized he was talking about the doughnut holes only when he offered the bowl to me, inviting me to take one. "I mean, the holes are what they leave behind, not what they are. It's like saying they're an absence. Identifying them with the space they once filled."

I wanted to say something insulting, but the rest of my day depended upon this techie's ability to recover my files. I needed his know-how, as did the students who were lining up behind me.

"A hole is a hollow space in a solid body." He tapped the escape button on the keyboard several times. FaceTime on his Mac rang. "Hang on, will you?" he said to his screen. "On the other hand, there are black holes, defined by such a strong gravitational pull that no matter can escape. They're interesting, don't you think?"

The phone in his pocket buzzed. He looked at the number and answered briskly: "Yeah, yeah, get Daryl down here, maybe Inez, too. Looks like a busy day ahead of us." He clicked off the phone and rested his chin in his hands, studying his own Mac. He poked at the screen, cocked his head to cast a sideways glance at my laptop, then shut his eyes for a long moment, as if giving up the effort to hide his boredom.

"Frankly, I don't know what's going on," he finally admitted.

"What do you mean? You can't fix it?" I asked.

"You have a Cloud account, right?"

"Yeah, of course."

"Then you're safe," he assured me.

"No, she's not," said the boy behind me. "Siri is saying Cloud files are inaccessible."

"My life is over," said a girl wearing cutoff shorts and a vintage Minnie Mouse T-shirt, marching toward us without bothering to take a place in line, her flip-flops angrily slapping the floor. "I give up."

"You're budging," another girl called from the back of the line.

"Look there—" The boy behind me directed our attention to the television on the wall. The subtitles at the top of the screen were garbled symbols; the bottom banner that usually circulated breaking-news headlines was blank. The sound was on mute, but we could see that the newscaster had stopped talking and was looking frantically in the direction of the teleprompter.

"Must be a malware offensive," said the techie, popping another doughnut hole into his mouth. "We'll have to wait for quarantine mandates and the updated firewall. Everyone got the same problem?" More students were arriving in search of help. The line was long and getting longer, with students groaning, complaining, jostling one another, reminding friends about the dance on Friday in the Field House. "Hey, guys," called the techie to the crowd. "Everyone got a problem with text?" There was agreement, cursing, and laughter in the crowd. The techie interlaced his fingers, cracking his knuckles. "Come back in five," he said to us. What did that mean? Five minutes? Five hours?

It would take a good five hours for most of us to become aware of the vastness of the attack, and five days or more to understand the extent of the loss: Everything written in English, new and old, every book that had been scanned (and, as was protocol back then, discarded), every document in a digital archive, every e-mail and text, everything involving the digital transmission of words, everything that provided our civilization with a record of its vast knowledge was gone, dissolved by a virus that had been lying latent in software from the beginning, programmed fifty years in advance to explode all at once, leaving only shreds of meaningless shapes floating with malicious wantonness on screens of English-speaking users around the world.

Luckily, the important diagrammatic programs that keep the infrastructure running, along with images and videos, were untouched by the attack. I suppose this might explain the current blasé attitude about it all. There's general consensus that the essential documents have been recovered, some located as rare hard copies, most supplied through costly translation. The American public has long since stopped fretting over missing materials. But let's not pretend that we've restored the full inventory. Not even close. We can't begin to know what we've lost. All we can do is keep searching, and advocating for funds for the National Archive Project. Where would we be without the NAP?

I'd be without income, for starters. If I weren't an NAP agent, I'd be unemployed. Truly, I'm thankful for the paycheck, but I also believe in the worth of the mission. This whole project is about memory. By remembering, we can avoid repeating the mistakes we made when we considered ourselves ingenious and invulnerable.

IV.

NAP Recovery Record: Cataloged July 17, 2052

1) *Treatise of How to Perceive from a Letter the Nature and Character of the Person Who Wrote It*, author unknown, 1622: translation.
2) *The Queensberry Rules*, London Amateur Athletic Club, 1867: found document, complete.
3) *Letter to Posterity*, Petrarch, 1351: translation.
4) *With Americans of Past and Present Days*, J. J. Jusserand, no date: found document, incomplete.
5) *A Tutor for the Renaissance Lute*, Diana Poulton, copyright page missing: donated by owner.
6) *Self-Portrait in a Convex Mirror*, John Ashbery, 1975: in summary.
7) *Book of the Prefect*, author unknown, 950: translation.
8) *Songs of Experience*, William Blake, 1794: translation.
9) *Horse-Shoe Robinson*, J. P. Kennedy, 1835: found manuscript.
10) *Gazette*, Rhinebeck, NY, from 1947–1949: donated by municipality.

V.

And lastly, No. 11, which I failed to supply but should have consisted of a summary of Eleanor Feal's first novel, as transcribed from our interview.

"You must talk to Olivia in person," she was saying. "Her work is difficult to describe."

Courtesy kept me from pointing out that I'd come in search of books written by Eleanor Feal, a writer whose existence I'd learned of only in my previous interview with the author Timothy von Patten, himself unknown to me until the prior interview with Leonard Dumaston—and so on.

"She was an Avanti?"

"Of course. Any writer worth the time it took to read was an Avanti."

Six months earlier, I'd set out with six Avanti writers to track down. The list had grown to include twenty-seven other lesser-known writers who, I was told, were not at all of lesser merit. That I had overlooked them when I'd been researching the movement for my dissertation now seemed inevitable. Avantism was an elusive prey, with its cohorts keeping a low profile. Like nocturnal animals, they spooked easily and melted into the nearest burrow when threatened, disappearing before they revealed much of anything about themselves, camouflaging their work with the work of a fellow author, as the centenarian Eleanor Feal was doing with Olivia Gastrell.

As far as I knew, all the Avanti books had been confiscated, scanned, and shredded over the preceding thirty years—there were no extant copies left in the world. I was still hopeful that someone somewhere would reveal a secret library. New recovery laws protected book collectors from the criminal charges they would have faced in the past, but no one had come forward with any valuable inventory. In the absence of an actual book or manuscript, I could at least provide a detailed recounting of the work that had once existed—this was the purpose of my interviews. But Avanti writers didn't appear interested in their own work. They wanted to talk about the books by their friends.

"Take Olivia's *Say What You Mean*—a central text for the rest of us," Eleanor Feal was saying. "It tells the story of a young woman . . ." She studied me, squinting, as if searching my face for a minute blemish. "She had green eyes," she said. "Yes." Her satisfaction suggested that she'd solved a difficult equation. "Like yours, the same shade." How could she be so sure? She was speaking of a fictional character as if she'd met her in person, and comparing her to me. Her scrutiny was making me increasingly uncomfortable. "A literary scholar, as it happens." I was beginning to wonder if she was using me as a model to fabricate the supposed main character in Olivia Gastrell's book. "Her name was Juliana. She finds herself living in a time much like ours, after the entire written record of the English language has been wiped out by a computer virus. In the contest of prescience, Olivia wins, hands down. Our young heroine takes it upon herself to . . . come in!"

I hadn't heard a knock, but there was the nurse again, standing in the doorway with a wheelchair, ready to escort Eleanor Feal to the dining room.

"Yumtime!" he said.

"Already? But we were having such nice conversation. I'm sorry, dear. They don't like it if we're late for meals around here!" She was suddenly cheery. "They aim to keep us in tip-top shape, you know, on

268

schedule and such! The longer we live, the more federal funding they receive, isn't that right, lovey?"

The nurse concurred. "It's a win-win," he declared. "Andiamo!"

I stood aside as she lifted herself into the wheelchair the nurse had slid toward the bed. In her eagerness to be done with our interview and take her place at dinner, she seemed transformed—deceptively so. She struck me as a woman versed at playing the part of a beloved grande dame who enjoyed being tenderly cared for. In reality, she was a woman who clearly preferred to take care of herself.

"What happens to Juliana?" I demanded, following the nurse as he briskly wheeled Eleanor Feal out of the room and up a carpeted corridor.

"You'll have to ask Olivia," she said, lifting her hand above her shoulder, bending her fingers in the shape of a python's flat head to signal a wave goodbye, a gesture that had a strange, chilling finality, as if scripted to bring an end to the whole story—this story, I mean, the one I've begun but will never finish. I could have predicted its incompleteness before I asked my first question.

I gave up trying to keep up with them. As I stood watching the nurse roll Eleanor Feal down the corridor, I thought about the pills she had secreted away in that box in her bedside table. I thought about the stepping-stones of my interviews, from one Avanti writer to the next, that had led me here. I wondered about the cost of a round-trip fare to Fort Worth. I thought about *Say What You Mean* by Olivia Gastrell. How could I be sure that it had ever existed? I wondered about all the other books that I would never read.

Nominated by Joyce Carol Oates and Conjunctions

WASTE

by AFAA MICHAEL WEAVER

from POETRY

Everything that was young went quickly,
the way his eyes met mine as soon as we

woke together in a room outside Nanjing,
feeling as if all the things that were falling

would fall and make their thunder, leave
us with the challenge of being happy,

all the things that felt given when gifts
were not just surprises, but what we

knew, what we hoped to take with us
to heaven, unbound by faults and sins,

not deceived the way we were when
the end came to what we knew of China,

landing me here. I am a wish in the skies
spun out from celestial space to be poor,

to be covered with black skin, a felt
quilt of a map with only one way to China—

through pain as big as hogs squealing
at killing time on black farms in Alabama—

the noise of death, the shrill needle
that turns clouds over to rip the air

above the cities where people are young
and all that is given is never taken away.

Nominated by Martha Collins

THE CHILDHOOD
OF THE READER

by JOYCE CAROL OATES

from CONJUNCTIONS

At the roadside fruit and vegetable stand on Transit Road, in Millersport, New York, I would sit reading. Head lowered, scarcely aware of my surroundings, which is the consolation of reading.

Comic hooks—*Tales from the Crypt, Superman, Classics Illustrated* (*Ivanhoe, The Last of the Mohicans, Moby-Dick, Robin Hood, Sherlock Holmes, The Call of the Wild, Frankenstein*)—*Mad Magazine*.

Or books from the Lockport Public Library in their crisp plastic covers—Ellery Queen, H. P. Lovecraft, Isaac Asimov. Bram Stoker's *Dracula*. Jonathan Swift's *Gulliver's Travels*. Illustrated editions of the *Iliad*, the *Odyssey, Metamorphoses, Oliver Twist*, and *David Copperfield. Great Dialogues of Plato.*

(Yes, it is bizarre: I was reading, trying to read, Plato as a young girl. More bizarre yet, I was writing my own "Platonic dialogues" on tablet paper—though perhaps Socratic irony was lost on me.)

(Often the librarians at the Lockport library would look at me doubtfully. Who is this girl? Is she really reading these books? *Trying* to read these books? Who is giving her such outsized ideas? But I'd been brought to the library by my grandmother Blanche Morgenstern, whom the librarians knew as a loyal patron with an impassioned love of books; since my grandmother had arranged for me to have my first library card there, the librarians may have felt kindly disposed toward me.)

Difficult to concentrate on any kind of reading in such circumstances! At a roadside farm stand you are distracted by vehicles approaching on the highway, and passing; for the majority of the vehicles pass by without slowing. There is an air of derision, mockery, repudiation in such circumstances that will linger in the memory for years.

Only now and then a vehicle will slow, and park at the roadside, and a *customer* will emerge, usually a woman.

"Hello!"

"Hello . . ."

"Is it—Joyce?"

A hopeful smile. Or is it a craven smile. When you are *selling*, you are *smiling*.

Quart baskets, bushel baskets of pears. How much did my parents charge for a bushel basket of pears? I have no idea; surely not much. Their prices had to be competitive with those of commercial vendors, if not lower. If you were a small-time farmer you could pitch your goods so low that you made virtually no profit and worked for nothing. (All of the farms in our vicinity employed "child labor"—the farm owners children. Hours of such employment are not negotiable.) Yet I remember the sting of embarrassment when a potential customer, frowning over our pears, or strawberries, or tomatoes, deftly turning back the tight leaves of our sweet corn to examine the kernels, decided that our produce wasn't priced low enough, or wasn't good enough in some way, returned to her car, and drove off.

Sitting at a roadside, vulnerable as an exposed heart, you are liable to such rejections. As if, as a writer, you were obliged to sell your books in a nightmare of a public place, smiling until your face ached, until there were no more smiles remaining.

Years later, as an undergraduate at Syracuse University, I was grateful to work as a "page" in the university library for as many hours a week as I could manage—for one dollar an hour. This was my first authentic job; I could consider myself now an adult. Alone, stationed on one of the upper floors of the library (which seemed immense to me, for whom a "library" was the Lockport Public Library), as I pushed a cart to reshelve books like an enthralled Alice in Wonderland, I could explore the stacks—rows upon rows of stacks—*English Literature, American Literature, Philosophy;* there was an open reading area with a long wooden table that was usually deserted and here I could sit and read with fascination what are called "learned journals" and "literary magazines"—an entire category of magazine utterly unknown to me before college. Discovering these journals was the equivalent of my discovery at age nine of the wonderful *Alice* books.

For here was Poetry—in which I read Hayden Carruth's harrowing autobiographical poem "The Asylum"—Epoch (the first literary magazine in which a story of mine would appear, under the name "J. C. Oates," in 1960)—Journal of Metaphysics (which I read avidly, or tried to read, as if "metaphysics" was as firm and respectable a discipline as physics)—Modern Fiction Studies (the first academic literary journal of my life). Equally intriguing were Philological Quarterly, PMLA, Romanticism, American Literature, American Scholar. A treasure trove of original fiction, poetry, essays, and reviews—Kenyon Review, Virginia Quarterly Review, Southern Review, Southwest Review, Kenyon Review, Paris Review, Hudson Review, Partisan Review, Dalhousie Review, Prairie Schooner, Shenandoah, Georgia Review, The Literary Review, Transatlantic Review, Quarterly Review of Literature—the very "little magazines" in which, over the next several decades of my life, my own work would appear.

(My first published story in a national magazine wasn't in one of these, but in Mademoiselle, in 1959. Like Sylvia Plath in a previous year's competition, I'd received an award from this chic fashion magazine in which, in those days, writing by such distinguished contributors as Tennessee Williams, William Faulkner, Paul Bowles, Katherine Anne Porter, Flannery O'Connor, Jean Stafford, and Truman Capote routinely appeared. How improbable this seems to us, by contemporary standards! Yet high-quality fiction appeared in many glossy magazines of the era—Vogue, Harper's Bazaar, Cosmopolitan, intermittently even in Saturday Evening Post and Playboy, as well as in the more likely Atlantic, Harper's, Esquire, and New Yorker. It did feel to me, at the age of nineteen, that my life had been magically touched, if not profoundly altered, by the Mademoiselle citation.)

One of the great reading moments in my lifetime—if it isn't more accurately described as a life-altering moment—occurred in the second semester of my freshman year when I entered a classroom in the Hall of Languages, and idly opened a book that had been left behind—a philosophy anthology in which there was an excerpt from the work of Friedrich Nietzsche. A sentence or two of this German philosopher of the nineteenth century, of whom I'd never heard, and immediately I felt excitement, and a kind of rapport; after class I ran to the campus bookstore, where, with reckless abandonment for one who had virtually no spending money, I bought paperback copies of Nietzsche—*Thus Spake Zarathustra, The Genealogy of Morals, Beyond Good and Evil*—which I have, heavily annotated, to this day.

For here was one who argued as if "with a hammer"—the very weapon to counter those years of enforced passivity as a quasi-Christian conscripted into an adult world of piety in which nothing was clearly explained, nothing was sincere, and all was obscured; my sense that the elders of my world were conspiring to convince me, as a child, and as a young person, of "beliefs" in which none of them believed, even as the pretense was *This is the way, the truth, the light. Only through this way shall you be saved.*

To counter such smug pieties, the devastating voice of the philosopher—*What is done out of love always happens beyond good and evil.*

As a freshman I lived not in a dormitory but in a less costly "cottage" on Walker Avenue with approximately twenty other scholarship girls, all of us from upstate New York. (We were "girls" and not "young women"—in age, experience, appearance. This was an era when "girls" were under a kind of protective custody at universities, subject to curfews that male undergraduates did not have. It is an accurate description of the "scholarship girls" of Walker Cottage that none of us minded in the slightest that we had to be back in our residence by 11:00 p.m. weeknights—we had nowhere else we'd have preferred to be than in our rooms, studying.) My room was a single room, cell-like, sparely furnished, where I could work uninterrupted for long hours; for the first time in my life, I was free of the surveillance of my parents, however benevolent this surveillance might have been. And I could work in the university library, until curfew, at the long oak table that seemed magical to me, surrounded by shelves of "little magazines" I came to revere and even to love; I wrote by hand in a spiral notebook, sketches for fiction, outlines, impressions, which I then brought back to the residence to convert into typed pages. Stories, novels—even poetry, and plays—hundreds of pages of earnest undergraduate work that I would not have known to identify at the time as "apprentice work"— much of it discarded, some of it reworked and refined into the stories that I would submit to the writing workshops I took at Syracuse and that would eventually appear in my first book, a story collection titled By the North Gate (1963).

If I open that book, composed and assembled so long ago, it's as if I am catapulted back into that era—I can shut my eyes and see again the oak table in the library, the displayed magazines on both sides; I can see again the room in which I lived at the time, the plain table desk facing a utilitarian blank wall.

As the Lockport Public Library had been a sanctuary for me as a child and young girl, and a hallowed source of happiness, so the library at Syracuse University would be its equivalent, if not more, in my undergraduate years. Over all, Syracuse was a young writer's paradise: my professors Donald A. Dike, Walter Sutton, Arthur Hoffman, among esteemed others, were brilliant, sympathetic, and unfailingly supportive. (Disclosure: Not once was I made to feel, by any of my professors, that as a young woman I was in any way "inferior" to my male classmates. However, it did not escape my awareness that there was but a single woman professor in the English Department and no women at all in Philosophy.)

If the university library was a treasure trove to a word-besotted undergraduate like myself, it was also, I suppose, a little too much for me. My memory of my workplace is of a labyrinth so dimly lighted—for stacks not in use were darkened: You had to switch lights on as you entered the aisles—as to inspire hallucination; here was a universe of books, overwhelming and intimidating and seemingly infinite as a library in a Borges fiction. One could never begin to read so many books—it invited madness just to think that each had been cataloged and shelved. Each had been conscientiously *written*!

One day, I would convert some of these experiences into prose fiction—quasi-memoirist fiction, titled *I'll Take You There*. But not for decades.

"Seventy cents? *Seventy cents?*"—it was a shock to me to receive my weekly paycheck for the first time, to discover that I wasn't even earning a dollar an hour but, after taxes, considerably less. My pride in attending Syracuse University and working in the library was undermined by such reminders of how desperate I was, or how naive.

When, after the first check, I expressed my dismay to one of the librarians for whom I worked, the woman said curtly: "It's the same for all of us, Joyce."

Yet I had no choice but to continue at the library. It has been the mantra of my life—I have no choice but to continue.

And years later, as a graduate student in English and American literature at the University of Wisconsin at Madison.

The pressure of graduate school, at least as first-year English graduate students experienced it, was unrelenting: hundreds of pages of reading each week, and these pages densely printed on tissue-thin paper—Old English *Beowulf, The Wanderer, The Dream of the Rood, Anglo-Saxon Chronicle*, works by Bede, Cynewulf, Caedmon; *Liturgical Plays of the Story of Christ, The Castle of Perseverance, Gammer Gurton's Needle, Damon and Pythias, Second Shepherd's Play, Everyman, Noah's Flood*. Chaucer's *Canterbury Tales* and *Troilus and Criseyde*, Spenser's *Faerie Queene*, witty John Skelton, Jacobean and Elizabethan and Restoration drama and more. Much more. One by one we discovered Sir Thomas Wyatt, and committed to heart the mysterious gem "They Flee from Me" (1557)—

They flee from me, that sometime did me seek,
With naked foot stalking in my chamber,
I have seen them, gentle, tame, and meek,
That now are wild, and do not remember
That sometime they put themselves in danger
To take bread at my hand, and now they range,
Busily seeking with a continual change . . .

The great works of English literature were monuments to be approached with reverence. Unlike my Syracuse professors, these older, Harvard-trained professors at Wisconsin did not regard literature as an art but rather more as historical artifact, to be discussed in terms of its context; there was little or no discussion of a poem as a composition of carefully chosen words. History, not aesthetics. The thrilling emotional punch of great art—totally beyond the range of these earnest scholarly individuals. One might lecture on Latin influences in pre-Shakespearean drama, or influences in Shakespeare, but the white-hot dynamic of Macbeth, for instance, the brilliant and dazzling interplay of "personalities" that is Shakespearean essential drama was unknown to them. If they were explorers, they'd been becalmed in an inlet, while the great river rushed past a few miles away.

277

Yet, at Madison, I did read, reread, and immerse myself in the work of Herman Melville. For a course at Syracuse I'd read the early, relatively straightforward *White-Jacket*, and the wonderfully enigmatic short stories—"Bartleby, the Scrivener," "The Paradise of Bachelors and the Tartarus of Maids," "The Encantadas." While still in high school I'd read *Moby-Dick*—our greatest American novel, which one might read and reread through a lifetime, as one might read and reread the poetry of Emily Dickinson. At Madison, I became entranced by the very intransigence, one might say the *obstinate opacity* of the near-unreadable *Pierre: or, The Ambiguities*—a pseudo romance written in mockery of its (potential, female) readers, as if by a (male) author who'd come to hate the effort of narrative prose fiction itself. (It isn't surprising that *Pierre* sold poorly, as its great predecessor *Moby-Dick* sold poorly. Tragic Melville—"Dollars damn me!") After a few pages of its curiously stilted, self-regarding prose I fell under the spell of the slightly more accessible allegory *The Confidence-Man*, as well as *Billy Budd*. I wondered what to make of *Benito Cereno*, with its perversely glacial-slow pace: In our racially sensitized era we expect that Melville will surely side with the slave uprising, and not with white oppressors like Captain Cereno, but Melville doesn't comply with our twenty-first-century expectations in this case in which "the shadow of the Negro" falls over everyone—including even the executed rebel Babo.

Writers who are enrolled in graduate programs soon feel the frustration, the ignominy, the pain of being immersed in reading the work of others—illustrious, renowned others—Chaucer, Shakespeare, Donne, Milton—Hawthorne, Poe, Melville, James—when they are themselves unable to write or even to fantasize writing. During these months of intense academic study when my head was crammed with great and not-so-great classic works, of course I had no time for fiction or poetry of my own (as I thought it) except desperate fragments in a journal like cries for help.

Suffocated by books. Crushed by books. Library stacks, tall shelves of books, books, books overturning upon the young writer groping in the dark for the overhead light to switch on.

Nominated by Joan Murray and Conjunctions

FROM *A TILT IN THE WONDERING*

by NICOLE BROSSARD

from VALLUM

LEXICON 1

my best buy of the year is an alarming *creativity*
a new concept for management so business becomes
a cute gentle occupation
almost a must for you and me to be creative so
everyone takes part in the *nyou* wealth

I left the office I left the bar with non-written words
just excitement *sur le voile du palais*
I wanted you not in fiction as art money love and war
where was my lexicon where were my written vowels
I left the office I left the bar not creative

❋

le verbe être allait dans toutes les directions
moving fast ignorant of etymology
but familiar with lemon or tulips or
such a blue sky this morning lavish thoughts
or so many slashes in meaning
dazzling jumps in connotation

❋

where the verb stands
authentic I have to be faster than
spontaneous explanations

like continents and planets
I need to move in time
au *figuré de l'intime*

VISUAL LEXICON 2

saw only 5 seconds of the kneeled woman about
to be throat cut by a male, saw a line of blood
from left to right on the neck
did not want to find out if it was true.
Suspect it was true. Could not watch. Would with one touch
of the finger on the screen not see IF IT WAS real if it was
                                                    not REAL
had time to not see though time expanded in my eyes
and nerves neutralizing all at the same time fear anger
and what's the w?ord? sadness gloom murk obscurity
what's the word uckingmademenreligion
what's the word if not repetition what's the word
uck uck uckf uck what's the word decapitated capitulating
capitals of blood what was that image again it was

HALF-WAY

half-way through the book
time came back with a question a trace
a spiral ready to expand meaning
a tilt in the wondering

how do you remove time from
meaning so meaning grows roots
in sound to exist beyond sounds

half-way through your notes:
you spoke louder in the mic
so as to hear new micro sobs in yourself

half-way like markers
des silences nous abordent
ready to crackdown on us
not so strange but possibly so
if I surrender with mourning sounds
when the mouth rocks *onelanguage*
with another

Nominated by Vallum

BURY ME

fiction by ALLEGRA HYDE

from THE MISSOURI REVIEW

> *Beware the pine-tree's withered branch!*
> *Beware the awful avalanche!*
> —Henry Wadsworth Longfellow

It was the strangest funeral I'd ever attended. Sun-soaked—on the old farm field behind Sally's house—the bereaved dressed in a rainbow of colors, the air sugared with cotton candy and the pangs of a string quartet. A downy white pony for children to ride.

Sally saw me and came sailing across the lawn, a loose yellow dress lashed to her body.

"My mother's," she said, hiking the dress past her knees, as if she were a little girl crossing a mud puddle. "I'm so glad you're here." She gave me a wet, splintering smile. "I almost thought you weren't coming."

"Sal—"

But already she was gone, engulfed by relatives, all of them echoes of her: lithe Nordic bodies, white-blond hair, long noses. Polished people who looked like they'd be cold to touch.

I had not wanted to come. It had been three months since I'd so much as grabbed coffee with Sally, and in those months I'd finally felt able to think straight. "It's my work," I'd told her, in the phone calls I answered. "I'm unbelievably busy." I said this despite living less than two hours away. Despite the fact that her mother was dying—for real this time, no more chance of remission—and that her father had been dead for eight years. I deliberately took on extra hours, extra projects, anything to stay longer in the white light of the lab, among whirring fans, trays of bladderwort and daffodils standing erect, in the place where I believed myself happy.

Notes 5/12—Characteristics

Native to New England, Pinus Strobus *is also known as* *White Pine, Soft Pine and Weymouth Pine. The evergreen tree takes a conical shape. Fast growing, given the proper climate.*

"Madeline," called a voice, and I peered out toward the other funeral attendees, like bright dashes of paint dotting the lawn. No sign of Sally. No sign that the voice belonged to anyone. A caterer lunged at me with a tray of little marzipan animals: zebras, penguins, a slumping chimpanzee. I felt dizzy.

"Madeline."

I turned to find Lou Crane, one of Sally's ex-boyfriends (always Lou Crane, never Lou. "Like Charlie Parker," he used to tell people). He'd gotten paunchy since college but still had the same foxy, glittering eyes. He beckoned from a half circle of young men, some of whom looked familiar. More of Sally's ex-boyfriends, I realized.

It surprised me, seeing them, though it shouldn't have. Sally had the uncanny ability to stay close after breakups. The boyfriends waved, a few hugged me—they all seemed to be getting along quite well— unaware, evidently, of their own oddity: a series of successive upgrades, each in turn abandoned.

"So," said Lou Crane, as he and the other boyfriends dismantled a tray of blue cheese canapés, "I got us some stuff for tonight." He exaggerated the word *stuff*.

"Tonight?" I echoed.

"We're having a party."

In college, Lou Crane had called himself a musician—played saxophone and wore his hair long—but even then you could detect a harshness, a bulldoggedness, beneath the smell of hash. How fitting that he'd since started working in finance.

"For Sally," he added, drawing close and raising his eyebrows, "to take her mind off things."

Despite the circumstances, I had enjoyed seeing Lou Crane—enjoyed jostling shoulders with my past—but now I wanted to shut that past out. I wanted to return to my clear-eyed life: the 6:00 AM jogs, the hissing cappuccino maker, a newspaper so fresh it smudged my palms black.

"Can't stay," I said, trying to sound disappointed. "Got to get back— work."

Lou Crane gave me a *come on* look, the other boyfriends following his gaze, as if it were a road leading from him to me. "Maddy," he said, like he owned the name. He looked at me, eyes brimming with remembrance, with the authority of having once watched me crawl across a frat room floor, of having once walked in on me blowing his roommate (I'd flipped him off and kept going), of having, perhaps more than anyone, witnessed the nights Sally and I seemed to float untouchable, reckless to the point of elegance.

"I think it would mean a lot to her if you stayed." The voice belonged to one of the other boyfriends, one I hadn't noticed at first. Carlton, I guessed. Sally's current beau. He wore a well-tailored jacket and had large, clean-looking hands. "She talks about you so often," he added, with the sort of sincerity I might have mocked in other circumstances. He was the kind of guy Sally and I had both avoided in college.

"What d'you think?" asked Lou Crane again, and, in the presence of Carlton, I felt a moment of allegiance. Maybe I could handle one night—just one—for the sake of the girl I'd once called my best friend. One night, and I'd drive home in the morning.

But even thinking this, my mouth went dry; I felt the breath siphoned from my lungs.

Notes 5/12—Growth Patterns
  White Pine seeds distributed by wind. Cone production peaks every three to five years, with two years required for full maturity.

The funeral service was about to begin. The cotton-candy machine was silenced, the pony held fast. Everyone gathered around a gazebo covered in ribbons and balloons. A passerby might have thought we were assembling for a birthday party or an unconventional wedding, if all the brightly dressed people hadn't looked so grave.

"Planned the whole thing on her deathbed," I overheard a woman tell the man at her elbow.

"She would, wouldn't she," the man answered. He might have said more, but their pious incredulity drifted out of earshot.

I had not known Sally's mother well. She visited campus only once or twice. An elegant woman, even with skin turned waxy from chemo, hair fallen away. And yet it had been her idea to get drunk on margaritas with Sally and me, in a dive bar three towns over. Drunk enough for us to sing bad renditions of "Baby One More Time," Sally's mother singing loudest of all, her bald head gleaming under neon lights. Even with the trappings of old New England money, she—like her daughter—had never been a stuffy woman.

That, or she had been a woman who always liked to get her way.

As the funeral got started, I found a seat apart from the boyfriends and most of the guests. I sat with my back against a tree, ignoring the root prodding my hip, the snag of bark. From there, I could see Sally. She sat near the microphone, yellow dress draped over her chair, hands folded in her lap. I tried to imagine how I'd arrange my face if she turned around and looked at me. I decided I would give her a strong smile, whatever that meant.

People spoke. The sunshine became heavy. Sally did not turn around, and I began wondering if I should speak. The facilitator was welcoming people up for a sort of open mic. This was something I could do, I realized, something I could do for Sally. She had not spoken herself. She was an outgoing person but hated public speaking. They called again for the open mic. The offer tickled my throat. I couldn't move—I was there for Sally, not her mother.

It was only Sally I could eulogize:

> *How unfortunate, we used to say, that the two of us weren't born lesbians.*
>
> *How unlucky.*
>
> *Sally and I, we met in an astronomy class both of us eventually dropped, but our connection, we decided, had always been in the stars. We could finish each other's sentences on the first day. By the second week we'd already mapped out our whole life: us, together after college in the farmhouse she'd inherit. There'd be yoga at sunrise, baskets of homegrown strawberries, stray cats, foreign lovers who flew in for weekends. We'd learn to sculpt, to play the accordion. We'd host outdoor concerts that would last for days.*
>
> *This is what we used to tell each other, even as we both stood peering into a bar's bathroom mirror, coating our mouths with lipstick, painting our eyes. The visions of our future like a lullaby before we slipped into darkness.*
>
> *She was a wonderful girl, Sally. A special girl.*
>
> *I'll miss her.*

"Where you off to?" said Lou Crane, catching sight of me when the service was over. I had assumed no one would notice if I left early.

Everyone was struggling to stand, stunned by the weight of their grief, half blind in the sunshine, in the confusion of ribbons and music. The band had started playing again. A little girl released a balloon.

I ignored Lou Crane and kept walking toward my car. I would send Sally a card, I'd decided. I would tell her I was sorry I hadn't been able to stay longer.

"Hey," said Lou Crane, jogging after me and grabbing my shoulder. "Hey, don't walk away." His grip became insistent. Knowing him, I couldn't help wondering if this was all part of some half-assed scheme to sleep with me.

"Let go," I said, tugging myself free, preparing to tell him off. But when I looked in his face again, the foxiness was gone. Instead I saw a strained gaze, pupils rimmed with white. Of course he still cared for Sally. They all did, all those boys. They were each here to save her.

Well, then, I told myself, *let them save her*

"Please stay." Lou Crane reached for me again. "She needs you, she—"

As he spoke, I realized what he, what all of them, thought I could do. He thought that with my history—the history I shared with Sally—I could give the girl a night of oblivion. A few hours, at least, of forgetting.

"I can't, I—"

Too late: the shrill bird-call of my name, the flash of a yellow dress.

"You ready to par-tay?" Sally draped an arm on each of my shoulders, so that for a moment her face eclipsed my whole vision. Oval and bone pale. She raised an eyebrow, meaning to be salacious, but the movement only made her appear more unhinged. It made me want to hide her. To put her away where she wouldn't be seen by anyone, by me.

"Madeline was just heading to her car," said Lou Crane. He gave me a dirty look, but I felt grateful that he had said it and not I.

Sally, though, appeared unfazed. In fact, she grinned and said, "Of course, Maddy was just going to grab supplies." Then she drew even closer, all earth-smells and bright blond hair, running her hands down my arms, pausing at my wrists, manacling them with her thin, cold fingers. "Right, babe?"

"Actually—" I murmured, but Sally sprang away.

"The house is all ours tonight," she exclaimed with steely joy. "We're going to have so much fun. It's been so long since I had any fun." She looked at me, at the boyfriends who had begun gathering around. "No parents, no rules!" She was trying to make a joke, but none of us laughed. Sally waited for a moment, then laughed for us, her voice clanging like a warning bell. Her mouth the darkest hole.

Notes 5/12—Potential Problems
Threats to Pinus Strobus *include Blister Rust and the White Pine Weevil, as well as strong winds, heavy snowstorms and air pollution.*
The tree, however, is relatively resistant to fire.

With the funeral guests packed away and gone, the night closing in, the boyfriends and I stood in Sally's kitchen taking small sips of whiskey. Sally gulped. We passed around a joint, mainly passing it to her. The boyfriends looked pleased. She was changing, we could all see that; she was blossoming, color coming into her cheeks, eyes sparkling.

Lou Crane clinked his glass with Carlton's. Everyone seemed to relax.

Then, without warning, Sally dropped to the floor. She rolled around for a moment, then began punching and kicking the air, blond hair thrashing, her face smeared with tears. The boyfriends stepped back, scared to touch her. They looked at me as if I might do something. It made me want to laugh, their scared faces. "It's just Sally," I wanted to say. "What did you expect?"

I knelt beside her, so that she flailed against me for a moment before going still. Then I eased myself down onto the floor and into her arms. Sally had kept her eyes closed, but now she opened them. "Remember," she said to me, still catching her breath, "remember the dean's lawn?"

"Oh, I remember," I replied, my solemnity giving her a little spasm of giggles. "We peed on it."

She went on like this for a while, remembering things while the boys stood stiff and silent around us. "The Goat Room," she'd say. Or "poker night!" And I'd nod, then add flesh to the memory: remind her of how we'd filled the Goat Room with candles and nearly burned the place down. How one poker night we'd won all her math tutor's clothes. Or, even better: our double date with a pair of lacrosse players—star athletes, campus studs—whom we'd ditched five minutes into the winter formal to watch movies in my room.

It was a strange feeling, recounting those stories. A tingling feeling. Almost like recognizing myself in photographs I'd forgotten I was in.

Eventually, Sally and I got up and started drifting through the house, from room to room. I don't know what happened to the boys. They didn't matter anymore; I convinced myself they had never mattered. As we drifted, Sally touched objects—a tall glass lamp, her mother's quilt—as if they were new to her.

"Remember," she said, "our wedding?"

She picked up a photo frame, held it to me, and I saw us: decked out in frothy white thrift-store dresses, holding hands on the college quad. It had been her idea, our sophomore year. By that time her mother's cancer still could have gone either way, but Sally wasn't taking any chances. "I want a wedding photo for my mother," she'd said, "and you're my one true love." So we held a ceremony on the quad, and some nearby Frisbee players officiated. A passing tour group stopped to watch. "You may kiss the other bride," our makeshift priest declared, and we'd made out like we sometimes did at parties, sloppily, half giggling, tongues sliding on teeth, loving how we could shock people.

After that, we'd honeymooned in the cafeteria.

"I wish," said Sally, "I'd kept that dress."

We were in the living room by then, on the couch. A tangle of limbs. I couldn't remember getting there. All around us: funeral bouquets. Bright bunches of white lilies. Lilacs, her mother's favorite. Azaleas. All piled in the room.

"It's been so good to see you," Sally murmured, nuzzling my arm.

Her words made my heart pound. This is what I'd feared most—her needing me more than I needed her—the moment when I'd have to explain that.

"Sally," I said. "Sally, the thing is—"

She placed a finger on my lips. "Shhh," she said. "Enough talking."

So we lay still, inhaling the flowers—their painful perfume, their last gasps—until a figure loomed over us: Carlton, announcing that it was late, that it was time for bed, as he scooped Sally up in his arms.

"No," Sally moaned, dizzy with tiredness. But even as she said it, she pressed herself against him.

"No," I echoed.

Toward the end of college, when I started retreating more often to the library, even staying until close on Friday and Saturday nights, Sally used to visit me. She'd come by, dressed for a party: short skirt, skin peppered with glitter, feet jammed into heels. By that time her mother's health was only getting worse, but that was never what she wanted to talk about.

"Plants," she'd say, perched on the end of my desk and making a little pout. "Tell me what you love so much about plants."

And I'd answer, "You don't really want to hear this," but she'd nod, her earrings tinkling, and say, "Yes, I really do." So, sighing, I would tell her about Hawaiian mosses that had been cloning themselves for 5,000 years. About the corpse flower that smells like rotting meat. Or the famous kadupul blossom, blooming only at night and withering before dawn. And I'd get carried away. I'd realize other people were looking up from their books, glaring over at me, but that Sally was still listening; she was trying so hard to listen. And that's when I'd start to feel angry. Angry, I told myself, that she could never understand why I needed to study so much. Growing up I'd had to fight my way through public schools for scholarships. I couldn't just graduate with good grades, I needed the best grades. How could that make sense to her? There was a building on campus named after her family.

But of course, my anger was never really for Sally. And, if I'd been honest with myself, I wasn't even that desperately poor.

The morning after the funeral, sunlight lanced through windows in dusty rays. The boyfriends lay sprawled asleep on couches and easy chairs, Lou Crane's chainsaw snores concealing the creak of stairs as I crept toward Sally's room. I'd woken clear-headed, resolute: I would invite Sally to stay with me. I would invite her down for the weekend, take her out for dinner, maybe even show her around the lab. The idea made me feel giddy, openhearted. This would be a fresh start for our friendship. A new chapter.

Upstairs, Sally lay on her bed next to Carlton, who still wore his clothes from the night before. Sally, though, was naked. It was how she liked to sleep. I had seen her naked plenty of times, but never so still. Never like that. It shocked me—the vulgarity of nude flesh—her flat chest, hipbones jutting forward, pubic hair shaved away. There was nothing I couldn't see.

Sally opened her eyes.

"Oh," I said, hastily looking away, then back again. "I'm leaving. I have to go."

Sally rolled languidly toward me. "Okay, 'bye," she said, yawning, her eyelids already fluttering closed, her breaths returning to long, easy measures.

Stunned, I remained unmoving. I could not believe that our conversation might end there, that it could end so quickly, that she would let me leave.

"Sally," I whispered. My hand hovered above her body. Two inches, maybe less. I wondered what it would mean to touch the white plain of her skin; what it would have meant, those years ago, to have crossed that threshold on the far side of friendship. "What a shame we weren't born lesbians," we used to say. And we'd meant it.

"Sally," I whispered again, this time a little louder.

We had loved each other, hadn't we? It had been a difficult kind of love—the kind that always stops short of fulfillment—but it had been love, nonetheless.

"Sal, wake up."

Carlton groaned and stretched, one arm falling across Sally's chest.

I fled. I tumbled back through the house, past the boyfriends just beginning to stir. Someone may have called out to me, but I pushed through the front door, out into the dazzle of a summer morning, gasping for air, choking on the realization that Sally hadn't been trying to pin me down or keep me in her life. She'd been trying to say good-bye.

Notes 5/12—Mechanisms for Survival

"But really," Sally had giggled in the library, even when I made an exasperated point of looking at my watch, made it clear there wasn't much else to say. We were close to finals, to graduation, and every minute felt precious: another drop of water, swallowed or lost. "Why," said Sally, twirling her hair, "why do you love plants so much?"

So I told her, in excruciating detail, about abscission. I had my botany textbook open—a section on White Pine—and I pointed to an image of the tree. *Foliage includes fascicles of five bluish green needles.* I told her how the plant would sometimes drop part of itself. *Abscission typically occurs in the colder months.* That it would excise its needles, its cones, even an entire branch in order to make the whole stronger. *This process of detachment furthers chances for survival.*

When I finished and looked at Sally again, there was something wrong with her face. Usually she listened with an expression of vague dreaminess, a smile lolling on her lips, but at that moment she showed complete understanding. Understanding mixed with something I couldn't quite place. It almost looked like pity.

I still think of that moment as I unwind hours in the lab, grinding plants down to their most essential parts, unlocking their secrets in the march of retrogression and reassembly. Chymopapain. Taxol. Podophyllotoxin. It makes me feel like a magician, an alchemist—though I'd never admit so to my colleagues—to find and conjure these substances from the paper thinness of a leaf, the frailty of a petal. It's hard to explain, but sometimes I still believe I could find anything.

Nominated by John Fulton

WHITE LILIES

by RACHEL ROSE

from PRISM

It is hard for the dying to leave us.
We make it hard for them. So they wait
for us to step outside before they cut
the cord. So the baby
in the cabin, lungs full of staph,
who had been fighting the infection
for long nights and days
waited until his mother went out
to chop firewood before he sighed
and stilled. How can I forget her
running across the wet pasture
with his body in her arms
as though my mother were a witch
who could bring back the dead?
I picked the thick white lilies from our garden
for his grave, but was not permitted to the place
where the mourners gathered. Instead I waited
in the silent house, unfolded
the image of his mother
with her hair wild as the wind
and the weight of him in her arms
a stone, a feather, a sunflower
as my mother rose to meet her
or what I have imagined, the map of memory
creased and softened

like a star repeating its trajectory into the sea,
the father who did not yet know
coming up the gravel driveway
with a shovel over his shoulder
whistling, kicking the mud off his boots
before he opened the door.

Nominated by Andrea Hollander and Prism

PAST THE ECONOLODGE

fiction by BRANDON HOBSON

from NOON

After all that, they told me to take out the trash and leave. I put everything into a duffel bag, including the lighter and book I stole from Whitefeather's dad. The little girl was crying but I couldn't bring myself to tell her good-bye. They wanted me gone. They called my social worker and made me wait outside in the yard. It was getting dark out and I could see road dust settling from a truck that drove by. But I didn't want to go back to the shelter, so I left on my own. I jumped the fence and walked all the way to Highway 51, past the EconoLodge and to the gas station across from it.

The woman I met there offered to take me to her home and feed me. She was old with gray hair that hung down in her face. She told me she was raised in an orphanage many years ago. She wore rings on every finger. When we got to her house she brought me soup on a tray and sat next to me while I ate. She wanted to put the spoon in my mouth but I wouldn't let her.

We stayed up late, drinking cheap wine and watching TV. She showed me photos of a boy with crutches. They were old black-and-white photos taken on a farm somewhere.

"His name was Arthur," she said. "He was crippled and walked with crutches until he died. He was born that way. He was only ten when he died."

I wasn't interested. She had this way of trying to laugh. She touched the burn mark on my arm and told me my eyes were gray. Did I know they were gray? Did I want her to look into my palm and tell me my future? She reached for my hand but I pulled away. She told me a story from the Bible about a woman at a well who gave water to Jesus. The next thing I knew it was almost midnight and rain was hitting the window.

I asked her where the bathroom was and she pointed to the hall. When I got in there I didn't close the door all the way. I left it barely open. Then I lifted the toilet seat and unbuttoned my pants. I pulled out my cock and masturbated, looking at the open door the whole time until I shot into the toilet. Some of it missed the water. Some of it ran down the side of the toilet, very slowly, and I didn't bother to clean it up.

When I returned to her living room she tried asking me about my mom and family but I didn't want to talk. I told her I needed to leave.

"I understand how you must feel," she said.

"You don't understand anything," I told her.

"If you stay I'll let you sleep in the bed."

I said, "Don't you get it? I don't have to stay anywhere. I can leave if I want."

She was sitting on the edge of the divan, staring at something on the floor.

"At least wait until it stops raining," she said.

I grabbed my duffel bag. She didn't get up or try to stop me. I waited for her to say something. I waited for her to do something, anything, but she wouldn't look at me.

All she was trying to do was help me.

Nominated by Elizabeth Ellen and Noon

A SINGLE DELIBERATE THING

fiction by ZEBBIE WATSON

from THE THREEPENNY REVIEW

It had been a long, rainless July and before that, a dry June. The pastures were brown, the grass chewed to stubs and coated in dust. The horses stayed in all day and if I tried to turn them out before dark, they stood by the gate and sweated and stamped. Most farms got the corn planted early enough that it grew shoulder-high and deep rooted, but the second cutting of hay would be late and small and the soy beans were doing poorly, their leaves chewed by the deer and withering on the stem. I was counting swallows and waiting for the letter from Kentucky that might let me know if you still loved me.

There were more swallows that summer than I can ever remember seeing. In spring there had been the usual number of mud-daubed nests—one under the eaves in the front of the barn, one in Otter's stall, and one on the side of the garage—but somehow, come July, the fields positively crackled with the glint of the sun off their blue-black backs. Most days I counted more than thirty of them. They would perch in a row on the telephone wire that ran up the drive, and when I passed under them, they'd peel off one by one in all directions, sleek and made of angles, to swoop across the fields and turn their wingtips vertical. Dad said it was because there was no mud for a second nest; there was nothing else for them to do.

When you told me you were enlisting, you said we should just break up then because you would probably be sent some place out of state. That made sense, but then the night before you left, when you came over to say goodbye, you hugged me on the front porch and pressed a folded paper into my palm with your address at boot camp and left without coming inside. I wasn't sure if that meant you wanted me to write or not, and if that was your way of letting me choose, I didn't get it at the time.

I wrote you mid-June. I think now that I shouldn't have, but what can I say, it was habit to want to tell you things. When I saw fox kits playing in the field, when I counted thirty-seven swallows on the wire, when Grace jumped her first full course without refusing a fence, I wanted to tell you. I also wanted to apologize for saying you looked dumb with your head shaved, you know it would have grown on me. And then I added that I didn't care if you were giving up college or if we would have to be apart a lot because I didn't need that much from you anyway. And I didn't get why you thought staying together would be hard when it had always been easy before. And finally I told you that I wouldn't mind waiting most of the time, which, I realize now, is funny, because after a couple weeks the waiting started to drive me crazy. I knew the mail would be slow but the relentless heat made the days longer and they eventually began adding up and summer dragged on indefinitely.

I should have kept busy riding but Mom and I were only riding in the late evening when the flies were more bearable. You know how grumpy the mares get in the heat, some days I didn't even bother. One night I was riding Grace behind the house and she was already so annoyed to be out that when a horsefly landed on her rump she bucked once and launched me right over her head. She was good for the most part, but that night not so much. Maybe I'd have ridden more if you were home to come out with me, my mom never wanted to. She's even less tolerant than the mares. I never told her I had written you but sometimes I swear she knew by the way she'd say *why don't you do something different with your hair*, or *you'll meet so many cute boys in college*. Other times it seemed like she'd forgotten, she didn't ask, as if hearing from you was never on the table to begin with. Family dinners were spent mostly just complaining about the lack of rain and worrying about Notes.

We took Notes in March from a friend of a friend. They told us he couldn't be ridden due to his age and his heaves, but as soon as the summer humidity set in, it was obvious that his breathing was so bad he should have just been euthanized. We saw that and acknowledged that but still he was already so dear and familiar and Otter, who in seventeen years had never bonded closely with the other horses, loved Notes instantly and fiercely. The two of them grazed nose to nose although Notes barely came up to Otter's chest, and Otter would chase the two mares if they came close to his pony. He lost weight quickly when summer came; he wasn't too thin when you saw him last, but by the end his ribs showed with every breath and his hollow neck tied into bony withers. My parents would talk about it every time the temperatures rose, watching in the late evening as Otter's tall dark shape moved in protective circles around Notes' small white one, and we were all guilty of too much hope. It became a pattern of *maybe this summer won't be too bad*, and then *we got him through the last heat wave, we can't give up now the humidity's broken a bit*. But July dragged on and I was still waiting for your letter and drenching Notes with cold water every afternoon to keep him cool.

I wish now that I could have just made a decision for him. That's a lot of afternoons in the barn with sweat between my shoulder blades and nothing to do but listen to Notes' wheezing and think about when your letter might come. I imagine that summer in Kentucky must have been even hotter than Virginia so I thought of you every time sweat soaked through the back of my shirt, knowing you were wearing combat boots and fatigues. I thought of how easily your nose and ears sunburned, and how dark your freckles would be. I thought that maybe it had taken a long time for you to get my letter, and that maybe you were too tired each night to write back. At some point I realized that I hadn't even told you to write back, I was just leaving it up to you to decide, I was only ever asking you to decide. My parents must not have known or else they would have kept saying things like *teenage love will die naturally anyway* or *you two would have eventually grown apart at college*. They assumed my worry was about Notes, which makes sense because he was the one I sat next to as I waited.

The day before he died, looking back, I think we knew. It was an unbearably heavy week, the air was so thick and the temperature barely dipped into the eighties at night. When Mom brought the horses in that morning, Notes ate his small handful of grain and lay down, already tired and heaving. I confess we were so used to his flaring nostrils that it didn't seem much worse than usual, but I could tell she was worried when she left for work. She asked me to check on him in the afternoon, reminding me about his medication, as if I didn't do it every day.

I checked on him every day but that day I avoided it, waiting until after lunch when it would be time for his medicine. I remember that I went out on the porch to water the plants and saw a dozen or so of the swallows gathered in a low dip in the driveway that would become a puddle were there any rain. They moved so unnaturally, their bodies stooped and narrow, it was striking. I watched them, amazed that some deep instinct drove them to this low place—that they knew if there were mud to be found it would be there—and yet somehow ashamed to see them that way. I loved the tiny sharpness of their hunched shapes when they perched, but on the ground they groveled, moved like bats in daylight, it made me feel so helpless. I took the watering can to soak the dust they were pecking and they scattered before me. It was a relief to watch them skim away across the pasture.

I went out to the barn after lunch. The place where I'd poured water for the swallows was dry; I hadn't seen them come back. The barn was dark and still, no air moving despite the open doors and windows. Notes was standing up eating his soaked hay, but I could hear the rapid pace of his breathing. Otter was napping with his head in the corner and a hind-leg cocked, bits of straw in his tail from having lain down earlier. Grace and Sassy were sleeping too. Their flanks were already dark with sweat despite the box fans in every stall that were always on those days. I refilled the water buckets then crushed Notes' Albuterol pills and mixed them with his Ventipulmin in a syringe. Otter woke up at the sound of the feed room door so I grabbed mints from the bag and gave him one. Notes came to the front of his stall and nickered. His nicker was an unbearable choking noise. His eyes looked bright though, glinting out from his thick forelock, his small, sculpted ears alert. I fed him a mint and his lips were damp and green from the hay, leaving slime on my palms.

He was used to the routine and allowed me to hold his head with an arm over his neck and squeeze the medicine into his mouth. I could feel the strain of his breathing through his whole body and he was drenched in sweat underneath his heavy mane. We'd clipped his coat twice already that summer, Mom did it in the spring and then I clipped him again in June since his hair was so thick, but he sweated and labored anyway. In that moment I felt suddenly desperate, as if all summer I'd been telling myself he was dying but didn't see it until then. It wasn't a decision, not really, I just grabbed scissors from the shelf and began to cut his mane off in chunks, twisting bunches of it in my fists and letting them fall to the ground. Otter watched us over his stall door and chewed his hay in tense, intermittent bites. Notes didn't move, just stood with his head low, looking out from behind that long white forelock. I cut that too.

I fetched the electric clippers from the cabinet, unwound the cord, and knelt down next to him, feeling the cool of the concrete spread up through my knees. I started between his ears and ran the clippers down the crest of his neck in one long stroke, watching the jagged tufts of hair pour off. I clipped more slowly down each side, evening out the edges, meticulously, my free hand over his neck and pulling him closer to me as I shore off the remains of his forelock, carefully moving between his ears and following the swirl of a cowlick. When I was finished, Notes' skin showed black and dusty through the stubble.

I sat back on my heels. Notes turned and nosed my hand for a treat and I gave him another mint. The roached mane did not flatter his thin neck. You know, he was actually only about twenty, but he looked so old and sick. I don't know what could have happened to make him that way. His grey coat was dingy and yellow from sweat and dust. I took him outside to the water pump, Otter watching us suspiciously, and washed him, spending a long time with my fingertips working suds into his coat and tail until he was clean. The swallows swooped and chattered in the sunlight as I worked. The medication had kicked in and Notes was breathing a little more freely when I put him back inside. I swept up the hair and threw it away.

I didn't even bother checking the mailbox that afternoon. I think my parents were used to me doing it because they asked me where the mail was but I just answered *Notes is bad today* and they forgot about the mail. I wish I'd added *we should do it tomorrow*, but I knew they'd realize that themselves. I heard them in the kitchen after dinner talking about him and they both came out to the barn that evening to help me feed and turn the horses out. They commented on how clean he was but didn't mention the haircut. He was clean; he glowed in the dim, late-evening light walking across the pasture with Otter shadowing his steps. As I washed my own hair that night, I thought that Otter should be with him when we put him down, and that you weren't going to write back.

Notes died sometime that night. We found him not far from the barn, in the spot where he and Otter always stood. His body looked very small. Otter was still next to him and wouldn't come to the gate, but when I took him in on a lead he didn't protest. Dad called a friend with a backhoe and they buried him on the edge of the field behind the house, by the woods, with two of Dad's old foxhunters and my first pony. I stayed in the barn while they did, watching Otter chew hay and feeding him mints. I didn't cry until Dad came back with a banded lock of Notes' tail he'd saved, and I thought about the feel of his mane in my fists as I cut it. Otter was quiet all day but when he went back

300

out at night, he whinnied once and looked back toward the barn as if waiting.

The next day, it finally rained, one of those wicked summer storms that can only come after weeks of relentless heat. The worse the weather, the bigger the snap, and this one broke with a rare violence. We could feel it coming, all morning the air crackled and the swallows were nowhere to be found. It finally came early afternoon, like something out of an ancient mythology. It was then that I realized I'd done nothing all summer but wait for rain, that I hadn't done a single deliberate thing. The electricity went out and we watched from the house as waves of rain swept through like fists, wind bowed the trees, and the sky flared a sick, tornado green in the distance. When it was over, I turned the horses out and they went like new colts, all high-kneed and quivering. Grace dropped right to her knees to roll, then ran off bucking and nipping at Sassy's flank. Otter sniffed the ground where Notes had lain, then trotted off after the mares.

The storm brought down trees all over the place. Dad and I were at the end of the driveway clearing branches a few days later when the mailman brought your letter. I took the bundle from the mailbox and rifled through it and when I saw my name in your handwriting, I didn't know what to do anymore. You'd decided to have your say after all, but I'd stopped waiting. Dad asked if there was any interesting mail and I answered *Nothing*. The swallows flitted from the wire one by one as I walked back up the drive to the house, my back sticky with sweat and your letter tucked between other envelopes in my hand. I wondered when you had sent it and why it took too long to arrive.

Briefly, I held the envelope over the trashcan, but that felt too impulsive. Instead, I put it in the bottom drawer of my desk, under some old school papers. Notes' tail was still on my dresser and I didn't know what to do with that either, so I put it in the drawer as well.

I just wanted you to know, that's what I did.

Nominated by Alice Mattison and The Threepenny Review

HOLI: EQUINOX APPROACHES

by RAENA SHIRALI

from QUARTERLY WEST

> "Young woman attacked on bamboo platform in front of entire village."
> The Independent, January 24, 2014

Palash, flame of the forest, unfurls
against morning: a signal as it begins.
If only to forget the women

we won't speak of, we toss
powder colored with spring crops
& watch our bodies eviscerate
the concentrated tone. If only to celebrate,

we look, for a day, past
the fire our kin have lit—blaze that chases
young women into alleys, or out

of this nation. If only to watch these bodies—only
ours. The town squares, the raised platforms
might have never been—

We could let the full moon & delicacies
fill us. We could trade
turmeric for bits of leaves, fungible entities
ground in marvelous clay pots bursting
with saturates—

      & not think of her hair:
Stygian, oiled, gripped or   ripped
by a thirteen-year-old boy. & then
by many boys as young as any of our sons.

If only blue hibiscus & not the hue
of her skin: color she turned at heat-sick

dawn. If only beetroot to decorate,
to complement the rare
green fleck of her eyes. The amla fruit pigment
flings out from my palms.

      If only I could tuck a jacaranda
flower behind her ear, place dried tea leaves
in her hands, ask that she color her flesh

back again. I hold the girl's absence
as though I could see her

nails stained red. I hear a woman, chasing
her sister, say, *Run all you want, I'll catch you,*
hear her sister shriek, hear the crowd—
that mass—   shriek.

      Someone hurls the color of flames
up, like a call to god.

A man approaches me, a blurred eddy
of tones. He mesmerizes. He wields
a fist full of saffron dye.

Nominated by Kathy Fagan

A RING OF BELLS

by CATHERINE JAGOE

from THE GETTYSBURG REVIEW

It is a frigid February night in snowbound Wisconsin, and the chamber choir I sing with is rehearsing Randall Thomson's anthem "Alleluia," which ends with a series of downward runs. They remind me of the sound of church bells in any English town on Sundays—those rills of notes spilling out, tumbling after one another down the scale, weaving in and out like dancers round the Maypole, calling people to church for Matins, Eucharist, and Evensong, for weddings and funerals and holy days. "Alleluia, alleluia," and I am taken back forty years to Shropshire: grass scent and thrush song.

The bells were ringing the day my siblings and I arrived in Ellesmere for the first time, in August, 1969, when I was eight years old. Our family's new home, called "St. Mary's Cottage," was a rambling old house adjacent to the parish church, St. Mary's, which was built by the Knights Hospitallers in the thirteenth century on a site where people had been worshipping for centuries. The town was founded by a Saxon chieftain on the edge of a mere and named after him: Elli's Mere, Ellesmere. It lay on the border between England and Wales, on the edge of water, and our house, too, seemed to occupy a liminal space—in our case between secular and religious life. It was once part of church lands, and both the entrance to the church and the path to the vicarage lay right next to our back gate. In the churchyard, eighteenth-century gravestones covered with lichen listed at odd angles among the thick, tussocky grass and starry flowers of orange hawksbit.

Church bells punctuated our lives, doling out information and instructions, for the church clock tolled every hour. Eight bells meant it was time to jump out of bed and get ready for school. One bell meant it was lunchtime. Six bells, and it was time for Dad to switch on the evening news. Bells at 7:30 PM on a Friday meant the ringers were holding their weekly practice. In the evening, ten bells meant it was time to switch out the light. On New Year's Eve, twelve strokes meant squeals, hugging, and one of the grownups popping a cork. Saturday bells signaled a wedding or a funeral.

Living so close to the church, I was soon drawn into its life. Because my mother helped "do" the flowers, we were often there at off hours, so it became familiar territory, an extension of St. Mary's Cottage. While she busied herself cutting stems and arranging blooms in bricks of green Oasis floral foam, I would wander around, playing in the high-backed choir stalls carved with heraldic birds and beasts, kneeling on the woven blue hassocks in the pews, pacing the uneven tiled floor, staring at the stained-glass windows, thumbing the hymn books with their soft leather backs and impossibly thin pages, fingering the sacred heart and pierced hands and feet on the baptismal font, or the cold brass wings of the great lectern eagle, with its giant Bible lying open at the gospel for Sunday, marked by a lanyard of frayed red silk.

I started taking organ lessons and would come in the evenings to practice, pulling stops so that the different voices would sound, my feet working the keys below me, sitting in a pool of yellow light in the dark transept. The organ was so much bigger than me, and so difficult to learn, with all the different keyboards and stops, but I loved the sound of the instrument more than any I had yet encountered. I felt a mixture of peace, happiness, and fear sitting there—joy at the music and fear of the looming dark spaces beyond the light. I was also afraid of the walk home through the dark churchyard, still enough of a child to be afraid of ghouls and ghosts rising from their graves, the lurking presence of beings from countless other centuries, the impenetrable dark of the country.

I was one of the first girls to sing in the choir; I was proud to be let into the vestry at the back of the church—a place off-limits to the congregation—and to don a wine-colored cassock and white surplice with the men and boys. I remember fighting attacks of the giggles during the sermon; once, before choir practice, I felt daring enough to climb the stairs to the high stone pulpit but was caught by the vicar and reprimanded terribly. I remember, too, smoothing the lilac print of my confirmation dress over my knees, and trying unsuccessfully to make sense of the gory business of eating Christ's body and drinking his blood. I loved the hymns and the Tudor language of the liturgy, even though some of the words—especially "womb," "virgin," "flesh," and "conceive"—made me squirm a little, seeming obscenely female and corporeal in that masculine, spiritual space.

The vicar of St. Mary's was a stolid and humorless man called Reverend Norman Fenn. He rather liked the sound of his own voice intoning, and I couldn't help admiring it too, since he got to use such lovely, weighty phrases. There was the opening prayer: "Almighty God, unto whom all hearts be open, all desires known, and from whom no secrets are hid," as well as the confession of having "erred and strayed like lost sheep" because we were following the "devices and desires of our own hearts." Midway through Holy Communion, in the Eucharistic prayers, Reverend Fenn's sonorous voice would start to rise, like a jet taking off, until he arrived at the mystical commands: "Drink ye all of this: for this is my blood of the new covenant, which is shed for you and for many for the forgiveness of sins." My favorite part came just before people went up to the rail to take communion: "We do not presume to come to this thy table, O merciful Lord, trusting in our own righteousness, but in thy manifold and great mercies. We are not worthy so much as to gather up the crumbs under thy table." It captured perfectly my own sense of being small and flawed despite all my attempts to be good, and my gratefulness at being allowed to participate, to be in the church and at the table.

Being present at all the services, I would see the bell ringers slipping into the back pews as the choir processed up the aisle to the Introit following the cross, the floor beneath our feet vibrating to the organ. They came in late because they had to ring right up until the service began, and it took them some time to get down from the tower. Around the time I was confirmed, at twelve, the ringers enquired if any of the choristers were interested in learning "the ropes." They were in need of new recruits; the older members were dwindling, and there was a dearth of new blood to continue the tradition. I was tall and strong for my age, and curious about the origin of the sounds that were so entwined with my home life. I began taking bell-ringing lessons, and thus began my initiation into another world.

We are following a man who has turned the great, black iron key and swung the small door inward, and we are ascending the narrow spiral stairs, with their pale sandstone steps hollowed out by the passage of centuries of feet. There is a musty smell of old stone, and the surface of the wall is rough to the touch as we lean into it, circling upward. Halfway up, over the little four-petalled rose window with the blue Star of David, there is a flat landing, a wooden passageway from which we can look down into the church. Then we ascend still further to the ringing chamber with its one dusty window set small and low in the foot-thick stone walls. This chamber is halfway up the tower, over the nave.

We have gathered here to ring the bells: old Arnold Whitehead, canal worker and head ringer; Hugh Thomas, the soft-spoken farm forehand; his wife, Pat, strong willed and stocky; Will Campbell-Wallis, the skinny mathematician at the local private school with his huge sideburns, bell-bottom jeans, and boundless enthusiasm; and three local youths who have faded now into anonymity in my mind.

We stand around in a circle, a rope dangling from the ceiling in front of each of us. At first all eight bells will be hanging "down," sleeping, so the fluffy red, blue, and white woolen grips called "sallies" are at roughly head height. We have to reach up to grasp them. Each bell has to be individually rung "up," set in motion by pulling the sally harder and harder so that the bell swings back and forth in ever-increasing arcs until it comes to rest mouth up, balanced against its "stay," a wooden bar at the top of the circle.

There are no carillons here, with their melodies tapped out by a carillonneur's hammer on a set of fixed, unmoving bells. British bells are free—free to swing a great circle, from the up position round to the other side, then back again, with the clapper striking once on each downswing. Each bell is a giant pendulum that has to be controlled by a ringer, its live weight—anywhere from 150 pounds for the smallest treble bell to three or four tons for the giant tenor—falling, rising, pausing, falling, rising, pausing. You can't see the bell—it is way above you in the louvered bell chamber. You have to control it by feel, by the counterweight of your own body, by the sensation you transmit to it and it transmits to you through the bell rope. A bell badly handled could swing wildly and break its stay, in a havoc of splintered wood. The rope could whip up or down and catch you and drag you up to the ceiling, knocking you out. Even when under control, the rope snakes up into the tower like a live thing. You have to work with its momentum, find the way to exert enough force to make the bell pause the length of time you want, and then fall again, in great arcs.

All of this takes years to learn. To make a bell ring is one thing, but to be able to control exactly when it sounds requires skill, strength, and good rhythm. Just to make a set of six to twelve bells ring a single downward scale with no clashes and equal gaps of a fifth of a second between each note requires exquisite timing and expertise. You need to be able to speed up or slow down as necessary, shortening the swing or holding the bell at balance.

My bell is number three, fairly light. Each bell has its own weight and character, and all but the most experienced ringers ring the same bell each time. It is like handling a horse. It takes about a year of practicing for several hours a week before you are allowed to ring on Sundays by yourself without anyone standing by. There is the conscious heave of effort with the shoulders and arms as you pull on the sally with both hands to set the bell in motion. The slap of the rope on the wooden floor as the bell swings down. The strain of reining it in exactly where you want it with your arms above your head as it reaches its peak, sensing when the bell will sound in your own body, wincing if you get the timing wrong, and it clashes with someone else's, pulling it back down, braking it gradually as the sally comes up to waist height. The faces, the presences, the dry texture of the rope, the novice's fear, the concentration, the old-timers' calm. The dim interior, smelling of vanished centuries. My back is to the door. A stone bench is recessed into the wall behind me. Faces in a dream, a ritual, a practice both commonplace and arcane. The sound of the distant organ preludes coming up through your feet before the services.

Mr. Whitehead calls the order of the bells. We always begin and end with plain "Rounds" (12345678). Then comes the familiar "Queens" (13572468), and the weirder "Tittums" (15263748). Then there is "change ringing," in which the head ringer changes the order of the bells by calling out individual permutations. If he calls "two to three," bells two and three switch place in the scale, so that two follows three and 1234 becomes 1324. "Treble to three" means that one follows three, so that 1234 becomes 2314.

For special occasions like weddings or jubilees, and for holy days like Candlemas, Ash Wednesday, and Whitsun, we do something special: a "peal," which involves following a "method." The methods have esoteric names like "Plain Bob Minor" and "Grandsire Doubles." In a method, the changes are not called out individually: each ringer studies and memorizes an algorithm, the pattern that his bell follows to advance toward the beginning of the line and go to the back. The bells weave in and out like the English country dance called "Strip the Willow." A quarter peal lasts forty-five minutes, and a full peal lasts three hours, during which time no bell ever strikes in the same consecutive order, ringing thousands upon thousands of changes.

Five minutes before the service, the bells are "rung down," so that their wide mouths and clappers are safely hanging downward. Then number four is chimed as a warning to latecomers. Its rope goes all the way down into the nave of the church where it is pulled three times by the altar boy during Holy Communion when the host is being raised. Out in the fields, you can hear the three strokes of the Sanctus bell and know. For funerals, we put felt hats on the clappers and ring the bells muffled. They speak dimly then, as if underwater.

My ten years of bell ringing precede and include my years of teenage love, of anorexia and clinical depression, of losing my virginity and my faith. The bells woke me every day and kept vigil in the long nights of my illness when I lay unable to sink into sleep. The bell chamber became a refuge where I could sink into rhythm and concentration and briefly escape the obsessions that tortured me. Not one of the ringers commented on the mass of Band-Aids occasionally visible under my long sleeves, where I had sliced my forearms with a razor. They kept mercifully mum as I became thinner and thinner, eventually losing half my weight; they did not know when I was dizzy and weak from vomiting, nor when my depression was so deep that I could barely speak. There, I didn't have to speak. All I had to do was show up, hang onto my rope, and sound my bell on time. Ringing anchored me physically, acting as a literal lifeline to a community of music making and faith at a time of radical isolation and silence in my life. I was one note in a communal instrument speaking to the town.

In my late teens, the gaps between reason and Christian dogma became too wide and too numerous for me to bridge any longer. Struggling to forge a healthier relationship to my own body, I couldn't accept what I saw as the denial of the human body in the Virgin birth, the magical resurrection of the dead, and the fact that torture and human sacrifice were supposed to redeem us. In this time of growing alienation, it was the bells, and music, that kept me coming to church. My routine of Friday night practices, Sunday morning and evening ringing, and studying for peals became an essential part of the fabric of my life, something that grounded me, gave me a sense of belonging to something larger than myself, something that was at once part of ancient tradition and the everyday life of Ellesmere.

On Ascension Day, forty days after Easter, the bell ringers and the vicar and the church wardens and choristers climb the spiral stairs beyond the ringing chamber, past the bells and up onto the tower itself, and we sing hymns looking out over the village, the Shropshire countryside, the mere, the old-people's home, the Tudor coaching inn and the Georgian houses and the eighteenth-century canal. "Of the Father's love begotten, ere the worlds began to be. . . ." Beneath us lie the Saxon preaching cross; the crusader's sandal and the vial of earth from the Holy Land in a glass reliquary; the rood screen; the Queen of Heaven with baby Jesus on one arm and the orb in her left hand; the Scrivener with his inkhorn and little dog; and the alabaster effigies of Lord and Lady Kynaston, lying side by side on their tomb, hacked at by Oliver Cromwell's troops during the Civil War in the seventeenth century, with the little statues of their seven children kneeling mutilated round them.

"All glory, laud and honor, to thee, redeemer, king . . . ," we sing to the landed gentry, the Jebbs and the Cholmondeleys and the Mainwarings; to the pinched children on the council-house estate, to the laborers drinking Wem Ales and smoking Woodbines in the Bridgewater Arms, the Red Lion, the Black Lion, the Sun, the Swan, and the White Hart; to the mothers cooking Sunday roasts; to the lines of washing in the gardens; to the Welsh hills rising green and vertiginous twelve miles away, with their lambs and their slag heaps; to the primary school with its silver-haired headmaster; to the raw teenagers at the Secondary Modern; to the well-heeled boys at Ellesmere College, where my father works; to the three ruddy butchers in their striped canvas aprons, in their separate shops, wiping their large hands among the carcasses and strings of sausages; to the ladies in the market on Tuesdays with their blocks of crumbly Cheshire cheese, their muddy potatoes and lettuces and leeks, their Cox's Orange Pippins in brown paper bags; to the greengroceries, where tulips and daffodils and freesias stand in buckets, and avocados are beginning to make their exotic appearance.

"Jesus shall reign where'er the sun doth his successive journeys run . . . ," we sing to the sleepy, tea-colored canal meandering toward Llangollen and to the dour fishermen on its banks with their umbrellas and Wellington boots; to cattle standing hock-deep in mire around five-barred gates; to stiles and sheep; to the Working Men's Club; to the red Royal Mail postboxes bearing the embossed crown and the letters *EIIR*; to bluebells in the coppices; to the newsagents with their dirty magazines on the top shelf and the *Shropshire Star* and jars of gobstoppers,

310

Pear Drops, and Liquorice Allsorts; to the greasy fish-and-chip shop; to the Indian takeout and its poppadoms; to the furniture-stripping shop and the opticians and the ironmongers and the dairy; to the dusty ladies' clothing store and the haberdashers; to the youths lounging on the steps of the Old Town Hall, fags drooping from their lips, who eye me up and down with furtive hostility and whistle like wolves; to the watch mender and the jeweler; to Rowlands, the chemists with the peroxide blonde lady whose skin is orange from tanning booths and whose made-up eyes are hard; to the postcards at Fred Roberts that say, "Welcome to Ellesmere."

"Crown him with many crowns, the Lamb upon His throne. . . . ," we sing to the bank clerks at Lloyds and Natwest; to the two policemen living at the station where I watch Princess Anne's wedding with my friend; to the New Town Hall and the roundabout; to the deep, secret ruts of Love Lane and Sandy Lane; to the farms with their sheepdogs; to the smell of coal fires burning in the grates of all the houses; to the uprooted train tracks, reverting back to field; to the Canada geese by the mere who have eaten all the grass; to the herons in the heronry; to the grimy old lorries thundering through the village on the main road to Shrewsbury under the walls of the church; to the castle whose motte is now a bowling green; to the garage on the corner that sells petrol and Walker's Salt 'n Vinegar crisps and Cadbury's chocolate bars; to the Convent of the Poor Clares, silent by the canal, with its vegetable garden and its invisible cloistered nuns; to the Methodists in their chapel down on Scotland Street; to the Cottage Hospital and the doctor's surgery; to the war memorial with its withered wreaths of poppies. "His the sceptre, His the throne . . ."

On Sunday evenings, after we finish ringing, I slip into Evensong at the back of the shadowy church, just as the vicar is intoning "O Lord, open thou our lips." I know the service by heart, so as I am walking into a pew, I join the first response: "And our mouth shall shew forth thy praise." I find the service comforting, especially the beautiful collects: "Lighten our darkness, we beseech thee O Lord; and by thy great mercy defend us from all perils and dangers of this night." I can still recite the collect toward the end, with its plea for "rest and quietness": "O God, from whom all holy desires, all good counsels, and all just works do proceed: Give unto thy servants that peace which the world cannot give; that both our hearts may be set to obey thy commandments, and also that by thee we being defended from the fear of our enemies may pass our time in rest and quietness." The *Nunc dimittis*, Simeon's words at the center of the service, also reenacts the granting of peace after a lifetime's wait: "Lord, now lettest thou thy servant depart in peace, according to thy word." I always imagined the old man's amazement, recognizing the six-week-old Jesus in the Temple as the Messiah; his tears of sudden joy, gratitude, and relief. The words transmit a sense of release, consolation, and safety that I take with me into my week.

Evensong ends with one of my favorite hymns:

> The day thou gavest, Lord, has ended
> The darkness falls at thy behest.
> To thee our morning hymns ascended;
> Thy praise shall sanctify our rest.

Afterward, the ringers and I walk out of the church, through the cemetery, and push open the heavy iron gate with its black bars and gold rosette. We cross the cobblestone alley, they to their cars and me to go up the gravel driveway of St. Mary's Cottage: home. The last thing I hear before falling asleep will be the sound of the bell in the tower, striking the hour: a link to the church's ongoing presence as I slip between worlds.

Nominated by Alice Mattison and Gettysburg Review

SONG FOR
PICKING UP

by TONY HOAGLAND

from THE SUN

Every time that something falls
someone is consigned to pick it up.

Every time it drops and rolls into a crack,
blows out the window of the car

or down onto the dirty restaurant floor
— a plastic bag, a paper clip, a cube of cheese
                                    from the buffet —

there somebody goes, down upon
                                    their hands and knees.
What age are you when you learn that?

After Dante finished the *Inferno*, someone
cleaned up all the ink and crumpled paper.

After the surgeons are done with the operating room,
someone makes it spic-and-span again.

After World War I, the Super Bowl,
a night at the ballet;

after the marching feet of all humanity
come the brooms and mops, the garbagemen

and moms, the janitors.
One day you notice them.

After that, then, no more easy litter. No more towels
on the hotel bathroom floor. You bend over

for even tiny bits of paper,
or, bitterly, you look back at your life—like Cain

upon the body of his brother.

Nominated by Marianne Boruch, Joan Murray, Charles Harper Webb

MEZZO

fiction by KATE PETERSEN

from THE KENYON REVIEW

Though it had been four years since she'd seen him, (since she'd been passed over), and they were predicting more snow for Boston, it was the right year to have lunch, so Martha took the commuter rail in from Worcester to meet her old teacher, Fred Holleman.

"We'll have lunch every year that has an extra day in it," he'd said at her last lesson before graduation. "It's extra so that old friends find time to have lunch."

It was his way of speaking—imaginary, in a way—but Martha believed in it, had ever since her fourth lesson ten years ago, when she was fifteen, her voice airy and breaking across the important phrases of the soprano audition piece. "Know this?" he'd said in the middle of the Italian aria, and began to play the low opening bars to "Send in the Clowns." Martha did, and sang. "It's rich," he'd said, stopping her after a verse, "that no one took you for a mezzo. But there it is, Day. You're home in B flat." And he'd let her sing on, to know it.

In the years since college, Martha had kept in touch, sending a note about a concert she'd gone to, a link to her thesis piece being performed by the Conservatory Chorale. Fred wrote back each time—small, well-worded encouragements, how it was nice to hear from her—and did again when she wrote in that certain October. He would be in Massachusetts at Christmastime, Cambridge, performing in a Vaughan Williams concert, and this was great timing re: lunch. Could she get to Cambridge?

Martha called the day before to confirm. They were to meet at noon in the lobby of the Charles Hotel in Harvard Square.

315

The snow started early Saturday morning. It broke Martha's sleep, ticking at the window, the first flakes green in the light from her clock radio. Martha took a train that left her an extra two hours, and the trip was slow, the conductor stopping several times on the tracks between stations. She arrived at the hotel twenty minutes early. Inside, the lobby was warm, ringing. Martha shook off the snow, then settled in a wing-backed chair to wait, bookbag leaned against her knee. A Christmas tree a story high stood in the corner, its boughs strung with amber and white lights and tied with little tourniquets of snowdrops.

"Martha, they weren't kidding," Fred said, as he stepped off the elevator. He hugged her. "So you made it. I was about to call you to give you an out."

"I made it," she said, hoping that was the right answer. Martha made things. She called people who said to call, and when she was asked for her number, which wasn't often, she gave it, the real one. It was a sort of hope, she supposed, and let her down as hopes did. Not this time, though. At Natick she put her finger in her book and just watched the snow coming down the rest of the way, imagining what they'd eat, wondering how different she looked since the last time he saw her.

Martha had thick pale lashes that made her eyes look lighter than they were, drowsy. *Pony lashes*, her mother had called them when she was a girl. Her mouth fit like a clasp and was as small as the rest of her; she could only play a ninth. She wore her hair cut below the shoulder, in plaits. It had been yellow-white when she was younger, but now the light in it was weak like autumn and gathered at the ends.

The tree lights cheered her. She'd give him the song score today. As they passed through the lobby to the restaurant at the west end, Martha thought about what she'd say. *Here.* Or just: *I wrote something and*—A woman in sweats and curlers was angling a five-foot submarine sandwich into the elevator.

"Prime spot," Fred said when the host left them at their table. "Put your coat here, and sit there." He had a formal overcoat and a small blue scarf, the kind that went around once, and he folded his coat and laid it across Martha's over the back of the chair. Still the standard blazer and white shirt he'd worn to every lesson. Fred's salt-and-pepper hair was now fully gray, white along his temple and collar, but his face looked younger than she'd remembered, wide open. *It's all that city*, she thought.

They sat facing into the dining room. The walls were dark mahogany and above the great hearth the brick was stamped with a faux Veritas.

The bartender was slicing celery on a board at the end of his bar, the knife ticking like a nail in a tire.

The server brought a little plate with two green onions, two carrot slices, and two radishes, set it down with a ramekin of salt.

"Should we have coffee?" Fred dipped a radish in the salt and put it on his plate.

"Two," Martha said to the server.

"And could I get some cream?" Fred asked. "Well, here we are in the middle of this," he said to Martha. "We should eat like it." He made a show of opening the menu and adjusting it back and forth in front of him, like a British spoof.

There was steak *au poivre*, Caesar salad, and a set of small fancy cheeseburgers. Fred ordered the Reuben, and Martha ordered the grilled cheese and tomato soup.

"That will be good," he said. "So, you're teaching piano now. In—"

"Worcester."

"Which is a few trains from here, I understand." The coffees came.

Martha took her cup. "One train," she said. "Ten students, and four of them who practice."

"Those are good odds!"

"Well, I don't know about odds," she said, "but the money's good enough and it leaves me time to compose." It was true: the cost of living in Worcester was modest enough that she didn't have to teach every day. Martha liked teaching, liked her students and the questions they asked, though lately she'd begun to resent the way it sounded like a different career, and composing only a hobby, some fancy of girlhood that had not quite worked out.

"So the link to that choral piece you sent me," he said. "You wrote that." Martha nodded, her mouth pressed, waiting. "That was a fine setting."

He had declared her, and she unfolded her napkin, shy with it.

Martha had studied voice with Fred through high school and college. He was a soloist with the Baltimore Choral Arts Society and director of choral programs at Loyola. She'd begun as a performance major there but switched to composing after two years of frustrating auditions. After she started in the composing track, Fred would have her bring in the pieces she was working on and they'd sing through them so she could get the baritone color right, or work out a tricky modulation.

"Are you working on something now?" he asked.

317

"A song cycle, art songs." Martha tried an onion. "I've just set the first one."

"Who's the poet?"

"Jaine Timson. 'Park Street,' it's called. I found it when I was here, at the conservatory."

"It sounds perfect. How does it go?" Fred's spoon tinged against the cup.

"Oh," Martha said, taking a radish and twisting it like a stamp on her plate. "I'm not good at recitation." Though she'd been walking around with it in her head for months.—*The world had gone blue, and dark seemed like another country.* And it's for you, she thought. I found that the thing I made was yours.

"Good, that's good," he said. "Never answer that." Fred smiled, looked down the way she remembered him doing when she'd sung a difficult melisma or phrase well.

"The setting's for piano, mezzo, and oboe," she said, as apology. "And you're in New York now?"

A light question that stung to ask. Each member of the Loyola music faculty could nominate one senior to compete for a graduate composing fellowship at Julliard, and Fred had nominated Britte Haines. Martha had heard it from others, but she wanted to have him say so. So she'd asked him at her weekly lesson, held onto the music stand when she did. "Day," he'd said, not turning from the piano. "What can I say but it's a dumb world that has an old teacher pick among bright unrelenting musicians, and it's a dumb teacher that falls for it." Part of her had wanted him to say he was sorry, and part of her was grateful he never had. And now, she'd read, he'd taken a job at the New School.

"Yes," he said now, shaking his head. "That city. I have this little apartment with one of those petite Manhattan fridges and my piano fits in a nook on the first floor, so I keep it there because I know the four people in the building—all upstanding—and upstairs I have a desk where the piano should be. And when I sit down to pay a bill, I look out over this little pocket of a park."

"The one with the pigeons?"

"That's the one."

"It sounds lovely," she said. Where the piano should be. She pressed her napkin into her legs, played two minor triads.

"It is just this side of lovely," he said, "but it's enough."

Strange to picture him living in a little walk-up like a student. Maybe it was penance after the separation.

The food came. Outside, two men were struggling under the hood of a van stalled in the deepening street.

"Here," Fred said, turning his plate so the chips were near her, "have one of these. I had eighty last night. They are so good."

"Salt and vinegar," she said, having two. "Are you doing the *Hodie* tonight?"

Martha was skipping the close questions. She had heard through another former student that Fred's oldest daughter had been killed in a car accident two years ago. He and his wife had separated soon after, which they said was common. Martha had met the daughter only once, but she knew they were about the same age.

"The *Hodie*, yes, and the O'Sullivan poems. If anyone gets to the church."

"Oh, New Englanders are tough," she said. "I'm here."

"You are," he said.

Why was she bragging? "I just mean, people will come. Those songs are real candles." Martha had heard them performed once in Baltimore, a cappella settings for solo baritone, thin and haunting. She dipped her sandwich in the hot soup.

"There was someone here for you at New England, right?" Fred asked. "Did you get married?"

The question caught Martha off. "Not married," she said, "but close." She wondered if that was true. "Or, we had a kitchen."

Sam. They'd had two wall calendars stacked, like a joke, and a little stovetop espresso maker. A shallow bowl of salt Sam called the Salt Canoe.

Fred held his sandwich with both hands and looked at her. "You had a kitchen," he said. "That's all you need to say. And did you play him your songs?"

"Not often." She was not prepared for this.

"Oh, see," he said. "Anyone you have a kitchen with should hear your songs."

Once, at a bar near the conservatory, Sam had asked to hear something she'd written, but when she demurred, out of habit, he'd said fine, and then seemed to forget, and had not asked again.

"But now?" Fred said. "Wait, we need more coffee for this." He signaled to the server.

"He was in a car wreck," she said, holding her spoon. "Last year." Martha's mouth cottoned up with the lie. Sam had been in a fender-bender, once, years before she knew him.

Fred brought his hand down to the bridge of his nose, but the server was already on her way with the carafe, so they both held their mugs out.

"Day," he said. "Martha."

Everything in her waited. The dull slap of the door to the kitchen, there, then again. The snow came down.

"Well, look at us," Fred said finally. "A real Lonelyhearts Lunch Bunch."

"I shouldn't have said anything." She smiled, then dropped her head, in case the shame and love did funny things to her face. Her bag rested against her knee and in it, the score.

"No, look. So now you keep your songs close," he said. "You wait with them." He touched her hand, and it belled her, hollowed her out.

"Do you know anyone else coming tonight?"

"Some of the musicians, ones here and there, you know. After this many notes, you know some people."

"But you said lonely." Did he know that she knew about his daughter, his marriage? Martha wanted him to tell her himself—admit how alone he was now. The way she was.

"It's a phrase," he said, signaling for more coffee. "Just a phrase they say."

"Of course," she said. Quick, send in the clowns.

The dining room was filling up. Martha checked the hockey game, a sport she didn't know. Save this thing, Day. "So what are your plans before the concert?"

"Oh, a little rest, and I have a few Christmas errands, if there's time."

"The Timson poem," she said. "It takes place at Christmastime." If she handed him the score after the concert, then she could leave, and he wouldn't have to say anything. But then he would take it back to his studio, or home, wherever that piano was, and play through it. He would think: this is true, and lovely for it. Would think, I have made a mistake.

"You won't try to go home again before the concert, I imagine," Fred said. She shook her head. Fred handed her the squat ketchup bottle. "Here, take this then, for the long afternoon before us."

"I don't need ketchup," she said, waving it off. "I know it's Worcester, but even we have ketchup."

"But these ones," he said, lowering his voice with the plan, "were made especially to fit in the pockets of young musicians. Don't worry. I'll tip for it."

He reached across to the chair with the coats and put it in the pocket of hers. Lunch or the snow had made him suddenly giddy, insistent, and Martha, brave with it, took sugar packets and stuffed them in his coat.

In answer, Fred took a few more sugars from the table and put them in his shirt pocket. The concert ticket he'd brought her was there, and its seriousness stopped him. She had always listened dangerously to him. He could see Martha sliding her train ticket into the slat above the head rest, her book mirrored against the snow. The quiet car. She had ridden in the quiet car to see him, and he had not considered that.

When the waitress came with the check, he asked for a to-go box and waved off Martha when she reached for her purse.

"I have this," he said. "You took several trains to see your old voice teacher."

"One, really."

"Yes, OK. One." He slid a card from his billfold into the check sleeve. Outside the snow was still falling heavily, and the men had left the van half in the white road.

The server returned with the sandwich and fries in a small paper bag.

"Do you need a hat?" Martha said. She didn't have an extra hat. It was the space she worked from so often, between offering something and having it to give.

"No, I have one in the room," he said. "It looks like a popover, but it works all right."

In the lobby, a group of women huddled near the fire. They wore peep-toe shoes and black dresses with little pearl accents. One was crying, and the others were trying to console her. Fred took Martha's coat sleeve.

"It's OK," one said. "Shayna said they have a back-up photographer." The woman gulped and blotted her face with the heel of her hand. Martha could see the glitter in their hair.

Fred moved toward the elevator, out of earshot. "Today's lesson." He took her coat sleeve for just a second. "Everyone should have back-up everything." He was telling her a secret now. This, the whole day, a confidence between them. "Back-up photographer, back-up bridegroom—"

"Back-up singers," Martha said.

"Back-up hearts." Fred was looking past Martha at the bridesmaids, so she couldn't read how much he meant it. Martha meant most everything, and that Fred probably knew that made her sad again, as if she were already on the train back with her one earnest heart, back to her earnest apartment on Avalon Place and the two earnest water glasses in the sink there, waiting.

"Here's your ticket," he said, handing it to her along with one sugar and one Splenda. "I'm going to go over early. But the kid at the desk said it's just a five-minute walk from here. I'm not sure he was counting this." He nodded out the window. The skating rink in front of the hotel was mounded over, a foot and a half at least, by the looks of it.

"I know where it is," she said, "it's not far. So break a leg." The old stage tradition sounded foolish to her, but she still found herself saying it. "I'll look for you after?"

"Yes, Martha. Do that," he said, and boarded the elevator.

The lobby was set for holiday tea and based on the dresses, it seemed that at least three wedding parties were coming in and out, so Martha took a seat out of the way, in the window of the darkened hotel bar. She took out her score again. The light from the snow blued the pages.

Park Street

When I came up from the train and into the park
when I saw the inns and churches, their upturned faces,
their doors and panes tinsel-browed, waiting
the world had gone blue, and dark seemed like another country.

A blue night is like a blue note:
not quite there, but close enough
the way I was almost inside those lobbies then, those
thick-lit rooms of people. Instead I stood, happily
shivering between
young beech trees not old enough
to hold the snow up off the ground
and I was not old enough for something else
but what was it?
and who
who, on this dark Christmas eve, would stop to tell me?

Martha was glad she hadn't said it earlier. She liked the words with the melody, the triplet pattern in the accompaniment she'd written to evoke the revolving hotel doors, but on the page she worried the poem was too broad with its wishes. She found her pencil and traced back over the dedication at the top of the score: *For Fred Holleman.*

By the time Fred called at two o'clock to say the concert had been cancelled because of the weather, the MBTA had stopped train service. Martha knew people in Boston from her time at the conservatory whom she could stay with, but the snow was coming faster now, and she couldn't see to the other side of the square. No one would be driving in this.

She left her coat and went to the desk. They'd pulled the plows twenty minutes ago, the concierge said. Nothing would be on the roads again till ten the next morning. Rooms were expensive, more than she made in a week, but it was a blizzard. Martha fished out her credit card and asked for a toothbrush and paste. She had nothing to take to her room, so instead she went back to her place in the bar and read.

The evening bartender came in around four and turned the lights on. Martha got up. "Oh, no—you can stay," the woman said, and set down the case of beer she was carrying.

"I was trying not to get roped into being a flower girl understudy," Martha said.

"I know," the woman said. "They've kept rooms aside for staff, I guess we'll have to stay here tonight. My daughter's at a sleepover, luckily. I've never seen snow like this."

A man came in and leaned on the bar.

"New bouncer, Tiffin?" he said, looking toward Martha. "I like the book thing. Harvard folks will love that shit."

"Something like that, Win," Tiffin said, and set a RESERVED plaque and a Newcastle down in front of him. He looked like he was in his late thirties. He wore a fine zip-front sweater and a good watch, and spoke at boardroom volume.

Martha kept reading, and when her book was done, she ordered a glass of house red and picked at the beer nuts the bartender set in front of her.

"I'll buy our bouncer this one," Win said, picked up his plaque and moved down toward Martha. Martha said that was OK, she would get it. He said she should call him Win, and he nearly lived in this hotel, and anyway, it was a fucking PBS blizzard. Let him pick this one up.

So Martha did, listened as he told them about the day's wedding disasters he'd overheard: one bride and groom stuck in a church with no pastor, a van of in-laws in a ditch somewhere near Medford. "Plus," he said, "everyone has the wrong shoes." They talked about the president's Chicago problem and debated who the best fake doctor was on cable news.

Win was a crisis management consultant, based in Chicago, but his main client was a pharmaceutical company that kept him in the Charles about four months out of the year. "So Tiffin lets me guest bartend sometimes, keep the customers happy," he said, pulling the label off his beer bottle and smoothing it down in front of Martha's glass. "Right, Tiff?" Martha couldn't read the bartender's smile.

Fred came in from outside, wearing his popover hat. "You're still here, Day," he said, walking into the bar. He had shopping bags and wore new snow boots.

"Everything's stopped," Martha said. "I had to get a room." Win got up and went across to talk to someone he seemed to know, leaving his sign.

"A room here?" Fred said, looking toward the lobby. "Must be nice to be rich."

Martha felt her lips part, stunned open. "Is it ever," she said finally, "if by rich you mean has a credit card and a cold cheese sandwich." She held up the bag with her leftovers in it.

"I'm joking," he said.

"I am, too."

He stepped up to the bar, next to her. She could smell the snow on him. "I'm sorry about the concert, you coming all this way for, what are these?"—he picked a cashew from the bowl and held it up to the light—"beer nuts." He placed it back on the bar, away from the bowl.

Isn't it rich? My fault, I fear . . . Maybe he'd meant it that way. Those early lessons, the songs by Quilter and Godard, the way she'd seemed to improve each week. Sometimes that first year, Fred would put a hand an inch or so away from her lower back to remind her where to engage the breath. "OK, right here—" he'd say before a high phrase, "breathe all the way to my hand." And she'd dug in.

"If you want to have a drink later," Martha said. "I've got a tab, of course." How far she still reached to absolve him.

Fred laughed. "Yes, good. Perhaps." He pushed back a sleeve and looked at his watch. "Why don't you call me at what, seven?" He looked at the RESERVED sign, pointed and smiled, then went to the elevator in his very thin scarf and funny hat.

Martha left the bar after the glass of wine and went to her room. She opened the TV cabinet. There was a wine key, three remotes, two water bottles wearing paper aprons that said ENJOY FOUR DOLLARS, and a row of old-timey jars filled with fruits and nuts. She took all three remotes back to the bed and flipped through bad movies.

324

At seven she looked outside. Fully dark and the snow had finally let up. She wondered where Sam was right then, wished suddenly that they were talking still, just talking, so she could tell him the one about the time she killed off an ex in lunchtime conversation. It was the kind of thing Sam would have found funny, made her laugh at herself about. Martha typed the first letters of Fred's name into her phone. Send.

"Hi, Fred," she said when he answered.

"Martha. Hi."

"Up for any more snow-camp?" She stood looking in the full-length mirror as she talked.

"That's good," he laughed. "Snow-camp." There was a pause, and she pursed her lips in the mirror, having known. "Oh you know, it is so rare to have a night and a book and nowhere to be."

"Yes, but this isn't nowhere. I came here." Nowhere to be was not rare, she wanted to say. For you, maybe.

"I should have given you that out," he said.

"OK. Well, have a good night, I guess. Sorry to have bothered you." She held the phone away from her, counted a silent beat, and tried not to hear his tinny goodnight as she hung up.

Martha put the phone down and looked at the sandwich bag on the desk, then back at the mirror. She was wearing a secondhand sweater that made her neck look long and trousers that went under her snow boots. For as much as she'd thought about this meeting, she was dressed as if she'd forgotten that she'd ever have to take off her coat. Certainly underdressed for dinner at the Charles by herself. Still, she was hungry, would have liked to be shored up by the noise of those wedding parties again, the various meltdowns and couplings.—*Those thick-lit rooms of people.*

But she couldn't bear seeing Fred down there after all—alone, or with someone else. Didn't need more proof of being passed over, or to risk outing his rough loneliness a second time that day. So she turned on the TV, took out her sandwich. Reaching for her coat on the other bed, she found the ketchup bottle and dabbed some into one of the Styrofoam compartments. There was half of a romantic comedy left that had a snowglobe in it, but that was the only thing that was the same at all.

The sky was predawn green when Martha woke in the Charles the next morning, clothes on, the TV droning its carousel of Boston attractions.

A wasted night in good sheets. She undressed and put her clothes on a chair, turned the TV off by hand. Pulled the curtains back. She hadn't even wondered what floor Fred was on, but now she did. Maybe he would set up the little coffeemaker and shave while it worked, without music. Maybe read the newspaper as he drank his first cup, sitting on the side of the bed, his shirt starched and hung on the closet door. Or over the chair. She grew wet. Her room faced east toward Boston, and she could see the river between, stilled beneath its pelt of snow, the light from the bridges just reaching. The carillons of Harvard Yard stood up from the snow like lighthouses. Across the river street, in a fir tree next to Kirkland House, a garland of crimson dress ties had been knotted together and tucked in the branches on the side nearest the widow's walk. "Oh, you old world," she said, the heat leaving as quickly as it'd come. She heard the bill scrape under the door. "What now?"

She'd slept too long to go back to bed, so she showered and put her clothes back on, dried her hair and brushed her teeth. She put the courtesy toothbrush back in its cellophane sleeve and tucked it into the pocket of her book bag with the pens and those matchbooks she'd nicked from No. 9 Park that time with Karen and forgotten to use. The face soap smelled nice, not like anything, but nice. She did not have weekend piano students, or pets. No one else knew she was here and not in her own bed, and that fact, a thin towel pressed to her face, made a certain life.

It was 10:30 when she got downstairs. The plows were just going out, the clerk said when she returned the key, and the trains would start again at 12. Martha checked the schedule in her purse. The next left from South Station at 1:16, and she would need to leave by 12 to get there with the Sunday schedule and the snow.

She sat near the tree, facing away from the elevator, and opened the newspaper left by her door.

"Hey, there's our librarian." Win sat down next to her and tapped her newspaper. "How did the book turn out?" he said.

"Oh, you know," Martha said, "spoiler alerts. Can't say."

"What are you doing now?" he asked. She said the trains would go soon.

"Because they have a world-ending brunch here." She could smell his cologne. "As in seriously there is no reason the apocalypse can't happen, once you've had these eggs Benedict."

"I'm all right," she said. "Thanks, but I have to leave for my train in an hour."

"Tell you what. Have brunch with me and I'll drive you to the train," he said. "I'm in the garage."

"Oh, it's OK."

"So you're just going to sit here reading about—" he squinted at the front page, "the Korean state visit till noon? Come on."

"Well, I'll get coffee," she said, looking around for Fred.

The host in the breakfast room seated them in a corner and handed them menus.

Win opened and closed his menu like applause. "Cape Codder," he said. "Crab cakes, bacon, eggs. But you should still have the Benedict."

Martha read the menu. It seemed late in the day, though nothing had happened.

"So you missed a night there," he said. "Tiffin and Joe from the hotel and I went over to the TenBar, and man, this woman from the purple wedding was on my lap the minute I sat down. Just, boom."

"Aren't you married?" Martha asked, trying not to look at his wedding band.

"I am," Win said. "Me and my wife both."

"I don't know what that means." The coffee didn't taste as good as she had remembered.

"We have an understanding," Win said, leaning back in his chair. "I travel. She travels." He was probably trained in such square-eye contact, Martha thought. "Enough about me. What's the story with you and the fellow in the hat?"

"The hat?"

"You know," Win said, and puffed out his cheeks and made a motion over his head. Martha giggled. The popover hat.

"Oh, him."

"Oh, him is right. You two have your nightcap?"

"No," Martha said. "I shouldn't have even asked, I guess. I took voice lessons from him, a long time ago."

"Whoa, whoa, whoa," Win said. "You're telling me that he's not just the second down this morning? An old student looks like you stuck in the Charles, and he not only has you get your own room, but won't take you up on a nightcap? What did you say to him?"

Martha almost told him: the lie, how it came, quick and unrepeatable, how Fred touched her hand after, sealing it. And how Sam had kissed her the last morning, then unpinned one of the calendars from the wall, leaving the other like a punch line told first, small and ruinous. "Well, he doesn't owe me anything," she said finally.

"Right, that's exactly what I ask myself on some occasions," Win said. "I say: Win, what do I owe this woman? Exactly zero. Everything here out"—he winked—"is a courtesy. I didn't do anything last night because this chick at TenBar was three in and maybe I wasn't the first that night, you know?" he said. "Besides, she wasn't married. I'm trying to stick with marrieds." He dropped three sugar cubes into his coffee.

"Marrieds?" The server came, a different one from yesterday, and they ordered. For some reason, Martha ordered food, the Benedict.

"Yah," Win said. "A, they're clean. B, they aren't going to call you in the middle of the night when you're home. C, they aren't going to call you. It's like getting glasses," he went on, "when you realize how many married women there are out there who want to find another bed, preferably one belonging to someone on the next flight to Chicago."

Fred came in. Martha folded at her napkin, which suddenly didn't seem made for a lap. Hers, anyway. He stopped at the host stand and looked over, waved, then took a newspaper from the rack and waited. She waved, too, and bumped her coffee, sloshing it on the tablecloth.

"You married?" Win said.

Martha shook her head. Her tongue felt big.

"Joking," he said, reaching across for her left hand, but she pulled it away.

"Oh."

"Half the women in this room would give me a key if they knew I was married," he said. "Two-thirds of the marrieds."

"You don't know that," Martha said, but it sounded like a question. She wondered if Fred was watching, but she couldn't look.

The plates came.

"Your friend knows this," Win said. "He knows what I am saying. What's his name?" He looked over toward Fred. "He knows. There are odds."

"He doesn't know those odds," Martha said, picking up her fork, putting it down. "Those are yours." *Widower*, her heart said.

It looked like something it was not; still, it looked like it. And how could she tell Fred otherwise? Say: This is not what I did when we hung up last night. What I did was fall asleep with my clothes on at ten and my train doesn't leave till twelve and what I wanted was just coffee, but even this is a mistake, these apocalyptic eggs. This man doesn't even take off his ring in other bedrooms and my Sam is gone, but not like that. There are ties in the Harvard trees, and your daughter is dead. I wrote you a song. There were nine things Martha could not say, but they filled her throat and kept her from eating.

"Look, this is brunch," Win said, "not honor court. Do I probably do this because I was not told early and often that my dick was of sufficient length and girth? Or because I married a woman who is also traveling half the year and can't go twice a day, at least with me? These are not bad hypotheses. All I am saying is I can tell pretty fast if there is a chance, and I have learned to do that while keeping my investment pretty low." He took a bite, set the fork down in the same place on his plate each time.

He is practiced, Martha thought. He belongs to himself.

"You know, if we have brunch and I'm giving you a ride to the train and that's all, fine. Gold, silver, fine. But say we're talking and it's going and then, hey, there's a three-o'clock train and you've still got the room till two. Then, see, I'm happy to oblige." He sawed into the second English muffin with his fork.

"Stop," Martha said. "Just stop." The snow had turned things lopsided, wrong. Her throat felt very small. "There were no chances here. I need to go." Fred probably couldn't hear them from where he was because the morning show was on, but maybe he could.

"OK, look," Win said. "Cool down. Just eat." He held up his hands. "Soapbox dismount."

"I need to go," Martha said again. She counted cash for her meal; she was two dollars short but figured he'd expense it anyway. There was not enough time for her to walk to the red line, and there were probably delays, but the day was lost, and she needed air.

She crossed the room. "Well, funny meeting you here," Fred said, setting his paper aside. His voice seemed quieter this morning.

"They didn't let you order the chips again?" she said.

"They said these were close," he said, nodding at his pancakes. "Same shape, anyway." He had not motioned her over, and Martha couldn't think what to do with her hands.

"Well, the trains are running again," she said, and looked at her watch, which seemed about to stop. "There's this tree, though. I think it's Kirkland House?" she pointed, though you couldn't see it from there. "You should go past, I mean, if you have time before your flight. To look at it."

Fred didn't say anything right away. Looked at her hands as if he, too, could tell they were lost. "All right, a tree," he said. "Well, we'll consult our calendars here again soon, Martha. Go get your train."

"Good-bye," she said and left, keeping her eyes down, though Win was gone.

Outside, she put her gloves on and wound her scarf around her mouth. The cold felt good, made tears in her eyes. The paths weren't shoveled yet so Martha walked toward the train station in the newly plowed streets. Only mounds of buried cars and newspaper boxes suggested where the sidewalk was. She checked the time on her phone but a missed call appeared. It was Fred, from 5:00 that morning.

With the snow, she could not hear Win's car until it was almost upon her. He leaned over and opened the passenger door. Martha kept walking, though she hadn't worn heavy enough socks and her toes hurt. He drove alongside her, saying something about her train or sorry, but all she could hear was the ajar doorbell ballad—*Don't Leave, Don't Leave*—one of those odd little songs that's pretty only to those who have sung it before.

Nominated by Idris Anderson, Sarah Frisch, Jill McDonough and The Kenyon Review

THE SOLDIER
OF MICTLÁN

by RIGOBERTO GONZALEZ

from FOUR WAY BOOKS

Once upon a time there was a soldier
who marched to Mictlán in his soldier
boots and every step was a soldier
step and every breath was a soldier
word. Do you know what this soldier
said? I'd like a piece of bread for my soldier
hand. I'd like a slice of cheese for my soldier
nose. And I'd like a woman for my soldier
heart. The mayor of Mictlán saluted the soldier
and bowed his head as he told the soldier:
We have no bread, oh honorable soldier,
we hold empty hands instead. Dear soldier,
let us take yours if we may. And the soldier
held out his hand to be taken. Oh brave soldier,
said the mayor, cheese is your soldier
wish, but we have none since the other soldier
left. We whiff empty hands instead. The soldier
let the mayor sniff the scent of his soldier
palm. And forgive us, oh strong soldier,
said the mayor, but no woman worthy of soldier
warmth lives in our empty town. Will your soldier
eyes teach us wonder and kindness and soldier
love instead? Silence stiffened the soldier
face as a search ensued in the soldier
head for a moment one moment of soldier

bliss. But all was dead. The longer the soldier
looked the more the streets of his soldier
mind resembled the streets that his soldier
feet had taken him to: where no lost soldier
finds bread or cheese or a woman to be a soldier
wife. This was no space for a soldier
life indeed. So off to the hills the soldier
fled to seek out the place where a soldier
sheds the rattle that beckons the soldier
to death to soldier to death to soldier.

Nominated by Mark Irwin

TRAIN TO HARBIN

fiction by ASAKO SERIZAWA

from THE HUDSON REVIEW

I once met a man on the train to Harbin. He was my age, just past his prime, hair starting to grease and thin in a way one might have thought passably distinguished in another context, in another era, when he might have settled down, reconciled to finishing out his long career predictably. But it was 1939. War had officially broken out between China and Japan, and like all of us on that train, he too had chosen to take the bait, that one last bite before acquiescing to life's steady decline. You see, for us university doctors, it was a once-in-a-lifetime opportunity. We all knew it. Especially back then.

Two nights and three days from Wonsan to Harbin the train clattered on, the lush greenery interrupted by trucks and depots manned by soldiers in military khaki. Despite the inspections and unexplained transfers, this man I shall call S remained impassive, shadowed by a dusky light that had nothing to do with the time of day or the dimness of the car's interior; he sat leaning against the window, face set, impervious to the din around him. Later, I would come to recognize this as a posture of self-recrimination, but at the time I had barely recovered from our initial journey by sea, and I was in a contemplative mood myself, in no condition to pause over the state of others, much less engage with my colleagues, who by now had begun drinking in earnest, liquor still being plentiful then, loosening even the most reticent of tongues. So I excused myself and must have promptly nodded off, for the next moment it was dawn, the day just beginning to break, the long length of the train still shrouded in sleep. I was the only one awake, the only one woken by the sudden cessation of rhythm, which drew me to the window, still dark except for my reflection superimposed on it.

We had apparently stopped for cargo, the faint scuffling I could hear revealing a truck ringed by soldiers, their outlines barely visible against the paling horizon. Later, I would learn the significance of this stop, but for the moment the indistinct scene strained my eyes, and I pulled back, hoping to rest for another hour.

Forty years later, this scene returns to me with a visceral crispness that seems almost specious, when so much else has faded or disappeared. Perhaps it is simply the mind, which, in its inability to accept a fact, returns to it, sharpening the details, resolving the image, searching for an explanation that the mind, with its slippery grasp on causality, will never be able to find. Most days I am spared by the habits of routine. But when the air darkens like this, turning the windows inwards, truncating the afternoon, the present recedes, its thin hold on consciousness no match for the eighty-two years that have already claimed it. If hindsight were more amenable, I might long ago have been granted the belated clarity that might have illuminated the exact steps that led me into the fog of my actions. But hindsight has not offered me this view; my options and choices are as elusive now as they had been then. After all, it was war. An inexcusable logic, but also a fact. We adapted to the reality over which we felt we had no control.

For what could we have done? After seven years of embroilment, followed by two years of open war, the conflict with China had begun to tax the everyday, with small signs of oncoming shortages—empty shelves, shuttered windows—beginning to blight the streets, so that even menus at the fanciest restaurants soon resembled the books and newspapers blatantly censored by the Tokko thought police. Then, when officials began making their rounds of sympathetic universities, seeking candidates disposed to patriotic service, our director submitted a list of names, eliciting more visits from other officials, this time escorted by military men. Were we alarmed? Some of us were. But the prospect of a new world-class facility with promises of unlimited resources stoked our ambitions, we, who had long assumed ourselves dormant, choked off by the nepotism that structured our schools and hospitals. If any of us resisted, we did not hear about it. Flattered and courted, we let ourselves be lured, the glitter of high pay and breakthrough advancements all the more seductive in the light of our flickering lives.

So the day we set sail, we were in high spirits, the early sky heavy

334

with mist, the hull of the *Nippon Maru* chopping and cleaving as the sound of rushing water washed away our coastline, leaving us to wend our way through our doubts and worries to arrive in Wonsan, stiff and rumpled, but clear in our convictions. After two turbulent days, we were grateful to be on steady ground, overwhelmed by new smells and sounds, the bustling travelers and hawkers broken up by the young, bright-eyed representative dispatched to meet us. This youth was energetic, if brashly so, and perhaps it was this, along with the sudden physical realization that we were no longer in Japan, that reminded me of my son, but it plunged me into a mood that would last the rest of the trip. Of S I have no recollection at this time, not until a few hours' gap resolves into the memory of that cold window of the stilled train, my eyes pulling back from the soldiers and the truck, their dark outlines replaced by the reflection of my face, above which I caught another face, its eyes watching me.

No doubt it was the hour, and the invasiveness of having been watched, but the shock colored all my subsequent encounters with S, so that even decades later I am left with an ominous impression of a man always watching as the rest of us adapted to our given roles and fulfilled them perfectly. Did we exchange words? I regret that we did not. For by the time I gathered myself, he was gone. Two hours later we pulled into Harbin, our Emperor's celebrated new acquisition.

From Harbin we were to head twenty-six kilometers southeast to Pingfang. But we were granted a few introductory hours in the famed city, and we set about familiarizing ourselves with the cobblestone streets flanked by European shops and cafes still festive with wealthy Russians and a few well-placed Chinese, all of whom politely acknowledged our entourage. If people were wary, they did not show it, and we, for our part, acted the tourist, taking turns deciphering the familiar kanji strung together in unfamiliar ways on signs and advertisements as onion domes and minarets rose beside church steeples and pagoda roofs, obscuring the city's second skyline: the "Chinese" sector of this once-Russian concession city. Once or twice unmarked vans stole by, but overall our impression was of wonder and delight as we strolled through the crowd, the hot sun on our backs coaxing out a healthy sweat despite the chill in the October air.

If not for a small incident, Harbin may have remained an oasis in my memory of China. But our young representative had irked me from the start, and the farther we walked the more he chatted, pointing out this or that landmark we *must* have heard of, and soon his loud voice, lilting with presumptions, began grating on me, and I snapped back with an energy that surprised even me.

My colleagues were quick to intervene, rallying around him like mother hens, clucking at my lack of magnanimity. But, you see, my son and I had been getting into it just like this, and I could not abide the youth's hooded eyes; I lashed out, admonishing his audacity, his misguided courage and naïve ideals—the very things that had pushed my own son to run away, presumably to enlist. I might have lost my head, save for the tether of my wife's face, her pleading terror checked by her refusal to blame me every day I failed to find him. I dropped my voice and let myself be pecked back, the sun-dappled street once again leading us on, this time, to our first proper meal in days.

The day's specialty was duck. Despite our meager group of thirty-one, the restaurant had been requisitioned, its large dining room conspicuously empty, its grand floors and walls imperiously echoing the stamps and scrapes of our shoes and chairs as we accepted the seats arranged around two large tables set in the center of the room. S was observing us, his stolid face highlighting the garishness of ours as our tables brimmed with plates and bowls, and our chopsticks swooped and pecked, securing a morsel, punctuating a quip, our cheeks glowing rosy as platter after platter crowded the wheel ingeniously fitted at the tables' centers. At last the duck was set before us, its dewy skin crisped and seasoned, the complex aroma of fruit and game emanating from it. For most of us, this was our first taste of the bird, and the pungent flesh, voluptuously tender, provoked our passions, prompting us to trade stories of our youthful lusts. But I for some reason found myself remembering the days I had spent toting siblings who never tired of feeding the ducks that splashed in the pond behind our house. I earned my title as the group's sentimentalist that day, but I believe it was at this moment that we fell in with each other, our shared pleasure piqued by our unspoken guilt at gorging on such an extravagance when our families back home had mere crumbs grudgingly afforded by the patriotic frugality demanded of them. Perhaps this is why Harbin has stayed with me, nostalgic and laden, edged with a hysteria I would come to associate with this time.

I believe few of us forget what we keep hidden in our memory's hollows. True, many of us are capable of remaining professionally set, tossing out facts of our wartime accomplishments the way we toss our car keys, casually and full of the confidence of important men who have worked hard and earned their keep, rightfully. But forgetting?

My two colleagues and I have been debating this point over our yearly meals taken here in the rural outskirts of F City, where by chance we converged fifteen years ago. They claim that, if not for these meals, they too might have forgotten, these memories, stowed for so long, buried by a present that discourages remembrances so that a trace of feelings, occasionally jostled, might momentarily surface, but nothing more. For why dig up graves from a banished past, selfishly subjecting all those connected to us to what can only amount to a masochistic pursuit? Isn't it better to surrender to a world populated by the young, who, taught nothing, remain uncurious, the war as distant as ancient history, its dim heat kindling the pages of textbooks and cinemas, occasionally sparking old men with old grudges, but nothing to do with them?

I would like to disagree. But life did move on, the war's end swallowing us up and spitting us out different men, who, like everyone else, slipped back into a peacetime world once again girdled by clear boundaries and laws meant to preserve lives, not to destroy them. And yet, for me, S has continued to tunnel through time, staying in my present, reminding me of our shared past, which we, whatever our excuses, have been guarding as tightly as the walls that surrounded us in Pingfang.

You see, you must understand something: We had always meant to preserve lives. A few thousand enemies to save hundreds of thousands of our own? In that sense, I hardly think our logic was so remarkable or unique.

What was remarkable was Pingfang. Its imposing structure looming in calculated isolation, its vast grounds secured by high-voltage walls, its four corners staked with watchtowers overlooking its four gates armed with guards whose shouts were regularly drowned out by the clatter of surveillance planes circling the facility. Approaching it for the first time in trucks bouncing along bumpy roads, we watched the walls of a fortress compound unroll endlessly before us, each additional meter contracting our nerves so that our faces, initially loose with excitement, began to tighten, eliciting a lustrous laugh from our young guide, who turned to remark, *Of course, we don't bear the Emperor's emblem here.*

Sure enough, when we stopped for authorization at the northern gate, we saw that the walls were indeed ungraced. In a world where even our souls were expected to bear the mark of the Emperor, the absence was terrifying, and perhaps this was when I *saw* Pingfang, its forbidding grandeur, cloaked by its unmarked walls, presaging what it was capable of. By then it was clear that the warning emanating from it made no exceptions, even as it opened its gates and saluted us in.

In increments we would become privy to the extent of Pingfang's ambitions. But first we were dazzled. Our days snatched away by seminars and orientation tours, we scarcely had time to unpack, our bodies as well as our minds collapsing into an exhausted sleep that always seemed white with sunlight, so that even the hardiest of us grew weary, dragging from conference room to auditorium, the occasional outdoor tour whisking us off in rattling trucks that clattered our teeth and fibrillated our brains, so that we soon developed an aversion to Pingfang's jumbled landscape. After a fortnight, we reached our threshold. We broke down, all of us mere husks of ourselves, our individual drive wrung out of us. Until then we had been accustomed to mild routines with little expectation; to be inducted into a life ruled by the exigencies of war proved transformative. We readjusted, our senses and sensibilities recalibrated to accommodate the new demand. After all, humans are remarkable in their ability to adapt. Time and again we would find ourselves reminded of this fact, which, I believe, was at the root of what came to pass at Pingfang.

Had I understood what I glimpsed that night from the train window, would I have turned back, returned to the circumscribed safety of my home and career? I would like to imagine so. And in my right mind I am certain I would have. But, you see, there is the problem, and I come back to the issue of "transgression." In peacetime lines are clearer; even if procedures are flawed and verdicts inconclusive, one generally can and does *know* if one has transgressed. But in war? Does transgression still require intent? Or is it enough for circumstances to conspire, setting up conditions that pressure one to carry out acts that are in line with, but not always a direct result of, orders? I do not know. Yet I find myself looping through memory's thickets for that exact bridge that let us cross our ambivalence to another side.

My two colleagues believe it happened in Harbin. They claim that, as tourists, we were set up to accept the exotic and so dismiss what would have been, in another context, obviously amiss. I do not dispute this view. Yet I wonder whether we hadn't been set up—inoculated—long before we set sail for Wonsan. By then the mood of war, long since gathered in the air, had precipitated into crackdowns, the once distant patter of the jingoists' tattoo pounding down doors, sending us scurrying under the official wing. Even our mandatory participation in the bucket brigade, as well as our patriotic duty to look the other way, had already become two more chores as seemingly unavoidable as the war itself. Resisting would have been foolhardy, the hard-line climate a meteorological fact, its terrorizing power mystical in effect. Yet I am a man of science; I have never been swayed by weather's mystical claims. Nor have I been captive to its blustery dramatics. So I was arrested. My son, Yasushi, was six then, a bright child already fiercely righteous. He never mentioned my arrest, but I believe it left an impression. He became rebellious, his childish disobedience erupting into full-scale mutiny by the time he was fourteen. My wife urged me to confront him; I did nothing of the sort. Because, you see, I recanted my beliefs. True, I was thinking of them, their torturous road if I refused to cooperate. But finally, I could not bear it, the dark shapeless hours sundered by wood and metal and electricity; in ten meager days, I gave in.

Four decades later I do not have reason to believe Yasushi is still alive, but every so often there is news of yet another Imperial Army straggler emerging from the jungles in Southeast Asia, and I am unable to let go.

The latest straggler, one Captain Nakahira Fumio, is currently on the run. His hut, discovered on Mindoro island two weeks ago, had evaded detection for thirty-five years. Widely speculated to be the last repatriate, the authorities finally released his picture.

What could I do? I bought up the newsstand. The image, a grainy reproduction of a school portrait, showed a hollow-chested boy with an affable face. A little thin-framed, he was nevertheless generic enough to be any youth. Could Yasushi have taken his identity? Because, you see, Yasushi had been too young for service. Needing my consent, he had approached me with the forms. I, of course, refused, taking precautions to prevent him from forging them. But forms are traceable; Yasushi, realizing this, opted to trade in his identity. What name he assumed we never found out. Even then the military was eager for soldiers, and I, despite my connections, had a record, an official charge of treason.

Comparing the images for quality, I tucked several newspapers under my arm and hastened into the street still burnished with morning light. That's when I saw him—S—his old man's shape bearing the shadow of his younger self, his rounded back craning as if beckoned by a destination. He did not see me; his ornithic neck bobbing forward, he sped up his once languid gait to a near footloose shuffle. I opened my mouth. But what could I have said? Had I been a different man, able to withstand the eyes of those eager to condemn me for what they themselves might have done in my position, I might have mustered the courage to catch the attention of the one man who may yet have the right to judge us. But I am not that man; I did not call out. Humans may be adaptable, but that has no bearing on our ability to change.

All told, I spent twenty-four months in Pingfang. Officially, we were the Boeki Kyusuibu, the Epidemic Prevention and Water Purification Department, Unit 731, a defensive research unit. Materially, Pingfang spanned three hundred hectares, its fertile land dappled with forests and meadows, its innumerable structures—headquarters, laboratories, dormitories, airfield, greenhouses, pool—luxuriously accommodated within its fold. Locally, we were known as a lumber mill, our pair of industrial chimneys continually emptying into threatening skies.

I remember the first time I stood beneath one of these chimneys. Having finished a procedure, we had followed the gurney out, the damp air white with frost, the bare earth crunching underfoot. S, like the rest of us, was in a morose mood. At the time our work, bacteriological in nature, was making useful gains, but we had not succeeded in developing the antidote we had been after, and I, for one, had become increasingly restless. By then the war, in gridlock in China, was beginning to fan southward, and I was convinced that if Yasushi had indeed enlisted, he would end up in the tropics, where the fruits of our work would be most vital.

I do not know why I risked airing these thoughts. Perhaps it was my way of acknowledging my son. I approached S. Until then we had all been careful to keep to the professional, repeating stock answers whenever we strayed. But S was sympathetic. He replied openly, agreeing with my prognosis, adding only that the war was likely to turn west before pushing farther south—an unentertained notion at the time. I was about to press him on the feasibility, indeed the audacity, of such a course, but just then a flare of heat drew our attention, and the gurney, now emptied of our maruta—yes, that's what we called them: *logs*—pulled us back to our duty.

Because, you see, that was what Pingfang was built for, its immaculate design hiding in plain sight what we most hoped to control: the harvesting of living data. For how else could we compete? Our small nation, poor in resources and stymied by embargoes egregiously imposed by the imperial West. Our one chance lay in our ability to minimize loss, the most urgent being that of our troops, all too often wasted by war's most efficient enemy: infectious diseases. But war spares no time. We found ourselves beating against the very wall that had always been the bane of medical science. In other words, our problem was ethical; Pingfang sought to remove it. Its solution was nothing we dared imagine, but what we, in medicine, had all perhaps dreamed of. All we had to do was continue administering shots, charting symptoms, studying our cultures—all the things we had always done in our long medical careers—except when we filled our syringes, it was not with curatives but pathogens; when we wielded our scalpels, it was not for surgery but vivisection; and when we reached for sample tissues, they were not animal but human. This was perhaps Pingfang's greatest accomplishment: its veneer of normalcy. We carried on; the lives of our soldiers, indeed our entire nation, depended upon us.

I do not know who came up with the term "maruta." It is possible that its usage preceded us, though I do not recall hearing it used in those introductory days. The first time we saw them we were in the hospital ward, where they looked like any patients, supine under clean sheets changed daily. The second time we saw them it was at the prison ward, where they looked like any prisoners, uniformed and wary. Both times, all I remember is the pause that settled between us as we registered exactly what we were being shown before we were briskly ushered away. By the time we were given full rein over our research, we were using the term, counting up the beds, tallying our maruta in preparation for our next shipment, always by train at night. Indeed, I believe it was a cargo transfer that I witnessed that morning on the train to Harbin.

I was asked to accompany the inspection of such a cargo just once. Woken abruptly, I was summoned by an officer who, for this occasion, had driven his private jeep. Throughout the ride, I had been bleary, my mind cottony with sleep, and once I gleaned the purpose of the trip—a preliminary health scan—I shut out the chatter and arrived unprepared for the secluded station, the small squadron of military guards patrolling the length of the curtained train, the cargo's white tarp peeled back to reveal twelve prisoners strapped to planks and gagged by leather bits.

My first reaction was morbid fascination, my mind unable to resolve the image of these people packed like this, and the term "maruta" acquired an appropriateness that struck a nerve. I began to laugh, a sputtering sound that elicited a disapproving glance from the officer who

341

pressed me forward. How they managed to survive I could not imagine. Trembling with exhaustion, they lay in their thin prisoners' clothes, wet and stinking of their own unirrigated waste, until one by one they were unstrapped, forced to stand, their movements minced by the shackles that still bound their hands and feet. No one protested, the only shouts coming from the guards as they stripped and prodded them, the tips of their knives shredding their garments, exposing them first to the cold, then to the water as a pair of soldiers hosed them down.

Had I been able to, I would have abandoned my post, and perhaps I had made as if to do so, for the officer gripped my arm, his placid face nicked by repulsion, though it was unclear by whom or what. As the water dripped away, and the maruta were toweled off, I was led to the nearest plank, where four women, now manacled together, sat shivering. All in their twenties and thirties, their eyes were black with recrimination and their bodies so violently pimpled by the cold I could hardly palpate them. The second plank was an all-male group, each man, wiry with work, radiating humiliation so primal my own hands began to shake. The third and final plank was a mixed group, perhaps a family. One woman grew so agitated by my attempts to minister to a limp girl, I barely registered the man pulled from the train and added to the cargo. This new prisoner was my age, in good health and spirited enough to have risked the curtains to "spy" from the train window. He was brought to me to be tranquilized; and though I must have complied, I remember nothing else, only the leering heat of the soldiers snapped to attention behind me, and then later, the vague relief that flooded me when the next day I stepped into my ward and did not recognize a single face.

Lumber mills?

I do not believe anyone was so naïve.

Pingfang's operation expanded with the war, its defensive function superseded by its natural twin: the development of biological weapons. This offensive capability had been pursued from the start, mostly in the form of small-scale tests surreptitiously deployed as creative endnotes to our ongoing anti-insurgency missions, but it did not peak until the war took that fatal turn west. By then, many of us had been dispatched to newly conquered regions or strategic teaching posts back home, but news continued to reach us, mostly as rumors but sometimes through odd details we recognized in otherwise ordinary news reports. As the war entered its last throes, Pingfang rose in importance. By the time Germany began its retreat, Pingfang, already anticipating a Russian offensive, had begun testing, for example, the human threshold for the northern freeze. How they planned to use the data I do not know. With so few resources and so little infrastructure left, there would have been no way to manufacture, let alone distribute, any new equipment. Why these tests struck me as crueler I also do not know. Perhaps the obvious brutality of the method touched my conscience. Or perhaps it was simply a defensive reflex, the mind's protective instinct that indicts another in the attempt to save itself. After all, had I been in their position, I too would have likely carried out these experiments, meticulously freezing and thawing the living body to observe the behavior of frostbite or assess the tactical viability of a literally frozen troop. While some of us still insist on our relative humanity, I do not believe we can quibble over such fine points as degree.

I, for one, return to the fact of the cargo inspection, and it was this that finally drove me from my practice, a quiet family clinic discreetly set up for me after the war. Having become an inconvenience for the university, the director had found ways of paying us off, and for a while the setup suited me fine. The clinic, bankrolled by the director, yielded enough to survive on, and I was able to keep to simple diagnoses and treatments. Even so, the body does not forget. A clammy arm, a quivering lip—my hands, once recruited for their steadiness, began to jump.

So fifteen years ago, following my wife's death, I ventured to F City. At the time China had just normalized its relationship with Japan, and my two colleagues and I, having respectively come to a similar juncture, found ourselves reunited at the K noodle shop known to connoisseurs for its duck. To say we were surprised would be an understatement. It took us a moment before we could attempt a greeting, our old hearts fluttering like scattered chickens. Once again we ate with a greediness we dared not explain and parted with a gaiety that consoled us. But I believe we would have preferred to have sat apart, if not for our curiosity and relief that this moment, dreaded and yearned for, had finally come to pass. Since then, we have had an unspoken agreement to reconvene on the same day every October, the fateful month we boarded the *Nippon Maru*.

Only once did S and I manage a sustained conversation. That day I had gone in search of a colleague, T, a man of considerable promise, who

343

had taken to visiting the female prisoners. Soft-spoken and decorous, he had become the most vicious among us, his increasing notoriety forcing us to take turns to restrain him. But T was not in the prison ward that day, and I made my way to headquarters, thinking he had gone to request more "materiel," but nobody had seen him there either. I was about to retrace my steps when I glimpsed S emerging from a restricted office, slipping a sheaf of papers into his laboratory coat. When he spotted me, he paused but made no attempt to explain himself. Instead he fell into step with me, convivially opening the door to the underground passage that connected all the buildings in Pingfang.

"Who knows what'll happen to him now," I said, trying not to glance at the papers.

"T?" S shrugged. "Who's going to miss him?"

"He could have had a whole career, a whole future."

"Future?" S looked at me. "You think this is going to last?"

"I don't think that's anything we're in a position to say."

"What? That we're going to lose?"

"Look." I lowered my voice. "We're just following orders."

"And you think the world's going to be sympathetic?"

"What choice do we have? T, on the other hand, is being excessive."

"And you think that makes you different from people like T."

"I'm saying the world will have to consider that."

"And if it doesn't?"

I was silent. It was true: the world had no obligations. What chance did we have in what was likely going to be a Western court? True, we were obeying orders, but we were the ones carrying them out; we could not look at our hands and plead innocence, dusting them off the way our superiors did, passing off their dirty work, expecting it returned to them perfectly laundered "for the sake of the medical community." From the start this had been an untenable situation we were expected to make tenable. Forced to be responsible for what I felt we should not be, I had become resentful. I began misnotating my reports. Small slips, easily dismissable, until the accumulation became impossible to ignore. Instead of 匹, the counter suffix for animals, I began writing 人, the counter suffix for humans. I worked systematically, substituting one for the other with a calculated randomness befitting Pingfang. "I suppose it all depends on whether anyone finds out," I said, glancing at his laboratory coat.

"We all have to do what we have to do, don't we?" S patted his coat, grinning.

"After all this, maybe they'll have no choice but to protect us," I said.

S did not disagree. "There may already be interest in the matter beyond our small military and government," he replied.

And he was right. That was more or less how it played out, with the Cold War descending on the infernal one, and the Americans, fearful of the Russians, agreeing to negotiate with our Lieutenant General for sole access to our research, the objective being the advancement of their own secret bio-program stymied by medical ethics. The result? Our full immunity in exchange for all our data, human and otherwise.

Few historians have unearthed, let alone published, evidence of Pingfang's abuses. Those who have have been divided over the problem of numbers. At one end, Pingfang's casualty rate has been estimated at several thousand. At the other end, the number hovers closer to 200,000, mostly Chinese but some Russian and Japanese deaths as well. I believe both figures tell a certain truth. While it is true that our furnaces saw no shortage of logs in their five years of operation, our goal was never mass extermination. Our tests, contingent on the human body, its organic processes and upkeep, were costly, and even our field tests, aerial or onsite, were limited to small villages and hamlets optimally secluded for tracking our data. But Pingfang cannot be confined to its five years of operation. Its construction took two years, 15,000 laborers, 600 evictions; and afterwards, when surrender triggered the destruction of the compound, whose walls were so thick special dynamite was needed, the final blasts were said to have released only animals, common and uncommon, the only witnesses to escape alive. And the gain? Militarily, history has shown the regrettable results, with reports of odd casualties surfacing now and again, if only in the half-light of prevarications. Medically, it is harder to assess, our research having pushed our field to the cutting edge, landing many of us influential positions in the pharmaceutical sector, where some of us are still directing the course of medicine, or the money in medicine, in not insignificant ways.

The irony of it all is how well we ate within those walls, our maruta fed better than us to maintain optimal biological conditions. This prurient coupling of plenitude and death, so lavish in its complicity, has lent a kind of heat to my memory of Pingfang, compressing its eternity into a vivid blur coalesced around two towering chimneys, their twin shapes always looming, gone the moment I turn to look. These days it is this collusion of the mind with Pingfang's irreality that terrorizes me, the fog of the entombed past threatening to release a hand, a face, a voice.

My colleagues are more fortunate. Our annual meals seem to have done them good, churning up old soil, mineralized by the years, the new exposure letting them breathe. I, on the other hand, find myself hurtled back to people and places lost in time but not lost to me. At my age it is time, not space, that is palpable, its physicality reminding me of the finality of all our choices, made and lived.

This morning they deemed the story of the straggler a hoax. Captain Nakahira Fumio, whereabouts irrelevant.

And so it goes, all of us subject to the caprice of time as it releases not what we hoped for but what it does before it closes in on us and draws back, once again withdrawing the past from the present. And perhaps that is as it should be. For what would I have done? Would I have risked showing myself, braving the eyes of idle journalists, braving those of my son? I have not even had the courage to visit my wife's grave.

I mentioned S to my colleagues for the second time last year. After the first time, I should have known better, but the urge had taken hold of me. Over slivers of duck prepared to our specifications, I gave my account, the papers he had stolen, the exchange we had had. As before, they listened patiently, commenting on his courage, his uncanny foresight and reckless integrity, wondering how they could have forgotten such a character. Again, I described his solitariness, the way he had observed us—so quietly, so persistently—until they finally remembered, not the man himself, but the previous time I had given this account. Should he have exposed the papers? I asked. As before, my colleagues turned on me, asking me why I returned to this, what stake I had in these moot moral questions, nothing but a masochistic exercise—was I certain I hadn't made him up?

I defended myself, reminding them that we had each mentioned one person the other two hadn't been able to recall, and frankly, I said, wasn't the point to see if we *could* imagine it, another life, another self, because look at us, I said, year after year, three old men uselessly polishing stones.

The silence was prickly. For the first time we parted uneasily, our forced gaiety failing to hide what we must have all been dreading. Indeed, the last few times we convened, we had gone through our menu of memories rather mechanically, and despite our appetites, our bodies had grown less tolerant of the fowl's fattiness, and I am not sure that we haven't lost our taste for the bird now that we have exhausted our staple of remembrances. Perhaps at our age it is only natural to want that release, to move once more in time with the clock.

As for S, he may as well have not existed the way things turned out; he never exposed those papers. Yet he had offered me a chance, and perhaps that is my final offense. I did not take that chance. Instead, I carried on, watching, as the world marched on—another war, another era—with fewer of us left every year to cast a backward glance.

So perhaps this is why I continue to return, tantalized by those moments during which it might have been possible to seize the course of our own actions. Because, you see, we all had that chance. That day, just before we walked to the chimney, we had performed a surgery. I was at the head of the table, logging the charts, while T glided the scalpel over the body's midline. Y, my noodle shop companion, was tracking the vitals, calling out numbers, the beat of the pulse measured against the ticking of the clock, as the body underwent all the characteristic spasms—the fluttering of the eyes, the shaking of the head—the once warm flesh rippling with tremors as the skin grew clammy, its tacky surface soon sliding beneath our gloved hands, as we wrestled the mutiny of the body. Perhaps if Y had stuck to procedure. But, you see, Y was monitoring the vitals; he was looking at the body, its special condition, and it occurred to him that he should be tracking not one pulse but two—the second, unborn beat. So he pressed his fingers in; the maruta bolted up. Fixing her eyes on us, she opened her mouth, stilling us. Few of us had acquired the language beyond the smattering of words we kept in our pockets like change, but we did not need language to understand her, her ringing voice a mother's unmistakable plea reminding all of us of our primary duty: to save lives, not destroy them.

Needless to say we did not save anyone's life in that room that day. Instead we went on to complete a record number of procedures, breaking down bodies, harvesting our data, the brisk halls and polite examination rooms only reinforcing the power of omission as we pushed to meet the demands of a war that had heaved us over one edge, then another, leaving us duly decorated but as barren as the landscape we left behind.

As for S, his story began irrecoverably to diverge from ours the day he slipped the papers. While the rest of us hunkered down, he continued to plan and plot, imagining a justice that seemed inevitable. When the war ended and the proceedings began, he too must have waited, hoping and fearing that justice would find itself. But the sentences never came, and he, more than any of us, must have felt its weight doubled back on him. Yet he never disclosed the papers. Instead he stowed them away, perhaps planning to donate them someday to one or another bookstore frequented by frugal university students. Then, fifteen years ago, he retired to a house in the rural outskirts of a city, where an old cedar gives its shade to a backyard visited by birds in the spring and blanketed by snow in the winter. There he spends his days tending to the saplings he has planted behind the shed, where he keeps the papers stashed in a crate of old textbooks. Now and again his mind wanders to the crate, and he marvels at his own resistance, the unrelenting human will to preserve itself.

But today, with spring softening the breeze, and the birds abundant in the yard, he finds himself compelled to visit the papers. After all these years, it is a wonder they have survived, slightly yellowed but otherwise intact, and he places them on a workbench he keeps outside the shed. In this light, the pages are clear, and the neat script, painfully familiar, has the power to jolt him, once again invoking the face of the woman, her wide eyes and gaping mouth, silenced by the wet sound of the fetus slapping the slop bucket. For days he had smelled it, the sweet scorched scent drifting beneath the common odors of cooking and laundry and disinfectant, and he inhales, filling his lungs, as he steps back into the shed, pausing to appreciate his rake and shovel, the long-handled hedge shears now corroding on the wall. Reliable for so many years, there is comfort in this decay, evidence of a long life granted the luxury of natural decomposition. He untangles a knot of rope, empties the crate that had held his papers. The rope is sturdy, as is the crate. He drags them to a spot beneath the arching cedar and sets the crate's open face squarely on the ground. He briefly wonders if his colleagues will meet this year. He hoists the rope, faces the wall. Once again creepers have scaled it, their dark leaves ruffled by a breeze eager to spread the fragrance of the neighborhood's peach and plum blossoms. He grips the rope; the crate momentarily trembles, and while I never tested the precise time it takes for air to be absorbed by the lungs, the brain to starve of blood, and the body to cease its struggle to save itself, I am hoping that, in that duration, I will be able to wrest from myself the snatch of consciousness necessary to remember once more my siblings and those ducks that swam in the pond back home.

Nominated by The Hudson Review

WAITING FOR RAIN

by ELLEN BASS

from THE SUN

Finally, morning. This loneliness
feels more ordinary in the light, more like my face
in the mirror. My daughter in the ER again.
Something she ate? Some freshener

someone spritzed in the air?
They're trying to kill me, she says,
as though it's a joke. Lucretius
got me through the night. He told me the world goes on

making and unmaking. Maybe it's wrong
to think of better and worse.
There's no one who can carry my fear
for a child who walks out the door

not knowing what will stop her breath.
The rain they say is coming
sails now over the Pacific in purplish nimbus clouds.
But it isn't enough. Last year I watched

elephants encircle their young, shuffling
their massive legs without hurry, flaring
their great dusty ears. Once they drank
from the snowmelt of Kilimanjaro.

Now the mountain is bald. Lucretius knows
we're just atoms combining and recombining:
stardust, flesh, grass. All night
I plastered my body to Janet,

breathing when she breathed. But her skin,
warm as it is, does, after all, keep me out.
How tenuous it all is.
My daughter's coming home next week.

She'll bring the pink-plaid suitcase we bought at Ross.
When she points it out to the escort
pushing her wheelchair, it will be easy
to spot on the carousel. I just want to touch her.

Nominated by Frank X Gaspar, Philip Levine

FOOD AND WORKER SAFETY ACROSS THE GLOBE: A NERVOUS AND INCOMPLETE CASE STUDY

by WENDY RAWLINGS

from CREATIVE NONFICTION

So the situation was: our niece—let's call her Amy—up at 4:20 a.m. with vomit out one end and diarrhea out the other, except diarrhea not so much diarrhea-y but rather small particles of waste in bloody slurry. Amy's parents and three sisters sleeping the profound sleep of the post-Christmas holiday-exhausted, so Amy, age eleven, procured old towels used to wipe off Lynx (Irish Setter) when he came in from yard with dirty paws, set them up as nest in bathroom, and just sort of bled and vomited until light of day. Not really so bad (it would, after all, get so much worse) other than nastiness of forced evacuation of Stouffer's lasagna consumed at dinner with large glass of orange juice and then the long stretch of dry heaving afterward. Amy grateful for one thing: had iPad for company.

One place iPads are made is Chengdu, China. Shifts run twenty-four hours a day. Blinding lights plague the eyes of Lai Xiaodong. Who is Lai Xiaodong? Well, in 2010, he left his home for the city of fourteen million to work at Foxconn's factory in Chengdu. Such a shy young man, yet he'd convinced a beautiful nursing student to marry him and wanted to earn money to buy an apartment. For now, Lai works twelve hours per day and earns about $22. Gets room in dorm just large enough for a mattress and desk and wardrobe. Works with thousands of others with swollen legs from standing all day. But still: a job! Sign on wall says, WORK HARD ON THE JOB TODAY OR WORK HARD TO FIND A JOB TOMORROW. Words to the wise. Some workers don't even have their own rooms. Twenty people stuffed into a three-room apartment. Rodent problems. Bummer for those workers. Things could be a lot worse, Lai tells himself. (Things will get a lot worse.)

And then the explosion. Super-downer. Or whatever Chinese phrase is the equivalent to "super-downer." One Friday evening in May, workers covered in sparkling aluminum dust stand there buffing iPad cases nonstop. Over there (difficult to ascertain exactly which worker Lai is, as all are wearing masks and earplugs, all have slight aluminum sparkle in hair even after showering), Lai buffs iPad case after iPad case. iPad 2 has been released in the United States just weeks ago, and so many cases needed! Important to polish as many iPad cases as possible. Get priorities straight. Buff buff buff. Sand sand sand. Okay, so giant explosion caused by dust and inadequate ventilation blows up factory. Poor skinny Lai taken to hospital, where beautiful nursing student girlfriend recognizes him only by his legs because most of skin seared away. Giant bummer for everyone involved when two days later Lai dies.

Back to Amy in west Michigan. iPad screen smudged with her desperate fingerprints. What a night of suffering. Who knew so much blood could come out of her? Small but significant source of comfort is the pet she invented on one of those sites where kids can invent virtual pets. Cat named Lana kept Amy company. If Amy spoke at Lana, Lana repeated what Amy said. For instance, "I am going to feel better soon." Cat said it right back to her. "Mom will get up soon and help me." That was a good one to play back again and again and again.

Sure enough, Mom up at six, and—wow!—what a distinct and upsetting surprise to find Amy on a nest of towels sort of bleeding to death.

Let's talk about shredded romaine lettuce for a minute. Too boring? Lettuce is boring. Let's talk about State Garden (Chelsea, Massachusetts) Organic Spinach and Spring Mix Blend. The company's Web page is currently under construction, but the slogan under the PLEASE EXCUSE US WHILE WE UNDERGO REDEVELOPMENT OF OUR WEBSITE is "Where Freshness Comes First." Let's talk about raw clover sprouts on sandwiches at Jimmy John's. No? How about industrial beef production process that results in workers sometimes nicking the intestines of cows during slaughter and thus releasing E. coli bacteria that have the potential to shut down little kids' kidneys and kill them?

Okay, but Amy's just lying here bleeding, so maybe time to stop talking about raw clover sprouts, time to load Amy into the car and get her to the nearest hospital.

Which Amy's mom and dad (my sister- and brother-in-law) did. Now there, you see Amy in the back of the car, insisting on clinging to iPad with Lana the cat on it.

Back to China. No, wait. Take a few minutes in Cupertino, California. Apple execs hold special meeting to discuss rumors about working conditions for Chinese in their factories. Dust causing explosion at factory a super-duper bummer, yes, but "working conditions in Apple's supply chain are safe." Also, all "workers treated with respect and dignity." Also, manufacturing processes "environmentally responsible." I'm quoting straight from official documents here. So: respect and dignity good. Environmentally responsible also good. However: explosion not good. However also: there are an awful lot of Amys in America desperately waiting to buy new iPads, and if Chinese workers are too busy playing mah-jongg or whatever it is Chinese workers like to do in their off-hours, there won't be enough iPads for all the Amys and sisters, brothers, cousins, etc. Granted, this particular Amy in Michigan is a good deal more desperate than some people, not even for an updated iPad (though in other circumstances she would certainly be thinking about/yearning for it), but for the comfort of Lana the cat with a pink bow around her neck on the screen Amy views as her parents rush her to Helen DeVos Children's Hospital.

Difficult moment ahead: in the ER, nurses will have to pry Amy's hands off the iPad so they can insert IV and perform a variety of tests to try to figure out why the hell an eleven-year-old is shitting blood. Shitting blood more something older people do. And what the hell with the insane exorcism-like vomiting? Particularly rough moment when Amy screaming for Lana the cat becomes Amy sort of scream-vomiting/choking. Then, not long after that—wow!—the kid beginning to fill with fluid so that she starts to look like a bloated, inflated version of herself. Doctors unable to diagnose her, so while sitting by daughter's bed, Amy's mother, trained as a nurse, grabs iPad and begins Googling symptoms such as "blood in stool" and "renal trouble." (Too scared to Google "kidney failure.")

Did you know that the Salinas Valley in California is known as "The Salad Bowl of the World"? I would like to live in a place known for being a salad bowl. One of the problems in the Salinas Valley is that forests abut fields where vegetables are grown. Now, why would that be a problem? Well, sometimes, feral pigs come wandering out of the forest and into the spinach fields. Feral pig takes a shit in the spinach fields and contaminates future salad. I'll give you another one: wild birds. And another: people hired cheap to pick produce have to go to the bathroom while working the fields. No place to wash hands. So, as one Internet commentator pithily put it: "Paco pooped on the produce." Poor Paco: illegally immigrated from Ciudad Juárez and all he wants to do is pick enough spinach to give him food/clothing/shelter. Middle of the day, he has to go to the bathroom. You think there's a shuttle bus that picks him up and brings him to a hygienic indoor facility where he can poop in peace? Think again. There's another Paco in the Dome Valley of Arizona, not a Paco-sized spot of shade in sight, and the dude has to go to the freaking bathroom. If you were picking spinach all day and trying to drink enough water to stay hydrated, you, too, would be dying to take a piss/shit. So that's what he does, between the rows of spinach, and the wily bacteria travel wherever wily bacteria will, and the bag of spinach Amy's mom tosses into her cart at Frandor contains *Escherichia coli*, a.k.a. *E. coli.*

So basically we are talking about commerce. Commerce in lettuce, spinach, and iPads. Also, at some point, there should be a conversation about knockoff Prada bags and prescription drugs (Oxycontin, etc.) that one can buy over the Internet. But before that, I want to talk about a product called n-hexane. First, though, meet Bai Bing. Also, meet Wu Mei (not their real names). Both are young workers in the city of Suzhou who were poisoned by n-hexane, used to make iPad touch screens shiny. At first, Wu Mei noticed she couldn't walk as fast as she was used to walking. She figured working long hours was tiring her out. But then her hands went numb, and then she had trouble rising from a squatting position. Hmm. Interviewed in her hospital bed, Bai Bing reported that she was suffering from dizziness and partial paralysis. Wow!—the n-hexane smelled pungent and nasty, but the workers had no idea it might cause paralysis and so on. But the thing about n-hexane is that it evaporates more quickly than rubbing alcohol—like, a lot more quickly—allowing workers to clean more iPad screens each minute. And the more iPad screens Bai Bing and Wu Mei can clean per minute, the more quickly they can be shipped out to eager American consumers like Amy.

Bai Bing was cleaning Apple logos when she fell ill. What a funny sentence, but I read it in a *Guardian* report. What would Jane Austen make of the words *Apple logo*? What's a logo? Jane might ask. And beyond that: What's an Apple logo? What does it have to do with apples? Furthermore, how does one clean an Apple logo? And how could one become sickened from cleaning an Apple logo? Apparently, it's important for logos to be kept clean. Right? Ever seen a dirty logo? Dirty logos not good for business.

I've heard it said, "The difference between the First World and everyone else comes down to Apple gadgets." What the First World really wants is gadgets, and we want them damn shiny. Oh, believe me, I understand how hard it is to connect the shiny surface of your most beloved gadget with some random Chinese workers you don't even know having trouble walking and having to go to the hospital because they're suffering from a little, er, paralysis. Plus that description of the Chinese workers with their skin and hair sparkling from aluminum dust sounds kind of magical, as if they're Santa's elves. And there's something almost amusing/absurd about the image of eighteen Foxconn workers leaping off buildings to their deaths (though, of course, they didn't all jump at once; they jumped alone, over a period of months). Not funny in a funny way but funny in that absurd Dada way when you think of poor Ma Xiang-qian and Zhu Chen-ming (such crazy names, these Chinese workers!) falling from the tops of buildings. And then even more absurd, how Foxconn installed safety nets afterward instead of, like, improving ventilation or shortening the workday. It's just very difficult to see any connection at all between these shiny gadgets that do things like talk to you and keep all your appointments straight, and poor Miss Hou hanging herself in the company's dormitory bathroom somewhere over there in China.

Another case (or three cases) in point: cantaloupe, sprouts, bagged spring mix. Each of these items caused an outbreak that completely messed up little kids and their kidneys. Also, Odwalla juice, which prided itself on being unpasteurized. So Mom gets an iced tea for herself at the airport, and her daughter wants an apple juice. Before you know it, the kid's in the hospital with kidney failure, having been diagnosed with hemolytic-uremic syndrome. Which is horrible. Which has a 5 to 15 percent mortality rate. Higher in children. Oh yes, it's about as difficult to imagine the lowly sprout or the bodacious but essentially quotidian cantaloupe causing your kid's kidneys to shut down as it is to imagine your shiny gadget screen being responsible for the numbness in Bai Bing's hands or the suicide of Zhu Chen-ming. Cantaloupes and sprouts are girly foods, foods for middle-aged women on diets. Cantaloupes and sprouts are about the furthest possible foods from undercooked hamburger (another *E. coli* culprit) one can imagine. It's not hard to picture how a worker slaughtering a cow might accidentally puncture its intestines and release *E. coli* into the slaughterhouse. But how could cantaloupe carry deadly listeria? It's fruit, after all. It has a goofy name. And sprouts! You generally don't even eat the sprouts in your sandwich but instead leave them on the side of your plate because they are not delicious.

A couple of weeks ago, one of my "friends" on Facebook (I put friends in quotation marks because she's not really my friend, just someone I knew in college, from which we graduated almost twenty-five years ago) posted a photo of "Minimum Wage Barbie." The doll's wearing a McDonald's uniform and carrying a tray with a Happy Meal on it. Across the top of the doll's box are the words GIRLS! THIS WILL BE YOU IF YOU DON'T STUDY. My "friend" added to her post, "I've been laughing about this all morning." Now, you will probably accuse me of being overly sensitive and politically correct, but I walked around for the rest of the day thinking about Bai Bing and Wu Mei, Ma Xiang-qian and Zhu Chen-ming and their shitty jobs and their shitty useless dumbass deaths. They didn't work in dangerous, low-wage jobs because they hadn't studied hard at college. And in fact, I remembered that my Facebook "friend" hadn't done much studying at the second-tier liberal arts school in the Northeast that the two of us attended. My most vivid memories of her include (1) Lilly Pulitzer pink-and-green pedal pushers and (2) a night in her dorm room when a bunch of us got drunk on Jell-O shots and ended up piercing each other's ears with a needle dipped in rubbing alcohol.

Mostly, said Facebook "friend" posts about "Quonnie," a preppy pet name for Quonochontaug, an area in Rhode Island composed of three beachfront communities. Apparently, this "friend" owns a beach house in the area that serves for her as a kind of emotional/spiritual polestar. So if she's having a bad day, she might post on Facebook a photo of the beach at Quonnie with the words GOING TO MY HAPPY PLACE superimposed on it. One imagines that the kind of bad day that might send my college friend to seek the solace of her HAPPY PLACE might involve something more serious than not being able to find slipcovers that match the living room sofa and something less serious than working really long days at an unventilated factory in China while being poisoned by n-hexane used to clean iPad screens.

If you've seen Lilly Pulitzer clothes once, you've seen pretty much what Lilly Pulitzer clothes have been about since Lilly herself married a businessman and moved from New York to Palm Beach, where she (no joke!) set up an orange juice stand. Legend has it that she began designing brightly colored and patterned dresses to hide juice stains when she was working. Even with the Internet's vast informational reach, it's hard to figure where the pink-and-green pedal pushers are being made now, though the company's Web site has a breezy line about how "From South America to the Far East, our product is made all over." The distribution center is in Pennsylvania, but all we know is "some of the garments travel a long way on a sea vessel and some others take a quick twenty-one-hour flight on a plane."

One time in college, I needed a dress for a formal, and a bunch of my sorority sisters and I were going to Hilton Head, South Carolina, for spring break. Now, the college I went to was very expensive, so my parents took out a second mortgage on their house to pay my tuition. To pick up the spending money I felt I needed in order to keep up with my wealthier sorority sisters, I'd gone off the meal plan. I used the refunded money to buy groceries, which mostly amounted to single-serving cans of Progresso lentil soup, cases of Diet Coke, and a weekly bunch of bananas. By the time we got to Hilton Head, I'd squirreled away enough money to buy a magnificent cotton dress, green with coral and white flowers. It wasn't a Lilly Pulitzer, but it was snazzy.

"A sweetheart neckline!" one friend exclaimed.

"Now you need peau de soie shoes!" another friend exclaimed.

I pretended I knew all about sweetheart necklines and peau de soie shoes.

Peau means "skin" in French, and *soie* means "silk," so I would've known the meaning if I'd taken French like everyone else at my college, rather than Spanish, language of Paco.

Somehow, I have gotten very far afield from Amy in Michigan, who has now been moved to pediatric ICU and placed on a ventilator. Her lungs are filling with fluid, which causes her to struggle to breathe. When the doctor suggests that he intubate her, get her on a ventilator, and sedate her, Amy turns to him and says, "Bring it on." Which reminds me: what *did* bring it on? Was it a fast food hamburger like the ones at Jack in the Box that poisoned children in Seattle in 1993? That outbreak resulted in the largest food-borne illness settlement ever made in the United States, to one Brianne Kiner, a nine-year-old who nearly died after eating a hamburger contaminated with E. coli. Or could it be the girly sprouts or the girly cantaloupe or the spring mix that comes in the big see-through plastic clamshell that has phrases printed on it like "triple-washed!" and "ready to eat!" The truth is that right now no one knows what the hell got into Amy and caused her kidneys to shut down. The bloody diarrhea and subsequent diagnosis of hemolytic-uremic syndrome (HUS) have been reported to the county health department, which faxed over to the hospital a questionnaire aimed at determining a possible cause of the *E. coli* infection. At the present time, the questionnaire sits in the waiting room, under a pile of papers under Amy's mother's winter coat, while Amy's mother, when she's not hovering over Amy, sits listening to Christian rock on her iPod headphones while rocking back and forth and moaning.

In short, when your kid's suddenly dying in the hospital with kidneys that aren't working, the last thing you're likely to do is fill out a questionnaire faxed over from health department about what and where said kid might have eaten the last ten days. Especially if said kid asked you just before they intubated her if she was going to die.

Fast forward. Amy's mom has now been in the hospital going on two weeks with Amy, her second oldest daughter, and has consequently lost time/date orientation. Is it day or night? Thursday? Sunday? Breakfast? Dinner? If Sunday, then must make effort to attend large evangelical church to which family belongs. No, not going to church even if it is Sunday. Instead, she remains by Amy's bedside with iPad in lap, reading scripture—for instance, Exodus 23:25: Worship the Lord your God, and his blessing will be on your food and water. Also, Hebrews 9:22: Without the shedding of blood, there is no remission of sins. There certainly has been a lot of shedding of blood, that's for sure, Amy's mom thinks, remembering Amy bleeding through the pile of Lynx's dog towels on the bathroom floor.

My husband's aunt, a sage who worked for the U.S. Public Health Service, once opined over a martini, "The key to a healthy populace lies in separating people from their poop." She had endeavored to do just this while being posted in Africa. Turns out that in Africa, *E. coli* is caused by feces being used as fertilizer or feces tracked into factories on shoes of workers or feces getting into water supply. Fecesfecesfeces. One thing Amy's mother would like to stop thinking about is feces. Another is pee, which Amy hasn't produced in days, thereby causing Amy's parents to find themselves praying for pee. Saying pee prayers. Kneeling in prayer for the promise of pee. Amy's father even spent some time combing an online Bible for references to pee production. The parents have been told that Shiga toxins are responsible for Amy's current state. The term sounds exotic, and in some sense, it is for Westerners, having been named for Kiyoshi Shiga, the Japanese bacteriologist who, in 1897, discovered the toxin that causes dysentery. Imagine having a toxin named after you! Wow!—even crazier, imagine your eleven-year-old on a ventilator in pediatric ICU when just two weeks ago she was hugging the iPad and the karaoke machine she received on Christmas morning. Hugging them, that's how excited she was. Funny to think about how kids get attached now to consumer electronics, whereas when Amy's mom was a kid, she hugged a Baby Crissy doll with a ponytail that grew when you pulled it. Did you know that karaoke is a portmanteau of the Japanese kara, meaning "empty," and *okesutora*, meaning "orchestra"?

The elite class in America—the Kennedys, the Rockefellers, the Vanderbilts, the Whitneys—has a thing for cotton print skirts and trousers with garish pink-and-green-flowered patterns splashed across them. Go figure.

I think I'm losing control of this story.

The empty orchestra of the burbling fountain in the pediatric ICU, designed to muffle the sounds of families communicating the intimate details of their children's illnesses or the intimate sounds of families weeping.

The empty orchestra of the street in Chengdu after aluminum dust produced from polishing iPad screens caused the factory to explode.

The empty orchestra of the shit the immigrant worker takes in the field of spinach.

Of *E. coli* in the slashed intestines of the cow hung upside down.

(Loss of iPad production from explosion could reach half a million units).

In college, for a while, to afford the sweetheart necklines and peau de soie shoes, I worked a morning shift in the dining-hall dish room. The work stank of burnt toast and bleach. After the breakfast rush, I would walk back across campus to my dorm and take a hot shower.

I read in *The New York Times*: "New screens began arriving at the plant near midnight. A foreman immediately roused 8,000 workers inside the company's dormitories, according to the executive. Each employee was given a biscuit and a cup of tea, guided to a workstation, and, within half an hour, started a twelve-hour shift fitting glass screens into beveled frames. Within ninety-six hours, the plant was producing over ten thousand iPhones a day."

Three weeks have gone by since Amy invented a screen cat and programmed it to tell her she would feel better soon. As she breathes more easily on her ventilator, her body ever more overwhelmed with toxins her kidneys can't filter, her father uses his daughter's iPad to send a Facebook update to friends around the world: "Praise the Lord. He shall guide us."

Thirteen days after Amy was discovered to be infected, her youngest sister, let's call her Ava, age five, manifested symptoms nearly identical to Amy's and was admitted to a room right beside her sister's in pediatric ICU. On his Facebook page, the girls' father posted a status update that said simply, "In what feels like a punch in the face, my youngest daughter has also been diagnosed with HUS."

Update: Amy and Ava were both close to death in January 2013 when their doctors convinced the insurance company to let them treat the girls with a drug called Soliris (generically, eculizumab), which was flown in on a special flight from Boston to Michigan. Soliris is one of the "11 Most Expensive Medicines in America"; in fact, it has been named by Forbes.com as the "world's single most expensive drug, coming in at $409,500 a year." Even more expensive, now.

After extensive dialysis, both girls were given a clean bill of health in March 2013.

The source of the *E. coli* infection has not been found.

Suicide nets installed two years ago after nine workers jumped to their deaths at the Shenzhen factory remain in place.

The only part of this essay I have invented is the dog Lynx.

Nominated by Jennifer Lunden and Creative Nonfiction

EVERY MACHINE
HAS ITS PARTS

by BOB HICOK

from THE GEORGIA REVIEW

My father can talk to him but that's about it—
a guy you could sit beside in a bar and never know
he's picturing the knife in his boot
in your throat because you remind him
people exist and make noise—he is what war does
to some, a twitch covered in skin—a jester
should follow him with a song of warning
for the citizens or a doctor come before him
and inject small doses of Vietnam
into the eyes of everyone he meets—whatever's
easier—I prefer the needle
into our seeing what we ask soldiers to do—
certainly for presidents and senators a foxhole
should be required—some bleeding—a bit
of brain in their coffee—but I'm a poet,
you can excuse anything I say as antithetical
to reason—let me end then on a pleasantly
aesthetic note—my uncle can't hold a job
or conversation but carves robins and cardinals
that look so much like the real thing
I expect them to fly—one after another—
and shoots them for practice instead of you or me.

Nominated by Richard Burgin, Ed Falco, Elton Glaser,
David Hernandez Fred Leebron, Rachel Rose

HOLLYWOOD AND TOADVINE

fiction by CHRISTIAN KIEFER

from SANTA MONICA REVIEW

The notion that there is something wrong with the new ruler of the Evil Empire does not take very long to sink in. The man's predecessor, Yuri Andropov, was difficult to work with, but at least he was predictable: the kind of hardline Soviet patriot that, in many ways, you could relate to, making him a good enemy to have, a man a guy like you could hate without second thought or ambiguity. But things fell apart there, as they often do. First there was the equally ancient Konstantin Chernenko, but that barely lasted a full year before he was in the grave. Then this new man with the disturbing birthmark that was like a cloud, seeming to take on the shape of whatever might be on the viewer's mind. A map of Japan. A rubber duck. Your wife's intimate parts. Try having a discussion where the future of the world teeters on the knife-edge of nuclear destruction with a man who has your wife's vagina emblazoned on his forehead. It is a difficult discussion to have.

It is this birthmarked man, Mikhail Gorbachev, apparently a big reader, who suggests you might enjoy reading something other than Louis L'Amour and that there are several American authors he himself reads with regularity, one of whom has penned a new Western.

"I will send you this book," Gorbachev tells you over the phone.

"That sounds fine and I'll look forward to reading it," you answer in return.

"I must tell you, Ron, that this book is unlike your Louis L'Amour."

"Well, as long as it's not Danielle Steele, that's fine."

He laughs. "Okay, no Danielle Steele then."

"That's women's reading," you say. "My wife reads that kind of thing. Not for men."

He pauses long enough that you begin to wonder if the line has been disconnected when he says, "Maybe I send her new book too. For Nancy."

Weird, you think, but you thank him anyway. Why he has access to stores of Danielle Steele novels at the Kremlin is not a question you feel comfortable asking, so you turn to other topics. Nuclear war. SDI. The Soviet invasion of Afghanistan. Foreign policy. That kind of thing.

"I look forward to seeing you in Reykjavík next month," Gorbachev says. "We can talk about the book."

"I look forward to it too," you say. You are beginning to wonder if you misread Gorbachev. He's a Soviet, but he's also a man. At least there will be something to talk about in Reykjavík if the heavy topics get too heated. You can talk about Westerns until the cows come home.

You can tell one thing about Mikhail Gorbachev: birthmark or no, the man is true to his word. Only a few days later a package appears via special messenger. It is wrapped as if for Christmas although it is only September. Inside are two hardcover books: Danielle's Steele's *Family Album* and the mysterious Western, *Blood Meridian or the Evening Redness in the West*, by someone named Cormac McCarthy. Cormac. Is that a Soviet name? You can't decide. Gorbachev has inscribed the McCarthy volume: "To Ron. Enjoy! Your friend, Mikhail." You do not look to see what he has written in the Danielle Steele novel, if anything.

Both books sit unread for a good long while, first on your desk, then on a side table upstairs. It is Nancy who moves them both to the bedside tables. As a joke she places the Steele novel on your nightstand and the Western on her own. There they sit for days until one night you pick up the book at hand, the Danielle Steele novel, as it turns out, and read the first few pages. "The sun was so brilliant," the book begins, "nearly everyone was squinting, though it was only eleven o'clock in the morning. The tiniest of breezes ruffled the women's hair." Herein lay the problem with such reading. Women's hair ruffling in the breeze. What's the point of such things if there's to be no payoff? No fast draw or gunfight or chase across the desert. What a waste. The scene describes a funeral of some kind. Ward Thayer, a rich old man, is at the funeral of the woman he loved, a woman famous enough to attract a retinue of reporters. Who cares? You don't.

You lean over and place the book on Nancy's nightstand and retrieve *Blood Meridian* and begin to read. Immediately you find yourself confused, although the confusion fades some as you continue to turn the pages. There's a boy and he's on some kind of weird Mark Twain trip down the river, although there are guns and knives and some shooting as early as the second page. And there's an oddness here too, a kind of Biblical voice that is frankly disturbing. There's only one voice qualified to speak that way, and that voice belongs to God the Father. You flip back to the cover. A strangely out-of-proportion cart being pulled through some wasteland. Is that what the Soviets think America looks like? Perhaps they do. Maybe the movies gave them such a vision. But even the Westerns you so love feature the amazing rock architecture of Monument Valley, not this flat and featureless moonscape. John Ford! John Wayne! No weirdness there. Kill or be killed. That is the law of the West, and it is the same law that exists everywhere on earth.

"You've got to read it," your Chief of Staff tells you the next day. "The whole thing."

You shake your head. "Don," you say, "I just don't think I can. It's just so dark. And weird. Everything is so weird."

"Weird how? You mean like science fiction or something?"

"No, not like that. I don't know. It's just *off* somehow."

"Maybe he's trying to send you a message," Don says. "Maybe we should call in Bill."

"If the CIA gets involved we'll never hear the end of it," you say. "Plus they'll want the other book too."

"What other book?"

"Danielle Steele," you tell him. "Nancy finally started it last night. Stayed up half the night reading. She's deep in already. If Casey takes it she'll be mad as a hornet."

"Well, we don't want that."

"No, we don't."

Don sits there for another moment, awkwardly. "You want me to read it for you?" Don says at last. "I could write a brief."

You consider this. Consider it carefully. What if Gorbachev wants to discuss it? Every conversation you've ever had with the Soviets has been like game of cat and mouse. These books are already part of the same game. In the end you simply say, "I appreciate it but I think I'm gonna have to do it myself."

"I think that's a good choice, Mr. President," Don says.

And so it is that you sit up late at night reading that infernal book, the pages filled with characters you do not understand committing acts of horror you cannot fathom. Even when a familiar event occurs—a shootout between cowboys and Indians, for example—the encounter quickly devolves into an unmitigated bloodbath with no identifiable hero or villain. Who is the reader to root for? Where's the John Wayne character? Where's Gary Cooper or Gregory Peck? Where's the excitement? The tension? The noble vision of American manifest destiny? Indeed where is America itself in such a book?

You give it your best, and Don asks each morning for your progress. He likes to see the book on your desk in the Oval Office—you understand that, for him, it is an issue of national security—and so you dutifully bring it down each morning and set it there as if you had just been turning its pages. And you tell him you are making your way through it, even though you've more or less bogged down in the middle. When he presses, you tell him that it's time to move on to more important affairs of state, and when he leaves the Oval Office at last you look at the volume and sigh so loudly that a moment later your secretary appears in the doorway to ask if you are all right.

That night you reach over to Nancy's bedside table and lift the Danielle Steele novel and sit for a time in bed with both volumes on your lap. The inscription in the romance novel reads, "To the First Lady from a distant friend, Mikhail." You read a page or two. Another. Soon you are twenty pages in. You listen for the hissing of the shower in the bathroom to stop, the signal of Nancy's impending return, for of course you do not want to be caught reading Danielle Steele. This is reading for women and homosexuals. Not for you. Certainly not for you. And yet you cannot help but feel that this book, this romance novel, is much more enjoyable than the weird horrible book Gorbachev sent your way. Less manly but more enjoyable. What does that say about you? What does that say about America and the Soviet Union? Is Gorbachev reading romance novels in the wee hours? You find the notion unlikely.

The next day Don asks you about the book again. It is again resting on the desk in the Oval Office.

"It's getting a little better," you say.

"Oh yeah?" Don answers. "That's good news."

He meanders over near the desk, and when he reaches for the book, you say, quickly, "Do you have those reports on Afghanistan?"

His hand pauses above the book. "Of course. Did you want to go over them?"

"I think we should," you say.

He looks at you, perhaps a bit quizzically, but then says, "I'll go get them," and leaves the office.

You rise as soon as the door clicks shut and move to the desk and slip the book into a drawer. Why you've been placing the book on the desk at all is beyond your reasoning. It's your book. You're the President of the United States. And yet you're trying to prove to your Chief of Staff that you're continuing to read. It suddenly seems absurd, so absurd that you actually chuckle to yourself even as the book flops open in your hand and you see the pages within, not the text of Cormac McCarthy's novel but the text of Danielle Steele's, the book covers swapped out so that you could continue your surreptitious reading of the romance, McCarthy's book upstairs, on Nancy's nightstand, sheathed in Danielle Steele's cover. Good lord! What kind of deviant have you become? A latent homosexual? A pansy? A queer? You've swapped out a blood-drenched Western for a romance novel. My God!

It is nearly impossible to focus on the various tasks at hand. Reykjavík looms. Geneva had been a start, but you have particularly high hopes for Reykjavík. Hopes and plans. Big ones. Ballistic missile disarmament. The end of the nuclear standoff. And yet now, on the eve before the summit, you cannot concentrate. Is that disgust on James Baker's face? Is Pat Buchanan's joke about "those homos" directed at you? It seems impossible, and yet you wonder.

That night your dreams are unsettled. It is as if both books have collided in your mind. It seemed impossible to believe when only yesterday . . . only yesterday they'd been in Paris . . . the South of France . . . New York . . . Guadalcanal, where it had been raining for sixteen days and when he met Toadvine and it was raining yet. He was still standing in the same saloon, and he had drunk up all his money save two dollars. Then a knife fight. But before that is done you're seated at a table with a woman in a silver lamé gown.

"I'm sorry I told you all that," you are saying. "I didn't mean to lay my troubles in your lap."

"Why not, Ward?" Faye answers. "What's so wrong with that? Who else do you have to talk to here?"

You do not answer. Your eyes are overbrimming with tears. Violins swell from some secret place.

"It's all right, Ward," Faye says. And in the next moment, her arms are wrapped around you and she is crying.

Ah the romance! The fuzzy focus! You are a movie star once more! Young again!

But then something changes. There are others in the room. The lights darken. On the table are piled a collection of slick black scalps. You pull her head away from your chest, and her eyes are as wide as the eyes of a deer, a rabbit.

And then it's all blood and gore. You take off her head. The severed stump pumping blood into the air. Around you are the others from the book, the romance: Lionel and Greg and Anne and Valerie. The men have slaughtered the women and are raping the bodies. Blood soaking into the sand.

In the distance comes the rumble of hooves. Then they are coming down Pennsylvania Avenue. A legion of horribles, hundreds in number, half naked or clad in costumes Attic or biblical or wardrobed out of a fevered dream with the skins of animals and silk finery and pieces of uniform still tracked with the blood of prior owners. They come through the lawn, Secret Service men falling everywhere in heaps, and when you reach the Oval Office the man who sits at the desk is huge and pale and bald, like a giant gently grinning child, on his forehead a distinctive and familiar birthmark.

You wake in a kind of panic. The clock reads 1:17. The center of night. You're leaving for Reykjavík in the morning, but that's still many hours away, and now the whole of the White House is dark and quiet. Nancy breathes softly beside you. Your heart racing in your chest. That son of a bitch, you think. You recall reading about psychological operations during Vietnam, but this is even more insidious, more ingenious. It proves something that you never expected: that the new Soviet ruler is a much shrewder man than you anticipated, that beneath the friendly demeanor is the Devil himself. The second coming. The birthmark is the mark of the beast and it is a challenge. A colossal middle finger to democracy. A smear of blood. (And again the images of the nightmare return, the two books smashed together in your mind. The bald grinning judge sitting in your chair.)

When you rise, Nancy stirs. "What is it?" she murmurs.

"I've gotta call Don," you say. "It's nothing. Go back to sleep."

She half-turns, as if she might say something more, but then falls silent. You collect both books—the McCarthy novel from your nightstand and the Steele novel from Nancy's—afraid she might wake when you touch the cover, but she does not wake. And then you pad quietly into the office.

"Don?" you say when he picks up the phone.

"Yes, Mr. President," he says. His voice is clear, seemingly wide awake. But that is one of Don's special talents, that eternal alertness. It was one of the reasons why you made him Chief of Staff.

"The Star Wars project," you say.

"Yes?"

"That's the priority."

"Really?"

"Yes, really. That's the priority. We're talking about the future of America. We're going to disarm and then those sons of bitches are going to rain fire down on our heads. I won't have it. Star Wars. That's what I'm talking about. If they won't agree to that then the whole thing's off."

"That's a big gamble," Don says. There is a challenge in his voice. You like this about Don when it is in the right moment. It has helped you zero in on exactly the correct argument, the sharpest rhetorical approach. But this is not the right moment.

"I don't give a crap," you say. "I'm not going to open us up to getting blown off the map. I don't trust him. I'll never trust him."

"What about the ballistic missile program?"

"They're setting us up, Don."

"You really think so?"

"I know so," you say. "They're getting ready to unleash hell upon earth. It's the second coming. I can feel it. No SDI, no deal."

"All right," Don says. He sounds suddenly exhausted. Disappointed. "I'll start preparing."

"I'll meet you in an hour."

Don pauses for a moment, unspeaking. You just wait for the words, and then at last they come: "Yes, sir, Mr. President," he says at last.

You hang up the phone and sit with hands trembling and heart racing in your chest. Your reflection in the mirror is that of an old man, your hair in a heap, like hay from the ranch. The images of the dream have faded except for one: that feeling of youth, of how you looked and felt when you were in Hollywood. For a brief instant, you had been that man again, sitting across from a woman as beautiful as any you have ever had, even if this one was a fictional heroine from a romance novel. What happened to the leading star you once were? You were Brass Bancroft! You were Knute Rockne! You co-starred with Bette Davis and James Cagney! And now you are the President of the United States. And what? You are overrun by a birthmarked charlatan and the two books you hold in your hands. What kind of man reads romance novels? And the answer stares back at you from the window glass. An old man.

And yet you are the leader of the nation. You did not fall for the trick, the two books as evil as any you could have imagined, one a violation of what America is, its history, its being, its self. And the other a violation of another kind. Of your understanding of what it is to be a man.

You look at the books. Their covers. Their heft and weight. *Blood Meridian or the Evening's Redness in the West. Family Album.* Evil books. Evil books mailed from the Evil Empire. And that bald son of a bitch thought you'd fall for his psychological operation. Just how stupid does he think you are? You'll show him what you're made of in Reykjavík. It'll be hardball. That's for sure. And if he asks what you thought of *Blood Meridian* you won't let it crack your armor at all. Instead, you'll simply say, "It's not really what America is about but I can see how it might fool you," and if he presses further you'll bring it back to SDI. You'll shield America in a dome of missiles. Nothing will get through. It will be impenetrable. Complete. Perfect. Just like America.

Then you crack open the window and toss both books out into the darkness of the night. You know the Secret Service men will retrieve them but you'll deny they are yours. Let them disappear into whatever incinerator turns the garbage to ash. Let them go back to the hell from which they came. Maybe you'll have Casey run down this McCarthy. But then you know that of course it's probably better to do nothing at all. With books like that, what kind of audience could he ever have? Who would want to see such a vision of America? Just let him fall into obscurity on his own.

You return to the bedroom and drop your pajamas to the floor. Nancy awakens midway through but she doesn't say a word. You're the President of the United States, after all, and just as virile as the day you were married. She knows that. You know that. And when you flip her over to take her from behind and you see the bald pate and ring of hair of the Soviet leader where your wife's head should be, that could only mean that you are focused on the future. On the protection of the free world. On the Star Wars missile shield. On the survival of democracy. Even as you pound away at him you tell yourself that you will protect your nation at all costs. That you will not be fooled. And you tell yourself that you are, and will forever remain, a man.

Nominated by Michael Newirts and Santa Monica Review

BOMB

by DANIEL LUSK

from NEW LETTERS

The night the atom bomb nicknamed "Fat Man" fell from a plane over Nagasaki in faraway Japan, Kay DeWitt got her first period. I know because I was outside her house, kneeling on a concrete block beneath the downstairs bathroom window, when she burst in.

Until that moment, I didn't know it was the bathroom window. The shade was pulled down almost to the sill. Suddenly the light went on and there she was, hiking up her plaid skirt to sit on the toilet, practically beside me. She made little hiccupy sounds. As she leaned over to peer at the inside of her thigh, I could see a trail of red all down her leg and onto her white bobby socks.

Suddenly a woman filled the doorway, and of course, I fell to the ground and took off, using the dark rows of sweet corn in their garden for cover. So that's all I know about it. This was something I didn't expect and had never even thought of, because I had no sisters, and sex education would not be invented for two more decades.

You can believe that this is true. So even if I admit that I've lied about everything but the bomb and not having sisters, the bomb is so big it would make you believe any small, human story I told you. Even if there was a Kay DeWitt having her first period, saying I was outside her window on that August evening in 1945 is still a lie. But hearing that the bomb killed more than 75,000 people, as it reportedly did, that would be unforgettable for anyone, even if they weren't alive yet when it happened. That part, the bomb part, is the truth.

Nominated by Gary Gildner, New Letters

VARIATIONS ON
A PSALM

by EDWARD HIRSCH

from FIVE POINTS

When I was in distress, I sought the Lord; at night I stretched out
untiring hands, and I would not be comforted. (Psalm 77:2)

And I would not be comforted
    When I was in distress
        I sought the Lord
I did not know why I did not believe

While I stretched out untiring hands
    And I would not be
        Comforted in my distress
I sought the Lord

I would not pray
    I would not call on Him
        Stretched out with my untiring hands
And comforted I would not be

When I was in distress
    Without the Lord
        I stretched out tireless on the bed
My hands were sleepless in despair

And I would not be comforted
    In my distress
        I sought the Lord
I could not find Him

At night I stretched out untiring hands
        Like a penitent
            O Lord of disbelief
And I would not be comforted

Nominated by Jeffrey Harrison, Charles Harper Webb

WHAT HAPPENED TO US?

fiction by DAN CHAON

from PLOUGHSHARES

Rusty Bickers went walking through the fields at dusk, Rusty Bickers with a sadness and nobility that only Joseph could see. Joseph dreamed of Rusty Bickers at the kitchen table, eating Captain Crunch cereal before bedtime, his head low, lost in thought; Rusty Bickers, silent but awake beneath the blankets on his cot, his hands moving in slow circles over his own body, whispering "Shh . . . shhh . . . hush now"; Rusty Bickers standing in the morning doorway of the kitchen, watching Joseph's family as they ate their breakfast, his shaggy hair hanging lank about his face, his long arms dangling from slumped shoulders, his eyes like someone who had been marched a long way to a place where they were going to shoot him.

Joseph heard his mother's bright voice ring out: "It's about time you got up, Rusty!"

Joseph was eight years old, and Rusty was fourteen—an orphan, a foster boy. All that summer, Rusty slept on a folding bed in Joseph's room, so Joseph knew him better than anybody.

Rusty was beginning to grow a man's body. His legs were long and coltish, his feet too big, hair was growing under his arms and around his groin. He had his own tapes, which he listened to through enormous spaceman headphones. He had a souvenir ashtray from the Grand Canyon. He had some books, and photographs of his dead family, and newspaper clippings.

Sometimes, late at night, when Rusty thought that Joseph was asleep, he would slip into Joseph's bed. He curled his long body against Joseph's smaller one, and Joseph stayed still. Rusty put his arm around Joseph as if Joseph were a stuffed animal. Joseph could feel Rusty quivering—he was crying, and his tears fell sharply onto Joseph's bare back. Rusty's arm tightened, pulling Joseph closer.

Rusty's family—his mother, father, and two younger brothers—had died in a fire. Some people, some of Joseph's older cousins, for example, some of them whispered that they heard that Rusty had started the fire himself. Anyway, he was weird, they said. *Psycho.* They stayed away from him.

Before Rusty had come to live with them, Joseph's father was in a terrible accident. He had been working as an electrician on a construction site when a roof collapsed. Joseph's father and his father's best friend, Billy Merritt, fell through three floors. Billy Merritt died instantly. Joseph's father broke both legs, and his right arm was severed. His fall had been softened because he landed on Billy Merritt.

Now Joseph's father had a prosthetic arm, which he was learning to use. The prosthesis looked like two hooks, which his father could clamp together. For example, he was learning how to grasp a fork and lift it to his lips. Eventually, he would be able to turn the pages of a book, or pick up a pin.

There had been a settlement for his father's injury, a large sum of money. The very first thing Joseph's father did was to go and speak with the people at County Social Services. He wanted to take in a foster boy, he said. This had been one of his dreams, something he'd always wanted to do. When he was a teenager, he had been sent away to a home for delinquent boys. After a while, he ran away from that place and joined the Navy. But he still vividly remembered that terrible time of his life.

Joseph's father loved Rusty Bickers. Rusty's story was so sad that perhaps it made the father feel better. He felt that he could help Rusty somehow. He wanted to provide an atmosphere of Love and Happiness.

There was so much money! Joseph had no idea *how* much, but it seemed bottomless. His father bought a new car, and a pool table, and a large screen TV; his mother got her teeth fixed; they began to plan an addition to the house, with a family room and a bedroom for Rusty.

When they went to town, to the big store at the mall, Joseph and his brother and sister and Rusty were allowed to pick out a toy—anything they wanted. While their father looked at tools and electronic devices, Rusty and Joseph and Joseph's younger sister, Cecilia, would lead the baby, Tom, through the rows of toys: the pink and glittery aisle for girls; the mysterious and bookish aisle of games and puzzles; the aisle of action figures and toy weapons and matchbook cars; the aisle of baby stuff—rattles and soft-edged educational devices that looked like dashboards, things that spoke or giggled when you pulled a string. Rusty wandered the aisle of sports stuff, the aisle of BB guns and real bows and arrows, as Joseph and his siblings chased one another. The children could have anything they wanted: the idea almost overcame them.

"Nobody knows what they want, not really," Rusty Bickers said, sometimes, when they were in bed at night. Joseph didn't know whether Rusty had made this up, or whether he was quoting some movie or song. He said this when he was talking about the future. He was thinking about becoming a drummer in a rock band, but he worried that it might be pointless, living out in western Nebraska. He thought that maybe he should live in New York or LA, but he was worried that if he was in such places, the black kids would be always trying to beat him up.

"They hate white people," Rusty told Joseph. "All they want to do is fight you."

Rusty had met black people. He had lived with some black boys in a group home, and he'd had a black teacher.

Joseph hadn't yet seen a black person, though he wanted to. There was a cartoon on TV called *Fat Albert and the Cosby Kids*, about a group of black children who lived in a junkyard. This was Joseph's favorite show, and he longed to make friends with a black child. He hoped that the child would teach him how to talk in that funky way.

"You can't *make friends* with them," Rusty said, scornfully. "All they want to do is kick your ass."

Joseph was silent and thoughtful.

But Rusty didn't even seem to notice. He was thinking of where he would like to go, if he could go somewhere. He leaned back, playing drums on the air above his head.

It was a summer of parties. They were happy times, Joseph remembered later. Friday. Saturday. People would begin to wander in around six or so, bringing coolers full of icy beer and pop, talking loudly—Joseph's uncles and aunts and cousins, his father's old friends from work and their wives and kids—thirty, forty people sometimes. They would barbecue, and there would be corn on the cob, bowls of potato chips and honey-roasted peanuts, slices of cheese and salami, pickled eggs and jalapeños. Music of Waylon Jennings, Willie Nelson, Crystal Gayle. Some people dancing.

Their house was about a mile outside of town. The kids would play outdoors, in the backyard and the large stubble field behind the house. Dusk seemed to last for hours, and when it was finally dark, they would sit under the porch light, catching thickly buzzing june bugs and moths, or even an occasional toad who hopped into the circle of light, tempted by the halo of insects that floated around the bare orange light bulb next to the front door.

Rusty hardly ever joined in their games. Instead, he would stake out some corner of the yard, or even a chair inside the house, sitting, quietly observing.

Who knew what the adults were doing? They played cards and gossiped. There were bursts of laughter, Aunt DeeDee's high, fun-house cackle rising above the general mumble; they sang along with the songs. After he got drunk, Joseph's father would go around touching the ladies on the back of the neck with his hook, surprising them, making them scream. Sometimes he would take off his arm and dance with it. Sometimes he would cry about Billy Merritt.

The nights grew late. Empty beer cans filled the trash cans and lined the counter tops. The younger children fell asleep in rows on the beds. If he was still awake, Joseph would sometimes gaze out the window, out to where the last remaining adults stood in a circle in the backyard, whispering and giggling, passing a small cigarette from hand to hand. Joseph was eight and wasn't supposed to know what was going on.

But Rusty told him.

At first, Joseph didn't want to believe it. Joseph had mostly heard frightening things about drugs—that wicked people sometimes put LSD in Halloween candy, to make the children go crazy; that if you took Angel Dust, you would try to kill the first person you saw; that dope pushers sometimes came around playgrounds and tried to give children marijuana, and that, if this happened, you should run away and tell an adult as soon as possible.

376

Rusty had smoked pot; he had also accidentally taken LSD, which someone had given to him in a chocolate bar.

Joseph wasn't sure he believed this either. The depth of Rusty's experience, of his depravity, seemed almost impossible.

Later, when Joseph's parents were out, Joseph and Rusty went through their dresser drawers. They found copies of pornographic magazines in Joseph's father's T-shirt drawer, at the very bottom; in his mother's bra-and-panty drawer, they found a small baggie full of what Rusty said was marijuana.

Rusty took a little for himself, and Joseph nearly started crying.

"Don't tell," Rusty said to him. "You're not going to tell, are you? You know your mom and dad could get in trouble with the police if they ever got caught."

"I won't tell," Joseph whispered.

Joseph's father seemed like a regular father, except for his arm. Sometimes, on Saturdays after breakfast, Joseph and his father and Rusty would drive up into the hills with Joseph's father's 10 gauge rifles. Joseph's father lined up beer cans and mayonnaise jars and such along a fence, and they would shoot at them. Joseph's father could not hold the gun well enough to aim it himself, but he showed Joseph and Rusty how.

The first time Rusty took the gun, his hands were shaking. "Have you ever handled a gun before, son?" Joseph's father said, and Rusty slowly shook his head.

Joseph's father showed Rusty where to hold his hands, how the butt of the gun fit against his shoulder. "OK, OK," Joseph's father said. He stooped behind Rusty, his chin right next to Rusty's ear. "Can you see through the cross hairs? Right where the lines meet?"

Joseph watched as his father and Rusty took careful aim, both their bodies poised for a moment. When the mayonnaise jar burst apart, Joseph leapt up. "You hit it!" he cried, and Rusty turned to him, eyes wide, his mouth slightly open in quiet wonder.

Joseph's mother was waiting with lunch when they got home. She made hamburgers and corn on the cob.

She seemed to Joseph like a typical mother. She was slightly overweight, and bustled, and was cheerful most of the time. When Rusty first came, she would sometimes give him hugs, but he would always become rigid and uncomfortable. After a time, she stopped hugging him. Instead, she would simply rest her hand on his shoulder, or on his arm. Rusty wouldn't look at her when she did this, but he didn't move away either. Joseph thought of what he was learning about plants at school. They drank in sunlight, as their food; they breathed, though you couldn't see it. He thought of this as he watched Rusty sit there, with Joseph's mother's hand on his shoulder. Her hand briefly massaged his neck before she took it away, and Joseph could see the way Rusty's impassive expression shuddered, the way his eyes grew very still and far away.

Rusty stood at the edge of the backyard and stared out into the distance: the fields, lined with telephone poles; the grasshopper oil wells, gently nodding their sleepy heads. At the edge of the horizon, a ridge of hills rose from the flatland, and Rusty watched them, though there was nothing there. Joseph sat on the back steps and watched what Rusty watched, wondered what Rusty was wondering. After a time, Rusty turned to glance at Joseph. Rusty's face was solemn, stiff with the weight of his thoughts.

"What are you staring at?" Rusty said, and Joseph shrugged.

"Nothing," he said.

"Come over here," Rusty said, and when Joseph did, Rusty didn't say anything for a while. "Hm," he said, considering Joseph's face. "Do you know what would happen if a kid like you got sent to a foster home?"

"No." And Joseph breathed as Rusty's eyes held him, without blinking.

"They do really nasty things to the little kids. And if you try to scream, they put your own dirty underwear in your mouth, to gag you." He stared at Joseph, as if he was imagining this.

Then, abruptly, Rusty gestured at the sky. He pointed. "You see that?" he said. "That's the evening star." He put his palms firmly over Joseph's ears and tilted Joseph's head, swiveling it as if it were a telescope. "You see it now? It's right . . . there!" And he drew a line with his finger from Joseph's nose to the sky.

Joseph nodded. He closed his eyes. He could feel the cool, claylike dampness of Rusty's palm against his head. The sound of Rusty's hands against his ears was like the whispering inside a shell. "I see it," Joseph said softly.

Sometimes, they all seemed so happy. Here they were, watching TV in the evening, Joseph's mother sitting on his father's lap in the big easy chair, laughing at some secret joke, his mother blushing. Here they were, camping at the lake, roasting marshmallows on sharpened sapling sticks over a campfire; Joseph and Cecilia climbing on their father's shoulders out in the lake and jumping into the water, as if he were a diving board; baby Tom running along the sand naked, laughing as their mother pretended to chase him.

At night, Joseph and Rusty would wade along the edge of the shore with a flashlight, catching crawdads. Rusty wasn't afraid of their pinchers. He would grin hard, letting them dangle like jewelry clamped to the lobes of his ears.

Joseph didn't know what the feeling was that filled him up in such moments. It was something about the way the flashlight's beam made a glossy bowl of light beneath the water; the way, under the beam, everything was clear and distinct—the bits of floating algae and tiny water animals, the polished stones and sleepy minnows flashing silver and metallic blue, the crawdads, sidling backward with their claws lifted warily. It was the sound of his parents' voices in the distance, as they sat around the campfire, the echoing waver as their father began to sing. Rusty was a silhouette against the slick, blue-black stretch of lake, and Joseph could see that the sky wasn't like a ceiling. It was like water too, deep water, depth upon depth, vast beyond measure. And this was something Joseph found beautiful. And he loved his young mother and father, laughing in the distance, and Cecilia and baby Tom, asleep in their tent, already dreaming—and Rusty himself, standing there silently in the dark. He was filled with a kind of awed contentment, which he thought must be happiness.

Later, deep in his sleeping bag in the tent, Joseph could hear his parents talking. Their voices were low, almost underneath the crackling of the fire, but he found that if he listened hard he could understand.

"I don't know," his mother was saying. "How long does it take to get over something like that?"

"He's all right," Joseph's father said. "He's a good kid. He just needs to be left alone. I don't think he wants to talk about it."

"Oh," his mother said, and breathed heavily. "I can't even imagine, you know? I think . . . What if I lost all of you like that? I don't see how I could go on. I'd kill myself, I really would."

"No you wouldn't," Joseph's father said. "Don't say stuff like that."

And then they were silent. Joseph looked over to where Rusty was lying and saw that Rusty was awake too. The tent walls glimmered with firelight, and the glow flickered against Rusty's open eyes. Rusty's jaw moved as he listened.

"Hey you," Joseph's mother said playfully, after a long pause. "You keep that hand to yourself!" She giggled a little.

Joseph woke in the night; he could feel something pressing against him, and when he opened his eyes, the tent's thin walls were almost phosphorescent with moonlight. Rusty's sleeping bag was rolled close to his, and he could feel Rusty's body moving. Inside their sleeping bags, they were like strange, unearthly creatures—thick caterpillars, cocoons. Rusty was rocking against him and whispering, though the words blurred together in a steady rhythm, rising and falling until Joseph could almost make out the words, like something lost in the winds:

"Waiting . . . I've . . . when are you . . . O I am waiting for . . . and you never . . ." and the rocking quickened for a moment, and he thought Rusty was crying. But Joseph didn't dare open his eyes. He kept himself very still, breathing slowly, as a sleeper would. Rusty was making a sound, a high thread of tuneless humming, which, after a moment, Joseph realized was the word "Mom," stretched impossibly thin, unraveling and unraveling. And Joseph knew that this was something he could never speak of, to anyone.

Yet even then, even in this still and spooky moment, there was a kind of happiness: something wondrous in Rusty's whispered words, in the urgent pressing of Rusty's body, a secret almost glimpsed. What was it? What was it?

He couldn't ask Rusty, who was more silent and sullen than ever in the week after they returned from their camping trip. He would disappear for hours sometimes, trailing a heavy silence behind him, and if Joseph did encounter him—lying face up in a ditch thick with tall pigweed and sunflowers, or hunkered down by the lumber pile behind the garage—Rusty would give him a look so baleful that Joseph knew he shouldn't approach.

When Rusty had first come to live with them, Joseph said, "Am I supposed to call Rusty my brother?" They were sitting at the supper table, and both his father and mother stopped short and looked up.

"Well," Joseph's father said cautiously. "I know we'd sure like it if Rusty thought of us as his family. But I think it's up to Rusty what you call him." Joseph felt bad at the way that Rusty shrank when they all looked at him. Rusty froze, and his face seemed to pass through a whole series of uncertain expressions.

Then he smiled. "Sure, Joseph," he said. "Let's be brothers." And he showed Joseph a special high-five, where you pressed your thumbs together after slapping palms. You pressed your thumb against the other person's, and each of you fluttered your four fingers. It made the shape of a bird, probably an eagle or a falcon.

It didn't really make them brothers. Joseph knew that Rusty had probably only said something nice to please Joseph's parents, just as he sometimes called them "Uncle Dave," and "Aunt Colleen" to make them happy. But that was OK. *Something* had happened. Something strange and unexplainable passed through the pads of their thumbs when they slid against each other.

This was what Joseph thought of as he watched Rusty. That day, Rusty was slouching thoughtfully near an abandoned house not far from where they lived. Joseph had traced him that far, but he kept his distance. He watched through a pair of his father's binoculars as Rusty picked up an old beer bottle and broke it on a stone, throwing back his arm with a pitcher's flourish. The windows in the old house were already broken out, but Rusty hit at the empty frames with a stick for a while. He lifted his head and looked around, suspiciously. He didn't see Joseph, who was hidden in a patch of high weeds, and after a time, feeling somewhat content, Rusty settled onto his haunches and began to smoke some of the marijuana he'd taken from Joseph's parents' dresser.

Joseph observed: the way his eyes closed as he drew smoke into his mouth, and the way he held it in his lungs, then exhaled in a long breath. For a moment, Rusty let the handmade cigarette hang loosely from his lips, like a movie detective. Then he inhaled again.

Rusty seemed more relaxed when he finally came back to the house, around dinner time. He even deigned to play a game of Super Mario Brothers with Joseph, which he almost never did. They sat side by side on the living room floor, urging Super Mario through obstacles, dodging and jumping, and when Joseph discovered a magic mushroom that would make him invincible for several turns, Rusty gave him the old high-five. He grinned at Joseph kindly. "Rock on," Rusty said.

But that night, as he and Joseph lay in bed, all Rusty wanted to talk about was leaving. New York. Los Angeles. Nashville. Learning how to play electric guitar. He was thinking of writing a letter to the rock band Judas Priest, and asking if he could work for them.

"I'll take you with me," Rusty said. "When we go. Judas Priest is very cool. I could tell them you were my little brother. And we were, like, homeless or something. They'd probably teach us to play instruments. So, you know, when they got older, we would take over. We'd be, like, Judas Priest, Part 2."

"What would I be?" Joseph asked. He wanted to see himself in this new world clearly, to imagine it whole, as Rusty had.

"Probably the drummer," Rusty said. "You like drums, don't you?"

"Yes," Joseph said. He waited, wanting to hear more about himself as a drummer, but Rusty merely folded his hands behind his head.

"We'd probably have to kill them, you know, " Rusty said.

"Who?" Joseph asked. "Judas Priest?"

"No, asshole," Rusty said irritably. "Dave and Colleen. Your parents. I mean, we could get the gun while they were sleeping and it wouldn't even hurt them. It would just be like they were asleep. We could take your dad's car, you know. I could drive."

Joseph thought of his father's new Jeep Rambler, in the driveway, still shiny from its carwash. He pictured sitting in the passenger seat, with Rusty behind the wheel. He didn't say anything for a minute. He didn't know whether Rusty was joking or not, and he was both scared and exhilarated.

He watched as Rusty drew his bare foot out from beneath the covers and picked at a knobby toe. "You could kill the little kids first, while they were sleeping. It wouldn't hurt them, you know. It wouldn't matter. And then, with the gunshots, your mom and dad would come running in, and you could shoot them when they came through the door . . . " He paused, dreamily, looking at Joseph's face. "And then if you lit the house on fire, no one would ever know what happened. All the evidence, all the bodies and everything would be burned up."

He said this steadily, but his eyes seemed to darken as he spoke, and Joseph felt his neck prickle. He watched as Rusty's mouth hardened, trying to tighten over a quiver of his lips, a waver in his expression. He said, "They'd think we died too. They wouldn't come looking for us, because," he whispered, *they wouldn't know we were still alive."*

Rusty stared at him, his face lit silver in the moonlight, and Joseph could feel a kind of dull, motionless panic rising inside him, as in a dream. A part of him wanted to shout out for his mother, but he didn't. Instead, he slid his legs slowly onto the tile of the floor. "I have to go to the bathroom," he said, and stood, uncertainly. For a minute, he thought he would start to run.

But the minute he stood up, Rusty moved quickly, catching him by the arm. He caught Joseph and held tightly; he pulled Joseph close to him. The sweet, coppery smell of feet hung on his bare skin, as he pulled Joseph against him.

"Shh!" Rusty's fingers gripped, pinching Joseph's arms. "Don't scream!" Rusty whispered urgently, and Joseph could feel Rusty's muscles tighten. They stood there in a kind of hug, and Rusty pressed his mouth close to Joseph's ear, so that Joseph could feel Rusty's lips brush against the soft lobe. Rusty didn't let Joseph go, but his grip loosened. "Shh," he said. "Don't cry, Joseph. Don't be scared." He had begun to rock back and forth a bit, still holding Joseph, still shushing. "We're like brothers, aren't we? And brothers love each other. Nothing bad's going to happen to you, cause I'm your brother, man, I won't let it. Don't be scared." And Joseph looked up at Rusty's face. He didn't know whether Rusty was telling the truth or not, but he nodded anyway. Rusty's eyes held him as they rocked together, and Joseph swallowed tears and phlegm, closing his mouth tightly. It was true. They did love each other.

For the next few days, or maybe weeks, Rusty paid attention to Joseph. There were times when Joseph thought of that night that Rusty had talked of killing, of lighting fires, and there were even times when he felt that it would probably happen, sooner or later. But when he woke from a bad dream, Rusty was always awake, sitting on the edge of the bed, saying, "It's OK, don't be afraid," passing his hand slowly across Joseph's face, his fingers tracing Joseph's eyelids until they shut. During the day, Joseph and Rusty would take walks, strolling silently out into the bare stubble fields. An occasional jackrabbit would spring up from a patch of weeds and bolt away, leaving little puffs of dust behind its large, fleeing feet. They turned over rocks and found sow bugs, centipedes, metallic-shelled beetles. Sometimes, Rusty found fossils, and he and Joseph took them home and examined them under a magnifying glass. After a while, Joseph's worries passed away; he stopped thinking he should tell his parents about what Rusty had said that night. Rusty himself never spoke of it again. Sometimes, as they looked at the fossils—imprints of fish bones and ferns and clam shells—Rusty would lean over Joseph, letting his face softly brush Joseph's hair. It was said that there had once been a great sea covering the land where they now lived. That was where the fossils came from.

In those days and weeks near the end of the summer, it seemed that something strange was happening to Joseph's family. They were not dead, not burned up, but they seemed to have taken on the qualities of ghosts, without knowing it. There was baby Tom sitting on the sofa, solemnly staring at Joseph, motionless, his mouth very small and stern. There was Cecilia, skipping at the edge of the lilac bush, talking to herself softly in different voices, the sun behind her, making her shadowlike, so it seemed for a moment that she disappeared, melting into the branches and leaves.

Once, at night, he opened his eyes and his mother had been standing over him, in her pale, silky nightgown. A flash of distant lightning made her glow for a moment, and when she reached across him to close the open window above his head, the nightgown rippled and fluttered in a sudden wind, as if she might be lifted up like a piece of ragged cloth.

In the morning, when Joseph came down for breakfast, his mother was kneeling on the kitchen floor, tying the laces of Joseph's father's boots as Joseph's father sat in a chair at the table. They had been talking softly, but they stopped when they saw Joseph standing there.

"Breakfast will be ready in a little bit," she said. Joseph's father's head was drooping, and he didn't look up, only rolled his eyes in Joseph's direction. "Why don't you go outside and play," Joseph's mother said. "I'll call you when breakfast is ready."

One day, not long later, Joseph and Rusty came across his father sitting at the kitchen table, practicing picking up a cup with his prosthetic hand. They watched as he lifted it, set it down, lifted it, set it down, over and over. He was mumbling to the cup, cursing it. "Bitch," his father whispered at the cup, and they were very quiet as the cup wavered in the air, liquid spilling over the trembling cup's edge as his father hardened his eyes, hating the cup. Joseph's father brought the cup to his lips and then it slipped through the metal pinchers and fell to the floor. "Dirty bitch," Joseph's father hissed as the cup broke into shards of porcelain and splashes of coffee. Rusty tugged Joseph's arm, pulling him back. They knew they must not be seen.

There were times, during that last month of summer, when it seemed that he and Rusty were the only ones alive. The rest of Joseph's family seemed to be in a kind of trance, sleepwalkers that he and Rusty moved among. Joseph imagined them jolting awake, suddenly, blinking. "Where are we?" they would say. "What happened to us?"

But the trance didn't break. Instead, the rest of Joseph's family often seemed like statues in a faraway garden, people under a curse, frozen, while Joseph and Rusty walked in the distance.

Across the stubble field, in the old abandoned house, they gathered wood together and made a little bonfire in the center of what must have been the living room. They pretended it was after a nuclear holocaust, and they were the only two people alive. The smoke rose in a sinewy column and crawled along the ceiling toward the broken windows. Joseph and Rusty took vegetables from the garden and put them in a coffee can with water and made a delicious soup, boiled over their fire. Later, they put one of Cecilia's Barbies in the can with a G.I. Joe. They watched as the dolls' plastic limbs melted together, drooping and dripping. Removed from the heat, the two were fused together in a single charred mass.

Kissing: on the floor of the old house, shirtless, Rusty on top of him, their hands clasped, Rusty's sticky skin against his own, their mouths open. When Joseph closed his eyes, it felt as if a small, eager animal was probing the inside of his mouth. It felt funny; he liked it.

It didn't mean he was a fag, Rusty said, and Joseph nodded. There were children at Joseph's school who were called fags. They were too skinny, or too fat; they were weak, or wore stupid clothes, or had funny voices. You knew to avoid them because their loneliness would stick to you.

"You can't tell anybody," Rusty said. "Ever." He traced his finger along Joseph's lips, and then down, along Joseph's neck, his chest, his belly button.

"I know," said Joseph, and when Rusty lowered his body, Joseph let his tongue move over Rusty's chest. *They wouldn't know we were still alive*, Joseph thought, and he closed his eyes. For a moment, it was true: his family was dead, and he and Rusty were on their way together somewhere, and it was all right. He wasn't scared anymore. His lips brushed against Rusty's nipple and he liked the strange, nubby way it felt. He pressed his tongue against it, and was surprised by the way Rusty's body jolted.

Rusty rolled off of him, pushing away, and Joseph's eyes opened. He watched as Rusty knelt in the corner of the old house, unzipping his jeans.

"What are you doing?" Joseph said, and Rusty hunched himself fiercely.

"I'm jerking off, you moron," Rusty said hoarsely. "What, do you want me to fuck you?"

Joseph took a step closer, trying to see what Rusty was doing to his penis, but Rusty gritted his teeth and glared, so he kept his distance.

"Would it hurt?" Joseph said, after a moment, and Rusty hunched even further, the muscles of his back tightening.

"Yes," Rusty hissed. "It would hurt." And he was silent for a moment. "Get out of here, you faggot! Get lost! I mean it!"

And Joseph had slowly backed away, uncertainly. He stood in the high weeds at the door of the house, waiting. There was the summer churr of cicadas; grasshoppers jumped from the high sunflowers and pigweed into his hair, and he shook them off.

"Rusty?" he called. "Rusty?" After a time, he went cautiously back into the house, but Rusty wasn't there. Though Joseph looked everywhere, Rusty didn't appear until supper time.

And then it was over. A week later, they returned to school. They didn't go back to the old house together, and, though they would wait together for the bus in the morning, Rusty was distant. Whatever had happened between them was gone. Why? Joseph thought. Why? But Rusty wouldn't say anything. When Joseph tried to talk to Rusty at night, Rusty would pretend to be asleep. Once, when he tried to get in bed next to Rusty, Rusty kicked him, hard—hard enough to send him across the room with a clatter that brought his mother running.

"Joseph fell out of bed," Rusty said solemnly, and Joseph just sat there on the floor, crying, while his mother stared at them.

"What's going on here?" she said, and Rusty shrugged.

"Nothing," he said, and Joseph crawled back into his own bed, silently.

"Nothing," Joseph said.

Joseph waited for a long time after his mother had left before he spoke. "Rusty," he said. "What did I do? Why don't you like me anymore?"

But Rusty was silent. His breath came out in a threatening sigh.

When Rusty killed himself, a month later, it seemed like a long time had unfolded. Joseph had become used to Rusty's silences. Joseph was involved in school, and the time in the summer had already begun to seem like a long time ago.

He found Rusty in the old living room of the abandoned house. A small bonfire was dwindling, and Rusty's body was splayed out, arms wide, legs spread-eagle, propped in a sitting position against the wall. Rusty had taken one of Joseph's father's guns, put it in his mouth, and pulled the trigger. Later, Joseph learned that it was the anniversary of Rusty's family's death. That was why they said he did it. The bottom half of his face had been blown off, but his eyes were still open. They seemed to have been coated with a thick, smoky film.

Joseph didn't remember leaving the old house. He must have made his way through the weeds, across the stubble field, to the kitchen, where his parents were sitting there, drinking coffee. He could hear the sound of the television. It was Saturday morning, and Cecilia and baby Tom were still watching cartoons.

Years later, Joseph thought there must have been something he missed. Some bit of unremembered time, something that would help him make sense of it all. But it was surprisingly blank. He recalled the moment in the tent, and the night Rusty talked of killing; he recalled the steady effort of his father to hold a cup, to pick up a pen from the bare slick table. He remembered kissing. He remembered waking up in the morning with Rusty pressed against him, holding him tight, feeling Rusty's warm breath against his shoulder blades. But he didn't know what had happened, really. And now he would never know.

He stood at the screen door, and the kitchen seemed to stretch out like a tunnel. It was as if his own life were being separated from him;

he would forever float outside it, a ghost hovering above himself. His mother looked at him, her eyes tired and sad. His father raised his prosthetic hand, clicking the hooks together, and then he gave Joseph a wink.

"Hey there, little man," Joseph's father said, as Joseph waved vaguely.

He wanted to tell them, but his throat was dry. "Rusty's dead," he wanted to say, and he watched as they turned to him, smiling: grown suddenly huge in their sweetness, in their lostness, in their gentle, helpless unknowing.

Nominated by Wally Lamb, Nancy Richard, Alice Schell, Jean Thompson

MIGRATION INSTINCT

by KEETJE KUIPERS

from CODEX JOURNAL

for Becky

Today the wife of the last man who made me lonely
is having a baby. Oh, October: we all want
to get up and leave, crawl out of our flesh sacks and fly
like mad. Back when I was someone else this would have been
a day for wallowing, for bumming a cigarette
off some hot, filthy man and downing gin at noon. I'd
have basted my eyelids with green shadow, tossed less-than-
delicate looks across the room at strangers still full
of all the sweet possibility I could muster—
something to drive the low growl of nostalgia away.
It would have been a tear-down-the-street-blowing-stop-signs
day, a roll-down-the-windows-full-volume afternoon.
But I've got diapers to wash, tiny sock-after-sock
to fold. The greatest sin I'm allowed is a sip of
coffee. Sadness is so much work. Angry takes too much
time. And there's my own daughter, winking in the lamp light,
her mouth to my breast, sucking it all right out of me.

Nominated by Fred Leebron and Codex Journal

CONSTANCE BAILEY IN THE YEAR OF MONICA LEWINSKY

by SARAH VALLANCE

from THE GETTYSBURG REVIEW

Constance Bailey is the poorest person on their list, the woman from Little Brothers tells me when I turn up at their office in Roxbury and offer to volunteer. At eighty-eight, she has no friends nor family.

"She hasn't thought much of the volunteers we've sent her in the past," the woman says, scrunching up her forehead. "She's picky. I'm not going to lie. The last few visitors didn't work out. She didn't take to them at all." The woman puts on a pair of reading glasses and looks down at a notebook in front of her. "There's a scribble here that says she doesn't want any more visitors. Never mind, let's try and see what happens." She peers over her glasses at me and shrugs. "Don't take it personally if she asks you to leave."

"I won't," I laugh.

The woman licks her thumb and flicks through an old manila folder. I look up at a poster behind her of the Little Brothers Friends of the Elderly logo with its single long-stemmed rose. A red rose seems like an odd symbol for a charity that matches volunteers with old people, but that thought leaves my mind almost as soon as it enters. "She hasn't left her apartment in more than five years now. They stuck her in a place on the fifth floor. Without an elevator. Can you believe it?" The woman shakes her head. "She can't get round without a walking frame. There was a fire twenty years ago. Destroyed the place she was staying. Constance nearly died, and the fire took everything. Now what else can I tell you?" She runs her index finger down the page of her notebook and clicks her tongue. "Oh, that's right, be careful of her cat," the woman says, her eyes widening. "He's been known to attack."

I giggle.

"I'm not kidding," she says.

"Okay."

"And don't mention God."

"That won't be a problem," I say.

"Well you two might get along after all," she says and smiles.

It is September 1997, and by some happy accident, I have won a scholarship to Harvard for a year to study the access of very poor elderly African Americans to healthcare. I have just arrived from Australia and know no poor elderly African Americans and almost nothing about the American healthcare system, so as a first step, I have signed up as a volunteer with Little Brothers. I spend more time than I should pondering the name Little Brothers Friends of the Elderly. Are they little in stature or little in age? It is a slightly creepy name for a charity.

I get off the bus the next day outside the women's hospital on Huntington Avenue and cross the road to Tremont. The woman from Little Brothers warned me about the neighborhood. "It's the roughest part of Boston," she said. All I know of Roxbury is that Bobbie Brown grew up here and watched his brother-in-law get shot dead in a gang fight the year before. I saw it on TV not long after arriving in Boston when I was holed up in bed with the flu.

Constance lives less than three blocks away from Harvard Medical School. I could have walked. I reach inside my pocket and check the address. It is a gray 1970s concrete public-housing block, stacked in a long line of gray 1970s concrete public-housing blocks. The only way to tell them apart is the large red numbers painted on the fronts of the buildings. In the street outside, a man tinkers under the bonnet of an old blue Pontiac. There is no one else in sight.

The glass door to the building has a fracture running from the top right hand corner of the frame to the middle, where it stops, as if not knowing which way to go next. Stuck to the glass is a ripped flyer with a picture of a tabby cat. "Missing since 1 Aug." It is the last week of September. I don't hold out much hope for that cat.

A brick of plastic-wrapped yellow pages props open the door. Inside, there is nothing but a wall of letter boxes, some with their doors missing, stuffed full of junk mail. Opposite the letter boxes, a doorway leads to the stairwell. I make my way up to the fifth floor, sidestepping bits of broken furniture, a twisted bicycle wheel missing a tire, shards of

391

broken glass, bags of moldering garbage. The building is eerily quiet. I wonder where everyone is.

Her front door is protected by a thick steel grate. I take a moment to catch my breath before pressing the buzzer. My heart thumps. Why am I even here? I am terrible at small talk. What if she doesn't like me? What if I don't like her? I give her fifteen seconds to open the door. I get to thirteen when the door cracks open.

"Who is it?" a voice shouts from inside.

"Sarah. I'm a volunteer with Little Brothers."

"How do I know that?"

"They called to let you know I was coming."

"What?"

I poke through my bag for my Harvard ID badge. "That's the only ID I have," I say, slipping it through the grate.

A bony, knotted hand reaches through the grate and takes the card. The door inches open, and an elderly woman stares at me through the safety chain for a few moments before deciding to open the door and unlock the grate. I hold out my hand. "Nice to meet you," I say.

"Connie," she says, taking my hand like it's a clump of wet cabbage.

I am barely inside when a huge black cat leaps at me from the top of the sofa, pinning himself to my chest. "Fuck!" I shriek, trying to fight him off. Connie shuffles bow legged over to the corner of the room.

"Mind the cat," she says, without turning around.

She folds herself into the old brown vinyl chair, its arms and headrest held in place with thick strips of silver duct tape. Pointing at the green vinyl two-seater sofa, she instructs me to sit. I sit perfectly still to avoid upsetting the creature that hovers above me on the back of the sofa. I am not a cat person, I remember, as the cat stalks the length of the sofa. Eager to make a good impression on Connie, I smile at him and pretend I am not terrified at the prospect of a second assault.

"He botherin' you?"

"No, not at all," I lie.

"He scratch you? On the way in?"

"I'm okay."

"Bathroom's over there if you need to clean up."

"Thanks."

"Leave her alone, Inky," she says. With those simple words, the cat hops off the sofa, walks toward the kitchen, and glowers at me from the doorway.

"He's good security," I say.

"What? Oh, yeah. He scratched and bit the social worker once. Never saw *her* again." A slight smile starts across her face. I smile back, and she catches herself and fixes her glare on the TV screen.

It is a warm day in Boston, and the tiny apartment has no fan or air-conditioning. A block of wood wedges the window open to capture whatever breeze it can through the maze of buildings outside.

"This apartment is the worst," she says, fanning herself with an old newspaper. "Boilin' in the summer, freezin' in the winter."

Connie is a tall woman, buckled by age, gout, arthritis. Her hair is silver and too sparse to cover her scalp. She wears a pale blue night-dress underneath a flimsy polyester dressing gown. Beneath the cut off arms of her gown, I catch glimpses of skin grafts, a patchwork of flesh across her arms and forearms. Sweat trickles down the sides of her face from her hairline.

The living-room walls of her apartment are hospital green, the floor tiled with swirly gray-and-white linoleum squares. Her chair looks like it spent its life in a nursing home, before being tossed out to make way for something newer. The room looks like the inside of a poorly stocked thrift shop. Nothing matches. No ornaments or photographs. The only thing that belongs to Connie is the large black cat with moss-green eyes that prowls around the apartment like an armed guard.

"He came from the MSPCA," she says. "A man from the housing department found rats under the sink." She nods in the direction of the kitchen. "He went to the MSPCA himself and got him. God knows what they done to him. Terrified of everythin'. He's a lot better now. I've had him five years."

"He's a very handsome cat," I say, and he is. He looks like a panther cub.

She nods her head. "Not many with eyes like him."

"True," I say. He looks psychotic.

"Anyway, he's all I got and I'm all he's got too. We're family."

"He's a very lucky cat," I say.

"What?"

"He's lucky."

"Oh, yeah. No one else'd take him. Not with all that scratchin' and bitin'."

I tell her I have a rescue dog at home in Sydney.

"What?"

I say it again, but she shoots me another blank look.

"You like Clinton?" she asks after a pause.

"I do," I say.

"You believe in God?"

"I do not," I say.

"Well we got *that* in common," she says and slaps her knees with her hands.

We pass an hour with strained conversation before she starts to pry herself out of her chair. "No need for you to come back," she says. "Me and Inky get along just fine. We don't need *nothin'*!"

I take that as my cue to leave.

"Can I come back the same time next Monday?"

"Monday?" She sounds deflated.

"See you then."

She nods once without speaking and shuts the door behind me.

On Monday I return with a large floor fan that I set up next to the TV.

"What do I owe you for it?" she asks.

"It's a gift," I say.

"Well it's a fine gift, let me tell you. Thank you!"

"I'll get you a heater when it starts getting cold. But no need for that now."

"Thank you. I appreciate it. I do. But you don't need to buy me *nothin'*."

"I wanted to. You can't sit here sweating all day."

"What? Ah, I've done it for years now." She leans in toward the fan, relishing the breeze.

It is the second time I have seen her smile.

Our first few visits are awkward. I speak, and she looks back at me and shrugs. Perhaps she is hard of hearing. I make a point of speaking slowly and loudly.

It takes another few visits before Connie leans forward in her chair and smiles at me.

"You know, your first coupla visits?"

"When you told me you didn't want me to come back?"

"Want to know why?"

"Yes!"

"I couldn't understand a damn word you said! That accent! I ain't never heard anything like it! Ever!"

I laugh.

"It's like we was speakin' two different languages!"

I tell her a lot of accents are stranger than mine. Or at least I think so.

"Not to me!" she says, before dissolving into fits of laughter, slapping her knee with delight.

I have made her laugh. I am happy.

"Can you understand me now?"

"Most of the time, but it's taken a month to work out what you're sayin'!"

"I don't have a problem understanding you," I say.

"That's because I speak *English*!" she squeals and slaps her knee again.

Connie has limited contact with the outside world. A homemaker visits twice a week to clean the apartment and do her laundry. Every three weeks a nurse from the Visiting Nurse Association comes to check her heart and her blood pressure. A doctor comes by every three months to check in on her too. Then there is the social worker who visits every month. Meals on Wheels is available if she wants it. She doesn't.

"You tried that food?" she asks.

No, but I tell her my mother used to deliver Meals on Wheels when I was in high school, and each time I got into the car after she had made her rounds, I had to wind down the window and hang my head outside. It didn't smell like food.

"It's not fit for humans!"

A week or so later, when Connie is fighting off a cold, I offer to cook for her.

She looks at me like I am crazy. "White people can't cook! Well that's what they say anyway. I ain't never eaten any white person's food."

"You think the reason I can't cook is because I'm white? You might be right. I'm a lousy cook," I say.

She laughs and thanks me for the offer. I ask her about her favorite foods: fresh roast chicken, baked potatoes, cookies, and Hershey's Kisses. "But don't go to any trouble!" she says.

"It's no trouble at all," I tell her, returning the next day with two bags full of food.

I had never heard of Hershey's Kisses, but Connie's face lights up like a small child's when I unpack the shopping and produce a large plastic bag full of them. She peels off the silver wrapping and places a chocolate on her tongue.

"Nothin' like it," she says, her eyes closed with pleasure. "Try one," she says.

They are possibly the most disgusting chocolates I have ever eaten.

I bring her real chocolate, a couple of days later, so she can taste the difference.

"No!" she says, screwing up her face and passing it back to me. "It don't taste right. You eat it!" she says. I do.

Connie's only other visitor is a retired postman called Teddy Corsalis. Teddy worked the Tremont Street route until he turned sixty. Knowing Connie had nobody else, he decided when he retired to look in on her every weekday, and any weekend he could manage, and to do her grocery shopping twice a week. Every morning from Monday to Friday, and often on the weekend too, Teddy leaves home for the hour-long bus ride to Roxbury. He turns up around eleven o'clock with the day's newspaper and anything else she needs. He helps pay her bills, change lightbulbs, replace old washers, unblock the sink. Occasionally our visits overlap. Teddy gets up from the sofa where he has been reading his paper to let me in. He always seems relieved to see me. One day, after he leaves, I ask Connie why she never talks to him.

"He's a good man, I ain't doubtin' that," she says, "but I ain't got nothin' to say to him!"

"Why?"

"All that God stuff, I just don't like it."

"What God stuff?"

"Oh, you know, sometimes on a Sunday he'll tell me he came from church."

"Well that's okay, he's trying to make conversation. Does he talk about God with you?"

She stops for a moment. "No," she says quietly, her head bowed. "Maybe once but that was years back. I told him I don't care for any of that stuff."

"He's a good man, Connie. Be nice to him!"

She nods like a small child that has just been scolded. "All right."

Connie is curious about life in Australia. "Is it like *Crocodile Dundee*? I loved that movie!"

"No," I say, and watch her face drop. She is disappointed to learn that kangaroos do not hop down the main streets of our cities, that we do not carry large knives and kill our own food, that I didn't grow up in the outback. But she is impressed to learn that George, my dog, is a good part dingo.

"Could George carry a baby?" she asks almost instantly.

"I believe he could," I say. "Although I'd rather not give him the opportunity."

"So she was innocent?"

"Well, I don't think she killed the baby."

"What was she? A Jehovah? One of them weird religions, wasn't she?"

"Seventh-Day Adventist," I say. "I mean they are weird, but I don't think that means she killed her baby."

Connie pauses for a moment and nods.

"The way you treat your black people is a *disgrace!*" she says.

"Yes," I say. "It's shameful."

"Worse than here!" she says.

"A lot worse than here," I say. "You can't even compare them."

She nods and stares at the floor.

It is not the first time since arriving in America that someone has taken issue with me about Australia's appalling treatment of our aborigines.

"You have a lot of sharks there!" she says, her eyes wide open.

"No more than you do," I tell her. "But our surfers are braver than yours." She laughs. The only stories from Australia that make the news in Boston these days are about surfers getting chewed up by sharks. I tell her the perception many Australians have of Americans is of gun-crazed rednecks and TV evangelists.

"Really?" she laughs. "I guess we do have more than our share."

Connie spends hours poring over the newspaper each morning with a small magnifying glass. Nothing escapes her attention. By the time I show up, she is ready to grill me on anything from Clinton's healthcare reforms to Somalia to climate change. The fuss the media make over Monica Lewinsky incenses her.

"He's the best president we ever had! They should just shut up and leave him alone!"

"I agree," I say.

"He's a man! That's what they do!" she says.

"But he should have been a bit more discreet," I say.

"Who cares?" she shouts. "It ain't none of our business what he gets up to!"

I am about to tell her he is the president, so he should have been more careful, but I stop. Connie is Clinton's biggest fan, and I don't want to upset her.

"Leave the poor man alone!" She slumps back into her chair, shaking her head. "He's got enough problems!"

"Well he does now," I say, and we leave it at that.

My research stalls. It takes so many wrong turns I want to give up. I volunteer with two other very poor elderly women, an African American and a Caucasian, and visit them twice a week. Alice is blind and stuck in a wheelchair, and her apartment feels like a cave. I take her a tin of International Roast coffee every Tuesday, and we talk about her schizophrenic niece who visits without warning and smashes up her furniture. Then she takes my hand and prays. Kitty, the Caucasian woman, has a twisted spine and an elderly poodle-cross named Terry, and we spend our visits walking up Beacon Street to Johnny's supermarket and buying groceries that I carry home. Kitty lingers over the rancid-meat freezer, choosing packs of meat with red stickers that say, "Use Today," and I, a vegetarian for more than fifteen years, hold my hand over my mouth to stop myself gagging. When the shopping is done, we walk home together, the shopping bags in one of my arms, Terry in the other. I help Kitty unpack the groceries and leave.

Connie and I become close friends. I find myself identifying with her in a way that even I don't fully understand. I see bits of myself in her. Our past lives couldn't be more different. I have no experience of poverty, discrimination, disadvantage, servitude. And she certainly has no experience of the privilege and opportunity I have known. But our perspectives on life and our dispositions are eerily similar. I look at her sitting in her chair, alone in this world but for Inky, and I see myself.

Connie and I share an odd worldview. Neither of us likes people very much, but we care deeply for their welfare. We talk about the contradiction and decide we are part misanthrope, part humanitarian. I tell her that my father, a geologist, preferred rocks to people. "A rock will never disappoint you," he used to say. "And they don't speak." Connie laughs and tells me she wishes she had met him. "He would have loved you," I say, and she smiles.

Connie has always preferred animals to people. We were both like this since we were little. "Animals are a lot easier to love," Connie says, and she is right. She would rather be alone with her cat than an old person in need of visitors. I am pretty certain I will be the same. We talk about the paradox of loneliness: that we are more likely to be lonely *with* others than without. We are picky when it comes to company, and neither of us makes friends easily. When I leave America after my year here, Connie will end up being the only friend I made.

One afternoon after I have known her for a couple of months, I hug Connie good-bye. I am an awkward hugger and can count on one hand the number of spontaneous hugs I have offered in my life to people I am not sleeping with. But one day it happens. I get up to leave, and she follows me to the door. I put my arms around her. I tell her I will see her tomorrow. She exhales loudly.

"No one has done that to me in years!" she says.

I wave good-bye and make for the door before she sees my eyes well up.

I visit her most days, and on the days I can't make it, I telephone. I introduce her to Laura, my girlfriend, who has joined me in America and is taking a couple of subjects for her master's degree while I do my research. Laura knows how fond I am of Connie and has been pushing me to meet her.

"Connie, this is my friend, Laura, from Australia." Laura holds out her hand, and Connie takes it with both of hers.

"Your girlfriend?"

This catches me off guard.

"Um, well, yes." Connie and I have discussed pretty much every issue but homosexuality.

She smiles at me and then at Laura.

"Well you girls are *smart*!" she says. "And lucky! If I was your age, I'd be the same way. Who needs men?"

We laugh. I am relieved. "Laura is going to visit you on the days I can't make it," I tell her. "She's good company. Not as good as me, but good company all the same. And unlike me she can cook, so if you want anything just ask her. One of us will come every day. Sometimes we'll come together."

Connie beams. "Fine by me!"

Weeks later Connie tells me she likes Laura a lot, that Laura is good for me. "But boy you girls are different!" I tell her that Laura is my polar opposite in almost everything, and that my pessimism and introversion drive her crazy. I tell her that sooner or later Laura will leave me for someone more sociable, that it is just a matter of time. "That'll be her loss if she does," Connie says, and I shrug.

"She might be happier" I say.

I fill Connie in on my fucked-up family. I tell her about my father's death six years earlier from cancer and the rudderlessness I have felt since losing him. My father was the person in the world I loved most. Less than a year after he died, I got thrown off a horse and suffered a traumatic brain injury. Brain damage led to anger and depression, and I fell out with my mother and brother and have barely spoken to them since. I tell her about the neurologist who said I would never be able to work again, never finish the PhD I was a third of the way through researching. I tell her I spent a year alone at home lying on my sofa before waking one morning and realizing I had no choice but to teach my brain to work again. I transcribed large slabs of text from books and journals and kept a notebook in which I recorded every word I didn't remember or understand and its meaning. Over time I retaught myself to think, to write, to remember. I got a job. I met Laura, and she made me apply for a scholarship. I tell her that getting a scholarship to Harvard felt like winning the lottery because I had spent two of the past five years on a disability pension, with an IQ almost half what it was when I was eleven. Then I tell her my current fear: that every time I walk around Harvard yard, I worry that someone will approach me from behind, tap me on the shoulder, and tell me I am an imposter. It wasn't me who won the scholarship after all. Could I please go home?

Connie tells me about her stepfather who told her when she was six that no one wanted her, no one loved her, and that the best thing she could do was run away from home. He never sexually assaulted her, but he did try to kill her a couple of times. One night when she was ten, she woke in the bed she shared with a sister to find him straddling her, a brand new razor held at her jugular.

"Move and I'll kill you," he said.

"I just lay still as I could. Pretended I was dead. He got bored soon enough. Left me for another drink."

By the time she was eleven, Connie was cooking dinner for twelve siblings while her mother was at work. Her stepfather showed up in the kitchen drunk one evening and told her he was going to kill her. He picked her up by the waist, turned her upside down, and speared her into the ground. Her collarbone snapped. "I told my mother what he done. He denied it. Said I fell. But she said there was nothin' she could do. She was scared of him too," Connie said. "There was no laws back then. He could do what he wanted."

When Connie finally escaped her stepfather, it was to take up a job as a domestic helper. It was 1923, and she was fourteen. It was her only option if she was to make the money her mother needed to feed and clothe her siblings. Her first employer, a Yankee named Clarrie who owned a clothing store in Swampscott, kept her for nine years until the Depression wiped out his business. He was the kindest employer Connie ever had. He loved her cooking and would sit in the kitchen talking to her about literature and music while she baked him apple pie. Clarrie encouraged her to listen to opera and to read books from his library. "That's how I learnt about music and readin'." Clarrie ended up in a mental asylum, and Connie went from family to family, each one treating her worse than the last.

One family hired Connie on account of her "light-colored skin." They didn't want anyone scaring their children. Connie's skin looked dark to me. "I was never light colored! Never. And one day I did scare them kids. Then they let me go."

Families followed with wives that beat her and made her work fourteen-hour days, seven days a week, in return for ten dollars. Then came a wealthy Jewish family that called her "Schwartz" and referred to her in the third person when they found themselves in the same room. "You can't understand us can you?" the woman of the household once asked. Connie looked at her blankly. "Good," the woman said. This family insisted she prepare cooked meat and vegetables for their dogs and allowed her to eat nothing but macaroni.

Apart from Teddy, I am Connie's first white friend. I sit on the edge of her sofa, listening to her stories, my chest heaving with rage and shame. Then one afternoon, while we are drinking iced coffee and chatting about Princess Diana and how her death is taking up a ridiculous amount of media attention, she says, "I ain't never met anyone like you, Sarah. I wish I met you years ago."

"Me too," I say, having a feeling that things might have turned out differently. For both of us.

Connie tells me about the accident that nearly claimed her life. "I wish it had," she says. The oil burner in the apartment under hers exploded. It was daytime, and she was the only person home. She had been working nightshift in the hospital laundry and had just fallen asleep. She woke in the burns unit of a different hospital with a broken jaw and a badly scalded upper body. When a nurse passed her a mirror, she didn't recognize herself. Bald, bandaged, with a jaw the size of an orange. Blinded by smoke, she had fought the fireman as he had dragged her to safety through her bedroom window. She spent two months in hospital after the grafts became infected and had to visit the hospital each month for a year.

"You ain't never had anything like that pain."

"I can't even imagine," I say.

The hospital needed the bed back. A Red Cross van came to collect her. The volunteer gave her an old dressing gown and a pair of slippers and drove her to a local women's shelter. Along with everything else, the fire destroyed her money tin and $500. The grand sum of her life's savings. After months in a dorm in the women's shelter, the apartment here became vacant. "Ain't nothin' more important than a roof over your head," she says.

I want to take her out for the day, to release her from this tiny box, but I worry about getting her down and up five flights of stairs. I toss this around in my head for a week before suggesting we hire a car for the day and go for a drive. She can choose where we go and what we do. It takes her a couple of days to warm up to the idea, but then she gets excited. She has a niece living in West Lynn whom she hasn't seen for nearly ten years. Maybe we can drive up to visit her.

The day we are due to go, Connie is ready by 4:00 AM. Laura and I arrive five hours later, as planned. We are shocked when she opens the door. Her face is made up with lashings of electric-blue eye shadow and bright red lipstick, which looks like it was applied by a small child. Covering her thin silver hair is a jet-black wig with tight curls down to the shoulders. I don't recognize her. The contrast between an old woman's made-up face and knotted body with a mane of thick, youthful hair makes me do a double take.

"Wow!" I say.

On the floor are thick clumps of hair.

"I had to chop some of it off," she says, adjusting her wig. "I can't go out lookin' like no teenybopper!"

I find a tissue and clean the smear of lipstick from her mouth. "There you go," I say. "Much better."

Five years stuck inside her apartment have left Connie with a pair of legs that can't support her. She hobbles defiantly down one flight of stairs before her legs fold. We manage to catch her before she hits the ground.

"This place is a dump! Look at all this garbage!" she snorts, catching her breath.

There are four flights left. "We're going to have to carry you. That okay?" I say.

"Okay," she says.

"By *we*, I mean Laura."

"Okay."

Laura, six foot tall and a lot stronger than me, scoops her up in her arms and carries her down to the car.

Connie settles into the backseat of our metallic-red rental car. "Sure you don't want to sit in the front?" I ask. "You'll see more."

"I like it better back here!" she says.

"Are you embarrassed because of the color? I am, but it was the only one they had," I say.

"No! It's a beautiful color!" she says. "But if you ain't used to drivin' on the right side of the road, then I think I'll stay back here!"

"Good call," I tell her. Connie straps herself in tightly and begins to sing.

In the five years Connie has been locked inside, the local neighborhood has changed a lot. We do a few blocks of Roxbury, and she stares out the window, her mouth hanging open. I watch her expression in the rearview mirror as we pass new shops, new buildings, and gaping vacant lots where buildings she remembers used to stand. One thing hasn't changed: a long line of homeless people huddled outside a soup kitchen. We leave Roxbury, pass new roads, new freeways, new apartment blocks.

"Boy! It all looks so different!" she says.

It is my first time driving in America, and driving on the other side of the road from what you are used to is not as much fun as it sounds. The highways and freeways aren't so bad, because no matter how hard you try, you can't go in the wrong direction. It is the smaller two-way streets that get you. You can drive along quite happily without seeing another car, before one pops up over a hill and nearly wipes you out.

I miss the turnoff to West Lynn. The absence of a map and the impulse to drift over to the left-hand side of the road mean I don't hear Connie's hushed words, "It's here on the right." That ends up being the last turn to the right for nearly twenty minutes. It is a pretty drive, but I am starting to wonder if we will ever find West Lynn. I finally find a turn to the right and hurtle down the road. In my rearview mirror, I see the flashing lights of a police car. I slow down to let him overtake me, thinking nothing more of it.

At the end of the road, I pull in to a shopping center, hoping to ask directions. As I enter the car park, I hear a loudhailer behind me: "Pull over to the curb!" I leap out of the car as we do in Australia and try to explain that I am lost.

403

"Get back in the car!"

The sight of two white women chauffeuring an elderly African American woman in a lurid red car attracts a large group of curious onlookers. Connie shrinks into the upholstery. My middle-class indignation at being stopped by a policeman is no match for her fear.

"Do you know why I pulled you over?" he asks, his head cocked.

"No." I am thinking one of two things: I was on the wrong side of the road, or our bright-red hire car has been used in a gangland killing and the plates have been traced.

"You were doing seventy back there in a forty zone. You from outta town?"

"Very much so," I say. I tell him we are driving our friend to West Lynn so she can see a niece she hasn't seen for ten years.

"May I see your license, ma'am?" the policeman asks. I hand over my New South Wales driver's license. He doesn't blink.

He peers into the back of the car and sees Connie recoiled against the door. And in one of those rare and unexpected acts of human kindness, he smiles at her and lifts his hat. "Hey, I like your accent!" he says to me, before offering directions. "Now you girls have a nice day, and remember to take it slow!"

Connie looks at me in disbelief. "He let you off?"

"Apparently," I say.

"And he told you how to get there?"

"He did." I smile.

She roars with laughter. "I ain't never seen a policeman like *that* before!"

Connie's niece opens the door without smiling and invites us in. She is a large woman who looks to be in her late forties, with a gap between her front teeth wide enough to hold a pencil sharpener. Her hair is held back tightly from her face with a pink plastic clip. She is barefoot with tracksuit pants and a brightly colored T-shirt. If she is happy to see her aunt, she shows no sign of it. Helping Connie up the front steps, I have a hunch things might not go smoothly. I tell her we will go for a walk and come back in a while and check on her.

We walk around the block. And another block. Some kids are using a slingshot and rock to hit a cat on a neighboring porch. I tell them to stop. They look at each other baffled. It must be the accent. The cat grabs the opportunity to scramble underneath the house. We return to Connie within an hour. The front door is propped open so I let myself in. Connie is perched on a wooden kitchen chair. Her niece, another woman, and a man sit slumped into a sofa drinking cans of Budweiser. Connie is without a drink. I wonder how long they have been sitting in silence, their eyes shifting across the floor. What was said that led to this?

"C'mon, Sarah. Let's hit the road," Connie says finally, and we leave without saying good-bye.

On our drive home, she sits quietly, hunched in the back of the car. I have never seen her look so frail. I don't know what to say, so I say nothing and watch her stare at the scenery through my rearview mirror. I try to imagine what has happened, what they might have said to her. Why would they want to crush an old woman? I can't keep quiet anymore.

"I'm sorry, Connie. Families are fucked."

"Don't say that!" Laura says.

"Well it's true!" I say.

"You can say that again," says a small voice from the backseat.

We pass a liquor store, and Connie pipes up.

"Can we go back?"

"I can stop around the next corner," I say. "What would you like?"

"Some port, please. Two bottles."

She fumbles through her wallet and finds a ten-dollar note.

"Our shout," I say. Laura offers to go inside.

Alone in the car, I turn around to Connie. "I'm your family, Connie. And you're mine."

I hold my hand out, and she squeezes it. "I'm glad," she says.

We get back to Roxbury late in the afternoon. Connie is exhausted. Laura and I link fingers to make a seat so we can carry her up the stairs to her apartment.

"You know that's probably the last time I'll ever leave here," she says when we have made it inside. "It's true," she says. "Next time they take me outta here I'll be dead." It is not a conversation I am ready for so I distract myself in the kitchen.

"Would you mind pourin' me a glass of that port before you go?"

I fix her a small glass and hand it to her.

"What's that?" she asks. "I'll have a tall glass please, with ice."

"This is Australian port, Connie. I don't know what crap you Americans drink, but this is strong stuff." I look closely at the bottle. "It's 22 percent alcohol. A tall glass will knock you out."

"A tall glass, please," she insists, and asks me to bring her the bottle.

"Be careful." I use my best stern voice. She nods.

I offer to spend the night on her sofa, but she won't have it. "I'll be fine," she says. "Don't worry about me."

I ring her at eight o'clock the next morning.

"Top of the mornin' to ya, Sarah!" she says. "Say, you don't think you could pick me up another couple of bottles of that wine, do you? It was wonderful!"

"Have you finished them?" I ask, realizing she is drunk. She doesn't answer.

"Lookin' forward to seein' you soon," she chortles.

She is nearly ninety and has just polished off two bottles of Australian port, I think to myself, hanging up the phone. Jesus. I had planned to visit her in the afternoon, but I shuffle things round and head there right away. Another thing we have in common, I think to myself as the bus lurches through the traffic of Massachusetts Avenue. We both like a drink.

By the time I reach her, she isn't so sprightly.

"I feel terrible. I made myself eight of them frozen hamburgers. I needed something to soak up that wine. I think I'd better put myself to bed."

I help her to the bedroom. "Oh, and Sarah, thanks so much for yesterday. I haven't enjoyed myself so much for years. The way you took those curves, girl! I'll never forget that. The way you drive! You're just my speed. You can take me out anytime. And Sarah, no one has ever been this good to me. I love you."

I hug her, hoping she won't notice I am crying, and tell her I love her too.

Six months later my visa ran out, and I was back in Sydney. Leaving Connie was one of the hardest things I had done. We had talked about her moving to Sydney, where she could stay in a spare bedroom in my house and I could care for her. We could arrange for Inky to join us. In my head I had it all planned. Immigration would not be a problem because she would never leave. No one would even have to know. But it is a long plane trip, and I had my doubts about whether she would make it. In the end, she thanked me but insisted she would rather not be a burden. She would never be a burden, I told her, but she wouldn't budge.

Her life would return to wordless visits with Teddy and hours in front of the TV. Mine would have a hole in it that no one would fill. I found a friend of a friend at Harvard I hoped might keep in touch for me. She visited Connie a couple of times but couldn't really spare the time. They never really "clicked" anyway, she told my friend later.

At nine o'clock Sydney time each Sunday evening, I rang Connie. Her response was always the same.

"Sarah! Is that *you*? I don't believe it! What time is it over there?"

"It's nine in the evening."

"Boy, isn't that *something*? It's only seven in the mornin' here!"

We spoke each week for the next few months. With each conversation her voice grew softer. She talked about what would happen to Inky when she died. Her social worker had promised to take him back to the MSPCA to have him euthanized. "They'll have to kill him. No one else'd take him."

Connie celebrated her ninetieth birthday with a visit from Teddy. He brought her a bottle of port. I rang her, and we talked for an hour. She sounded flat.

"I don't know why I'm still alive, Sarah," she said. "What's the point?"

When I called the following Sunday, the phone rang out. I held my breath and waited. Maybe she was in the bathroom. I waited five minutes and called again. And again. And again. I called Teddy's number, but he wasn't home. By eleven o'clock in the evening Sydney time, I rang the Visiting Nurse Association in Boston. They gave me an after-hours number to ring. The after-hours number I called gave me another number. And another. I spoke to five different people, and all they could tell me was that Connie wasn't due a visit for another three weeks. I asked for the manager. I was calling from the other side of the world. Something had happened to Connie. She must have fallen. She might still be alive but out of reach of the phone. I was the closest thing Connie had to family. I told the woman about Inky and the social worker's pledge. A nurse would be there within an hour, she promised.

I waited an hour before calling again. A nurse had visited. Connie had fallen and broken a hip. It was hard to say when it happened but probably in the last twelve hours. Inky was tearing around the place like a lunatic. The nurse opened a tin of cat food for him and left it in the kitchen. An ambulance was on its way to collect Connie's body. The MSPCA would visit the next day to collect Inky. I got off the phone and sobbed. The prospect of dying alone had never bothered Connie. She just wanted to die. Ninety years had been more than enough of life for her. She knew how it would happen. A broken hip, a day spent on the floor. Then this hell would finally be over.

I called Teddy. This time he picked up.

"She's gone," I told him. "But we should be happy. It's what she wanted."

We chatted for a while about Connie, and I thanked him for being such a good friend to her.

"Well, you were a lot closer to her than I was," he said. "She loved you."

"I loved her too," I said.

I told him to take good care of himself, and he asked me to keep in touch.

"I hope we can stay friends," he said.

"Of course we will," I said.

But it took me another two years to get round to calling Teddy, and by that time he didn't answer the phone. I searched for him through the phone directory, but they had no record of him. He was gone too.

Nominated by Michael Waters and The Gettysburg Review

HOLY NIGHT

by DAN ALBERGOTTI

from CRAB ORCHARD REVIEW

My father said he wished the child were dead.
He didn't say it in so many words,
but he said it. And it was Christmas Eve.
I breathed in silent tension next to him.

The news anchor said that of the seven
born to a black couple three nights before
the weakest child had gathered strength and would,
the doctors said, most likely now survive.

I'm sorry to hear that, my father hissed.
That's just what this country needs, seven more—
of course he used the word. You know he did.
The television screen blurred to pastels.

I sat in silence next to him, the man
whose blood was my blood, whose eyes looked like mine,
and tried to breathe the thick air between us.
He was my father. This was Christmas Eve.

Lord of this other world, what will you make
of this? And reader, what will you accept?
That I stood up without a word and left
the house, got into my car, and then drove

to the pizza place as he expected
me to, picked up our order, and drove back
to that goddamned house to join my mother
and sister, who'd been singing Christmas hymns

by candlelight at the evening service
while my father wished death upon a child?
Will you accept that I wept on that drive,
listening to Radiohead's "The Tourist,"

wishing I could stop the world's spinning cold,
drive off its surface and take to the sky,
break its gravitational hold, sever
myself from it forever then and there?

Reader, I hear your silence now, hear it
like I heard silence that night in the space
between my father's words and the night sky
I could see through my windshield, one bright star—

impossibly distant, already dead—
pulsing its pure light through millennia
of utter void to meet my aching eyes.
Maybe it's better that you have no words,

that I have no answer. Maybe better
to just recall the peace of that short drive,
its brief respite where music and silence
were one blessing and the dark night holy.

Nominated by Colette Inez, Crab Orchard Review

LONG BRIGHT LINE

fiction by JOSH WEIL

from THE VIRGINIA QUARTERLY REVIEW

Through the window Clara could see the men: dark still hats huddled together. The only thing moving was their pipe smoke. It curled in lamp-lit clouds. Then—a whoop!—the clouds blew, the huddle burst, the hats were flying.

Out in the street the gaslights seemed to feel her father's cheer; on her mother's face she watched them gutter.

"Look at him." The woman's grip was strong as any man's. "How happy!" But the fingers were bonier, worn to hooks. "Look," she commanded, "and tell me where he sets his heart." Then the grip became a shove. Her mother's *fetch your father*, and *that damn club*.

The Society for Aeronautical Enthusiasm. Sometimes, when she was sad, or scared, or simply felt the inexplicable weight of herself, she would intone the strange words like an incantation: *Aeronautical enthusiasm, aeronautical enthusiasm, aeronautical* . . . She said it now . . . *enthusiasm* . . . starting up the station steps . . . *aeronautical.* . . shoe-clacking through the empty lobby . . . *enthusiasm* . . . to the shut door . . . *aeronautical enthusiasm.* She knocked.

Inside it was all smoke and suit backs, elbows at her head level, her father bending down, face flush as drunk, but eyes clear, grin pure, *whoop* a straight shot of glee. He scooped her up.

"Fifty-nine seconds!"

How long had it been since her father had held her like that?

"Eight hundred and fifty feet!"

Lifted her so high? With each hoist and drop she felt her years shake off, seven, six, five, her brother's age, Larry in the corner watching, *this is what it's like to be him.*

Before her face: a piece of paper, some smiling stranger lifting and lowering it for her to read. At the top, the stationmaster's name. At the bottom, that of the man her father called *their father*: Bishop M. Wright.

"The Flyer!" Her father raised her high again. Near the ceiling the air made her eyes water. "The Flyer!" He lifted her into the pipesmoke clouds.

But she wasn't, wouldn't be. The balloon ride he'd won—best guess at time and distance of the first flight—was a prize he unwrapped on the cold walk home: how they would scale the sunset, skim beneath the stars, a Christmas present more miracle than gift. Just not for her. *Why?* The basket size, the limits on weight. *Besides*, he said, *ascending so high would surely swell that head of yours.* He tugged her braid. *No doubt big as the balloon itself.* Laughed. While around them little Larry ran in circles, whooping.

On Christmas Eve all she wanted was to stay up late enough to watch them float by above. But if she did, her mother told her, putting her heavy shoulders into the rolling pin, how could Saint Nick bring her her gifts? She spoke in sentences choppy with work: What did Clara think they were doing up there, her father, her brother, in that balloon? Airborne beside the sleigh, pointing out good children's houses, steering the reindeer toward the right roofs. Why else would they have had to do it on Christmas Eve? The last word pressed out by a hard push. Why else leave their women alone this one night a year she liked to share a little brandy with her husband, squeeze beside him on the chair, sing carols, hear *that sweetness in your father's voice*, let her own loose just a little. . . .

"But what about Larry? *He* won't be asleep."

Her mother set the pin down, crouched: her face suddenly level with her daughter's, her eyes strangely soft, her brow smooth as the dough she'd rolled, her hand ice cold on Clara's cheek. From her forearm flour fell like snow. "You know," she said, "they won't see anything. Going up at night. Sweetie, out there it'll just be cold and dark and not one damn thing to see."

There was the whole world. Edge to edge. Lit by the stark stare of a full Yule Moon. And, out in the white-bright yard, at the verge of the snow-glowing fields, a seven-year-old girl illumined, looking up. Behind her: the sleeping house. Above: the starry sky. In it: nothing moving. She watched until her eyes stung. No tear-drop silhouette slipped across the luminescent globe. Would the men up there have lit a lantern? Would she see its wink? The stars had fled the moon for the rest of the sky, piled so thick upon one another she had no hope of picking out the one she wanted. . . . But there! Could it move so fast? Careen across like that? Disappear in a blink before. . . . And she was running, running in the direction the light had shot, running for the place on the horizon where she was sure she'd seen it come to earth.

Sometime in the night her father found her. She woke to his hands unclamping her huddled curl, hauling her up. In his arms she shook so much the stars seemed to rattle. The moon was down. His stumbling, his breath: He was drunk.

"Did you see us?" His quaking grin. "We went right over."

"No, you didn't."

"Yes!" His teeth a pale tremulous strip. "Your brother waved! I showed the house to Saint Nick. His sleigh landed right there!"

"No, it didn't."

"You missed it? All that commotion? The hooves on the roof? Us caroling while we circled above? You truly missed it, truly?"

Had she? His breath fluttered against her face, or her face shuddered beneath it. *Had she?* Inside they waited for her: the presents, lurking beneath the tree, irrefutable.

Papa, what did it look like?

Oh, magnificent! The white balloon, the light of the moon, the stars so close!

No, Papa, what did it look like down here?

Oh, so vast, so small, so strange to think we all live out our lives down there!

No, Papa.

The world! Astounding!

What did *I* look like? Papa, what was it like to look down and see me?

Like this, next Christmas Eve, had he been ballooning again: A small girl sneaking out after supper, out past the last light of the candle-lit

413

windows, beyond the hay barn, the silo, the snow-blown fields, away from the dwindling singing, the laughter—mother, father, brother, home—his eight-year-old daughter disappeared in the blackness beneath the sky. And then: a spark. A golden bloom. Like this, Clara: A little fiery face looking up out of all the darkness of the fields, your little face flickering with the light of the oil lamp you brought, your breath a sunset's clouds, your eyes two glittering stars.

Aeronautical enthusiasm, aeronautical enthusiasm. . . .

All the winter of '05 she chanted it, silently, to herself, a spell to melt the snow, a wish for the rush of spring, and had he looked for her that March, that April, May, on the days when she skipped school, shirked chores, left her brother to play their well-house echo game alone, her mother on her knees wringing out the wash, had he looked her father would have found her here: in the Scotch broom behind the split-rail fence that bordered the cattle paddock they called Huffman Prairie, here, on her belly, behind a scrim of reeds, watching him.

Watching him watch them. Two men in tweed coats and flat caps obsessed with some giant machine. Day after day, they worked on it, trained it like a horse, except—when one at last would mount it, and the other, joined by a helper, would give it a mighty running push—it flew. Its muslin wings stock still, its engine roaring like a mudstuck truck, its driver clinging to the controls, and yet it flew surely as any bird. A bird aloft with a man on its back. Its shadow swept the stampeding cows, the whooping men. Her father, too. (*Tell me where he sets his heart.*) He seemed to shiver in his clothes. *Here*, Clara thought. Rose on tiptoe, raised a hand to his eyes. *Here.*

Sometimes he would join the others running down the field after the roaring bird. Sometimes he would help push it off the earth. If they were far away, she might not manage to tell him from the rest. She might imagine it was him up there guiding that flying machine. How she wanted to ask him! What did it feel like? What *would* it: That wind in *her* hair; that sudden lift below *her* belly? But all June she lay flat on the ground, behind the weeds, keeping quiet.

Until, one day in mid-July, she screamed. How he heard her over the crash, she didn't know. But when she peeled her palms from her eyes, there was the wreckage slammed against the ground, and two far figures running: one toward the crumpled machine, the other toward her.

"No, no, no, no," her father said, and, "can't" and "daughter" and "not how the world works. Don't you ever think of anyone but yourself?

414

How could you make her do your work, your mother worry, poor sick woman!"

She was? How had Clara not noticed it till now? She would have crouched beside the bed and shut her eyes and said the incantation, but learning what the words meant had leeched the magic from them. *Enthusiasm*: merely eagerness. *Aeronautical*: only relevant to things that lifted off the earth, took to the air, soared for the heavens.

This was the last thing her mother said to her, one word: *selfish*, or *selfless*. She wasn't sure. She only knew her mother had turned in bed, clutched her daughter's face, held her gaze, said the word with such vehemence Clara flinched at the flecks of spit. Her mother's fingers gripped her skull, eyes bore into hers. But did she mean herself or Clara? Was it an apology or reprimand? Warning or wish?

She was at Huffman Prairie the day her mother died. September, windless. No figures in the field, no Flyer for them to push. She walked out there alone. At the end of the narrow track, a launching dolly lay overturned. Behind it, in the wet green grass, the bleached board looked white as bone. She lay down on it, aligned her spine with the rail. Stared up at the sky. Spread her arms.

That evening, returning to her father's stricken silence, her brother's sobs, a home whose walls had become more thin, she would wonder if it was something you could see: the soul ascending. If that day she had simply been watching the wrong place in the firmament.

Fall had come by the time her father brought her back to the field. He told her it was her mother's dying wish.

"To see the Flyer?" she asked.

"For you to see it," he said.

Huffman was crowded. Farmers and friends, the entire Society, even the old man her father called *their father*, came out to watch the flight. That day, the machine made it above the windbreak and kept on, became a hawk, a kite, a sparrow, a speck, was gone. But she could hear the sound somewhere, coming back around, circling her, homing in.

Her father seemed to have forgotten how to steer. She would hear his footscuffs wandering the house, floor to floor, gliding room to room, his tail rudder busted, blown by winds only he could feel. Her brother: a brooding boy, so serious—seven years old and up first to fry the bacon, last in from the barns—so careful cleaning the plow horse's hooves, so watchful over the hung tobacco for the slightest sign of rot. He spent his eighth birthday on the back of a cart, alone in the cold, forking fresh hay to the shivering Jerseys, worry frozen on his face.

While Clara spent her tenth in her room writing a letter to a woman she'd never met: *Dear Mrs. Miller, Can you please describe your ride in the dirigible? How long before you will go up again? And would you consider taking along a girl? I'm still quite small, and very light . . .* By the time she was a teen, the walls around her were plastered with clippings, posters, photographs: Lieutenant Lahm alighting from his balloon in the field at Fylingdales Moor; the Wright brothers on the racetrack at Le Mans; the note she got back from Hart O. Berg (*You never know . . . I'll ask Orville . . . Maybe one day you'll pilot your own!*), the first American woman ever lifted off the earth inside an aeroplane signing her name with an "O" bold as a daredevil's loop. And the daredevils themselves! Glenn Curtiss of that lush mustache; sly-eyed Arch Hoxsey with his wry smile. Her first pack of cigarettes she purchased solely for the Ralph Johnstone card inside: goggles raised, chin-strap sharpening his jaw, that slight swerve she so loved in the cock of an eyebrow above his steady gaze. At school, the girls talked of which boys they'd like to date. She smoked her Meccas, kept quiet. The boys discussed their options for careers, mocked her when she mentioned Raymonde de Laroche. (*Her license!* she shouted; *That's France!* they jeered.) *Why do you even bother?* her few friends asked, when, already fourteen, she fought for a seat in the science class. *You know this is your last year, anyway.*

Still, the day her father sat her down it was a shock. She had tried her best to bring him back, curled beside him on the couch reading aloud the news (Blériot across the English Channel! Latham breaks a thousand meters!), hoping to rekindle the heart her mother had heard in his whoop that long-ago first flight. Hadn't she brought him into her room to show him each poster she put up—the Los Angeles expo, the Grande Semaine d'Aviation de la Champagne? Hadn't they gazed together at the mademoiselle in her windblown dress waving at the silhouetted planes, daydreamed of standing beneath a sky aswirl with aviators thick as bees? All spring she'd tutored boys in science class, saved just enough: two tickets to the aero meet in Indianapolis that June!

But here was her father shaking his head. "You're a woman now," he told her.

Her brother, across the table: "We need you here."

"And what," she demanded, "if I go anyway?" To Indianapolis that June, or back to school that fall, or away forever.

416

"This isn't New York," her brother said.

"This is your home," her father told her.

"Sis," Larry reached over, touched her arm, "can't you see this is your job?"

In the last year, he had become taller than her.

"There isn't any union," he said. "You can't go on strike."

And, on his lip, she thought she could see a hint of hairs.

When summer came she stole away to Asbury Park. Walked to the train station, bought a seat east, saw the ocean for the first time, the boardwalk, the beach, slept on sand, discovered the affect her shoulders had on men, her smile, snapped up a ride, attained a ticket, was there on the field when Brookins crashed into the crowd, when Prince plummeted 6,000 feet, held her breath with everyone else, praying for his parachute to open (*open! open!*), felt the spectators' communal shudder, would sometimes feel it again, back home, alone in the kitchen cracking the back of a bird, or serving a spatchcocked half to her brother, or sewing a split in her father's yellowed longjohns, or stepping off the train onto the platform of her small Ohio town the day that she returned. But for one August night, at the edge of the Atlantic, looking up, she had been struck by a sudden sureness that it would be all right. The moon. The Milky Way. The Stardust Twins swooping through. That was what the papers called them after that first night flight, Johnstone and Hoxsey circling each other in the lunar glow, their pale-winged biplanes soaring smooth as owls. And her, beneath them, swept by the peace of certainty. Neck stretched back, face flat to the sky, she knew it: She was not meant to be up there; she was meant to be down here, here like a cairn seen from above, a landmark, her.

Let Bessica Raiche climb behind the controls that October.

Let Harriet Quimby claim her license from the Aero Club.

Here is Clara Purdy, standing far out in her father's field, surrounded by electric lamps. All these months she has collected them, repaired ones given her for free, purchased others with earnings made from sewing piecemeal, stolen the rest from her own home. Here is the cord she's spliced, snaking away to the windmill her brother installed just this past September. It is November now, cold and clear and night. She stands in the high grass, waiting for wind. Behind her the turbine is still, the generator asleep. Above, the sky is breathtaking. What is the chance someone flies over tonight? What does it matter? For the first time she understands what she felt in August: It doesn't. The wind will gust, the turbine will whir, the charge will shoot through the cord, the

417

lamps will all light up, and she will know how it would look from high above—the concentric circles, bright bulbs swirling inward to her here at the center—and that will be enough. The dry grassheads stir against her shins. The filaments await the spark. Here it comes.

After the fire, they lived in a fourth-floor flat in Dayton, the three of them cramped close, her father and brother away all day in the old bicycle building, assembling engines for the new Model B. The intricacy of understanding, the advanced industry: The Wrights wouldn't hire her. Instead, she spent her sixty-hour weeks on the National Cash Register line, setting small round buttons—red number five, red number five, red number five—in their place on the machine. At home, her father ate whatever she cooked in his usual silence. Her brother, chewing, wouldn't even look her way, ever unforgiving of the conflagration she had caused. That spring, when flames consumed a shirtwaist factory in New York, he slid the *Daily News* across to her (*a hundred and a half dead*, jabbing his finger at the newsprint, *most of them women*). . . . Beside it, her eyes took in a different headline: In India, a Sommer biplane had delivered the first air mail. *What*, she thought, flushed with excitement, *would come next?* Her father, reading aloud one night, his voice aghast: a ship, an iceberg. He couldn't stand it, handed her the paper. She drew in breath. Was it true? Quimby had piloted across the Channel? Alone, a woman! *Eight thousand suffragists*, her brother announced, slapping the paper, shaking his head, *marching on the capital like a bunch of Albanians trying to overthrow the Turks.*

Nearly a thousand days went by before the flood of 1913 gave her a whole week off. Alone with herself for the first time in years, she climbed the stairs to the roof, thunked down a satchel bulged with buttons. Every shift she'd swiped one round red number five and now, crouched high above streets deep with water, she lay them out with a typersetter's care. Above, surveying aeroplanes circled. She wrote them notes in big red letters: Come closer! Lower a rope!

In Austria-Hungary an airship floated, testing photographic tools. An army aviator tried out his loop-de-loops. Biplane, dirigible: ball of fire erupting in the summer sky. A few weeks later Archduke Ferdinand took a bullet to the throat. A month after that, all of Europe was at war. In a few years, her brother, too.

Mid-September, 1918: 2,000 planes aswarm over Saint-Mihiel, blasting thick as scattershot across the sky. It was the biggest air battle the world had ever seen, and the next night, while her new husband finalized what that afternoon had wrought, Clara stared up past the strange shoulders (later, she couldn't recall if he'd removed his undershirt, if he'd still worn his glasses) at the ceiling of waterstain clouds and watched the dogfight in her mind: a welkin of dark specks swirling, the opposite of stars. If Abner Lowell noticed (later she would know of course he had), he said nothing (of course he wouldn't), just as the few guests—his family, his friends—had looked at her drained face and silently assumed it must be grief (her fallen brother, her heart-felled dad). A few whispered she must have married out of desperation (her new husband's bony chest, his paltry schoolteacher's wage), but they were wrong. Clara had married the man for his location.

"Near Toledo," he'd told her, shelling a hot peanut, slipping it into her palm. "A little town you wouldn't know."

She'd chewed, flashed him a look of *try me*.

"Maumee," he'd said.

"On the Maumee River?"

Laughing, he'd coughed out, "You!" It was what he would later say was their first date. "You've got to be a bargeman's daughter!"

Smiling, she'd swallowed, held out her empty hand.

"A little land," she told him, a few months later, after they'd moved up north. "A little place of our own out in the country."

"But Dear"—he called her *Dear* and *Sweets* and *Mrs. Lowell*—"We have a house already. Right here, right around the corner from the school."

"Abner," she said, "I grew up on a farm."

"But why so far?"

"I want our children—"

"Why pick a place near precisely nothing?"

It was true: the plot she'd found sat equally far from even the tiniest of towns. Grand Rapids, Whitehouse, Waterville. It wasn't even on the routes between them. But it was beneath the one she wanted, right below the one up there.

Mornings, she made him hot cornmeal muffins, liver and onions the way he loved, helped carry his schoolbooks out to the car, stood in the dirt drive waving. She kept the bills in order, the mousetraps empty, the dust down, herself up, a wife he'd want to come home to, a home he'd be happy to find her in. Except he wouldn't.

Afternoons, after everything else was done, she'd change into her coveralls, head for the tractor shed. Alone in all the horse-worked county, the Allis-Chalmers had cost her every cent of life savings her father had left, and every day before dusk she would crank its engine over, hitch its thresher on, rumble out into her field. Or, as Abner called it, her canvas. The tractor he called her Big Bad Brush. In the summer, she painted with it, mowed her pictures into high grass. In the fall, she ploughed pen-lines, the overturned topsoil dark as ink. Winter found her bundled in the aviator's coat and hat her husband gave her, long leather earflaps whipping in the wind while she made her etchings on the earth, her shovel a chisel, snow peeling away like curls of wood. She planted daffodils. Dug up the bulbs each fall, stitched them back into the dirt like needlework, watched her embroidery bloom sun-bright each spring.

From the sky, the airmail pilots watched it, too. Twice a day they flew the route, eastward in morning, westward late afternoon. Perched atop the Allis-Chalmers, or kneeling in the new-turned dirt, or simply standing still in a swirl of snow, she would listen to the hum, scan the sky, smile up, wait for the dip of a wing, the tiny stick arm flung back and forth in a far-off wave. She would watch them dwindle away to Cleveland, morning awhirl in their propeller blades, watch them disappear toward Chicago, sunset on their struts.

And home from his day at the Maumee Secondary School, hunched over the kitchen table doing his preparatory work, her husband would catch a flutter in the corner of his eye, look out the window: his wife in that distant field of daffodils, her breeze-swept hair all auburn fire in the late light, her cap lifted into the last of the sun, waving, waving. She always left his supper warming in the oven. He always let it warm till she was done, would come clomping in, shuck her boots, sit down to eat beside him. Sometimes, he'd go out to her. In winter storms, if visibility was bad, the pilots, searching for landmarks along the route, might fly so low their wheels seemed close enough to grab, the silver belly suddenly there tearing through the all-white sky, the aviator's face a flash of goggles, the airplane roaring by. He'd stand behind her, arms around her, feel the gust, the rush, the thrumming of the engine in the air.

"What's it this time?" Abner would ask.

She'd tell him: President Roosevelt on his first flight, Von Richthofen shot down over the Somme, the new airmail stamp. "See there's the biplane, there's the '24,' over there the cents.' "

And Abner would gaze at the indecipherable arcs in the grass, the random squiggles in the snow, the mystifying daffodils, and fill his face with what he hoped conveyed belief in her, faith that from above it would all be clear. Until she began digging portraiture in dirt. Eddie Rickenbacker. Bert Acosta. Jack Knight. Airmail pilots that might *right then* fly over on the Chicago-Cleveland route. "Do you think," Abner said, his voice very level, his eyes somewhere off in the field, "that they might . . . I mean, that they really . . . That they could actually really recognize themselves?"

She meant to nod, but instead found herself starting to shake inside his arms. Against her back, his chest shook too. Their laughter filled the field.

Once, after a fight (Him: Weren't kids the entire reason they'd moved out there? Her: That's just the way people without meaning in their lives try to make some. Him: And didn't she want that, too? Her: What did he think she did all afternoon?), she'd asked him, "Why did you marry me?" Because, he said, he loved her. "What does that mean?" He'd told her then he'd never seen someone so consumed by what most moved them, never been that close to such a burning need, wanted to assuage it or be burned up in it, to feel even a little of it in the warmth of what he felt for her.

Abner was the one who brought her books—Klee, Kandinsky, Mondrian—who suggested they drive four hours to Cleveland just to see a room bedeviled by Kazimir Malevich's strange bars and slabs. She didn't understand what stirred behind it, no more than she understood what stirred in her. But dragging the thresher in wild swaths, plowing scattered squares of earth, planting bulbs in shapes that seemed to suggest themselves, she was sure of this: It was a style that far better fit her tools. A tool itself that let her grasp at last at what she had begun to conceive of as a gift. A gift Abner had wrapped for her. The way he wrapped himself around her the night the postal service flew its first transcontinental flight.

That night in February of '21 the snow spilled down as if to douse their fire. They had lit it in the middle of her field, at dusk, no telling when—or *if*—the plane would hurtle overhead. All day she'd waited for news, pulled open the Ford's door to retrieve the evening paper from her husband's outstretched hand: The last heard from the airmail pilot, he was headed straight into a storm above Cheyenne. Cheyenne to North Platte to Omaha to Iowa City to Chicago to right overhead: At night the only thing to guide him would be a few post-office workers' flares, nothing to mark the path between but what bonfires a few farmers might keep alight. Abner helped her haul out the half-rotted boards, pour on the gasoline. They brought blankets, a bottle of bootleg, sat close to the fire. All around her: Abner's enfolding coat, his enveloping arms, the warmth of his breath on her cheek, of his cheek against her ear, of him waiting all the long night with her. Sometime after midnight, they lay down together between the blankets. Sometime before dawn, he fell asleep. Sometime after first light she woke her husband, straddling him with her heat, tenting him with her body, the bottom blanket rough on her knees, the top blanket blocking his view of the sky, her own eyes focused only on his face. "I hear it," he said. "Darling, I hear it." She shook her head, rocked on his hips, kissed him quiet.

So why did she still daydream pilots down? That they would see her wave, circle round, land in her field, take her up. In a De Havilland with a scooped-out second seat? Or curled on her knees in the bin behind the engine, the mail hatch sprung? A gloved hand on her cheek (she could smell the leather), the twist of her neck as she turned to see (she could feel her whipping hair) his goggled eyes, his chapped lips, her first kiss at five hundred feet, six, seven, a thousand. . . . Why, when she first heard of the postal-service beacons—fifty-foot towers erected all across the country, a trail of landlocked lighthouses flashing their specific signal (me, me, me) to pilots plying a sea of stars—did she feel betrayed? They built one five miles away. At night she could see its blinking flare (here, here, here). Why when all those women (only one aviatrix shy of a hundred) came together in Curtiss Field to make their mark in the history of flight did Clara turn with even more determination to her own canvas?

Now, she worked at night. She spent all the allowance Abner gave her on a single headlight for her Big Bad Brush, ate her suppers sitting on the tractor's seat, stayed out past the last window gone dark in her house. What sent her to the shed to sharpen thresher blades at the news of Earhart's first Atlantic flight? What about word of the woman's solo crossing kept Clara up till dawn mapping out her next work of art? Each one, each season, outdid the last, pushed her abilities to new feats of skill, scaled the atmosphere of her imagination. She clipped grass by hand, cut staggered banks in sweeping slopes, accomplished tricks of shading by varying stalk heights. She incorporated color in the spring, in winter watered carefully considered ditches to show the sky fleeting paintings made of glinting ice.

And when, one summer morning in '37, the kitchen radio reported that the Queen of the Air had gone down over the ocean, was feared drowned, she found she couldn't breathe. She stood up from the table. The house was empty. The news announcer's voice seemed to cinch her throat. And, even before she heard the airplane's purring approach, she was fleeing into the field. Maybe it was her frantic waving, maybe the desperation in her shout: This time the pilot swung around, returned, roared down to her.

A Boeing Monomail, army drab, no room to sit anywhere but in his lap. The leather of his jumpsuit creaked. He had to reach between her legs to take hold of the controls. The noise was deafening, the treeline rushing. The earth dropped.

There was her world: the house, the empty driveway, the field where she did her work. The flesh on the back of her neck urged her *look at the sky*, the giddy slide of her stomach told her *you're flying*. But she couldn't take her eyes off the small, and smaller, square of landscape that was her canvas below.

At her cheek, the aviator was saying something. His chapped lips brushed her ear. For a second, she pulled her stare away, glanced at him: His goggles were so smeared with engine grease she couldn't see his eyes, just the rawness of his sunburned nose, the wetness of his grin.

"Take me back," she said.

"Down?" he shouted.

She shook her head. "Back around, back over, I want to see it again."

It was the first time that she ever had. Till then, it had all existed solely in her mind. There, *there*, if she concentrated hard enough she could forget the feeling of his hand creeping across her chest, if she fought the wind in her eyes and focused hard enough, she could imagine that there was nothing around her but air, that she was up there, flying, looking down, alone.

Maybe it was the depression. Early on she'd offered to plow her canvas under, grow vegetables instead, but Abner insisted. No: Even when parents lost their jobs, students still needed teachers. Though when, that autumn after her first flight, Lucas County consolidated its schools and proved him wrong, her homebound husband spent his days gazing at her field, his nights commenting on her progress, his energy in coming up with ways that he could help—*Observe you from the roof, shout when you're about to lose the line. I know: a business in balloon rides! Listen, I'll write a letter to* LIFE *Magazine, to* Art News, *get you noticed!*—his whole self seeming to clutch at her work as if it could become in some way his. Maybe it was the fact that all his attempts to garner her attention finally did. Late in '41 rumors began to go around: Her flowers sprouted in secret patterns, her tractor furrowed code, Mrs. Lowell was planting messages for Japs. That winter, at Abner's urging, she undertook a radical revision of her aesthetic. He brought home images of Far Eastern art, read her haikus. And in the fresh snow of the new year's first storm, he helped her shovel a field full of brushstrokes:

見えるかな
野原の上の
流雲

There it was, black shovel lines in white, giant characters carved beneath the January sky. Two days later an army corporal showed up at their door, watched them while, with the Big Bad Brush, Clara plowed their work away. Afterward, Abner admitted it was probably time to stop. He looked so sad, sitting there in his coat, his pants wet to the knees, his head hanging forward, his hands hiding his face. His fingers were all knuckles and loose skin. He was going bald. How had her husband become a man of fifty? How had she become a wife of forty-five?

And maybe it was simply that: so much time together, so many years gone by.

At first, she didn't think of the separation as something that might last. Just a few months away from each other, Abner working at his new job in Bowling Green, her in Toledo, working thirty miles from him, doing her part to keep the country stocked in B-17s, apart only until the war was over, maybe a year at most. But it was four. Four years living in her own room in a single-sex boardinghouse, four years in which she found she liked working alongside other women, liked earning enough on her own, liked the feeling of finishing the nose cone of a behemoth bomber, assembling the canopy of something that would one day soar over Hamburg, Dresden, Mainz. She was the oldest woman working at Libbey-Owens-Ford. *Gran Gunner* the others called her, smoking cigarettes, snapping gum. On their lunchbreaks they laughed about messages for airmen slipped into secret cracks, read aloud the *Blade's* dispatches from the fronts, passed around pamphlets by the old Birth Control Federation of America, debated its new milquetoast moniker—Planned Parenthood—and whether General Spaatz was right to bomb Jerry's oil before his rails, and if it made sense to join a dying Women's Trade Union League, shared home-canned pickles, packs of cigarettes, wondered what they would do after all this was done.

On Fridays, after work, she would wonder the same. Abner would pull into the Libbey-Owens lot, take her back to a home that, all weekend, they would pretend still felt like theirs. The wall calendar Allis-Chalmers always sent her, now swapped for one his students made. The sink corner that had once held her hand cream, now crowded by his shaving mug. He'd move it over, turn the month. Sometimes by Sunday they could almost feel like them again. Though more and more she worked the weekend shifts—overtime, extra pay, Saturday night out with the girls—Sunday coming every other week, then once a month, then not. On the phone, Abner would speak things he'd never said before—how much he'd wanted children; how he used to lose himself in his guitar; all he'd given up for her, would, still wanted to—as if the distance between them made him brave. But it was just distance. Close was this: the cigarette smoke of the women she worked with, their laughter around card tables at night, her own eyes caught in the curved reflection of a bomber's canopy, looking back. Sometimes the smile she saw saddened her. Sometimes, wiping a rag at the glass, she tried to see her husband instead. Sometimes she simply stared through herself until she saw the driveway, the house, some new shape coming up in the field.

Weeds, scrub willows, the driveway buried somewhere beneath the grass. She stood in the sun, seedheads scratching at her stockings, looking at the house. He'd written her—moved out, a simple flat nearer the school he worked at now, she could stay in the house, or sell it, *it's up to you*, he'd transferred the deed to her. But not the car. She'd walked the last two miles. Such flat land: The whole way she'd watched the house grow near, the road to town slip out of sight, its treeline dwindling to distant shakings, far-off Toledo disappearing from her life. The air grew thin. Her stomach dropped. Her juddering heart: She might have been taking off, climbing up, seeing the earth fall away below. Except she wasn't looking down. Instead, on every side it seemed the world was drawing itself away from her. Once, long ago, in a dim Dayton stairwell, her arms beneath her father's arms, dragging him down, flight after flight, fast as she could, she had felt it—in his eyes on her, in the *thud thud thud* of his heels on the steps, in the desperate heartbeats of his departing life—had felt the world withdraw like that. There, on the landing where they'd stopped, he had watched her with such hurt, such hope, so much understanding (*selfish? selfless?*), such loneliness suddenly inside her.

Standing in the hot sun in front of the abandoned house, she set her suitcase down. Hiked up her skirt. Peeled away her stockings. They ringed her shins like thick black shackles. But God the breeze on her legs felt good.

It gusted all the time. Flat fields like runways for the rushing wind, windbreaks bent by its launch against them, the stolid brick house huddled close to the ground, Clara leaning forward, dress and coat and hair afloat behind her, her whole body seeming about to lift off into the sky. These days no more mail planes flew by. Just clouds and birds and the bellies of DC-4s, their fuselages perforated with passenger windows, their cargo holds carrying the mail alongside luggage now. How high up they flew! How far away they seemed! How fast they grew—Comets and Constellations and Stratocruisers—big as blue whales swimming through the sea above. Sometimes it struck her as strange: the way their shapes—so much larger than the biplanes of before, but so much higher, too—seemed, from below, to stay the same size to her. She hung tobacco in the barn to dry, stuffed advertisers' envelopes all winter, barely scraped by. Even with the checks Abner still sent her. She knew he couldn't afford to give so much, knew she should tear them up, just as the one time she'd seen him in Maumee she'd known she should leave him alone. But she had crossed the street to the lunch-counter window, watched his shape stiffen at sensing her, his face furrow with the effort of staring into his shake. She'd turned away, gone farther down the street, glanced back: There on the sidewalk her still-husband stood, his hat pushed up from his eyes as if to keep the brim from blocking even a sliver of her in his sight.

And the next time an envelope came from Abner it contained not just the usual check but a story clipped from *LIFE*. *Is he the greatest living painter in the United States?* the caption read. Photographs of splattered paint, scattered color. To Clara they looked like her field when she'd first come home: a bird's-eye view of what nature could do without her. Sometimes at night lying alone in her bed she could hear the airliners droning overhead. Sometimes, midday, sun-bright rooms

426

would dim for a second, go bright again. Their shadows passed over her there in her field, and she watched them sweep away, disappear, didn't even look up.

But look down. Out that oval window. There, on the ground—what is that?

"I'd like to buy it," the gentleman said. He stood on her doorstep, pinstripe pants aflutter in the breeze, voice like the news on CBS. News of a collector out in California who'd sent this man to hunt out art.

She looked past him to the field, the barn, the shadow of the plane. She'd stitched the tar paper together scrap by scrap, covered it with black-painted muslin that wavered, rippled, gave the sense of the shape moving. Though it was nailed down, glued, painted mid-pass atop the barn, the yard, the plowed-under field, its wingspan 900 feet long, its fuselage distorted as a real shadow's would have been by the slant of the sun. It had taken her three years.

"The barn?" she asked.

"That, too," he said, in his Edmund Chester voice.

Now Chester was off the radio and everyone was watching television instead and her barn was gone to some hangar outside Los Angeles, and she was in a magazine. Some writer spurred by word of the sale had done some digging, discovered a defense-department file, photographs of her early-forties shovelings, revealed the message she and Abner had sent the Japanese:

Clouds drift back and forth
Over my fields—I wonder:
Can you see them too?

Clara Lowell. There on the page her name seemed like another person's. She read the story of herself as if from far away, from before she'd taken Abner's name, a Purdy girl again who might tear out a page, pin it to her bedroom wall. She read it all until, halfway, she hit a thing she'd never heard: *soldier, bullet*, how her brother had died. *Face down in a ditch*, it said. Shot from the air by a strafing ace. Her eyes kept moving along the page, her mind making out the words, but she was seeing Larry again: running, running, engulfed by the onrushing shadow of the plane.

And there went her phone again, ringing, ringing. The Garner Agency,

427

the Fineman Gallery, funding from an arts foundation in San Francisco where she spent the first year of the new decade peering down from the Golden Gate or up from a boat beneath it, devising a way to make the bay look as if the shadow of fuselage and wings had been painted on its waves. Across the ocean, over Pyongyang, jet fighters screamed into the sky. She couldn't hear them. No more than Jackie Cochran, three years later, could have heard the sonic boom she left behind along with all the other aviatrixes still shackled to sound. Clara was in New York City, affixing the faux reflection of an onrushing airliner to the steel and glass of the Empire State—a tragic trompe l'oeil. Haunting, critics called it, heart-stopping. They said her work rang of the grim reaper, contained a sense of the moment made permanent, and yet seemed fleeting, too, as if to offer a possibility of reprieve. And so was also hopeful. And so when, high above the Colorado Plateau a DC-7 struck a Constellation, she was commissioned to commemorate the lost souls, spent the fall of '57 marking the Grand Canyon with two immense shadows facing each other across the chasm, their shapes distended exactly as the sun had stretched them the morning of that last day.

It would be known as Clara Lowell's final shadow piece. Even in the moment, hovering above in the helicopter the Park Service pilot flew, she knew it: The silhouettes were old shapes cut from the woman she used to be, not who she had become. Down in the station everyone else had moved on, too. They were crowded 'round a short wave radio, listening to a faint, steady beep. *That's it*, one of the rangers said. *It must be passing over us right now.*

Back in Ohio she stood in the spot where her barn had once been and watched the tiny glint arc along its orbit. She had seen pictures of the Soviets' sphere. She wondered what, from that height, it could possibly see down here.

Old ovals found in dusty bureau drawers, age-spotted hand-me-downs, rearviews salvaged from crashed cars, cast-off skyscraper panes from construction lots in Cleveland: She collected shards of any size, from all over, carted them back to her small square of earth, slowly, piece by piece, resurfacing her old canvas in glass. Ten entire acres. Half as many years. Hundreds of thousands of seamless fits found from a million broken sides. By the time John Glenn radioed down *Oh, that view is tremendous!* he might have meant the flash of glinting land she'd covered.

Or the sight of all the others who'd come to help. From the beginning she had watched in wonder—these young seekers fleeing their old lives, stopping by on their way to wherever, stepping out of dusty cars, parking in her driveway for a day, a couple, crashing in her guest room, on her couch, men on motorcycles with their plaid shirts unbuttoned, wind-wild hair, women wearing jeans, scarves in colors more vibrant than anything for miles—but as they crouched by her side, helping find a fit for a piece, holding a glued edge together, she had begun to think of them as somehow akin to her. These kids who were a third her age! Who drove up blaring bands with names like the Del-Tones, the Animals, the Stones. "Can't you hear my heartbeat?" The girls sang it while they worked. Girls who said things like *out there it's trying to bury us alive*, and *can't let it stifle your voice within*, who laughed when she insisted she was still married. Well, she said, *it's true I haven't seen him in, let's see, oh jeez. . . .* And they told her she couldn't continue like that, it was a new era—*all that matters now is what will make you happy, what's the point in living if your life isn't true to you*—an age of self-fulfillment, of our own happiness not just pursued but caught, kept, held perpetually near all our hearts. They could have been her children, her grandchildren, but standing amid a group who'd helped her put the last broken piece of glass in place, she felt as if she had at last found her generation, kindred spirits, a moment in time in which she fit.

Only the babies gave her pause. The ones brought into her home on the hips of girls younger than Clara had been when she'd first entered the house herself. In their sounds she would hear her long-gone husband's late-night voice, his telephone pleas. And, watching the stare the babies settled on their mothers, she would wonder if Abner—another's husband now?—had felt enlarged by that enamored gaze. She hoped he had. Though whenever an infant was handed to her, she felt the opposite: the child's need tight as its fist around her finger, squeezing her down to fit its purpose, herself made small as the reflection in its unblinking eyes.

Instead, she kept her sights on the work before her. There, in the field of mirrors, the sun shone up out of a sky in the ground. Clouds crept through the grass along the edge, floated into twin squares of blue, followed themselves. Soon, she knew, a contrail would cut across like a line of chalk. A 727 on its way to Chicago, or coming east, a hundred and more passengers peering out their windows. Staring down at the sky beneath herself, she tried to imagine what they would see.

A blinding glare, according to the FAA. Clear the mirror off the ground: the agency's order that at last turned Clara Purdy into a house-

429

hold name. The destruction on the evening news, the documentary about the flood of youth answering the artist's call, the image censored around the world: all that mirror-cleared ground blanketed now by a thousand bodies stripped bare, a ten-acre square of naked flesh flashed upward in a *fuck you* so communal it seemed to capture the entire decade's mood. By the sixties' end she had lit an entire rural county's roads, spidering bright veins across the nighttime dark; she made a color photograph of one square mile of the Earth, shot from a mile high, then blew it up to actual size, printed it in pieces, put them back together over the spot, so from the air it almost looked like life, but not.

Still, it was her "Long Bright Line" that Clara meant to be her masterpiece. She had convinced the postal service to loan her the antiquated airmail beacons for one night. Coast to coast, every twenty miles, they stood rusting, signals extinguished long ago, last remnants of an idea once pioneering, now obsolete. Until, for sixty seconds on the night of July 20, 1969, she would bring it back to life. All her funding had gone into the purchase and installation of 140 first-order Fresnel lenses, powerful as any lighthouse beam, mounted atop the towers, aimed straight up. The volunteers who manned the stations wanted only to share in what would happen at her signal: Starting in New York the first would flare on, followed by a second to its west, and the one that was next, and the one after, a constellation untangled across the country into a single strand of terrestrial stars, a gleaming necklace laid atop the Earth's dark breast. Seen only by the moon. And the astronauts on it.

Sometime early that afternoon, the TV would show the lander touch down. Around sunset it would show Armstrong or Aldrin stepping onto the surface. By dark they were supposed to be done. And she would call the beacon in New York and start her signal to them.

But in between the landing and the moon walk, her phone rang instead. She picked it up, heard breathing.

"Wasn't that incredible?" the voice on the other end said.

Even after all these years she knew him. While he talked all out of breath about the surface of the moon seen coming close, and closer, the shadow of the lander growing (*that beep, beep, beep,* he said, *can you still hear it?* and, for some reason, laughed), she slid open the deck doors, let the scent of the ocean in. She stood there trying to smell it, trying not to let him hear her inhale. Her old nose. Her old mind. Him?

He must have been approaching eighty. He must have been becoming senile:

How else could he have just now asked her to come see him?

"I'm sorry," she told him.

"Tonight," he said.

"I live in Los Angeles now."

"Clara . . ."

"I'm busy, Abner."

"I'm dying," he said.

Isn't this something, Cronkite exclaimed.

And it was. It was like nothing she'd ever seen.

From two hundred forty thousand miles out there. . . .

She sat on the couch, in the salt-sticky breeze, feeling it on the loose skin of her neck, her scalp beneath her thinned-out hair, remembering the scent of peanuts, engine oil, the soft fleece of the aviator cap, the warmth of the earflaps—on winter days his fingers had brushed her chin, buckling the straps, just so she wouldn't have to shuck her gloves—how he'd gazed up at her astride him that winter night, his face full of bonfire light, the way he'd looked at his new wife in the picture he'd sent so many years ago to share the birth of his first child. A daughter? A son? She sat in the breeze, trying to remember (*what do you think I do all afternoon?*), listening to Armstrong speak from the moon.

There seems to be no difficulty. . . . Definitely no trouble. . . .

Gee, Cronkite said, *that's good news.*

And she leaned forward, turned the volume down. She sat in silence, staring. A gray, grainy picture. A pale blur she knew was the shape of a man but might have been anything that moved. The longer she watched, the more strange and beautiful and unworldly, unreachable, it seemed. The longer she looked, the more it broke into its parts—stillness, shadow, something stirring—the more she felt her own shape blurring, too. If anyone had looked away from the TV, glanced up at her window, aglow with the light broadcast off the moon . . . but who on Earth would?

She was still watching the fuzz of the screen when, a long time later, the broadcast done, the window for her beacons passed, the phone rang again.

"What happened?" The volunteer's voice came all the way across the country. Some young woman high up in her tower, finger on the switch. "We're waiting," the voice said, crackly with distance, beginning to doubt.

In the hospital she meant to tell him it hadn't been his fault, but stepping into his room, she found herself unable to utter the words *work*, or *self*, or *matter*. Instead, she sat gazing again, this time at her once-husband's face. Someone had turned his sound off, too. When the nurse told her he could no longer speak, Clara asked what his last words had been. The nurse didn't know. She wondered: Would they have even been meant for her to hear? She wondered: Would she have even been able to? There was just the beeping of the EKG. The blinking of his eyes. Even when they were open, she could tell they didn't see her. But she watched them: blink, blink, blink.

Flying home, she could not stop feeling her own lids opening and closing, even as she leaned toward the window, looked down. The lights of Dayton dwindling. The lights of its outskirts spread as far as she could see. Somewhere down there, it struck her, was what used to be her father's farm. It was smothered by suburbs now, buried beneath the unrelenting burn of each house's separate star, but once it would have been unlit, all of it, house and barns and trees and field and a little girl looking up, all indistinguishable, dark as sleep. When the moon went behind the clouds, the balloon must have seemed suspended in pure blackness, they must have held the basket tight, peered over its edge, thought *how beautiful!* So strange, she thought now, what we have done to the surface of the world. She shut her eyes—simply paused her lids, stopped them from opening. And, taking in the emptiness before her, wondered how many seconds of each minute she'd spent like that, how many minutes of each day, how many hours, how many years.

Nominated by Don Waters, Virginia Quarterly Review

A COTTONY FATE

by JANE HIRSHFIELD

from THE PARIS REVIEW

Long ago, someone
told me: avoid, *or.*

It troubles the mind
as a held-out piece of meat disturbs a dog.

Now I too am sixty.
There was no other life.

Nominated by Jim Moore, Susan Terris

THE ORANGE PARKA

fiction by E. A. DURDEN

from GLIMMER TRAIN STORIES

Ten minutes before closing time, Rakesh sees his daughter enter the store. He is not in his own section, Kitchen Appliances, but in the neighboring section, Surveillance, where he has been fiddling with a pair of binoculars. He happens to be looking through the instrument's wrong end and gets a miniature view: glossy black hair falls to the waist of a well-rounded figure; a piece of clothing throbs the color of tangerine. As he removes the lenses from his eyes, he finds it hard to breathe.

The jacket of tangerine is the same, but the girl is not. He holds his mistake against her. He wonders if her parents know of the makeup she caulks over the beauty she was born with, or the insufficiency of her skirt; of the pair of youths who follow her into the store, and how they attend with jocular competition the promise of her hips. He wonders if the girl has two parents, which seems every child's right; and if she doesn't—if her mother has died—he wonders whether the girl's father knows where she is tonight.

He sets down the binoculars and looks again at his watch, although he knows the hour. The trio of teenagers will browse and joke and not buy. Marge the manager, also of the unwrinkled, will let them linger past closing time. Galaxy's employees are used to her haphazardness, but tonight, every minute of delay is a doubloon kicked down a drainage grate. It has been fifteen hours since he knew where his daughter was.

The day started in the dark.

Since the beginning of Prithi's sophomore year, when she began to attend a charter school in another part of Brooklyn, Rakesh has accompanied his daughter to the city bus stop where her route begins. Snow scraped by the night plows formed banks that winnowed the sidewalks, and reflected, in their dingy crystals, green and red at intersections, and orange from the streetlights in between. At this sleepy hour, *Don't Walk* signs blinked without authority; to leave the curb was to step into a river of space. Gusts sallying south from Canada found these channels and tried to conscript Rakesh's ratty blue scarf. Prithi fared worse. The only shelter she offered her legs from the cold was a pair of fuschia tights and a wisp of denim she called a skirt. At least she loved her snow boots, a pricey pair she had paid for with babysitting money, of buff-colored suede she tended in the evening with brushes and spit. She loved, too, the bright orange parka her mother had given her the previous winter, before she died.

Though the girl had always been careful to stay several paces behind, her distaste for him lately had grown, and so too had the distance she kept. Rakesh reached the bus stop first. Half a dozen people were already waiting. From where they had emerged, along those empty streets, Rakesh did not know. Yet there they huddled, slim slashes in the lids of the cups they clutched unleashing chains of steam. He took his place in the straggly line, which would have appeared informal to anyone who did not join it, but he felt all eyes note his position, just as he would register that of whoever came next.

When Prithi finally appeared, he bequeathed to her the spot he had been saving and retreated across the street to a bench.

As a mutinous boy, Rakesh had been slapped. His mother's right hand had found the swiftest route to his left cheek so often, the air came to hold its arc, even when she was not around. The worst such corrections were those she applied in the theater of the streets and the market, for then he felt, too, the brute hands of every grownup who happened to catch sight. It was as though every one of them became an auxiliary mother. It was as though they had conspired to cow any child elected at any time.

In this city, now, shame was reserved for parents. It seemed a status symbol—the more money one had, the more time one had to indulge in mortification, to speak of how awful a parent one was (the more time one had to be an awful parent). He had seen it on the seamless faces of certain mothers and fathers at the orientation meeting at Prithi's new school: leggy parents in tailored blue jeans and jackets of mountaineering fleece, who clustered near the principal during the tour, who interrupted to ask questions from lists they had prepared, who jotted notes on legal pads swaddled in supple leather. Such displays suggested that they were trying to prove something; that they were trying to prove something suggested the esophageal blockage of shame. Shame of what? Of sending their children to a charter school instead of one that was private? After the tour, when they filed into the auditorium for the "Open Forum on Student Life," these same parents asked the guidance counselor such questions as, *What if my son comes home drunk? What if my daughter becomes sexually active?* He had thought the questions rhetorical, until he realized what they were actually asking: *Am I allowed to punish my child?* As though to teach one's child that poor actions had painful consequences were the act of a primitive—like the singeing of cave roofs with cooking fires, or the pulling of feathers from one's teeth after a meal.

Recently, while he was fixing his daughter a late dinner, she flounced into the kitchen and said, "Why do you do that?"

He fluffed the pot of rice with a fork, as he had watched his wife do.

"You need real food," he said.

Prithi crossed her arms. "Why do you wait at the bus stop? It's like you think I'm not getting on."

"That never occurred to me."

"Mom never did it."

"You weren't attending that school—you were not taking any bus."

"She wouldn't."

Onto her plate, he dropped a spoonful of rice. "Wrong."

"How do you know?"

He didn't. Sandhya had been strict with their daughter, and lax. She had insisted on healthy food, fresh vegetables and legumes, until the girl's birthday, when she dumped from her shopping bag every manner of sugary treat. She forbade Prithi from spending the night at her friend Angela's house, until, one weekend, she encouraged it; what had changed, in Prithi or Sandhya—or, for that matter, Angela—he could not discern. At such times, he had felt like a novice cricket fan, scrutinizing the slightest twitch of every player in a vain attempt to glean the rules.

He dropped peas on top of the rice. He pushed the plate of food across the counter, in front of his daughter. He got from the drawer a fork and a spoon.

She sniffed at what the dish exhaled. "Weird."

"I followed the directions." He held up the card covered in Sandhya's scrawl.

She took the evidence.

"This isn't how she did it."

He retrieved the card. "This is your mother's hand."

"She didn't use that recipe."

"Show me the one she did."

Prithi shrugged. She was wearing an old gray sweatshirt of Sandhya's. The name of the hospital where she had worked as a nurse was peeling off. Every turn in the laundry clawed from the red letters more of their ink. When he looked at the frayed shirt, he could still read the words, but only because he had known each letter whole.

Prithi pushed peas around with her fork. "You always try so hard," she said, scraping the plate with the metal.

He did not know what to say. Once, Prithi had asked him questions to which he had known the answers. Now her statements were like questions that had no answers.

"If you would just eat," he said.

"You're not."

What had he had? A cigarette for breakfast; a dented apple during break. His new stomach, aloof since Sandhya's death, accepted only the essential. To eat was to shovel and snort, to gurgle with gas, to give off waste.

He opened the cabinet. He burdened a plate. A fork felt like cheap tin, apt to slip from his grasp. The tines were crooked. He sunk them into the grains and mash; they made their deposit between his arid cheeks. The girl was right: the dish bore no sign of Sandhya's flavors. The recipe card, he now noticed, was curiously clean.

Across the street from the bus stop this morning, he found it hard to sit still in the cold. He gave up the bench and paced. Prithi wrote text messages without her gloves on. He regretted every day that he had allowed her to buy that phone. Perhaps her obsession with the new gadget explained the parent-teacher conference he had been asked to schedule, and which, in a few hours, he would attend. He had not told Prithi about the upcoming meeting. He claimed to himself that he did not want to worry his daughter, before he found out the issue. In truth, he desired secret knowledge: a packet of indisputable facts to surprise her with.

The bus appeared too full to accept a single new passenger, but it began to swallow the dozen it found waiting, one by one, like a goat bound to chomp every low-hanging lemon. Rakesh imagined the daily scene onboard. The driver would shout, "Move back! Move back! Let the new passengers on," and his captive cargo obeyed. They squeezed their bags beneath their arms and between their feet; they brought reading materials closer, like a race of myopics. Prithi negotiated the center aisle, parti-colored with the uniforms of nurses and security guards, those who worked in mailrooms and daycares and doughnut shops; the neon green of a safety vest; the lacquered canary of a hard hat. The doors closed. The laden vessel cleaved from the curb. His daughter's dimpled paw skipped its way down the overhead handrail, from one empty spot to the next, as she joined the momentary village that moved.

Prithi used to go to school four blocks from where they lived, but its proximity had been its sole advantage—it was a troubled institution with a ham-fisted principal. Sandhya had entered the girl into a lottery for the new school. When her name was picked, Rakesh could find no good reason to object.

Five minutes before closing time, a blond weather girl appears on the two hundred televisions that line the store's back wall. She upgrades the snow storm expected tonight in Brooklyn to the status of "extreme weather conditions."

Of all the days Prithi chooses to vanish from school.

He has left several messages already on Prithi's unanswered cell phone. In the midst of hawking toasters and microwaves, he scours his moth-eaten memory, trying to scare up her friend Angela's last name. No doubt Sandhya had written it down, along with the girl's mother's phone number, and added it to one of her piles, but the one time he had tried to find something—a utilities bill—her system of organization had proven more baffling than he had supposed. Mingled with memos from her work and from Prithi's new school were such things as ticket stubs from the first movie they had seen in America, in the jobless weeks after they had arrived, when they were young enough not to allow the sense of wasting money to spoil the pleasure of what they were wasting it on.

Of those piles in plain view—on such places as the kitchen counter, the coffee table, atop her dresser, beside the TV—he counted eight: eight traps of quicksand. Midway through the second, he stopped. He has not disturbed them since.

When Prithi comes home—when this gnashing of teeth is over—he will get from her Angela's phone number. Until then, he will try to take succor from two known facts: Prithi has her parka, and she dislikes precipitation of any kind. Perhaps the storm will drive her home.

Meanwhile, Marge, the person with the keys, the one who can determine when they leave, shows off to the three teenagers a digital camera. She peers at the LCD to frame the shot. Prithi's impostor, the girl in the orange jacket with the dark hair, hooks one arm around the neck of each boy. The boy's ogle her out the side of their eyes as they mug for the picture. Do they look at Prithi that way? He sees his daughter as a pink-clad kindergartner, barreling down a gymnastics mat, bound for a springboard that will launch her miniature self into the air.

He hurries over to Televisions. Giovanni, their keeper, has a way with Marge.

He finds the boy performing some contraband activity on his contraband computer, a freakish model almost tiny enough for the lap of a doll.

"Can you believe those geese who just came in here?" Rakesh whispers. "If you kill the televisions, perhaps Marge will take the hint."

Giovanni's lugubrious eyes leave the screen of his toy and begin to search the store, skimming over Kitchen Appliances and Stereos, until they light upon Cameras and zero in on Marge. Apparently their manager has become pals with Prithi's twin and her consorts—after having brandished the most opulent camera to take the trio's picture, now she allows them to fondle the import.

"Slut," Giovanni says.

He returns to the keyboard of his diminutive computer, apparently unperturbed that it is closing time and their manager seems to have lost whatever sense she had. The boy's unwitting confidence in Time's coffers reminds Rakesh of Prithi, who has taken to spending sunny Saturdays squirreled away in her room, as though sunny Saturdays were a given, rather than a gift.

"Giovanni, I recall that you commute from New Jersey. If this blizzard comes in, the trains will stop."

439

The mute whelp continues to tap at his tooth-sized keys.

"You won't be able to get home," Rakesh tries again. "If we leave now, though, you'll still have a chance."

"Who wants to go home? My roommate's picked up a coke habit from his girlfriend. Really? Coke? What the hell am I supposed to do with that?"

The boy looks at him. Pimples flourish in the oil field between his eyebrows. The boy seems to be waiting for him to speak. Was the question an actual question? He is not used to the sort of confessions his adopted countrymen are comfortable with, and apparently comforted by.

He points to the screen of Giovanni's laptop. "Do you think you might postpone the game you're playing, so that we could get out of here?"

"It's not a game." The boy holds up the screen to eye level. "It's a conlang."

On the computer screen is a box. Inside the box, Giovanni has typed letters, but they amount to no recognizable language. He feels a rush of anger, that the boy would show him balderdash and expect him to care. It reminds him of the young woman in his building, often in the elevator with her toddler, who expects Rakesh to find the child amusing. He made the mistake once of mentioning this annoyance to Sandhya, who called him a grump, and pointed out that he had once loved babies, and had wanted many more. He conceded all counts: he was a grump, he still loved babies, and he had wanted more (they had tried for years). But that was not the point: the baby did not irritate him—the little fellow, now two years old, simply did the things that children his age do. It was the baby's mother who irked him. Her assumption that Rakesh will see the world as she does leaves him no breathing room. Brooklyn is crowded enough. Add to all the bodies three million such oblivious egos, and it would be a marvel if any elevator door were ever able to squeeze shut.

After Prithi had boarded the bus that morning, he retraced his route back home (he was not due at Galaxy Electronics until two in the afternoon). As he picked his way down the sidewalks narrowed by snow, he tried to imagine how his daughter appeared to her fellow commuters. If they noticed her, she must have seemed another pretty teenager poorly dressed for the weather—poorly dressed for any reasonable occasion; another of the ill-pierced, with a silver hoop that straddled her eyebrow.

The ornament she had acquired a week ago. She came home from visiting a friend, it was ten o'clock at night, and he met her at the door to their apartment.

"Why are you looking at me?" she said as she strolled in.

As though he had not spent the past fifteen years looking at her.

"There is a piece of metal sticking out of your face."

"Mom had a nose ring."

"That was tradition—this is trash. You were raised to know the difference."

"Just because it's not your culture doesn't make it bad."

She tried to skirt past him, down the hall. He would not let her. He reached out to touch the garish tinsel.

"Tell me what it's supposed to mean," he said. If she believed that it meant something, perhaps he could begin to understand.

She veered away. "It is just a piece of jewelry."

"It's poked through your skin."

"Don't yell at me. It's my body. I make my own choices."

Choices. She was fifteen. "Where did you learn to talk that way?"

"What way?"

"You sound like you're a character on a TV show." His mouth felt dry, but he was spitting. His throat burned.

Someone knocked on their door. A neighbor must have heard.

"What were you thinking?" Prithi whispered.

She slid past him, into her bedroom. The lock clicked.

Rakesh crept into the living room and looked out the window. The street in front of their building, a service road separated from Eastern Parkway only by a median, offered nothing unusual—no cops, no red and blue spiraling lights. Only cars hunkered curbside; the ice that mottled the sidewalks; the homeless man who stood often at the entrance to the subway, always in the same soiled T-shirt and ripped jeans (they referred to him as Crazy Man). A woman in a white fedora trailed a yellow dog.

Someone knocked again.

He slunk back and stared through the peephole. It was elderly Mrs. Gomez, who lived below. She resembled a fragile vase, protected by her plush blue robe.

"*Hola*, Señor Dabydeen," she said, when he opened the door. "*¿Está Prithi aquí?*"

He nodded. "She's fine."

Mrs. Gomez began to talk quickly. He had known Spanish as a young man. He was studying it again, on a lark, from a textbook he had bought for a dollar, but no language came to him now.

She touched her fingertips and thumbs together, and made the shape of a circle. "My stove—broken. *Prithi habla español, ¿sí?*"

"Oh—well—she studies it in school."

Prithi was already on her way to the door. She brushed past him. She gave the old lady a hug. They exchanged spirited phrases. Mrs. Gomez reached up and cradled the girl's chin. At the sight of Prithi's eyebrow ring, she pulled back. Prithi's smile began to wilt.

Rakesh could not intervene—the girl and the woman shared currents he did not receive. He wanted, though—he surprised himself by wanting—Mrs. Gomez not to make a fuss.

The old neighbor said something about *las reinas*, something about *Egipt antigno*—queens of ancient Egypt? Rakesh could not be sure. The girl laughed. In the muddy light of the hallway that ran the length of the sixth floor, amid the tiles with their dingy grout, the door to the elevator painted a skunky blue, his daughter's teeth were the white of a seabird.

He left Mrs. Gomez and Prithi to their visit.

Not knowing where to go, he retreated to the bathroom. The black-and-white-tiled chamber had no radiator. It was like a cold house of former days, where people preserved meats.

He did not need to urinate, and he had already brushed his teeth. He looked in the mirror; he focused on his eyebrow, and tried to imagine punching a hole there, and stringing through it a dubious alloy peddled by a sidewalk swindler. *It's my body*, Prithi had said, but was it? Who owned the flesh they inhabited?

He flipped the lever that closed the tub's drain and turned on both taps. He had never taken a bath in this apartment—that had been Sand-hya's ritual. The beat of the water against the porcelain was her sound, and he had not heard it since she died.

Every night, when he came home from eight hours on his feet, he would remove his shoes and leave them in the hallway, beside his daughter's boots and his wife's white nurse's clogs. In socks, he would move quietly through the apartment to the bathroom door, closed except by a crack. The aroma of spiced soaps containing such fruits as he used to eat at home, before America, overwhelmed him as he nosed his way into the steam-filled closet, where his wife lay immersed, jet hair clipped into a peasant's knot atop her sleeping head.

She was not actually asleep. She opened her eyes and made a great flap.

"One moment of solitude, that is all I ask," she said. "I am a tired nurse in need of a plunge. Mr. Dabydeen, can't you see my weariness?"

He loved when she called him Mr. Dabydeen. He leaned down and kissed the corona of frizz that marked where her forehead ended and her hair began. This annoyed her, too—that he would strain his back.

"When you can no longer walk because of such silly moves, I'm not going to be the one to drag you around, or fetch your every desire," she said, and ran a sea sponge up and down each arm. Bubbles streamed and popped. "I will be gone by then—I'll be retired, sunbathing on a beach, and our daughter will be with me, as well as our grandchildren, and whatever son-in-law the gods have asked us to tolerate. So you can keep yourself in tip-top shape and come with me. Or you can ignore my advice, break your back, and find yourself alone."

She looked up from her bathing and caught him in her tawny gaze.

The taps squeaked as he turned them off. The steamy water smelled like wet metal. He did what he used to do, those nights with Sandhya: he peeled off his socks and dropped them in the hamper; on the chilly porcelain edge he balanced, and dunked his tired dogs into the pool.

"Look, Giovanni—Marge is done talking with her new friends. Ask if she needs help closing the register."

"You ask."

"She likes you."

"Not since we did it. Those fingernails—Jesus Christ."

"I don't want to hear it," Rakesh says.

In fact, he does. The shame clouds him. A blizzard bears down, his daughter is missing, and yet he does want to hear of Marge's predation. Marge, of the mown bleached hair, the spectacles she wears only—as she admitted once to Giovanni—to look smarter, lumbers into Heating/Cooling, giving pendulous life to a pair of blue jeans obviously purchased for a former figure or in hopes of future slimness. Yellow strips of plastic tied to the grill of a window fan lick at her exorbitant hips. When he first met her, she had asked if he spoke English without so much as a glance at his application. Upon being told that Guyana was a former British colony, where English was the official language, she had flicked her green eyes over him in a way that titillated as much as disturbed.

He is a man of fifty—surely it is time for no such thoughts to rule him.

More mumbo jumbo appears on Giovanni's computer. The youth chuckles as he reads it.

"Constructed language, Dabydeen—conlang, for short."

"That alien business you were learning?"

"Klingon? No. Me and my buddy made this up."

Rakesh checks his watch: it is one minute past ten. On the weather girl's map, red welts stream south, Brooklyn-bound.

"Giovanni, I'm presently more interested in how you communicate with Marge."

"Haven't you ever wanted to be able to speak to just one person?" the boy says. "To use some kind of code no one else gets?"

"The world is full of such codes."

"That's why you gotta make your own. Get it?"

"I do not understand why you are learning—what did you call it?—Cling On. So that you might sell a television to an alien? They likely have models better than ours."

"If Klingons invade, we'll have way bigger problems."

"They are the dark ones, aren't they?" Rakesh says. "The ugly ones who make things messy for the white men?"

"Sulu's Asian. The chick is black. There's a Scot, too: Scotty. What do you want, Dabydeen? It's a fucking rainbow."

"I should never have come in today."

"Hey, does your building have any vacancies? I'm looking around." The youth's question disarms him.

"You would want to live where I live?"

Giovanni shrugs. "As long as it's cheap. No more roommates."

"Of course." Rakesh nods. "You are a man in search of a suitable home."

"I'm talking rock bottom."

"Understood. Coax Marge to free us, and I will see what I can find."

"Done," Giovanni says, and lopes off in search of his lady with the keys.

When Rakesh arrived for the conference with Prithi's teacher, the loud halls of the brick high school smelled of sneakers and luncheon meats. Children Prithi's age made outlandish promises with their bodies as though to caricature adults. They pinched and hugged and took flirtatious offense; they carried textbooks like odd props they had been handed. In corners, they formed clans and named overlords. Short girls laced themselves up in the arms of lofty boys. The bell dispersed them, much more quickly than Rakesh would have thought.

Rakesh caught no sight of his daughter, which was both a disappointment and a relief. He was not eager to have her ignore him.

"Mr. Dabydeen," her teacher said, as he took a seat in front of her desk. "I'm afraid I don't have much time today, but I wanted you to know as soon as possible that Prithi—"

"Pree-thee," he corrected. "One pronounces her name Pree-thee."

The white lady blushed. "Preethi, then. Mr. Dabydeen, your daughter hasn't been coming to class. She has missed six periods in the past two weeks. Do you have any idea what she's been up to?"

She was mocking him, when he was raising the girl by himself. "I would appreciate it if you would just tell me," he said.

Her brow dropped. "That's just it—I don't know. I'm asking you."

Astonishing: she wanted to learn about Prithi. His wife Sandhya would have known how to cultivate the teacher's harried concern. A girl from a muddy farm in Guyana did not become a nurse in Brooklyn without knowing how to woo. He had stood by and watched as she did the near impossible: convinced power to cede power, at least by a little, enough to get them a modest break on rent, or on Prithi's late fees at the library, or at Key Food, where she would offer to pay half price for a dusty can of coconut milk. She would manage it coolly—that seemed the trick. She had masked the demands of their overtaxed budget as a matter of principle, to pay exactly what was fair.

Prithi was no cut-rate grocery, however. It was not enough, that he could describe Sandhya's talents; it was not enough, to recall a cleverness here, or a frugality there, if he could not put her habits into practice for himself. He should have paid more attention. What man expects to bury his wife?

"Mrs. Tyler, Prithi has always liked mathematics. Do you know if she has missed other subjects?"

Before the teacher could answer, the door to the classroom opened. A splotchy-faced boy with a backpack barely tethered to his shoulder began to enter, until he saw Rakesh staring, and then he tarried. Mrs. Tyler gestured for the student to come in.

"I'm sorry, Mr. Dabydeen—my freshmen are about to arrive. We can schedule another conference—please email me." She handed him a business card with her address on it. It was of flimsy stock.

"How about tomorrow?" he said.

She glanced down at a day planner. She flipped a page. "Maybe the end of next week. Let me know. And tell Prithi she needs to get to class, please."

Once back in the hallway, he looked at his watch: their conference had lasted all of three minutes. Were he a parent of the leggy, fleece-wearing set, would he have pushed for more of the teacher's time? Would he have gotten it?

The secretary in the principal's office asked to see identification. He showed her his green card. She consulted a computer through a pair of bifocals.

"Prithi Dabydeen has not come to school today." She spoke into the machine's glowing face.

"Preethee."

She did not reply.

Where else did that bus go? What other buses might she have transferred to? Then there were the trains and the ferries. The map of the transit system flickered before him like the veins of his eyeballs caught in a questing beam. All she needed was $2.50 and she could reach any cankerous hamlet within the five boroughs; with a little more, she could hopscotch out of state.

Sandhya would have removed the piercing from her daughter's eyebrow. She would have dropped it in the garbage without ceremony. She would have repealed TV and phone privileges; she would have insisted the girl do more of the vacuuming, keep a cleaner room.

Theirs had been a love match, not arranged by their parents. In so breaking with custom, he had been asked to explain himself. The girl held the secret to many a curry, he had told his mother; to his father, he had described the sense of loyalty she had been raised with. Yet what young man knows the real reasons he is drawn to his bride? For the luster of her long hair, for the way her arms smelled of shea butter—

yes, he had wanted the privilege of her beauty as his daily meal. Others were pretty, too; yet, for them, he felt a raindrop; for Sandhya, a monsoon.

Now, he was starting to understand a bit more about the storm his bride had inspired. While his lust had gone into tumult at every turn of her mocking eyes, some speechless part of him, hewn from millennia, must have chosen his wife for all of the ways that she was different from him. Were she still with him, he might tell her that he admired, even more than her hair (and at this, she would have shaken her head in disbelief), the skepticism with which she regarded her own moods. She was not without feeling. After her father had died from a heart attack in the midst of chores on the family farm, Rakesh had found his wife crying into a washcloth at the kitchen sink. Yet she had the presence to know when her own emotions were beside the point. She did not insist on cherishing a point of view.

He had no such distance. He could not point to a tree and say, simply, "That is a tree." Whatever he was feeling engulfed whatever he came upon. The name of a thing was merely a kind of buoy, colorful but forlorn, a marker indulged by an immensity.

"Might I use your telephone, at least?" he said to the lady in the principal's office.

For once, he was glad Prithi carried a cell phone. He was due at work in forty minutes. He did not have time to track down his lawless vagabond.

"School business only."

"This is school business—I need to call my daughter, who is not in school."

The phone rang. The lady answered it. In Rakesh's direction, she made an unintelligible gesture with her purple fingernails. It was either a shooing motion—*Please leave now*—or a sign of resignation: Whaddya want, mister? *What do you expect me to do?*

Adolescent faces crowded the hallway, all either ecstatic or miserable. Where was her locker? He had been here only once, months before, at orientation. He looked up and down the corridor for something familiar, but the hundreds of metal boxes were identical, neat rows in stoic contrast to their skittish owners, like palace guards harassed by tourists.

En route to the subway, he searched for a pay phone. He wished he

447

had noticed when they had all disappeared. Certainly he would be getting a cell phone now.

The neighborhood around Prithi's new school was strange: no trees, squat warehouses, a factory where they canned maraschino cherries that smelled of some cloying booze-brew he would have snuck when he was young. Hewing close to the edge of industry were blocks of row houses, all two stories, sided with aluminum panels that were, in the case of most, about to tumble.

If he did not show up for the start of his shift in thirty minutes, Marge would brook no excuse. The only sign of him that would remain, after she fired him over the phone, would be the coconut sweets he kept in his employee locker. He could see it perfectly: Marge will prod them with her twisted fingernails and pronounce them "wack." Without offering to Rakesh's colleagues any of the homemade delicacy—sent to Rakesh by his arthritic aunt in Guyana—Marge will turn the bag over the garbage bin. The pink squares will crumble. She will make fun of how dry they are, but that's just it—they are the texture they are meant to be. Not every treat has to be unctuous and American.

She will grant his locker to his replacement, whatever sot happens to apply that day. *That very same day.* Consider the training video: a troop of animated humanoids, sporting the blue uniform of the sales force—genderless figures sprung from software, with skin the pinkish-brown of a sickly sow. If Galaxy Electronics could replace all of its employees with pixilated uncomplainers, it would. He could not give Marge a reason to start with him.

On the elevated subway platform—in this neighborhood, the tracks ran over the street, at a height taller than most rooftops—he spotted a man around his age, possibly Indian, or Guyanese, or even American, completing a call on his cell phone. As he was folding it closed, Rakesh approached him from the side, so as not to cause alarm.

"Excuse me—may I ask you a favor?"

"I have no cigarettes." The man was from India. "I quit three months ago."

"I was wondering if I might make a call on your phone."

The man glanced around the platform. A girl with a barcode tattooed on her cheek was cooing to a rat-faced dog in a rhinestone collar.

"You see, I left mine at home." Rakesh could not admit the truth. "My wife is in the hospital. I need to tell her that I am coming."

"Well, in that case." The man unfolded the phone. "Before the train gets here. If I'm late for work again . . ."

The numbers were small and glowed blue. He had to remove one of his gloves in order to press Prithi's exchange. While he clutched the phone to one ear and held his hand over the other, the man turned away and looked down the length of the tracks, as though to watch for the train. From the awkwardness of his stance, it was clear that he was acting: he was trying, with the means available, to give Rakesh a private field.

"Hello?" Prithi said.

"Hello, indeed! Why aren't you in school?"

There was static.

"Who is this? Father?"

She laughed like the heroine of a noir. She had never called him "father."

"Of course it's me. Where are you? Why aren't you in school?"

The static stopped, as though someone had closed a door. A loud bleating began. *Call failed.*

They heard the train before they saw it.

"This is mine," the man said, jutting his thumb toward the track as the lead car swayed into view. He kept talking, but the train's bluster obliterated what he was trying to say.

It was not Rakesh's route, not if he was to go straight to work.

The man took the phone. He slid it into the pocket of his coat. Over the screech of the brakes, the man shouted, "My daughter has not spoken to me for three years."

The subway halted. Sixty sets of doors, on twenty cars, sprang open. He felt his shoulders curl forward, as though to shield his heart from the man's bad luck. The superstitions of his grandparents told him that the stranger was tainted. Three years without Prithi, and with Sandhya already dead? It was a curse not to be imagined. How this man could still stand, and walk around, and go to work, all while his daughter became more of a wraith, Rakesh did not know. He did not want to know. The man could be his future self, sent back in time as a warning.

The computerized conductor announced the name of the stop.

The man offered his hand as he was boarding. Rakesh did not take it.

He finally escapes the store at ten fifteen. As he gets off the bus at the end of his block, the snow begins. When he enters the lobby of his building, flakes snagged on his blue scarf melt into beads. Mrs. Gomez and another neighbor, a plump woman around his age named Jill, are

449

installing their annual holiday decorations. Jill teeters on the top level of a stepladder, set next to the mantel of what was once a fireplace, long bricked-in. She holds an oversized cardboard menorah, silver with yellow flames, dotted on the back with duct tape. Mrs. Gomez, in a pair of lavender high heels, attempts to steady the ladder with her knotty hands. Where is Bella, her daughter, to allow this? It is all he can do to keep moving through the lobby; it is all he can do not to intervene.

"Oh, Mr. Dabydeen," Jill says, "we could really use your height."

"Have you seen Prithi?" He does not stop on his way to the elevator.

"*¿Está Prithi okay?*" Mrs. Gomez says.

"I have to get upstairs. Terribly sorry. Leave me some job to do."

Through the small, diamond-shaped window cut into the outer door of the elevator shaft, it is evident that the car is busy. He runs up the stairs. The last time he asked such a feat of his lungs was the night Sandhya died.

His daughter's boots are not where she usually leaves them; the orange jacket is not on its hook.

In the apartment, he does not sit down. He leaves the lights off; his coat, scarf, hat, and gloves, he leaves on. His messages grow more ragged as the hour limps by. He sings happy birthday to her voicemail, though her birthday is not for two weeks. He describes the black curls she was born with. "When I saw that hair, I knew you would be trouble. Your mother would say—"

The digital lady interrupts: *You have exceeded the time limit.*

Outside the living room window, street lamps tell him the weather: snow passes through their peach-colored beams on its way to the world that attracts it. Fire hydrants begin to disappear.

The mailbox of the person you are calling is full.

The neighbors have left him no job in the lobby. The high ceiling and vast girth are silent, on his way out. Small bulbs cast hundreds of gleams, nestled in the shadows of the ill-lit room like emerald caches, diamond, amethyst, ruby. These holidays do not belong to him, but he sees that the ladies have done what ladies know how to do: transformed bargain hoopla—the menorah, a grinning Santa face, kentei-patterned letters that spell Kwanzaa—into a kind of good cheer.

When he emerges into the frenzied flakes, the service road that runs parallel to Eastern Parkway wears snow the plows have yet to disrupt. It keeps a record of his footsteps as he crosses over to the subway station he and Prithi use, almost directly in line with the front door of their building. In the corridor of wind coursing down the Parkway, he says "Good evening" to Crazy Man, who paces around the entrance to the subway as though the weather were beneficent. The man appears not to notice Rakesh.

One descends into the subway station via a stairwell, around which a city planner of long ago had installed a fanciful metal balustrade painted civic green. From this railing, Rakesh sweeps off with his gloved hand a swath of snow. He leans his elbows on the cleared-off patch and looks down the stairs into what he can see of the station. From this vantage point, he might watch as passengers ascend. It is shortly before midnight, the point when the trains switch, in their frequency, from sluggish to scarce. He does not believe that his vigilance will bring her closer, but it seems his duty to be in the storm. He is the one who brought her to this weather.

A subterranean grumbling begins at a distance. The roar starts to sharpen into distinct rhythms, the clacking of wheels against tracks. It so overwhelms, that Rakesh cannot tell—he can never tell, those times when he's running late, and dashing downstairs to meet the train—from which direction it is coming, and thus, which direction it will go. Tonight, he does not know which to hope for.

The train's brakes squeal loudly enough to be heard from the street. By this point, the top steps have collected windrows of snow, which will make climbing difficult for those passengers who get off at this stop. Rakesh crouches and makes a plow of his hand and begins to sweep the snow to the side. It is sodden. The cold moisture soaks through his imitation-leather gloves and turns his fingers dumb. A passenger coming up the stairs, a middle-aged woman in what looks like nurse's whites beneath her long blue coat, gives him a puzzled look as she steps around him, but she does not slow. Rakesh finds himself breathless as he finishes the job. He rises and claps his hands together, to knock off the extra flakes, but this stuff is heavy and wet, not like flour or sand, and he is stuck with it.

Crazy Man interrupts his perambulation to come to the head of the stairs. He eyes Rakesh's work. It is the first time Rakesh has seen him standing still. He is not an old man, after all. His deep brown skin, beneath his tangled beard, has the poured-on quality of youth. The shape of his eyes is wide and stately, the flesh around them smooth. His hair, though matted, the tips of his curls catching snowflakes, is shiny and lavish. The boy is not more than twenty-two. He could be Manuel

451

who works at the corner bodega; he could be Q'asim who stocks the shelves at Key Food. He could be Giovanni. His bare neck, wet with snowmelt, glistens in the street light.

Rakesh unwinds his blue scarf. "Here." He holds out the ragged specimen.

The boy does not look at him. He resumes his orbit of the balustrade.

When the boy's route brings him closer, Rakesh offers the scarf again. When this second attempt is ignored, he throws the skimpy fabric over the boy's neck. The youth flinches at the touch of the wool and slithers out from under it. The scarf falls into the snow. Rakesh begins to bend down to retrieve it. His lower back twinges with pain. He must right himself slowly. Fatigue hardens in his joints like cooled wax.

He will go down into the station and ask the person in the ticket booth if she knows when the next train is supposed to arrive.

"Come into the station," he says to the boy. "That's where I'm going. Out of the weather."

The boy shakes his head regretfully.

"All right, then," Rakesh says. "Don't trust me."

The staircase he swept clear is already slick again, and he must hold onto the banister to keep from slipping as he descends. The fluorescent lights of the station are too insistent; he must squint through their cloud. Inside the ticket booth, someone has taped a red foil star to the bulletproof Plexiglas, just over the crooked sign that says, *Attendant not available.*

There is meant always to be an attendant at this ticket booth. Other stations have switched over to machines, but the manned post at this one has been kept, supposedly for safety. What of a young girl coming home at night by herself—what if someone were to follow her off the train? The emergency phone would be useless. By the time the transit police arrived, she would be gone, dragged away by a maniac.

As Prithi would say: *What were you thinking?* He never should have gone to work that day, after he had found out about the skipping of school, but he would have been fired. He sees every day in the store men his age who cannot find jobs, who wander the aisles pretending to appraise the gadgets they cannot afford, all so that they might have a place to go outside of the home, as they once did. If he loses his job, Prithi will suffer. With his late hours, the fact that he scarcely sees her, she suffers already.

Kind souls, like Mrs. Gomez, her daughter Bella, and Jill, would have helped, had he asked—they had made their sympathy clear: to raise a

452

child calls for more than one pair of hands. They were like Sandhya. Sandhya had treated their building as though it were a ship floating on an unknown ocean, with stores of favor and obligation every passenger must partake of, in order to survive. To him, such dependence on others had a whiff of country mud, of handmade tunics made from unprocessed animal hairs. He wanted the clean cottons of American life.

No train comes. He mounts the snowy stairs. As he has done countless times, he emerges onto Eastern Parkway and glances up at the top floor of his building, at the four dark windows on the left. A yellow cab, marooned in this unlikely borough—could it be Prithi?—spits up snow as it trundles down the block. It makes an illegal left turn onto Washington Avenue, fishtails slightly, and disappears.

He might not see his daughter tonight. Nothing good will come of a fifteen-year-old girl adrift in a city made desolate by a snowstorm. At best, such freedom might seem fun to her, now, but she is sifting through the masks of some harrowed place, trying to choose which to wear, not realizing the residue every guise she ever dallies with will leave behind.

He will wait. He will wait for the moment when she is grown enough to understand that he is the one to blame for whatever happened to her this snow-dead night of her sixteenth year.

On a bench near the entrance to the subway, the homeless boy sits on top of snow. His jeans look saturated; surely he no longer can feel his legs.

"You must have someplace to go," Rakesh says.

The boy's teeth are chattering. His dark eyes, as handsome as any Rakesh has seen, begin to close. It is nineteen degrees, and the boy is on the verge of sleep.

Rakesh finds in his wallet exactly three dollar bills—enough for the boy to feed the ticket machine.

"Ride the next train," he says. "It will be warm and dry."

He holds the money near the boy's face. The boy slides away from his outstretched hand and gets up and walks behind the bench, as casually as if he were distancing himself from an unpleasant smell. He leans against the back of the bench, turns away from Rakesh, and crosses his arms.

"I'm supposed to be cold," the boy says.

"What?" It is the first time that Rakesh has heard him speak.

"It's a test."

"A test of what?"

The boy shakes his head. "You won't get it."

Rakesh has one more chance before the boy disappears—before he falls asleep on some other block, to be found when a dog digs up his icy body. He circles the bench and grabs the boy's wrist. The boy, apparently amused, tries to pull away. Rakesh crumples the cash into the boy's palm and closes the resistant fingers around the greasy paper.

The boy opens his hand and prods the crushed money, as though to see if it's alive. He hunches over and smooths out the bills along the top of his knee.

"Can't pay you back."

From one direction or the other, a train begins to thunder.

"Just get on the goddamn subway."

Flakes of snow cling to the boy's eyelashes. He turns and begins to slink down the stairs into the station.

The slurry from the sky adds its weight to the Parkway—to asphalt, to sidewalks, to the roofs and hoods and door handles of parked cars. He slogs through it, across the service road, toward his building. He will call 911—for whatever it is worth—to report the boy's precarious position, in case he does not get on the train. He should have found help for him a long time ago, but he had assumed that the wanderer was a man, not a boy, and he had been lazy. He had been annoyed and repulsed, too.

Before he reaches his building, he hears a shout. He turns around.

It's the boy. He slides across the service road toward Rakesh like a child mimicking an ice skater. In his hands is the old blue scarf, soaked and speckled with snow. *You keep it*, Rakesh is about to insist, but the boy's breathless excitement stops him. The boy grins as he presents the scarf, as though to say: here is what you have been searching for.

Nominated by Glimmer Train Storier

IMMIGRATION

by KEVIN PRUFER

from THE SOUTHERN REVIEW

When the wheels came down over Miami,
the stowaway in the landing gear,
half-frozen and unconscious,
slipped from the wheel well into blue air.
How amazed he must have been
to wake to that falling sensation
and the rapidly approaching sodium lamps
of the airport parking lot.

The couple that owned the car his body crushed
was astonished at the twist of fate
that brought his life so forcefully into theirs.
Their young son would always remember it,
how just then the cold shadow of another airplane
passed over him, how the bits of jewel-like glass
lay strewn across the asphalt
like the dead man's thoughts.

Nominated by David Baker, Richard Burgin, Martha Collins,
Mark Irwin, Alan Michael Parker, Anis Shivani

HELL

by MEGHAN O'GIEBLYN

from THE POINT

A couple of years ago, a Chicago-based corporate-identity consultant named Chris Herron gave himself the ultimate challenge: rebrand hell. It was half gag, half self-promotion, but Herron took the project seriously, considering what it would take in the travel market for a place like hell to become a premier destination. The client was the Hell Office of Travel and Tourism (HOTT), which supposedly hired Herron in the wake of a steady decline in visitors caused by "a stale and unfocused brand strategy." After toying with some playfully sinful logos—the kind you might find on skater/goth products—Herron decided that what the locale needed to stay competitive in the afterlife industry was a complete brand overhaul. The new hell would feature no demons or devils, no tridents or lakes of fire. The brand name was rendered in lowercase, bubbly blue font, a wordmark designed to evoke "instant accessibility and comfort." The slogan—which had evolved from "Abandon Hope All Ye Who Enter Here" (1819) to "When You've Been Bad, We've Got It Good" (1963) to "Give in to Temptation" (2001)—would be "Simply Heavenly." The joke was posted as a "case study" on Herron's personal website and quickly went viral in the marketing blogosphere—a testament to the power of effective branding.

I grew up in an evangelical community that wasn't versed in these kinds of sales-pitch seductions. My family belonged to a dwindling Baptist congregation in southeast Michigan, where Sunday mornings involved listening to our pastor unabashedly preach something akin to the 1819 version of hell—a real diabolical place where sinners suffered for all eternity. In the late 1980s, when most kids my age were performing interpretive dances to "The Greatest Love of All" and receiving enough gold stars to fill a minor galaxy, my peers and I sat in Sunday school each week, memorizing scripture like 1 Peter 5:8: "Be self-controlled and alert. Your enemy the devil prowls around like a roaring lion looking for someone to devour."[1]

I was too young and sheltered to recognize this worldview as anachronistic. Even now as an adult, it's difficult for me to hear biblical scholars like Elaine Pagels refer to Satan as "an antiquarian relic of a superstitious age," or to come across an aside, in a magazine or newspaper article, that claims the Western world stopped believing in a literal hell *during the Enlightenment.* My parents often attributed chronic sins like alcoholism or adultery to "spiritual warfare," (as in, "Let's remember to pray for Larry, who's struggling with spiritual warfare") and taught me and my siblings that evil was a real force that was in all of us. Our dinner conversations sounded like something out of a Hawthorne novel.

According to Christian doctrine, all human beings, believers included, are sinners by nature. This essentially means that no one can get through life without committing at least one moral transgression. In the eleventh century, Saint Anselm of Canterbury defined original sin as "privation of the righteousness that every man ought to possess." Although the "saved" are forgiven of their sins, they're never cured. Even Paul the Apostle wrote, "Christ Jesus came into the world to save sinners—*of whom I am the worst.*" According to this view, hell isn't so much a penitentiary for degenerates as it is humanity's default destination. But there's a way out through accepting Christ's atonement, which, in the Protestant tradition, involves saying the sinner's prayer. For contemporary evangelicals, it's solely this act that separates the sheep from the goats. I've heard more than one believer argue that Mother Teresa is in hell for not saying this prayer, while Jeffrey Dahmer, who supposedly accepted Christ weeks before his execution, is in heaven.

I got saved when I was five years old. I have no memory of my conversion, but apparently my mom led me through the prayer, which involves confessing that you are a sinner and inviting Jesus into your heart. She might have told me about hell that night, or maybe I already

---

1 *I think evangelicals are under the impression that any scriptural passage with an animal reference is kid-friendly. In fact, this verse once inspired my Christian camp counselors to have our second-grade class sing a version of the doo-wop classic "The Lion Sleeps Tonight," as "The Devil Sleeps Tonight," which we performed for our parents, cheerily snapping our fingers and chanting "awimbawe, awimbawe," etc.*

knew it existed. Having a frank family talk about eternity was seen as a responsibility not unlike warning your kids about drugs or unprotected sex. It was uncomfortable, but preferable to the possible consequences of not doing so. Many Protestants believe that once a person is saved, it's impossible for her to lose her eternal security—even if she renounces her faith—so there's an urgency to catch kids before they start to ask questions. Most of the kids I grew up with were saved before they'd lost their baby teeth.

For those who'd managed to slip between the cracks, the scare tactics started in earnest around middle school. The most memorable was *Without Reservation*, a thirty-minute video that I was lucky enough to see at least half a dozen times over the course of my teens. The film (which begins with the disclaimer: "The following is an abstract representation of actual events and realities") has both the production quality and the setup of a driver's ed video: five teens are driving home from a party, after much merrymaking, when their car gets broadsided by a semi. There's a brief montage of sirens and police radio voice-overs. Then it cuts to four of the kids, Bill, Ken, John and Mary, waking up in the car, which is mysteriously suspended in space. Below them is a line hundreds of people long, leading up to a man with white hair, stationed behind a giant IBM. When a person reaches the front of the line, this man (who's probably supposed to be God or St. Peter, but looks uncannily like Bob Barker) types the person's name into a DOS-like database, bringing up their photo, cause of death, and one of two messages: "Reservation Confirmed," or "Reservation Not Confirmed." He then instructs them to step to either the left or the right.

At this point, it's pretty clear that this isn't a film about the dangers of operating under the influence. The kids begin to realize that they're dead. One of them, Bill, a Christian, uneasily explains to the others that what they're seeing is a judgment line, at which point Mary loses it, shaking uncontrollably and sobbing "I want to go back! Why can't we all just go back!" The rest of the film consists of a long sequence showing their memorial service, back on earth, where some kind of school administrator speaks in secular platitudes about death being a place of safety and peace—a eulogy that is inter-spliced with shots of Ken, John and Mary learning that their reservation is "not confirmed," then being led down a red-lit hall and violently pushed into caged elevators. The last shot of them is in these cells—Mary curled in the fetal position, Ken and John pounding on the chain-link walls—as they descend into darkness. There's a little vignette at the end in which the fifth, surviving, passenger gets saved in the school cafeteria, but by that point I was always too shell-shocked to find it redemptive.

It's difficult to overstate the effect this film had on my adolescent psyche. Lying in bed at night, I replayed the elevator scene over and over in my head, imagining what fate lay in store for those kids and torturing myself with the possibility that I might be one of the unconfirmed. What if I had missed a crucial part of the prayer? Or what if God's computer got some kind of celestial virus and my name was erased? When you get saved young, when you have no life transformation—no rugged past to turn from—the prayer itself carries real power, like a hex.[2]

This anxiety was exacerbated by the fact that, around junior high, youth leaders began urging us to "re-invite" Christ into our lives. They insinuated that those of us who had been saved early might not have *actually* been saved—particularly if we were just repeating obediently after our parents. Some said the childhood prayers had been provisional, a safety net until we reached the age of accountability (traditionally believed to be twelve). Apparently, the words weren't enough—you had to mean them, and, at least to some extent, you had to live them. Good works couldn't get you into heaven, but if your life showed no sign of the Holy Spirit working in you, then this was a pretty good hint that you might not have been completely genuine when you asked Jesus into your life.

One of the most obvious ways of living your faith was through evangelism. I recently re-watched *Without Reservation* and realized that, as a kid, I'd totally missed the intended message. The film was not a scare tactic meant to trick teens into becoming Christians; it was very clearly designed for the already-saved, a dramatized pep talk urging us to get the word out about hell to our non-Christian friends. The most dramatic sequence of the film (apart from the elevators) is when John, before being carried off to hell, asks Bill, the believer, why he never said anything about eternal damnation. "We rode home from practice

---

2 At one point during my early teens, before I understood the concept of eternal security, it occurred to me that if I could ask Jesus into my heart, I could just as easily ask him to leave. Once this fear lodged itself in my brain, it became impossible not to think the prayer "Jesus, go out of my heart," the way it's impossible not to visualize a purple hippopotamus once someone tells you not to. For weeks, I found myself mentally replaying this heresy, then immediately correcting it with the proper salvation prayer, all the while terrified that something would happen to me (a car accident, a brain aneurysm) in the seconds in between, while I was technically unsaved.

together every day," he pleads. "We talked about a lot of stuff, but we never talked about this." Bill can only offer feeble excuses like "I thought you weren't interested!" and "I thought there was more time!"

That this message never got across to me might have had something to do with the fact that, as a homeschooled junior-high student, I actually didn't know any unbelievers. In my mind, the "lost" consisted of a motley minority of animal-worshipping tribesmen, Michael Jackson, Madonna, and our Catholic neighbors. It wasn't until I started going to public high school that I began to feel a gnawing guilt, spurred by the occasional realization that my evolution-touting biology teacher, or the girl who sat next to me in study hall reading *The Satanic Bible*, was going to spend eternity suffering. Despite this, I never got up the courage to share my faith. Part of it was a lack of personal conviction. But I was also becoming aware that the gospel message—which depends on convincing a person he's a sinner in need of God's grace—sounded seriously offensive and self-righteous. Our pastor always said that we needed to speak about hell in a spirit of love, but he clearly didn't know what it was like to be a teenager in the 1990s. I went to a high school that didn't publish the honor roll for fear of hurting those who weren't on it. The most popular yearbook quote among my graduating class was Tupac's "Only God can judge me." And most of those kids didn't even believe in God.

In retrospect, *Without Reservation* looks to me like a last-ditch effort, one of the church's final attempts to convince the emerging generation of the need to speak candidly about eternity. Over the course of my teenage years, Christians began to slip into awkward reticence about the doctrine of damnation. Believers still talked about the afterlife, but the language was increasingly euphemistic and vague. People who rejected Jesus were "eternally separated from God." We were saved not from an infinity of torment, but from "the bondage of sin." Back then, nobody in ministry had the hubris—nor, probably, the sophistication—to rebrand hell à la Chris Herron. Rather, hell was relegated to the margins of the gospel message, the fine print on the eternal-life warranty.

In the King James Bible, the English word "hell" serves as the translation of four different Greek and Hebrew terms. The Old Testament refers exclusively to *Sheol*, the traditional Hebrew underworld, a place of stillness in which both the righteous and the unrighteous wander in shadows. There's no fiery torment, no wailing or gnashing of teeth. The devil had not yet been invented (though Satan, a trickster angel with whom he would later be conflated, pops up now and then). Sinners seem remarkably off the hook—so much so that Job laments that the wicked "spend their days in prosperity and in peace they go down to Sheol." For many of these writers, the word simply denotes its literal translation, "grave," or unconscious death. The psalmist prays, "For in death there is no remembrance of thee: in Sheol who shall give thee thanks?"

In the New Testament, several writers refer to this place under its Greek name, *Hades*. There's also a number of passages about *Gehenna*, literally "the Valley of Hinnom," which was a real area outside Jerusalem that served as the city dump. Fires burned there constantly, to incinerate the garbage; it was also a place where the bodies of criminals were burned. The Jewish rabbinical tradition envisioned Gehenna as a purgatorial place of atonement for the ungodly. This is the word Jesus uses when he gives the hyperbolic command that one should cut off the hand that is causing one to sin: "It is better for thee to enter into life maimed, than having two hands to go into Gehenna, into the fire that never shall be quenched." Another Greek term, *Tartarus*, appears only once, when the author of 1 Peter writes about the angel rebellion that took place before the creation of the world. Drawing from the Greek myth of the Olympians overthrowing the Titans, he relays how Lucifer and his allies were cast out of heaven into Tartarus. In the *Aeneid*, Virgil describes Tartarus as a place of torment guarded by the Hydra and surrounded by a river of fire to prevent the escape of condemned souls. Except in the 1 Peter version, there are no human souls there, just bad angels.

The most dramatic descriptions of hell come from the strain of apocalyptic literature that runs through the New Testament, as well as the Old Testament prophets. Apocalypticism was a worldview that arose during the sixth century BCE, when Israel was under Syrian domination. It involved the belief that the present era, which was ruled by evil, would soon give way to a new age here on earth in which God would restore justice and all evildoers would be punished. The authors of Daniel and Ezekiel were apocalyptists—so was John of Patmos, the author of Revelation. It's these authors who provide us with passages such as, "They will be tormented with burning sulfur in the presence of the holy angels and of the Lamb. And the smoke of their torment will rise for ever and ever." This was a belief system born out of persecution. The Book of Daniel was written in response to the oppressive monarch Antiochus Epiphanes; the Book of Revelation came about during the rule of Domitian, who had Christians burned, crucified and fed to wild animals. As Nietzsche noted in *The Genealogy of Morals*, these passages are essentially revenge fantasies, written by people who'd suffered horrible injustices and had no hope of retribution in this life. In fact, many of the fantastical beasts that populate these books were meant to represent contemporary rulers like Nero or Antiochus.

I didn't learn any of this at church. As a kid, it never occurred to me that Solomon and Daniel had drastically different views about the afterlife. Christian theology, as it has developed over the centuries, has functioned like a narrative gloss, smoothing the irregular collection of biblical literature into a cohesive story written by a single, divine author. Secular scholars refer to this as "the myth," the story that depicts all of human history as an epic of redemption. Paul came up with the idea of original sin, transforming the Crucifixion into a voluntary sacrifice that brought salvation to the world. Drawing from his background as a Pharisee, he connected Hebrew scripture to the life of Christ. Just as sin entered the world through one man, Adam, so can the world be redeemed by the death of one man. As time went on, Satan, Lucifer and Beelzebub were consolidated into a single entity, the personification of all evil. Likewise Sheol, Gehenna, Hades and Tartarus came to be understood as physical representations of the darkest place in the universe. By the time the King James Bible was published in the sixteenth century, each of these words was translated as simply "hell."

The various depictions of hell over the centuries tend to mirror the earthly landscape of their age. Torture entered the conception of hell in the second century, when Christians were subjected to sadistic public spectacles. Roman interrogation methods included red-hot metal rods, whips and the rack—a contraption that distended limbs from their joints. The non-canonical *Apocalypse of Peter*, a product of this era, features a fierce and sadistic hell in which people are blinded by fire and mangled by wild beasts. Dante's *Divine Comedy* has traces of the feudal landscape of fourteenth-century Europe. Lower hell is depicted as a walled city with towers, ramparts, bridges and moats; fallen angels guard the citadel like knights. The Jesuits, who rose to prominence during a time of mass immigration and urban squalor, envisioned an inferno of thousands of diseased bodies "pressed together like grapes in a wine-press." It was a claustrophobic hell without latrines, and part of the torture was the human stench.

Today, biblical literalists believe hell exists outside of time and space, in some kind of spiritual fifth dimension. Contemporary evangelical churches don't display paintings or stained glass renderings of hell. It's no longer a popular subject of art. If hell is represented at all, it's in pop culture, where it appears as either satirically gaudy—like animated Hieronymus Bosch—or else eerily banal. In *The Far Side*, Satan and his minions are depicted as bored corporate drones who deal with the scourge of the post-industrial earth. ("There's an insurance salesman here," Satan's secretary says. "Should I admit him or tell him to go to Heaven?") One of the most popular diabolical archetypes in recent years has been the effete Satan. He shows up in episodes of *The Simpsons* and appears in Tenacious D videos, whining about the fine print of the Demon Code. He makes cameos in *South Park*, where he's usually involved in petty domestic squabbles with his boyfriend, Saddam Hussein. Satan has become an unwelcome nuisance, an impotent archetype occasionally dragged out for a good laugh. In an episode of *Saturday Night Live* from 1998, Garth Brooks plays a struggling musician who tries to sell his soul to the devil for a hit song, only to find that Satan (Will Ferrell) is an even more pathetic songwriter than he. When Satan finally gives up and asks if he can leave, Garth shows him out and tells him to lock the door behind him.

Although the sermons of my childhood were often set against the backdrop of hell, I wasn't introduced to the theological doctrine of damnation until I enrolled at Moody Bible Institute at the age of eighteen. Known within evangelical circles as the "West Point of Christian service," Moody is one of the most conservative Christian colleges in the country. When I was there, students weren't allowed to dance, watch movies or be alone in a room with a member of the opposite sex. The campus was downtown, occupying a purgatorial no man's land between the luxurious Gold Coast and the Cabrini-Green housing projects, but most of the students rarely left campus. The buildings were connected by subterranean tunnels, so it was possible to spend months, particularly in the winter, going from class to the dining hall to the dorms, without ever stepping outside. We spent our free time quizzing one another on Greek homework, debating predestination over soft-serve ice cream at the Student Center, and occasionally indulging in some doctrinal humor (Q: What do you call an Arminian whale? A: Free Willy).

Ideologically, Moody is a peculiar place. Despite the atmosphere of serious scholarship, the institute is theologically conservative, meaning that we studied scripture not as a historic artifact, but as the Word of God. Most of the professors thought the world was created in six days. Nearly all of them believed in a literal hell. One of the most invidious tasks of the conservative theologian is to explain how a loving God can allow people to suffer for all of eternity. God is omnipotent and Paul claims it is his divine will that all people should be saved—yet hell exists. Before taking freshman Systematic Theology, I'd never given this problem much thought, but once I considered it, it seemed pretty significant. In layman's terms, the argument our professors gave us went something like this: God is holy by nature and cannot allow sin into his presence (i.e. into heaven). He loves all humans—in fact, he loves them so much that he gave them free will, so that they could choose to refuse salvation. In this way, people essentially condemned themselves to hell. God wasn't standing over the lake of fire, laughing uproariously while casting souls into the flames. Hell was simply the dark side of the universe, the yin to God's yang, something that must exist for there to be universal justice.[3]

There were still a number of problems with this formulation, but for the most part I was willing to suspend my disbelief and trust that God's ways were higher than my own. What bothered me was the numbers. Freshman year, every student was required to take a seminar called Christian Missions. It was basically a history of international evangelism, taught by Dr. Elizabeth Lightbody, a six-foot-three retired missionary to the Philippines who sported a topiary of gray-blonde curls, wore brightly colored wool suits and smiled so incessantly it seemed almost maniacal. During the first week of class, we watched a video that claimed there were currently 2.8 billion people among "the unreached"—that is, people who had never heard the gospel. Dr. Lightbody, like the rest of the faculty, adhered to exclusivism, the belief that only those with faith in Jesus Christ can be saved (as opposed to pluralism, the belief that people of all religions will be saved, regardless of the name they use for God). Jesus said that "no man comes to the Father, but by me," and we had to take this word for word as the truth,

3 There's a widespread misconception that biblical literalism is facile and mindless, but the doctrine I was introduced to at Moody was every bit as complicated and arcane as Marxist theory or post-structuralism. There were students at the institute who got in fierce debates about infralapsarianism vs. supralapsarianism (don't ask) and considered devoting their lives to pneumatology (the study of the Holy Spirit). In many ways, Christian literalism is even more complicated than liberal brands of theology because it involves the sticky task of reconciling the overlay myth—the story of redemption—with a wildly inconsistent body of scripture.

meaning it included those who had no idea who Jesus was.[4] Technically, I'd known this since I was a kid (after all, if the unreached could get to heaven some other way, what would be the point of sending missionaries?), but I'd never paused to consider the implications. If you took into consideration all the people who'd ever lived—including those centuries upon centuries when entire continents were cut off from the spread of Christianity—then the vast majority of humanity was going to spend eternity in hell.

I tried to feel out other students to see if anyone else was having similar thoughts, but it was a dangerous subject. Our communal language was so rigid and coded that there was very little vocabulary with which to express doubt. I had to frame my questions as technical doctrinal queries, or else pretend I was seeking evangelism advice (e.g. "Say an unbeliever were to ask you to defend the existence of hell . . ."). One evening, in the cafeteria, I suggested that it seemed kind of unfair that people were going to suffer for eternity simply because we believers hadn't managed to bring them the good news. On this point, I got nothing more than a thoughtful nod or a somber "hmm." A few students gave me knowing smiles and little shoulder squeezes, as though I was in the midst of some revelatory spiritual experience that would lead me to the mission field.

On Friday nights, I went down to Michigan Avenue with a dozen other students to do street evangelism. Our team leader was Zeb, a lanky, pimpled Missions major who probably would have been into LARPing or vampirism if he weren't a Christian. Instead, he memorized Luther and Zwingli and made vivid chalk drawings illustrating the plan of salvation, all of which made him kind of popular on campus. We'd set up an easel in front of Banana Republic, and Zeb would draw the abyss that lies between mankind and God, which can only be bridged by the cross, telling the story of redemption as he drew. The rest of us handed out tracts to tourists and businesspeople. We usually drew a small crowd—mostly men who were waiting for their wives to finish shopping and seemed to view us as a zany sideshow. It wasn't one of those vicious "turn or burn" productions, but Zeb's chalk narrative referred to sin and repentance, and the tracts, which had the reason-

4 One day, a student asked about children who died without being saved. Dr. Lightbody gave an answer so tortured and evasive that I had no clue what she was implying until she closed with the caveat "Now, don't ever say that to a mother who's lost a baby." I later found out that Augustine also believed unbaptized infants were sent to hell.

able title "How to Become a Christian," mentioned hell only once or twice. These terms were the water we swam in, but out on the street, against the softly lit backdrop of window displays, they sounded ancient and fierce.

I knew how ridiculous we looked. These people already knew who Jesus was. They'd grown up watching Jerry Falwell spaz out on TV, or sneering at Ned Flanders on *The Simpsons*. They didn't know all the theological reasons why God was good, and would probably never give us the time of day to explain them. We were speaking a foreign language. In a just world, they wouldn't be held accountable for their refusal of the gospel any more than an unreached person who followed his culture's belief in ancestral worship. When Zeb gave the call to come forward and find forgiveness in Jesus Christ, our audience awkwardly glanced at their watches, put their headphones back on, or yawned.

While I was attending Moody, the most controversial church in the Chicago area was Willow Creek Community Church, out in the northwest suburbs. I'd heard students raving about it—and others railing against it—ever since orientation week. It was popular amongst the Pastoral, Youth Ministry and Sports Ministry majors. The critics were mostly in the theology department. Willow Creek's pastor, Bill Hybels, was a well-known author and something of a celebrity in the evangelical world, but the big draw was apparently the size of the church. There was a $73 million "Worship Center," a food court and a parking lot worthy of an international airport. Every Sunday morning, a school bus would pull up to the Moody campus and dozens of students would climb on board to be bused out to South Barrington for the 9 a.m. service. I had been attending a fledgling Baptist church in Uptown that year, and when I got back to the school cafeteria on Sunday afternoons I was routinely confronted with students fresh off the Willow Creek bus, all of whom were visibly charged, as though they'd just gotten back from a rock concert. One blustery Sunday morning in February, as I was walking to the "L" station to catch the train to Uptown, faced with the prospect of another 65-minute sermon about gratitude or long-suffering, I found myself suddenly veering across the campus to get on the Willow Creek bus.

I'd always associated megachurches with televangelists, those bottle-tanned preachers with Southern accents who addressed the cameras from palatial churches with fountains out front. Willow Creek was different. The Worship Center seated 7,000 people, but it was sleek and spare, more convention hall than cathedral. Hybels preached in a simple oxford shirt, and his charisma was muted, reminiscent of the gentle authority assumed by dentists and family physicians. The sermon was based in scripture. At first, it just seemed like the traditional gospel set to a brighter tempo. According to Hybels, God's love was not an unearned gift granted to sinners, but proof that we mattered on a cosmic scale. Our primary fault was not our sinful nature, but our tendency to think too little of ourselves. We needed to expand our vision, to stop doubting that we could do amazing things for God. It took me several more visits, over the following few months, before I was able to put my finger on what was off. One Sunday, as I was riding back on the bus, staring out at the mirror-plated corporate headquarters along the freeway, I realized that I couldn't recall anyone at Willow Creek ever mentioning sin, repentance or confession. I never once heard a reference to hell.

I wasn't aware of it at the time, but Willow Creek was on the front lines of a movement some described as a "second Reformation," with the potential to remake the Christian faith. Hybels was one of a handful of pastors—including, most notably, Rick Warren of Saddleback Church in California (author of *The Purpose Driven Life*)—who pioneered what would become known as the "seeker-friendly church," a congregation targeting the vast population of Americans who had little to no experience with Christianity ("unchurched Harry and Mary," in ministry lingo). The goal was to figure out why this demographic was turned off by the gospel, and then to create a worship service that responded to their perceived needs.

Essentially, this is consumer-based management.[5] During Willow Creek's inception, Hybels—who studied business before entering the ministry—performed preliminary market research, surveying the unreligious in his community to find out why people weren't going to church. Unsurprisingly, the most common responses were "church is boring," "I don't like being preached down to" and "it makes me feel guilty." Harry and Mary were made uncomfortable by overt religious symbolism and archaic language. They didn't like being bombarded by welcome committees. The solution was a more positive message: up-

---

5 Hybels keeps a poster in his office that reads: "What is our business? Who is our customer? What does the customer consider value?" Rick Warren's Saddleback motto is "Let the target audience determine the approach."

beat tunes, an emphasis on love and acceptance. There would be respect for anonymity—visitors wouldn't be required to wear name tags or stand up and introduce themselves. Everything was designed for the visitor's comfort and leisure.

It goes without saying that pastors who are trying to "sell" God won't mention hell any more than a Gap ad will call attention to child labor. Under the new business model, hell became the meatpacking plant, the sweatshop, the behind-the-scenes horror the consumer doesn't want to know about. Once I became aware of what was missing, it was almost a game to watch the ministers try to maneuver around the elephant in the room. One strategy was to place the focus exclusively on heaven, letting people mentally fill in the blank about the alternative. Another was to use contemporary, watered-down translations of the Bible, like *The Message* (reviled around Moody's theology department, where it was better known as "The Mess").

Some Moody students accused Hybels of being a Universalist—a charge lodged against Rick Warren as well, based on his refusal to mention the h-word. But away from the pulpit, these ministers were surprisingly traditional. In his book *Honest to God?* Hybels writes, "I hate thinking about it, teaching about it, and writing about it. But the plain truth is that hell *is* real and real people go there for eternity." Warren admitted essentially the same thing when pressed in an interview: "I believe in a literal hell. Jesus believed in a literal hell. And once you're in, you can't get out." This raises the obvious question: How ethical is it to stand up each week before an audience who you believe are going to suffer for all of eternity, and not talk about hell because you "hate thinking about it," or are afraid people will be offended?

At the same time, I realized that Hybels and Warren were responding to the problem we'd noticed down on Michigan Avenue. Most of my friends at Moody disagreed with their approach, but our only other option was to be the ranting voice in the wilderness. It was a hopeless effort, and we all knew it. People looked at our street evangelism team like we were Jesus freaks. (In fact, a number of passersby felt compelled to say as much.) Every Friday night, we'd ride back to campus on the subway in silence, each of us staring slack-faced at the crowd of people hooked up to MP3 players and engrossed in fashion magazines. Many of my friends were planning to leave the States after graduation to become missionaries to the developing world. Apparently it was easier to convince people of the existence of hell and the need for salvation in places like Uganda and Cambodia, where the human capacity for evil was more than an abstraction. Zeb was planning to go to Albania after graduation to plant churches, though he said he worried this was taking the easy way out, like Jonah jumping the boat to Tarsus to avoid bringing the news to the more affluent Nineveh. He said the U.S. had become so rich and powerful we'd forgotten our need for divine grace.

I started my sophomore year at Moody in September 2001. On the morning of the 11th, I'd overslept and woke up to my roommate—a soprano in the women's choir—shrieking that we'd been "bombed." There was one television in my dorm, on the second floor, and I made it down there to find the entire female student body crowded around it, watching the footage in silence. An hour later, we were filing into the eeriest chapel service of all time. The overhead lights were off and the television footage was projected onto a large screen at the front of the auditorium. The school president announced that instead of the regular session, we were going to hold a prayer hour, so we split off into circles, holding hands and whispering in the dark, beneath the muted apocalyptic footage. Nobody knew what to say. We were Bible school students—the closest thing to professional pray-ers out there—and yet people stumbled over common phrases and veered into awkward anachronisms like "keep us from evil" and "bestow thy grace." When it was my turn, I squeezed the hand of the girl next to me, signaling for her to go ahead. After the service, they turned the sound back on, but it seemed like the newscasters were just as dumbstruck as we were.

Once the initial shock wore off, you could sense people groping around the cultural junk drawer for appropriate terminology. Newscasters and witnesses referred to Ground Zero as an "inferno" and "hell on earth." In his address to the nation, George W. Bush said, "Today, our nation saw evil." It was a rhetorical choice designed "deliberately to seek an antique religious aura," as a writer for the *New York Times* noted. Biblical prophecy was revived by conspiracy theorists who tried to prove that the disaster was predicted in the Book of Daniel, or who claimed that the architect of the Twin Towers resided at 666 5th Avenue. A handful of people said they saw the face of Satan in the smoke billowing out of the World Trade Center. Very quickly, a makeshift theology of good and evil was patched together. The terrorists were "evildoers" who, as Colin Powell put it, were "conducting war against civilized people."

Evangelicals responded with similar vitriol. Billy Graham called the acts "twisted diabolical schemes," and the Church of the Open Door's David Johnson preached from the Book of Revelation, insinuating that the terrorists were a "demonic force in the earth." Around Moody, our professors and administrators kept talking about how the pilots must have been surprised when they woke up expecting to be welcomed by Allah and instead found themselves face-to-face with Jesus and the prospect of eternal suffering. This was said with a belabored sigh that often concealed, I suspected, a note of vindictive satisfaction.

That Sunday, Willow Creek was one of many American churches filled to the brim with newcomers. The Moody bus arrived a little late for the morning service, and we ended up sitting in the uppermost balcony, looking down at the crowd of people seeking spiritual comfort. I was eager to see how Bill Hybels would handle the event—whether he would demonize the enemy or invoke safe platitudes about the brevity of life. As it turned out, he did something completely different. One of the biggest lessons of the past week, he began by saying, was that "evil is alive and well." It was the first time I'd heard the word from his pulpit.

Hybels then did something even more unexpected. He proposed that the evil we'd experienced was not limited to the men who flew the planes. He alluded to the terrorists' accomplices and the people in other countries who were shown celebrating the tragedy. Those actions were evil as well, he said. He talked about the gas station owners who'd tripled their prices to capitalize on the hysteria and the people who attacked Arab Americans out of rage. At this point, the audience hummed in collective disapproval.

The pastor paused for a moment, and then said, "Let's bring it close to home—what about the evil in me? Because boy, I felt it this week." Hybels then described his own anger when he was watching the news footage, his immediate craving for revenge. "What is it in us that makes some of us want others to pay a hundred times over for the wrong done to us?" he asked. "Well, that would be evil, and I felt it in me. Did you feel it in you?" With regard to the military response, he argued that Jesus's teaching to not repay evil with evil was just as relevant at a national level. Think about the retaliation that happened all over the world, he said: How was that working out for Sudan? How was it working out for Northern Ireland? The vindictive rage we felt watching the attacks from our kitchen televisions was the same emotion that was creating hell all over the world.

I hadn't felt that rage myself—not because of virtue or self-discipline, but because I was too immature to grasp the full scope of what had happened. It all seemed removed, cinematic. But I did know the feeling he was talking about. It was the same thing I felt when our evangelism team got called Bible-thumpers and Jesus freaks.

I don't know what prompted Hybels to diverge from the market-tested optimism that day, but it was a powerful sermon—people at Moody were talking about it all week. In fact, in a study on the evangelical response to 9/11, this sermon was cited as the only one that questioned the compatibility of military action with Jesus's command to love one's neighbor. The pacifism of the political Left seemed inert and self-flagellating by comparison. Their hesitance to condemn the terrorists, the insistence on the passive voice when describing what had happened, often made it seem as though the attacks had been an act of God, divine punishment for Western imperialism. That Sunday was the only time that someone had asked me to examine myself and my response to the attacks without dismissing their severity, or the reality of the human intention behind them. The next Sunday, Hybels preached a message entitled "Religion Gone Awry," about how the backlash against American Muslims ran counter to Christian principles. The following week, he invited Imam Faisal Hammouda to speak at the Sunday service, giving the congregation the opportunity to exercise "discernment" in understanding Islam.

One of the most perplexing things about 9/11, for me, was how swiftly the event congealed in and then dissipated from the national consciousness. Half a century ago, when Roosevelt addressed the country after Pearl Harbor, he underscored the severity of the offense by declaring that the nation would not forget it: "Always will we remember the character of the onslaught against us . . . There is no blinking at the fact that our people, our territory and our interests are in grave danger." Since then, it seems we've come to see prolonged meditation on this kind of horror as a sign of weakness and a threat to the market. Less than two months after the attacks, Bush noted with pride, "People are going about their daily lives, working and shopping and playing, worshipping at churches and synagogues and mosques, going to movies and to baseball games."

Willow Creek soon got back to business as usual as well, mostly due to the huge backlash against Hybels's decision to "share his pulpit" (as his critics phrased it) with an imam. Apparently the honeymoon was over. People began to find tolerance tedious. Although Hybels didn't apologize for his decision to bring in the imam, he seemed, like any good CEO, to take note of the negative response. In the first sermon of 2002, he encouraged us to put the past year's events behind us and adopt, instead, "an optimistic hope-filled attitude for the year." It was the first message of a sermon series that included titles such as "Wellness," "Family" and "Surviving a Financial Storm." In the end, his radical sermons about collective evil turned out to be aberrational—like many noble acts inspired by the tragedy and then quickly forgotten.

At the time, I didn't appreciate just how radical Hybels's 9/11 sermon was. In speaking about his own capacity for revenge and hatred, he had opened up a possibility, a way of talking about evil that felt relevant and transformative. It wasn't fire and brimstone; it wasn't condemning the sinner as some degenerate Other. Rather, he was challenging his congregation to exercise empathy in a way that Jesus might have, suggesting that he among us without sin should cast the first stone.

Back at Moody, though, I was still staying up late at night, thinking about all those people who would suffer for eternity for never hearing the gospel. By the end of the semester, the problem of hell had begun to seriously unsettle my faith—so much so that I had lost the ability to perform the basic rites. When I stood in chapel with my classmates, I was unable to sing along to the hymns in praise of God's goodness; and when we bowed our heads to pray, I pantomimed that act of supplication. I left Moody the summer after my sophomore year and took a volunteer position with some missionaries in Ecuador, which was just an elaborate escape plan—a way to get away from Moody and my parents. Three months into the commitment, I moved to a town in the south of the country where I didn't know anyone and got a job teaching ESL. I ditched my study Bible at a hostel book exchange and stopped going to church entirely.

But people who've gotten that far into the faith never totally shake it. To be a former believer is to perpetually return to the scene of the crime. It's been ten years since I left Moody, and I still find myself stalling on the Christian radio station to hear a call-in debate, or lurking around the religion section of chain bookstores, perusing the titles on the Christianity shelves like a porn addict sneaking a glance at a Victoria's Secret catalog.

In the spring of 2011, I was browsing through a crowded airport newsstand when I glimpsed an issue of *Time* with the headline "What

If There's No Hell?" The subhead elaborated, "A popular pastor's best-selling book has stirred fierce debate about sin, salvation, and judgment." The book in question was the modestly titled *Love Wins: Heaven, Hell, and the Fate of Every Person Who's Ever Lived*, and the pastor, it turned out, was Rob Bell. Back when I was at Moody, Bell was known primarily as the pastor of Mars Hill Bible Church in Grandville, Michigan—one of the more groundbreaking "seeker churches" in the Midwest. If Hybels was the entrepreneur of the seeker movement, Bell was its rock star. He wears hipster glasses and black skinny jeans and looks strikingly like Bono, if you can imagine the laconic machismo replaced with a kind of nerdy alacrity. Most of Bell's congregants were Gen Xers who had difficulty with the Bible's passages about absolute truth, certainty and judgment. His first book, *Velvet Elvis: Repainting the Christian Faith* (2005), was purportedly aimed at people who are "fascinated with Jesus but can't do the standard Christian package."

I found a copy of Bell's new book at that same airport and blew through it during my three-hour flight to Michigan. It was a light read. Bell lineates his prose like a free-verse poem, and roughly half the sentences are interrogative, a rhetorical style that seems designed to dampen the incendiary nature of his actual argument. He does not, as the *Time* headline suggests, make a case against the existence of hell. Rather, he argues that hell is a refining process by which all of the sins of the world, but not the sinners, are burned away. Those who are in hell are given endless chances throughout eternity to accept God's free gift of salvation and, because this gift is so irresistibly good, hell will eventually be emptied and collapse. Essentially, this is universal reconciliation—the idea that all people will be saved regardless of what they believe or how they conduct themselves on earth.

Love Wins created an uproar in the evangelical community. Zondervan (basically the Random House of Christian publishing), which had published Bell's previous books, dropped him upon reading the proposal, stating that the project didn't fit with their mission. After it was published, Albert Mohler, Jr., a prominent reformed pastor, called the book "theologically disastrous" and conservative John Piper tweeted "Farewell Rob Bell," as if to excommunicate him from the fold. Closer to home, Bell watched as thousands of his congregants left Mars Hill in protest. At the same time, a lot of evangelicals who seemed to have been harboring a private faith in universal reconciliation came out of the woodwork and defended the book. And in the secular media, the theology of *Love Wins* was lauded as the radical conception of a vision-

473

ary. Bell was the subject of a long profile in the *New Yorker*, and *Time* named him one of the most influential people in the world. "Wielding music, videos and a Starbucks sensibility," the magazine wrote, "Bell is at the forefront of a rethinking of Christianity in America."

"Rethinking" is not as accurate as "rebranding." Throughout *Love Wins*, it's obvious that Bell is less interested in theological inquiry than he is in PR. At one point in the book, in order to demonstrate the marketing problems many congregations unwittingly create, he gives a sampling of "statements of faith" from various church websites, all of which depict a traditional Christian understanding of hell (e.g. "The unsaved will be separated forever from God in hell"). Instead of responding to these statements on a theological basis, he remarks, sarcastically, "Welcome to our church." Later on, he reiterates his warning that even the most sophisticated seeker churches won't succeed in attracting unbelievers unless they revamp their theology: "If your God is loving one second and cruel the next, if your God will punish people for all eternity for sins committed in a few short years, no amount of clever marketing or compelling language or good music or great coffee will be able to disguise that one, true, glaring, untenable, unacceptable, awful reality."

Despite Bell's weak hermeneutics and the transparency of his motivation, there was one moment while reading *Love Wins* where it seemed as though he might initiate a much-needed conversation about the meaning of hell. Toward the end of the book, he begins to mobilize a more radical argument—that heaven and hell are not realms of the afterlife but metaphors for life here on earth. "Heaven and hell [are] here, now, around us, upon us, within us," he writes. He recalls traveling to Rwanda in the early 2000s and seeing boys whose limbs had been cut off during the genocide. "Do I believe in a literal hell?" he asks. "Of course. Those aren't metaphorical missing arms and legs." Here, I brightened at the idea that perhaps Bell was out to make a statement as bold and daring as Hybels's 9/11 sermon, using hell as a way to talk about the human capacity for evil.

But no such moment came. As I read on, it became clear that Bell wasn't actually looking for a way to talk about the darker side of human nature. Soon after he posits the possibility of a metaphorical hell, he glosses over its significance by suggesting that the "hells" of this earth are slowly being winnowed away as humans work to remedy social problems like injustice and inequality. He suggests that Jesus's allusions to the Kingdom of God were referring not to an eternal paradise, but rather to an earthly golden age (a claim with which few—if any—evangelicals would agree, even if it is commonly accepted among secular scholars). In his discussion of Revelation, Bell skims over most of the apocalyptic horrors to note that the book ends with a description of "a new city, a new creation, a new world that God makes, right here in the midst of this one. It is a buoyant, hopeful vision of a future in which the nations are healed and there is peace on earth and there are no more tears." Traditionally, evangelicals have read the "new city" as representing heaven, but Bell's insistence that this new creation is "right in the midst of this one" suggests a kind of Hegelian linear-progressive history, a vision of the future in which humanity improves itself until we've engineered a terrestrial utopia. It's an echo of the contemporary narrative of technological solutionism—the gospel of human perfectability that is routinely hyped in TED talks and preached from the Lucite podiums of tech conferences across the country.

Love Wins succeeded in breaking the silence about hell, and its popularity suggests that a number of evangelicals may be ready to move beyond a literalist notion of damnation, reimagining hell just as God-fearing people across the centuries have done to reckon with the evils of their own age. At the same time, the book demonstrates the potential pitfalls of the church's desire to distance itself too quickly from fire and brimstone. Bell claims to address the exact theological problem that motivated me to leave the faith, but rather than offer a new understanding of the doctrine, he offers up a Disneyesque vision of humanity, one that is wholly incompatible with the language biblical authors use to speak about good and evil. Along with hell, the new evangelical leaders threaten to jettison the very notion of human depravity—a fundamental Christian truth upon which the entire salvation narrative hinges.

Part of what made church such a powerful experience for me as a child and a young adult was that it was the one place where my own faults and failings were recognized and accepted, where people referred to themselves affectionately as "sinners," where it was taken as a given that the person standing in the pews beside you was morally fallible, but still you held hands and lifted your voice with hers as you worshipped in song. This camaraderie came from a collective understanding of evil—a belief that each person harbored within them a potential for sin and deserved, despite it, divine grace. It's this notion of shared fallibility that lent Hybels's 9/11 sermon its power, as he suggested that his own longing for revenge was only a difference of degree—not of kind—from the acts of the terrorists. And it's precisely this acknowledgement of collective guilt that makes it possible for a community to observe the core virtues of the faith: mercy, forgiveness, grace.

The irony is that, at a time when we are in need of potent metaphors to help us make sense of our darkest impulses, the church has chosen to remain silent on the problem of evil, for fear of becoming obsolete. The short-term advantages of such a strategy are as obvious as its ultimate futility. Like so many formerly oppositional institutions, the church is now becoming a symptom of the culture rather than an antidote to it, giving us one less place to turn for a sober counter-narrative to the simplistic story of moral progress that stretches from Silicon Valley to Madison Avenue. Hell may be an elastic concept, as varied as the thousands of malevolencies it has described throughout history, but it remains our most resilient metaphor for the evil both around and within us. True compassion is possible not because we are ignorant that life can be hell, but because we know that it can be.

Nominated by Lydia Conklin, Barrett Swanson, The Point

THE CLOUD

fiction by ANN BEATTIE

from SALMAGUNDI

Back in the town where she'd graduated from the university five years before, Candace waited at the inn to be picked up by Uncle Sterling. This was a business trip, paid for by her company in D.C., and they were amenable to putting her somewhere other than the DoubleTree out on the highway. Sterling was able to drive his car again, after finishing the last round of chemo three weeks earlier. The prognosis was good, but Candace's mother Claire still wept about it on the phone, and Candace was worried, herself. Sterling was her favorite relative, even if he did maintain contact with her father. *For sure* he understood that Hank was an untrustworthy liar, but the two former brothers-in-law still occasionally golfed together, belonged to the same gym—not that Sterling had been seeing much of that place lately. *For sure* Claire deserved better than a dry drunk ex who'd married a woman barely older than his daughter. He lived in Keswick now, courtesy of his buy-out and early retirement, with his newly acquired young wife with whom he had twin boys. Candace had seen them once, about a year before, on Saturday at the City Market, her father descending the steep incline of the parking lot, guiding the babies in a double stroller, Claire ascending hand-in-hand with her fiancé Daniel, who'd graduated from Darden last May. That day, also, she and Daniel had stayed at the inn, a charming place not too historically oppressive, with comfortable furniture, good sunlight, and damp, warm cookies in late afternoon.

But today she was on her own, Daniel now working for Sapient in Boston, though they hoped the job he really wanted would become available in D.C. after the first of the year. Her only reason to come back to town was a business meeting she'd volunteered to attend because she wanted to see Sterling. She might also visit a couple of places that might be nice venues for their wedding reception–they'd decided on a City Hall marriage and a big party soon afterwards–though more and more she was thinking of having the party at his parents' house in Sperryville. Everything could seem a bit too university connected, sometimes, even if the town was quite various, with its Street o' Liberals (as Sterling called Park Street), its horsey crowd, the arts community.

She walked to Mudhouse and ordered a café au lait. While others had gotten through school on caffeine, she'd primarily existed on milk (milkshakes; skim milk with Hershey's chocolate added, along with a packet of powdered vitamins, in late afternoon), though a café au lait was the perfect combination of the two. The person behind the counter (her ears with many piercings) gave her a cup to put in the amount of coffee she wanted, then hand it back for the hot, foamy milk to be poured in. "Do you like foam?" the barista asked. What a question. Who did not like foam except those people who did not like foam, though they might have thought it an important component of waves, or of laundering clothes, or shampooing. It was one of those questions you couldn't trust to convey the right meaning if you put it in a time capsule.

Her new leather boots had cost five hundred and fifty dollars. She'd admitted to three, to Daniel. If Sterling commented at all, he wouldn't have any idea what they cost–he lived alone and cared nothing about fashion–so she wouldn't have to lie. She'd noticed that the woman checking her in earlier in the day had eyed the boots; since the woman had already commented on her ring, though, she wasn't about to keep complimenting her. Candace was wearing her favorite black skirt, with black tights and a cashmere sweater slightly silver tinged, a gift from Daniel's mother. She didn't look like a college girl, and she certainly didn't look like a faculty member, either. They wore sensible shoes and rectangular glasses and weighed either too much or much too little. She was just right. At least, that was what Daniel thought.

She checked her cell and saw that Sterling had called while she'd been in the coffee place. The message said he'd pick her up at six, unless she told him otherwise. He'd be taking her to the restaurant in Belmont she'd suggested for dinner–not too fussy or expensive, and Sterling was always interested in changing neighborhoods. He wasn't like her mother, who thought nothing ever changed for the better; he was appreciative of old buildings being saved, of new energy coming into the community.

On the porch of the inn, Sterling gave her a big hug—he felt thin—and commented on her boots first thing. "New shoes?" he said. They were, and there was no reason to wear them yet during this late, mild October, but they made her feel good. "You and your mother, always fashionable," he said.

He was driving his old Lexus with a crooked back bumper with an Obama/Biden decal and a patch of paint gone from around the door handle on the passenger's side. '93, he told her proudly, as he opened the door from one of the few still-operating features, the button that unlocked all doors. The last time she'd been in his car, the window wouldn't go down on the passenger's side, but what did that matter on a chilly October night? She settled back into the slightly cracked seat, pulled on her seatbelt. No place to park in front of the restaurant; thirty minute limit by the convenience store. Sterling made a right turn, then a left, then saw a place on the opposite side of the street. He made a u-turn and parallel parked and turned off the engine. She opened her door, wondering whether it was okay that the bumper slightly overhung the white line by a driveway. He saw her looking. "Okay to park here?" he called to a man she hadn't seen, sitting on his front porch in the near dark.

"Yessir, that's fine," the man replied. From his voice, it was obvious he was old. There was another man sitting with him. Sterling gave a little salute and walked around to give Candace his arm. It felt bony. She wanted to talk about what he'd been through, but later, when they were in the restaurant and more comfortable, after they'd had a drink, not right off, which would seem aggressive. If her mother was forty-eight, Sterling was fifty-one, though he acted younger than his sister. Not immature younger, but tentative, without Claire's easy way of conversing, a little preoccupied and twitchy, like a young boy. He did hate to sit still.

The restaurant was crazy, and she hadn't thought to make a reservation: a young woman with a top knot at the corner table was shrieking; some blowhard was hectoring a table of fat, middle-aged people in suits and ugly dresses who looked at him puzzled, as if firecracker after firecracker failed to ignite; waitresses made themselves mouse-thin to slide through the small holes in the crowd of people with their barstools pushed back into the aisles, or headed to the bathroom, or on their way to the second floor, or to the roof, from which they'd take flight and clutter the night sky, for all she knew. "Let's go somewhere quieter," she said. It was too chaotic in the restaurant. All wrong.

They walked back to the car, Sterling's hand guiding her elbow. Her mother had said, "Sterling got Papa's cancer and I'm going to get Leigh's breast cancer, you watch." Her mother was in Florida tonight, visiting her best friend who'd moved there from Pennsylvania a year ago. They'd be drinking too much wine and doing other unhealthy things sure to lessen her mother's chances of escaping "the family curse," though as far as Candace knew, only one woman in the family had had breast cancer, and she'd survived it.

"Wait a minute, hold on, folks," came the old man's voice. They stopped outside the car, turning in his direction. "I've got something for you. It was polite of you to ask about parking near my driveway." He was tall and his lanky arm was outstretched. Both reached out to shake his extended hand, but instead of shaking, he dropped something into each of their palms. There was enough lamplight that she could see hers was a dark origami bird. Two smaller birds sat in Sterling's hand: one white; one that seemed to have been made out of some lightweight cardboard.

"For us?" she said. "How did you do this?"

"I fold," the man said. "I hope you like 'em."

"This is very nice of you," Sterling said, staring at the little birds in his hand but not touching them. Actually, he seemed quite taken aback.

"Origami!" she said, realizing Sterling probably didn't know the word. "What a lovely present. Origami birds."

"That one's a swan," the man said, though the sentence was uninflected, not proud at all.

"Thank you very much," she said. "I can't believe you're giving these to us."

"More where they came from, sailing up and down Mother Nature's river," the man said. "You have a nice night."

"Really, thank you," Sterling said. "I've never seen anything like this."

"I'm a veteran," the old man said flatly. "You have a nice evening."

Sterling handed her his bird so he could insert the key into the lock on the passenger's side. The three birds, with big beaks and lovely wings, really looked like treasures in her hand. She stepped into the car carefully off the steep curb, a little awkward about settling herself gracefully when one hand was useless.

She looked back at the porch in time to see the light extinguished, though it seemed the two men were still seated, in the dark. She dumped the birds on her lap and reached across quickly to unlock her uncle's door, but he'd already inserted the key. The door swung open. "I don't know why he did that," Sterling said. "Do you think he took you for my girlfriend, or something?"

"Of course not!" she said. "That's ridiculous, Uncle Sterling."

"Or he seemed to think I'd been in the military," Sterling said.

"Not with your asthma," she said.

"Honey, I never had asthma. I had pneumonia twice when I was a teenager, and your mother never got over it. I never tried to enlist. One idiot doing that in the family was enough. Cousin Coop going to fight in Desert Storm. Nobody in our family had anything to do with the military since the Second World War, when they had to. Coop—he'd do anything it took to push his old man's buttons. I guess he did, too, coming back with a blown off pinkie and a lifetime of migraines."

"Mom said you tried to enlist but they wouldn't take you because of asthma."

"Your mother lives in her head," he said.

"Really? She completely made that up? I've always thought it was strange that you felt so patriotic, but you never vote."

"Like I said: she lives in her head."

"But you did finish with chemo, right? And everything's looking good?" Why had she blurted that out now. *Why?*

"It's not a good kind of cancer to get. Without treatment, something like forty, fifty percent chance of recurrence, pretty quick. I think it halves it, something like that, if you do chemo."

"Oh. Well—I think mom might have told me that, but I was just feeling very optimistic."

"She didn't tell you. I'll bet you anything."

"No, I don't think she did, actually. So now are you going to tell me my father's not such a bad guy, that with all her bitterness about money and broken promises, she was just living in her head?"

"Honey, I don't want to say anything about your parents' divorce. They're divorced. That's that."

"*Are* you going to vote?"

"America's run by a big machine, and we're not even a splinter of a

481

cog in the wheel. They fixed the election the year Al Gore had it. I'm not gonna vote, I'm not gonna avoid having a beer tonight in spite of my medicine, and also, just to keep you fully informed, since a few weeks ago I've taken on my girlfriend's car payments, which makes me a chump and a fool, because her husband's just waiting in the shadows, and when that car's paid for, you can bet he'll be back behind the wheel."

"You have a girlfriend?"

"Yeah, what? Your mom told you I was gay?"

"She never said that."

"Maybe she did, and you were just optimistic."

"Stop it!" she said, shoving his shoulder. A bird fell from her lap to the floor. She picked it up, wiped it carefully, unnecessarily, on her jacket. Its finely pointed beak resembled the toes of her Italian boots. She dropped it on top of the others.

"So you e-mailed you were going to check out some wedding places? What kind of places you thinking of?"

"You know, now I'm thinking about having the party at his parents' weekend place in Sperryville. It might be easier for our friends in D.C., and it's really pretty there."

"But your poor afflicted uncle would have to drive farther. Think about that. And now I've got a pet—now I've got a wild swan—so going north might mess up its migration."

"We could eat dinner at that place out 250," she said. "The one that's like a family restaurant?"

"That's for old folks," he said.

"No it isn't. I used to go there with my friends."

"Old people vegetables. Brussels sprouts. Mashed potatoes."

"So where do you want to go?"

"I'll take you to my girlfriend's and we can order pizza," he said. "She lives in a cliff-hanger of a so-called townhouse on the way to the entrance onto 64, with crappy wall-to-wall carpeting and an addict daughter who comes and goes, who can't even make it through beauty school. I was reaching for a plate the other night, and the cabinet door came off in my hand. Particleboard."

"Why would I want to go there?"

"Because she cares about me," he said. "Because I shouldn't compartmentalize. It would be good for her to meet somebody from my family."

"This is someone you're serious about, Sterling?"

"The love of my life. At least, up to this point."

"Well, sure. It would be nice to meet her then. Sure."

"Her name's Lana. She's vegetarian, but she smokes. You okay with that?"

"With smoking? Will she absolutely have to smoke?"

"She lives there," he said.

He glanced in the rear-view mirror and made a quick u-turn: they were suddenly headed away from town, past a Food Lion and a Dollar Store. So her uncle wasn't asthmatic, he had a girlfriend, and he knew in detail his chances for survival. Since that was true, what else might he tell her? She'd probably hear more about her mother before the night was out, and that it wouldn't just have to do with her cowardice about pneumonia thirty years ago. Claire had always been phobic about catching colds. She kept Ivory soap, which she maintained was much better than hand sanitizer, in not one but two soap holders on both sides of the sink in her bathroom and in the kitchen.

"You know what happened to Lana a week or so ago? She'd been working on the story of her life, a memoir thing, about being kidnapped when she was a teenager and made to work on a ranch out west, and this one horse that she said saved her life. She had eighty pages, and it all just disappeared. We took her Mac to a place in town but they couldn't get it back. She said it was like the horse dying all over again, working so hard on something and having it desert her, it just made her crazy. She'd been taking this course up at Piedmont at night, along with her nursing course: people's stories about how they got where they are in life. Not the kind of thing you probably studied over at the university, but —"

"Uncle Sterling, she didn't have it backed up in any way she could retrieve it? Do you mean the hard drive crashed, or —"

"The one thing I know, I convinced her to keep the machine, to print the story every time she had a new part. She didn't have a printer before. Anyway, this guy who was teaching the course told us that for very little money, she could have everything backed up and it could go to heaven."

"*What?*"

"A service you pay for, where everything you write—"

"Automatic back-up? It goes to the cloud?"

"That's it! I told you, up to the sky, like a moonbeam bouncing back! Goes to the clouds."

"Cloud," she corrected. "It's an abstraction, but—"

" 'Buckets of moonbeams, buckets of tears!' "

She looked at him, confused. It was like having a conversation with a crazy person. "Buckets of moonbeams, buckets of tears . . . blah, blah, blah, honey, when you go," he sang, in a good imitation of Bob Dylan. Aha! She smiled with relief. "He was at JPJ. I saw him with Elvis Costello when I was here. Did you see that concert, Sterling?"

"Don't go to concerts," Sterling said. "Those days are behind me."

Sterling was pulling into a new development–she'd imagined the girlfriend living in some old, outdated place from the way he'd described the dreary interior–with bathmat-sized balconies off the front, bordered in metal railings. On one, someone stood in front of a glowing grill that puffed steam into the night's cooling air. Romney signs were draped over a few of the rails. In front of them, a boy pedaled slowly up the incline, the light underneath his seat weakly blinking as his bike moved up the steep hill.

"This feels good. This seems like just the right thing to do," Sterling said, and she realized by the way he spoke that he was perplexed by his actions, not certain. Had he been drinking before he picked her up? Or was the medicine having some bad effect on him? She could hardly ask. He'd turned on the radio and they were listening to Radiohead–Radiohead!–as he pulled into an empty carport that looked as flimsy as an opened tin of sardines and turned off the ignition. "You'll like her," he said. "Even if you don't, you can tell your mother and she'll be shocked. She won't believe I introduced you to someone I've been dating, who lives in a housing development with a bunch of Republicans."

She pulled her jacket more tightly around her as she got out of the car. It was a part of town she didn't know existed; it had been a field the last time she'd driven past this big outcropping of buildings on the hillside of bare earth, with what looked like the devil tending his fire with a pitchfork just above them, as they ascended the stairs.

The door Sterling was heading toward was on the third level, right in front of the stairs, a Coke machine making noise beside it. It was the sort of room you'd ask not to have in a motel. There was no light inside, but two doors down, she could see a little boy in boxing gloves hammering his father's leg as he tended the grill. Sterling knew someone who'd been kidnapped? Like that girl the crazy couple took in Utah? A large, long-haired cat arched its back and darted around the man and the boy, playing with something it batted between its paws.

"It's me, Lana!" he said, staring into the peep-hole as if it would allow him to see inside. "I want you to meet my niece, open up, darlin'!"

"Jee-*zus*," a young Hispanic woman said, peeking through the door opened only a crack, its safety chain pulled on. "Did you ever think of calling first?" She slid back the chain and stepped aside. Sterling preceded Candace into the apartment without an entranceway and gave the young woman a quick, one-armed hug. "Where's your mother, darlin'?" he said.

"I thought you were sick," she said. "Who's this?"

She spoke as if Candace weren't present. The young woman seemed about her age, maybe younger. She was wearing three gigantic hair rollers and was dressed in black: black sweatpants; black turtleneck; black shoes with white laces. "Ooh la la," she said, whistling through the space between her front teeth. "Those are million dollar boots," she said. "This the way you dress your other girlfriends, Sterl?"

"She's my niece. The only family member who's willing to make a visit to her uncle. I'm feelin' fine now, darlin'. Where's your mother?"

"Community college," the girl said. "In case you forgot she was working toward her nurse's aide credentials."

"I didn't forget, but since when does she have classes on Wednesday night?"

"Since they cancelled classes on Tuesday because there was a bomb scare," the girl said. "Pleased to meet you." She extended her hand. There was a tattoo of a spider's web on the back of her hand. "Somebody got a credit card? We can call Dominoes," she said. Candace gripped the girl's hand, looking at Sterling for guidance. He gestured toward the single piece of furniture: a sofa in the living room. He took his credit card out of his wallet and handed it to the girl. "I like extra cheese," he said.

"You?" the girl asked Candace.

"Just . . . what he has will be fine," she said.

"What exactly is a niece?" the girl said to him. "It's the daughter of your brother or sister, right?"

"Sister," Sterling said, as if this was an often asked question.

"College girl?" she asked, still not looking at Candace.

"Used to be," Candace said. "Now I work in Washington."

"Ooh, la la," the girl said. She texted the pizza place on the phone she'd been holding in one hand all the time, the motion of her thumb rippling the spider's web, then placed the phone on the table. "Pepperoni on half, extra cheese on the other," she said. "It comes with a free bottle of Dr. Pepper tonight." She sat on the floor and stared at them. "That's not your niece, is it?" she said to Sterling.

485

"Candace, my niece," he said.

"Cool," the girl said, lightly fingering a hair roller. "It's between you and Lana." She picked up a magazine and twirled a bit of loose hair around a finger. "I been irradiated like you, I might do whatever I had a mind to do, myself," she said. "You drink your protein shake today? I heard her call you this morning to remind you."

"I drank it," he said.

"Sounded like a little love buzz going on, maybe? She didn't tell you about the make-up class tonight?"?

"No," he said.

"Well, maybe because you're not part of the family, proof being that you got a credit card that works," she said. "So I'm glad you've got your niece there, and your very own family."

"I am his niece," Candace said. "I love him very much."

"I've had some loving very much," the girl said, "so don't go claiming no superiority in that department."

Sterling sat on the sofa. He reached up and turned on the floor lamp, and his already pale face blanched white. He hardly had any eyebrows, Candace saw for the first time. Instead, there were a few scraggly hairs; above them, his skin was wrinkled like a Shar-pei. How could she not have noticed before? His hair was sparse, his thinness quite obvious, with his long legs stretched in front of him. He'd looked healthier before he took off his jacket. Candace's jacket was still pulled tightly in front of her, her arms folded over her chest. It seemed colder in the apartment than it did outside. She glanced to the side and looked into the small kitchen. There was a child's highchair. Every door to every cabinet seemed to be open. Piles of dishes sat on either side of the sink. She was thirsty, and wished for a drink of water, but not enough to get up and walk in there.

"I'm nobody," Sterling said to Candace, as if he were saying "Good morning" to a colleague who meant nothing to him.

"That's not true," she said. "You're my favorite relative. Somebody took a liking to you tonight and gave you a very nice present this evening, remember that? Things are going to be okay. I really feel like they are."

The girl was twirling her hair, listening to them talk and pretending not to.

"I'm a coward," he said, "but not in the way you think. They make me see a shrink in order to get my pain meds refilled. Every Friday I have to report in. He told me not to compartmentalize, to open myself up more. If that's what it takes, me making my report of success, I guess you came along at a good time for me, maybe not such a good time for you."

"It's fine," she said.

"Everybody understands everybody. I'll be back when the pizza shows up," the girl said, getting up and walking out of the room. They both stared after her. She went into another room and quietly closed the door.

"She's looking after her friend's kid," Sterling said. "She's got a good heart."

"There's a child in there?" Candace said.

Sterling nodded. "Asleep, I guess. Maybe it's better if I sit by the window and watch for the pizza guy. Maybe that way he won't wake up."

"Why would she walk out of the room like that?" Candace said.

"Not sure," Sterling said. "Not 100% sure she's telling me the truth about her mother and where she is tonight, either."

Candace looked into the kitchen. "Maybe we should go," she said. "Let's go back to the inn and I'll order us a pizza," she said. "To be honest, I wouldn't mind having a beer from the honor bar. It's quiet there, maybe somebody in one of the rooms, but quiet. Warm."

"A perfect place, complete salvation," he said. "A cloud."

He took a twenty dollar bill out of his wallet and put it on the table next to *Allure*. He picked it up, creased it, put it down again, folded so it looked like a little roof.

"Is it your child?" Candace said quietly.

"Mine? No. What would make you think that? Mine? It's her best friend's two year old, Jake. She took the train to Albany to visit the kid's father. He's in jail. She apparently always takes her time getting back to Virginia." Sterling looked at his watch. "Dominoes usually gets here fast, because they're just down the street," he said. "Maybe it would be nicer to wait for the pizza guy. Have a slice with her, then leave."

"I think he's here," Candace said, looking past his shoulder to the stairs. She saw the top of someone's head, coming nearer. But it wasn't the delivery person, it was two EMT's. Below, in the parking lot, a white light blinked atop the ambulance. The pizza delivery person was, however, coming up the stairs as the two men returned, carrying an empty stretcher. She could hear them greet the Dominoes guy as if it was all in a night's work, as Sterling stood with the door thrown open, his wallet removed from his pant pocket, another few bills pulled out to put in the delivery guy's hands. Some leaves blew into the room and she thought: autumn! Not the most colorful autumn, but autumn! Next, winter. Then her wedding in early spring, six months from now, May. She looked at her diamond ring. At her uncle. Who must have ordered from Dominoes before, because he was on good terms with the delivery guy. They exchanged a quiet joke as the two men carrying the stretcher moved past them. Into the middle of it all streaked the big cat, but with fancy footwork the man carrying the back of the stretcher avoided tripping on the animal. She looked at the twenty dollar bill on the table. Had he forgotten it, or did he mean to leave it? He'd walked past Candace, box in hand, and when he returned from the room, minus the box, he pulled on his coat and said, "You're right, Candy. Let's go."

She exited behind him, relieved that when the door was pulled closed, you could hear it lock. From the landing, the cat's eyes flashed as it stared down. She stopped briefly before following her uncle down the stairs. Somewhere, she'd scuffed the toe of one boot. There was a scratch, though there'd been nothing in the apartment but the ugly rug she'd heard about, so how had she done that? She followed Sterling down the stairs, into the driveway where the doors of the ambulance were open, and she saw inside an old woman being transferred onto a gurney. She instantly looked away, followed Sterling to his car, eyes averted, shivering a little as she waited for the click of the button that would allow her to open the door. She felt ashamed. Because she hadn't been nice to the girl who, she'd decided, was much younger than she. Because she hadn't even had the courage to go get a drink of water. Why had she felt humiliated, why had the thought of eating the same pizza she'd eaten for years, all through college, washed down with milk, why had the thought of oily residue on her fingers depressed her so much? Sterling had left the apartment because of her, hadn't he? She didn't think she was better than other people. She really didn't. Even when she'd been in school, she'd realized there was animosity in the community because of the haves and the have-nots. If Obama won, maybe there was still a chance that people would pull together. He was a decent person, an intelligent man, he'd known hardship first-hand. Above her, a Romney/Ryan sign flapped in the breeze.

"I married her," Sterling said across the roof of the car, "but she kept thinking about her ex-husband, she was a lousy actress, so I said, Hey, I'll continue to make your car payments as a wedding present, and we can get this annulled. Four days? What's four days? So I called a frat brother of mine, a big-shot lawyer in Ivy. But now Lana's daughter pretty much hates me. She thought I was a real improvement over him. She was a bitch tonight, but she's got her worries, taking care of that kid for however long she'll have to take care of him this time. She flunked out of the same program her mother's going to, and I guess she's flunking out of beauty school too. What the hell must that be like? She's twenty-two, and she hasn't pulled off one thing in her entire life."

"Sterling . . ."

"I *do* consider them family. Lana picked me up all but one time from the hospital, and she sent a guy who's a friend of hers the time she couldn't be there. Who knew all that cancer shit was going to broadside us? It's okay. It was a big mistake, a big mistake, but we've put it behind us, we're still friends. The ex-husband's got his nose out of joint, but maybe they'll work it out. I don't know."

"This is hard to believe," she said. "Did you know this is where we were going to end up, or was this just —"

"Impulsive?" he said. "Yeah, I'm a little impulsive sometimes."

She sat in the passenger's seat, mutely. Had they even been inside for half an hour? She thought back to the last time she'd seen her uncle. It had been at the zoo. They'd gone to the reptile house, which had been her favorite when she was a child. Her mother had been with them. What was it—three years ago, more? March or April? He'd bought her a balloon, saying that she could let it go any time she wanted, none of that little-girl fumbling, none of those clumsy attempts to tie it around her wrist, no little girl tears if the balloon got away from her: it would be liberating to deliberately let it go high into the cloudy sky. And so she had; she'd released the string, her mother frowning, disapproving. Later, they'd had Chinese food on Connecticut Avenue, Claire sulking a bit as Sterling and Candace toasted liberation. Of course people became more mature with age, her mother had protested: Candace had grown up; of course a balloon didn't mean the world to her anymore. She just didn't get her brother, really she didn't. So her daughter's being happily in collusion with Sterling—she didn't get that, either. The day would have been better if Claire hadn't been along, though it was likely neither of them would have thought of a balloon if she hadn't been there as a witness. What was she going to say to her mother about this night?

Of course, nothing. The next time she saw her uncle, he'd be dancing at her wedding party. While all this had been going on, had Daniel tried to call? She wondered, but she didn't reach for her purse. Neither did she spit on her finger and hope against hope that the mark on her boot was dirt, not a scratch. Her throat was too dry to swallow, anyway. Dinner? Who wanted that? But a drink of water. . . .

She opened the window–it rolled down–picked up the little cluster of birds, and extended her hand until the wind sucked them out the window. She thought of the eerie cat, of how it would find its perfect moment on Halloween. How it would have liked to pounce on the pretty birds. How much it would have liked to kill them.

Autumn leaves spun in the breeze under the street lamps.

"I'm so sorry," he said, not speeding, but not braking for a yellow light, either. "Here, Sperryville, I'm not going to be able to come to your party." He reached down and gave her hand a squeeze, and again she realized that his hand was bony, much too light. *Daniel*, she thought. *I'm engaged to a man named Daniel?* The wind was whipping her hair across her face. It stuck to her lips, chapped from being bitten. Tears rolled down her cheeks. Her hands fluttered uselessly.

Nominated by Joyce Carol Oates

DEATH DEFIANT BOMBA OR WHAT TO WEAR WHEN YOUR BOO GETS CANCER

fiction by LILLIAM RIVERA

from BELLEVUE LITERARY REVIEW

Paseo Basico/Basic Step

His snoring will wake you. You'll be pissed off at first but then you'll welcome the snoring over the clock set to go off in an hour. It's still dark outside and although it's warm next to him, you'll get up, your bare feet searching for your slippers. You'll say a short prayer and move the bed a bit to get him back into regular breathing. It won't work.

If the doctor's appointment is early, at 9 a.m., pull out the red sheath dress, the one that you bought on sale at Nordstrom with the famous but unpronounceable designer label. The red will wake the reception- ist up like a motherfucker and cause her to send you hate for daring to outshine her that morning. The receptionist will think you're tacky, loud, too much. In the bloodshot color, the doctor will notice that you wore the equivalent of a flag and think you're stately and in charge. You'll wear red, definitely red.

If the doctor's appointment is later, say at 3 p.m., then the only color you should wear is . . . red. Late in the afternoon the receptionist has not had time to eat the Snickers bar hidden in the drawer right next to some Orbit chewing gum, flavor piña colada, and the small box of "just- in-case" feminine napkins. The receptionist will be hungry and crabby from arguing with the old man with Alzheimer's who keeps forgetting that his appointment is not today but was last week. She can't curse at the old man but she's on the verge. When she sees the red dress, she'll think how presumptuous you are for wearing it like a drag queen, like a *telenovela* star, like a *Nuestra Belleza Latina* of the Month. But she'll remember you and that's all that matters.

You'll wear five-inch black pumps because they make that annoying noise that alerts everyone everywhere in the whole wide world that you're arriving. What you really want to wear are your red high-top Nikes, the ones that makes you feel like you're rolling back in the day with your crew of girls. You want to wear them with your baggy track jacket and a sports bra, tummy baring, all defiant. With your hair pulled up in a tight-ass ponytail and large gold hoop earrings dangling from your ears. This is what you wore when you first saw him, when he was playing handball, smacking that spaldeen like he owned it, like it was his bitch. *Toma.* If only you could reach for that outfit in your closet like an old friend, but no, you can't go back. You will wear your red, expensive-looking sheath dress and black pumps. You'll tuck in your nameplate necklace underneath the dress so that you can have some sort of protection.

Your makeup will be subtle because you're not going to El Coyote with your girlfriends to toast someone's bullshit promotion, engage-ment, divorce, wedding. No, your makeup will be almost drab except for the lips. The lips are going to be making a lot of moves and there's no question they have to be painted. At first, you'll make the rookie mistake of going for lip gloss like some fourteen-year-old Lolita trying to lure some *papi* in the corner. No. That won't do for today. Instead, you'll grab the orange-red lipstick. So what if it clashes with your red dress. You don't care. This is war. You're going to double up on the red.

As for your man, your boo, *tu negrito*, he's going to wear baggy jeans that are falling off his ever-thinning hips. He'll wear the dingy white T-shirt at first, but you'll force him out of that and beg him to wear a suit. When he yells at you to stop nagging, you'll give in and let him wear the Mets shirt and matching Mets baseball hat that will cover the unruly hair that you held tight last night when you guys were tearing into each other like tomorrow would never come, like the appointment would never happen, hungry for each other. Last night, when you ig-nored how his hips are now bones and how they're pushing up against you, hurting you. Not like before when you wanted his bulging stomach to squash you. I like my man with meat, that's what you used to say. But you don't say that anymore. You'll let him wear what he's wearing, al-though he's rooting for a losing team. You'll convince yourself that at least you both match. Red on red. Blue on red. Red.

You'll take your car and do the driving even though he hates that more than anything. He doesn't like to feel like a weakling. This is what he'll say but he'll give in to your driving. You'll drive to the city and curse at all the cars getting in your way. The drive will be quiet, minus your cursing. No salsa. No smooth jazz. No NPR. Nothing to distract and take away from your bleeding dress. You'll pay to park your car in the hospital's overpriced parking lot and shove your mid-sized car into a compact space. Because you are nice, you'll drop him off in the front of the building so that he won't have to walk all through the parking lot. You won't expect a thank you for this generous move. There's too much pride in him. You'll convince yourself that this is what you like about him. Two strong people doing their own thing, no questions asked, anchoring each other.

You'll surprise yourself and take his hand while walking towards the elevator. His hand is cold although it's hot outside. You will squeeze his cold hand but only slightly, only enough to let him know.

Saludo/Greeting

Your stomping heels will arrive first at the doctor's office. You'll immediately go up to the glass window, the one that resembles the *bodegas* back in the day when you would pay a dollar for a loosey in the middle of the night. The receptionist will smile and say good morning. You will not smile. You will say good morning and let her know why you are there. Why you are both there. You'll say it all angry because that's how you feel. Like everyone is at fault all the time, even the person that held the elevator door for you seconds ago. You'll say thank you but the thank you will sound more like a fuck you.

You'll fill out papers while your boo grabs the *Sports Illustrated* magazine. You'll fill out the medical history. You have it memorized but you'll pull out your iPhone and pretend to look up the information like an executive assistant. You'll have insurance. If you don't have insurance, you're not wearing red; you're not waiting for an appointment. You and your man are fucked. But you'll have insurance and when you get to that part where they'll ask you who is the emergency contact person, you will feel good knowing that your name goes in that slot. Your number goes in there. And you'll feel secure because this is your weapon of choice. You are the one for emergencies.

There is the waiting game and you hate playing that game but you know the rules already. You give them a few minutes, maybe more, but usually less. Then you'll get up and ask them when they're going to call you. It doesn't matter that there are others waiting. It doesn't matter that the old man with Alzheimer's is still at the window trying to figure out how to get back home. It doesn't matter. You will approach the window and demand to know a specific time, right down to the second. And your man will shift his bony ass uncomfortably in the sunken leather brown sofa but he won't tell you to stop.

And then they'll call his name. You'll grab everything and rush out to the door because you don't want them to change their mind and call the Alzheimer guy. No, *viejo*, you want to tell him, this is mine. You will walk so closely to the nurse who is leading you to the office that you will almost trip her. You are doing this on purpose. You want to watch her fall, to create a distraction, an obstacle you can use to climb over and show your man that whatever comes your way, you know what to do. But he is only looking at the nurse's tight ass. You will make a mental note to start working out again. You'll squeeze your butt and keep it squeezed.

When you are led to the doctor's office, you'll glare at all of the diplomas. If he got his degree from some city college, you will look at him like he's your cousin who got his degree at DeVry Institute. If the doctor got his degree at any of the Ivy League schools, you will still look at him like he's your cousin but you will do so only for a second. If the doctor is older than your own father, you will listen to him respectfully, taking down notes while he speaks, nodding when the moment is right. If he is younger than you, you will listen to him but know that you will get a second opinion because no first-year-at-my-damn-job doctor is going to know what he's doing. Hell no.

The doctor will have graduated from Columbia University. You will shake the doctor's hand firmly and will look carefully at your man to make sure he does the same. When you feel that your man's handshake was too weak, ended too quickly, you will be embarrassed by him and wish he had worn the suit. The suit would have given him the allure of power but now he looks like a punk. You'll notice that his baseball hat is almost covering his eyes and you'll fight the urge to slap it off of his face.

Piquetes/The Exchange
You will bring out your file first and lay it on your lap. One folder in it is composed of all the photocopies you insisted on making after each appointment with your man. There are annotations and articles you've

torn out. Another folder has pages of your notes and a notepad. The file is marked with his name. It's your very own dossier, the type of file given to Jim Phelps of *Mission: Impossible* on the TV show, not the movie with Tom Cruise. There are images of doctors and specialists attached to the copies. It took you hours to organize this file and you're already eager to update it tonight with new notes, new revelations, new whatever.

The doctor will follow your lead and spread out his files on his large mahogany desk. He will ask for your man's name and medical history and this will piss you off because he should know this already. You will let your man speak, for once, but will interject to clear dates, episodes, dramas. You know more than he does and he's tired of repeating it over and over. But you enjoy this part. You know more than the doctor. For now.

You will look out the window and notice that the hospital is building another facility and you will ask the doctor what the building will focus on. And you will laugh when the doctor mentions the price tag like money is some funny punch line.

You will pull out an expensive pen, not a cheap Bic and not a Number 2 pencil. A pen with black ink that you will use to highlight, jot down, and mark up your file after every word the doctor utters.

The doctor will not use a pen but his ring finger will display a rather large wedding band that you will find hard not to stare at. And you will wonder how many diamonds are in that band and how much it costs. You will absentmindedly search for your nonexistent wedding band, the one your man promised to give you but instead you both ended up in city hall with his stupid friend Manny as the only witness and no ring. An idiot is what your Mami called you when you told her what you did. And you didn't argue with her.

You will lead by asking a question first because you are in control, because you are wearing red, because you're burning up. The question will be a timid question, a starter question, just something to test the waters. You don't want to start off the bat with the big question, no, that can wait. Start slow, then build up from there.

The doctor will answer your question quickly. His lips are dry and you wish he would use Blistex. His breath stinks of coffee and not the good kind. You will sit back and make a note into your file.

The doctor will change the subject and you'll hold your breath because the moment of truth is coming and there's nothing more to do but wait for the doctor to speak.

You will notice that you have accidentally placed a pen mark on the right-hand corner of your dress. This will cause you to have a mini-panic attack. No one in the room will notice. The mark will grow larger with every passing minute until you feel as if the pen mark is now standing over you, reprimanding you for not being more careful. The pen mark is breathing down your neck and you feel your head being pressed down to your lap. And you look at your man but your man is nodding at you like nothing is happening.

When the doctor dares to say the words, when he finally utters them, birthing exactly what you and your boo were afraid to even utter, when he finally says that word, you will not cry. Not even when it hurts your throat, when your eyes feels like burning. You will not cry. Not even when he says words like, 'we will try all we can, it's growing at a rapid speed, it's an aggressive disease.' You will not cry. You will be stone cold, just like the doctor who is spurting out statistics like he's trying to impress some dumb bitch at a bar. You are impressed but he will never know that. Those same statistics you will find on Web MD and utter them to your friends later when you will all meet for tea or something stronger. No, definitely something stronger.

You will insist on asking about the trial clinics. And you will not accept the doctor's answer that he is not qualified. You'll believe it has something to do with his last name or the fact that you didn't donate money for that new building.

The doctor will start to close the file.

You must not let that happen. The file must stay open.

The doctor will close the file and will start to stand.

You will not stand and you will place a hand to stop your man from leaving. You are not done yet.

Your voice will crack.

The doctor will look nervously at your man. He won't meet your eyes. He'll excuse himself, something about having to pull up another chart. He is running away.

The desk has expanded somehow, taking over the whole room, pressing your body up against the wall. You can't breathe. There's no air. You can't move.

Despedida/Goodbye

Your man will call you by his secret nickname, the name he christened you that night at the handball court. He will call you this name, the same name he whispered in your ear last night. And you will learn how

496

to breathe again. You will breathe and lock eyes with him. And for a moment, that's all you'll do.

Then you will take the lead again.

When the doctor returns, you will alert him of his next steps, not the other way around. The doctor will agree with you. You will firmly shake the doctor's hand goodbye. You will take his card.

When the receptionist tells you that she likes your dress, you will thank her.

Tomorrow, you will take the dress and give it your cousin. Better yet, you will donate it. You will never wear that red dress again.

Nominated by Kathleen Hill, Bellevue Literary Review

WINTER, 1965

fiction by FREDERIC TUTEN

from BOMB

In the few months before his story was to appear, he was treated differently at work and at his usual hangouts. The bartender at the White Horse Tavern, himself a yet unpublished novelist, called out his name when he entered the bar and had twice bought him a double shot of rye with a beer backer. He had changed in everyone's eyes: He was soon to be a published writer.

And soon a serious editor at a distinguished literary publishing house who had read the story would write him, asking if he had a novel in the works. Which he had. And another one, as well, in a cardboard box on his closet shelf that had made the tour of slush piles as far as Boston. Only twenty-three, and soon, with the publication of his story in *Partisan Review*, he would enter the inner circle of New York intellectual life and be invited to cocktail parties where he, the youngster, and Bellows and Mary McCarthy, Lowell and Delmore would huddle together, getting brilliantly drunk and arguing the future of American Literature.

On the day the magazine was supposed to be on the stands, he rushed, heart pounding, to the newspaper shop on 6th Avenue and 12th that carried most of the major American literary magazines, pulled the issue of *PR* from the rack, opened it to the table of contents and found his name was not there. Then turning the pages one by one, he found that not only was his story not there, but neither was there any breath of him.

Maybe he was mistaken; maybe he had come on the wrong day. Maybe the delivery truck had got stuck in New Jersey. Maybe he had picked up an old issue. He scrutinized the magazine again: Winter,

1965—the date was right. He went up to the shop owner perched on a high stool, better to see who was pilfering the magazines or reading them from cover to cover and call out, "This is not a library!" He asked the man if this was the most recent issue of *Partisan Review*, and it was, having arrived that morning in DeBoer's truck, along with bundles of other quarterlies that in not too many months would be riding back on that same truck—bound in stacks, magazines no one would ever read.

He took a day to compose himself, to find the right tone before phoning the editor. Should he be casual? "Hi, I just happened to pick up a copy of *PR* and noticed that my story isn't there." Or very casual? "I was browsing through a rack of magazines and remembered that there was supposed to be a story of mine in the recent issue but it doesn't seem to be there, so I wondered if I had the pub date wrong."

With the distinguished editor's letter in hand—typed and signed and with the praising addendum, "Bravo," he finally got the courage to call. The phone rang a long time. He hung up and tried again, getting an annoyed, don't-bother-us busy signal. He considered walking over to the office but then imagined how embarrassed he would be, asking: "Excuse me, but I was wondering whatever happened to my story?" Maybe Edmund Wilson would be there behind a desk with a martini in each fist, or maybe the critics Philip Rahv and Dwight Macdonald would be hanging out at the water cooler arguing over the respective merits of Dreiser and Trotsky. What would they make of him and the unimportant matter of his story?

Months earlier, he had written the editor thanking him and now he wrote him again: "Might I expect to see my story in the next issue?" To be sure his letter would not go astray, he mailed it at the post office on 14th and Avenue A. And for the next two weeks, he rushed home every day after work to check his mailbox but found no response, just bills and flyers from the supermarket. He knew no one to ask, having no one in his circle remotely connected to *PR* or to any of its writers. For those at the White Horse *he* was *their* ticket to the larger world.

The news that his story had not appeared quickly got around. His colleagues at the Welfare Department—avant-garde filmmakers, artists without galleries, and waiting-to-be-published poets and novelists— where he was an Investigator since graduating from City College in '63, gave him sly, sympathetic looks. "That's a tough break," a poet in his unit said, letting drop that he had just gotten a poem accepted in the *Hudson Review*.

His failure made him want him to slink away from his desk the instant he sat down. It was painful enough that he had to go to work there. As it was, it made him queasy the moment he got to East 112th and saw the beige, concrete hulk of the Welfare Department with its grimy windows and its clients lining up—eviction notices, termination of utilities letters in hand. His supervisor, who had been at the Welfare Department ever since the Great Depression and who now was unemployable elsewhere, tried to console him, saying he was lucky to be on a secure job track and with a job where he could meet so many different kinds of people with a range of stories, some of which could find their way into his books.

But he didn't need stories. What he needed was the time to tell them. And he had worked out a system to do that. He rose at five, made fresh coffee or drank what was left from the day before, cut two thick slices from a loaf of dark rye, which he bought at that place on 8th off 2nd Avenue that sold great day-old bread at half price, and had his breakfast. Sometimes he would shower after breakfast. But the bathtub in the kitchen had no shower, so he had to use a handheld sprinkler that left a dispiriting wet mess on the linoleum floor, which added cleanup time to the shower itself. Thus, he had a good excuse to cut down on the showers and to use that time at his desk to write.

Usually, by 5:45AM, he was dressed and at his desk, the kitchen table he made from crate wood that almost broke the saw in the cutting. He sat at his typewriter for two hours and no matter what resulted from it he did not leave the table. At 7:45 he was at the crosstown bus stop on 10th and Ave D and if all went well he was at the Astor Place station before 8:15 and, if all still went well, he would catch the local and transfer for the express at 14th, get off at 96th Street and take another local to 114th. Then he'd race to clock-in—usually a minute or two before nine. It was not good to be late by even a minute. He was still a provisional and had to make a good impression on Human Resources.

When he got upstairs to his desk and had joined his unit, he'd look over the list of calls to see if any were urgent. They were all urgent: Someone never got her check because the mailbox had been broken into. Someone was pregnant again. Someone needed more blankets. Someone had had just enough and jumped off the roof on 116th and Park Avenue—her children were at her grandmother's.

Today, he finished all his deskwork and phone calls by noon and clocked out for lunch, which he decided to skip. Instead, he finished four field visits very quickly, with just enough time to solicit the information needed to file his reports. He had looked forward all morning to his final, special visit.

He was alarmed when he saw a cop car parked in front of her building. An ambulance, too, with its back doors wide open. He was worried that something bad had happened to her, blind and alone. But the medics were bringing a man down in a stretcher. He was in his eighties, drunk and laughing. The cop spotted his black field book and came over asking, "Is he one of yours?"

"Not mine," he said.

"Maybe not even God's," the cop said. "His girlfriend shot him in the hand," he added. "Jealousy, at that age!" He laughed. As he was being lifted into the ambulance, the wounded man laughed, "Hey! Take me back. I haven't finished my homework."

He rang her doorbell only once before he heard footsteps and then the "Who is it?"

"Investigator," he answered. She opened the door, smiling. She wore white gloves worn at the tips and a long blue dress that smelled of clothes ripening in an airless closet. Her arm extended, her hand brushing along the wall, she led him through a narrow, unlit hall. From her file, which he had reviewed that morning for this visit, he knew it was her birthday. She was eighty-five.

"It's your birthday," he said.

She laughed. "Is that so! I guess I forgot," saying it in a way that meant she hadn't. "I have tea ready," she said.

She poured tea from a porcelain teapot blooming with pink roses on a white sky. Its lip was chipped and stained brown, but the cups and sugar bowl that matched the teapot were flawless and looked newly washed. So, too, the creamy-white oil-cloth that bounced a dull light into his eyes. It was hot in the kitchen; the oven was on with the door open, though he had told her several times how dangerous that could be. A fat roach, drunk from the heat, made a jagged journey along the sink wall.

"Do you need anything today?" he asked. "Maybe something special?" He wanted to add, "for your birthday," but he did not want to press the obvious point. He could put in for a clothes or blanket supplement for her, deep winter was days away. Or a portable electric heater she could carry from one room to another, so she would not have to use the stove. But how would she locate the electric sockets? "Oh! Nothing at all," she said, as if surprised by the question. "Thank you, but what would I need?"

Not to be blind, he thought. Not to be old. Not to be poor. "Well, if anything comes to mind, just call me at the office," he said, remembering that she had no phone.

"Well," she said shyly. "If you have time, would you read me that poem again?"

She already had the book in hand before he could answer, "I'm very glad to."

She had bookmarked the Longfellow poem he had read to her in his previous visits. He read slowly, with a gravity that he thought gave weight to the lines. He paused briefly to see her expression, which remained fixed, serene.

When he finished, she asked him to repeat the opening stanza. " 'Tell me not in mournful numbers, / Life is but an empty dream! / For the soul is dead that slumbers, / And things are not what they seem. // Life is real! Life is earnest! / And the grave is not its goal . . .' "

She thanked him and asked, "Do you like the poem?"

"Yes," he said, to please her. But he disliked the poem because of what he thought was its cloying, sentimental uplift. He did not want to be sentimental but he had to admit how much the lines had moved him anyway.

They sipped tea in silence. He did not like tea but accepted a second cup, commenting how perfectly she had brewed it. "Come any time," she said, "It's always nicer to drink tea in company."

She walked him to the door, picking up a cane along the way. He had never seen her use a cane before. He suddenly worried that should she fall and break her hip, alone in the apartment, she could not phone for help. He made a note in his black notebook to requisition a phone for her.

"The cane is very distinguished," he said.

"It helps me hop along." She smiled. "Thank you for reading to me. You have a pleasing voice, do you sing?"

"My voice is a deadly weapon," he said, surprised by his unusual familiarity. "Birds fall from the sky on my first note."

"Does it kill rats?" She laughed. "I hear families of them eating in the hall at night."

He fled down the stairs, having once been caught between floors by three young men with kitchen knives who demanded his money but when they saw his investigator's black notebook they laughed and said they'd let him slide this time—everyone knew that investigators never carried cash in the field. He sped to the subway where he squeezed himself into a seat so tight that he could not retrieve his book, Malamud's *The Assistant*, from his briefcase. He tried to imagine the book and where he had left off reading. It was about an old Jewish man who ran a failing grocery store and his assistant, a young gentile who lugged milk crates and did other small jobs and who stole from him. It was a depressing novel that pained him, but that had, for all its grimness, made him feel he had climbed out of the grocery store's dank cellar and into a healthy sunlight.

The train halted three times. The fourth might be the one that got stuck in the blackness for hours and he thought to get off at the next station and take a bus or run home or, better, close his eyes and magically be there. But finally the train lurched ahead and when he exited at Astor Place, a lovely light early snow had powdered the subway steps. He waited for the bus.

He waited only eight minutes by his watch but it seemed an hour, two hours—that he had been waiting his whole life. Finally, he decided to walk and hope to catch the bus along its route. But he still did not see it by the time he got to First Avenue, so he decided to save the fare and walk the rest of the way home to 8th between C and D. By Avenue A, it began to be slippery underfoot and the snow came down in fists. Now the thought of going home and leaving again in the snowy evening to travel all the way on the snail's pace bus to the White Horse Tavern for dinner seemed a weak idea. Anyway, he was still smarting from the bartender's faraway look and the wisecracks from the bar regulars when he walked in. He decided to eat closer to home, a big late lunch that would keep him through the evening and keep him at home, writing.

Stanley's on 12th and B was almost empty, the sawdust still virgin. It was still early and still quiet, with just a few old-timers, regulars from the neighborhood—the crowds his age came after eleven, when he would be in bed. He ordered a liverwurst sandwich on rye with raw onions and a bowl of rich mushroom soup, made in the matchbox kitchen by a Polish refugee from the Iron Curtain, an engineer who had to turn cook. A juniper berry topped the soup. That, the engineer told him, was the way you could tell it was authentically Polish. He always searched for the berry after that—like a pearl hiding in the fungus. Stanley, the owner, balder than the week before, brought him a draft beer without his asking. "It's snowing hard," he pronounced. "Should I salt the street now or later?" He did not wait for an answer and went back to the kitchen to shout at the cook in Polish.

He took two books from his briefcase, so that he could change the mood should he wish: *Journey to the End of the Night*—for the third time—*Under the Volcano*, which he had underlined and made notes in the margins. "No one writes the sky as does Lowry, with its acid blues and clouds soaked in mescal." He was proud of that note. One day he would write a book of just such notes. Note upon note building to a grand symphony. Then he voted against ever writing such a book, pretentious to its core—worse, it was facile, a cheat. He wanted to write the long narrative, with each sentence flowing seamlessly into another, each line with its own wisdom and mystery, each character a fascination, a novel that stirred and soared. But what was the point of that? What had become of his story?

A girl he liked came in with a tall man in a gray suit. She smiled a warm hello. He returned with a friendly wave and a smile that he had to force. Now he was distracted and pained and could not focus on reading his book or on his sandwich, which, anyway, was too heavy on the onion. He had met the girl at Stanley's several times, never with a plan, although he had always hoped he would find her there; they talked without flirting, which he was not good at anyway, going directly to the heavy stuff of books and paintings.

The first time he saw her there months earlier, she was reading a paperback of Wallace Stevens poems. He imagined her sensitive, a poet maybe. She was from upstate, near the Finger Lakes with their vineyards and soft hills that misted at dawn and had the green look of Ireland. He had never been upstate or to Ireland. He had never been to Europe. She had been, several times, and had spent a Radcliffe year abroad in Paris, where she had sat at the Café Flore educating herself after the boring lectures at the Sorbonne on the rue des Écoles. She had learned how to pace herself by ordering *un grand café crème* and then waiting two hours before ordering another, and then ordering a small bottle of Vichy water with *du citron à côté*. By then, she was more than twenty pages to the end of *La nausée*. What did he think of Sartre's novel, she had asked him as if it were a test. He hated it, he said. It crushed him, written as if to prove how boring a novel could be.

"That's smart," she said. "If you were any more original you'd be an idiot."

They kissed one evening under a green awning on Avenue A. He kissed hungrily, her lips opening him to a new life. After he had walked her to her doorway and gone home and got into his bed, he felt as if he just had been released from years in prison, the gates behind him shut, and "the trees were singing to him." He did not have her phone or her address and, over the next few weeks, when he went to Stanley's hoping to find her she was not there.

He buried himself in the Céline and tried not to look at her. But then she was beside him. "Come over, I want you to meet someone," she said, sweetly enough to almost make him forget that there was a someone he was supposed to meet.

"This is George", she said, "my fiancé." He extended his hand and George did the same, a hand that spoke of a law office or some wood-paneled place of business high up and far downtown, maybe in the Woolworth building.

George asked him if he'd like a drink and, before he could answer, George called out to Stanley and ordered two double Scotches, neat. "Johnny, Black Label," he said. She was still on her house wine, white, from grapes in California, fermenting under a bright innocent sky. The drinks came. They had little to say to each other or, if they did, they said little. He made a toast: "Best wishes for your happiness," he said. Not much of a toast, not very original. It would take him a day to think of one better; under the circumstances, perhaps never. He looked at his watch and remembered he had to meet a friend for dinner across town: they all shook hands again, and he wished them both good luck. "You too, fella," George said.

The snow fell in wet chunks that seemed aimed at him. When he got home, his head and jacket were wet and he had to brush off the snow married to his trousers. He was worried his jacket would not be dry by morning when he went to work, and he was on the second landing before he realized he had not checked the mail. He thought it was not worth the bother of going back and checking, but he could not stand the thought that he would be home all night wondering if *PR* had finally written him. There was a letter in the mailbox. But it was not from the magazine. But it was also not from Con Edison or Bell Telephone or Chemical Bank, announcing the fourteen dollars in his savings account. When he got to his apartment, he closed the door behind him with a heavy, leaden clunk and slid the iron pole of the police lock into place. "Home is the sailor, home from the sea and the hunter home from the hill," he announced.

He noticed that his cactus was turning yellow. He had overwatered it, and now it was dreaming of deserts—the old country—as it died slowly, ostentatiously. He thought of getting a cat. It would be great to have company that would be the same as being alone. A black cat that would melt in the night when he slept. He picked up the letter cautiously when he saw there was no return address. It may have come from a disgruntled client who had wanted to spew hatred and threats. But it was not. The note was handwritten with lots of curls that announced Barnard or Sarah Lawrence or some grassy boarding school in Connecticut. "Sorry," it said, "that your story did not appear in the new issue as you were led to expect. Do call, if you like." There was a phone number, each digit inscribed as if chiseled in granite and the seven was crossed. For a moment he thought it a prank by one of the White Horse crowd, hoping he would call and find he had dialed a funeral parlor or a police station or a suspicious, jealous husband. But what if it was for real?

He washed his face in cold water, brushed his teeth, combed his hair, took four deep breaths and dialed, holding back for a moment the last digit. At first he thought, with a little lift in his spirits, that it was the girl from the bar. Maybe, after comparing him to her beau, she had decided to call off the engagement. But then, he realized how absurd that was since the girl in the bar had nothing to do with his story. He let the call go through and on the second ring a woman answered. "I've been calling for a week," she said. "Don't you have a service?"

"I let it go," he said. "Looking for a better one."

"Well, I gave up and wrote you."

"Sorry for the trouble," he said and then in an anxious rush and hating himself for the rush, asked, "Are you an editor at *Partisan Review*?"

"Something like that," she said. Then cautiously added, "We can meet if you like." He wanted to ask if she could tell him right now, over the phone, tell him what had happened to his story but he held back not wanting to seem anxious and unsophisticated.

"Sure," he said, adding as casually as he could, "When?"

"How's tonight? I live just across town. You name the place."

"You don't mind coming out in all this snow?" he said, immediately regretting he had asked. What kind of man is afraid of the snow? "I mean, I could come to you if that's easier."

"I'll just grab a cab. How's 8?"

He wondered if she had dinner in mind. He would have to offer to pay for it, and he began calculating his finances. But to his relief, she said, "I'll already have had dinner."

"Okay, then, how's the De Robertis' Pastry Shop, the café on First, between 10th and 11th, next to Lanza's?"

"Is that the café with the tile walls that looks like a bathroom?"

He didn't like his café being spoken of that way. "I guess some may see it like that."

They fixed the time at 8:30. Just as he was about to ask whether they were going to publish the story in another issue, the line went dead. There were still some hours to go before meeting her and he had time to write or to review the morning's work. The portable Olivetti, shiny red, hopeful, was quietly where he had left it, waiting patiently on the kitchen table; the two pages he had written beside it, like accomplices. He read over the pages. They were absurd, stupid, illiterate, worthless— and worse, boring. He was stupid and boring, a failure. The Welfare building sailed at him like an ocean liner in the night. "Life is real, life is earnest," he sang, as the ship loomed larger.

He did not want to meet her hungry and he did not want to spend money for another sandwich at Stanley's. He scavenged the fridge. The crystal bowl heaped with Russian caviar was not there so he settled for the cottage cheese, large curd, greening at the top, which he spooned directly from the container. Then he considered taking a nap so he would be refreshed and alert and not stupid or dull but bright when he met her. He practiced a smile but it was strained and pathetic. He tried napping, leaving on the kitchen light so he would not wake in the lonely darkness. The Welfare building pressed full steam toward him but he blinked it away and tried to clear his mind of all troubling thoughts but without much success. So he rose with the idea of making himself presentable. He brushed his teeth and gave himself a sponge bath; he cleaned his fingernails and brushed his teeth again. He had reached the limit of his toilette and returned to his desk; maybe his pages would brighten at the cleaned-up sight of him; maybe his Olivetti would regard him more favorably and let him turn out some astonishing gems.

By the time he arrived at the café, he had to shake off the heavy snow twice from his umbrella. His shoes were soaked. He had not changed them for fear of getting his second pair drowned as well and thus having to spend the next day at work in wet shoes.

She was easy to spot, sitting in a booth with a pot of tea and a half-eaten *baba au rhum*. Her black hair was pulled tight in a ponytail, gold hoops dangled from her earlobes; kohl rimmed her eyes; her yellow sweater was the color of straw in the rain. What was she, twenty? She was more Café Figaro on Bleecker with its Parisian hauteur than someone who usually came into his neighborhood. He was sure he had spotted her at the White Horse, men hoping to catch her eye circling her table, where she sat in among other men chattering for her attention. She had never once looked up at him, even when he was ostentatiously clutching *Under the Volcano* in his hand.

She smiled in an anxious way that relaxed him and he took his seat and said, "I hope I haven't kept you waiting." He was ten minutes early, but he had no better introductory words. He felt foolish for having said them.

"I liked your story," she said, as if she too had mulled over her first words to him and now had let them burst.

"I'm very pleased," he said. Pleased seemed tempered and not over anxious, showing a proper balance of self-esteem and of professional dignity. But then he overrode his self-control and said, "Are they still going to publish it?"

She forced a little laugh. "I doubt it."

This was bad news, indeed. But before he could ask the cause of this doubt, she said: "He hates me now." She made a high-pitched sound like a young mouse broken in a trap.

"I read him in college. We all did. I never thought I'd become his assistant! Anyway, he has a new assistant now," she said, her eyes glistening.

Johnny, the café owner, brought over the cappuccino, with a glass of water and a cloth napkin. He looked at the young woman and smiled and turning to him said, "*Hai fatto bene.*"

"You know, it's just one of those crazy things that happens. Maybe not so crazy when people work so closely all the time," she added, as if talking to herself.

He wanted to ask, "Please, what thing that happens?" But he was afraid that pressing her would only make him seem unworldly. Instead, he said: "Yes, crazy things do happen," thinking he would offer, as a current example, the story of the shot man who said he hadn't finished his homework.

The café was foggy, steaming up like the baths on 10th Street he went to once and hated, all that wet heat boiling his blood—and the absurd thing was that he had to pay for it too. He could leave now, as he had then, with the steam stripping the skin from his bones. But he was listening to her story and was not ready to run. She looked down. "I suppose you can fill in the rest," she said. And then with a little pinched laugh, added, "After all, you're the writer." He waited for her to add, "and as yet unpublished." But he realized it would have been his addition and not hers and that he was bringing to the table the same feeling of defeat as when he went to the White Horse, where the greetings had gone stale.

"Oh! I don't know," he said, with some affected casualness, "I'm not good at realism or office fiction." He was thinking of a popular novel some years back, *The Man in the Gray Flannel Suit*, which he had not read but understood had to do with office politics and unhappy commuters with sour marriages and lots of scotch and martinis before dinner. He knew nothing of that world, making him wonder in what America he lived and if he was an American writer or any kind of writer at all.

She gave him a studied look and in a brisk, business-like tone said, "Of course, I know that. That's what I like most about your story. I loved that part where a dying blue lion comes into the young blind woman's hut and asks for a bowl of water and how she nurses him to health."

"That sounds a bit corny," he said. "Maybe I should be embarrassed instead of flattered that you remembered it."

He himself had forgotten the passage as well as most of the story. It had seemed so long ago and somewhat like a friend who, for no reason that he knew, had turned on him.

"Don't be silly," she said. "It's an archetype, all archetypes seem corny."

"So," he asked, as if he had not already been told, as if, finally, to invite the *coup de grâce*, "why won't he publish it?" The steam was clouding him and the wall's white tiles were oozing little pearls of hot water and bitter coffee.

"Look," she said, with an edge in her voice, "I just came to tell you that I'm sorry it didn't work out."

"Excuse me," he said, "I'm a bit slow, more than usual tonight—the steam's getting to me." He wished he could close his eyes and find himself home and, once there, obliterate all memory of the sent story or of having received the acceptance letter that was to have changed his life. The espresso machine was screaming. She looked about the room and then back at him and smiled. "And frankly, I was curious to know what you were like."

"I hope I met your expectations," he said. That was so lame. He started to revise but she did not give him time.

"My boyfriend also thinks you're a good writer. And he studied with Harry Levin at Harvard."

"Harry Levin's *The Power of Blackness* is a great book." He wanted her to know he knew.

She offered to pay her share of the bill—and a little extra because she had had those two *babas au rhum*—but he said, in what he thought was a worldly fashion, "Not at all, you are my guest."

He walked her to 9th and First Avenue and waved for a cab. "Thanks," she said, "I don't believe in cabs, do you? They're so bourgeois." They stood on the corner shivering, and waited until the bus skidded to the stop; snow blanketed the roof and the wipers swiped the windshield with maniac fury. He wanted to kiss her on both cheeks, as he had seen it done in French films, but thought it was too familiar too soon. In any case, the hood of her slicker covered much of her face. She smiled at him very pleasantly, he thought. On the second step of the nearly empty bus, she turned and said, "I don't have a boyfriend." He waited until he saw her take her seat. He waved as the bus moved into the traffic, but she was facing away and did not see him.

He thought of returning to the café, but he was sick of coffee and the screaming white tiles, or of going back to Stanley's bar for a beer, but was afraid he would run into the girl he had liked—still liked—and she would ask what he had thought of her fiancé and he would have to be brave and swallow it and say how solid he seemed and how he was happy for her if she was happy.

He went home and climbed the stairs. A dog barked at him behind a door on the second floor—Camus, *The Stranger*, the mistreated, beaten dog; the Russian woman on the third floor was boiling cabbage and the hall smelled of black winter and great sweeps of bitter snow, a branchless tree here and there dotting the white expanse—Mother Russia, Dostoevsky, *Crime and Punishment*, the bloody axe, a penniless student. On the fourth floor, not a peep. Then suddenly, a groan followed by a cry like a man hit with a shovel: "*Welt welt,* kiss *mein tuchas.*"

On the fifth floor, he thought about the groan and the cry on the fourth. He had seen the tattooed numbers on the old man's wrist and knew what had given them birth—hills of eyeglasses, mounds of gold teeth, black black smoke rising from an exhausted chimney. When he finally reached the sixth and last floor, he stopped at his door, key in hand, thinking to turn and leave the building again for a fresh life in the blizzard. But he was already shrouded in snow and was chilled and wanted to take off his clothes and lie in bed and be whoever he was. There was a song coming from the adjacent apartment: Edith Piaf, who regretted nothing.

His playboy neighbor had returned from Ibiza with a sack full of 45s and a deep suntan. He always had visitors, beautiful girls from Spain and Paris and London, who came to crash and who sometimes stayed for a week or two. One had knocked at his door at two in the morning and asked if he had any coke. He apologized, he did not drink soda; she made a face and said, "Where're you from?" Another banged at his door at five in the morning blind drunk; she had mistaken his apartment for the playboy's. "You have the wrong door," he said, his sleep shattered. "Who cares," she said, staggering into his room.

He was down to his shorts and T-shirt and had pulled a khaki surplus army blanket to his knees. He sat up in bed with Céline and read. Ferdinand was working in an assembly line in Detroit. Molly was his girlfriend. Ferdinand was a young vagabond and she was a prostitute. She loved him. There was no loneliness in the world as the loneliness of America. And the two had made a fragile cave of paper and straw against the loneliness. He read until he no longer knew what he was reading. Then he gave up. His mind was elsewhere and nowhere. The day had been fraught with distractions. He was a distraction. He thought of phoning someone. Maybe the assistant he had just left at the snowy bus stop—to find out if she got home all right. Maybe he would call some friends, but he did not know whom and, finally, he did not have anyone he wanted to talk with or who would welcome his call. He thought again of getting a cat. A white one he could see in the dark. The cactus looked healthier in the lamplight; maybe it had had second thoughts and decided to give life another try. "Goodnight," he said to himself and switched off the light.

But he quickly turned it back on, thinking again of calling the assistant, thinking that perhaps they could soon become friends. They could go to poetry readings at the Y—Auden and other great poets read there, or take in a movie at the Thalia on Broadway and 95th—he was sure she liked foreign films, like Fellini's *La Strada*, or Bergman's *The Seventh Seal*. Maybe on the weekends they would sit over coffee under the bronze shadow of Rodin's giant *Balzac* in MoMA's tranquil garden, and he would read to her his latest work. She would immediately recognize what was excellent and what was not and, with her as his editor and muse, he would write beautiful, original stories and novels. She had already been his champion. Now they would collaborate, nourishing each other on life's creative adventure and they would never be lonely in Detroit or anywhere else. He tried to remember if he had found her attractive, but she was a blur with a messenger's voice.

Maybe he had neglected to see that she was beautiful, desirable. He suspected that she was both. He was sure of it. Maybe he'd invite her for a dinner of spaghetti and salad and house red at Lanza's, where whatever you wanted on the menu they did not have. Maybe at dinner together there, under the frescos of Sicilian villas grilling in the sun, she would find its *prix fixe* and soiled menus louche and seductive and thus find him equally, if not more so. Maybe one morning they would wake together in his bed, the raw light from the window on her beautiful, bare, straight shoulders. Maybe one midnight, after a movie and over coffee and a plate of rolls at Ratner's on 2nd Avenue and under the eyes of the shaking old Jewish waiters, retired from the Yiddish Theatre, they would realize they were in love. Maybe they were already in love.

He could hear the scraping of a snow-shovel in the distance—maybe on Avenue C. His own street would not be cleared for days. He went to his window. The synagogue across the way had been locked tight for two years; its smashed windows covered with sheets of fading plywood. The grocery three buildings to the east of him was closed, the two brothers who owned it were still in Rikers Island for fencing radios, so the whole way to Avenue D might be snowed over, impeding his walk to the crosstown bus on 10th and D. The snow was building on his window ledge and he would let it mount, better to gauge how much of it was piling up below in the street he could no longer clearly see. With all this snow, the morning bus might be delayed and the subway, too. He would have to get up extra early to get to work, and budget himself the time to shovel Kim's sidewalk. The laundry was still dark: Kim was in the back recovering from a mugging and beating three days earlier. "Where is your gold?" the robbers had demanded. "Chinks always have gold," one said, giving Kim a whack on the knee with a blackjack. He would have to shovel the snow for him before he went to work or Kim would get a summons or two. When would he find time to write? Who cared if he did? He would go down in the street and sleep there in the blanketing snow, Céline in hand. Or maybe the Lowry.

He went back to bed, tossing and turning and sleeping a dozen minutes at a time, then waking. He returned to Céline. Ferdinand was still miserable in cold Detroit, but he had no luck in focusing and no better luck with *Under the Volcano*, whose drunken protagonist still reeled about in the hot Mexico sun. He went to the window again. The snow had piled a quarter way up the window and was whirling in the sky like it owned the world. He might be late to work or never get there no matter how early he left his house.

There was a knock at the door, alarming at that hour, but then he thought it was his playboy neighbor or one of his wandering drunk girlfriends, or the one always prowling for drugs. He opened the door to the limit of the chain. It was the neighbor, drink in hand.

"I heard you puttering about and thought it was not too late."

He opened the door, feeling vulnerable in his underwear.

"Just wanted you to know I'm moving out and want to sublet for a year or so. Thought you might like it for your office." He could not afford two apartments scraping by on one, but he said, "Thanks, give me a day or so to think about it."

"The rent's the same thirty-two a month—I'm not trying to make anything on it."

"I wouldn't have thought so." It was cold in the hallway and he thought to invite him in but was embarrassed that he would see three days of dishes still piled up in the sink. And then, feeling he was not cordial enough, he added, "Where're you going?" expecting him to say Ibiza or Paris or San Francisco.

"Uptown, closer to work."

"Sorry you're leaving," he said.

"Well, me too. But Dad thinks it's time to put on the harness and he got me something in publishing."

"Oh!"

"It should be okay. I'm told editors mostly go to lunch."

"I've heard that," he said. He wanted to add, "I'll send you my novel, maybe you'll like it." But he felt humiliated and hated himself for the thought that he would ask. "Come and lunch with me one day!"

"I'd like that," he said. They shook hands. He shut and locked the door but felt he was on the outside, in the hall, freezing. He checked his Timex. How had it ever become midnight? No wonder he was freezing—at that hour the boiler was shut off and all the radiators turned to ice. He lit the oven, setting it on low, and left the door open. Maybe he would buy a portable heater and one for the blind woman. Maybe he'd drag out the Yellow Pages from the back of the closet and look up the closest animal shelter, like the ASPCA, which he heard was respectable. He would go there on Saturday and would come home that very day with a cat. He wondered what kind of cats they had there. Old ones, sick ones, mean ones, dirty and incontinent ones who would pee on his bed, all ready to be gassed. He would save ten and herd them in a train to follow him as he went from room to room. He'd circle them around his bed at night and keep away Bad Luck. He had Bad Luck. He'd save fifteen. Seven white ones; seven black ones. The other would be marmalade. Would they let him take that many at one time?

He could not sleep. But he could not stay awake another minute. Better than chancing a morning bus and subway failure, maybe he'd get dressed and start walking to work now, fording the snow drifts so to be sure to get there on time. He'd show up at first light, half-frozen, waiting for the doors to open. He would be exemplary. He would be made permanent. He would be promoted and never have time to write again or wait for rejections in the mail. Or maybe he would be found icy dead at the foot of the Welfare Department's still closed doors. The editor of *Partisan Review* would eventually learn of it and publish his story, boasting that he had been their promising discovery.

The snow had bullied the streets into silence. The building slept without a snore. In the distance, the tugboats owlishly hooted as they felt their way along the blinding snow. He closed his eyes. He stayed that way for several minutes, chilled under his blanket. But then the oven slowly heated, sending him its motherly warmth. He rose and went to the kitchen table and to the gleaming red Olivetti waiting for him there.

This story is dedicated to Tom McCarthy.

Nominated by Bomb

PROJECT FUMARASE

fiction by APRIL L. FORD

from NEW MADRID

After the last St. James Lacop congregant passed away, the State repurposed the church as a meeting place for members of AA and other damned populations, but no one is damned enough to travel one hour northwest of Palmyra to a dirt cul-de-sac of six boarded-up farmhouses whose front porches are sunken and splintered open in places where people once rocked on chairs and smoked corncob pipes; the church's disrepair is a statement about how little twenty-first century God participates in the lives of the dysfunctional and insolvent. St. James once contained twenty hand-carved pews, an ornate pine lectern, and a gold-tasseled Persian rug, above which Christ smiled onto the priest during his late hours of worship and self-flagellation. It once boasted a blocky white cross on its roof; now, a wire forced into the approximate shape of an angel serves as a beacon for the lost.

Today, the lost are forty-seven children. They've arranged themselves from youngest to oldest, smallest to biggest: infants and toddlers at the front, harnessed to a carousel of mechanical arms designed to rock them to sleep; a row of schoolchildren, both sexes; two rows of prepubescent boys; a row of teenage girls against the wall at the very back. Like organ pipes, the girls lift up and down on their toes to keep sight of their young. Except when a mother visibly suppresses the instinct to tend to her fussing baby, no one from the group has retaliated, even mildly, against confinement to the church basement since eight o'clock this morning. Refusal to engage is the only way they know how to behave toward Outsiders. Any child who might know other possibilities— from sources prohibited within compound boundaries—must keep quiet in case He's listening through the mouthpieces clipped to the Outsiders' belts.

The group is of one oily complexion, which becomes overwhelmed by acne with age. The schoolchildren wear John Lennon-style glasses with thick, dirty lenses that make their eyes bulge as if from thyroid disease. The boys are gaunt and the girls are stout, and all of them, even the infants and toddlers, are dressed in white baptismal garments. Someone from the compound learned of the impending raid, and at dawn this morning the community was ready. The mothers had just finished preparing the Flock when the convoy of Child Protective Services transport vans arrived. CPS encouraged the mothers to accompany their children to St. James church, a discrete location where the children would be separated from one another and sent to transitional homes, but the mothers stood back, linked arm in arm in a neat crescent as their children, lifting the skirts of their garments in fists to avoid rain puddles, were herded into one set of vans. The Fathers, smelling of tobacco and other pre-dawn immoralities, filed into the other. "Do not allow the Outsiders to remove your garments!" the Fathers warned. "Your garments are all that will protect you!"

It is noon. The children's excruciating docility has spread anxiety among the CPS team and church volunteers, who pace and crack their knuckles, waiting for something to happen. No one had anticipated a delay between the children being moved from one location to the next, but the unmarked black vehicle parked across from the church, likely media, has forced CPS into a waiting game.

Laird Fullerton, the intelligence behind Project Fumarase and a man with ten years experience working on unusual cases, can't look at the group any longer; what has driven him for the last two years now makes him want to puke. The faces all watch him in the same unblinking, iron-deficient way. Do their eyes *have* any color? The closest he can guess is gray, except even gray has something to it, a highlight of blue, green, or gold. Laird has seen what a child looks like after being locked in a cupboard for eighteen months. He has watched nanny-cam footage of a seven-year-old solemnly dissecting a toy poodle. Once, undercover, he was solicited by a mother looking to rent out her little girl for a bump of meth.

Peggy Galvin, the newest addition to Project-F, walks the length of the group with a tray of juice boxes and crackers. She has offered snacks to the children regularly since they arrived. "You guys must at least be thirsty by now!"

The schoolchildren eye the snacks more desirously than their seniors do, but their fingers, curving and curling, remain at their sides.

Peggy must win the group's trust by the end of the day; otherwise, Laird will transfer her back to the windowless office filled with reports of missing persons. He was frank about why he invited her on board: "We need someone with a soft touch." She is the only woman on the team.

A girl speaks from the back row. "Ma'am? I need to feed my son."

When Peggy starts toward her with the tray, the girl huffs and points at her breasts. "I need to *feed* my son."

Her son could be any baby on the carousel; they're all genderless in their matching white garments. They've been supplied with a steady stream of formula since they arrived, and the church volunteers have been timely and efficient about diaper changing and burping. Except for one baby, who has rejected the bottle every time and writhes whenever anyone touches him. A fusty odor like wasps in the last days of summer hangs in the air around him.

"Bring a fresh bottle, please," Peggy tells a volunteer.

Mother and son's matching flat noses are lost in the fleshiness of their faces, and their earlobes remind Peggy of scrotums. There's an absence of curiosity and intelligence about the young mother, but also an absence of the wrath stewing in the other children's expressions. Maybe this one will talk.

Project Fumarase, as the public understands it, is about rescuing children and prosecuting criminals. Few people know about its sinister purpose: to collect certain evidences before the State-issued warrant expires in three days and the children and Fathers have to be released. After that, the group will relocate like it did in 2005 and 2008. The men will continue to espouse their twelve-year-old half-sisters and nieces, the recessive gene will continue to proliferate, babies will continue to be stillborn or severely deformed. The group will breed itself out of existence, but that could take another century.

"What do you mean, 'certain evidences?' " Peggy asked Laird when he first spoke to her about the project.

"Blood tests. We're looking for a specific enzyme."

"I mean the sexual abuse. How will you prove it if the kids won't talk?"

"They won't talk, Galvin. We know that already."

"I don't understand."

"We need the State to think it's about child sexual abuse or else we

517

won't get funding. What we're really after is evidence of fumarase deficiency. Once we prove it's in these kids, we'll be able to do a lot more than arrest a few zealots and pedophiles. It'll be big, Galvin. Big."

"Who else breastfeeds?" Peggy asks the back row. Only the one girl breaks rank; the others close in on her empty space, eyes training after her with disapproval and envy.

"I want privacy." She puffs Her torso against the scorn from the back row. Her right shoulder sags, like a dislocation never corrected.

"You can use the bathroom. I'll have to accompany you, but I'd like your consent."

"I don't consent."

"Charlie!" Peggy calls to the volunteers idling by the exit door. A scoliated man with pattern baldness steps forward. "Would you accompany this young lady to the bathroom?"

The girl looks at Charlie and scowls. "You said you needed my consent. You lied."

"I said I'd *like* it, and I thought you would appreciate the opportunity. It's up to you. If you're old enough to be a mother, you're old enough to make lesser choices."

Charlie, the other volunteers, even Laird, stare at Peggy like she's announced that a bomb is strapped to her chest and everyone's going to die. Her pulse speeds, pruritus spreads under her clothes. Why did Laird insist she come dressed for a business meeting? These children won't identify with her simply because she's female! In her black wool power-suit, she must look like Satan compared with the image surely looming in their minds right now: soft, safe mothers in pastel blue and eggshell pink floor-length dresses buttoned to the chin. Fathers in jeans and plaid shirts. Everyone, on days like today, in white.

Peggy feels her confidence shake; she must prove her competency to Laird. She clicks her tongue like the disappointed older sister. The girl considers her, and beyond the bovine dish of her face, Peggy sees a person who understands compromise. Perhaps CPS will use this girl against her own people. The community of outliers is already vulnerable: the children have been separated from their mothers, the women from their husbands, and everyone from the Voice, who did not, like the rest of his community, draw from the strength of faith and heavenly love. He's probably in Canada by now.

Peggy dismisses Charlie and unhooks the infant from the carousel. Above his congested protests, she asks once more if anyone else breastfeeds. The back row responds with furious silence. She passes the baby to his mother, and it's as though the group suddenly realizes what's happening; everything before now belonged to a reality that couldn't touch them under their white garments. It starts when a schoolgirl whispers, "Your son is going to Hell." A few more join her and it graduates to a controlled chant. "Your son is going to Hell. Your son is going to Hell." In the short time it takes Peggy to lead the girl away, it escalates to a unanimous cry, with Laird and the volunteers watching in awe as the children point their index fingers toward the bathroom. "YOUR SON IS GOING TO HELL. YOUR SON IS GOING TO HELL."

The bathroom is miniscule and as malodorous as an outhouse. There's a plastic hand-mirror duct-taped to the wall above the sink. A sticky note on top of the toilet seat reads *lift flapper to flush.* Water from exposed, mold-covered pipes overhead drips into a tin wastebasket. Peggy empties it into the toilet and lifts the flapper; the toilet belches and spits until all that remains is a tampon applicator floating in slow circles.

The girl clutches her baby to her chest and stares at the plastic mirror. Peggy wonders which is more devastating to her: being locked up with an Outsider, or seeing herself, probably for the first time in her life, removed from her reality. She flips the wastebasket over and sits down, then closes the toilet seat and invites the girl to do the same. "I won't look. I understand how uncomfortable you must be feeling."

The girl does as instructed, her son quiet in her arms. She pats his head the way a five-year-old pats her teddy bear in pretend consolation, presses her fingertips gently over his lips, which are bunched and ready to receive the nipple.

Even though Laird warned her not to get on a first-name basis with any of the children, Peggy wants to with this girl—just to diminish the horrible awkwardness of the situation. Laird claimed the community teaches its children to give aliases, but as Peggy and the girl face each other with absolutely nothing in common, an exchange of false names would be something.

Peggy turns away to give the young mother some privacy. The waist of her slacks scoops below her tailbone, and she wonders if the girl notices her scorpion tattoo. Does she even know what a tattoo is? "Let me know when you're done, okay? If you have personal needs, I'll take your son and wait outside."

"I need help."

"Help?"

"With my son."

When Peggy turns back, the girl huffs and extends her arms until they lock at the elbows. The baby is balanced dangerously on the pads of her fingers. "I can't feed him." Her voice is pliant, like she's about to either wail or laugh hysterically. The baby gazes up at his mother through glassy eyes. She looks pointedly at her breasts. "I don't know how to make Bailyn take it. Bridger does that."

Peggy has an impulse to burst out of the bathroom and urge the children to retaliate, to run back to their mothers—to return to a world that wants them. Instead, she taps a finger three times below her right collarbone, on the small microphone Laird taped to her skin this morning.

"Bailyn and Bridger. Good work, Galvin." He sounds pleased. There's a crackle in the receiver in Peggy's right ear, and then silence and nausea.

The girl puts Bailyn on the floor between her white ballerina slippers and hugs her arms around her shins; she is vulnerable without her group. She is Project-F's best chance. Peggy's big chance. And while Laird and the other team members are doing the easy stuff, listening, taking notes, making plans, she has to engage with a teenager who doesn't know how to breastfeed her own baby. Bridger does that. Is Bridger the father? The Voice? Both?

The girl starts to weep. She squeezes her arms more tightly around her shins, fingers interlaced, hands bruised on the middle knuckles. Peggy lays a hand on the girl's shoulder and time both suspends and becomes elastic, the way it does when you catch your lover screwing someone.

Laird shouts into her ear. "Why so quiet, Galvin? What's happening? Keep her talking. Keep. Her. Talking!"

Bailyn squirms on the floor at his mother's feet, grabbing tiny fistfuls of his white blanket, opening and closing his mouth around them. As though being guided in a dream, Peggy reaches into her breast pocket for her kerchief. Before the girl can react, she touches the kerchief to her face and pats it dry. The girl smells of overripe bananas and rubbing alcohol. Her pulse labors through the vein across her forehead.

"There's a better way to give little Bailyn a bath, here," Peggy whispers. "You're gonna have to cry a lot more to get the job done right."

It's the stupidest thing she could possibly say, but she has to connect with this girl, transform her from genetic horror show to human being.

"Bridger said you all were coming."

Peggy tucks the girl's hair behind her ears and examines the lobes, two hazelnut-sized knobs of loose, wrinkled flesh. She'll never be able to pierce her ears. Something so basic will never be an option for this girl. Blood tests aren't necessary to prove she's suffering from fumarase deficiency and carries the recessive gene; she has passed it onto her baby with the Dumbo ears.

Laird rushes in once more. "Get her talking more about Bridger. Ask subtle questions to keep her on topic—*don't* bring up the Voice."

"Is Bridger the Voice?"

A series of curses grace Peggy's ear.

The girl stands and smooths the fabric of her starchy baptismal garment, peers down at her ankles to make sure they're covered, runs her hands over her face and re-braids her hair. Peggy feels hypnotized watching her preen in the mirror like a perfectly normal, well-adjusted teenager getting ready to meet friends at the mall.

The girl picks Bailyn up off the floor and kisses his forehead. "Bridger is my Voice. We each have a Voice."

The incongruity of her behavior is so dramatic Peggy can't focus. It's Laird, buzzing madly in her ear, who enables her to respond. "You mean each person has a Voice?"

"Only men are Voices, and only mothers and children obey them. I would like to feed Bailyn now."

"Good, Galvin. Good! Keep her talking about Voices. Keep that filthy vixen talking."

After Galvin went into the bathroom, he stepped outside so he could speak to her without unsettling the children. No doubt their mutiny is as intolerable as their silence—worse than a B-rated horror movie. He has left the door ajar in case the situation in the basement becomes unmanageable, and when he peers in now he oddly wants to inflict pain on the children. The school-aged ones seem to be daring him to hurt them. He turns away and kicks the desiccated rosebush around which he's been walking fast, tight circles; it explodes like bones from the impact of his Oxford shoe. He thumbs mud off his black trouser cuffs, pats the graying tufts at his temples, makes a mental note that it's time

521

for a trim. Most women in their twenties think gray is sexy, as long as it's neat.

He presses the headset microphone to his mouth. "What the fuck, Galvin? I don't hear anything."

In the same way he can't help hating the children for their ugliness, Laird can't help punishing Galvin for being who she is. The day he stopped by her office to invite her onto Project-F, he expected the woman to crawl out of her skin at the chance for an "upstairs job." Everyone at CPS knows that basement jobs, like missing-persons cases more than two years old, are terminal. And yet Galvin has been in that windowless office so long she commissioned her friend *Frédérique*, or something fruity like that, to paint an ocean scene mural facing her desk, an orange and pink sunset with a fleet of piping plovers skimming the saltwater surface. Better than seeing your boss's face every time you look up, or the clerks whom he's fucking, Laird supposes.

He presses the headset to his ears. "Galvin? Galvin, when you think you have something for me, sneeze twice, okay? Achoo-achoo. Tell me you hear me."

He waits for the blunt sound of finger-tapping then steps back inside, staying by the exit door while he considers the scene before him: flies circling around the babies on the carousel, feasting on the opaque nasal discharge; CPS team members and volunteers shielding their noses with the backs of their hands, dipping their mouths behind their shirt collars. The breathing air has become toxic like in the basements of old people's attics, but the children continue to hold their ground.

The light bulb above the toilet is so Goth dark blue that the young mother and her son look like Asiatic glassfish. Twenty minutes ago, Peggy could have left for lunch and returned unable to distinguish the pair from the group.

"Get that baby fed, Galvin." Laird's voice sounds constricted.

Without thinking, Peggy asks, "Everything all right out there?"

Laird screams into her ear and Peggy reaches for the wall and touches the girl by accident. The girl touches her back, her socketless eyes seeming to communicate that she understands, that she's sorry. Bailyn is back on the floor, his cries of hunger the only natural thing about this whole situation.

"Get me that baby, Galvin, and you'll never have a windowless office again," Laird croons.

If she succeeds in taking Bailyn from his mother then turns him over to the nurses and doctors waiting in the medi-van parked behind the church, the State will be in a position to begin making arrests, to rescue women and children from sexual slavery. If Project Fumarase succeeds, the State could become famous—nationwide, states have been plotting and planning and failing at capturing hosts of the recessive gene that first seized the public's attention. In 2004, a teenage mother snuck into a doctor's office with her hours-old baby and begged someone to help the little girl breathe. The baby had no nose, just two slits above her harelip, and the slits had filled and clogged, causing her to suffocate. Over the next two weeks, a dozen more babies and children with varying degrees of bone-chilling physical and mental retardation were snuck into the office by trembling adolescent mothers and the deficiency was named. Then, as suddenly as the young mother had appeared with her choking newborn, the entire community vanished. The only life that remained on the compound, once it was located, was a flourishing root vegetable garden. CPS has been tracking a group reported to be protecting the same gene discovered in the west of the country—the gene of "celestial will." Laird knows it, Peggy knows it, everybody on Project-F knows it; but without confessions and scientific evidence, they will have to release the children and Fathers, and then the group will vanish once more.

"Okay," Peggy says, rubbing her hands up and down the girl's arms in a vigorous, affectionate way. "Let's get this baby fed."

The girl smiles, a broad, spontaneous smile, and just like that the trance is broken; she is missing gaps of teeth, and those she has are nubs the color of rubber bands, poking out of gums so tight with swelling they're almost white. Peggy's heart breaks, the girl reads it on Peggy's face, and intimacy evaporates. The girl turns away, touching her hands to her arms where Peggy touched, mimicking the motion while considering the famished infant at her feet.

"I need to feed my son. Can you please undo my zipper?"

"Yes, of course."

So swiftly the girl has no time to change her mind, Peggy clasps her shoulders and turns her around. The girl allows herself to be manipulated without flinch or struggle, as though she is back on the compound, where women behave like robots. The zipper on the back of her dress is split open, but Peggy imitates the gesture of opening it properly. Peggy doesn't let her eyes train on the quarter-sized welts along the girl's spine; she has to tuck her thumb against her palm to keep from touching them; even though it doesn't matter whether they are hard or soft, she wants to know. She wants to feel them the way kids want to touch dead things. In all her imagined scenarios of how she would react to the horror of finally seeing the children, she imagined she would cry. This is the most comforting thing about her windowless office job: no real horror to contend with. In the rare event a missing person is found, the body is barely bones; it's a blessing for everyone involved, as dust is so rarely the provenance of nightmares.

Peggy shoves the girl aside and hurls into the toilet, deluging the cardboard tampon applicator in coffee and bile. As she heaves, the receiver dislodges from her ear and falls into the toilet. She lifts her hand, but her fingers won't open to trap the tiny black device; they defy her, coil into a fist, which punches her thigh over and over again, until she is crouched over, dry heaving, her tongue seizing from the strain, her eyes wide and wet.

Now she is alone with the girl.

A yellow school bus backs up behind the church. The driver honks and Laird comes running out, sweat pearled across his brow and upper lip. He directs the driver closer to the exit door and then waves his arms; the children will load more easily like this. They've grown belligerent in the last half hour, since that girl and her baby left them. One of the prepubescent boys wet his pants on purpose, while a girl of about five picked her nose until it bled.

Laird walks up to the driver, a lissome brunette no older than thirty who should be playing volleyball on a beach or animating cruise ship activities. "Laird Fullerton, Assistant Director, Child Protective Services. Thank you for coming on such short notice." He makes sure to extend his hand that showcases his gold pinky ring with the black onyx monogram.

"Adina Michaels. If you wouldn't mind, I'd like to smoke a cigarette and then get back on the bus."

"Of course. We should be ready to leave soon." Laird extracts a gleaming, inscribed cigarette case from his pants pocket and flips open the lid. He smiles. "Please, try one. They leave a slightly sweet taste on the lips."

Adina chooses a cigarette from the center of the row, sliding it neatly from the case and turning away to light it before Laird can offer his

Zippo. "I'd really prefer not to see them, if you understand. I'm not involved, okay?" She exhales smoke as she talks, and then walks around to the other side of the bus.

Laird chooses a cigarette for himself, holds it up to appraise as though it's an expensive cigar, and then drops it unlit on the ground and destroys it with his Oxford. He hears the commotion in the basement, the sound of CPS and the church volunteers failing at getting the children to migrate to the bus. They're chanting again—"You're all going to hell! You're all going to Hell!"—and they've formed a circle around CPS and the church volunteers. Laird pretends not to notice when one of his team members signals frantically above the chaos for backup. He can't bring himself to call for backup because of principle. This is *his* project. Project Fumarase is his, and it will succeed.

He takes another cigarette from the case, lights it, holds his exhalation in his mouth and counts to ten before emitting a series of perfect blue smoke rings. He repeats this down to the filter and then flips open his cell phone. "Fullerton here. I need some backup . . . yes, transport is here, but I need some squad—loaded."

Everything has been distilled to this moment for Peggy. The noise outside the bathroom is rocking the walls, quaking the foundation. She has no sense of how long it's taken her to steady herself, to stop the gagging and spinning and heart palpitations. The girl has been silent all this time, and Peggy expects she will turn to find mother and son gone. Instead, the girl watches her levelly.

"I must go with them, but I would like you to help me feed Bailyn first."

Her edict makes Peggy shudder: how can so much composure exist in a person who has been denied the world? The girl's confidence wavers when she leans over to gather her son and the bodice of her dress falls to her waist. "I don't usually wear this. It fit me better before I was joined with Bridger." She balances her son precariously atop her palms once again. His pouchy lips smack and suck at the air. The girl's eyes open in wonderment, then horror, and she thrusts her baby at Peggy.

Peggy draws Bailyn to her collarbone and pats his back. His mouth roots along the neckline of her blouse. "What have they done to you?"

The girl's front is a labyrinth of scar tissue. The tissue is so thick in places it looks like objects have been tunneled underneath. A scar that

525

runs diagonally from her navel to under her left breast looks fresher than the others—a recent, sutured wound. The skin has barely fused together and appears crisp and faintly blue, though it's difficult to tell under the Goth light. But the swelling is a definite sign of infection. On the girl's right side, in the spot where a nipple should be, is an older wound—a hole with an inch of tube sticking out of it. Yellowish fluid, Bailyn's overdue meal, oozes from the tube.

"You poor goddamn thing." Peggy lifts Bailyn higher on her shoulder and embraces the girl.

Outside the bathroom, Laird cracks his authority like a bullwhip, but the project will ultimately register as a failure. He knows it and has already begun to make everyone pay. Peggy hears it as the children are rounded up with police batons. The frenzy is reaching into the bathroom, and she knows time is up. They have run out of time—the girl, Bailyn, herself. She has accomplished nothing: the baby is unfed; the girl has made no confession.

"I want to help you," she speaks into the top of the girl's head. "I wish I could help you." She teases a knot from the girl's long braid, tightens her arms around the bare torso and rocks back and forth, side to side; the girl hiccups then begins to rock with her.

"Do you know what Bridger told me, the day Bailyn was born?"

Her scent, under that of unwash, is of limes. Bright green limes, full and healthy, and Peggy entertains a desperate fantasy. She imagines the girl standing beside her at the kitchen counter while she explains how limes can flavor almost any meal in the most delightful way. *You can marinate fish in lime juice, squeeze some on a bowl of white jasmine rice, or—now don't tell Him I said this!—drop a wedge into your vodka on a hot summer day.* "What, sweetheart? What did He tell you the day Bailyn was born?"

The girl reaches up with both hands to cradle Bailyn's head. " 'Kara-leen,' he said to me, 'as your Father, I will always protect you as long as you lie with me and pray every night. They won't treat you nice out there because you are special. You are on this Earth for bigger reasons.' "

Karaleen pulls away and takes her son; her movements are soft, swift, confident. Bailyn squawks loudly and gazes up at his mother with a tiny baby smile. Peggy nods, agrees to something she can no longer find a reason to contest, and gives Karaleen space—it's the only thing she can give.

"Maybe you are special," Karaleen says. "It was nice to know you."

She waits for Peggy to open the door, even though it was never locked, then breathes in the chaos before her and hugs Bailyn to her chest. Her group is loading the bus, and she will follow. Peggy stays behind and counts the number of scars on Karaleen's back, guesses how old they are, the reason for each one. She watches Laird's frustration escalate as he screams into his headset at her, and she feels relief at no longer hearing his voice.

Nominated by Fred Leebron

THE TRUE SEER HEARS

by BARBARA HURD

from THE FOURTH RIVER

Most of the ninety thousand species of insects on this planet use sound to court and to warn. The horned passalus, a kind of beetle, rubs one of its legs against a textured part of its own abdomen. Picture your torso as a washboard you can strum with your knees so adroitly that you end up not with cramping back muscles or whatever other damage such contortions might cause us, but with the music of seventeen different sounds floating through the evening air. Or under the water. That's the setting for an arthropod the size of paper clip whose mating call rivals the decibel level of motorcycles. Water must muffle the female's sound receptors. Or maybe she forgives the noise of his antics for the chance to mate with a bug whose gestures she can't resist. How many females, after all, wouldn't sidle up to a male floating across the pond with his right paramere's *pars stridens*—something like a penis with a hand— stroking his own abdomen?

Insects outnumber humans by two hundred million to one. Most of them hear, most of them make noise—clicking grasshoppers, stridulating dung beetles, head-banging termites, fruitflies who flirt by waving one wing, crickets who rub their legs together and un-silence the night. They reproduce prodigiously, millions of them cranking out two or three, or up to twenty-five generations a year, and except for the usual crickets and cicadas, most of them do it out of audible reach of the likes of me, who rose early this morning to sit with my granddaughter Samantha on a downed hemlock at the overlap of forest and field and test the truth of a poem I loved many years ago. *You will never be alone*, William Stafford wrote, *you hear so deep / a sound when autumn comes*. Autumn—with its sounds of coherence?—has clearly come to Appalachia—the hills are yellow and bronze. Except for a woolly bear caterpillar inching across the log by Samantha's leg, we're by ourselves in this pre-dawn darkness. She's poking her fingers in the dirt. I'm listening. Overhead, the stars are silent. Across the valley nothing moves. I don't hear a thing.

In the fable that opens Rachel Carson's *Silent Spring*, what's been silenced are song birds, poultry flocks, honeybees, fruit, fish, voices—human and otherwise. Vitality, in other words, has been leached from the land. It's a fable that warns about the dangers of pesticides, a warning so well heeded for a while that it launched, as we know, the modern environmental movement. As a little girl traipsing through the woods around her Pennsylvania home, Carson had not only seen but listened to a world full of the sounds of small creatures, listened so carefully she knew herself as part of that world, a sneezing, breathing, sighing, humming human being, a body, even when language-less, alive among the small splashes of river pools and fox yips in wooded hills. When those sounds were poisoned to silence, she heard that, too. Dying of breast cancer while the pesticide industry unleashed a well-financed and vicious assault against her, Carson wrote this near the end of her life: "I never hear these [bird] calls without a wave of . . . many emotions—a sense of lonely distances, a compassionate awareness of small lives controlled by forces beyond volition or denial, a surging wonder at the sure instinct for route and direction that so far has baffled human efforts to explain it."

Nose-deep in insect books for the past few weeks, I've been reading about bugs' ears. This woolly bear caterpillar next to us on the log, for instance, has none. No amount of my shouting or singing or reciting poems would make it turn its charred-looking head. But if Samantha stood up and stomped on this log we're sharing—as I worry she's about to do—, hundreds of the brown and copper hairs—setae—on its bristly body would act like tuning forks. Set in motion by the sound waves exploding from her foot, the ruffling tufts would translate as danger. The woolly bear would curl into a tight ball, wait out the storm like a furry nugget of amber.

Peril averted, it will spend this part of its life crawling silently over the ground, munching what it can, surviving the winter coiled under bark or log or rock. There, its heart will stop beating. As temperatures drop, its guts will freeze, then its blood, then the rest of its body. Its tissues soaked with a cryoprotectorant, the frigid body will know nothing of cold snaps or January thaws, the blizzard we're likely to get in March. It will weather the winter in icy motionlessness.

Read almost any of the major creation myths—Judaic, Christian, Islamic, Maori—and see what precedes the beginning: Cold, dark voids, motionless calm, black boundless vacancy, interminable stillness, perhaps what this woolly bear will feel in a few weeks. See, too, that Genesis, for example, means rupturing that stillness with the Word. From there, it's a free-for-all of noisy creation: ripened fruit drops, wings flap, beasts multiply. The whole shebang unleashed, the world becomes a place of niches and noise, teeming profligacy and a million tongues, the origin of both blather and song. From then on, sustained silences—personal, ecological, political—have worried some of us: do they precede some kind of creative explosion or do they signal yet another kind of death?

They do neither, of course, for those who haven't listened. There is, in fact, no such thing as silence—ominous or rewarding—to those who've never heard the sounds that surround them. Rachel Carson not only taught us to pay attention but to distinguish between blather and song, and between the quiet of mornings like this one and that other quiet, which means something vital has vanished. The quality of her listening has also trained me to hear both large and small losses. Remembering The Lettermen can turn me, a middle-aged woman, into a teeny bopper at a make-out party in George Toder's basement. Some Saturday mornings, listening for the routine phone call my mother will never make to me again, I'm forty, thirty-five, twenty-two, in need of her advice, even if I'm not.

Because of Rachel Carson, I think I'm learning how to listen stereophonically. At a certain point in one's life, the mind isn't really a blank slate; it has its positions and predispositions. But she has taught me to ready myself, anticipate, somewhat unfocused, turning this way and that. Grateful for ears on both sides of the head, I try to collect what's out here by listening for what isn't.

If Carson had not sounded the alarm fifty years ago, the silence of this early autumn dawn might be disturbing. I might be thinking about Stafford's poem while overhead the crushed confetti of DDT-thinned eggshells litters the nests and underfoot earthworms move the poisoned dirt in and out of their bodies, make themselves plump targets for doomed robins, while nearby a barred owl (I've heard it hundreds of times: *who cooks for you? who cooks for you?*) twitches on the forest floor. The fields and woods might be as she described: blighted, silent, withered and fruitless, without birdsong, chipmunk chatter, cricket calls. My listening would be full of worry and lament.

Instead, these mountains are, for now, reasonably robust. There's a moratorium on fracking; healthy trout in the nearby Savage River; at least a few wetlands preserved. I'm listening for what's underfoot at this moment, what's in the air, for any of the lip-smacking, tongue-hissing, panted-breath sounds of evolution and adaptation that have landed us here, two humans on a log, watching this earless woolly bear go about its daily rounds in the early dawn while overhead, a bat swoops among tree tops.

Seventy to eighty percent of the creatures alive out here are insects. Though most of them stake their ability to eat, survive, and mate on their ability to hear, none of them have ears like ours—sound-trapping projections on both sides of our heads. In fact, so separately have we developed from them, their ears—evolutionarily speaking—are not even related to ours. Remember the tuning fork setae of this woolly bear that are not vibrating at the moment because Samantha's not stomping her foot? They are its "ears." Hinged at their base to the caterpillar's cuticle, they respond to sound waves, especially from the rear, especially as a bat, sonar blipping, closes in with open mouth.

Other insects sport their hearing organs wherever they can—on the tips of their antennae, inside their mouths, on their knee caps or chest, behind their heads. Those "ears" take the forms of sound-sensitive drums made up of levers and pistons, sensitive membranes and tiny cavities of air. The fruit fly has a feathery wand; the cockroach, a set of bristles. The male mosquito, a complicated system of lever and shaft on his head. If he's awake now in this pre-dawn light, he's likely listening for the low frequency sounds a female emits via wing beat. When his tiny hairs begin to quiver—i.e. when he hears her with his body— he'll lift his wings and fly toward her, the vibrations on his head triggering him to seize her and clasp.

Between Samantha and me, the woolly bear caterpillar has turned north on the log and begun to inch toward my thumb. If it survives the winter and spins its pupae next spring, it will emerge as a moth with newly-grown tympanic membranes on either side of its head, which is not much bigger than a big grain of sand. Then the moth and the bat, now circling overhead, will listen hard for one other. If the moth, flitting from tree to tree, detects the oncoming echolocating cries of its number one predator, it will, in midair, activate its tymbal, the drum-like structure stretched over a small cavity on its chest, emitting its own rhythmic pulse. The bat, aimed for a direct hit, will be thrown off course. Unable to find its prey in the dark, it will continue its high-pitched cries, flying erratically in search of the moth, which, also flying erratically, will continue to pulse its tymbals—jamming the bat's radar—until the bat gives up and heads elsewhere. The moth, of course, isn't thinking about jamming frequencies or ultrasonic clicks. In fact, so reflexive is its defensive pulsing that its body will continue to emit the pulse for a good three hours after that tiny head has been severed in a lab.

Scientists love this stuff. So do I. Imagine devoting your life to listening to what can't easily be heard. Researchers have, in fact, filled millions of pages and thousands of websites with studies of every part of insects' body structure and functions, including auditory. They've dribbled water on insect "ears," dolloped them with shellac and flour, smeared them with Vaseline, corralled the bugs in boxes with recordings of crows, plucked the hairs off their backs, serenaded their lab cages, barraged them with low frequency tones. Trying to discover hearing thresholds, impairments, purposes, they arm themselves with tiny weight scales, electron microscopes and sophisticated amplifiers, recording the hisses of Madagascar cockroaches and the squeaks of Death's-head hawkmoths.

Sitting here on this silent autumn morning, waiting for the sun, we, of course, can hear no such commotion. Which is, in many ways, a blessing. Who could bear that kind of cacophony? But to ignore what we cannot hear may be worse. It's what Carson railed against: the silence that's born of hubris.

I see now I must listen not so much with lament or anticipation but with a better sense of limitations. Though I close my eyes and concentrate, the tympanic membranes inside my immovable, flat-against-my head-ears aren't dainty enough to pick up the zillions of sound waves I know are, at this very moment, pulsing across the field, through the trees, along this log where the woolly bear has turned again and headed away from my thumb. We sit here, as if deaf, as if we've been booted from the world of hearing, backed into a soundproof room in which the only noise comes from us—the scrape of my pants on the bark and the occasional sniffle from Samantha's nose.

Carson's job was to anticipate the silence that could follow damage—to eggs in nests, reproductive capabilities, liver functions, small lungs, nervous systems, and children's brains. She was a seer who, armed with careful research, heard her way into the future. When she published *Silent Spring* many dismissed it as the work of a hysterical woman. Unable—or unwilling—to distinguish between the scientific basis of her passion and the outcries of apocalyptic kooks who claim the world will end next week, critics—many of them allied with chemical industries—carped for decades. Some continue even today. The silent spring she warned about was averted only because wiser minds prevailed, minds informed by the accuracy of her work.

Can we simultaneously hear what's not yet come, what's here, and what's gone? Polyphonic silences, like polyphonic music, demand deep listening. Such listeners historically have been called seers, or fools—the difference is sometimes very slight. Is a fool someone whose listening has not yet led to truths? Or someone who hears sounds that do not and never have existed, nor ever will? And can one hear too much? Perhaps to truly hear the world requires both heightened sensitivity and a fair amount of filtering and skepticism. Balance, in other words.

Given the physical limits of my paltry hearing, the least I can do is to make a stab at knowing what I don't know, to risk being a fool, to sit here in this early morning silence with my granddaughter and realize that across the fields and up in the woods, even here on this log, hundreds of small creatures are vibrating their vocal chords, smashing their wings, strumming their abdomens, filling their lungs with pre-song, drumming their tymbals, all their zillions of attempts to survive, to eat, to mate—and we can hear none of it. Meanwhile, the woolly bear has silently rounded the log, begun to descend the opposite side.

Perhaps what Stafford means after all is not that we can literally "hear so deep/a sound when autumn comes" but that if we can imagine or imagine remembering that sound—*all* those sounds—maybe then "the whole wide world pours down." Or at least the whole wide world might inch a little closer, click by strum by belly-scraping song. And if it doesn't, maybe then we'll know, as Rachel Carson certainly did, which silences prevent that pouring down, which ones, in other words, mean we could be increasingly alone.

Nominated by Jack Driscoll, David Jauss, BJ Ward

NIGHT MOVERS

fiction by PERRY JANES

from GLIMMER TRAIN STORIES

The month my stepbrother Tony died in a ball of gas-lit flame, the Sarychev Peak volcano erupted in Russia and changed the Michigan sunset. It was all over the news: particles blown into the atmosphere and diffusing across the continents. The way they interfered with the refraction of light over the Mississippi, the Chattanooga, the Detroit River. It turned the sky true lavender, no pinks or reds or blues.

I watched the sunset spread and dim from the back patio of a poorly kept yard, corralled by a privacy fence the way a length of cord restrains a crowd: tightly fit, grass busting from the earth, limbs sprawling from stooped trees to stretch over the perimeter. I was only just waking as the sun was setting, readying myself for another long shift through the night. The son of an insomniac, sleeping through the day was never a problem for me. My brother Tony and I, when we were young, spent the weekends with our dad, where we became nocturnal: sleeping until ten p.m., eating breakfast at all-night diners, playing hide-and-seek while the TV's midnight infomercials droned through the walls. Now, years later, the routine comes as easy as a handshake. Shower, stretch, eat my eggs, and sit out back while drinking my coffee and watching the sky go dark.

The way I saw it, I opened each night with a show of what the day had offered. Red meant the day had been a mild one. Orange, the city had run itself hot, and overflowed. Those stripey motherfuckers that looked like a stack of multicolored pancakes, filled with pinks and all the rest, meant the day had been a tired one.

But that lavender had me stumped. Purple trawled along the sky

534

combing out every shade of blue. And because I couldn't predict for myself what the day had been like, what it had brought, I couldn't safely say what the night had in store for me either.

Which was a dumb conclusion for me to reach, since some things in this world are as consistent as earthworms in the rain. Tye was one such consistency. I had only just pulled into the mansion's gravel-paved parking lot in the company vehicle when he leaned out the side of a duplicate white moving van and yelled, "You're a whole five minutes late."

I steeled myself in the car, set my jaw and opened the door.

"Don't sweat it, Tye. I'll work extra hard to make up for it," I said. Outside the van now, he smirked as he edged his slight hands into a pair of black, fingerless gloves.

"I know you will. That's why I like you, Zeke. It's in you—the plow horse. This city could use more like you." His voice, which had been smoother when I met him, now sounded like a wood chipper: layered and grinding.

Each night Tye's voice buzzed in my ears like a bad idea, nagging and repeating the same talking points. Which is not to say that he was wrong. But at a certain point a man can be too right, too caught in how wrong the rest of us are to see his own mistakes. Tye was part of a new migration of suburbanites to Detroit, enamored with the idea of *rebuilding what was left behind.* Born and bred an intellectual, he'd graduated college and fled as far from his own roots as possible: construction, painter, mover. He'd eased his way into the city until, eventually, it defined him. That was Tye. Idealist. Bulldog. Part colleague, part friend.

Tye's keyring was stuffed with enough brass that I thought someone might leap from the shadows and rob him for it, but the lot was quiet while he fumbled for a key at the mansion's back door. Above us chimneys spun up and away with a memory of former majesty, but were now canted at an angle, blown sideways by wind and wear. The brick looked to be running the way ink does in the rain. The steps, even, scuffed with rubber that looked like scribbles.

Tye and I were night movers, grunts who moved furniture and boxes across empty street-lit highways for clients in a rush to leave the city. I was surprised, after taking the job, at the demand for work like ours: military families with short-notice transfers; the lucky few to land well-paying jobs in the northern suburbs; those unfortunate enough to run afoul of local hoods and dealers. By and large, though, our clients were the tough-as-nails folk who had stubbornly refused to flee until absolutely necessary. Most were evicted, families who spent their ninety-days' notice warring with the courts to save their homes until, on night eighty-nine, they hired us to get them out. Some were simply worn down, overcome with grief or shame as the city sucked still more bodies into its earth. I liked to imagine the time-lapse photo of Detroit from overhead; that it looked like fireworks maybe, filled with taillights blurring as they streamed from the city, burning embers that landed across the country, where they slowly cooled to ash.

There were others, though, who demanded we didn't ask questions about the job. Landlords who had us strip homes clean and leave what we gathered at the dump. Dealers who ducked surveillance cops by hiring us to move their product. Once, Tye and I emptied a garage filled with double-sealed barrels and left them sitting in the woods. Drugs, I figured. We never met the clients. Just cashed our checks each morning before returning home to sleep. The job didn't pay well, and there were days I wondered why I didn't quit. Whenever I asked myself this question, though, I knew that Tye and I had found work like this for reasons other than money.

We were a two-man operation. Tye started the business as a one-man startup, but when I responded to his *Help Wanted* ad in the paper, I knew I had the job if I wanted it. And what logo do you think Tye had painted on the side of our moving vans, printed on the backs of our jackets? Fucking raccoons, the universal symbol for burglars. Call it portent, then, but it wasn't just once we were mistaken for thieves. Got to the point we had a routine for run-ins with the law: hands in the air, calmly explain, "We're movers. I have papers, in my coat. No, I won't reach for them. Pull them out yourself." This, of course, wound up with us on the ground in cuffs until the cops slipped two shaky fingers inside our jackets to pull out our paperwork. Then followed the usual apologies, the gruff, *Just doing our job.*

Tye and I tried to stay small-scale, moving apartments or flats or duplexes if we had to. But when we stepped inside that mansion's mudroom, I could tell we'd set ourselves a challenge. "Haven't had to move a place like this one," I said, climbing what I was sure had been a servants' staircase to and from the kitchen. I'd seen places like this in the suburbs but hadn't ever been inside one. It wasn't the extravagance that got me, but the size. I'd been the chore-runt as a kid, and standing in that hallway, I tried to imagine how long it would take to vacuum a house that big.

The living room yawned at our approach: gold trim along the ceiling like yellowed teeth, blood-red runner down its middle like a tongue. All of it as seamless and elastic as a piece of modern art. Even the couch cushions were unstitched in the front, their cotton-fluff insides splayed across the floor, mist.

Old news. I had seen this kind of blight before. But Tye—he lived for it. He was enamored with the absence of abandoned houses, factories, warehouses. Absence, not emptiness. People get that wrong all the time. You can find emptiness in the night sky in northern Michigan staring at the constellations. Emptiness is a vacuum; absence is a memory. Its presence crowded the rooms we worked in night after night. Which was, I knew, why Tye had taken the job. But I also knew what all he'd given up for it. The normalcy of a relationship, a home, the daytime. To him, the city's hollow spaces existed to be filled with his imagination.

To me? I'd made it through high school. I'd survived my first few years of adulthood. I had a paying job. Right then, that felt like enough.

"Get a load of this place," he said.

"That's exactly what this place is going to be—a fucking load," I replied.

Tye walked a circuit of the room. Ran his hands over the folded afghan on the easy chair; examined an empty vase on the mantel; blew coal dust across the floorboards with an old, accordion bellows. Then, as he turned the corner, a squeak. He kicked a dog's chew toy into a pool of light coming through a crack in the boarded-up windows.

"Look at this," he said.

Bending over, he squeezed the toy, bad tempered. "Jesse used to have a squeaky just like this," he said, holding its green, dinosaur body up to the light. "She loved it, tossed it all over the room before I fed her. You know a town's really going to shit when . . .," but he trailed off. "You know I went back to that alley last week? Know what I found? A rifle casing, of all things. I mean—a rifle?"

Ever since Tye's dog Jesse died, Tye took her ashes with him everywhere. They rode in the passenger seat of the van, tucked tight into his pack. When Jesse had been alive, that dog had gone everywhere with him, too. She romped around the houses while we sweated out to nothing, running under our feet at the worst possible moments. Once, while leaping up the steps, Jesse had taken Tye's legs right out from under him. Tye's head cracked on the stairwell railing like an electric trans-former going down. But up he got. I thought at first that he might kick her—or yell, at least—but he went right back to work as though the whole thing hadn't happened.

It broke him when Jesse died. As Tye told the story, it went down during the daytime hours. He had worked well into the morning and left the side door open before crashing into bed. While he was asleep, Jesse wandered outside and into the city, sniffing her way down alleys near the house. If it had happened differently, Jesse would have come back, of course. Tye was adamant about that. But when a cold draft woke him in his bed, the house was empty.

Tye called in sick and took to the roads, cruising the nearby streets yelling Jesse's name. Didn't she always come when called? Turned out Jesse hadn't wandered far. Tye, sweeping his flashlight down a back street two blocks away, found the body on the pavement. Shot.

I had spent whole nights with Tye rehashing this moment, imagining how he must have felt pulling Jesse from the dried blood, tufts of fur left stuck to the alley pavement. But right then I didn't have the pa-tience, wanted him to keep that shit to himself. What was his dog to my brother?

The toy in Tye's hand gave a feeble whine, its rubber body punctured and deflated. He stooped back toward the ground and left it gently at his feet. I looked around the room for a change of subject.

"How are we s'posed to move all this shit in time?" I asked.

"Same way we move everything else," he said. "Back breaking, ball busting, and bitching."

Tye and I spent the early hours of each night working in complete silence. No music, no conversation. Just shuffles and grunts. We moved the big stuff first—sofas, bed frames, pianos—and the exertion it took just persuading our muscles to spring load, fire up, and cool down kept us stony quiet.

Two and a half hours in and we'd managed to maneuver most of the heavy objects inside the vans, puzzle-pieced together in lopsided pat-terns that maximized our space. Once the heavy lifting was behind us, we split up. Wandered into dark, emptied corridors of the house. Work-ing alongside another man—tearing at our muscles, pulling faces to keep from giving in—made us feel vulnerable. Not unlike the feeling you get when, after lying in bed with a woman, you throw back the sheets and come back to yourself. Stupid, to feel that way with another man. So we receded into the dark corners of different rooms to compose ourselves, returning moments later to exchange head nods or elbow bumps.

It didn't click with me how large the house really was until, halfway down a dark offshoot of the living room, I came upon a set of double doors with the words *East Wing* engraved on its woodwork. The letters' deep grooves still had shreds of gold foil in the bottom-most curves, scraps that hadn't completely peeled away.

I pressed open the doors. On the other side: three rooms. Three doors, all ajar. The room immediately to my left was an old, egg-shaped conservatory. Its glass-paneled ceiling bent fluidly into window walls. Outside, a flickering street lamp stuttered in the room like a strobe light.

Behind the second door was a bedroom. Had everything inside it except for a bed: dresser with the drawers left open, photos on the wall, boyish wallpaper patterned with basketballs and hoops. I grew up in rooms like that. When we were young, Tony, my friends, and I spent damn near every day after school rotating from house to house, chilling out on one another's floor and watching muted pornos. Flicks handed down to us from older cousins who had moved on to the real deal. Those shows taught us how to talk. "Look at that pussy!" we'd whisper, but it took us years to grow into those words.

They're all I remember: Jamaal, my neighbor; Mark, my oldest friend. I don't see them any longer. I think of them as my boys on the other side. They live lives parallel to mine, now. No longer intersecting. They'd known Tony from our childhood when, smaller and younger than the rest of us, he'd tag along pretending to be streetwise. When he died, I hadn't answered their calls. Taking a job working nights was a choice. It took the teeth out of their arguments. *You don't ever hang with us no more.*

I hate nostalgia. I continued on.

I was beginning to think that, despite the house's size, there wasn't anything more interesting than dust between its walls when I approached the third door. Big, dadoed with a tarnished silver panel in its center, it was twice the size of the other doors, and heavy. Swung only a couple inches when I kicked it, so I leaned a shoulder against its weight and muscled my way inside.

I allowed myself one ridiculous thought: that I had just walked into the belly of a beached submarine. I stood on the topmost step of a stout stairwell that led to the bottom of a room big enough to house a space missile.

Of course. It would be the biggest, scariest motherfucking doorway that housed a room like this. Sometimes the real world lacks serious originality. And then I spotted it, a carved out shadow dead ahead.

"Ay! Yo! Tye!" I yelled. "Tye!"

I heard him huffing down the hall, then stop short. "Where the hell are you?" he yelled.

"Big imposing son of a bitch, third door down," I called back. "Check this out."

There was a creak behind me, Tye standing at my shoulder.

A beat.

"I hope they don't expect us to move that thing," he said.

In the center of the room, standing upright but tipped sideways against the wall, was a giant school bell. Brass body the size of a boat. Knotted tongue lolling dumbly on the floor. It rose from a mess of furniture littered wall to wall, much of it tipped sideways or stacked end on end.

The room looked to be an old wine cellar that, during renovations on the house, had been sealed off from its other half. To my left just past the stairwell, a partition of poorly spackled plaster—distinctly newer and less ornate than the rustic brickwork of the other three walls—was warping in the middle. All throughout the room, metal pillars had been bolted to the ceiling for foundational support. And it wasn't hard to guess why. A thin film of water rippled strangely along the floor, leaked from some unseen network of cracks in the masonry. White powder from the plaster had dusted on its surface, made the water look eerily concrete, some pulsing ground that lapped at the bell's metal rim and left it stained with wavebands.

I knew bells like that, had gone to an antique but beat-up school in Detroit where they hung from a low-slung belfry overhead. Tony and I, we used to hang out in that tower after school, dangling our feet over the four-floor drop until we heard Mark's car honking from the street.

Tye shifted weight behind me, eager to get a closer look. "What is this place?" he asked.

"Hell if I know," I said. Which was just about the truth. I had learned long ago that the world distinguishes itself by detail. I told myself to take a closer look. A closer look at that bell and I could get rid of the familiar shakes creeping up my hands.

I tested the stairwell first before descending. With the state the place was in, I wasn't taking anything on faith. "Move it," Tye said. "I want to see what we're dealing with here." But I kept moving slowly. The only light in the room passed through a series of window wells opposite where I stood. What little light that made it in was streetlight blue.

When I reached the bottom of the stairwell, the floor was spongy, moss-like, as ocean bottom as the murky light suggested. Water came up just past the soles of my shoes. I could already feel my socks squelch as I walked.

"This is really something," I said. I knew because Tye had shut right up. Didn't make a sound. Now that was something.

I wound around the room's little hills of junk toward the bell. Up close, I ran a thumb over the chipped surface, where deep grooves in its exterior smoothed down to rounded hills. Tipped the way it was, I ducked beneath its bottom rim.

The bell's interior was a worn gray color with two polished brass circles on either side where the tongue's knot had rubbed the metal clean. Light seemed, impossibly, to fill the space with a dull glow that slapped flatly against the rounded walls. Looking down, I saw a web of picture frames carried and trapped beneath the bell by some unseen tide or angle in the floor. Their glass surfaces caught the light outside and sent it reflecting up.

I leaned down and grabbed a frame knocking against my ankle.

There was always at least one photo left behind, usually some kind of family portrait, kids and their parents gumming smiles at the lens. These pictures were comforting. I looked at the flash-washed faces and told myself I knew exactly who they were, where they'd gone, why they'd left. And each and every night I held these stories close to my chest the way one holds a lie: wide eyed, blood sore, afraid of the slip that loses you for good.

It wasn't hard to see the stories in those frames. A boy on a tenement roof, sprinkler running on the tarmac, goggles hiding his eyes from view; a willowy girl, brightly colored hair clips hanging from her braids; a woman, the mother, her black hair like a voice from the radio. Her hair was freckled the way most faces are, with dusty bits of golden blond as stark as flecks of paint. Her eyes wavered between squinty and knowingly round, and I could imagine the way she flickered her lids for the picture.

I used to be able to look at Tony this way. No photographs, I'm talking real life. He could sit across the dining room table from me and I would pick apart the coloration on the outsides of his lips, knew he'd been chewing them, something on his mind. I pried too much, pressed too hard. There was a little of my mother in me, and hadn't I rebelled as well?

Floating the frame back into the water, I ran a hand along the bell's flaking metal dome. Its smoothness uninterrupted except for the lightest catch on my callus. I paused. I could feel grooves on my palm, old scratches. I lifted my hand. There in front of me were the initials *T.U.V.* Tony's initials: Tony Underwood Victors. He used to scratch them into everything: desks, walls, windows. He had hated his name, used to laugh that our dad *didn't know nothing but the alphabet*. I could remember him scraping them inside our school's bell.

The nostalgia was rushing back. How Jamaal had left for Cleveland— *Getting the fuck out*, as he put it, but who the hell escapes Detroit to go to Cleveland?—and Mark had gone upstate for college, leaving Tony and me alone. Three years younger than the rest of us, Tony wasn't home free yet. Hadn't made it out of high school.

Maybe it was in his blood to finally push against me, against how I had become more like a parent that last year than a brother. Without my friends and me to hang with, he hunted for a substitute, someone who, if not older, carried equal weight with the boys his age. A threat.

Had Mark, Jamaal, and I been that mean? Had we scared the younger boys in class? We'd fronted, sure, to keep the bangers off our backs, but no one truly hard stayed in school. I'd assumed Tony understood that.

He dropped out with only weeks left until graduation. Which is when we almost killed each other.

I got the call, was the only one who ever answered the phone in our house, unafraid of bill collectors. "With whom am I speaking?" the voice had said.

"Ezekiel," I replied, using my full name.

"Ah, Zeke," the voice said then, and I recognized the weary tones of my school principal, his city accent slipping beneath the affected proper English. "It's Tony," he said. "Hasn't shown for three days straight. Is he sick?"

The line was quiet, not even static from the receiver. "Sick. Yeah," I said.

"One more day and he flunks. Every class."

"Tomorrow," I said. "I'll get him there tomorrow."

I knew who Tony had latched on to, a group of boys whose jeans, when they stood from chairs, smelled not so faintly of gunpowder.

No car to speak of, not then, I walked two miles to their hangout, a townhouse re-wired with pirated gas from the place next door and kicking music like a bass drum. When I arrived, there was a boy leaning on the stoop I recognized from school, two years younger. His lazy stare was unsteady as he sized me up, slipping from my face to fists to jeans, as though unable to catch hold. "Yeah, we're holding," he said, as though I were a junkie.

I could have punched him right then. Fuck his guns, his boys eyeing us from the window. I wanted to tear his teeth out with my fingers.

I let it slide and replied in even tones, "I'm here for Tony."

"You're, here," he said, rocking each word on his tongue, "for, Tony?" He stood, then, got right in my face. He was tall, matched me eye to eye, shoulder to shoulder. His arms were lined with sinew like the grooves cut in highways. "Who the fuck are you?"

"Tony!" I yelled past him. The boy didn't take his eyes off me. There were footsteps inside, laughter as a chair clattered to the floor. Then, in the doorway, Tony. I could see the surprise register in his eyes, in how his shoulders dropped the way they used to when, as a boy, he weathered Dad's tirades, those late-night shouting fits that came after days of sleeplessness.

"What are you doing here, Zeke?"

"We need to talk," I said.

Maybe it was the anger in my voice, still chest to chest with the boy in front of me, or maybe it was the leering faces in the window, but I watched his shoulders swell as he crossed his arms and said, "So—talk."

"Your principal called." Well, that was the wrong thing to say. Shoulders bobbed with laughter all around me. Heads cocked to the side in a *who-the-hell-do-you-think-we-are?* stare.

I couldn't believe it. These kids had me feeling like a house cat. I clenched my fists as Tony came down the steps, shrugged past his boy who had me blocked, got so close to my face I could feel the breath from his nose on my chin. "So?"

I swung.

I was never a tough guy—fact. But people act like putting hands to another man is difficult to do. In reality, it's just like throwing yourself into the surf. The cold water hits you in places so personal you withdraw at first. But once you grow accustomed to its temperature you reach even beyond your limbs. You are lifted and crushed, in turns, by

543

the pitching of the moment, brought back to your body only when the skin on your knees and knuckles begins to peel.

There was a loud gong of vibrating metal. Shaken, I covered my ears, felt for the gap, and ducked back out. Stepping into the room, I saw Tye kick a steel-toed shoe against the brass that gave a tinny ring, far quieter than the noise inside it.

"How did they ever get this thing in here?" Tye asked. "It's huge."

That one had me stumped. I cast my eyes around the room, from the shallow basement windows to the double doors we'd come in from. It was as though the bell had always been there. All I could think of was the wall behind us, its papery plaster surface the only thing out of place in the house's architecture.

"You think it'll fit?" Tye asked, staring at the doors we had come in from.

"There's no way," I replied.

"No way to know until we try."

I gave him a look that could bleach car paint. "Call the owners," I said. "Ten bucks says we leave it here."

"They didn't give me any contact information," he said. "Just a check, a key, and instructions."

"It stays, then," I said. "Look at this stuff." I kicked a waterlogged journal floating at my ankles. "I wonder if they even meant for us to find it."

The room felt even larger now, cavernous, and just a fraction of the house. It moaned with its own throaty growl. Then I realized that the bell was humming. A note so low it almost went unnoticed. The ringing peaked and quieted like my echo talking back.

"Fuck that," Tye said. "I've never come up against a thing I couldn't move."

I didn't know how the bell had gotten there. Sold for school revenue, maybe, or salvaged from renovations. The homeowners had been pack rats, citizens who collected debris from abandoned buildings, who fancied themselves preservationists. Either way, I didn't want to move that bell, it was sealed inside. I liked it that way.

But Tye wouldn't hear it. Throwing his arms out like a boxer stretching before a spar, he took up position on the other side of the bell's bottom rim, where it leaned sideways and met the floor. I slipped my

544

hands inside a pair of padded leather gloves and hooked my hands beneath the sharp brass lip.

I gave it everything I had, and wouldn't you know? It lifted—just—and as it did, the frames from underneath began to fan out on the water. More, even, than I had thought. They floated like vessels filled with pools all their own that caught the light and held it.

After the fight with Tony I'd turned over every frame in the house that held his picture, but even months after the two of us fell out, the dreams just wouldn't stop. I'd fall asleep and imagine the many ways his body could take the bullets: from behind, like a hand that reaches to grab you by the shoulder; in the chest, walking right into them; from above, spilled like nails from a roof.

The insomnia got worse. Couldn't hardly get out of bed until two in the afternoon—if that. For a while, my boy Mark suggested I *take something for it. Depression does just that*, he'd say, *keeps you down, in bed.* He was wrong, of course. Time had just turned over. Sleep at day, wake at night. But I could live like that. Nighttime, Tony's absence was logical. Everyone was asleep. Of course he wouldn't be around.

I had beaten Tony right in front of his boys who held on to their guns but refused to pull them, some code or rite of passage. I'd made it certain he wouldn't ever leave. At one point, my knuckles split his cheek and cracked the bone. I could hear it happen. When I stood upright, my left eye bleeding beneath the lid, I saw a tall boy in the doorway pull his knife. But just then, from the pavement, Tony waved his hand and said simply, "Nah." His cheek was split like a pair of lips. His knuckles were nearly skinned. I hadn't wanted to put him in the ground, but I'd damned near done it.

Turned out Tony wasn't dropped by gang members. He went out with a bang. The house, with gas lines jerry-rigged through the windows, blew itself all to hell. No details were salvaged from the wreck. They could have been smoking joints, could have been firing clips into the baseboard, could have just been cooking breakfast.

When I went by the house the day after the explosion, the street-corner lamppost was covered with stuffed animals, prayer tokens, photos framed in doilies. I stared closely at each picture, surprised to find I recognized each boy's older, meaner face hidden in his childhood photos. They didn't look any different than Tony had, young kids playing commandos on the playground or football in the street. I went home that night, carved an *RIP* from my favorite piece of driftwood,

and went back the next day to leave it at the shrine. But nearly every-
thing was gone, all the teddy bears ripped from their staples, just a flare
of fuzz left behind.

What kind of asshole steals stuffed animals from a street memorial?
Isn't that just like this piece of shit city I keep trying to defend? Steal
our boys and steal their memories, too?

In the mansion's cellar, with Tye still struggling to keep his balance,
it was all I could do to tear my eyes away from the photos as they floated
past. I could feel my muscles' pistons begin to misfire, the weight of
the bell cutting my finger pads, my shoulders shaking with effort. Tye's
grunts traveled through the metal's nerves to my fingers and I knew,
then, that he wouldn't give it up.

I did the only thing that made sense. I wound up, heaving sideways,
hoping to toss it over.

"Whoa whoa whoa!" Tye called as the bell began to tip.

I heard Tye drop the bell as it rolled, like a cup turned over, on its
rim. Its weight shifted away from me, then back, trying to find its bal-
ance.

I couldn't break Tony to himself. I'd only cut him open. But this bell,
I could take in my hands, could lean my weight against it, could break
it if I wanted.

I let go and kicked.

"Zeke!" Tye yelled and grabbed me by the shoulders.

I kicked again, again, found that both my feet were off the floor. I
felt my weight in Tye's arms, back pressed to his chest. I fought to get
free but Tye had always been the heavy lifter. The stronger I struggled,
the more resolute he became. It felt good being held like that. Con-
tained. Letting-rip.

My boot connected with the brass. Another groan. A creak.

Tye threw me like a medicine ball and jumped just clear of the metal
as it crashed. Didn't matter how soft the floor felt beneath our soles,
that bell made a noise like the city coming down.

Water splashed me head to foot. The liquid in my mouth was stale,
pasty. I could feel it sticking to my teeth. Waves rocked between the
walls and dislodged piles of rubble across the room. Their small splashes
were nearly drowned out by the bell's throaty hum. On its side, now, its
round mouth looked like a cave or tunnel in the room.

I stood, soaked and streaked with plaster. I looked at Tye and began
to feel embarrassed. I tried to catch his eye but could feel my voice
stuffed way far down, out of order. Tye didn't even glance at me. He

stood and walked to the bell that rocked on its side, all its shadows gone gray in the dim light. Like that, the bell didn't look to be much bigger than a man with his arms outstretched.

Tye bent, picked a piece of metal chipped away from the rusty rim. "Souvenir," he said. I met his eyes. Bumped his elbow.

The night was already winding its dark threads back around its spool as light busted through the basement windows, and I was reminded of Tony as a boy, stubbornly refusing sleep until the sun began to peak. In the cellar, Tye and I looked around the room, understanding that work would take us well into the late morning hours, maybe even afternoon. I didn't mind, though. It had been months since I'd been up past morning. Outside, the sunrise was a screen of purple being lifted in the sky. Somewhere in Russia the same shock of lavender slid away as the night began to dim. Tye and I rubbed the dirt from our knuckles, pressed our knuckles to our eyes, awake to endure the first bright pieces of the day.

Nominated by Timothy Hedges, Glimmer Train Stories

SPECIAL MENTION

(The editors also wish to mention the following important works published by small presses last year. Listings are in no particular order.)

FICTION

Isabelle Deconinck — Road Trip With A Dead Therapist (Five Points)
D.R. MacDonald — Blueberries (Epoch)
Kirstin Valdez Quade — The Manzanos (Narrative)
Tom Paine–Bagram (Glimmer Train Stories)
Stephen Dixon — Feel Good (Southern Review)
Jack Driscoll — The Alchemist's Apprentice — (Prairie Schooner)
Tony Eprile — City of Words (Agni)
Laird Hunt — Algeline (Ploughshares)
Jonathan Lee — Before The Bombing (Tin House)
Chantel Acevedo — Strange And Lovely (Ecotone)
Ben Hoffman — The Only Place the Blood Goes (Missouri Review)
Joy Williams — Revenant (Idaho Review)
Debbie Urbanski — Not Like What You Said (Alaska Quarterly Review)
Bret Anthony Johnston — Young Life (Southampton Review)
Jaquira Diaz — Ghosts (Kenyon Review)
Lilliam Rivera — Death Defiant Bomba (Bellevue Literary Review)
Gina Frangello — The Yuppie Threesome Next Door (Ploughshares)
Joyce Carol Oates — High-Crime Area (Boulevard)
Mary O'Connell — Limbo! Limbo! (Idaho Review)
Gary Gildner — Timmy Sheean Is A Prime Example (Southern Review)

Angelica Baker — The Feather Trick (One Teen Story)

Alexander Weinstein — The Cartographers (Chattahoochee Review)

Brenda Peynado — The History of Happiness (Cimarron Review)

Stephen O'Connor — Con (The Common)

Christy Jordan-Fenton — Ghost Dance (Water-Stone Review)

Reid Maruyama — Buzzard Lagoon (Berkeley Fiction Review)

Louise Erdrich — tinywriter (Brick)

Steven Swiryn — The Unicycle (Bellevue Literary Review)

Chika Unigwe — Happiness (Transistion)

Emma Smith-Stevens — An August In The Early 2000's (Wigleaf)

Ursula K. Le Guin — The Jackson Brothers (Catamaran)

Melissa Yancy — Dog Years (ZYZZYVA)

Willer de Oliveira — The Urologist (Chicago Review)

Jo Lloyd — My Bonny (Zoetrope)

Jaimy Gordon — Mysteries of Lisbon (Mississippi Review)

Regina Marler — Glendale Gumshoe and the CH*EAP VI*A*GRA (Cimarron Review)

Phil Sultz — Sauce (Doctor T.J. Eckleburg Review)

Isaac Blum — Cassie Two Kids (One Teen Story)

Aurelie Sheehan — The Three Graces (Southern Review)

Ann Pancake — Rockhounds (Agni)

Jamel Brinkley — Infinite Happiness (A Public Space)

Maria Kuznetosova — The Accident (Iowa Review)

Gretchen Van Wormer — Fake Barn Country (The Pinch)

Lauren Groff — Abundance (Ecotone / Lookout Books)

Jesse Goolsby — Sometimes Kids Bleed for No Reason (Redivider)

Katie Cortese — Welcome to Snow (Epiphany)

Lydia Davis — The Letter to the Foundation (Threepenny Review)

Andy Mozina — Martha and Her Dulcimer (River Styx)

Kent Nelson — Lucky (Sewanee Review)

Karl Taro Greenfeld — Zone of Mutuality (American Short Fiction)

John J. Clayton — The Old Gentleman (Sewanee Review)

Karen E. Bender — Candidate (Ecotone/Lookout Books)

David James Poissant — Zugzwang (Tweed's)

Monica McFawn — The Chautauqua Sessions (Missouri Review)

Pamela Painter — Look, See (Green Mountains Review)

Patrick Lawler — The Meaning of If (from *The Meaning of If*, Four Way Books)

Carmen Maria Machado — The Husband Stitch (Granta)

Richard Burgin — The Raided (Per Contra)

Ariel Dorfman — The Last Word (The Common)
Julie Diamond — Birds (Threepenny Review)
Arna Bontemps Hemenway — Helping (A Public Space)
Kelly Cherry — The Starveling (Blackbird)
Anna Vodicka — Sirens (Sweet)
Joan Wilking — Clutter (Elm Leaves Journal)
Linda McCullough Moore — On My Way Now (The Sun)
Melissa Yancy — Consider This Case (Missouri Review)
Kawai Strong Washburn — What The Ocean Eats (McSweeney's)
Ammi Keller — Isaac Cameron Hill (America Short Fiction)
Alyssa Knickerbocker — The Uncertain Future of the Body (Alaska
    Quarterly)
Maegen Poland — Spores (Pleiades)
Kate Petersen — Ice (Epoch)
Peter Gordon — The Water's Edge (Antioch Review)
Jane Gillette — The Trail of the Demon (Missouri Review)
James Yeh — Nice House, Nice Car, Nice Children, Nice Clothes (Noon)
Janet Kim Ha — The Box Where Songs Lived (Mississippi Review)
Kenneth Calhoun — Ultraviolet (Post Road)
LaShonda Katrice Barnett — Graf (Juked)
Cathy Adams — Asphalt Chiefs (Upstreet)
Rob McClure Smith — A Man At Banna Strand (J-Journal)

NONFICTION

Peggy Shinner — Berenice's Hair (Bomb)
Paul Zimmer — Secret Information (Georgia Review)
Brenda Miller — Spin Art (River Teeth)
D.L. Mayfield — The Rule of Life (Image)
Kate Washington — Abide With Me (Ninth Letter)
Jacob Mikanowski — Noma (The Point)
George Saunders — On Process (Kenyon Review)
Doug Crandell — The Last Harvest (The Sun)
Pearl Abraham — For the Sins We Have Committed Before You
    Through Hard-Heartness (Michigan Quarterly Review)
Kent Russell — Enforcers (n+1)
Jill Storey — A Clutch of Eggs (Gettysburg Review)
James Winter — A Very Small Frame (One Story)
Alison Hawthrone Deming — The Pony, the Pig, and the Horse (Ecotone)
Lee Martin — A Month of Sundays (Zone 3)

Jessamyn Hope — The Reverse (Prism)

Sarah de Leeuw — Soft Shouldered (Prism)

Barrett Swanson — This Swift and Violent Forgetting (Ninth Letter)

Robert S. Brunk — Selling Everything (Iowa Review)

Rachel Kaadzi Ghansah — We A Baddd People (Virginia Quarterly Review)

H.G. Carrillo — Splaining Yourself (Conjunctions)

Howard Tharsing — The Visible and the Invisible (Threepenny)

Mako Yoshikawa — The Veterans Project Number Two (Missouri Review)

J.B. McCray — Blue Magic (The Sun)

Joan Wickersham — An Inventory (One Story)

Patricia Smith — Holy War (Broad Street)

Richard E. Cytowic — Teaching Death (Southampton Review)

Yepoka Yeebo — The Bridge To Sodom and Gomorrah (Big Roundtable)

Heather Sellers — Breathless (Brevity)

B.J. Les — Dale Flynn's Blood (Broad Street)

David Harris-Gershon — Transformative Reconciliation (Tikkun)

Sylvia Bowersox — This War Can't Be All Bad (O-Dark-Thirty)

Zachary Lazar — We Forgive Those Who Trespass Against Us (Brick)

Dawn Davies — Confessions of A Stay At Home Mom (Brain, Child)

Eva Saulitis — Listening And Seeing With All That I Am (Catamaran)

Andrés Felipe Solano — The Nameless Saints (World Literature Today)

Frances De Pontes Peebles — The Crossing (Zoetrope)

Leonora Smith — Locate Mercy (4th Genre)

Eva Saulitis — Wild Darkness (Orion)

Carol Ann Davis — The One I Get and Other Artifacts (Georgia Review)

Kris Saknussemm — Listen To The Lizards (World Literature Today)

Thaddeus Gunn — Slapstick (Brevity)

Mark Strand — On Nothing (Salmagundi)

Kathleen Blackburn — Wing Trace (The Pinch)

Gordon Lish — Für Whom? (Antioch Review)

Robert Sullivan — Forest Farewell (Orion)

Robert Anthony Siegel —Gourmets (Tin House)

Tony Kushner — Eugene O'Neill: The Nature of Eloquence (Provincetown Arts)

Camille T. Dungy — Differentiation (Ecotone)

Kate Petersen — Ice (Epoch)

Ron Clinton Smith — A Pilgrimage to Dennis Hopper (River Teeth)

David Samuels — Justin Timberlake Has A Cold (n+1)

Mark Gustafson — Bringing Blood to Trakl's Ghost (Antioch Review)

Justin Cronin — My Daughter And God (Narrative)

Darcey Steinke — Frankenstein's Mother (Granta)

Larry I. Palmer — The Haircut (New England Review)

Sarah Vallance — The Pockmark on the Wall (The Pinch)

William McPherson — Falling (Hedgehog Review)

David Naimon — Third Ear (Fourth Genre)

Floyd Skloot — Let The Dark Come Upon You (Boulevard)

Mark Brazaitis — Pepe and I (Under The Sun)

Leslie Jamison — The Empathy Exams (The Believer)

Stacey Richter — Mrs. Max Siegel's Rules for Jewish Women (Willow
Springs)

Antonio Muñoz Molina — On The Inner Lives of Ghosts (Hudson Review)

Lisa Knopp — Still Life With Peaches (Georgia Review)

Tom Ireland — Brother Bomb (Missouri Review)

Judy Rowley — Light (Agni)

Melissa Febos — Call My Name (Prairie Schooner)

POETRY

Josephine Yu — If I Raise My Daughter Catholic (Southeast Review)

Frank Giampietro — Dear Daphne (Southern Review)

Phillis Levin — Anne Frank's High Heels (Poetry)

Thomas Reiter — Drought Fishing (Epoch)

Derek Sheffield — A True Account of Wood-getting from *Up the
Chumstick* (Hampden-Sydney Review)

Stephen Dunn — Mrs. Cavendish and the General Malaise (Five Points)

Ellen Bass — What Did I Love, from *Like a Begger* (Copper Canyon Press)

Colette Inez — Sunday, the War (Saranac Review)

Melissa Kwasny — Counting the Senses (Gettysburg Review)

Bob Hicok — Amen (Poetry Northwest)

Jane Hirshfield — The Orphan Beauty of Fold Not Made Blindfold
(Tin House)

Wendy Rainey — Girlie Show (Chiron Review)

Bobby C. Rogers — Junk (Cimarron Review)

X.J. Kennedy — Hopes (The Hudson Review)

Kevin Prufer — Monkey Lab (Agni)

Michael Robbins — Sonnets for Ed Snowden (Prelude)

Franny Choi — Chinky (Radius)

Bianca Stone — Vow (Jai-Alai)

Charles Harper Webb — Frogman (Hotel Amerika)

PRESSES FEATURED IN THE PUSHCART PRIZE EDITIONS SINCE 1976

A-Minor

The Account

Agni

Ahsahta Press

Ailanthus Press

Alaska Quarterly Review

Alcheringa/Ethnopoetics

Alice James Books

Ambergris

Amelia

American Circus

American Letters and Commentary

American Literature

American PEN

American Poetry Review

American Scholar

American Short Fiction

The American Voice

Amicus Journal

Amnesty International

Anaesthesia Review

Anhinga Press

Another Chicago Magazine

Antaeus

Antietam Review

Antioch Review

Apalachee Quarterly

Aphra

Aralia Press

The Ark

Art and Understanding

Arts and Letters

Artword Quarterly

Ascensius Press

Ascent

Aspen Leaves

Aspen Poetry Anthology

Assaracus

Assembling

Atlanta Review

Autonomedia

Avocet Press

The Awl

The Baffler

Bakunin

Bamboo Ridge

Barlenmir House

Barnwood Press

Barrow Street

Bellevue Literary Review

The Bellingham Review

Bellowing Ark

Beloit Poetry Journal

Bennington Review

Bilingual Review
Black American Literature Forum
Blackbird
Black Renaissance Noire
Black Rooster
Black Scholar
Black Sparrow
Black Warrior Review
Blackwells Press
The Believer
Bloom
Bloomsbury Review
Blue Cloud Quarterly
Blueline
Blue Unicorn
Blue Wind Press
Bluefish
BOA Editions
Bomb
Bookslinger Editions
Boston Review
Boulevard
Boxspring
Briar Cliff Review
Brick
Bridge
Bridges
Brown Journal of Arts
Burning Deck Press
Butcher's Dog
Cafe Review
Caliban
California Quarterly
Callaloo
Calliope
Calliopea Press
Calyx
The Canary
Canto
Capra Press
Carcanet Editions
Caribbean Writer
Carolina Quarterly
Cave Well

Cedar Rock
Center
Chariton Review
Charnel House
Chattahoochee Review
Chautauqua Literary Journal
Chelsea
Chicago Review
Chouteau Review
Chowder Review
Cimarron Review
Cincinnati Review
Cincinnati Poetry Review
City Lights Books
Cleveland State Univ. Poetry Ctr.
Clown War
Codex Journal
CoEvolution Quarterly
Cold Mountain Press
The Collagist
Colorado Review
Columbia: A Magazine of Poetry and Prose
Confluence Press
Confrontation
Conjunctions
Connecticut Review
Copper Canyon Press
Cosmic Information Agency
Countermeasures
Counterpoint
Court Green
Crab Orchard Review
Crawl Out Your Window
Crazyhorse
Creative Nonfiction
Crescent Review
Cross Cultural Communications
Cross Currents
Crosstown Books
Crowd
Cue
Cumberland Poetry Review
Curbstone Press
Cutbank

Cypher Books

Dacotah Territory

Daedalus

Dalkey Archive Press

Decatur House

December

Denver Quarterly

Desperation Press

Dogwood

Domestic Crude

Doubletake

Dragon Gate Inc.

Dreamworks

Dryad Press

Duck Down Press

Dunes Review

Durak

East River Anthology

Eastern Washington University Press

Ecotone

El Malpensante

Eleven Eleven

Ellis Press

Empty Bowl

Epiphany

Epoch

Ergo!

Evansville Review

Exquisite Corpse

Faultline

Fence

Fiction

Fiction Collective

Fiction International

Field

Fifth Wednesday Journal

Fine Madness

Firebrand Books

Firelands Art Review

First Intensity

5 A.M.

Five Fingers Review

Five Points Press

Florida Review

Forklift

The Formalist

Four Way Books

Fourth Genre

Fourth River

Frontiers: A Journal of Women Studies

Fugue

Gallimaufry

Genre

The Georgia Review

Gettysburg Review

Ghost Dance

Gibbs-Smith

Glimmer Train

Goddard Journal

David Godine, Publisher

Graham House Press

Grand Street

Granta

Graywolf Press

Great River Review

Green Mountains Review

Greenfield Review

Greensboro Review

Guardian Press

Gulf Coast

Hanging Loose

Harbour Publishing

Hard Pressed

Harvard Review

Hayden's Ferry Review

Hermitage Press

Heyday

Hills

Hollyridge Press

Holmgangers Press

Holy Cow!

Home Planet News

Hudson Review

Hunger Mountain

Hungry Mind Review

Ibbetson Street Press

Icarus

Icon

Idaho Review
Iguana Press
Image
In Character
Indiana Review
Indiana Writes
Intermedia
Intro
Invisible City
Inwood Press
Iowa Review
Ironwood
Jam To-day
J Journal
The Journal
Jubilat
The Kanchenjunga Press
Kansas Quarterly
Kayak
Kelsey Street Press
Kenyon Review
Kestrel
Lake Effect
Lana Turner
Latitudes Press
Laughing Waters Press
Laurel Poetry Collective
Laurel Review
L'Epervier Press
Liberation
Linquis
Literal Latté
Literary Imagination
The Literary Review
The Little Magazine
Little Patuxent Review
Little Star
Living Hand Press
Living Poets Press
Logbridge-Rhodes
Louisville Review
Lowlands Review
LSU Press
Lucille

Lynx House Press
Lyric
The MacGuffin
Magic Circle Press
Malahat Review
Manoa
Manroot
Many Mountains Moving
Marlboro Review
Massachusetts Review
McSweeney's
Meridian
Mho & Mho Works
Micah Publications
Michigan Quarterly
Mid-American Review
Milkweed Editions
Milkweed Quarterly
The Minnesota Review
Mississippi Review
Mississippi Valley Review
Missouri Review
Montana Gothic
Montana Review
Montemora
Moon Pony Press
Mount Voices
Mr. Cogito Press
MSS
Mudfish
Mulch Press
Muzzle Magazine
N + 1
Nada Press
Narrative
National Poetry Review
Nebraska Poets Calendar
Nebraska Review
New America
New American Review
New American Writing
The New Criterion
New Delta Review
New Directions

New England Review
New England Review and Bread Loaf
    Quarterly
New Issues
New Letters
New Madrid
New Ohio Review
New Orleans Review
New South Books
New Verse News
New Virginia Review
New York Quarterly
New York University Press
Nimrod
9X9 Industries
Ninth Letter
Noon
North American Review
North Atlantic Books
North Dakota Quarterly
North Point Press
Northeastern University Press
Northern Lights
Northwest Review
Notre Dame Review
O. ARS
O. Bl k
Obsidian
Obsidian II
Ocho
Oconee Review
October
Ohio Review
Old Crow Review
Ontario Review
Open City
Open Places
Orca Press
Orchises Press
Oregon Humanities
Orion
Other Voices
Oxford American
Oxford Press

Oyez Press
Oyster Boy Review
Painted Bride Quarterly
Painted Hills Review
Palo Alto Review
Paris Press
Paris Review
Parkett
Parnassus: Poetry in Review
Partisan Review
Passages North
Paterson Literary Review
Pebble Lake Review
Penca Books
Pentagram
Penumbra Press
Pequod
Persea: An International Review
Perugia Press
Per Contra
Pilot Light
The Pinch
Pipedream Press
Pitcairn Press
Pitt Magazine
Pleasure Boat Studio
Pleiades
Ploughshares
Poems & Plays
Poet and Critic
Poet Lore
Poetry
Poetry Atlanta Press
Poetry East
Poetry International
Poetry Ireland Review
Poetry Northwest
Poetry Now
The Point
Post Road
Prairie Schooner
Prelude
Prescott Street Press
Press

Prism

Promise of Learnings

Provincetown Arts

A Public Space

Puerto Del Sol

Quaderni Di Yip

Quarry West

The Quarterly

Quarterly West

Quiddity

Radio Silence

Rainbow Press

Raritan: A Quarterly Review

Rattle

Red Cedar Review

Red Clay Books

Red Dust Press

Red Earth Press

Red Hen Press

Release Press

Republic of Letters

Review of Contemporary Fiction

Revista Chicano-Riqueña

Rhetoric Review

Rivendell

River Styx

River Teeth

Rowan Tree Press

Ruminate

Runes

Russian *Samizdat*

Salamander

Salmagundi

San Marcos Press

Santa Monica Review

Sarabande Books

Sea Pen Press and Paper Mill

Seal Press

Seamark Press

Seattle Review

Second Coming Press

Semiotext(e)

Seneca Review

Seven Days

The Seventies Press

Sewanee Review

Shankpainter

Shantih

Shearsman

Sheep Meadow Press

Shenandoah

A Shout In the Street

Sibyl-Child Press

Side Show

Sixth Finch

Small Moon

Smartish Pace

The Smith

Snake Nation Review

Solo

Solo 2

Some

The Sonora Review

Southern Indiana Review

Southern Poetry Review

Southern Review

Southwest Review

Speakeasy

Spectrum

Spillway

Spork

The Spirit That Moves Us

St. Andrews Press

Story

Story Quarterly

Streetfare Journal

Stuart Wright, Publisher

Subtropics

Sugar House Review

Sulfur

Summerset Review

The Sun

Sun & Moon Press

Sun Press

Sunstone

Sweet

Sycamore Review

Tab

Tamagawa
Tar River Poetry
Teal Press
Telephone Books
Telescope
Temblor
The Temple
Tendril
Texas Slough
Think
Third Coast
13th Moon
THIS
Thorp Springs Press
Three Rivers Press
Threepenny Review
Thrush
Thunder City Press
Thunder's Mouth Press
Tia Chucha Press
Tiger Bark Press
Tikkun
Tin House
Tombouctou Books
Toothpaste Press
Transatlantic Review
Treelight
Triplopia
TriQuarterly
Truck Press
Tupelo Press
TurnRow
Tusculum Review
Undine
Unicorn Press
University of Chicago Press
University of Georgia Press
University of Illinois Press
University of Iowa Press
University of Massachusetts Press
University of North Texas Press

University of Pittsburgh Press
University of Wisconsin Press
University Press of New England
Unmuzzled Ox
Unspeakable Visions of the Individual
Vagabond
Vallum
Verse
Verse Wisconsin
Vignette
Virginia Quarterly Review
Volt
Wampeter Press
Washington Writers Workshop
Water-Stone
Water Table
Wave Books
West Branch
Western Humanities Review
Westigan Review
White Pine Press
Wickwire Press
Wig Leaf
Willow Springs
Wilmore City
Witness
Word Beat Press
Word-Smith
World Literature Today
Wormwood Review
Writers Forum
Xanadu
Yale Review
Yardbird Reader
Yarrow
Y-Bird
Yes Yes Books
Zeitgeist Press
Zoetrope: All-Story
Zone 3
ZYZZYVA

THE PUSHCART PRIZE FELLOWSHIPS

The Pushcart Prize Fellowships Inc., a 501 (c) (3) nonprofit corporation, is the endowment for The Pushcart Prize. "Members" donated up to $249 each. "Sponsors" gave between $250 and $999. "Benefactors" donated from $1000 to $4,999. "Patrons" donated $5,000 and more. We are very grateful for these donations. Gifts of any amount are welcome. For information write to the Fellowships at PO Box 380, Wainscott, NY 11975.

563

James Breeden
Rosellen Brown
Jane Brox
Andrea Hollander Budy
E. S. Bumas
Richard Burgin
Skylar H. Burris
David Caliguiuri
Kathy Callaway
Bonnie Jo Campbell
Janine Canan
Henry Carlile
Carrick Publishing
Fran Castan
Chelsea Associates
Marianne Cherry
Phillis M. Choyke
Suzanne Cleary
Linda Coleman
Martha Collins
Ted Conklin
Joan Connor
John Copenhaven
Dan Corrie
Tricia Currans-Sheehan
Jim Daniels
Thadious Davis
Maija Devine
Sharon Dilworth
Edward J. DiMaio
Kent Dixon
John Duncklee
Elaine Edelman
Renee Edison & Don Kaplan
Nancy Edwards
M.D. Elevitch
Failbetter.com
Irvin Faust
Tom Filer
Susan Firer
Nick Flynn
Stakey Flythe Jr.
Peter Fogo
Linda N. Foster
Fugue
Alice Fulton
Alan Furst
Eugene K. Garber
Frank X. Gaspar
A Gathering of the Tribes
Reginald Gibbons
Emily Fox Gordon
Philip Graham
Eamon Grennan

Lee Meitzen Grue
Habit of Rainy Nights
Rachel Hadas
Susan Hahn
Meredith Hall
Harp Strings
Jeffrey Harrison
Lois Marie Harrod
Healing Muse
Alex Henderson
Lily Henderson
Daniel Henry
Neva Herington
Lou Hertz
William Heyen
Bob Hicok
R. C. Hildebrandt
Kathleen Hill
Jane Hirshfield
Edward Hoagland
Daniel Hoffman
Doug Holder
Richard Holinger
Rochelle L. Holt
Richard M. Huber
Brigid Hughes
Lynne Hugo
Illya's Honey
Susan Indigo
Mark Irwin
Beverly A. Jackson
Richard Jackson
Christian Jara
David Jauss
Marilyn Johnston
Alice Jones
Journal of New Jersey Poets
Robert Kalich
Julia Kasdorf
Miriam Poli Katsikis
Meg Kearney
Celine Keating
Brigit Kelly
John Kistner
Judith Kitchen
Stephen Kopel
Peter Krass
David Kresh
Maxine Kumin
Valerie Laken
Babs Lakey
Linda Lancione
Maxine Landis
Lane Larson

Dorianne Laux & Joseph Millar
Sydney Lea
Donald Lev
Dana Levin
Gerald Locklin
Linda Lacione
Rachel Loden
Radomir Luza, Jr.
William Lychack
Annette Lynch
Elzabeth MacKierman
Elizabeth Macklin
Leah Maines
Mark Manalang
Norma Marder
Jack Marshall
Michael Martone
Tara L. Masih
Dan Masterson
Peter Matthiessen
Alice Mattison
Tracy Mayor
Robert McBrearty
Jane McCafferty
Rebecca McClanahan
Bob McCrane
Jo McDougall
Sandy McIntosh
James McKean
Roberta Mendel
Didi Menendez
Barbara Milton
Alexander Mindt
Mississippi Review
Martin Mitchell
Roger Mitchell
Jewell Mogan
Patricia Monaghan
Jim Moore
James Morse
William Mulvihill
Nami Mun
Carol Muske-Dukes
Edward Mycue
Deirdre Neilen
W. Dale Nelson
Jean Nordhaus
Ontario Review Foundation
Daniel Orozco
Other Voices
Pamela Painter
Paris Review
Alan Michael Parker
Ellen Parker

Veronica Patterson
David Pearce, M.D.
Robert Phillips
Donald Platt
Valerie Polichar
Pool
Horatio Potter
Jeffrey & Priscilla Potter
Marcia Preston
Eric Puchner
Tony Quagliano
Barbara Quinn
Belle Randall
Martha Rhodes
Nancy Richard
Stacey Richter
James Reiss
Katrina Roberts
Judith R. Robinson
Jessica Roeder
Martin Rosner
Kay Ryan
Sy Safransky
Brian Salchert
James Salter
Sherod Santos
R.A. Sasaki
Valerie Sayers
Maxine Scates
Alice Schell
Dennis & Loretta Schmitz
Helen Schulman
Philip Schultz
Shenandoah
Peggy Shinner
Vivian Shipley
Joan Silver
Skyline
John E. Smelcer
Raymond J. Smith
Joyce Carol Smith
Philip St. Clair
Lorraine Standish
Maureen Stanton
Michael Steinberg
Sybil Steinberg
Jody Stewart
Barbara Stone
Storyteller Magazine
Bill & Pat Strachan
Julie Suk
Sun Publishing
Sweet Annie Press
Katherine Taylor

Pamela Taylor
Elaine Jerranova
Susan Terris
Marcelle Thiébaux
Robert Thomas
Andrew Tonkovich
Pauls Toutonghi
Juanita Torrence-Thompson
William Trowbridge
Martin Tucker
Jeannette Valentine
Victoria Valentine
Hans Van de Bovenkamp
Tino Villanueva
William & Jeanne Wagner
BJ Ward
Susan O. Warner
Rosanna Warren
Margareta Waterman
Michael Waters

Sandi Weinberg
Andrew Weinstein
Jason Wesco
West Meadow Press
Susan Wheeler
Dara Wier
Ellen Wilbur
Galen Williams
Marie Sheppard Williams
Eleanor Wilner
Irene K. Wilson
Steven Wingate
Sandra Wisenberg
Wings Press
Robert W. Witt
Margo Wizansky
Matt Yurdana
Christina Zawadiwsky
Sander Zulauf
ZYZZYVA

SUSTAINING MEMBERS

Agni
Betty Adcock
Dick & L.N. Allen
Russell Allen
Jacob M. Appel
Philip Appleman
Renee Ashley
Alec Baldwin Foundation
Jim Barnes
Ann Beattie
David S. Caldwell
Bonnie Jo Campbell
Carrick Publishing
Dan Chaon
Suzanne Cleary
Martha Collins
Linda Coleman
E.L. Doctorow
Daniel L. Dolgin & Loraine F. Gardner
Wendy Durden
Elaine Edelman
Ben & Sharon Fountain
Alan Furst
Robert L. Giron
Susan Hahn
Alexander C. Henderson
Genie Henderson
Lila Henderson
Helen & Frank Houghton
Mark Irwin
Diane Johnson
Don & René Kaplan

Edmund Keeley
Peter Krass
Wally Lamb
Linda Lancione
Sydney Lea
William Lychack
Maria Matthiesson
Alice Mattison
Robert McBrearty
Rick Moody
John Mullen
Neltje
Joyce Carol Oates
Daniel Orozco
Pamela Painter
Horatio Potter
David B. Pearce, M.D.
Barbara & Warren Phillips
Elizabeth R. Rea
James Reiss
Stacey Richter
Sy Safransky
Valerie Sayers
Schaffner Family Foundation
Alice Schell
Dennis Schmitz
Aaron Schultz
Cindy Sherman
Charline Spektor
Maureen Stanton
Raymond Strom
Jody Stewart

CONTRIBUTING SMALL PRESSES FOR PUSHCART PRIZE XL

(These presses made or received nominations for this edition.)

A

A-Minor Magazine, 7C, 42 & 42A Hollywood Rd., Hong Kong
A Narrow Fellow, 4302 Kinloch Rd., Louisville, KY 40207
A Public Space, 323 Dean St., Brooklyn, NY 11217
aaduna, 144 Genesee St., Ste. 102-259, Auburn, NY 13021
Abenbook, P.O. Box 80708, Baton Rouge, LA 70898-0708
Able Muse Review, 467 Saratoga Ave., #602, San Jose, CA 95129
ABZ Press, PO Box 2746, Huntington, WV 25727-2746
Abyss & Apex, 1574 CR 250, Niota, TN 37826
Academy of American Poets, 75 Maiden Lane, New York, NY 10038
Accents Publishing, P.O. Box 910456, Lexington, KY 40591-0456
The Account, 4607 N. Campbell Ave., Apt. 2, Chicago, IL 60625
Acorn, 115 Conifer Lane, Walnut Creek, CA 94598
Ad Lumen Press, 4700 College Oak Dr., Sacramento, CA 95841
Adastra Press, 16 Reservation Rd., Easthampton, MA 01027-1227
The Adirondack Review, 107 1ˢᵗ Ave., New York, NY 10003
The Adroit Journal, 3910 Irving St., Philadelphia, PA 19104
The Aerogram, P.O. Box 591164, San Francisco, CA 94159
African American Review, Saint Louis University, Adorian Hall 317, 3800 Lindell Blvd., St. Louis, MO 63108
Agave Magazine, 3729 Monterey Pine St., #H-101, Santa Barbara, CA 93105
Agni, Boston University, 236 Bay State Rd., Boston, MA 02215
Airlie Press, P.O. Box 82653, Portland, OR 97282
Airways, P.O. Box 1109, Sandpoint, ID 83864
Akashic Books, P.O. Box 46232, West Hollywood, CA 90046
Alabaster & Mercury, 5050 Del Monte Ave., #6, San Diego, CA 92107

Alabaster Leaves Publishing, 1840 West 220th St., Torrance, CA 90501

Alaska Quarterly Review, 3211 Providence Dr., Anchorage, AK 99508

Aldrich Press, 24600 Mountain Ave., #35, Hemet, CA 92544

Aleph Book Company, 161 B/4, Ground Floor, Gulmohar House, Yusuf Sarai Community Centre, New Delhi, 110049, India

Alexandria Quarterly, 29 East Atlantic Ave., Audubon, NJ 08106

Alice Blue, 4019 NE 39th Ave., Vancouver, WA 98661

Alice James Books, 114 Prescott St., Farmington, ME 04938

All Due Respect, 2300 Oakdale Rd., #27, Modesto, CA 95355

Alligator Juniper, Prescott College, 220 Grove Ave., Prescott, AZ 86301

Alligator Press, 1953 S. 1100 E Unit 526368, Salt Lake City, UT 84152-5015

Alternating Current, P.O. Box 183, Palo Alto, CA 94302

Ambril's Tale, 301 Hillcrest Rd., San Carlos, CA 94070

American Arts Quarterly, 915 Broadway, Ste. 1104, New York, NY 10010

American Athenaeum, P.O. Box 2107, Lusby, MD 20657

American Chesterton Society, 4117 Pebblebrook, Minneapolis, MN 55437

American Circus, 330 E. 6th St., NY, NY 10003

The American Literary Review, Creative Writing Program, Dept. of English, University of North Texas, Auditorium 112, 1155 Union Circle #311307, Denton, TX 76203-5017

The American Poetry Journal, P.O. Box 2080, Aptos, CA 95001-2080

The American Poetry Review, University of the Arts, 320 So. Broad St., Hamilton 313, Philadelphia, PA 19102

American Poets Magazine, Alex Dimitrov, Academy of American Poets, 75 Maiden Lane, Ste. 901, New York, NY 10038

The American Reader, 779 Riverside Dr., Apt. A40, New York, NY 10032

American Scholar, 1606 New Hampshire NW, Washington, DC 20009

American Short Fiction, 109 W. Johanna St, Austin, TX 78704

Amoskeag, 2500 No. River Rd., Manchester, NH 03106-1045

Ampersand Books, 5040 10th Ave. So., Gulfport, FL 33707

Ampersand Communications, 2901 Santa Cruz SE, Albuquerque, NY 87106

Anaphora, 1803 Treehills Parkway, Stone Mountain, GA 30088

Anatomy & Etymology, 1915 Maple Ave., Apt. 809-A, Evanston, IL 60201

Ancient Paths, P.O. Box 7505, Fairfax Station, VA 22039

anderbo.com, 270 Lafayette St., Ste 705, New York, NY 10012

Animal, 264 Fallen Palm Dr., Casselberry, FL 32707

Annalemma Magazine, 112 Second Ave., Ste. 30, Brooklyn, NY 11215

Annapurna Magazine, 4408 Sayre Dr., Princeton, NJ 08540

Anomalous Press, 1631 Muscatine Ave., Apt. A, Iowa City, IA 52240

Another Chicago Magazine, 602 So. Morgan St., Chicago, IL 60607-7120

Anti- , 4237 Beethoven Ave., St. Louis, MO 63116-2503

The Antioch Review, PO Box 148, Yellow Springs, OH 45387-0148

Antrim House Books, 21 Goodrich Rd., Simsbury, CT 06070

Anvil Press, 278 East First St., Vancouver, BC V5T 1A6. Canada

Any Puppets Press, 6065 Chabot Rd., Oakland, CA 94618

Apeiron Review, 1173 Ridgeview Dr., Waynesboro, PA 17268

Apercus, c/o Henley, 423 S. Ash, Redlands, CA 92373

Apology, Jesse Pearson, 679 Durant Place, NE, Apt. F, Atlanta, GA 30308

Appalachia North, P.O. Box 57, East Dixfield, ME 04227

Appalachian Heritage, Berea College, CPO 2166, Berea, KY 40404-0001

Apple Valley Review, 88 South 3rd St., #336, San Jose, CA 95113

Apryl Skies, 13547 Ventura Blvd., Sherman Oaks, CA 91423

apt, 2643 Maryland Ave., #3, Baltimore, MD 21218

Aquarius Press, P.O. Box 23096, Detroit, MI 48223

Aqueous Books, P.O. Box 170607, Birmingham, AL 35217

Arcadia Magazine, 9616 Nichols Rd., Oklahoma City, OK 73120

The Archstone, 250 W. 50th St., 15L, New York, NY 10019

Arctos Press, P.O. Box 401, Sausalito, CA 94966-0401

Arizona Authors, 6145 West Echo Lane, Glendale, AZ 85302

Arkansas Review, P.O. Box 1890, State University, AR 72467-1890

ArmChair/Shotgun, 377 Flatbush Ave., No. 3, Brooklyn, NY 11238

Arnolfini, 16 Narrow Quay, Bristol BS1 4QA, United Kingdom

Arroyo Literary Review, C.S.U. 25800 Carlos Bee Blvd., Hayward, CA 94542

Arsenic Lobster, 1830 W. 18th St., Chicago, IL 60608

Art Night Books, 3348 N. Dousman St., Milwaukee, WI 53212

Art Times, c/o Barragan, Weinstein, 142 Brentwood Dr., Iowa City, IA 52245

Arte Publico Press, 452 Cullen Performance Hall, Houston, TX 77204-2004

Artichoke Haircut, P.O. Box 22541, Baltimore, MD 21203

Artifact, 1139 N. Harrison St., Stockton, CA 95203

The Arts Fuse, 100 Bay State Rd., 3rd Flr., Boston, MA 02215

Arts & Ideas, P.O. Box 1130, West Tisbury, MA 02575

Arts & Letters, Campus Box 89, Milledgeville, GA 31061-0490

Arts Journal, 2340 14th Ave. E, Seattle WA 98112-2103

Ascent, Concordia College, 901 8ths St. S., Moorhead, MN 56562

Asheville Poetry Review, P.O. Box 7086, Asheville, NC 28802

Ashland Creek Press, 2305 Ashland St., Ste. C417, Ashland, OR 97520

Asian American Review, 1110 Severnview Dr., Crownsville, MD 21032

Askew, P.O. Box 559, Ventura, CA 93002

Asymptote Journal, 40 Butler St., 3rd Floor, Brooklyn, NY 11231

At Length, 716 W. Cornwallis Rd., Durham, NC 27707

At the Bijou, 71 Bank St., Derby, CT 06418

Atelier26 Books, 4207 SE Woodstock Blvd., #421, Portland, OR 97206

Atherton Review, 1000 El Camino Real, Atherton, CA 94027

Atlanta Review, PO Box 8248, Atlanta, GA 31106

The Atlas Review, 54 India St., Apt. 3, Brooklyn, NY 11222

Atticus Books, 20 Waverly Pl., 2ⁿᵈ Floor, Madison, NJ 07940
Augury Books, 305 E. 12ᵗʰ St., Apt. 1, New York, NY 10003
Augusta Heritage Press, 123-C North Orlando, Los Angeles, CA 90048
The Austin Review, 4700 Hilwin Circle, Austin, TX 78756
Autumn House Press, 87 1/2 Westwood St., Pittsburgh, PA 15211
The Awakenings Review, P.O. Box 177, Wheaton, IL 60187-0177
The Awl, 875 Avenue of the Americas, 2ⁿᵈ Floor, New York, NY 10001

B

Backbone Press, P.O. Box 51483, Durham, NC 27717-1483
The Backwaters Press, 3502 North 52ⁿᵈ St., Omaha, NE 68104-3506
The Bacon Review, 19 S. Emerson St., Denver, CO 80209
Bacopa, P.O. Box 358396, Gainesville, FL 32635-8396
The Bad Version, 2035 W. Rice St., Chicago, IL 60622
The Baffler, 200 Hampshire Street, No. 3, Cambridge, Mass 02139
The Bakery, A. Abonado, 12 Strathallan Pk., #2, Rochester, NY 14607
Ballard Street Poetry Journal, 124 Alvarado Ave., Worcester, MA 01604
The Baltimore Review, 6514 Maplewood Rd., Baltimore, MD 21212
Bamboo Ridge Press, PO Box 61781, Honolulu, HI 96839-1781
Barbaric Yawp, 3700 County Route 24, Russell, NY 13684
Barely South Review, Old Dominion University, Norfolk, VA 23529-0091
Barge Press, 3729 Beechwood Blvd., Pittsburgh, PA 15217
Barn Owl Review, 275 Melbourne Ave., Akron, OH 44313
Barrelhouse, 793 Westerly Pkwy., State College, PA 16801
Barrow Street, PO Box 1831, New York, NY 10156
Bartleby Snopes, 2219 Grimm Rd., Chasta, MN 55318
basalt, One University Blvd., La Grande, OR 97850-2807
Baseball Bard, Box 90923, San Diego, CA 92169
Baskerville Publishers, 9112 Camp Bowie Blvd., Fort Worth, TX 76116
Bat City Review, 208 West 21ˢᵗ St., Stop B 5000, Austin, TX 78712
Bayou Magazine, U.N.O., 2000 Lake Shore Dr., New Orleans, LA 70148
Bear Star Press, 185 Hollow Oak Dr., Cohasset, CA 95973
Beaten Track Publishing, 11 Manor Crescent, Burscough Lancashire L40
    7TW, United Kingdom
Beatlick Press, 1814 Old Town Rd., NW, Albuquerque, NM 87104
Beecher's Magazine, K.U. Graduate Creative Writing Program, 1447 Jayhawk
    Blvd., Lawrence, KS 66045
Being and Becoming, Sein und Werden, 9 Dorris St., Levenshulme, Manches-
    ter M19 27P, United Kingdom
The Believer Magazine, 849 Valencia St., San Francisco, CA 94110
Belle Reve Literary Journal, PO Box 324, Georgetown, GA 39854

Bellevue Literary Review, NYU School of Medicine, 550 First Ave, OBV-A612, New York, NY 10016

Bellingham Review, MS-9053, WWU, 516 High St., Bellingham, WA 98225

Beloit Fiction Journal, 700 College St., Box 11, Beloit, WI 53511

Beloit Poetry Journal, 271 N. Gorham Rd., Gorham, ME 04038

Benicia Literary Arts, 356 E. 2nd St., Benicia, CA 94510

Bennett & Hastings Publishing, 2400 NW 80th St., #254, Seattle WA 98117

Berfrois, Russell Bennetts, 23 Rochester Rd.. London NW1 9JJ, UK

Berkeley Fiction Review, MC 4500, UCB, Berkeley, CA 94720-4500

Berkeley Poetry Review, 2718 College Ave., #2, Berkeley, CA 94705

Bernheim Press, 5809 Scrivener, Long Beach, CA 90808

Best New Writing P.O. Box 11, Titusville, NJ 08560

Bicycle Comics, 555 Mission Rock St., #617, San Francisco, CA 94158

The Bicycle Review, 1727 10th St., Oakland, CA 94607

Big, Big Wednesday, 13 Munroe St., Apt. 1, Northampton, MA 01060

Big Fiction, 7907 8th Avenue NW, Seattle, WA 98117

Big Lucks, 3201 Guilford Ave., #3, Baltimore, MD 21218

Big Pulp Publications, c/o Oliver, 116 Greene St., Cumberland, MD 21502

Big River Poetry Review, 4550 North Blvd., #220, Baton Rouge, LA 70806

The Big Roundtable, 310 West 106 St., #10A, New York, NY 10025

Big Table, 383 Langley Rd., #2, Newton Centre, MA 02459

Big Time Books, 4826 Agnes Ave., Valley Village, CA 91607

The Binnacle, 19 Kimball Hall, 116 O'Brien Ave., Machias, ME 04654

bio Stories, 175 Mission View Dr., Lakeside, MT 59922

Birch Brook Press, P.O. Box 81, Delhi, NY 13753

Birdfeast, 656 Old Lincoln Highway, Ligonier, PA 15658

Bird's Thumb, 19806 Wolf Rd., Apt. 207, Mokena, IL 60448-1387

Birds, LLC, 207 Bertie Drive, Raleigh, NC 27610

The Birds We Piled Loosely, 2017 East Genesee St., Apt. 4, Syracuse, NY 13210

Birkensnake, 559 30th St., Oakland, CA 94609-3201

Birmingham Poetry Review, UAB, Birmingham, AL 35294-1260

Bizarro Press, 20 Noble Ct., Ste. 200, Heath, TX 75032

BkMk Press, UMKC, 5100 Rockhill Rd., Kansas City, MO 64110-2446

Black Clock, CalArts, 24700 McBean Parkway, Valencia, CA 91355

Black Hills Writers Group, P.O. Box 1539, Rapid City, SD 57709

Black Lantern Publishing, P.O. Box 1451, Jacksonville, NC 28541-1451

Black Lawrence Press, 326 Bigham St., Pittsburgh, PA 15211-1463

Black Scat Books, 930 Central Park Ave., Lakeport, CA 95453

Black Warrior Review, P.O. Box 870170, Tuscaloosa, AL 35487-0170

Blackbird, P.O. Box 843082, Richmond, VA 23284-3082

Blacktop Passages, 15420 Livingston Ave., Apt. 3009, Lutz, FL 33559

Blank Slate Press, 2528 Remington Lane, St. Louis, MO 63144

BlazeVox, 131 Euclid Ave., Kenmore, NY 14217

Blinders Journal, 6324 Cameron Forest Lane, Apt. 1C, Charlotte, NC 28210

blink-ink, P.O. Box 5, North Branford, CT 06471

Blip Magazine, 2158 26th Ave., San Francisco, CA 94110

Blood Lotus, 307 Granger Circle, Dayton, OH 45433

Blood Orange Review, 1495 Evergreen Ave. NE, Salem, OR 97301

Bloodroot, P.O. Box 322, Thetford Center, VT 05075

Bloom, 5482 Wilshire Blvd., #1616, Los Angeles, CA 90036

The Blotter Magazine, P.O. Box 2153, Chapel Hill, NC 27515

Blue Cubicle Press, P.O. Box 250382, Plano, TX 75025-0382

Blue Earth Review, 230 Armstrong Hall, Mankato, MN 56001

Blue Fifth Review, 267 Lark Meadow Circle, Bluff City, TN 37618

Blue Heron Review, N66W38350 Deer Creek Ct., Oconomowoc, WI 53066

Blue Hour Press, 640 NE 10th St., McMinnville, OR 97128

Blue Lyra Review, 275 West Main St., Forsyth, GA 31029

Blue Mesa Review, UNM, MCS 03-2170, Albuquerque, NM 87131-0001

Blue Print Review, 1103 NW 11th Ave., Gainesville, FL 32601

Blue Scarab Press, P.O. Box 2803, Pawleys Island, SC 29585

Blue Unicorn, 22 Avon Rd., Kensington, CA 94707

Blueshift, 29 Ivana Dr., Andover, MA 01810

Bluestem, Eastern Illinois Univ., 600 Lincoln Ave., Charleston, IL 61920

Blunderbuss Magazine, 113 Stockholm St., Apt. 2A, Brooklyn, NY 11221

BOA Editions, 250 North Goodman St., Ste 306, Rochester, NY 14607

Bodega Magazine, 451 Court St., #3R, Brooklyn, NY 11231

Body, Mezivrsi 87/17, 147 00 Praha 4, Czech Republic

The Boiler Journal, 1818 Leicester St., Garland, TX 75044

Bold Strokes Books, P.O. Box 249, Valley Falls NY 12185

The Bollard, P.O. Box 17765, Portland, ME 04112

BOMB Magazine, 80 Hanson Place, Ste. 703, Brooklyn, NY 11217-1506

Bona Fide Books, P.O. Box 550278, Tahoe Paradise, CA 96155

Bone Bouquet, 317 Madison Ave., #520, New York, NY 10017

Book Thug, 260 Ryding Ave., Toronto ON M6N 1H5, Canada

Booktrope Editions, 1019 Esplanada Circle, El Paso, TX 79932

Boone's Dock Press, 235 Ocean Ave., Amityville, NY 11701

Booth, English Dept., Butler Univ., 4600 Sunset Ave., Indianapolis, IN 46208

Border Crossing, 650 W. Easterday Ave., Sault Sainte Marie, MI 49783

Border Press, P.O. Box 3124, Sewanee, TN 37375

Border Senses, 1500 Texas St., #up, El Paso, TX 79901

Borderlands: Texas Poetry Review, P.O. Box 33096, Austin, TX 78764

Borderline, 1915 Maple Ave., Apt. 809-A, Evanston, IL 60201

Bordighera Press, 25 West 43rd St., 17th Floor, New York, NY 10036 bosque, 163 Sol del Oro, Corrales, New Mexico 87048

Boston Literary Magazine, 383 Langley Rd., #2, Newton Centre, MA 02459

Boston Poetry Magazine, 15 Beal St., Winthrop, MA 02152

Boston Review, P.O. Box 425786, Cambridge, MA 02142

Botticelli Magazine, 5982 Goode Rd., Powell, OH 43065

Bottom Dog Press, P.O. Box 425, Huron, OH 44839

Boulevard, 7507 Byron PL (#1) St. Louis MO 63105

Bound Off, P.O. Box 821, Cedar Rapids, IA 52406-0821

Box of Jars, 453 Washington Ave., #5A, Brooklyn, NY 11238

Box Turtle Press, 184 Franklin St., New York, NY 10013

Boxcar Poetry Review, 630 S. Kenmore Ave., #206, Los Angeles, CA 90005

Brain, Child, 341 Newtown Turnpike, Wilton, CT 06897

Brevity, English Dept., Ohio University, Athens, OH 45701

The Briar Cliff Review, 3303 Rebecca St., Sioux City, IA 51104-2100

Brick, P.O. Box 609, Stn. P, Toronto, Ontario, M5S 2Y4, Canada

Brick Books, 431 Boler Rd., Box 20081, London, Ontario N6K 4G6 Canada

Brick Cave Media, P.O. Box 4411, Mesa, AZ 85211-4411

BrickHouse Books, 306 Suffolk Rd., Baltimore, MD 21218

Brigantine Media, 211 North Ave., St. Johnsbury, VT 05819

Brilliant Corners, 700 College Place, Williamsport, PA 17701

Brink Media, P.O. Box 209034, New Haven, CT 06520-9034

Broad! Magazine, 1518 Old Ranch Rd. 12, Apt. 603, San Marcos, TX 78666

Broad Street, Virginia Commonwealth Univ., Richmond, VA 23284

Broadkill Review, P.O. Box 63, Milton, DE 19968

The Broadsider, P.O. Box 236, Millbrae, CA 94030

Brooklyn Arts Press, 154 N. 9th St., #1, Brooklyn, NY 11249

The Brooklyn Rail, 845 Hancock St., Brooklyn, NY 11233

The Brooklyn Review, English Dept., Brooklyn College, 2900 Bedford Ave., Brooklyn, NY 11210

Brothel Books, 116 Ave. C, #17, New York, NY 10009

Buffalo Almanack, 606 E. Sheridan St., Laramie, WY 82070

Bull, 343 Parkovash Ave., South Bend, IN 46617

Bull City Press, 1217 Odyssey Dr., Durham, NC 27713

Bull Spec, P.O. Box 13146, Durham, NC 27709

Burnt Bridge, 6721 Washington Ave., 2H, Ocean Springs, MS 39564

Burntdistrict, 2016 S. 185th St., Omaha, NE 68130

Burrow Press, P.O. Box 533709, Orlando, FL 32853

Butcher's Dog, c/o Live Theatre, Board Chare, Quayside, Newcastle upon Tyne NE1 3DQ, United Kingdom

C&R Press, 812 Westwood Ave., Chattanooga, TN 37405
C4, 17 Cameron Ave., Cambridge, MA 02140
Cactus Heart Press, 97 South St., Apt. 1C, Northampton, MA 01060
Cadence Collective: 4763 Deeboyar Ave., Lakewood, CA 90712
The Café Irreal, P.O. Box 87031, Tuscon, AZ 85754
Café Review, c/o Yes Books, 589 Congress St., Portland, ME 04101
cahoodaloodaling, 1802 W. Maryland Ave., #3067, Phoenix, AZ 85015
Cairn: The St. Andrews Review, 1700 Dogwood Mile, Laurinburg, NC 28352
Caketrain Journal, PO Box 82588, Pittsburgh, PA 15218-0588
Caitlin Press, 8100 Alderwood Rd., Halfmoon Bay, VON 1Y1, BC Canada
California Quarterly, 23 Edgecroft Rd., Kensington, CA 94707
Callaloo, 4212 TAMU, Texas A&M Univ., College Station, TX 77843-4212
Calliope, 2506 SE Bitterbrush Dr., Madras, OR 97741-9452
Calyx Inc., Box B, Corvallis, OR 97339-0539
The Camel Saloon, 11190 Abbotts Station Dr., Johns Creek, GA 30097
Camera Obscura, P.O. Box 2356, Addison, TX 75069
Carbon Culture Review, P.O. Box 1643, Moriarty, NM 87035
Cardus, 185 Young St., Hamilton, ON, L8N 1V9, Canada
The Caribbean Writer, Univ. Virgin Islands, RR #1, Box 10,000, Kingshill, St.
    Croix USVI 00850
The Carolina Quarterly, Box 3520, UNC, Chapel Hill, NC 27599-3520
Carrick Publishing, 32 Thimble Berryway, Toronto, ON M2H 3K7, Canada
Cartagena Journal, 3727 Monroe St., Columbia, SC 29205
Carve, P.O. Box 701510, Dallas, TX 75370
Casa de Snapdragon, 12901 Bryce Ave. NE, Albuquerque, NM 87112
Cascadia, 8017 Lee Blvd., Leawood, KS 66206
Casperian Books, P.O. Box 161026, Sacramento, CA 95816-1026
Caspian Press, P.O. Box 302, Hardwick, VT 05843
Catamaran Literary Reader, 1050 River St., #113, Santa Cruz, CA 95060
Catch & Release, Columbia University, 415 Dodge Hall, Mail Code 1804, 2960
    Broadway, New York, NY 10027
Catfish Creek, Box 36, Loras College, 1450 Alta Vista St., Dubuque, IA 52001
Cave Moon Press, 7704 Mieras Rd., Yakima, WA 98901-8021
Cave Region Review, 1515 Pioneer Dr., Harrison, AR 72601
Cave Wall Press, PO Box 29546, Greensboro, NC 27429-9546
CCLaP Weekender, 4157 N. Clarendon Ave., #505, Chicago IL 60613
Cease, Cows, 20300 Burr Oak Dr., #B, Coupland, TX 78615
Central Recovery Press, 3321 N. Buffalo Dr., Ste. 200, Las Vegas, NV 89129
Cerise Press, 10510 Parker St., Omaha, NE 68114
Certain Circuits, 1315 Walnut St., Ste. 309, Philadelphia, PA 19107
Cervena Barva Press, PO Box 440357, W. Somerville, MA 02144-3222

Cha: An Asian Literary Journal, OEW 1115, Ho Sin Hang Campus, 224 Waterloo Rd., Kowloon Tong, Hong Kong

The Chaffey Review, 5885 Haven Ave., Rancho Cucamonga, CA 91737-3002

The Chattahoochee Review, 555 N. Indian Creek Dr., Georgia Perimeter College, Clarkston, GA 30021

Chatter House Press, 7915 S. Emerson Ave., Indianapolis, IN 46237

Chautauqua, 601 South College Rd., Wilmington, NC 28403

Chelsea Station Editions, 362 West 36th St., #2R, New York, NY 10018

Cherokee McGhee, 124 Peyton Rd., Williamsburg, VA 23185

Cherry Castle, 7240 Lasting Light Way, Columbia, MD 21045

Chicago Poetry, 2626 W. Iowa, 2F, Chicago, IL 60622

Chicago Quarterly Review, 517 Sherman Ave., Evanston, IL 60202

Chicago Review, 935 E. 60th St., Chicago, IL 60637

China Grove, 280 Magnolia St., Magnolia, MS 39652

Chiron Review, 522 E. South Ave., St. Johns, KS 67576-2212

ChiZine Publications, 67 Alameda Ave., Toronto, ON M6C 3W4, Canada

The Chrysalis Reader, 1745 Gravel Hill Rd., Dillwyn, VA 23936

Cider Press Review, P.O. Box 33384, San Diego, CA 92163

Cimarron Review, 205 Morrill Hall, Stillwater, OK 74078

Cincinnati Review, PO Box 210069, Cincinnati, OH 45221

Cincinnati Writers Project, 79 W. Broad St., Hopewell, NJ 08525

Cinco Puntos Press, 701 Tenth St., El Paso, TX 79901

Citizens for Decent Literature, 5 Morningside Dr., Jacksonville, IL 62650

Citron Review, 933 Pineview Ridge Ct., Ballwin, MO 63201

The Claudius APP, 220 20th St., Apt. 2, Brooklyn, NY 11232

Cleaver Magazine, 8250 Shawnee St., Philadelphia, PA 19118

The Cleveland Review, 1305 Andrews Ave., Lakewood, OH 44107

Clock, 1203 Plantation Drive, Simpsonville, SC 29681

Clockhouse, 352 9th St., Brooklyn, NY 11215

Clover, A Literary Rag, 203 West Holly, Ste. 306, Bellingham, WA 98225

Coach House Books, 80 bpNichol Lane, Toronto, Ontario M5S 3J4, Canada

Coal City Review, English Dept., University of Kansas, Lawrence, KS 66045

Cobalt Review, 5511 Pilgrim Rd., Baltimore, MD 21214

Codex Journal, English Dept., Eastern Illinois University, 600 Lincoln Ave., Charleston, IL 61920

Codhill Press, One Arden Lane, New Paltz, NY 12561

Codorus Press, 34-43 Crescent St., Ste. 1S, Astoria, NY 11106

Coffee House Press, 79 Thirteenth Ave. NE, Ste. 110, Minneapolis, MN 55413

Coffeetown Enterprises, P.O. Box 70515, Seattle, WA 98127

The Coffin Factory, 14 Lincoln Place, Ste. 2R, Brooklyn, NY 11217

Cold Mountain Review, ASU – English Dept., Boone, NC 28608

Cold River Press, 11402 Francis Dr., Grass Valley, CA 95949

The Collagist, Warren Wilson College, CPO 6205, Ashville, NC 28815

Colorado Review, Colorado State Univ., Fort Collins, CO 80523-9105

Columbia Magazine: A Magazine of Poetry and Prose, 622 West 113th Street, MC 4521, New York, NY 10025

Columbia Poetry Review, 600 South Michigan Ave., Chicago, IL 60605-1996

Comment, 185 Young St., Hamilton, ON Canada LN8 1V9

The Common, Frost Library, Amherst College, Amherst, MA 01002-5000

Common Ground Review, 40 Prospect St., #C-1, Westfield, MA 01085-1559

Compass Flower Press, 315 Bernadette, Ste. 3, Columbia, MD 65203

Complicity, McClelland & Stewart, One Toronto St., Unit 300, Toronto, Ontario M5C 2V6, Canada

Conclave, 4800 Foster Rd., #88, Oklahoma City, OK 73129

Concrete Wolf, PO Box 1808, Kingston, WA 98346-1808

Confrontation, English Dept., LIU/Post, Brookville, NY 11548

Conium Press, 4753 Eagleridge Circle, #302, Pueblo, CO 81008

Conjunctions, Bard College, Annandale-on-Hudson, NY 12504-5000

Connecticut Review, 39 Woodland St., Hartford, CT 06105-2337

Connecticut River Review, P.O. Box 516, Cheshire, CT 06410

Connotation Press, 714 Venture Drive, #164, Morgantown, WV 26508

Consequence Magazine, P.O. Box 323, Cohasset, MA 02025

Constellations, 127 Lake View Ave., Cambridge, MA 02138

Conte, Arts & Humanities, 32000 Campus Dr., Salisbury, MD 21804

Copper Canyon Press, PO Box 271, Port Townsend, WA 98368

Copper Nickel, Campus Box 175, P.O. Box 173364, Denver, CO 80217

Corium, P.O. Box 2322, Richmond, CA 94802

The Cossack Review, 15810 Cherry Blossom Lane, Los Gatos, CA 95032

Counterexample Poetics, 13 Sixth St., Englewood Cliffs, NJ 07632

Counterpoint Press, 2560 Ninth St., Ste. 318, Berkeley, CA 94710

The Country Dog Review, P.O. Box 1476, Oxford, MS 38655

Court Green, 600 South Michigan Ave., Chicago, IL 60605-1996

Cowfeather Press, P.O. Box 620216, Middleton, WI 53562

Crab Creek Review, PO Box 247, Kingston, WA 98346

Crab Fat Literary Magazine, 5485 Woodgate Dr., Columbus, GA 31907

Crab Orchard Review, SIUC, 1000 Faner Drive, Carbondale, IL 62901

Crack the Spine, 29 Park Place, #1506, Hattiesburg, MS 39402

Crannóg Magazine, 6 San Antonio Park, Salthill, Galway, Ireland

Crazyhorse, College of Charleston, 66 George St., Charleston, SC 29424

The Cream City Review, UW-Milwaukee, P.O. Box 413, Milwaukee, WI 53201

Creative Nonfiction, 5501 Walnut St., Ste. 202, Pittsburgh, PA 15232

Creative Cellogny, 3114 N 26th St., Tacoma, WA 98407

Cross-Cultural Communications, 239 Wynsum Ave., Merrick, NY 11566-4725

Crosstimbers, 1727 W. Alabama, Chickasha, OK 73018-5322

Cultural Weekly, 215 S. Santa Fe Ave., Studio 19, Los Angeles, CA 90012

Cumberland River Review, 333 Murfreesboro Rd., Nashville, IN 37210-2877

The Curator, 227 16th St., Seal Beach, CA 90740

Curbside Splendor, 2816 N. Kedzie, Chicago, IL 60618

Curbstone Press, 321 Jackson St., Willimantic, CT 06226-1738

CutBank, 1626 Mason Lane, Charlottesville, VA 22903

Cutthroat, A Journal of the Arts, PO Box 2414, Durango, CO 81302

The Cyberpunk Apocalypse, 5431 Carnegie St., Pittsburgh, PA 15201

Cyberwit.net, HIG 45, Kaushambi Kunj, Kalindipuram, Allahabad – 211011 (U.P.) India

D

Dahse Magazine, 80 Leonard St., #2C, New York, NY 10013

Daniel & Daniel Publishers, P.O. Box 2790, McKinleyville, CA 95519-2790

Dappled Things Magazine, 600 Giltin Drive, Arlington, TX 76006

Dark Moon Books, 3412 Imperial Palm Dr., Largo, FL 33771

Dark Valentine Press, 4717 Ben Avenue, Valley Village, CA 91607

Dart Society, 1601 Barnum Rd., Kaycee, WY 82639

The Darwin Press, P.O. Box 2202, Princeton, NJ 08543

Deadly Chaps, 673 Classon Ave., #1R, Brooklyn, NY 11238

december, P.O. Box 16130, St. Louis, MO 63105

decomP, 726 Carriage Hill Dr., Athens, OH 45701

Deep Kiss Press, 101 Stafford St., Staunton, VA 24401

Deep South, 203 Iris Lane, Lafayette, LA 70506

Deerbrook Editions, P.O. Box 542, Cumberland, ME 04021-0542

Defunct, 1028 Earlville Rd., Earlville, NY 13332

The Delmarva Review, PO Box 544, St. Michaels, MD 21663

DemmeHouse, P.O. Box 2572, Brentwood, TN 37024

Denver Quarterly, University of Denver, 2000 E Asbury, Denver, CO 80208

The Destroyer, 3166 Barbara Court, L.A., CA 90068

Devil's Lake, UWM, 600 North Park St., Madison, WI 53703

Devilfish Review, 200 Willard St., #201, Mankato, MN 56001

Diagram, New Michigan Press, 8058 E. 7th St., Tucson, AZ 85710

Dialogist, Michael Loruss, 14172 Sacramento St., Fontana, CA 92336

DIG, P.O. Box 608, Wainscott, NY 11975

Diode, 421 S. Pine St., Richmond, VA 23220

District Lit, 2016 N. Adams St., #312, Arlington, VA 22201

Divinity Press, 1203 Hurlock Court, Bear, DE 19701

The DMQ Review, 16393 Bonnie Lane, Los Gatos, CA 95032

DNA Ezine, P.O. Box 746, Columbia, CA 95310

The Doctor T. J. Eckleburg Review, 1717 Massachusetts Ave., NW, #104, Washington, DC 20036

Doire Press, Aille, Inverin, County Galway, Ireland

Dos Gatos Press, 1310 Crestwood Rd., Austin, TX 78722

Drafthorse, Lincoln Memorial University, 6965 Cumberland Gap Parkway, Harrogate, TN 37752

Dragoncor Productions, 12530 Culver Blvd., #3, Los Angeles, CA 90066-6622

Dragonfly Press, P.O. Box 746, Columbia, CA 95310

Drash, 2632 NE 80th St., Seattle, WA 98115-4622

Dreams & Nightmares, 1300 Kicker Rd., Tuscaloosa, AL 35404

Driftwood Press, 851 SE 13th Court, Pompano Beach, FL 33060-9526

The Drum Literary Magazine, 19 Pelham Rd., Weston, MA 02493

Drunk in a Midnight Choir, 4416 NE 10th Ave., Ste. B, Portland, OR 97211

Drunken Boat, c/o Wendt, 147 Rosedale Apts., Hershey, PA 17033

Drunken Monkeys, 5016 Bakman, #110, No. Hollywood, CA 91601

Duende, 4914 43rd Ave. So., Seattle, WA 98118

Dunes Review, P.O. Box 1505, Traverse City, MI 49685

Dzanc Books, 1334 Woodbourne St., Westland, MI 48186

E

ECW Press, 2120 Queen St. East, Toronto, Ontario, M4E 1E2, Canada

East Jasmine Review, 601 N. Barranca Ave., Glendora, CA 91741

Echo Ink Review, 9800 W. 83rd Terrace, Overland Park, KS 6621

Eclectica Magazine, 67 W. Etruria St., Seattle, WA 98119-1916

Ecotone, UNCW, 601 S. College Rd., Wilmington, NC 28403-3201

Edgar & Lenore's Publishing, 13547 Ventura Blvd., Sherman Oaks, CA 91423

Edge, PO Box 101, Wellington, NV 89444

Educe Journal, 712 ½ W. Franklin, Boise, ID 83702

Edwin E. Smith Publishing, 199 Clark Rd., McRae, AR 72102

Eiso Publishing, 3450 Wayne Ave., #12P, Bronx, NY 10462

Ekphrasis, PO Box 161236, Sacramento, CA 95816-1236

ELT Publications, LLC, P.O. Box 904, Washingtonville, NY 10992

El Zarape Press, 1413 Jay Ave., McAllen, TX 78504

Electric Literature, 147 Prince St., Brooklyn, NY 11201

Elephant Rock Books, P.O. Box 119, Ashford, CT 06278

Eleven Eleven Journal, 1111 Eighth St., S.F., CA 94107

Emby Press, 3675 Essex Ave., Atlanta, GA 30339

Emerge Literary Journal, 9 Waterford Circle, Washingtonville, NY 10092

Emerson Review, Emerson College, 120 Boylston St., Boston, MA 02116

Emprise Review, 2100 N. Leverett Ave., #28, Fayetteville, AR 72703-2233

Empty Sink Publishing, 2330 Boxer Palm, San Antonio, TX 78213

Encircle Publications, P.O. Box 187, Farmington, ME 04938

Engine Books, P.O. Box 44167, Indianapolis, IN 46244

The Enigmatist, 104 Bronco Dr., Georgetown, TX 78633

Enizagam, Oakland School for the Arts, 530 18th St., Oakland, CA 94612

Epiphany, P.O. Box 2132, Sag Harbor, NY 11963

Epoch, 251 Goldwin Smith Hall, Cornell University, Ithaca NY 14853-3201

The Equalizer, P.O. Box 272, North Bennington, VT 05257

Equus Press, 22 rue Claude Lorrain, 75016, Paris, France

Erie Times News, 205 West 12th St., Erie, PA 16534-0001

Escape Into Life, 108 Gladys Drive, Normal, IL 61761

Espial, 12401 SE 320th St., Auburn, WA 98092

The Evansville Review, 1800 Lincoln Ave, Evansville, IN 47722

Evening Street Press, 625 Edgecliff Drive, Columbus, OH 43235

Event, PO Box 2503, New Westminster, BC, V3L 5B2, Canada

Every Day Publishing, P.O. Box 2482, 349 W. Georgia St., Vancouver BC, Canada V6B 3W7

Exit 7, 4810 Alben Barkley Dr., Paducah, KY 42001

Exit 13, P.O. Box 423, Fanwood, NJ 07023

Expressions, 1 Barnard Dr., Oceanside, CA 92056

Exter Press, 116 Greene St., Cumberland, MD 21502

Extract(s), 464 Rockland, Manchester, NH 03102

Eye to the Telescope, 1300 Kicker Rd., Tuscaloosa, AL 35404

F

F Magazine, 3800 DeBarr Rd., Anchorage, AK 99508

FM Publishing, P.O. Box 4211, Atlanta, GA 30302

The Fabulist Words & Art, 1377 Fifth Ave., San Francisco, CA 94122

failbetter, 2022 Grove Ave., Richmond, VA 23220

Fairy Tale Review, English Dept., Univ. of Arizona, Tucson, AZ 85721

Falling Star Magazine, 1691 Tiburon Court, Thousand Oaks, CA 91362

Fantastique Unfettered, 21 Indian Trail, Hickory Creek, TX 73065

The Farallon Review, 1017 L St., #348, Sacramento, CA 95814

Faultline, English Dept., UC Irvine, Irvine, CA 92697-2650

Feile-Festa, 15 Colonial Gardens, Brooklyn, NY 11209

Femspec, 1610 Rydalmount Rd., Cleveland Heights, OH 44118

Fender Stitch, 9301 Fairmead Dr., Charlotte, NC 28269

The Feral Press, P.O. Box 358, Oyster Bay, NY 11771

Festival Writer, 688 Knox Road 900 North, Gilson, IL 61436

Fiction Advocate, Oxford Univ. Press, 198 Madison Ave., New York, NY 10016

Fiction Fix, 1909 Maiden Lane SW, Roanoke, VA 24015

Fiction International, SDSU, San Diego, CA 92182-6020

Fiction Week Literary Review, 887 South Rice Rd., Ojai, CA 93023

Fiddleblack, P.O. Box 78, Peninsula, OH 44264

The Fiddlehead, Univ. New Brunswick, Fredericton, NB E3B 5A3, Canada

Field, 50 North Professor St., Oberlin, OH 44074-1091

Fifth Wednesday, P.O. Box 4033, Lisle, IL 60532-9033

Fiktion, Gallus, Sredzkistr. 57, 10405 Berlin, Germany

The Filid Chapbook, 16-6828 Rue Clark, Montreal, QC, H2S 3E9, Canada

Finishing Line Press, P.O. Box 1626, Georgetown, KY 40324

The First Line, PO Box 250382, Plano, TX 75025-0382

First Step Press, P.O. Box 902, Norristown, PA 19404-0902

Fithian Press, P.O. Box 2790, McKinleyville, CA 95519

5 AM, Box 205, Spring Church, PA 15686

Five Chapters, 387 Third Ave., Brooklyn, NY 11215

580 Split, Mills College, English Dept. 5000 MacArthur Blvd., Oakland, CA 94613

Five Oaks Press, 6 Five Oaks Dr., Newburgh, NY 12550

Five Points, Georgia State University, P.O. Box 3999, Atlanta, GA 30302-3999

Fjords, 2932 B Langhorne Rd., Lynchburg, VA 24501-1734

Flame Flower, 3322 King St., Apt. B, Berkeley, CA 94703

Flash Fiction, University of Missouri, 107 Tate Hall, Columbia, MO 65211

Flash Frontier, P.O. Box 910, Kerikeri 0245, New Zealand

Flashquake, 804 Northcrest Dr., Birmingham, AL 35235

Fledgling Rag, 1716 Swarr Run Rd., J-108, Lancaster, PA 17601

Fleeting, 125 Lower Green Rd., Tunbridge Wells, TN4 8TT, United Kingdom

Fleur-de-Lis Press, 851 S. Fourth St., Louisville, KY 40203

The Flexible Persona, 3000 Bissonnet St., Ste. 6206, Houston, TX 77005

Flint Hills Review, 1 Kellogg Circle, Emporia, KS 66801-5415

The Florida Review, English Dept., Univ. of Central Florida, 4000 Central Florida Blvd., Orlando, FL 32816

Flycatcher, 5595 Lake Island Dr., Atlanta, GA 30327

Flying House, 1622 Hatch Pl., Downers Grove, IL 60516

Flyleaf, 6627 Old Oaks Blvd., Pearland, TX 77584

Flyway, English Dept., 206 Ross Hall, Iowa State Univ., Ames, LA 50011

Folded Word, 79 Tracy Way, Meredith, NH 03253-5409

Foliate Oak Literary Magazine, UAM Box 3460, Monticello, AR 71656

Fomite, 58 Peru St., Burlington, VT 05401-8606

Foothill, Jagels Bldg., 165 East Tenth St., Claremont, CA 91711-6186

Fordham University Press, 2546 Belmont Ave., Bronx, NY 10458

Forest Avenue Press, 6327 SW Capitol Hwy, Portland, OR 97239

Forge, 1610 S. 22nd, Apt. 1, Lincoln, NE 68502

Fort Hemlock Press, P.O. Box 11, Brooksville, ME 04617

Fortunate Childe, P.O. Box 130085, Birmingham, AL 35213

Found Poetry Review, 4400 East West Highway, Bethesda, MD 20814

Four and Twenty Poetry, P.O. Box 61782, Vancouver, WA 98666

Four Chambers Press, 1005 E. Moreland, St., Phoenix, AZ 85006

4 Stops Press, 225 S. Olive, #101, L.A. CA 90012

Four Way Books, P.O. Box 535, Village Station, New York, NY 10014

Fourteen Hills, S.F.S.U. 1400 Holloway Ave., Humanities 372, S.F., CA 94132

Fourth Genre, 235 Bessey Hall, East Lansing, MI 48824-1033

The Fourth River, Chatham University, 1 Woodland Rd., Pittsburgh, PA 15232

Free Scholar Press, P.O. Box 206, Sparkill, NY 10976

Free State Review, 3637 Black Rock Rd., Upperco, MO 21155

Freedom Fiction Journal, Nirli Villa, 7, Village Rd., Bhandup west, Mumbai
  – 400078, India

Freelancelot Publishing, 7001 Seaview Ave., NW, Seattle, WA 98117

The Freeman, 600 Merrimon Ave., Apt. 18B, Asheville, NC 28804

Freight Stories, Ball State University, Muncie, IN 47306-0460

Freshwater, Asnuntuck Community College, 170 Elm St., Enfield, CT 06082

Fringe Magazine, 93 Fox Rd., Apt. 5A, Edison, NJ 08817

Front Porch Journal, Texas State University, 601 University Dr., San Marcos,
  TX 78666

Fugue, University of Idaho, 875 Perimeter Dr., Moscow, ID 83844

Full Grown People, 106 Tripper Ct., Charlottesville, VA 22903

Full of Crow, P.O. Box 1123, Easton, PA 18044

Full of Crow Fiction, 2929 Nicol, Oakland, CA 94602

The Furious Gazelle, 55 Waldorf Court, Brooklyn, NY 11230

Future Cycle Press, 313 Pan Will Rd., Mineral Bluff, GA 30559

Fwriction, 519 E. 78th St., Apt. 3G, New York, NY 10075

G

Gallaudet University Press, 800 Florida Ave. NE, Washington, DC 20002-3695

Garden Oak Press, 1953 Huffstatler St., Fallbrook, CA 92028

Gargoyle Magazine, 3819 13th St. N., Arlington, VA 22201-4922

Gaspereau Press, 47 Church Ave., Kentville, Nova Scotia, Canada B4N 2M7

Gemini Magazine, PO Box 1485, Onset, MA 02558

The Georgia Review, University of Georgia, Athens, GA 30602-9009

Gertrude Press, P.O. Box 83948, Portland, OR 97283

The Gettysburg Review, Gettysburg College, Gettysburg, PA 17325

Ghost Ocean Magazine, 5234 N. Wayne Ave., #1, Chicago, IL 60640

Ghost Town Literary Review, 1516 Myra St., Redlands, CA 92373

Gigantic, 250 Adelphi St., #16, Brooklyn, NY 11205

Gigantic Sequins, 2335 E. Fletcher St., Philadelphia, PA 19125

Gilbert Magazine, 4117 Pebblebrook Circle, Minneapolis, MN 55437

Gingerbread House, 236 Lake Ella Dr., Tallahassee, FL 32303

Gival Press, PO Box 3812, Arlington, VA 22203

Glass Lyre Press, P.O. Box 2693, Glenview, IL 60026

Glen Hill Publications, P.O. Box 62, Soulsbyville, CA 95372

Glimmer Train Press, P.O. Box 80430, Portland, OR 97280-1430

Glint Literary Journal, 1200 Murchison Rd., Fayetteville, NC 28301

Globe Light Press, 8411 Cienega Rd., Mentone, CA 92359

Gobshite Quarterly, 338 NE Roth St., Portland, OR 97211

Gold Gable Press, 1405 Michaux Rd., Chapel Hill, NC 27514

Gold Man Review, P.O. Box 21391, Keiser, OR 97307

Gold Wake Press, 5108 Avalon Dr., Randolph, MA 02368

Golden Handcuffs Review, 1825 NE 58th St., Seattle, WA 98105.

Good Men Project, 83 Beech St., #3, Belmont, MA 02478

Good Sheppard Press, 110 Landers St., #2, San Francisco, CA 94114

Goose Lane Editions, Ste. 330, 500 Beaverbrook Court, Fredericton NB, E3B 5X4 Canada

Goreyesque, 1637 W. Olive Ave., Unit 3, Chicago, IL 60660

Gorse, 48 the Poplars, Monkstown Valley, Monkstown, Co., Dublin, Ireland

Grandma Moses Press, 331 Linda Vista Rd., Las Cruces, NM 88005

Grain, Box 67, Saskatoon, SK, S7K 3K1, Canada

Granta, 12 Addison Ave., Holland Park, London W11 4QR, United Kingdom

Gravel, University of Arkansas at Monticello, Monticello, AR 71655

Gray Dog Press, 2727 S. Mt. Vernon #4, Spokane, WA 99223

Graywolf Press, 250 Third Avenue No., Ste. 600, Minneapolis, MN 55401

The Great American Literary Magazine, 11621 Deerfield Dr., Yucaipa, CA 92399

Great Lakes Review, 2050 Kingsborough Dr., Painesville, OH 44077

Great River Review, PO Box 406, Red Wing, MN 55066

great weather for MEDIA, 515 Broadway, #2B, New York, NY 10012

Green Bay Group, 793 E. Foothill Blvd., San Luis Obispo, CA 93405-1615

Green Hills Literary Lantern, Truman State Univ., Kirksville, MO 63501

Green Lantern Press, 1511 N. Milwaukee Ave., 2nd Floor, Chicago, IL 60622

Green Mountains Review, 337 College Hill, Johnson, VT 05672

Green Poet Press, P.O. Box 6927, Santa Barbara, CA 93160

The Green Silk Journal, 221 Shenandoah Ave., Winchester, VA 22601

Green Writers Press, 34 Miller Rd., West Brattleboro, VT 05301

The Greensboro Review, UNC Greensboro, Greensboro, NC 27402-6170

Greenwoman, 1823 W. Pikes Peak Ave., Colorado Springs, CO 80904

Greta Fox Publishing, P.O. Box 571, Coarsegold, CA 93614

Grey Sparrow Press, P.O. Box 211664, St. Paul, MN 55121

Grey Wolfe Publishing, P.O. Box 1088, Birmingham, MI 48009

Grist, 301 McClung Tower, Univ. of Tennessee, Knoxville, TN 37996

Grolier Poetry Press, 6 Plympton St., Cambridge, MA 02138

Groundwaters, PO Box 50, Lorane, OR 97451

The Grove Review, 1631 NE Broadway, PMB #137, Portland, OR 97232

Guernica Magazine, 106 Borden Ave., Wilmington, NC 28403
Gulf Coast, Dept of English, University of Houston, Houston, TX 77204-3013
Gypsy Shadow Publishing, 222 Llano St., Lockhart, TX 78644

H

H.H.B. Publishing, 9550 S. Eastern Ave., Ste. 253, Henderson, NV 89123
H.O.W. Journal, 12 Desbrosses St., New York, NY 10013
The Habit of Rainy Nights Press, 900 NE 81st Ave., #209, Portland, OR 97213
Hackwriters, 7 Cromwell Rd. Cleethorpes. N E Lincs, DN 35 0AL, UK
Haight Ashbury Literary Journal, 558 Joost Ave., San Francisco, CA 94127
The Hairpin, 111 River St., Hoboken, NJ 07030
Hamilton Arts & Letters, 92 Stanley Ave., Hamilton ON, L8P 2L3, Canada
Hamilton Stone Review, P.O. Box 457, Jay, NY 12941
Hampden-Sydney Poetry Review, Box 66, Hampden-Sydney, VA 23943
Hand Fashioned Media, 300 South Central Ave., #C55, Hartsdale, NY 10530
Hand Type Press, P.O. Box 3941, Minneapolis, MN 55403-0941
Harbor Mountain Press, Box 519, Brownsville, VT 05037
Harbour Publishing Co., P.O. Box 219, Madeira Park, BC V0N 2H0 Canada
The Harlequin, 2001 Westheimer Rd., #255, Houston, TX 77098
Harpur Palate, PO Box 6000, Binghamton University, Binghamton, NY 13902
Harvard Review, Lamont Library, Harvard University, Cambridge, MA 02138
Harvard Square Editions, 851 E. Belmont Ave., Salt Lake City, UT 84105
Haunted Waters Press, 1886 T-Bird Drive, Front Royal, VA 22630-9038
Hawaii Pacific Review, 1060 Bishop St., LB 7A, Honolulu, HI 96813
Hawkins Publishing Group, P.O. Box 447, Bellflower, CA 90707
Hawthorne Books, 2201 NE 23rd Ave., 3rd Floor, Portland, OR 97212
Hayden's Ferry Review, A.S.U., P.O. Box 870302, Tempe, AZ 85287-0302
Headmistress Press, P.O. Box 275, Eagle Rock, MO 65641
The Healing Muse, 618 Irving Ave., Syracuse, NY 13210
Heavy Feather Review, 4416 Grayson St., Kettering, OH 45429
The Hedgehog Review, UVA, PO Box 400816, Charlottesville, VA 22904-4816
Hedgerow Books, 71 South Pleasant St., Amherst, MA 01002
Helen: A Literary Magazine, 6650 S. Sandhill Rd., #231, Las Vegas, NV 89120
Hen House Press, 506 Mountainview Ave., Valley Cottage, NY 10989
Hennen's Observer, 9660 Falls of Neuse Rd., Ste. 138, Raleigh, NC 27615
Heron's Nest, 476 Guilford Circle, Marietta, GA 30068
Heyday, P.O. Box 9145, Berkeley, CA 94709
Hidden Clearing Books, 6768 Real Princess Lane, Baltimore, MD 21207
High Coup, P.O. Box 1004, Stockbridge, MA 01262
High Country News, 119 Grand Ave., PO Box 1090, Paonia, CO 81428 (970-527-4898

High Desert Journal, P.O. Box 8554, Missoula, MT 59807

High Hill Press, 2731 Cumberland Landing, St. Charles, MO 63303

Hip Pocket Press, 5 Del Mar Court, Orinda, CA 94563

Hippocampus, 1 Alpha Dr., Elizabethtown, PA 17022

Hiram Poetry Review, PO Box 162, Hiram, OH 44234

Hither & Yahn, P.O. Box 233, San Luis Rey, CA 92068

Hobart, PO Box 1658, Ann Arbor, MI 48106

Hobble Creek Review, PO Box 3511, West Wendover, NV 89883

Hobblebush Books, 17A Old Milford Rd., Brookline, NH 03033

The Hollins Critic, P.O. Box 9538, Roanoke, VA 24020-1538

Home Planet News, PO Box 455, High Falls, NY 12440

Homebound, P.O. Box 1442, Pawcatuck, CT 06379

Honest Publishing, 21 Valley Mews, Cross Deep, Twickenham TW1 4QT, UK

Hoot, 1413 Academy Lane, Elkins Park, PA 19027

The Hoot and Hare Review, 309 Sarabande Dr., Cary, NC 27513

Hopewell Publications, P.O. Box 11, Titusville, NJ 08560

The Hopkins Review, John Hopkins Univ., 081 Gilman Hall, 3400 N. Charles St., Baltimore, MD 21218-2685

Horror Society Press, 6635 W. Happy Valley Rd., Glendale, AZ 85310

Hot Metal Bridge, University of Pittsburgh, English Dept, 4200 Fifth Ave., Pittsburgh, PA 15260

Hotel Amerika, Columbia College, 600 S. Michigan Ave., Chicago, IL 60605

Hub City Press, 186 West Main St., Spartanburg, SC 29306

The Hudson Review, 684 Park Ave., New York, NY 10065

Huizache, 3007 N. Ben Wilson, Victoria, TX 77901

Hulltown 360, 7806 Sunday Silence Lane, Midlothian, VA 23112

Humber Literary Review, 205 College Blvd., Toronto, ON M9W 5L7, Canada

Hunger Mountain, 36 College St., Montpelier, VT 05602

Hustle, Sarabande Books, Inc., 2234 Dundee Rd., Louisville KY 40205

Hyacinth Girl Press, 312 ½ Lenox Ave., Forest Hills, PA 15221

Hydeout Press, 1262 Fry Ave., Lakewood, OH 44107

I

I-70 Review, 5021 S. Tierney Dr., Independence, MO 64055

iARTistas, 604 Vale St., Bloomington, IL 61701

Ibbetson Street Press, 25 School Street, Somerville, MA 02143

Ice Cube Press, 205 North Front St., North Liberty, IA 52317-9302

The Idaho Review, Boise State Univ., 1910 University Dr., Boise, ID 83725

ideonics, 40 Central Park So., New York, NY 10019

The Idiom Magazine, 2739 Woodbridge Ave., Edison, NJ 08817

Ideomancer Speculative Fiction, 141 Howland Ave., Toronto, Ontario, M5R 3B4, Canada

Ilanot Review, Shaindy Rudoff Graduate Program in Creative Writing, Bar-Ilan University Ramat Gan, 5290002 Israel

Illuminations, College of Charleston, 66 George St., Charleston, SC 29424

Illya's Honey, PO Box 700865, Dallas, TX 75370

Immagine&Poesia, C. Galileo Ferraris 75, 10128, Torino, Italy

Image, 3307 Third Avenue West, Seattle, WA 98119

In Other Words: Merida, Calle 58, #301A, X25A Y27, Colonia Itzimna, Merida, Yucatan 97100, Mexico

In Posse Review, 11 Jordan Ave., San Francisco, CA 94118

Incubator, 15 Cairndore Vale, Newtownards, BT23 8PF, Northern Ireland

India Currents, 1885 Lundy Ave., Ste. 220, San Jose, CA 95131-9983

Indian Literature, Sahitya Akademi, Rabindra Bhawan, Ferozeshah Rd., New Delhi, 110001, India

Indiana Review, 1020 E. Kirkwood Ave., Bloomington, IN 47405-7103

Indiana Voice Journal, 3038 E. Clem Rd., Anderson, IN 46017

InDigest, c/o Nelson, 2815 34th St., 3A, Astoria, NY 11103

The Inflectionist Review, 11322 SE 45th Ave., Portland, OR 97222

Inkwell, Manhattanville College, 2900 Purchase St., Purchase, NY 10577

Inlandia, 4178 Chestnut St., Riverside, CA 92501

The Intentional Quarterly, 267 Clifton Place, #5C, Brooklyn, NY 11216

Interim, UNLV, 4505 Maryland Pkwy, Box 455011, Las Vegas, NV 89154-5011

International Poetry Review, P.O. Box 26170, Greensboro, NC 27402-6170

Intranslation, 85 Hancock St., Brooklyn, NY 11233

iO, 1402 N. Valley Pkwy, #404, Lewisville, TX 75077

Ion Drive Publishing, 6251 Drexel Ave., Los Angeles, CA 90048

The Iowa Review, 308 EPB, University of Iowa, Iowa City, IA 52242

Iris G. Press, 1716 Swarr Run Rd., J-108, Lancaster, PA 17601

Iron Horse, English Dept., Texas Tech Univ., Lubbock, TX 79409-3091

IsoLibris, 4927 6th Pl., Meridian, MS 39305

Isthmus, 4701 SW Admiral Way, #386, Seattle, WA 98116

J

J Journal, 524 West 59th St., 7th fl, NY, NY 10019

Jabberwock Review, Mississippi State Univ., Mississippi State, MS 39762

Jacar Press, 6617 Deerview Trail, Durham, NC 27712

Jaded Ibis Press, P.O. Box 61122, Seattle, WA 98141-6112

Jelly Bucket, 521 Lancaster Ave., Case Annex 467, Richmond, KY 40475

Jersey Devil Press, 1507 Dunmore St. SW, Roanoke, VA 24015

Jet Fuel Review, Lewis University, #1092, Romeoville, IL 60446-2200

Jewish*fiction*.net, Editor, c/o Nora Gold, Weiss International Ltd., 378 Walmer Rd., Ste. 1000, Toronto, ON, M5R 2Y4, Canada

Jewish Women's Literary Annual, 40 Central Park South, Apt. 6D, New York, NY 10019

jmww, 2105 E. Lamley St., Baltimore, MD 21231

John Gosslee Books, 2932 B Langhorne Rd., Lynchburg, VA 24501

John M Hardy Publishing Co., 14781 Memorial Dr., Houston, TX 77459

The Journal, 17 High St., Maryport, Cumbria CA15 6BQ, UK

The Journal, Ohio State Univ., 164 West 17th Ave., Columbus, OH 43210

Journal of Experimental Fiction, 1110 Varsity Blvd., DeKalb, IL 60115

Journal of New Jersey Poets, 214 Center Grove Rd., Randolph, NJ 07869-2086

Jovialities Entertainment Co., 521 Park Ave., Elyria, OH 44035

Joyland, 302 Nassau Ave., 3R Nassau Ave., Brooklyn, NY 11222

Juked, 3941 Newdale Rd., #26, Chevy Chase, MD 20815

Junk, 16233 SE 10th St., Bellevue, WA 98008

K

Kartika Review, 934 Brannan St., San Francisco, CA 94103

Kattywompus Press, 2696 W. Saint James Pkwy., Cleveland Heights, OH 44106

Kelly's Cove Press, 2733 Prince St., Berkeley, CA 94705

Kelsay Books, 24600 Mountain Avenue 35, Hemet, CA 92544

Kelsey Review, Mercer County Community College, 1200 Old Trenton Rd., West Windsor, NJ 08550-3407

Kentucky Review, 3351 Cove Lake Drive, #152, Lexington, KY 40515

Kenyon Review, Finn House, 102 W. Wiggin St., Gambier, OH 43022

Kerf, 883 W. Washington Blvd., Crescent City, CA 95531-8361

Kestrel, 264000, Fairmont State Univ., 1201 Locust Ave., Fairmont, WV 26554

Kin, 425 S. 5th St., Brooklyn, NY 11211

Kind of a Hurricane, Press, 1817 Green Place, Ormond Beach, FL 32174

Kitsune Books, P.O. Box 1154, Crawfordville, FL 32326-1154

Kiwi Publishing, P.O. Box 3852, Woodbridge, CT 06525

The Knicknackery, 170 Carroll St., Brooklyn, NY 11231

Knot Magazine, 721 East 8th, Springfield, CO 81073

Kolob Canyon Review, Southern Utah Univ., English Dept., 351 West University Blvd., Cedar City, UT 84720

Kore Press, P.O. Box 42315, Tucson, AZ 85733-2315

Korean Expatriate Literature, 11533 Promenade Drive, Santa Fe Springs, CA 90670

Kudzu House Press, 299 Commerce St., Montevallo, AL 35115

Kweli Journal, P.O. Box 693, New York, NY 10021

KY Story, 2111B Fayette Dr., Richmond, KY 40475
KYSO Flash, 1810 Stone Mason Court #2, Fayetteville, NC 28304

L

La Muse Press, 1 East University Pkwy, Unit 801, Baltimore, MD 21218
Labello Press, Unit 4C Gurtnafleur Business Park, Clonmel, County Tipper-
ary, Ireland
The Labletter, 3712 N. Broadway, #241, Chicago, IL 60613-4235
Lafayette Press, P.O. Box 40831, Lafayette, LA 70504-0831
Lake Effect, Penn State Erie, 4951 College Drive, Erie, PA 16563-1501
Lalitamba, 110 West 86th St., #5D, New York, NY 10024
Lamberson Corona Press, P.O. Box 1116, West Babylon, NY 11704
Lamar University Press, 400 MLK Blvd., Beaumont, TX 77710
Lana Turner Journal, 2309 Pearl St., Santa Monica, CA 90405
Lantern Journal, 15001 East 44th St., Independence, MO 64055
Lanternfish Press, 22 N. 3rd St., Philadelphia, PA 11975
Lapham's Quarterly, 33 Iriving Place, New York, NY 10003
Lascaux Review, Parrish, Lessingstr 27, 55543 Bad Kreuznach, Germany
Lavender Review, P.O. Box 275, Eagle Rock, MO 65641-0275
Lay Bare the Canvas, 99 Cranberry Terrace, Cranston, RI 02921
Leaf Press, Box 416, Lantzville, BC, V0R 2H0 Canada
Ledgetop Publishing, P.O. Box 105, Richmond, MA 02154
Legas, P.O Box 149, Mineola, NY 11501
Levellers Press, 71 S. Pleasant St., Amherst, MA 01002
Levins Publishing, 2300 Kennedy St., NE. #160, Minneapolis, MN 55413
Light, 500 Joseph C. Wilson Blvd., CPU Box 271051, Rochester, NY 14627
Lighthouse, 3003 SE 53rd Ave., Portland, OR 97206
Lilly Press, 510 Braddock Ave., #2, Daytona Beach, FL 32118
Lime Hawk Literary Arts Collective, E. 4th St., #9, New York, NY 10003
The Lindenwood Review, 209 S. Kingshighway, St. Charles, MO 63301-1695
Lines + Stars, 1801 Clydesdale Place NW #323, Washington, DC 20009
Lips, P. O. Box 616, Florham Park, NJ 07932
Liquid Imagination, 7800 Loma Del Norte Rd. NE , Albuquerque, NM 87109
Literal Latté, 200 E. 10th St., STe. 240, New York 10003
The Literarian, 17 East 47th St., New York, NY 10017
The Literary Bohemian, Po Vode 381 01 Cesky Krumlov, Czech Republic
Literary Imagination, ALSCW, 650 Beacon St., Ste. 510, Boston, MA 02215
Literary Juice, 511 Travers Circle, Apt. C, Mishawaka, IN 46545
The Literary Lunch Room, 209 Riggs Ave., Severna Park, MD 21146
Literary Orphans, 7307 N. Greenview Ave., Chicago, IL 60626
The Literary Review, 285 Madison Ave./M-GH2-01, Madison, NJ 07940
The Literati Quarterly, 1441 Leah Ave., #2705, San Marcos, TX 78666

Little Balkans Review, 315 South Hugh St., Frontenae, KS 66763

Little Fiction/Big Truths, 353-24 Southport St., Toronto, ON M6S 4Z1, Canada

Little Patuxent Review, 5008 Brampton Pkwy, Ellicott City, MD 21043

Little Red Tree Publishing, 635 Ocean Ave., New London, CT 06320

Little Star, 107 Bank St., New York, NY 10014

The Lives You Touch, P.O. Box 276, Gwynedd Valley, PA 19437-0276

Livingston Press, Station 22, Univ. of West Alabama, Livingston, AL 35470

Local Gems Press, 408 7th St., East Northport, NY 11731

Long Hidden, 330 Cochituate Rd., #1433, Framingham, MA 01702

Long Story, 18 Eaton St., Lawrence, MA 01843

Long Story, Short Journal, 39 Upper Cork St., Mitchelstown, Co. Cork, Ireland

Lookout Books, 601 South College Rd., Wilmington, NC 28403

Loose Leaves Publishing, 4218 Allison Rd., Tucson, AZ 85712

Lorimer Press, PO Box 1013, Davidson, NC 28036

The Los Angeles Review, P.O. Box 2458, Redmond, WA 98073

The Los Angeles Review of Books, 4470 Sunset Blvd., #115, Los Angeles, CA 90027

Los Angeles Poets' Press, 24721 Newhall Ave., Santa Clarita, CA 91321

The Los Angeles Review of Los Angeles, 1316 Lemoyne St., #22, L.A., CA 90026

Lost Coast Review, 41 Shearwater Place, Newport Beach, CA 92660

Lost Horse Press, 105 Lost Horse Lane, Sandpoint, ID 83864

Louffa Press, 1750 2nd Ave., Apt. 4S, New York, NY 10128

The Louisiana State University Press, 3990 Lakeshore Dr., Baton Rouge, LA 70803

The Louisville Review, 851 South Fourth St., Louisville, KY 40203

Love + Lust, Open to Interpretation, 599 Laurel Ave., #6, St. Paul, MN 55102

Loving Healing Press Inc., 5145 Pontiac Trail, Ann Arbor, MI 48105-9279

low key/slate, #262, Street 31, F-10/1, Islamabad, Pakistan

Lowestoft Chronicle Press, 1925 Massachusetts Ave., Cambridge, MA 02140

Loyal Stone Press, 13549 36th Ave. NE, Seattle, WA 98125

Lucid Moose Lit, 1386 E. Hellman St, #1, Long Beach, CA 90813

Lumina, 1 Mead Way, Bronxville, NY 10708

Luminis Books, 13245 Blacktern Way, Carmel, IN 46033

Lunch Ticket, 400 Corporate Pointe, Culver City, CA 90230

Lynx House Press, P.O. Box 940, Spokane, WA 99210

M

The MacGuffin, 18600 Haggerty Rd., Livonia, MI 48152

Madcap Review, 3030 Verdin Ave., Cincinnati, OH 45211

The Madison Review, English Dept., 600 North Park St., Madison, WI 53706

Magnapoets, 13300 Tecumseh Rd. E., Tecumseh, Ont. N8N 4R8, Canada

Main Street Rag, P.O. Box 690100, Charlotte, NC 28227

MAKE, 2229 W. Iowa St., #3, Chicago, IL 60622

make/shift, PO Box 2697, Venice, CA 90294

The Malahat Review, PO Box 1700 STN CSC, Victoria BC V8W 2Y2 Canada

Mambo Academy of Kitty Wang, P.O. Box 5, North Branford, CT 06471

The Manhattan Review, 440 Riverside Dr., #38, New York, NY 10027

Manic D Press, P.O. Box 410804, San Francisco, CA 94141

Manifest Station, Linda Loewenthal, Black Inc., 335 Adams St., Ste. 2707, Brooklyn, NY 11201

Manoa, English Dept., University of Hawai'i, Honolulu, HI 96822

Many Mountains Moving, 1705 Lombard St., Philadelphia, PA 19146-1518

Map Literary, William Paterson College, 300 Pompton Rd., Wayne, NJ 07470

Marathon Lit Magazine, 362 Dupont St., Philadelphia, PA 19128

Marco Polo, 153 Cleveland Ave., Athens, GA 30601

Marin Poetry Center, P.O. Box 9091, San Rafael, CA 94912

Marriage Publishing House, 800 SE 10th Ave., Portland, OR 97214

Martha's Vineyard Arts & Ideas, P.O. Box 1130, West Tisbury, MA 02575

Mary Celeste Press, 393 Pinewood Dr., Wyckoff, NJ 07481

The Massachusetts Review, 211 Hicks Way, Amherst, MA 01003

The Masters Review, 1824 NW Couch St., Portland, OR 97209

Matchbook, 31 Berkley Place #2, Buffalo, NY 14209

Matter Press, P.O. Box 704, Wynnewood, PA 19096

Maudlin House, 1463 N. Winslowe Dr., Palatine, IL 60074

Mayapple Press, 362 Chestnut Hill Rd., Woodstock, NY 12498

Mayhaven Publishing, 803 E. Burcthorn Circle, Mahomet, IL 61853

The McNeese Review, MSU Box 93465, Lake Charles, LA 70609-2655

McSweeney's Publishing, 849 Valencia, San Francisco, CA 94110

Mead Magazine, 720 Fort Washington Ave., #T, New York, NY 10040

The Meadow, VISTA B300, 7000 Dandini Blvd., Reno, NV 89512

Measure, University of Evansville, 1800 Lincoln Ave., Evansville, IN 47722

Meat for Tea: The Valley Review, 27 Knipfer Ave., Easthampton, MA 01027

The Medulla Review, 612 Everett Rd., Knox, TN 37934

Memoir Journal, 1316 67th St., #8, Emeryville, CA 94608

Memorious, 409 N. Main St., 2A, Hattiesburg, MS 39401

Menacing Hedge, 424 SW Kenyon St., Seattle, WA 98106

Menu, 87-16, #501, Daejo-dong, Eunpyong-Ku, Seoul, South Korea 122-030

Meridian, University of Virginia, P.O. Box 400145, Charlottesville, VA 22904

Metazen, Ulrich-von-Huttenstr. 8, 81739 Munich, Germany

Michigan Quarterly Review, 915 E. Washington St., Ann Arbor, MI 48109-1070

Michigan State University Press, 1405 S. Harrison, E. Lansing, MI 48823

Mid-American Review, Bowling Green State Univ., Bowling Green, OH 43403

Middle Gray Magazine, 88 Washington St., Brighton, MA 02135

Middlewest, 5821 N. Winthrop Ave., #25, Chicago, IL 60660

Midway Journal, 8 Durham St., #3, Somerville, MA 02143

Midwestern Gothic, 957 E. Grant, Des Plaines, IL 60016

The Mighty Rogue Press, P.O. Box 19553, Boulder, CO 80308-2553

Milkweed Editions, 1011 Washington Ave. So., Minneapolis, MN 55415

The Millions, 107 Birch Rd., Highland Lakes, NJ 07422

The Milo Review, 1820 Milo Way, Eugene, OR 97404

Milspeak Books, 3305 Lightning Rd., Borrego Springs, CA 92004

Mina-Helwig Company, 8732 Nottingham Place, La Jolla, CA 92037

The Minnesota Review, Virginia Tech, ASPECT, Blacksburg, VA 24061

Minnetonka Review, P.O. Box 386, Spring Park, MN 55384

MiPOesias, 604 Vale St., Bloomington, IL 61701

Miramar, 342 Oliver Rd., Santa Barbara, CA 93109

Misfit Magazine, 143 Furman St., Schenectady, NY 12304

Misfits' Miscellany, 28 Edward Rd., Hont Bay, Cape Town, 7806, South Africa

The Missing Slate, #262, Street 31, F-10/1, Islamabad, Pakistan

Mississippi Review, 118 College Dr. #5144, Hattiesburg, MS 39406-0001

The Missouri Review, 357 McReynolds Hall, Columbia, MO 65211

Mixed Fruit, 925 Troy Rd., Edwardsville, IL 62025

Mixer.com, 3013 Woodridge Ave., South Bend, IN 46615-3811

MMIP Books, 416 101st Ave., SE, #308, Bellevue, WA 98004

Mobile Album International, Montagne Froide, 89 Grande rue, 25000 Besancon, France

Mobius, the Journal of Social Change, 505 Christianson St., Madison, WI 53714

Mobius, the Poetry Magazine, W5679 State Road 60, Poynette, WI 53955-8564

Modern Haiku, PO Box 33077, Santa Fe, NM 87594-9998

Mojave River Press, 7516 SVL, Victorville, CA 92395

mojo, WSU, English Dept., Box 14, 1845 Fairmount St., Wichita, KS 67260-0014

The Monarch Review, 5033 Brooklyn Ave., NE, Apt. B, Seattle, WA 98105

Monkeybicycle, 206 Bellevue Ave., Floor 2, Montclair, NJ 07043

Moon Maiden Productions, P.O. Box 70, La Pryor, TX 78872

Moon Pie Press, 16 Walton St., Westbrook, ME 04092

MoonPath Press, P.O. Box 1808, Kingston, WA 98346

Moonrise Press, P.O. Box 4288, Los Angeles – Sunland, CA 91041

Moonshot Magazine, 416 Broadway, 3rd Floor, Brooklyn, NY 11211

Mootney Artists, 213-B Main St., Woodbury, TN 37190

The Morning News, 6206 Wynona Ave., Austin, TX 78757

Moss, 377 Baltic St., Ste. 4, Brooklyn, NY 11201

MotesBooks, 89 W. Chestnut St., Williamsburg, KY 40769

Mount Hope, Roger Williams Univ., One Old Ferry Rd., Bristol, RI 02809

Mountain Empire Publishing, P.O. Box 613, 10 Main St., Clifton Forge, VA 24422

Mountain Gazette, P.O. Box 7548, Boulder, CO 80306

Mountain State Press, 2300 MacCorkle Ave. SE, Charleston, WV 25304

Mouse Tales Press, 19558 Green Mountain Dr., Newhall, CA 91321

MousePrints, 43200 Yale Ct., Lancaster, CA 93536

Mouthfeel Press, 15307 Mineral, El Paso, TX 79928

Mozark Press, P.O. Box 1746, Sedalia, MO 65302

Muddy River Poetry Review, 15 Eliot St., Chestnut Hill, MA 02467

Mud Luscious Press, 2115 Sandstone Dr., Fort Collins, CO 80524

Mud Season Review, 1283 Snipe Ireland Rd., Richmond VT 05477

Mudlark, Dept. of English, University of North Florida, 1 UNF Drive, Jacksonville, FL 32224-2645

MungBeing Magazine, 1319 Maywood Ave., Upland, CA 91786

Murder Slim Press, 29 Alpha Rd., Gorleston, Norfolk, NR31 0LQ, UK

Muskrat Press, P.O. Box 13064, Portland, OR 97213

Muse-Pie Press, 73 Pennington Ave., Passaic, NJ 07055

Muumuu House, Tao Lin, 229 E. 29th St., 4K, New York, NY 10016

Muzzle Magazine, 412 S. Albany St., #10, Ithaca, NY 14850

Mythopoetry Scholar, 16211 East Keymar Dr., Fountain Hills, AZ 85268

N

N + 1 Magazine, 68 Jay St., #405, Brooklyn, NY 11201

NaDa Publishing, 1415 Fourth St. SW, Albuquerque, NM 87102

NANO Fiction, P.O. Box 2188, Tuscaloosa, AL 35403

NAP, 5824 Timber Lake Blvd., Indianapolis, IN 46237

Narrative, 2443 Fillmore St., #214, San Francisco, CA 94115

A Narrow Fellow, 4302 Kinloch Rd., Louisville, KY 40207

Nashville Review, 6425 Henry Ford Dr., Nashville, TN 37209

Nat. Brut, 5995 Summerside Dr., Unit 796032, Dallas, TX 75379

The National Poetry Review, P.O. Box 2080, Aptos, CA 95001-2080

Natural Bridge, English Dept., One University Blvd., St. Louis, MO 63121

Naugatuck River Review, PO Box 368, Westfield, MA 01086

Nazar Look Journal, Luntrasului 16, 900338 Constanta, Romania

Negative Capability Press, 62 Ridgelawn Drive East, Mobile, AL 36608

Neon, 8 Village Close, Wilberforce Rd., Norwich, Norfolk NR5 8NA, UK

NeoPoiesis Press, P.O. Box 38037, Houston, TX 77238-8037

New American Writing, 369 Molino Ave., Mill Valley, CA 94941

The New Criterion, 900 Broadway, Ste. 602, New York, NY 10003

New Delta Review, 15 Allen Hall, L.S.U., Baton Rouge, LA 70803

New Directions Books, 80 Eighth Ave., New York, NY 10011

New England Review, Middlebury College, Middlebury, VT 05753

The New Guard, P.O. Box 866, Wells, ME 04090

The New Inquiry, 747 Baker St., San Francisco, CA 94119

New Issues, 1903 W. Michigan Ave., Kalamazoo, MI 49008-5463

New Letters, UMKC, 5100 Rockhill Rd., Kansas City, MO 64110-2499

New Libri Press, 4230 95th Ave., SE, Mercer Island, WA 98040

New Lit Salon Press, 513 Vista on the Lake, Carmel, NY 10512

New Madrid, Murray State University, 7C Faculty Hall, Murray, KY 42071

New Michigan Press, 8058 E. 7th St., Tucson, AZ 85710

New Mirage Journal, 3066 Zelda Rd., #384, Montgomery, AL 36106

New Native Press, P.O. Box 2554, Cullowhee, NC 28723

New Ohio Review, Ohio University, 360 Ellis Hall, Athens, OH 45701

New Orleans Review, Loyola University, Campus Box 50, 6363 St. Charles Ave., New Orleans, LA 70118

The New Orphic Review, 706 Mill St., Nelson, B.C. V1L 4S5 Canada

New Plains Press, P.O. Box 1946, Auburn, AL 36831-1946

New Pop Lit, W3868 Smock Valley Rd., Monroe, WI 53566

New Rivers Press, MSUM, 1104 Seventh Avenue S., Moorhead, MN 56563

New South, Campus Box 1894, Georgia State Univ., Atlanta, GA 30303-3083

New Southerner Magazine, 375 Wood Valley Lane, Louisville, KY 40299

New Urban Review, Box 195, Loyola University, New Orleans, LA 70118

New Verse News, Les Belles Maisons H-11, Jl. Serpong Raya, Serpong Utara, Tangerang-Baten 15310, Indonesia

New York Tyrant, 676 A Ninth Ave., #153, New York, NY 10036

Newfound Journal, 6408 Burns St., Apt. 209, Austin, TX 78752

News Ink Books, 22848 State Route 28, Delhi, NY 13753

NewSouth Books, P.O. Box 1588, Montgomery, AL 36102

Newtown Literary, 91-31 Lamont Ave., #2D, Elmhurst, NY 11373

Night Ballet Press, 123 Glendale Court, Elyria, OH 44035

Nightblade, 11323 126th St., Edmonton, AB T5M 0R5 Canada

Nightwing Publications, 19746 61st Place NE, Kenmore, WA 98028

Nightwood Editions, Box 1779, Gibsons, BC, VON 1VO, Canada

Nimrod, University of Tulsa, 800 South Tucker Dr., Tulsa, OK 74104

Nine Mile Magazine, 4451 Cherry Valley Turnpike, LaFayette, NY 13084

918studio, 918 N. Cody Rd., Le Claire, IA 52753

1966 One Trinity Place, San Antonio, TX 78212-7200

94 Creations, 6706 Crossmoor Lane, Louisville, KY 40222

Ninety-Six Press, English Dept., Furman University, 3300 Poinsett Highway, Greenville, SC 29613

Ninth Letter, University of Illinois, 608 S. Wright St., Urbana, IL 61801

Niteblade, 11323-126 St., Edmonton, Alberta, Canada T5M 0R5

No Tokens Journal, 300 Mercer St., #26E, New York, NY 10003

Noble/Gas Quarterly, P.O. Box 44043, West Allis, WI 53214

The Noise, P.O. Box 1637, Flagstaff, AZ 86002

noisivelvet, 2057 W. Berwyn Ave., #3, Chicago, IL 60625

Nomos Review, 28900 Lakefront Rd., Temecula, CA 92591

NonBinary Review, 101 Cooper St., Santa Cruz, CA 95060

Noon, 1324 Lexington Ave., PMB 298, New York, NY 10128

The Normal School, 5245 N. Backer Ave., M/S PB 98, Fresno, CA 93740

North American Review, Univ. of Northern Iowa, Cedar Falls, IA 50614-0516

North Carolina Literary Review, ECU Mailstop 555, Greenville, NC 27858

North Dakota Quarterly, 276 Centennial Drive, Grand Forks, ND 58202-7209

North Star Press of St. Cloud, Inc., P.O. Box 451, St. Cloud, MN 56302

Northwest Review, 5243 University of Oregon, Eugene, OR 97403-5243

Northwestern University Press, 629 Noyes St., Evanston, IL 60208-4170

Northwind, 4201 Wilson Blvd., #110-321, Arlington, VA 22203

Not One of Us, 12 Curtis Rd., Natick, MA 01760

Notre Dame Review, B009C McKenna Hall, Notre Dame, IN 46556

Now Culture, 90 Kennedy Rd., Andover, NJ 07821

O

O-Dark-Thirty, 6508 Barnaby St. NW, Washington, DC 20015

Oberlin's Law, P.O. Box 27, New Hampton, NH 03256

Obsidian, 2810 Cates Ave., Raleigh, NC 27695-7318

Ocean State Review, 60 Upper College Rd., Kingston, RI 02881

OCHO, 604 Vale St., Bloomington, IL 61701

Off the Coast, PO Box 14, Robbinston, ME 04671

The Offending Adam, 1319 11th St., #5, Santa Monica, CA 90401

Ofi Press, 4821 Calz. Tlalpan, Tlalpan, D.F., CP 14000, Mexico

Ohio University Press, 19 Circle Dr., The Ridges, Athens, OH 45701

Old Mountain Press, P.O. Box 66, Webster, NC 28788

Old Red Kimono, 3175 Cedartown Hwy. SE, Rome, GA 30161

Old Seventy Creek Press, P.O. Box 204, Albany, KY 42602

Omnium Gatherum, 9600 Tujunga Canyon Blvd., Los Angeles CA 91042

One Co., P.O. Box 517, Oneco, CT 06373

One Eye Two Crows Press, 4335 SE Hawthorne Blvd., Portland, OR 97215

1/25, (one of twenty-five), 151 Applegate Lane, East Brunswick, NJ 08816

1110, (One Photograph, One Story, Ten Poems), 54 Lower Rd., Beeston, Nottingham, NG9 2GT, United Kingdom

One Story, 232 3rd St., #A108, Brooklyn, NY 11215

One Teen Story, 232 3rd St., #E106, Brooklyn, NY 11215

One Throne Magazine, P.O, Box 1437, Dawson City, YT, Y0B 1G0, Canada

One Trick Pony Review, 42540 W. Bunker Dr., Maricopa, AZ 85138

Ooligan Press, Portland State Univ., P.O. Box 751, Portland, OR 97207

Orange Quarterly, 3862 Hidden Creek Dr., Traverse City, MI 49684

Orchises Press, George Mason University, Fairfax, VA 22030

Oregon Humanities, 813 SW Alder St., #702, Portland, OR 97205

Organic Weapon Arts, c/o Tarfia Faizullah & Jamaal May, 10000 Desquindre St., Hamtramck, MI 48212

Origami Poems Project, P.O. Box 1623, E. Greenwich, RI 02818

Orion Magazine, 187 Main St., Great Barrington, MA 01230

Orphiflamme Press, P.O. Box 4366, Boulder, CO 80306

Osiris, PO Box 297, Deerfield, MA 01342

Other Voices Books, 2235 W. Waveland Ave., Apt. 1, Chicago, IL 60618

Otoliths, c/o Mark Young, PO Box 531, Home Hill, QLD 4806, Australia

Out of Our, 1288 Columbus Ave., #216, San Francisco, CA 94133-1302

Outpost, 301 Coleridge, SF., CA 94141

Outside In Literary & Travel, 1475 SW Charles St, Dundee, OR 97115

Oversound, c/o Samuel Amadon, Univ. South Carolina, Dept. English & Literature, 1620 College St., Columbia, SC 29208

Overtime, PO Box 250382, Plano, TX 75025-0382

OVS Magazine, 32 Linsey Lane, Warren, NH 03279

Oxford American, P.O. Box 3235, Little Rock, AR, 72203-3235

Oyez Review, Roosevelt Univ., Literature & Languages, Chicago, IL 60605-1394

P

P.R.A. Publishing, PO Box 211701, Martinez, GA 30917

PAC Books, 72 Tehama St., San Francisco, CA 94105

The Packinghouse Review, 1030 Howard St., Kingsburg, CA 93631

Painted Bride Quarterly, 3141 Chestnut St., Philadelphia, PA 19104

Palabra, P.O. Box 86146, Los Angeles, CA 90086-0146

Palettes & Quills, 330 Knickerbocker Ave., Rochester, NY 146155

Palm Beach ArtsPaper, P.O. Box 7625, Delray Beach, FL 33484

Palo Alto Review, 1400 W. Villaret Blvd., San Antonio, TX 78224

Palooka, P.O. Bo 5341, Coralville, IA 52241

PANK Magazine, 1230 W. Polk Ave., Apt. 107, Charleston, IL 61920

Papaveria Press, 145 Hollin Lane, Wakefield, West Yorkshire, WF4 3EG, UK

Paper Crane Books, 2110 Beatrice St., Springfield, OH 45503

Paper Nautilus, 41 First Avenue, Enfield, CT 06082

Paperbag, 255A 19th St., Top Floor, Brooklyn, NY 11215

Parallel Press, 728 State St., Madison, WI 53706

Parcel, 6 E. 7th St., Lawrence, KS 66044

The Paris-American, P.O. Box 167, Tomkins Cove, NY 10986

The Paris Review, 544 West 27th St., New York, NY 10001

Parody, P.O. Box 404, East Rochester, NY 14445

Parthenon West Review, 1516 Myra St., Redlands, CA 92373

Passages North, 1401 Presque Isle Ave., Marquette, MI 49855

Paterson Literary Review, 1 College Blvd., Paterson, NJ 07505-1179

Pea River Journal, P.O. Box 2211, Midland, MI 48641

Pear Noir, P.O. Box 178, Murrysville, PA 15668

Pearl, 3030 E. Second St., Long Beach, CA 90803

Peg Leg Publishing, 1612 NW 20th St., Oklahoma City, OK 73106

PEN America, 588 Broadway, Ste. 303, New York, NY 10012

Pen & Anvil, Boston Poetry Union, 30 Newbury St., Boston, MA 02216

Pen-L Publishing, 12 W. Dickson St., #4455, Fayetteville, AR 72702

Penduline Press, 14674 SW Mulberry Dr., Portland, OR 97224

Penmanship Books Poetry, 593 Vanderbilt Ave., #265, Brooklyn, NY 11238

Pentimento, P.O. Box 615, Lambertville, NJ 08530

Perceptions, Mt. Hood Community College, 26000 SE Stark St., Gresham, OR 97080

Perimeter, 410 Fifth St., #3, Brooklyn, NY 11215

Permafrost, Univ. of Alaska, P.O. Box 755720, Fairbanks, AK 99775-0640

Perpetual Motion Machine Publishing, 152 Dew Fall Trail, Cibolo, TX 78108

Perugia Press, PO Box 60364, Florence, MA 01062

The Petigru Review, 4711 Forest Dr., Ste. 3, PMB 189, Columbia, SC 29206

Petrichor Review, 2 Short St., New Market, NH 03857

Phantom Drift, P.O. Box 3235, La Grande, OR 97850

Philadelphia Review of Books, 304 Glenway Rd., Glenside, PA 19038

Philadelphia Stories, Sommers, 107 West Main St., Ephrata, PA 17522

Phoenicia Publishing, 207-5425 de Bordeaux, Montreal QC H2H 2P9, Canada

Phoenix in the Jacuzzi, 19 Maple Dell, Saratoga Springs, NY 12866

Phrygian Press, 58-09 205th St., Bayside, NY 11364

The Pickled Body, 16 Capel St., Apt. 5, Dublin 1, Ireland

PigeonBike, 611 Wonderland Rd. N. Ste. 379, London, Ontario N6H 5N7, Canada

Pilgrimage, Colorado State University, 2200 Bonforte Blvd., Pueblo, CO 81001

Pilot Light Journal, 3809 Cliffside Dr., #4, La Crosse, WI 54601

The Pinch, English Dept., 467 Patterson Hall, Memphis, TN 38152-3510

Ping-Pong, 48603 Highway One, Big Sur, CA 93920

Pink Narcissus Press, P.O. Box 303, Auburn, MA 01501

Pink Petticoat Press, P.O. Box 130085, Birmingham, AL 35213

Pinwheel, 733 Summit Ave. E., Apt. #415, Seattle, WA 98102

Pinyon Publishing, 23847 V66 Trail, Montrose, CO 81403-8558

Pirene's Fountain, P.O. Box 2693, Glenview, IL 60025

Pithead Chapel, 3091 E 4430 S, Holladay, UT 84124

Pixelhouse, P.O. Box 1476, San Mateo, CA 94401

Plain View Press, 1101 W. 34th St., Ste. 404, Austin, TX 78705

Plan B Press, P.O. Box 4067, Alexandria, VA 22303

Pleiades, Univ. of Central Missouri, English Dept., Warrensburg, MO 64093-5069

Plenitude Publishing Society 102-2507 Wark St., Victoria, BC V8T 4G7 Canada

Ploughshares, Emerson College, 120 Boylston St., Boston, MA 02116-4624

Pluck, University of Kentucky, Lexington, KY 40506

Plume, 740 17th Ave. N, St. Petersburg, FL 33704

PMS - poemmemoirstory, UA-B, HB217, 1530 3rd Ave. So., Birmingham, AL 35294

Poecology, 109 McFarland Court, #418, Stanford, CA 94305

Poem a Day Academy of American Poets, 75 Maiden Lane, New York, NY 10038

Poem Sugar Press, 50 N. George St., York, PA 17401

Poems and Plays, MTSU Box 70, Murfreesboro, TN 37132

Poems In Which, 14 Colyton Rd., Flat 2, London SE22 0NE, England, UK

Poet Lore, 4508 Walsh St., Bethesda, MD 20815

poeticdiversity: the litzine of Los Angeles, 6028 Comey Ave., LA., CA 90034

The Poetry Bus, 40 The Pines, Sea Road, Arklow Co. Wicklow, Ireland

Poetry Center, CSU, 2121 Euclid Ave., RT 1841, Cleveland, OH 44115-2214

Poetry for the Masses, 1654 S. Volustia, Wichita, KS 67211

Poetry In the Arts Press, 5110 Avenue H, Austin, TX 78751-2026

Poetry Kanto, 3-22-1 Kamariya-Minami, Kanazawa-Ku, Yokohama, 236-8502, Japan

Poetry Magazine, 61 West Superior St., Chicago, IL 60654

Poetry Northwest, 2000 Tower St., Everett, WA 98201-1390

Poetry Pacific, 1550 W. 68th Ave., Vancouver, BC V6P 2V5 Canada

The Poetry Porch, 158 Hollett St., Scituate, MA02086

Poetry South, MVSU 7242, 14000 Hwy 82 West, Itta Bena, MS 38941-1400

The Poet's Billow, 6135 Avon, Portage, MI 49024

The Poet's Haven, P.O. Box 1501, Massillon, OH 44648

Poets and Artists, 604 Vale St., Bloomington, IL 61701

Poets Wear Prada, 533 Bloomfield St, Apt. 2, Hoboken, NJ 07030

The Point, 2 N. LaSalle St., Ste. 2300, Chicago, IL 60602

Pool, 11500 San Vicente Blvd., #224, Los Angeles CA 90049

Pomeleon, 5755 Durango Rd., Riverside, CA 92506

Port Townsend Poetry Press, Box 1514, Port Townsend, WA 98368

Posit, 245 Sullivan St., New York, NY 10012

Possibilities Publishing, 6320 Buffie Court, Burke, VA 22015

Post Mortem Press, 601 West Galbraith Rd., Cincinnati, OH 45215

Post Road, 140 Commonwealth Ave., Chestnut Hill, MA 02467

Postcard Poems and Prose Magazine, 14605 Lafernier St., Baraga, MI 49908

Postscripts to Darkness. 144-195 Cooper, Ottawa, ON K2P 0E6 Canada

Potomac Review, 51 Mannakee St., MT/212, Rockville, MD 20850

Prairie Journal Trust, 28 Crowfoot Terrace NW, P.O. Box 68073, Calgary, AB, T3G 3N8, Canada

Prairie Schooner, UNL, 201 Andrews Hall, Lincoln, NE 68588-0334

Precipitate, 1576 Portland Ave., Apt. 10, Saint Paul, MN 55105

Prelude, 589 Flushing Ave., #3E, Brooklyn, NY 11206

Presa Press, PO Box 792, Rockford, MI 49341

Press 53, PO Box 30314, Winston-Salem, NC 27130

Pressure Press, 2407 Raspberry St., Erie, PA 16502

Prick of the Spindle, P.O. Box 170607, Birmingham, AL 35217

Primal Urge Magazine, P.O. Box 2416, Grass Valley, CA 95945

Prime Mincer, 401 N. Poplar, Carbondale, IL 62901

Prime Number Magazine, 1853 Old Greenville Rd., Staunton, VA 24401

Printed Matter, 910 T St., Vancouver, WA 98661

Printer's Devil Review, 74 Park St., Apt. 2, Somerville, MA 02143

Prism International, UBC, P.O. Box 1957, Buffalo, NY 14240-1957

Prism Review, ULV, 1950 Third St., La Verne, CA 91750

Profane, 93 Ridge Ave., Homer City, PA 15748

Progenitor, Arapahoe Community College, 5900 S. Santa Fe Dr., P.O. Box 9002, Littleton, CO 80160

The Prompt, P.O. Box 293, Kansas, IL 61933

The Prose-Poem Project, Equinox Publishing, P.O. Box 424, Shelburne, VT 05482

Prospect Park Books, 969 South Raymond Ave., Pasadena, CA 91105

Proverse Hong Kong, P.O. Box 259, Tung Chung Post Office, Lantau Island, New Territories, Hong Kong, SAR

Provincetown Arts, 650 Commercial St., Provincetown, MA 02657

Provo Canyon Review, 4006 N. Canyon Rd., Provo, UT 84604

Proximity Magazine, 4 Ohio Ave., Athens, OH 45701

Psychopump Magazine, 3506 W. Tulara Dr., Boise, ID 83706

Publication Studio, 717 SW Ankeny St., Portland, OR 97205

Pudding Magazine, 5717 Bromley Ave., Worthington, OH 43085

Puerto Del Sol, N.M.S.U, P.O. Box 30001, MSC 3E, Las Cruces, NM 88003

Pulp Literature, 8336 Manson Ct., Burnaby BC V5A 2C4, Canada

Q

Qarrtsiluni, P.O. Box 8, Tyrone, PA 16686

Quail Bell Magazine, 6166 Leesburg Pike, #B06, Falls Church, VA 22044

Quarter After Eight, 360 Ellis Hall, Ohio University, Athens, OH 45701

Quarterly West, 255 S. Central Campus Dr., Salt Lake City, UT 84112

Queen's Ferry Press, 8622 Naomi St., Plano, TX 75024

Qwerty, University of New Brunswick, P.O. Box 4400, Fredericton, NB E3B 5A3 Canada

Quaint, 2824 Banks St., New Orleans, LA 70119

Quiddity, Benedictine University, 1500 N. Fifth St., Springfield, IL 62702

Quiet Lightning, c/o E. Karp, 734 Balboa St., San Francisco, CA 94118

Quiet Mountain Essays, Box 261, Scotland, SD 57059

Quill and Parchment Press, 1825 Echo Park Ave., Los Angeles, CA 90026

The Quotable, 4311 Rockbridge Rd., Portsmouth, VA 23707

Qwerty, UNB Fredericton, P.O. Box 4440, Fredericton, NB, Canada E3B5A3

R

r.kv.r.y quarterly, 72 Woodbury Dr., Lockport, NY 14094

R. L. Crow Publications, PO Box 262, Penn Valley, CA 95946

Radar Poetry, 19 Coniston Ct., Princeton, NJ 08540

Radius, 65 Paine St., #2, Worcester, MA 01605

The Rag, c/o Reilly, 411 West 44th St., #18, New York, NY 10036

Ragazine, Box 8586, Endwell, NY 13762

The Rain, Party and Disaster Society, 9 Third St., Holbrook, NY 11741

Raintown Review, 5390 Fallriver Row Ct., Columbia, MD 21044

Raleigh Review, Box 6725, Raleigh, NC 27628

Rampike, c/o Karl Jirgens, English Dept., University of Windsor, 401 Sunset Ave., Windsor, ON Canada N9B 3P4

Rappahannock Review, UMW, 1301 College Ave., Fredericksburg, VA 22401

Raritan: A Quarterly Review, Rutgers, 31 Mine St., New Brunswick, NJ 08901

Rathalla Review, Creative Writing, Rosemont College, 1400 Montgomery Ave., Rosemont, PA 19010

Rattle, 12411 Ventura Blvd., Studio City, CA 91604

The Rattling Wall, 269 S Beverly, #1163, Beverly Hills, CA 90212

The Raven Chronicles, 15528 12th Avenue NE, Shoreline, WA 98155

Ray's Road Review, P.O. Box 2001, Hixson, TN 37343

Read Short Fiction, 249 Great Plain Rd., Danbury, CT 06811

REAL, P.O. Box 13007-SFA Stn, Austin State Univ., Nacogdoches, TX 75962

Rebel Satori Press, P.O. Box 363, Hulls Cove, ME 04644-0363

Red Alice Books, P.O. Box 262, Penn Valley, CA 95946

Red Bone Press, P.O. Box 15571, Washington, DC 20003

Red Bridge Press, 667 2nd Avenue, San Francisco, CA 94118

Red Rock Review Journal, English Dept., College of Southern Nevada, 3200 East Cheyenne Ave., North Las Vegas, NV 89030

Red Fez, 304 W. 15th St., Georgetown, IL 61846

Red Hen Press, PO Box 40820, Pasadena, CA 91114

Red Lightbulbs, 4213 S. Union Ave., Floor 2, Chicago, IL 60609

Red Luna Press, 2616 West Verdugo Ave., Burbank, CA 91505

Red River Review, 4669 Mountain Oak St., Fort Worth, TX 76244

Red Savina Review, 305 S. Nickel, Deming, NM 88030

Red Truck Review, 1831 N. Park Ave., Shawnee, OK 74804

Red Wheelbarrow, 528 Windham St., Santa Cruz, CA 95062

Redactions, 604 N. 31st Ave., Apt. D-2, Hattiesburg, MS 39401

Redivider, Emerson College, 120 Boylston St., Boston, MA 02116

Reworked Press, 3215 Windshire Lane, #415, Charlotte, NC 28273

Reed Magazine, English Dept., 1 Washington Sq., San Jose, CA 95192

Referential Magazine, 21-B Morton Rd., Bryn Mawr, PA 19010

Regent Press, 2747 Regent St., Berkeley, CA 94705

The Republic of Letters, Apartado 29, Cahuita, 7032, Costa Rica

Requiem Press, 4501 42nd Ave. S.. Seattle, WA 98118

Rescue Press, 605 Center St., Iowa City, IA 52245

Resource Center for Women & Ministry, 1202 Watts St., Durham, NC 27701

Resurrection House, 310 N. Meridian, Ste. 204, Puyallup, WA 98371

Revolution House, 516 N. 6th St., #3, Lafayette, IN 47901

Rhino, P.O. Box 591, Evanston, IL 60204

Right Hand Pointing, 3433 Old Wood Lane Vestavia Hills, AL 35243

Riprap, CSULB, 1250 Bellflower Blvd., Long Beach, CA 90840

River Otter Press, P.O. Box 211664, St. Paul, MN 55121

River Styx, 3547 Olive St., Ste. 107, St. Louis, MO 63103-1024

River Teeth, Ashland University, 401 College Ave., Ashland, OH 44805

River's Edge Media, 6834 Cantrell Rd., Ste. 172, Little Rock, AR 72207

Riverhaven Books, 18 Pearl St., Whitman, MA 02382

Roanoke Review, 221 College Lane, Salem, VA 24153

Rock & Sling, Whitworth Univ., 300 W. Hawthorne Rd., Spokane, WA 99251

Room Magazine, P.O. Box 46160, Station D., Vancouver BC V65 5G5, Canada

Rose House Publishing, P.O. Box 3339, Grand Rapids, MI 49501

Rose Red Review, 13026 Staton Drive, Austin, TX 78727

Rougarou, PO Box 44691, Lafayette, LA 70504-4691

Ruminate, 1041 N. Taft Hill Rd., Ft. Collins, CO 80521

Rumpus, c/o Marisa Siegel, 742 Halstead Ave., Mamaroneck, NY 10543

Rust + Moth, 2409 Eastridge Ct., Fort Collins, CO 80524

The Rusty Toque, 680 Shaw St., Toronto, ON M6G 3L7, Canada

S

S.F.A. Press, P.O. Box 13007, SFA Station, Nacogdoches, TX 75962-3007

2nd & Church, P.O. Box 198156, Nashville, TN 37129-8156

2nd Wind Publishing, 931-B S. Main St., Box 145, Kernersville, NC 27284

Sacramento News & Review, 1124 Del Paso Blvd., Sacramento, CA 95815-3607

Saint Julian Press, 2053 Cortlandt, Ste. 200, Houston, TX 77008

Saint Paul Almanac, 275 East Fourth St., Ste. 735, Saint Paul, MN 55101

Sakura Publishing, P.O. Box 1681, Hermitage, PA 16148

Sakura Review, 1727 Sena St., Denton, TX 76201

Salamander, English Dept., 41 Temple St., Boston, MA 02114-4280

Salmagundi, Skidmore College, Saratoga Springs, NY 12866-1632

The Salon, 294 N. Winooski Ave., Burlington, VT 05401

Salt Hill, 401 Hall of Languages, Syracuse University, Syracuse, NY 13244

San Diego City Works Press, 1313 Park Blvd., San Diego, CA 92101

San Francisco Peace and Hope, P.O. Box 8057, Berkeley, CA 94707

San Pedro River Review, P.O. Box 7000 – 148, Redondo Beach, CA 90277

Sand Hill Review, 1076 Oaktree Dr., San Jose, CA 95129

Santa Monica Review, 1900 Pico Blvd., Santa Monica, CA 90405

Sarabande Books, Inc., 112 West 27th St., Ste. 607, New York, NY 10001

Saranac Review, SUNY, 101 Broad St., Plattsburgh, NY 12901-2681

Saturnalia Books, 105 Woodside Rd., Ardmore, PA 19003

Sawyer House, 721 Dean St., Floor 3, Brooklyn, NY 11238

Scapegoat Press, P.O. Box 410962, Kansas City, MO 64141-0962

Scarlet Literary Magazine, 1209 S. 6th St., Louisville, KY 40203

Scarlet Tanager Books, 1057 Walker Ave., Oakland, CA 94610

Scarletta Press, 10 South 5th Street, #1105, Minneapolis, MN 55402

Scars Publications, 829 Brian Court, Gurnee, IL 60031

Schuylkill Valley Journal, 240 Golf Hills Rd., Havertown, PA 19083

Scribendi, 1 University of New Mexico, Albuquerque, NM 87131-0001

Sea Haven Books, P.O. Box 61, Tolovana Park, OR 97145

Sea Storm Press, P.O. Box 186, Sebastopol, CA 95473

Seal Press, 1700 Fourth St., Berkeley, CA 94710

The Seattle Review, Univ. of Washington, Box 354330, Seattle, WA 98195-4330

Second & Church Press, P.O. Box 198156, Nashville, TN 37129-8156

Seems, Lakeland College, PO Box 359, Sheboygan, WI 53082-0359

Sein und Werden, 9 Dorris St., Manchester M19 2TP United Kingdom

Serving House Journal, 29641 Desert Terrace Dr., Menifee, CA 92584

Serving House Books, 6 Hannover Rd., Florham Park, NJ 0792-1819

Seven Circle Press, 744 N. 104th St., Seattle, WA 98133

Seven Hills Review, 2910 Kerry Forsest Parkway, Tallahassee, FL 32309

Seventh Quarry, Dan-y-bryn, 74 Cwm Level Rd., Brynhyfrd, Swansea SA5 9DY, Wales, UK

Sewanee Review, 735 University Ave., Sewanee, TN 37383-1000

SFA State University Press, 1036 North St., Nacogdoches, TX 75962-3007

Shabda Press, 3343 East Del Mar Blvd., Pasadena, CA 91107

Shade Mountain Press, P.O. Box 11393, Albany, NY 12211

Shadow Mountain Press, 14900 W. 31st Ave., Golden, CO 80401

Shadowgraph Magazine, P.O. Box 31339, Santa Fe, NM 87594-1339

Shanti Arts, 193 Hillside Rd., Brunswick ME 04011-7355

She Writes Press, 1563 Solano Ave., #546, Berkeley, CA 94707

Shenandoah, Washington & Lee University, Lexington, VA 24450-2116

The Shit Creek Review, 90 Kennedy Rd., Andover, NJ 07821

Shock Totem, 107 Hovendon Ave., Brockton, MA 02302

Shoppe Foreman Co., 3507 Homesteaders Lane, Guthrie, OK 73044

Short Story America, 2121 Boundary St., Ste. 204, Beaufort, SC 29907

Showcase Magazine, 753 Main St., #3, Danville, VA 24541

Sibling Rivalry Press, P.O. Box 26147, Little Rock, AR 72221

Siena Press, 8306 Wilshire Blvd., Ste. 882, Beverly Hills, CA 90211

Sierra Nevada Review, 999 Tahoe Blvd., Incline Village, NV 89451

Signal 8 Press, P.O. Box 47094 Morrison Hill Post Office, Hong Kong

Silk Road Review, 2043 College Way, Forest Grove, OR 97116-1797

Silver Birch Press, P.O. Box 29458, Los Angeles, CA 90029

Silver Pen, Inc., 9841 Hickory Lane, Saint John, IN 46373

The Single Hound, P.O. Box 1142, Mount Sterling, KY 40353

Sinister Wisdom, 6910 Wells Parkway, University Park, MD 20782

Sink Review, 95 Graham Ave., 2nd Floor, Brooklyn, NY 11206

Six Three Whiskey Press, 1234 6th St., #403, Santa Monica, CA 90401

Sixfold Review, 28 Farm Field Ridge Rd., Sandy Hook, CT 06482

Sixteen Rivers Press, P.O. Box 640663, San Francisco, CA 94164-0663

Sixth Finch, 95 Carolina Ave., #2, Jamaica Plain, MA 02130

67 Press, P.O. Box 933, Winston Salem, NC 27101

Skidrow Penthouse, c/o Rob Cook, 68 E. 3rd Street, Apt. 16, New York, NY 10003

Skive Magazine, 86/1 Laman St., Cooks Hill NSW 2300 Australia

Slake Media, 3191 Casitas Ave., Ste. 110, Los Angeles, CA 90039

Slant, 201 Donaghey Ave., Conway, AR 72035-5000

A Slant of Light, SUNY New Paltz, 1 Hawk Dr., New Paltz, NY 12561

Slapering Hol Press, 300 Riverside Dr., Sleepy Hollow, NY 10591

Sleet Magazine, 1846 Bohland Ave., St. Paul, MN 55116

Slice, P.O. Box 659, Village Station, New York, NY 10014

The Sligo Journal, Montgomery College, Takoma Park, MD 20912

Slipstream, Box 2071, Niagara Falls, NY 14301

Slope Editions, 34 Juckett Hill Dr., Belchertown, M 01007

Slough Press, Texas A&M University, College Station, TX 77843-4227

Small Doggies Omnimedia, 4432 SE Main St., Portland, OR 97215

Small Print Magazine, P.O. Box 71956, Richmond, VA 23255-1956

Smartish Pace, P.O. Box 22161, Baltimore, MD 21203

SmokeLong Quarterly, 5708 Lakeside Oak Lane, Burke, VA 22015

Smoking Glue Gun, 2845 B San Gabriel St., Austin, TX 78705

Snail Mail Review, 1694 Augusta Pointe Drive, Ripon, CA 95366

So to Speak, 4400 University Dr., MSN 2C5, Fairfax, VA 22030

Sock Monkey Press, 58 Garfield Pl., #1, Brooklyn, NY 11215

Solas House, 2320 Bowdoin St., Palo Alto, CA 94306

Solo Café, 5625 Continental Way, Raleigh, NC 27610

Solo Press, 5146 Foothill Rd., Carpinteria, CA 93013

Solomon & George Publishers, 108 S 8th St, Opelika, AL 36801

Solstice, 5 Damon Park, Arlington, MA 02474

Song of the San Joaquin, PO Box 1161, Modesto, CA 95353-1161

Sonora Review, University of Arizona, Tucson, AZ 85721

South Dakota Review, USD, 414 East Clark St., Vermillion, SD 57069

South Loop Review, Columbia College, 600 S. Michigan, Chicago, IL 60605

The Southampton Review, 239 Montauk Hwy., Southampton, NY 11968

Southeast Missouri State University Press, 1 University Plaza, MS 2650, Cape
    Girardeau, MO 63701

The Southeast Review, Florida State Univ., Tallahassee, FL 32306

Southern Humanities Review, 9088 Haley Center, Auburn, AL 36849-5202

Southern Indiana Review, USI, 8600 University Blvd., Evansville, IN 47712

Southern Poetry Review, 11935 Abercorn St., Savannah, GA 31419-1997

The Southern Review, L.S.U., 338 Johnston Hall, Baton Rouge, LA 70803

Southwest Review, PO Box 750374, Dallas, TX 75275-0374

Southword, Frank O'Connor House, 84 Douglas St., Cork, Ireland

Sou'wester Magazine, Southern Illinois Univ., Edwardsville, IL 62026-1438

Sow's Ear Poetry Review, P.O. Box 127, Millwood, VA 22646-0127

sPARKLE & bLINK, 215 Precita Ave., San Francisco, CA 94110

Sparks & Echo Arts, Attn: Jonathon Roberts, 9 Pocket Rd., Beacon, NY 12508

Specter, One Market St., Apt. 417, Camden, NJ 08102

The Speculative Edge, 149 W. Trottier Rd., S. Royalton, VT 05068

Spider Road Press, 1135 Allston St., Houston, TX 77008

Spillway, 11 Jordan Ave., San Francisco, CA 94118

Spirituality & Health, 444 Hana Highway, Ste. D, Kahului, HI 96732

Split Lip Magazine, 10906 Braewick Dr., Carmel, IN 46033

Spoon River, Illinois State Univ., Campus Box 4240, Normal, IL 61790-4240

Spork Press, 216 N. 3rd Avenue, Tucson, AZ 85705

Spout Hill Press, 440 Ferrara Ct., #110, Pomona, CA 91766

Spudnik Press Coop, 1821 W. Hubbard St., Ste. 302, Chicago, IL 60622

Squalorly, 1210 18th St., Apt. #2, Bay City, MI 48708

St. Andrews College Press, St. Andrews University, 1700 Dogwood Mile, Lau-
    rinburg, NC 28352

St. Petersburg Review, Box 2888, Concord, NH 03302

Star Cloud Press, 6137 East Mescal St., Scottsdale, AZ 85254-5418

Star 82 Review, P.O. Box 8106, Berkeley, CA 94707

Star°Line, W5679 State Road 60, Poynette, WI 53955-8564

Steel Toe Review, 1521 16th Avenue So, #J, Birmingham, AL 35205

StepAway, 2, Bowburn Close, Gateshead, Tyne & Wear, NE10 8UG, UK

Austin State University Press, 1936 North St., Nacogdoches, TX 75962

Still, P.O. Box 1121, Berea, KY 40403

Still Crazy, P.O. Box 777, Worthington, OH 43085

Stillwater Review, Sussex County Community College, Newton, NJ 07860

Stirring, 1031 Ashwood Place, Knoxville, TN 37917

Stone Canoe, 700 University Ave., Ste. 326, Syracuse, NY 13244-2530

Stone Highway Review, 1606 South 27th St., St. Joseph, MO 64507

The Stone Hobo, 16 Holley St., Danbury, CT 06810

Stone Telling Magazine, 200 Nebraska, Lawrence, KS 66046

Stoneboat, Lakeland College, P.O. Box 359, Sheboygan, WI 53082-0359

Stoneslide Media, 4 Elm St., Guilford, CT 06437

Stonewood Press, 97 Benefield Rd., Oundle, PE8 4EU, United Kingdom

Storm Cellar, 212 Ames St., Northfield, MN 55057

Story, 441 Country Club Rd., York, PA 17403

Story Quarterly, Armitage Hall, 4th fl., 311 N. Fifth St., Camden, NJ 08102

Storyscape Journal, 407 S. 51st St., #1, Philadelphia, PA 19143

storySouth, 3302 MHRA Bldg., UNC Greensboro, Greensboro, NC 27402

The Storyteller, 2441 Washington Rd., Maynard, AR 72444

Strange Worlds Publishing, 45 Westview Dr., Bergenfield, NJ 07621

String Poet, 10 Tappen Drive, Melville, NY 11747

Structo, 2 Lawns Cottages, Witherslack, Cumbria, LA11 6SD, UK

Stymie, 1965 Briarfield Dr. Ste. 303, Lake St. Louis, MO 63367

subTerrain, P.O. Box 3008 MPO, Vancouver, BC V6B 3X5, Canada

Subtropics, PO Box 112075, University of Florida, Gainesville, FL 32611-2075

Sugar House Review, PO Box 13, Cedar City, UT 84721

Sugared Water, 5425 Philloret Dr., Cincinnati, OH 45239

Summerland Publishing, P.O. Box 41323, Santa Barbara, CA 93140

The Summerset Review, 25 Summerset Dr., Smithtown, NY 11787

Summertime Publications, 7502 E. Berridge Lane, Scottsdale, AZ 85250

The Sun, 107 North Roberson St., Chapel Hill, NC 27516

Sunday Lit, 641 N. Highland Ave., #8, Atlanta, GA 30306

Sundog Lit, 641 North Highland Ave., #8, Atlanta, GA 30306

sunnyoutside, PO Box 911, Buffalo, NY 14207

Sun's Skeleton, 274 Bay Rd., #1, Newmarket, NH 03857

Super Arrow, 121 N. Normal, #3, Ypsilanti, MI 48197

Supermachine, 388 Myrtle Ave., #3, Brooklyn, NY 11205

Superstition Review, Arizona State Univ., Mesa, AZ 85212

SwanDive Publishing Company, 236 Pulaski St., Wilkes-Barre Twp., PA 18702

Swarm, www.swarmlit.com, c/o 43 Country Walk Dr., Manchester, NH 03109

Sweet, 110 Holly Tree Lane, Brandon, FL 33511

Swimming with Elephants, 513 14th St. NW, Albuquerque, NY 87104

Swink, 1661 10th Ave., Brooklyn, NY 11215

Switchback, 2130 Fulton St., San Francisco CA 94117-1080

Sybaritic Press, 12530 Culver Blvd., #3, Los Angeles, CA 90066

Sycamore Review, 500 Oval Dr., West Lafayette, IN 47907

Syracuse University Press, 621 Skytop Rd., Ste. 110, Syracuse, NY 13244-5290

T

TAB: The Journal of Poetry & Poetics, Chapman University, One University Drive, Orange, CA 92866

Tahoma Literary Review, 10234 132nd Ave NE, Kirkland, WA 98033

Tampa Review, University of Tampa, 401 West Kennedy Blvd., Box 19F, Tampa, FL 33606-1490

A Taos Press, P.O. Box 370627, Denver, CO 80237

Tar River Poetry, East Carolina University, MS 159, Greenville, NC 27858-4353

Taurean Horn Press, P.O. Box 526, Petaluma, CA 94953

Tawani Foundation, 104 S. Michigan, Ste. 525, Chicago, IL 60603

Tayen Lane, 2663 Telegraph Ave., #407, Oakland, A 94612

Tayler and Seale Publishing, 2 Oceans West Blvd., Unit 406, Daytona Beach Shores, FL 32118

Teflon Magazine, Vas. Voulgaroktonou 73, 11473, Athens, Greece

Telling Our Stories Press, 185 AJK Blvd., #246, Lewisburg, PA 17837-7491

Ten Thousand Tons of Black Ink, 716 Columbian Ave., Oak Park, IL 60302

10 X 3 Plus, 1077 Windsor Ave., Morgantown, WV 26505

Terminus, P.O. Box 54423, Atlanta, GA 30308

Terrain.org, 12786 Shore St., Leavenworth, WA 98826

Texas Review Press, Box 2146, Sam Houston State Univ., Huntsville, TX 77341-2146

Texas Christian University, TCU Box 298300, Fort Worth, TX 76129

The2ndhand, 1430 Roberts Ave., Nashville, TN 37206

Third Coast, Western Michigan University, Kalamazoo, MI 49008-5331

Third Flatiron, 4101 S. Hampton Circle, Boulder, CO 80301-6016

Third Wednesday, 174 Greenside Up, Ypsilanti, MI 48197

13th Floor, Univ. of Nebraska, Omaha, 6001 Dodge St., Omaha, NE 68182

32 Poems Magazine, Valparaiso University, 1320 Chapel Drive South, Valparaiso, IN 46383

THIS Literary Magazine, 315 W. 15th St., #12, Minneapolis, MN 55403

this Magazine, 417-401 Richmond St. West, Toronto, Ontario M5V 3A8, Canada

Thought Publishing, 73 Alvarado Rd., Berkeley, CA 94705

Thoughtcrime Press, 4716 North Talman Ave., Chicago, IL 60625

3: A Taos Press, P.O. Box 370627, Denver, CO 80237

Three Coyotes, 10645 N.Oracle Rd., Ste. 121-163, Tucson, AZ 85737

3 Elements Review, 4328 Ingersoll Ave., Des Moines, IA 50312

Three Mile Harbor Press, Box 1951, East Hampton, NY 11937

3QR: The Three Quarter Review, 528 Park Ave., Towson, MD 21204

Three Rooms Press, 51 MacDougal St., Ste. 290, New York, NY 10012

Threepenny Review, PO Box 9131, Berkeley, CA 94709

Thrush Poetry Journal, 889 Lower Mountain Dr., Effort, PA 18330

Thunderclap!, 1055 Thomas St., Hillside, NJ 07205

ThunderDome. 6655 Esplanade #3, Playa del Rey, CA 90293

Tia Chucha Press, 13197-A Gladstone Ave., Sylmar, CA 91342

Tidal Basin Review, P.O. Box 1703, Washington, DC 20013

Tiferet, 211 Dryden Rd., Bernardsville, NJ 07924

Tiger Bark Press, 202 Mildorf St., Rochester, NY 14609

Tiger's Eye Press, P.O. Box 9723, Denver, CO 80209

Tightrope Books, 167 Browning Trail, Barrie, Ontario, L4N 5E7, Canada

Tikkun Magazine, 2342 Shattuck Ave., Ste. 1200, Berkeley, CA 94704

TimBook Tu, 400 Capital Circle SE, Ste. 18236, Tallahassee, FL 32301-3839

Tin House, 2601 NW Thurman St., Portland, OR 97210

Tinderbox Poetry Journal, 1897 Grand Ave., #2, St. Paul, MN 55105

Tipton Poetry Journal, PO Box 804, Zionsville, IN 46077

TL Publishing Group, P.O. Box 151073, Tampa, FL 33684

Toadlily Press, PO Box 2, Chappaqua, NY 10514

The Toast, c/o Nicole Cliffe, 4246 Little Cottonwood Rd., Sandy, UT 84092

Toasted Cheese, 44 East 13th Ave., #402, Vancouver BC V5T 4K7, Canada

Tongue, 14 Thornhill House. London, N1 1PA, United Kingdom

Topside Press, 70 Leno Rd., #3B, Brooklyn, NY 11226

Torrey House Press, 21 Eldridge Rd., Jamaica Plain, MA 02130

The Toucan Literary Magazine, 6156 W. Nelson St., Chicago, IL 60634-4043

Trachodon, P.O. Box 1468, St. Helens, OR 97051

Transcendent Zero Press, 16429 El Camino Real, Apt. #7, Houston, TX 77062

Transition, 104 Mt. Auburn St., 3R, Cambridge, MA 02138

Transmission, 8582 Trenton Falls Prospect Rd., Remsen, NY 13438

Transom Journal, 185 Vernon Ave., Apt. 4, Louisville, KY 40206

Traprock Books, 1330 E. 25th Ave., Eugene, OR 97403

Travelers' Tales, Solas House, 2320 Bowdoin St., Palo Alto, CA 94306

Tree Killer Ink, 33 Sioux Rd., Sherwood Park, Alberta, Canada T8A 5T4

Tree Light Books, 5234 N. Wayne Ave., #1, Chicago, IL 60640

Treehouse Magazine, 113 S. Front St., Wilmington, NC 28401

Treehouse Press, P.O. Box 65016, London N5 9BD, UK

Trinacria, 220 Ninth St., Brooklyn, NY 11215-3902

Trio House Press, 1055 30th St., Apt. 4, Boulder, CO 80303

Triptych Tales, 8 Shaw Court, Kanata, Ottawa, ON, K2L 2L9, Canada

TriQuarterly, Northwestern Univ., 339 E. Chicago Ave., Chicago, IL 60611

Truman State University Press, 100 E. Normal Ave., Kirksville, MO 63501

Tuesday, PO Box 1074, East Arlington, MA 02474

Tule Review, Sacramento Poetry Center, 1719 25th St., Sacramento, CA 95816

Tupelo Press, P.O. Box 1767, North Adams, MA 01247

Turbulence, 29 Finchley Close, Hull, East Yorkshire, HU8 0NU, UK

The Tusculum Review, 60 Shiloh Rd., P.O. Box 5113, Greenville, IN 37743

The Tusk, 1419 NE 21st Avenue, Unit 1, Portland, OR 97232

Tweeds, c/o The Coffin Factory, 14 Lincoln Place, Ste. 2R, Brooklyn, NY 11217

Twelve Winters Press, P.O. Box 414, Sherman, IL 62684-0414

20 Something Magazine, 4429 Ebenezer Rd., Perry Hall, MD 21236

Twenty-four Hours Press, 39 W. 30th St., #G, Bayonne, NJ 07002

A Twist of Noir, 2309 West Seventh St., Duluth, MN 55806-1536

2 Bridges Review, 300 Jay St., Brooklyn, NY 11201

Two Hawk, Antioch Univ., 400 Corporate Pointe, Culver City, CA 90230

Two Lines Press, 582 Market St., Ste. 700, San Francisco, CA 94104

Two of Cups Press, P.O. Box 38095, Greensboro, NC 27410

Two Serious Ladies, 31 Maxwell Rd., Chapel Hill, NC 27517

Typhoon Media, P.O. Box 47094, Morrison Hill Post Office, Hong Kong

Tyrant Books, 676A Ninth St., #153, New York, NY10036

U

URJ Books, 633 Third Ave., New York, NY 10017-6778

U.S. 1 Poets' Cooperative, PO Box 127, Kingston, NJ 08528-0127

U.S. 1 Worksheets, P.O. Box 127, Kingston, NJ 08528-0217

Umbrella, 5620 Netherland Ave., #2E, Bronx, NY 10471-1880

Umbrella Factory Magazine, 2540 Sunset Dr., #125, Longmont, CO 80501

unboundCONTENT, 160 Summit St., Englewood, NJ 07631

Under the Gum Tree, 1617 18th St., Sacramento, CA 95811

Under the Sun, 1622 Edgefield Ct., Cookeville, TN 38506-7444

Underground Voices, 4020 Cumberland Ave., Los Angeles, CA 90027

Undertow, 1905 Faylee Crescent, Pickering, ON L1V 2T3, Canada

Unicorn Press, 1310 Glenwood Ave., Greensboro, NC 27403

University of Alabama Press, Box 870380, Tuscaloosa, AL 35487-0380

University of Arizona Press, 1510 E. University Blvd., Tucson, AZ 85721-0055

University of Chicago Press, 11030 South Langley Ave., Chicago, IL 60628

The University of Georgia Press, 320 So. Jackson St., Athens, GA 30602-4901

University of Hell Press, 0524 SW Nebraska St., Portland, OR 97239

University of Louisiana Press, P.O. Box 40831, Lafayette, LA 70504-0831

University of Massachusetts Press, P.O. Box 429, Amherst, MA 01004

University of Nebraska Press, 1111 Lincoln Mall, Lincoln, NE 68588-0630

University of Nevada Press, MS 0166, Reno, NV 89557-0166

University of North Texas Press, 1155 Union Circle, Denton, TX 76203

UNO Press, University of New Orleans Publishing, New Orleans, LA 70148

University of Tampa Press, 401 West Kennedy Blvd., Tampa, FL 33606

Unsaid, 3521 Pheasant Run Circle, #5, Ann Arbor, MI 48108

Unshod Quills, 39391 SE Lusted Rd., Sandy, OR 97055

Unsplendid, 169 Mariner St., #2, Buffalo, NY 14201

Unstuck, 4505 Duval St., #204, Austin, TX 78751

Unthank Books, P.O. Box 3506, Norwich, NR7 7PQ, United Kingdom

Unthology, P.O. Box 3506, Norwich, NR7 7PQ, United Kingdom

Up the Staircase Quarterly, 716 4th St., SW, Apt. A, Minot, ND 58701

Uphook Press, 515 Broadway, #2B, New York, NY 10012

Upstairs at Duroc, 52, rue du 8 Mai 1945, 94240 L'Hay les Roses, France

upstreet, P.O. Box 105, Richmond, MA 01254-0105

Uptown Mosaic, E Swan Creek Rd., Ft. Washington, MD 20744-5200

Utah State University Press, 3078 Old Main Hill, Logan UT 84333-3078

V

Vagabondage Press, P.O. Box 3563, Apollo Beach, FL 33572

Valley Voices, MVSU, 14000 Hwy 82 W, Box 7242, Itta Bena, MS 38941-1400

Vallum, 5038 Sherbrooke West, PO Box 23077 CP Vendome, Montreal, QC H4A 1T0, Canada

Valparaiso Fiction Review, Valparaiso Univ., Valparaiso, IN 46383

Vandal, 526 Cathedral of Learning, 4200 Fifth Ave., Pittsburgh, PA 15260

VAO Publishing, 4717 N. FM 493, Donna, TX 78537

Vector Press, 226 Ella St., #2, Pittsburgh, PA 15224

Vending Machine Press, P.O. Box 172, Glenbrook, NSW 2773, Australia

Vered Publishing, 1352 W. 25th Ave., Anchorage, AK 99503

Versal, 334 Oxford St., #2, Rochester, NY 14607

Verse Wisconsin, P.O. Box 620216, Middleton, WI, 53562-0216

Vestal Review, 127 Kilsyth Rd., #3, Brighton, MA 02135

Victorian Violet Press, 1840 W 220th St., Ste. 300, Torrance, CA 90501

Vine Leaves, c/o Jessica Bell, Konopisopoulou 31, Athens, 1152, Greece

Vinyl Poetry, 814 Hutcheson Dr., Blacksburg, VA 24060

The Virginia Quarterly Review, 5 Boar's Head Lane, P.O. Box 400223, Charlottesville, VA 22904

Virgogray Press, 2103 Nogales Trail, Austin, TX 78744

VoiceCatcher, 14388 SE Christenson Court, Clackamas, OR 97015

Voices, PO Box 9076, Fayetteville, AR 72703-0018

The Volta, 1423 E. University Blvd., 472, Tucson, AZ 85721

vox poetica, 160 Summit St., Englewood, NJ 07631

W

Waccamaw, Coasta Carolina University, Conway, SC 29528-6054

Wag's Revue, 786 Prospect Pl. 4F, Brooklyn, NY 11216

Wake: Great Lake Thoughts & Culture, 1 Campus Dr., Allendale, MI 49401

Wales Art Review, 62 King Rd., Cardiff CF11 9DD, Wales, United Kingdom

Walkabout Publishing, P.O. Box 151, Kansasville, WI 53139

The Walrus, Suite 101, 19 Duncan St., Toronto, ON M5H 3H1, Canada

The Wapshott Press, P.O. Box 31513, Los Angeles, CA 90031-0513

War, Literature & the Arts, 2354 Fairchild Dr., USAF Academy, CO 80840

Washington Square Review, 58 W. 10th St., NY, NY 10011

Water~Stone Review, MS A1730, 1536 Hewitt Ave., St. Paul, MN 55104-1284

Water Street Press, 108 Fifth St., Ste. 2, Healdsburg, CA 95448

The Waterhouse Review, 105 E Barnton St., Stirling, FK8 1HJ, UK

Watershed Review, CSU-Chico, 400 W. 1st St., Chico, CA 95928

Wave Books, 1938 Fairview Ave. East, Ste. 201, Seattle, WA 98102

Waxwing Magazine, 220 S. Humphreys St., Flagstaff, AZ 86001

Wayne State University Press, 4809 Woodward Ave., Detroit, MI 48201-1309

Weasel Press, 4214 Norton Dr., Manvel, TX 77578

Weave Magazine, 7 Germania St., San Francisco, CA 94117

The Weeklings, 43 N. Manheim Blvd., New Paltz, NY 12561

Weighed Words, 1326 Sleepy Hollow Rd., Glenview, IL 60025

Welter, 1420 N. Charles St., Baltimore, MD 21201

Wesleyan University Press, 215 Long Lane, Middletown, CT 06459

West Branch, Stadler Center for Poetry, Bucknell Univ., Lewisburg, PA 17837

West End Press, P.O. Box 27334, Albuquerque, NM 87106

West Marin Review, P.O. Box 984, Point Reyes Station, CA 94956

West Trestle Review, 1315 Merry Knoll Rd., Auburn, CA 95603

The Westchester Review, Box 246 H, Scarsdale, NY 10583

Western Humanities Review, Univ. of Utah, Salt Lake City, UT 84112-0494

Westland Park Press, P.O. Box 9594, Canton, OH 44711

When Women Waken, 133 Sharp Top Trail, Apex, NC 27502

WhiskeyPaper, P.O. Box 701452, Louisville, KY 40202

Whispering Prairie Press, P.O. Box 410661, Kansas City, MO 64141

Whistling Shade, 1495 Midway, Saint Paul, MN 55108

Whit Press, 4701 SW Admiral Way, #125, Seattle, WA 98116

White Dot Press, 707 Carl Drive, Chapel Hill, NC 27516

White Pelican Review, P.O. Box 7833, Lakeland, FL 33813

White Pine Press, P.O. Box 236, Buffalo, NY 14201

The White Review, 243 Knightsbridge, London SW7 1DN, United Kingdom

White Violet Press, 24600 Mountain Ave., #35, Hemet, CA 92544

White Whale Press, 2121 Cleveland Pl. 1-N, St. Louis, MO 63110

Wicked East Press, P.O. Box 1042, Beaufort, SC 29901

Wigleaf, University of Missouri, 114 Tate Hall, Columbia, MO 65211-1500

Wild Goose Poetry Review, 838 4th Avenue Dr. NW, Hickory, NC 28601

Wilderness House Press, 145 Foster St., Littleton, MA 01460-1541

Willow Springs, 668 N. Riverpoint Blvd., 2 RPT - #259, Spokane, WA 99202

Willows Wept Review, 17313 Second St., Montverde, FL 34756

Wilson Quarterly, 1300 Pennsylvania Ave., NW, Washington, DC, 20004-3027

Wind Publications, 600 Overbrook Drive, Nicholasville, KY 40356

Wind Ridge Books, P.O. Box 636, Shelburne, VT 05482

Window Cat Press, 80 Corey Rd., Apt. 3, Brighton, MA 02135

Wings Press, 627 E. Guenther, San Antonio, TX 78210

WinningWriters.com, 351 Pleasant St., PMB 222, Northampton, MA 01060

The Winter Anthology, 414A Altamont St., Charlottesville, VA 22902

Winter Goose Publishing, 2701 Del Paso Rd., 130-92, Sacramento, CA 95835

Winter Tangerine Review, 3820 E. McCracken Bloomington, IN 47408

Wiseblood Books, P.O. Box 11612, Milwaukee, WI 53211

Wising Up Press, P.O. Box 2122, Decatur, GA 30031-2122

Witness, Box 455085, 4505 S. Maryland Pkwy, Las Vegas, NV 89154-5085

WMG Publishing, P.O. Box 269, Lincoln City, OR 97367

WomenArts Quarterly, UMSL, One University Blvd., St. Louis, MO 63121

Woodley Memorial Press, 2518 W.View Drive, Emporia, KS 66801

The Worcester Review, 1 Ekman St., Worcester, MA 01607

Word Palace Press, P.O. Box 583, San Luis Obispo, CA 93406

Word Riot Press, P.O. Box 414, Middletown, NJ 07748

Wordcraft of Oregon, P.O. Box 3235, La Grande, OR 97850

Wordgathering, 7507 Park Ave., Pennsauken, NJ 08109

Wordrunner eChapbooks, 333 N. McDowell Blvd., Petaluma, CA 94954

Words without Borders, 154 Christopher St., #3C, New York, NY 10014

Work Literary Magazine, 8752 N. Calvert, Portland, OR 97217

Workers Write!, P.O. Box 250382, Plano, TX 75025-0382

World Literature Today, 630 Parrington Oval, Ste. 110, Norman, OK 73019

World Weaver Press, 215 W. Lake St., Alpena, MI 49707

Write Bloody Books, 2306 E. Cesar Chavez, Ste. 103, Austin TX 78702

Writecorner Press, PO Box 140310, Gainesville, FL 32614-0310

Writers Ink Press, 1104 Jacaranda Ave., Daytona Beach, FL 32118

The Writing Disorder, P.O. Box 93613, Los Angeles, CA 90093

Writing Knights Press, 2520 Market Ave., #2, Canton, OH 44714

Writing on the Edge, Writing Program, UC Davis, Davis, CA 95616

Written Backwards, 1325 H St., #11, Sacramento, CA 95814

Wyatt-MacKenzie Publishing, 15115 Highway 36, Deadwood, OR 97430

Wyvern Lit, 271 Dartmouth St., Apt. 4l, Boston, MA 02116-2828

Y

The Yale Review, Yale University, PO Box 208243, New Haven, CT 06520

Yarn, 26 Hawthorne Lane, Weston, MA 02493

YB, 401 Zanzibar, Billings, MT 59105

YU News Service, P.O. Box 236, Millbrae, CA 94030

Yellow Flag Press, 224 Melody Dr., Lafayette, LA 70503

Yellow Medicine Review, SMSU, 1501 State St., Marshall, MN 56258
Yemassee, English Dept., USC, Columbia, SC 29208
Yes Yes Books, 4904 NE 29th Ave., Portland, OR 97211-6361
Your Impossible Voice, 2099 Luka Ave., Apt. B, Columbus, OH 43201

Z

Zephyr Press, 50 Kenwood St., Brookline, MA 02446-2413
Zoetrope: All Story, 916 Kearny St., San Francisco, CA 94133-5107
Zone 3, APSU, P.O. Box 4565, Clarksville, TN 37044
Zymbol, 14 Cedar Lane, Bow, NH 03304
ZYZZYVA, 57 Post St., Ste. 604, San Francisco, CA 94104

CONTRIBUTORS' NOTES

DAN ALBERGOTTI's latest poetry collection *Millenist Teeth* was published by Crab Orchard/Southern Illinois University Press. He teaches at Coastal Caroline University.

POE BALLANTINE's *Guidelines for Mountain-Lion Safety* is just out. His *Things I Like About America*, an essay collection, is a "Cult classic."

ELLEN BASS is published by Copper Canyon Press. She teaches in the MFA program at Pacific University. *Like A Beggar* is her recent collection.

RICHARD BAUSCH's most recent books are *Before, During, After*, and *Something is Out There*, both from Knopf. He is the editor of the *Norton Anthology of Short Fiction* and teaches at Chapman University.

ANN BEATTIE is the author of several novels and story collections, most recently *The State We're In: Maine Stories*. She lives in Maine and Florida.

WENDELL BERRY's recent books include *This Day* (poetry), *A Place In Time* (fiction) and *Our Only World* (essays) from Counterpoint press.

CHANA BLOCH's *Blood Honey* is just published. She teaches at Mills College and lives in Berkeley, California

MARIANNE BORUCH is the author of *The Book of Hours* (Copper Canyon) and other poetry collections. She has appeared in the Pushcart Prize four times.

TIFFANY BRIERE holds a PhD in genetics from Yale and an MFA in fiction from Bennington. She received a 2013 Rona Jaffe award.

NICHOLE BROSSARD is a much honored poet, novelist and essayist and has published over thirty books, many translated into English and other languages. She lives in Quebec.

KURT BROWN was author of many books of poetry and chapbooks. He was editor of the *Aspen Anthology* and founder of the Aspen Writers' Conference. He taught at Sarah Lawrence College and Georgia Tech. He died in 2013.

JOHN CHALLIS lives in England where he has just completed a PhD at Newcastle University. His work has been published in various journals and has been broadcast on BBC radio.

DAN CHAON's new novel is due to be published in 2016. *Stay Awake*, his short story collection, was published in 2012. His *Among the Missing* was a finalist for The National Book Award.

KATIE COYLE's debut novel *Vivian Apple at the End of The World* was named one of the best YA novels of all time by *Rolling Stone*. She blogs at katiecoyle.com.

ANTHONY DOERR's essays appeared in *Pushcart Prize XXX* and *XXXVII*. His fiction was featured in *Pushcart Prize XXXIII*. He received the Pulitzer Prize in 2015. His novel *All the Light We Cannot See* is out from Scribner.

E.A. DURDEN lives in Seattle. Her stories have appeared in *Painted Bride Quarterly*, *Border Crossing* and elsewhere.

APRIL L. FORD teaches at SUNY Oneonta, New York. She is managing editor of *Digital Americana*.

MARGARET GIBSON authored ten books of poems and a memoir. She lives in Preston, Connecticut.

RIGOBERTO GONZALES is the author of thirteen books of poetry and prose. He is the editor of *Camino del Sol: Fifteen Years of Latina and Latino Writing*. Among his many awards are the Lenore Marshall prize and the Lambda Literary Award.

JAMES HANNAHAM is the author of the novels *Delicious Foods* (2015) and *God Says No* (2009). He teaches at Pratt Institute.

BOB HICOK's *Sex & Love* will be published by Copper Canyon in 2016. His *Elegy Owed* (2013) was a finalist for the National Book Critics Circle Award.

EDWARD HIRSCH has published eight books of poetry and five books of prose. His most recent work is *Gabriel: A Poem*.

JANE HIRSHFIELD's two new books are *The Beauty* (poems) and *Ten Windows: How Great Poems Transform the World*, both from Knopf. She has won four Pushcart Prizes.

TONY HOAGLAND's *Application For Release From The Dream* is published by Graywolf Press. He teaches at the University of Houston.

BRANDON HOBSON's novel *Deep Ellum* was published in 2014. He lives in Ponca City, Oklahoma.

ANDREA HOLLANDER lives in Portland, Oregon where she conducts writing workshops at the Attic Institute. She taught for many years at Lyon College and has published several poetry collections.

CHLOE HONUM grew up in Auckland, New Zealand. She received a Ruth Lilly Fellowship from the Poetry Foundation.

BARBARA HURD's *Listening to the Savage/River: Notes and Half Heard Melodies* is due soon from the University of Georgia Press. Her many awards include a Guggenheim Fellowship and the Sierra Club's National Nature Writing Award.

ALLEGRA HYDE received a 2015 Fulbright Fellowship. She is prose editor for *Hayden's Ferry*.

CATHERINE JAGOE authored two poetry chapbooks, plus essays and poetry in *Atlanta Review*, *North American Review* and *Athenaeum*.

PERRY JANES is a filmmaker and writer living in west Hollywood. His short film "Zug" toured Internationl Film Festivals recently.

CHARLES JOHNSON is a MacArthur Fellow and winner of a National Book Award for his novel *Middle Passage*.

LALEH KHADIVI was born in Iran and has lived many places since. Her two books in her Kurdish trilogy received many awards and were widely translated.

CHRISTIAN KIEFER is an actor, poet, and song writer. His novels are *The Animals* and *Infinite Tides*.

JORDAN KISNER lives in Brooklyn. This is his first appearance in The Pushcart Prize.

KEETJE KUIPERS has been a Wallace Stegner Fellow at Stanford and is the author of *Beautiful In The Mouth* (BOA, 2010) and *The Keys To The Jail* (BOA, 2014). She is editor of *Southern Humanities Review*.

DOROTHEA LASKY teaches at Columbia University. Her most recent book is *Rome* (Liveright/WW.Norton).

LISA LEE's story is an excerpt from a novel in progress. She lives in Los Angeles.

DANIEL LUSK has authored seven poetry collections. He is a Pablo Neruda Poetry Prize winner and lives in Vermont.

MICHAEL MARBERRY's work has appeared in *Sycamore Review*, *West Branch*, *Bat City*, *Thrush* and elsewhere. He lives in Michigan.

COLUM McCANN is the author of six novels and two story collections. He has received many international honors and teaches at Hunter College, New York.

EDWARD McPHERSON is the author of two nonfiction books plus essays and short stories in *Paris Review*, *Granta*, *Gulf Coast* and others.

SCOTT MORGAN received an MFA at the University of Missouri. He lives in Fenton, Missouri.

JOYCE CAROL OATES is a Founding Editor of the Pushcart Prize. She teaches at New York University and lives in Princeton.

MEGHAN O'GIEBLYN lives in Madison, Wisconsin. Her work has appeared in *The Guardian*, *Oxford American*, *Guernica* and *Boston Review*.

MORGAN PARKER's *Other People's Comfort Keep Me Up At Night* was published by Swtchback Books in 2015. She is a Cave Canem Fellow and co-curates "Poets With Attitude" reading series in Brooklyn.

LUCIA PERILLO is author of *Luck is Luck* (2005) and other books. This is her fifth Pushcart Prize.

KATIE PETERSEN is a recipient of a Wallace Stegner Fellowship. She is a Jones lecturer of Stanford University.

KEVIN PRUFER is co-editor of *New European Poets*. His books include *National Anthem*, *In A Beautiful Country* and *Churches*.

WENDY RAWLINGS is the author of a novel and a short story collection. Her work has appeared in *Agni, Tin House* and elsewhere.

LILLIAM RIVERA is a 2013 PEN Emerging Voices Fellow. She lives in Los Angeles.

RACHEL ROSE is the Poet Laureate of Vancouver. A chapbook is just out from Book Thug and a new poetry collection, *Marry & Burn* is due from Harbour.

MAXINE SCATES is the author of three poetry books from *New Issues*, *Cherry Grove* and the University of Pittsburgh Press. She lives in Eugene, Oregon.

JOANNA SCOTT's most recent novel is *De Potter's Grand Tour*. She lives in Rochester, New York.

ASAKO SERIZAWA received a writing fellowship from the Fine Arts

Center in Provincetown, Massachusetts. Her stories have appeared in *Antioch Review*, *O'Henry Prize Stories*, and elsewhere.

RAENA SHIRALI won the 2013 "Discovery"/*Boston Review* poetry prize and was a finalist for the 2014 Ruth Lilly Fellowship. She teaches at the College of Charleston in South Carolina.

GEORGE SINGLETON is a Guggenheim recipient and a member of the Fellowship of Southern Writers. He has published seven collections of stories, two novels and a book of writing advice.

ZADIE SMITH lives in England. She has published four acclaimed novels and won the Orange Prize. She was elected a fellow of the Royal Society of Literature.

LISA RUSS SPAAR teaches at the University of Virginia, This is her first Pushcart Prize selection.

JULIA STORY is the author of *Post Moxie* (Sarabande Books) and a chapbook, *The Trapdoor* (Dancing Girl Press). She lives in Massachusetts and Dorset, England.

SUE ELLEN THOMPSON is the author of five books of poetry. She received the 2010 Maryland Author Prize. Her selection here is from her new book *They*, just out from Turning Point.

FREDERIC TUTEN is the author of five novels and a short story collection *Self-Portraits*: *Fictions*. He grew up in the Bronx and lives in Manhattan.

DUBRAVKA UGRESIC is a Croatian writer living in the Netherlands. Several of her novels and essay collections are available in English.

SARAH VALLANCE lives in a small beach town outside Sydney, Australia with three rescued dogs and two rescued cats. She holds an MFA from City University, Hong Kong.

ZEBBIE WATSON lives in Athens, Georgia. This story is her first print publication.

AFAA MICHAEL WEAVER received the 2014 Kingsley Tufts Award. His current collection is *City of Eternal Spring* (University of Pittsburgh Press)

JOSH WEIL is the author of the novel *The Great Glass Sea* and the novella collection *The New Valley*, which received several honors. He lives with his family in the Sierra Nevadas.

INDEX

The following is a listing in alphabetical order by author's last name of works reprinted in the *Pushcart Prize* editions since 1976.

630

633

634

635

636

638

640

647

648

654